MURDERER OF
DREAMS

© Paul Taffinder 2020

Published by Xiphax Press

Printed in the United Kingdom

The right of Paul Taffinder to be identified as the author
of this work has been asserted by him in accordance with
the Copyright, Designs and Patents Act 1988.

Paperback 978-1-8380902-0-3
Hardback 978-1-8380906-2-3

Cover design and layout by www.spiffingcovers.com

Book One of The Dream Murderer Cycle

MURDERER OF DREAMS

PAUL TAFFINDER

THE CRITICS PRAISE PAUL TAFFINDER'S VISIONARY NOVELS OF THE DREAM MURDERER CYCLE

"Stunningly entertaining… this epic story of power struggle—and for the highest of stakes: the future of humanity…a gripping narrative"
– The European

"…an epic and enthralling future Earth trilogy packed with peril and pathos that keeps one foot firmly in the real world as it dives deep into the human condition… you'll be screaming for the conclusion."
– Reader's Digest

"A bold, ambitious story of future history driven by timeless human truths."
 – Timothy Arden, The London Economic

"Epic in scale, meticulous in detail, and grounded with the author's profound insight into the human psyche, this trilogy is a dream come true for all sci-fi and fantasy fans."
– Female First

"Author Paul Taffinder fuses artistic vision with intellectual keenness to deliver a stand-out epic work."
– MaleXtra

THE EASTERN
FLATS

SALAS FORESTS

GUNG'L
KOEST
WAW
WAW HEAD

BAY OF
MARSHESE

DESDANG
FORTRESS
CORCORAN

SMALLHAM

M
MAM
S
ELOY

BILJAN
SEA

AMSAV RIVER

SAV RIVER

KACIA LOWLANDS

SOHANYUN

LORANG
DOMITA
INGEN
LORANG STEPPES

DONIRA
DEKA

HONAM

BOLCOM CLIFFS

LIPHAN PLAINS

ELI

SSU-AM
THE GREAT HARRENHAM

ROSK

SHAD
KOVAL
KU

LADORE

HAGGAR

WEST
SUHL
RUS

LADORE STRAITS

BIRE

SUHL

WARK

NEG

THESSUAM SPILL

THE GAP

THE CORAN

LADORE

LADORE KEN

SOUTH
BILL
NORTH
BILL

CHEBOU

Kellax Cartographical Printing, AT CHISUA, IYE 1870

THE NORTHERN PASSAGE

MAW
UVAOL
R'MAN
ALLPO

WISIB POINT

A Chart of the

KIANGSU
REALM

0   MILES   200
0   KEMS   320

WOEL   RUN

KIANGSU
NORTH

SERO

PAUKEN   ENLUN RIVER   SAEN   KEI HEAD

LEE CISE RIVER

ESA'MIL   KEI

NG   ENLUN BASIN   XO

KIANGSU

KIANG   XERU

SYCHOMO

BOUR OCEAN

BIABARO STRAITS
SHAK   CISE   THE BILLOWS   FAR
BIABARO   NEYICH
CHULIEN   GRIV   FORMA
HISUA   TZINAMPO   OLED
GIRD   OLED LEE
ACHEEN   NOKING
ATHO
KIARININ

KIARIN

N
NW   NE
W   E
SW   SE
S

CEAN

The Royal City of CHISUA
Map & Key

1. Mera (The Old Palace)
2. The Hall at Mera
3. Ehri (The New Palace)
4. Monvar Hill
5. The Parvis
6. The North Gate
7. Chisuan Gate
8. Temple Gate
9. The Temple at Cise Hook
10. Lovar Rock
11. Ta-Shih Garrison (Headquarters)
12. The Roneca (The Academies)
13. Echrexar Inscription
14. The King's Way
15. Becon-ni Way
16. Higher Dirndorc
17. Kuo Square
18. West Onax
19. Ta-Shih Flat
20. Onax
21. The Council at Mera
22. Strad Place (The Maze)
23. The Sea Gate (Quay Road)
24. The Dirndorc

PORT CHISUA

NORTH RAMPART

WEST RAMPART

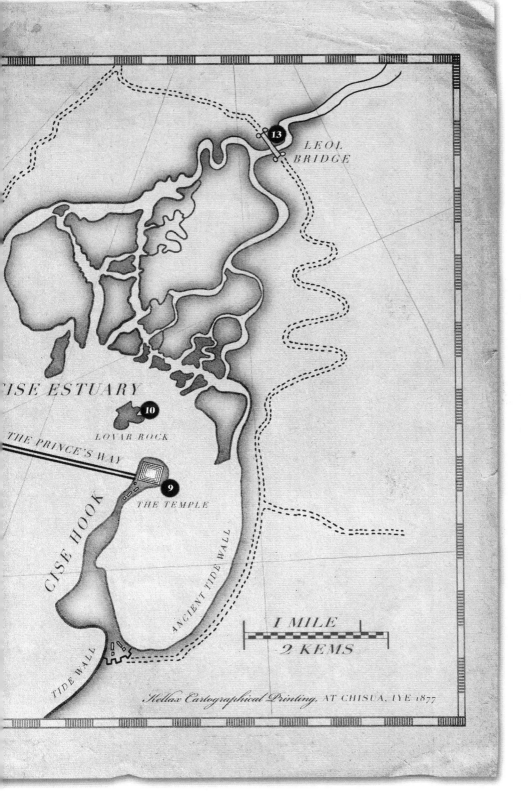

LEOL BRIDGE

CISE ESTUARY

LOVAR ROCK

THE PRINCE'S WAY

CISE HOOK

THE TEMPLE

ANCIENT TIDE WALL

TIDE WALL

1 MILE
2 KEMS

Kellax Cartographical Printing, AT CHISUA, IYE 1877

*To Nick, for his enthusiasm, critique,
nerdish attention to detail and great ideas.*

PROLOGUE

EC /2084 RE X/

Temporary designation by IAU (Committee on Small Body Nomenclature after Discovery):
  E: Eccentric orbit
  C: Comet
  X/: no reliable orbit has been established
  RE: Roger Ellwood

In the Year of Echrexar (IYE)

Eslin was five when she heard her parents first use the name. She was in the narrow concrete corridor outside the steel door of their equally narrow living quarters. They did not know she was there, but they spoke in muted whispers anyway, as if the truth were too awful to express aloud. Even so young, Eslin could feel their terror, a terror far beyond the daily anxiety that troubled the whole of the Svalbard refuge. Something had changed.

"Echrexar," came the voice of her father, strained and hoarse. "The media are calling it Echrexar, because of the IAU designation. Started as a joke on social media. Now everyone's picked it up."

To Eslin, the word was strange, but she was smart and she understood instantly that it was the name of the horror that was coming.

"The main body will miss, they say, but the dogs might hit," her father went on. "A direct strike…probably one. But there could be four hits. Maybe more…"

He meant the six large fragments strung out and trailing the comet. The news feeds were full of such portrayals. Colourful graphic animations needed a compelling narrative, and the 'dogs' stuck. The other children her own age – she could not call them friends – wondered why the comet had dogs, because they were nice and fluffy and small and they were told the comet was large. Eslin listened to them and thought they were stupid. The *dogs* were rock and ice, she informed them, and probably iron; but they giggled and whispered to each other and teased: how could dogs be made of rock and ice and *iron*? All she could do was repeat herself, but realized almost at once she had been defeated by the logic of their limited comprehension.

There was a pause and Eslin, standing alone in the cold corridor under pale strip lights, her hands clasped in her yellow mittens, held her breath. Inevitably, she knew, her mother would ask the hard question. Her mother was the one who would not shade the truth, where her father put on a smile and patted his daughter's auburn curls and spoke loudly and confidently that it was all fine and the government were merely taking precautions. Eslin had no idea what 'precautions' were, but she assumed they had something to do with leaving her home in the city and moving here to Spitsbergen, across the seas, and living underground for weeks with hundreds of other families. Just in case.

So her mother asked the question, as Eslin expected she would: "When?"

Her father had not answered at first. But she'd expected that too. He was a man whose genial, open face would shut, as firmly as a door, when a question demanded a serious answer, and he would look at you with deep hazel eyes as he gauged the precise response to give.

"Two days," he murmured at last. "Monday. The troops have sealed the doors."

"It will be bad," her mother stated, and that word 'bad', falling from her lips, resonated threat. Her mother spoke the truth. "We need to tell Eslin."

"No…she's too young," her father demurred at once. "And it might miss," he added, but could not protest further with any conviction. He sounded scared, Eslin thought.

"Do you think it will miss?" came the challenge.

Her father hesitated. "No," he admitted.

A single word, but appalling.

"Then we have to," her mother insisted. "With what's coming, what if something happens to us? She needs to know."

"If something happens to us," came the grave reply, "we shall all be gone, including Eslin."

"Yes, Monday or the day after," was her mother's sharp retort. "It won't matter if Svalbard is anywhere near the impact. But if the refuge is intact in six months' or a year's time? What if we get ill or we have an accident or…"

So, that afternoon, they sat her on her bed and told her. There were tears in her father's eyes. She watched the drops form on his lashes and run down his cheeks, and she understood that he grieved for a loss that was yet to happen. Abruptly he hugged her, and she clasped him hard as he lost control and wept. When he broke away, sitting beside her, head down, fists balled, her mother, dry-eyed and intent, cupped Eslin's face. It seemed there was only her blue gaze and nothing else.

"We will be fine," she said. "The refuge under the mountain is deep. We are safe here. We have food and water supply and the animals and the seed and gene vaults and the archives. We will be fine."

The word 'fine' was what struck Eslin hard. From her mother, *fine* meant bad, difficult and unpleasant; it was the word she had always used when she was upset and would say no more, especially to her husband. It was spat out to bring an end to speaking. So Eslin was not reassured and, in that, her mother had succeeded: better to worry and expect the worst while making the right noises to pretend otherwise.

But then, while those blue eyes held her own, and the warmth of slender fingers embraced Eslin's cheeks, her mother said a strange thing. It was so odd that only later did Eslin realize this was the truth her parents really wanted to impart: the imminent cataclysm she could not yet comprehend was only a horrifying stage for the personal drama in which she somehow would play a part.

"Do you remember the hospital last year, Eslin?" asked her mother.

Eslin nodded. It was a recollection of clean and ordered spaces, doctors and nurses and unfathomable machinery. And pain, inescapable and enduring. Afterwards, it seemed more dream than reality.

"You had a procedure, you recall. Something called NCR…" Her mother shook her head, a moment of irritation or frustration at Eslin's blank expression. She was a scientist, a biologist – though Eslin only half understood what that was – and she was impatient explaining things to a child. "It doesn't matter what it's called. It fixes any injuries, or makes you well when you get sick. You never get sick, do you?"

Again, Eslin nodded. That had never occurred to her, but she could take it as true. Other children had coughs. People did talk about getting sick. The moment stretched, in near silence, only a pipe ticking somewhere in the corridor as it warmed. Looking at her mother, it seemed there was more to come. And her father had turned his face towards her.

"You will live," said her mother, "a long time, Eslin."

This meant nothing to Eslin. A long time was unfathomable, although the trip on the ferry over icy seas to Spitsbergen had been a long time. The ship had pitched and rolled and people were being sick and the smell was horrible. A long time. And yet, she knew her mother was telling her something profound. She tried to understand.

"You will live a long time…but it will be hard. There are not many like you. None here at Svalbard, but others across the world. It will be hard, in years to come, but…you are our hope. You are our hope if things are very bad on Monday. If things are bad and there is chaos… Still, you will live through it, and you will thrive. You *must*."

Her father clutched at her small hand and she looked up at him. Through the creased pain of his features she saw his eyes light with hope too. She knew what hope was, but not how *she* could be their hope. *Must* be their hope. It was confusing. And then her mother said the thing that was strangest of all, and in a tone of such certainty and conviction that Eslin could only nod again, once, though she understood nothing at all: "You will be like Gilgamesh, two-thirds god…" she whispered, quiet and secret, so no one might hear, though only the three of them were in the room.

***

On Monday, after a subdued breakfast in the main dining hall where conversation among the collected families was hushed, fearful and expectant, the trio returned to their quarters. Her father absently closed the heavy steel door, then opened it again. The protocol was to keep it open during the *event*, in case the walls moved and it got jammed. Everyone, including the children, had been briefed on this. At the time it had seemed rather remote, like some school lessons; but now it was real. Her father had opened the door.

Their room had three beds, curtained for what passed for privacy. Three armchairs and a table occupied the centre. The walls, where three dark umber wooden wardrobes stood proud, old-fashioned and incongruous, were grey concrete, but Eslin and her father had stuck pictures up: lakes, forests and animals, like two-dimensional windows onto the world. Eslin sat in an armchair and stared at the galloping gold palomino horses beside the sea, white spray exploding from their hooves. She wanted to ride a horse, but knew it was unlikely now.

Her mother sat and her father stood. He was pale, almost grey like the walls. He wore a blue tracksuit. Some of the men and women had dressed in protective gear this morning and carried their sealed helmets with them. They were the duty troops if there was a breach to the paired external airlock doors. But her parents were dressed like any other day. Both of them were staring at their smartphones. They had taken Eslin's device from her.

"Entry trail," her father croaked. "Pacific…"

Eslin could imagine the bright streak across the skies. She ventured a question: "Is it the dogs?"

"Yes." This from her mother, a sharp hiss, eyes glued to the screen of her smartphone.

They waited. Then her father said bleakly, "Another."

Eslin closed her eyes. She could see, in her mind's eye, the second searing yellow wound across the pale blue of sky and sea, falling, falling, falling. Stillness for a long time. Perhaps nothing would happen; but a peculiar knot of fear had gripped her stomach and she thought that it was where she wanted to bury her mounting terror, as if doing so would stop this thing from happening. Finally, the room trembled. A low reverberation rose in frequency and it seemed to Eslin, as she opened her eyes, that the floor, rough polished solid sandstone, rippled like water. She could feel it through the thick rubber of her winter boots. It reminded her of the ship, ponderously climbing and rolling, again and again.

"WiFi's out," her mother said, grim and matter-of-fact, but kept looking at her phone, gripped in white-knuckled hands, as if it were the only remaining anchor to the world they had known.

Her father murmured, "I still have a signal…"

A second, deep trembling. Then a third, Eslin thought, and possibly a fourth. The dense shuddering seemed to have no sound, just a *feel* that was inside everything, until the strange waves of juddering merged into a continuous vibration.

"Four," confirmed her father. He seemed both stupefied and relieved. "Equatorial perhaps. Nothing too close…" He was a planetary geologist, Eslin knew. He studied rocks and planets…and comets.

The vibration picked up and seemed now to resolve into secondary surges, several seconds apart, very much like the rolling convulsion of the seas under the ship.

"Are you sure…" asked her mother, with forced but cool detachment, "that the main body will miss?"

"Echrexar will miss." He used that name again, as if the comet was more than a thing, a giant perhaps, followed by ferocious spectral dogs across the black infinity of space. Eslin suddenly longed to be like those children with their talk of fluffy dogs.

The shuddering did not cease, but later an abrupt pressure squeezed at Eslin. Her ears were blocked, painfully so. She swallowed to clear the pressure, but it returned. A creaking, grinding noise at the edge of hearing rose in pitch.

"Air blast," said her father. "It will pass, but the four impacts will create unpredictable vortices."

Eslin had seen this simulated online. It was not hard to imagine the vast cliff of wind slamming across Spitsbergen, blasting snow and ice and scouring the sandstone peaks and permafrost down to bare rock.

Her mother was staring intently at her husband. It was the first time Eslin had seen her look anything other than confident. Now she wanted reassurance: they were alive and the agony of hope was alive with them. "If it's four hits…this could be bad. The tsunamis?" she asked, slowly, cautiously, as if she dreaded the answer.

"Hours yet."

"But are we OK here?"

"Should be. We're one hundred and thirty metres above current sea level…"

"On projected surges of one hundred metres *minimum*. You know the upper range is three hundred. Will we be swamped?"

Her father might have shrugged. Eslin could see his shoulders almost shaping to do so, but he caught himself and spoke levelly: "I'm guessing the impacts are all Pacific and southern hemisphere. The amplitude will be smaller this far north, the energy less. And the vault is sealed."

"If the airlocks hold."

"We'll know if they don't. We'll feel the pressure shift."

"There *was* a pressure shift," her mother countered. "We felt it."

"There was, but that was…not significant."

Eslin imagined she could hear a dim roaring, like a summer rainstorm but all-encompassing and powerful enough to make the rock floor and concrete walls vibrate. She looked at her hands, fists pressed against her thighs. The taut knot that was her stomach seemed have become the centre of her terror. She wanted to go to her mother but she was rigid and blank-eyed, lost in her own dreadful world. Eslin had thought, in a vague way, that this would all be quick, but it seemed endless and full of unknowable menace. Unconsciously she lifted her knees to her chest and hugged herself, head down on her thighs but, with her eyes tight closed, it seemed much worse.

"Pappa," she said, voice quavering. "Make it stop."

He came to her, bent down to pick her up, cheek against hers, the rasp of his shaven stubble on her face a sudden reminder of home and her bed and the security of Pappa come to say goodnight, in another lifetime. "Hush, baby," he murmured. "It will stop. It will stop."

But it did not. Later, that night, when the trembling had died down, the bumping came, irregular and violent like some huge giant was hammering the sides of the mountain trying to get in. Eslin imagined a towering colossus, streaming searing yellow flames, smashing the great doors of the vault with titanic fists.

"Shock waves and debris falling," her father intoned, as he did whenever some new horror intruded. Her parents spoke, from time to time, guessing, Eslin thought, what was happening out there. She understood some of what they said, but had learned quickly that they did not know. No one knew.

"Will we get satellite feeds back again?" Her mother, taut but calm.

"Unlikely. The plasma bloom from each strike will have punched through the top of the atmosphere. Even the smaller dogs will cause massive damage. Together they may have wrecked telecoms and maybe those satellites in high orbits. The problem is also that the plume debris will fall again, maybe planet-wide because of the four impacts. If it's really bad, at terminal velocity so much debris will superheat the atmosphere. There will be massive regional fires. I can check maybe…later…"

"Anders," her mother murmured and, because she had used his name, Eslin knew the imminent question was not for her ears. Head down against her knees, she listened intently. "How many…?"

Anders was pacing. Eslin heard him pause. "What?" he then asked.

"If it's bad, how many casualties?"

Another pause, filled with deep tremors in the rock. "I don't know, Asta," he replied in a gentle voice, pitched to express regret and sadness and respect. "Billions in the first days. But I really don't know."

They both fell silent. It seemed to Eslin to be a silence heavy with guilt. She reflected on the words her parents used. They were all so vast.

Echrexar was vast. And she felt very small.

IYE 11

Eslin was sixteen when Anders died. People were careful how they talked about it, and her mother went along with the conceit, but Eslin knew he had taken his life. She had watched his confidence fail, in spite of his ready smile and his forced laughter.

The gloom of the impact winter affected people in different ways. Some ignored it, stiffening their resolve with light-hearted banter about the cramped conditions and food rationing, and the pervasive smell of animal urine and ordure. The young adapted; after all, most of their lives had been lived underground. But some despaired and, in spite of the community's support, the strain was carved in the marmoreal lineaments of their faces. What people had come to call the *in-between time,* in the perpetual hope that it would soon end, barely lifted. It was dark, always dark, and easy to believe they would never see sunlight again. Eslin learned to distinguish a multitude of greys in the shifting penumbra of the sky when the sun was somewhere above. The limited distances they could safely travel showed only a lunar landscape, polluted by acid rain and sustained heating from the original infernos. Her father told her with a sombre knowing look that volcanic activity across the planet had been intensified by the depth of impacts, pumping more soot, dust and gases into the skies. Echrexar was not finished with the planet yet. And it was warmer, warm enough that even this far north the permafrost had not returned. It was winter only because of the gloom.

Spitsbergen was smaller now. Although the expected tsunamis of the first impacts had never threatened Svalbard, dissipating their violent energies against the tangle of wave-fronts thrown up in huge storms across the world, the Arctic ocean had risen year after year as the vast meltwater process continued. Because at least two of the impacts had been in the oceans, throwing up a stupendous volume of water vapour, they were living in a greenhouse, perpetuated by the dense moisture, carbon dioxide and volcanic ash still circulating across the planet. The seas rose, and

21

Eslin and her father had measured the increments every month, taking readings from one rocky peninsular and another in the ashen light. In all directions, the island was grey, the curving foreshore thick with a covering of soot and dust like a monochrome dump of dirty snow. Mixed with the regolith were tiny glass ejecta of pulverised rock, almost invisible to the eye. Anders had shown them to Eslin under a microscope, spherules like tiny moons with their own craters from the rapid superheated re-entry through atmosphere back to earth. Eslin had held the inoffensive miniscule glass ejecta in the palm of her hand. Here were the murderous culprits that created the immense firestorms to incinerate the surface of the planet – trillions of them, the deadly offspring of Echrexar. It seemed impossible, but she knew the science to be true and wondered, time and again, what could have been done to prevent all this. It ignited an anger in her, a restless impatience to take action – although in truth she knew the fury that trembled below the surface of the cool detachment she presented had long been a part of her, the legacy of those early terrors. She hid the horror and the anger in a crucible at her core, tight and rigidly contained lest she do something precipitate, like her father.

All around, the sea was tempered steel, oily and sluggish as breakers heaved ponderously up beaches black with oozing regolith and dangerous to the inexperienced. Two of Svalbard's citizens had been careless enough to get mired in the deeper flows. One had drowned as the tide turned. The Citizens Council issued new directives for safety, and movement outside required the carrying of mud-hoppers, adapted from snow-shoes.

One behind the other, observing strict discipline, Eslin and her father had traversed the island, sticking to the known routes and the familiar landmarks, but noting the disappearance of features submerged by the waves. Even through linen masks, the air was distinctive, a chlorine-ozone pungency, like after an electrical storm, and redolent of burnt spicy bitterness that caught at the back of the throat so that everyone felt the compulsion to cough. Through it all, Anders maintained meticulous records, both electronic and paper. He had seemed optimistic. The graphs would peak, the inexorable flooding would reverse, he would say. That moment would be hugely significant for it would mark a *return*. He used that word with special emphasis, much as did all citizens; it was proof of hope, the promise of an end to the in-between time and the rebirth of the world…before it was too late.

And yet, he had given up. In her life one day, and gone the next. His body was not recovered. He had gone out alone and without a radio. The batteries for all the portable devices were failing now anyway. The Council recorded 'death by misadventure'. Perhaps, they reflected, he had slipped or become mired, and then the sea, the slick, seeping steel sea, had stolen his life. Eslin had listened to all this in silence. It would not do, she readily surmised, for the Council to admit that one of its senior scientists had committed suicide: the psychological welfare of the refuge was more important than the truth. The archivists recorded the Council verdict and stored the death certificate. Her mother, Asta, did not speak of it, but Eslin heard her crying in the night, bitter tears of loss and regret and, yes, anger too.

Eslin threw herself into reading, studying everything she could lay her hands on. It was as if her father had left her with a rushing urge to pack her head with all the learning and knowledge of the world – a vast store of it here in the Svalbard library and archives, but still merely a fragment of what had been lost. As some of the computers and digital hard drives failed, she picked up paper files and physical books on science, history, philosophy, medicine and literature, and pored over them, thrilling to the anticipation of finding something new. A thick tome of the collected works of Shakespeare was a favourite. She could speak English fluently, but this was a different experience entirely; an astonishing journey of imagination, and the wrench and lure of human emotion rendered through the immense power of words. She absorbed it all: the neat verses, the precise decasyllabic beat of each line of poetry, and the whole thing charged with potential.

And she re-read the *Epic of Gilgamesh*, again and again. She had never forgotten her mother's words, that moment on the eve of Echrexar's devastation. The sceptic in her scoffed, but still she searched the words of that most ancient of human stories for meaning, made more profound by the vast gulf of time and forgotten language. She had wanted to ask Asta what she had meant, but hesitated each time, as if uttering the question aloud might destroy some secret truth. Gilgamesh, the seeker of eternal life, condemned by the gods never to attain it.

It was an unspoken, unanswered challenge between her and Asta, like a foretelling, or a curse. Or both.

With no interruption, Eslin took over her father's work, accompanied now by Lars, a young man two years older than her, blond, blue-eyed and striking. Together they worked the island in the grey gloom and, inevitably, fell for each other. Eslin believed she was in love, but perhaps it was just youthful lust and opportunity. Alone out in the murk, it was easy to find a quiet clean cleft in the mountainside where the ubiquitous sooty regolith had been washed away by rain. It was exciting, breathless passion, the taste of his mouth on hers, his muscled body clutched to her breasts and their legs entwined. It felt timeless. On occasion, standing outside the tall vault doors of the refuge entrance as they prepared their kit for another excursion, Eslin would study Lars. He moved with easy grace, hands sure and accomplished as he tightened belts to secure safety harness and mud-hoppers to his backpack. Even in the dim light of mid-morning he looked beautiful, and she wanted to touch him, to feel the warm life of his arms and thighs, the need in him and in her...

While they negotiated the shores of the island, they talked. And argued. On the first occasion they were high up, picking their way across the slopes. They stopped, boots planted firm into the regolith, where bedrock gave purchase. Towards the east, the swell of the greasy smear of the ocean heaved across their eyeline. But there was something different. Eslin knew it but was cautious to give voice. It was Lars who pointed upwards, his arm outstretched.

"It's lighter," he said, with a breathless excitement.

It was. The overcast seemed thinner and one could almost see the disk of the sun halfway between horizon and zenith. Almost... There was a roseate glow, like a hesitant sunrise or the strawberry ice-cream Eslin remembered from her childhood, all deep pinks and magenta, shifting back to nickel grey then brighter again. These were colours no one had seen in the outside world in more than ten years.

"Yes!" he cheered, an outrageous sound of joy here in the rocky desolation of their island home. They hugged, somewhat awkwardly, stiff in attempting to keep their footing. "The first sign!" he shouted in triumph. "Let's get back and tell everyone!"

He let Eslin go and she replied, "But, Lars, we should finish the survey. It's not far to the Lasberg point—"

"What for?" he laughed. "Come on."

She stood still, and perhaps it was her father's discipline, but this felt important. "The record is vital, Lars," she argued. "It's fact. We rely on facts."

He was still ecstatic and laughed again, waving madly at the uncertain ochre gleam overhead. "Forget it. We won't need all that stuff anymore. We need to get on with moving out of the refuge. It's getting lighter now. We need to start *living* again!"

"I still think—"

But he was off, making his way downslope, and she was confronted with a dilemma. Citizens Council rules required that they work in pairs and it was sensible. It had saved lives. Reluctantly she followed.

The quarrels did not end there. One day, on one of their regular excursions, the sky overhead slowly brightening and giving promise of an end to the in-between time, Lars abruptly stopped. They stood on a high promontory, and the sky was appreciably lighter, a bleached coffee colour which changed the regolith to something less dead, a dense mud perhaps. Lars reached out and held her forearm, gazing out over the mountain ridge. She looked at him, thinking that he was alerting her to some danger. But his face was wistful.

"The cove there," he said, pointing now to a flat tract of land in the saddle of the ridges. "It's protected from the run-off and the wind. We could begin clearing it and experiment with crops from the vault. We could build terraces and a few houses and workshops. The overcast is clearing every day. In six months, we might have sunshine…" Eslin shrugged. He caught her look, his eyes level. "You think it's too soon?" he asked.

She shrugged again. "No. But I think we should try for the mainland.

Get to the other refuges."

Lars snorted. "Forget it," he grunted. "We lost contact years ago. Why risk life and limb and precious resources on foolhardy adventures?"

Eslin was accustomed to his bluntness. But this time she bridled and bit back. "Because we might pool any remaining technology and knowledge and rebuild *quicker*. Our library is limited. We have the animal husbandry, crop and seed databases and 13,000 years of agriculture history in the samples in the vaults. But we have very limited energy knowledge or machine technology or experts who can advise us. We forget that getting Svalbard extended and turned into a refuge was a rush job: the government only had a few months and we survived but, Lars, we have three diggers for earth-moving – and small ones at that – some outboard motors, a few generators, and the nuclear-powered heat-lamps for the crops. They will all break down and fail, sooner or later."

Lars looked uncomfortable, his face drooping in that way she knew meant he did not agree and wanted to get back to his topic. "Listen, Essie," he said, releasing her arm and using her diminutive name either to appeal to their intimacy or put her in her place, or maybe both. "You need to grow up. You're a dreamer, you know." Eslin fought back a biting response as he went on, "The planet is wrecked. Billions dead. Maybe everyone but us. No coastal city survived the mega-tsunamis, and inland the firestorms incinerated everything else. The communities that did make it through could never survive famine, unless they were in refuges like Svalbard."

"So you say," she responded with cold disdain.

"I do say." He jerked his chin at her, showing as much aggression as his Scandinavian upbringing and living in a tight community would allow. "Eslin, you need to be practical. Svalbard saved us. Agriculture, farming and fishing is our future. We can't survive or grow our population unless we get that right – and soon. Pretending otherwise is stupid."

Eslin drew herself up, shoulders back. She was nearly as tall as Lars, despite the difference in gender and age. "So we should just be farmers?" She said it with contempt because she intended it to hurt. Then she relented, feeling guilty, and conceded: "I get it, Lars. Yes, we have to solve food production. Of course. But there's a wider need. The skies may clear, the sun may shine and the new world dawn, but it's now a dangerous place. Disease, viruses, flooding, you name it. We need the refuges to work together and we need shared knowledge to solve all the challenges. We've already had too many immune system problems from lack of sun. The health of this refuge is not good – not to mention the population bottleneck we face. There are two thousand people here. It's barely enough for genetic variation, especially if we get hit with some virus."

He bridled. "It's enough to get started!"

"No, it isn't," she snapped back. "For a few generations, maybe, then we're in trouble as genetic diversity falls."

He glared at her. He hated to be on the wrong side of her arguments. He knew she was smarter, much smarter, and more articulate. He looked away. "You could help, you know," he muttered.

She knew instantly what he meant, but asked anyway: "What does that mean?"

"You know…"

"Do I?"

He swung round, eyes blazing, almost feral. "Settle down! Stop dreaming! Have children! For God's sake, Eslin, you know what you have to do!"

He was embarrassed, but he reflected the mood of the refuge. Eslin was sixteen, but she had felt the growing pressure, the expectation from the majority. When it came to sex with Lars, she had insisted on protection and, with the condoms now in short supply, she had been careful with her cycle. It was like some bad movie quoting ancient scripture: 'You will repopulate the earth… Go forth and multiply.' At one level she could understand it, here in their tiny tribe, isolated from any hope except their own. It was, moreover, essentially Scandinavian, Viking even, this impervious, dogged self-reliance, clinging to the rocky fjords to eke out an existence. She hated it, even though she knew, deep down, that she was made from the same stuff.

He was still glaring and she glared back, refusing to back down until he flushed, actually flushed and couldn't speak, so she barked, "Fuck you," just to finish things off.

IYE 13

Eslin hauled the bows of the small cutter another metre up the shingle. The keel was shallow enough that Eslin could get the boat onto most shores without either damage or trouble getting off again. She hammered in two tethering spikes, allowing enough give in the ropes, then picked her way up the slick pebbles beyond the seaweed-green tidemark. There she sat down to dry her feet, tingling from the cold water, and put socks and boots back on. She was alone, in defiance of Council rules, but unrepentant. She had sailed to a nearby island to explore – before Echrexar, this had been a high ridge on Spitsbergen, but the rising seas had inundated the peninsular.

Looking back at the cutter, she smiled. Sails had been neatly furled and secured. The rocky bay was calm and protected. She had navigated in *The Hope* from the new quayside at Svalbard across four kilometres of sea and, having done the trip solo, she could call herself an accomplished sailor now. Lars would probably call her a fool, and her mother would disapprove. What matter? She had the world to explore and nothing would stop her.

Boots on and tied, Eslin strode up the rocky tumble of folds and crevices that brought her to the highest point of the island. Fitful sunlight played across the slopes. The browns, citron greens and reds of algae and mosses painted the world around her in the vibrancy of spring. Some fifty metres away two grey and white arctic skuas rose from their perch on a flat outcrop and flew downwind, alighting once more to scrutinize this stranger in their domain, black caps bobbing in agitation. Eslin clambered the last tumble of broken rocks and gravel to stand on the flat eggshell-smooth pinnacle the skuas had abandoned. Exposed now, the wind tugged at her, fitful but persistent. She smiled again, turning her face to the gusts, her shoulder-length auburn hair streaming and twisting across her cheeks. A trembling excitement filled her: she was free. The rules and rigidity of the refuge were gone, for a time. Even the taste of the wind had a warmth about it, a promise of soft, healing rain and rebirth. Eslin thrilled to the *potential* in the world. And it was here, away from Svalbard, away from the small ambitions of her community.

Hand to her temple, she held back the unruly flicking of her hair across her eyes. There, east across a thousand kilometres of the bronze and silver swell of the ocean, was the mainland. What possibilities might there be? Was it all gone? Had the gigantic firestorms and earthquakes obliterated everything? Had the survivors starved? Or were there small populations of hardy folk with stored technology and knowledge of science rebuilding, making their mark on the world again? After all, the signs of returning life were everywhere: the skuas, black sea kelp, smaller fish, some in abundant shoals glimpsed under the surge of the eternal ocean. Fishing, indeed, was fast becoming the dominant economic activity of Svalbard. Eslin lifted her face to the scudding strips of dirty cloud slashing wide slate-grey cuts across the deep blue of the bruised sky. This felt like a beginning, an almost religious moment of truth, ineffable but profound. Destiny…

Eslin laughed, a barking snort of sardonic self-mocking humour. *Discipline*, her father would have said. *Science, facts and logic.*

She turned, intending to step down from the outcrop and go further across the island, but her explosive laugh and perhaps her sudden movement startled a nesting skua, hidden in the tundra below the outcrop. With a defiant screech it flew straight at her head. Instinctively, Eslin ducked, flinging up a hand. In that instant she lost her footing, her right boot meeting space where she had expected firm rock. She fell, the backpack swinging her weight sideways and back. There was a moment of abrupt physical shock as her head took a glancing blow from the edge of the outcrop, then numbing pain when her left arm struck hard against sandstone in the tumbling drop two metres onto the scree below.

Dazed, she groaned but did not move. Something was very wrong. Her arm was under her but the feeling was unnatural and her first attempt to shift her weight detonated an explosion of pain. A sprain, she thought, and at once dismissed this as wild optimism. It was broken. A wave of fear made her thoughts race: she was alone, no one knew where she had gone; there was no way to track her and, she realized with horror, it would be nigh on impossible to handle the cutter. Moreover, if she could not get off the shingle in the next few hours, the rising tide might rip *The Hope* from its mooring spikes. She had been a fool, overconfident and arrogant. Dismissing Council rules was folly. In that moment, her dearest wish was to be surrounded by the comradeship and support of her community. Tears pricked hot in her eyes. Panic threatened to rise unchecked.

And then something changed. She mastered herself, denying the growing terror a foothold. Here were echoes of Echrexar's impact – the violent horror of the assault, depersonalized and utterly random, and then her parents' rehearsal of the facts, the discipline of science and calm understanding of what it meant and how to survive. Despite the gathering pain, she managed to think clearly. Her pack held rations for a day – easily that could be stretched to three. Her canteen was full, two litres of water, so two to three days at best. But there was also standing water in gullies, even if it was brackish.

An unexpected calm came over her. Her body felt odd, like a quiet vibration coursed through her blood vessels. The pain in her arm had subsided too, so she levered herself off her shoulder, using her knee, and managed to sit upright, backpack wedged behind her against the base of the outcrop. She had expected more pain, but had no point of reference to judge. Hesitantly she examined her left arm and saw the horrible angle of her forearm under the tough green nylon coat. It looked like she had two elbows. A fracture, possibly ulna and radius. Very nasty. Was there blood? She couldn't tell, so carefully unzipped the wrist cuff and pushed up the sleeves of coat and shirt. No blood. That was good, she decided: no bleeding to weaken her and no infection if the skin was not broken. Should she reset the bones? She knew that rapid action was important in a dislocation of the shoulder. It had happened to a young man recently, and the medic had expertly manipulated the shoulder back into the socket. Speed had been critical: leave it too long and the damage would be worse. As she stared at the weird shape of her arm, thinking all the while about a rising tide and the difficulties of refloating *The Hope*, she came to a decision. Gently, her fingers probing the swelling around the break, she began to straighten the arm bones, wincing as she felt the clicking and grinding. Heat and perspiration broke out on her body, but the pain was surprisingly manageable. Eventually, her arm was straight and she fashioned a sling to immobilize it across her chest by pushing her fingers under the right strap of her backpack. She really needed a short splint, but nothing was to hand. Now, to stand up…

She struggled to her knees, then drew herself upright. Her entire arm throbbed, but in a remote way, and the odd vibrating rush through her body seemed to be stronger now, making her more alert and filled with energy. Step by cautious step, she eased her way round the outcrop, right arm against the sandstone to steady herself on the loose scree underfoot, until she reached the tundra on the leeside. The skua was perched a few metres away, protesting loudly and flapping. But, this time, Eslin was unmoved.

"Piss off," she grated. And the bird took flight.

Getting *The Hope* off was difficult, but she managed it. Even raising the mainsail was fairly straightforward, as was cruising directly back across the bay. Tacking, however, was painful. With only her right arm serviceable, she had to scramble between tiller and mainsheet as she came about, losing way until she braced the sail and it tautened in the stiff wind. Back at the Svalbard quay, a rough sandstone construction built some forty metres out into the bay, she could see a number of people watching her come in. One of them was Lars.

"Oh, shit," she muttered: a welcoming committee.

They helped her tie up as she came alongside. Lars was first to speak: "Where have you been?" Like he was her father…

She elected to play nonchalant. "Mapping the islands offshore…"

She climbed onto the quay and the three young men stared at her in what seemed to be shock. It made no sense, the weird overreaction. She jerked her chin at her arm, held close to her chest and fingers still tucked into the backpack. "I think I broke it…"

But they were not looking at her arm.

"Your eyes, Eslin!" Lars exclaimed.

She regarded him with incomprehension. "What?"

"Your eyes – what happened to your eyes?"

She was starting to get annoyed, imagining that this was their idea of a wind-up, some kind of cheap payback for going off alone… Or having a mind of her own.

"Fuck off, Lars," she snapped, and took a step towards the road up to the refuge.

Peter, one of the other youths, put a gentle hand on her shoulder, careful to avoid her injury. "Eslin, wait. It's true," he said. "Your eyes – they're weird. They're bright yellow…"

Later, when the medic had examined her, things got even more weird.

"Eslin," Dr Johansen announced, standing before her with a deep frown and lips pursed behind his beard. "The good news is that the yellow in your eyes is fading. It's a biochemical reaction from a build-up of bilirubin in your bloodstream. Bit like jaundice – although I've never seen the effect so bright yellow before. Quite startling."

He quirked his lips in a half smile.

Unamused, Eslin glowered at him: "I have jaundice?"

Johansen's smile vanished. "Not exactly."

"But the broken arm triggered something like jaundice?"

"Not really."

Eslin's glower deepened.

Johansen pressed on before she could snap at him. Her reputation for impatience was widely known. "Your NCR treatment when you were little promotes rapid healing. We don't understand it fully, I don't have the background to explain it properly, and I can't study it because the detailed research isn't on our database. Also, we've never seen a serious injury in Svalbard from…uh…someone like you… Well, you."

"Hmph."

"In addition," he went on, gesturing at her now splinted arm, "the fact that you managed to straighten that break without passing out is extraordinary. Also, the two fractures and the trauma around them should be much worse. I would guess that when you straightened the breaks, the nano-tech in you worked rapidly to start the healing. The speed is… well…amazing, but it will undoubtedly take time to heal completely. I hypothesize that the NCR is 'programmed' to flood the damaged area, fixing trauma directly and accelerating natural healing – which goes into overdrive, as it were. The bilirubin build-up is a side-effect, but incredibly fast."

"I look like a damned cat," Eslin complained, thinking that it was yet another thing to mark her out as different, or difficult, and therefore someone who needed to be controlled.

Johansen laughed. "It will be gone in a few days."

And it was.

IYE 15

Eslin was now twenty, and cut an isolated figure in the Svalbard community. She was respected for her work around the island, mapping the new geography and confirming the slow drop in sea level as the skies cleared and some of the northern ice returned each winter. She had initiated a boat-building programme, using a mix of materials, including driftwood, which had become more plentiful, signalling a gradual recovery of forests on the mainland. Unexpectedly, for years after the impacts, old shipping containers washed up on the shore, their submerged carcases, under the mass of barnacles and weed, battered into distorted shapes. Their contents were mostly long gone, although a cargo of steel-belted radial tyres was once recovered, the rubber a welcome substitute for repairing and making boots. The steel containers made strong hulls and, at twelve metres in length, supplied a lot of material. All around Svalbard, the ocean was vomiting up the detritus of human civilization killed off in a matter of hours. The citizens of the community were fishing folk and farmers but, in truth, scavengers first and foremost. Melted plastic, the most plentiful of flotsam, was largely ignored or, where it accumulated in the coves and threatened sea life, collected and buried inland.

Lars, revelling in his dream of farming, had married, moved into a new stone house on the slopes near the refuge and was now a father of twins. Eslin was relieved, if truth be told. It spared her his grimaces and crestfallen disapproval. Anyway, he was busy, dawn until dusk. Agriculture was not a simple challenge on Spitsbergen, or Svalbard island as most now called it, even with the much higher average temperatures. Eslin barely saw him. And her gaze was fixed beyond the community: she and a small crew had visited all the Svalbard archipelago, mapping carefully, researching the animal populations and how the flora was recovering. Chiefly they observed and recorded the range of fish stocks, since the survival of the community depended on it. Cod and other small species were recovering fast. Larger fish were an unusual sight.

That same year, Council agreed an expedition to the mainland. Eslin, long an enthusiast, was permitted to go: she was now the most proficient navigator and sailor, so her presence was essential. The decision to make the journey had not been without controversy. Ten men and women, even in a large cutter, were at considerable risk on a 1,000-kilometre trip in Arctic seas, and the community, for the greater part, was averse to undertakings that were not pragmatic and aimed at securing food or security. A few voices, Eslin's most vehemently, urged an expedition to try to make contact with surviving communities on the mainland, or at the very least to find out what might be left of their old world. More objected, citing the prospect of toxicity and poisons still remaining on the mainland, either from acid rain or ruptured nuclear power plants and buried weapons. Eslin had learned to understand people's underlying motivations and to persuade them to a course of action that, in a roundabout way, might satisfy them: Tromso, northernmost city of Norway, she argued, might still be standing, could offer shelter, possibly a foothold for a new community, to assure that the Svalbard people would endure. Council reluctantly approved the expedition.

Through the clearing fog off the mainland, Eslin could see the snowy peaks of the mountains around the fjords. The journey had taken six days, largely uneventful, although remarkable to the crew aboard for its duration: no one had sailed out of sight of land since arriving at Svalbard fifteen years ago. Even having missed their destination by twenty kilometres, and needing to hug the coast down from the north, making landfall was exhilarating. They embraced each other and even Eslin, little given to sentimentality, celebrated with her fellows. The fog lifted, just enough.

"There's the bridge!" cried out one of her fellow crew, Aneta. She had elected to come on this trip because she was a one-time resident of Tromso and, ten years older than Eslin, had been fifteen when she left.

More excitement gripped the crew. The fog cleared a little more and the cutter, *The Penguin*, glided closer on a calm silvery sea, while the jutting superstructure of the Tromso bridge revealed itself as a single black span, standing on broken concrete stumps, the whole like severed fingers clutching at the heights on Tromso island. It had burned and the rest was gone, reduced by wave and earthquake and fire. The city was ruin, a tumble of moth-grey mounds and spruce trees growing in oddly neat lime-green stands, intersected by the gaps of what had been roads. Most bizarre of all, large swathes of rhododendron were in flower on the higher ground, dark pinks and purple decorating the land like a floral tablecloth. Along the new higher shoreline hulked the inevitable broken shipping containers, a couple stranded far above the tidemark like the teeth of the giant that had consumed Tromso. Twisted, rusting cargo ships and half a dozen smaller vessels littered the bay and, in their midst, twenty metres offshore, the towering bows of a trawler, vertical in the swell of ocean as if it had been dropped stern-first from the sky. The blackened road bridge, reaching perhaps sixty metres into the straits, towered over it all and commanded *The Penguin* crew's attention. The mood was suddenly subdued. Desolate reality had crushed even the most prosaic of dreams.

Bendt, one of the older crewmen, gave voice to all their thoughts: "And Tromso was not hit that hard."

Silence answered him. Eslin had the deepest knowledge of planetary geology and Echrexar's impact, but she was as reluctant as the others to smother hope.

Per Landvik, Council's designated leader of this expedition, was up near the bows. He looked straight at all of them in a single sweeping glance. Sunlight was filtering through the last candyfloss-pink and white of the fog. His face was lit by the sun and framed by the dark timbers of *The Penguin*. The cutter was not a large vessel, but all ten of her crew were on deck and they were all looking at him, standing in the prow, one hand on the gunwale. He was a sceptical, down-to-earth sort, calm and revelling in his impartiality when disagreements aboard needed resolving. Eslin frowned, suddenly aware that the foreshore wreckage was a vivid symbol of catastrophe for the crew rather than a signal for hope. After all, she had been vociferous in her arguments that this expedition would help the community to get a foothold on the mainland – but it was a deeply shocking reality check.

As usual, Per would tell the fucking truth as he saw it. She could see him mentally rehearsing his speech and, in a flash of understanding, she realized he had been ready for this, ready to use the disappointment of finding the old world utterly obliterated to undermine any further ventures to find other refuges. Council was foursquare behind him. Who could blame them? The world was dangerous. Even this venture across the seas, once so unremarkable and routine, was a real risk to the lives of everyone aboard. With people desperate for hope and guilty about surviving in equal measure, it seemed right to be cautious.

But Eslin could not accept it. She strained against the mood of prudence and isolation and the way her fellow citizens preferred to avoid risk. Bitterly she watched Per. He gave the bay another slow examination, pulled at his beard as if assessing the weight of his words, then spoke: "Yes, that's true. Pacific Rim and southern oceans, coastal Africa and the whole of the Atlantic seaboard: bad, very bad. If there was even one hit to landmass, the firestorms would have been…terrible."

And there had probably been two land impacts, Eslin thought, because of the significant deposit of black regolith sediment *everywhere*.

Per was still talking. "We were lucky—" He shrugged in half apology for using that word, and he was right: the ocean strikes threw up an enormous volume of water vapour, which eventually washed out the dry deposition. It could have been much worse: an impact winter of decades not the greenhouse in-between time of eleven years. He swept his arm out to encompass the fractured stain of the city around them on the two shorelines of the straits. "You know coastal cities were inundated. No one survived that. Tromso was submerged in the first days by the fringes of the tsunamis."

"So there's no hope," said one of the crew.

Per turned his head and favoured them all with a serious look. "The old world is gone…"

"Of course, there's hope!" Eslin, unable to restrain herself, interjected. "Inland or high up. Any protected refuges or even deep caves with sufficient food supplies. How the fuck do you think *we* survived?"

Per turned his back on the broken sepulchre that had been Tromso. He was facing Eslin now, looking at her down the length of the cutter where she stood with one hand on the wheel. If he was Council's formal leader on this venture, she was its emblematic heart: the motive force.

"I think, Eslin," he responded in that maddeningly tolerant manner, "that our chances of finding anyone or anything left from before are minimal and not worth the effort or danger of straying too far…"

Eslin grunted, tossing her head. "We *know* small populations like ours will have survived. Refuges, deep military bunkers, that sort of thing. We had radio contact from at least three communities in central Europe and one in Britain."

"Then we need to go south," Aneta suggested, fired suddenly by hope. Of all the crew, she was the most closely aligned with Eslin. "Oslo, or Denmark or France–"

"Not on this expedition," cut in Per. The latitude granted by Council had been tight: explore Tromso and immediate surroundings, no more. "And, as you know all too well, the last of those radio transmissions ceased six years ago."

Eslin squeezed down on her anger. It would never work with Per. "Aneta's right," she said levelly. "If they survived nine years, then they'll have survived the last six."

"I don't deny it. But you seem to be proposing a madcap expedition when we've not even set foot on the mainland."

There was no easy retort to that, so Eslin stayed quiet. *The Penguin* cut through the waves and a steady northerly swelled the mainsail to drive them to landfall in Tromso.

Later, standing in the warm sun on a promontory overlooking the straits, Per moved up beside Eslin. They shared the viewing point with a jumble of burned out, corroded cars, six of them tossed together like a haphazard monument to Echrexar's raging hurricanes; no tyres, no trace of paint, just the warped fiction of what they were supposed to be. Soon they would be nothing, reduced by rust, salt and weed. The mood of the crew was more sombre yet. Aneta had come across human bones, stark white in the dark soil. In a silent circle, the ten of them had stood in contemplation, and most of them wept openly.

Sunlight sparkled off the straits below, and the scene might have been idyllic were it not for the blackened skeleton of the bridge looming over it all, and the shattered heaps of overgrown buildings that lay tumbled and half-submerged down below the water's edge.

"You were right to persuade Council to do this, Eslin," Per started. "We needed to know what's out here and we needed to extend our vision."

It was a peace offering.

Eslin nodded, but a part of her drew back, waiting for the other shoe to drop.

Per put a hand on her shoulder, overly familiar with his authority and his age. He was forty and he probably thought it was sensitive, supportive. "We could build here, eventually. The farming would be easier, that's for sure. And there's plenty to salvage, if we bring the right tools – the wrecks, the container steel, maybe some engine parts and pumps, even some of the buildings. Might even be fuel, if it didn't burn. And it's a good anchorage for a fishing fleet."

Eslin decided to call his bluff. She turned, forcing his hand from her shoulder. "Yes," she acknowledged, "and we could organize expeditions from here."

He frowned, hurt probably that she was unyielding to his concessions. After a moment he said, "What is it you want to find, Eslin? What is it we need to be doing that we aren't already?"

"Making contact –" she began but he cut her off.

"You keep on about this. But it's impractical. Where would we head? Would we walk? We have no transport. We could sail, but then what? The coastal cities were drowned."

"Straight up the rivers, like our Viking forbears," Eslin countered.

"Then walk."

"But why?"

She gave him a hard stare.

He was not going to relent.

"Really, why? Let's say we make contact with another refuge. In France, maybe. The distances are huge. What then? How can we cooperate?"

"We can't cooperate," she argued, "if you just want to farm or fish. But for God's sake have some ambition, Per. The knowledge of the entire world could have been preserved in communities all over the planet. We specialize in agriculture, and we have the seed vaults. Just sharing the seeds would be a massive boost to other people and could transform food production for populations everywhere. Other refuges will have technology – or at least the records to help us accelerate learning and rebuilding. To share knowledge and rebuild is why we need to explore and make contact."

He looked at her for a long time; a long, level gaze. Then, reaching a decision, he shook his head. "Too many 'ifs' and 'coulds', Eslin. You have huge faith in a lost world. All that knowledge didn't help us when Echrexar hit. We're a tiny community on the edge of survival—"

"That's my point exactly—"

"Let me finish. We need to focus on *us* first, Svalbard first, then gradually we can move out into the world. Here, for instance." He gestured to the hills. "But you will persuade no one, Eslin, to go against the community. We pull together. You should too."

The expedition, despite its emotional downs, was hailed a triumph when they returned to Svalbard. It had united the community in a dramatic success, made all the greater by the genuine peril of crossing the ocean. Per got the plaudits, but of course deflected it to the crew in a way that, if anything, enhanced his leadership stock. He had been a young, aspiring politician in that previous life that no one talked about now, and he knew his present-day constituency. Even Eslin received credit for her navigation. She was disappointed, though. In contrast to everyone else, the success of the expedition made her feel that they had not been ambitious enough. Their Viking ancestors, in ancient vessels not much larger than

The Penguin, had crossed to North America and the Mediterranean, for God's sake. And worse, much worse, was the sense that this expedition had been more like a chapter ending than beginning. Somehow, it defined not the possibilities but the limits of Svalbard's aspirations.

IYE 20

A month after her twenty-fifth birthday, Eslin was summoned to Council. To no one's surprise, Per Landvik's ambition had been rewarded. He was the chair, the top man in Svalbard. Beside him in a half-circle sat the five men and six women who governed with him. And around all of them was the new Svalbard Town Hall, built in carved sandstone with tall, narrow windows, shuttered in black repurposed steel against the worst of storms, an edifice to defy the perils that the world might visit upon the community here at the edge of the Arctic. By design it was imposing, whilst uncomfortably democratic, set aside for community events and Christian church services, but increasingly the governing of the island and, at a remove, the small expeditionary enclave across the sea in Tromso. The curving table, carved as three sections from seasoned driftwood, was almost too heavy to move, so there it remained, a mute obstacle to the communal activities of the folk of Svalbard. Without irony, it amused Eslin to wonder that this room was usually called the 'commons'.

She was directed to sit, facing the half-circle of Council members. Dressed in their most formal clothes – ties and jackets for the men; high collars and jackets for the women – they looked rather serious, Eslin decided, and, as they regarded her, she wondered what *they* saw: a young woman, auburn hair flowing in ringlets where it touched her shoulders and framing a sun-tanned, freckled face of blunt, pokerfaced detachment, made pretty only if she deigned to smile. As she took the indicated seat, folding one long leg over the other, black and white twill trousers tucked into her heavy boots, she reflected that they would interpret this as rather casual; but they knew her well enough and it would go unremarked. It was her eyes, pale hazel eyes with a flash of golden fire deep behind them, that threw people. Her balanced insouciance was made a lie by those lambent eyes. She had seen folk flinch when she glanced sharply at them. Hers was a gaze of anarchic challenge; a promise – almost – of violence that nowadays she did not care to soften.

"Eslin Kristiansen," Per intoned. It was the usual opening in Council, but he said it in a way that was ominous, even to someone as fearless as Eslin.

"Chair, Council members," she immediately responded, matching his formality with a sardonic smile and looking directly at each of them in turn.

If it irritated him, he was too composed to show it.

"Thank you for attending," he continued. "Council must convey to you a matter of some importance, a matter of *duty*."

Eslin liked the direction of this less and less. The faces that looked back at her were uncompromising. It was as if she had committed a crime. She could not, even in her quick mind, fathom what this was all about. And that word 'duty' was heavy with portent: it was a word that had grown in weight over the years in this community; a word to use with children to insist on good behaviour; an encouragement to the fainthearted and the lazy, and an insult or accusation to those who flirted with disobedience to Svalbard's rules, codified and unwritten alike.

"Eslin," Per said, leaning forward on his elbows. "You are twenty-five—"

"*There was a star danced,*" Eslin cut in with a quirk of her mouth, "*and under that was I born…*"

Per did not even blink. They had heard Shakespeare from her often enough. "You have not married," he went on evenly, "and you have no children yet."

Eslin curled her lip, but held tight a cutting remark. This was a well-trodden path. It bored her. But there was undoubtedly more to come.

"Your mother, Asta," Per went on in the same flat, high-handed tone, "confided something to Council last week. We need to tell you of this. And she says you do not know…"

A flush of heat suffused Eslin's face. Suspicion and understanding unfolded at the same time as feelings of embarrassment, shock and betrayal fought to gain expression. Her mother had never been close to her and the distance between them had grown to an unbridgeable chasm after Anders' suicide – but to have kept something from her! Asta had spoken to these people first? had betrayed her, had exposed her to this… this inquisition? She uncrossed her legs, sat straight and square, and glared at her tormentors. For the first time in a long time she was on the defensive, bereft of words. Wounded dignity threatened to break open the iron crucible of her fear and fury.

Per had softened his expression, as if he saw all too well her discomfort. That made it worse.

"We do not mean to embarrass you, Eslin," he apologized. "But Asta asked us to tell you this…thing. And it is a matter of duty – for you. That is why Council sits."

Finally Eslin found her voice: "Then spit it out." Hearing herself, she sounded hurt and petulant, like a teenager, and hated herself for it.

Now there were murmurs and a disapproving shake of the head from one councillor. Per raised a hand, emollient. "Of course," he conceded, but made it sound like pity. Eslin wanted to run, to get out of this place. It was a violation, dressed up in the pomp and authority of Council. "Eslin," Per explained, "you are different because of your medical condition…the procedure. We know that it protects you from disease, illness and injury. We know, and you know, that it will, apparently, enable long life. How long, no one can say. The procedure was new and now the science is lost."

"So everyone keeps telling me," Eslin retorted. Embarrassed fury was quickly turning to quivering impatience, a flood of rash impulses wrenching her control. With an effort she suppressed it and declared, "This 'long life' thing is mere theory – no, less than theory, because there is no body of evidence to justify it. And if I'm the only one like this on Svalbard, we can all call it true when I'm a hundred and fifty…"

Her sardonic humour did not land well. She realized too late that it sounded like a boast. *Well, fuck you*, she thought, and the stern, closed faces around the table closed up even more.

Per raised both hands, palm outwards in a gesture that seemed to say her point was moot. Then he replied softly, "There is one thing Asta did not tell you, but she says it was a stipulation of the treatment. It was designed into the nanotechnology of cell replication. The scientists who built this technology believed that with long life there should be a counterbalancing limit. A limit on reproduction."

That word hung in the air. Then Per continued, in a rush to get it said: "Asta tells us that at age thirty you will no longer be able to conceive. The nanotech will…trigger a switch. You will be barren, sterile. I'm sorry for my bluntness."

And there it was, the matter of 'duty'. A thousand angry protestations and complaints pressed for instant utterance but not a single word could she speak. She glowered at the pale faces before her, red heat suffusing her cheeks. She realized that Per was speaking, his tone still carefully officious, secure behind Council governance.

"No one disputes your great contributions to our community, nor your courage in your work around our island and our new settlement at Tromso but, more than anything, Eslin Kristiansen, your duty to Svalbard is the duty of bearing children. We fail this generation and our future if we do not fulfil this most fundamental and sacred of duties. It is…" – and Per's voice quavered momentarily with the grief and guilt that was the lot of all Svalbard's survivors – "an obligation to the lost generations of the world. We owe them. In this matter, it is specifically important for you to do this soon. You have, perhaps, as Dr Johansen and your mother have attested, five years, but it may be less. Council is unanimous in this determination."

Per fell silent. The hall was silent. There was only the mad seething of screaming voices in her head, raging at everything and nothing. With shocking abruptness she realized how separate she was from these people, like an embarrassing secret always in public view, different, awkward and disruptive. The promise of extended life had no name that they would dare use, so they called it 'her condition' as if it were a threat or a curse that might bring bad luck. Her mere existence reminded them of a world that was gone and that they would rather forget, confining it to a ghostly, ancestral mythology to assuage their own guilt, the guilt of having been randomly chosen, alone among the *billions* of humanity, to survive. With growing clarity Eslin realized they must either enslave her, make her one of them, uniform and obedient or, like a scapegoat, drive her from the community to carry away their collective guilt. In that instant she could see the shocking lucid truth of the path of her life – different, separate, privileged and cursed. *Gilgamesh.* Two-thirds god and cursed by the gods.

The taut crucible of pain and fury deep inside her did not break. Eslin would not speak. Instead she rose to her feet, turned her accusing eyes on them all, one by one, and then strode from the hall.

***

Later that afternoon, as the sun westered towards the molten copper of the vast ocean horizon, Eslin stood silent at the far end of the stone mole that sheltered Svalbard harbour. She had helped build this, stone by stone in a concerted communal effort characteristic of Svalbard's discipline and determination. Moored up against the stone wharf, rested two dozen vessels of wood and remodelled steel, large and small, fishing smacks, barges, sloops and cutters. Among them was *The Hope*, the vessel she regarded as her own, though distinctions of ownership were complex and mostly frowned on by her fellow citizens. The dog days of summer had brought a calm to the ocean, broken only by the white horses of wind-blown spume speckling the waters as far as her eye could reach. Near at hand, the breakers made their grumbling complaint against the stone blocks, crashing and surging along the length of this latest tiny human incursion into the Arctic ocean. A clot of Svalbard's citizens worked the dock, unloading the latest catch with shouts and good humour.

Eslin leaned on the stone sea wall of the mole, arms folded under her chin. She gazed east, towards Tromso and the distant, invisible mainland and, though a myriad emotions and thoughts might have crowded her consciousness, she was singular in her objective. The immense curve of the earth under pallid sunlight seemed invested with melancholy and a sad, sweet mood was on her, like regret at the passing of something significant and valuable. With a lift of her head she put it behind her, looked up into the high ivory cirrus above and then smiled. The air tasted of salt and the clean tang of ozone, ever-present since Echrexar. She smiled again and a thrill of fear and excitement coursed through her body.

She was ready. *The Hope* rode her moorings rhythmically in the placid bay, provisioned, prepared as always for voyage and expedition. She had stowed additional food aboard and a large canvas carry-all, heavy with the most important of her few books and possessions. Her course would take her to Tromso, where her arrival would excite no suspicions, and then... And then... She did not know. The vast earth awaited, with all of its secrets and unknown promises, thrilling, terrifying and immanent. She turned away to step down onto the aft deck, released the moorings, raised the jib and guided *The Hope* away from Svalbard.

CHAPTER 1

The stars fell.
The oceans boiled and flooded the land.
A darkness descended.
ECHREXA/ murdered our dreams.
Ancient inscription carved in bas relief, to the height of two men, high on the granite cliff face of the Chisuan Gorge.

1,890 Years After Echrexar

The hour before dawn. Time for the killing to begin. There was a campfire, yellow and brittle in the wet gloom. And for some inexplicable reason it had sparked a flashback and she was Eslin again, a name she had not used in a time too long to measure. So much time…*lifetimes.*

Gilgamesh.

Gilgamesh. You will be like Gilgamesh, two-thirds god.

She could hear her mother's voice speaking those words. It was remote, across the distance of the ages, but it was still that tone of disapproval and unreasonable hope.

Have I done and been what you dreamed?

Her mother had no answer but Eslin did. The misfortune of being a god, or nearly a god, was the ennui, the awful black despair. The gift of immortality was itself a curse of futility and blighted dreams. Her body and brain might be those of young woman, but the harsh wisdom of centuries told her she should be dead and what's the fucking point of it all?

Maybe it wasn't the fire triggering all this. Maybe it was the killing. Skava did not flinch from what was needed, even if the woman who had been Eslin shifted uncomfortably on the cold, damp ground, with a thousand ugly memories pouring in on her like a thousand spectral faces and a thousand thousand insistent screams.

After a febrile blaze of concentrated effort, the moment was gone, and Eslin was gone, and Skava was here and the world was simple and quiet and filled with purpose.

A whisper at her side. Maki had joined her, lying flat, silent and invisible in the night. "Boss," he murmured, barely more than a sigh, "all set."

She said nothing. She looked at the fire and the silhouette of the sentry. He wore chainmail and a helmet that winked polished firelight onto an ornate halberd grounded in one hand, more ceremonial than practical, the sort of thing the bodyguard of a lord would carry to impress. The distance was perhaps forty strides. Good for a crossbow. But they could not use a crossbow. They had to use a bow so that the arrows from this particular slaughter were the same as Shur-Shur nomads might have used. A stratagem that would work, if everyone did his job. But a bow required a bowstring, which did not like the rain, being prone to stretch and misbehave – a small complication she had planned for. Maki had the string in a pouch and would have to attach fast in the darkness. His credentials on that score were impeccable, even in this rain-veiled night. The rain made it even darker, and the darkest hour is just before the dawn and all that…when everyone is at a low ebb. The best time for an ambush. The best time for killing. What was the murder of a lord of the Realm? Regicide? An imperial assassination near as makes no difference.

A spark leapt outwards from the fire, a brief comet spat in an arc of fluorescent bile to die in the mud. Skava curled her lip. It was like a cosmic signal, if you believed in that sort of thing. So she nudged Maki with her elbow and he rose smoothly to one knee, bending the bow against his boot and looping the string onto the limb ends – all by feel alone. The bow swung up and level in a fluid movement, arrow nocked. A snap, like a knuckle crack, and the sentry spasmed and twisted, falling backwards behind the fire.

"Go!" Skava yelled.

And the killing began.

The troops emerged from all sides, moving very fast, no bows now, just swords and foot-long poniards, rippling amber and red in the firelight, bare steel stabbing bare flesh. Men waking from sleep, without armour, are so much meat to cut and hew. But they shouted defiance and some few made a defence of it. Near the fire, two silhouettes were hacking at something on the ground, the downed sentry or, it might be, Lord Shenri's own spymaster, the bastard, making a run for the horses. Blades high, then falling, winking winking gold and red-black, then high again and falling. Someone yelled loud and clear above the screams and the sickly wet hacking of blades, "Strath! Strath! To me!" Lord Shenri himself perhaps. Or his guardleader. Skava could not tell. She crouched, sword point down, alert and watching it all unfold, the bloody fulfilment of a plan – her plan. She had not wanted this slaughter. It was too blatant, too brazen, too *theatrical*. It required that she step out of the shadows to accomplish it like an audacious shout for unwelcome scrutiny. It was not her way. But it was her plan.

A knot of defenders had formed, most with shields tight-packed and overlapping, a last redoubt of bleeding muscle and hammering hearts. Surrounded. Fighting. But this was the critical time. The plan mattered. How they died mattered. These soldiers wanted to kill and die with honour, but honour was *not* the plan.

Skava bellowed, "Hold!" She used a voice that rang with male authority, pitched just so.

There was a shuffling; men stepped back. Stillness. Except for the knot of defenders, the shields and weapons shifting nervously, shocked wide eyes jumping.

"You fuckers!" came a hoarse challenge, probably, Skava reckoned, from Kalan, Lord Shenri's troopmaster. A small, wiry fellow, a good man, a fine soldier and bodyguard. She knew all about him. Minutely. It always pays to know. That was why her plan would work.

"Where is your honour?" Kalan yelled again. And he spat. Credit to him: he had worked it out. He knew they had one option only – face to face, hand to hand, an honourable fight – and then in the melee maybe a couple of them could get Shenri to a horse and away. Yes, credit to him, the insult worked. Her own regular troops started to mutter, an ugly riposte; they wanted it, their blood was up, it was how they did things. Honour. But it was not the plan.

So she spoke again, quieter now, but loud enough to stop any stupidity: "Withdraw!" Then in the same breath: "Bows! Mark!"

Kalan screamed, an incredulous animal wail, "Where is your *honour?*"

Maki's bow twitched and snapped and another, from Yan, at a wider attack angle joined his, again and again, and the knot of men collapsed slowly, like a building knocked down in stages. The shields caught a couple of arrows, but Maki and Yan were Skava's assassins, the best in the business. It was over in heartbeats. The wall of shields became a pile of shields and bare heads and bloody flesh, a spear still gripped and pointing skywards and the shafts of the arrows dark splinters, all angles and tumbled shapes.

Miraculously Kalan, crouching low behind his shield, was unscathed. "Fight me, you fucking cowards! Face to face! Man to man!" he screamed; but to Skava's ears it was the shriek of the cornered animal that knows it is dead, the final howl of unspeakable denial. A shaft took Kalan from the side in the throat, probably into the spine, and his head tipped over and he sat, a bit like a frog, the shield perhaps propping his body upright as if he was too tired even to fall down. The camp was silent, except for one of the tents where flame had caught and the fabric snarled and spat in the drizzle like a reluctant golden chimaera.

That was the start of the killing. But it was unfinished.

"Make sure," Skava called out. This was a job for Maki and Yan. The regular soldiers would not do it. You might call it a mercy, that final cut to the neck and spinal cord and the bubbling gush of red blood, but the regulars saw no honour in it, so Skava hadn't even asked them.

Maki and Yan moved quietly through the camp, bending and grunting and counting corpses as they did so. Eighteen. And that included the spymaster – very satisfying, the only satisfying thing about this carnage. If it was eighteen, then the killing was finished. And the theatre could begin.

"Eighteen," came the call. Maki, making his way back to Skava past the campfire, and cleaning his long knife with a square of linen. Fastidious was Maki.

Riders had come up slowly into the quivering light from the flames. The mounts were nervous, impatiently high-stepping because of the coppery smell of blood and the tension in the men. First the killing and now the theatre, Skava thought, and a line from Macbeth came to her: *The instruments of darkness tell us truths.* An officer dismounted, throwing back his cape to draw a blade, squelching through the mud to the collapsed redoubt of arms and legs.

"Skava. Spymaster!" came his voice, matter-of-fact, searching her out. "We are secure?"

He had used her name. Fool. They did not use names, even surrounded as they were by corpses.

"Have a care with naming," she replied, her voice all sharp edges; then, in answer to his question: "Eighteen. All of 'em."

He found the corpse he wanted, pushed a body aside with his boot, then hacked at the neck. Skava smiled. The theatre was only half a triumph: the fucking sword got stuck, as they tend to when you're trying to remove a head. The officer jerked and twisted, freed his blade and had another go. *Jophan, you arrogant bastard of a noble,* she mocked him silently. *You wanted this slaughter, this piece of theatre. Cut the fucking head off!*

Success this time. Glorious.

He picked the grisly object up by its hair, tossed it towards the horses, making them turn on their haunches again. "The fate," Jophan announced, "of your enemies, my lord."

The Lord of Honam, of Clan Ouine, Skava's employer, was near invisible at the edge of the camp, a black outline of horse and rider, his own bodyguards to either side. There was no acknowledgement. He simply urged his mount forward to step over the sightless remains of Lord Shenri and out of the camp. In short order, Jophan and then all the regular troops were mounted and gone in his wake.

Skava sniffed. The stench of killing was invariant; a nauseating thick smell of sweet blood and spilled intestines and shit. Yan joined Skava and Maki. Yan was young, twenty-three maybe, but dependable. Also, he didn't talk too much, which Skava liked. And he loved horses, had a way with them which made up for Skava's contempt of the stupid creatures.

"Clean up," she muttered, with a glance to the eastern horizon, lighter now like dirty ivory.

Killing. Theatre. Art. And now time for her to add the final flourish on the canvas.

***

"Make sure."

The voice had transfixed trooper Adaim, lying broken and bleeding in the mud. It was wrong, reverberating with an immanence that seemed to suck attention towards it and swallow it whole. It was as if the loose veil of the in-between had been ripped and a god had stooped, primal and ageless, into the world with all the terrors of Echrexar trailing behind.

Two men had picked their way among the bodies. Adaim heard daggers hiss from scabbards. *Now I die…and in the in-between time.* The thought had hit him with rising panic. His soul would be lost, abandoned with his comrades and torn to shreds by Echrexar's iron dogs. The soldiers had bent down, hunching over the still, awkward shapes in Adaim's tumbled world. A groaning plea and a horrible gurgle and the wounded squirmed briefly in the mud, dispatched by thrust and cut. A boot had kicked hard at Adaim's back, but his nerveless body registered only a remote sensation, as if his eye alone were still alive. Then there was a blade – glinting poisonously – near enough to see the wicked serrated edge, pausing above his face in a moment that had prolonged this insane intimacy. Incredulous, he still understood what was coming. The blade dipped, sliced into his throat. Deflected perhaps by the fractured, segmented steel of his spaulders, it had met his collarbone and was withdrawn, searing him with yellow heat. So he had screamed his silent scream but never once closed his eye.

There had been the voice: "Skava! Spymaster! We are secure?"

And the response in a tone of cold authority, but with an edge of contempt that made a pitch that might have been a woman's: "Have a care with naming… Eighteen. All of 'em."

Me! Me! Can you not see me! Perhaps he was already dead and his soul was falling into the madness of the next world. Perhaps the god's iron dogs already clamped sharp fangs upon his terrified soul. Details had seemed important. He felt mud against his neck – a section of steel plate was bent up from his shoulder where it should not be – and one eye was covered and blind, by mud or blood he did not know. The other blinked away drops of rain, and around him he saw the camp as if on its side.

Adaim had watched, crumpled and motionless, his single eye darting with the fury of action that his motionless body could not offer. He remembered he cursed these enemies. *May the Shae eat thy souls!*

Then, as his own guilt threatened to overwhelm him, the words of a dream-spell had come, a terrible curse on himself: *Do not despoil my soul in witness of my failure! Tear out my eyes so I cannot see!*

But, as if the gods surely mocked him, in the instant the riders left the ruined camp, Adaim's eye had fixed on a pennon folded about the tip of a lance gripped in the mailed fist of the last horseman. Careless work, by a nervous soldier, probably done in the darkness before battle and not secured properly, a flap of linen fluttered with a momentary flare of clarity as twilight abruptly became dawn – red and gold! Through half-felt agony and numbness, Adaim's crushed body trembled and in his solitary eye there burned a new intensity.

Skava, Skava, Skava, he had repeated to himself, the name like another dream-spell, this one against Echrexar. And, as the red and gold of the lance flickered in the pale light and was gone, in the distance the bloated sun crawled through mist to meet his unwavering gaze.

***

The sun, spectral and attenuated by the veil of mist and thin grey cloud, had risen directly behind the pyramid of corpses. From Adaim's vantage, it seemed as if everything, including the sun, had bled white. The fires that had burned in the dawn twilight had died and now only wisps of smoke and steam curled, drifting across the bleak tumble of bodies, obscuring a twisted arm or coiling under a bare leg protruding from the mass of bodies packed together in mutual degradation. If there was the merest comfort, it was that the angle of the feeble sun limned the severed head of Lord Shenri and threw his disfigured face into dark anonymity. For this, Adaim was thankful: the heavy-lidded accusation of lifeless eyes would have driven him mad.

The three remaining attackers had gone. For a while, before the light grew, they had moved around the camp, in and out of tents and, it seemed to Adaim's enfeebled mind, had busied themselves carefully opening strongboxes and then moving corpses. It was so incomprehensibly mad that, unable to move, cheek pressed into the mud and with the crushing, half-numb pain that consumed his torso, he wondered whether this was indeed death. As a boy, at his parents' side, he had listened open-mouthed to the exarchs' sermons, imagining in his child's way the terrors of the afterlife were he to stray from the path of righteous obedience. *Perhaps this is it*, screamed his thoughts. *Trapped in the circumstances of your demise for eternity, surrounded by your failures and their terrible allegations.* There was a horrible, perfect symmetry to it. He had transgressed and the gods had punished him – or, worse, had left him to the torment of this grey, unchanging nowhere. Perhaps his offence had been pride: the arrogance of a peasant boy taken into the service of the great household of the Lord of Strath, escaping the anonymous, grinding life of the tenant farmers; of believing he had become more than he was, a boy who could dare to be tempted by his Lord's daughter and she a princess, as far above him as the sun above the mud. On one knee, he had bowed before Lord Shenri, had taken the oath and pledged his life, had felt a surge of devotion towards Strath and his comrades-in-arms that had never diminished. He had been proud. His parents, in their simple, smiling, devoted way, had been proud too. Young Adaim, tall, agile and handsome, admitted to be a man-at-arms in the lord's estate at Mamoba – and ahead of his fellows, even the older boys in the village. They had looked at him sideways, the boys, envious and, among the eldest teenagers, wondering at his luck that he should receive such gods-given fortune, whilst they turned back to their toil, and their futures were no more than the histories of their fathers.

Such fortune! Here he lay in this netherworld of grey and white, surrounded by the dead. Did the boys envy him now? Despite the pain, a pang of guilt stopped the relentless plunge of his thoughts. In four years he had learned more and travelled further than anyone in his village. Yes, he realized, those boys would trade their lives for four such years, even to lie in this place at the end, broken, bleeding, soon to be dead. There was comfort in that.

And then, of course, there was the Lady Che Keleu. This thought he feared more than any other. It was the fulcrum of his joy and his shame. She had chosen him, secretly. She had given herself to him, in secret. The passion and excitement burned within him, even now. But he had done nothing to stop what had happened. She was a princess and he was no one. His obligation was to his lord, and he had betrayed this trust twice, illicitly loving his daughter and failing in his duty to defend his lord's life. A good death was a blessing he ill deserved.

A voice whispered to him, calm, persuasive, urging him to compose himself and pray to the gods, in all their many forms, and Holy Eslo, defender of the Faith, for his life to drain quickly, to take him from this world, grateful for what he had been given… He closed his eye, but the prayers he offered were sluggish and his thoughts scattered like broken yellow glass. Something tugged at his attention, making him look at the perfect disc of the pale white sun. *Colour*, the thought came to him, *my world has no colour*. And the idea of colour seemed important, something out of reach but that must be remembered – like the cornflower blue blanket on which Che Keleu had knelt up near the high ravine. As if in tune with his thoughts, the sun brightened, amber through the mist, faded a little then strengthened once more. He could see blue sky, a wedge above the black mud and corpses – the limit of his vision.

What is it that I am trying to remember?

In a short time the mist burned away and the orange sun threw a golden haze across the wreckage of the camp.

And then: Skava. What did that name mean? Adaim's twitching eye could find no answers.

***

He remembered… Or perhaps he dreamed? Dreams were dangerous, but they were also truth.

The first time she touched him, he was holding the horses. She had stepped close to pat the piebald neck of her mount, and her bare arm, perhaps her breast, brushed against him. Adaim was startled, instantly fearing he had brought trouble down on himself. But then she looked at him, her gaze direct, and, despite himself, he looked back, then dropped his eyes – he was barely more than a peasant after all, not the son of an officer, not even the son of a soldier. The hammering of his heart told him more though: to be this close, to actually feel the touch of her skin…

"You are beautiful," she had said, her breath hot against his cheek, their bodies close, impossibly close, and an urgent stirring at his crotch.

That morning under clear blue skies – late spring, he recalled – he had been assigned to Che Keleu's small retinue: two handmaidens, both a few years older than their mistress, and Adaim himself younger even than that, the youngest soldier in Lord Shenri's household. The little party rode out, slowly, in a manner that would not be indecorous for a princess, to take the air in the hills around Lord Shenri's vast estate. It would be untrue to say that Trooper Adaim had not stolen glances at the princess in the years he had been in the household; she was beautiful, a lithe, graceful woman of nineteen, dark-haired, pale-eyed like all in the lineage of Strath. In the formal setting of the household, she seemed to glide rather than walk, the silks of her long dresses clean, straight lines against her body, demure and hardly revealing…except once when she turned, in company with her father in the gardens, and an incautious breeze smoothed the lilac material against her waist, outlining the swell of her breasts, the secret curve of her hip – a moment for Adaim of hot fascination and terrifying self-reproach.

His face aflame, he had locked his eyes upon the old red bricks of the garden walls, withdrawing into his accustomed anonymity as the invisible sentry, cursing himself and determined to believe his interest had been that of a servant fascinated by his betters – a distant relationship, governed by centuries of rigid hierarchy and profound observance of etiquette and all its forms. She was, to Adaim and any man like him, irredeemably out of reach. But he was unable to get the delicious image out of his mind.

"Bring me wildflowers."

She commanded her handmaidens with the easy authority of a noblewoman, and they were obedient, as true to their status as she to hers. The nearest flowers, Adaim realized, were some way distant down the side of the valley, near the ravine and the rushing peril of the high waterfall that they could still hear even in this secluded pasture. Through the broad stand of leaning whisper trees where Che Keleu, contemplative and still, knelt on a cornflower blue blanket, her handmaidens followed the trail, walking with purpose but not quickly, and certain to be gone at least a full turn of a water-clock. He stood, unmoving, beside the four horses, and watched the women make their way down the gentle, grassy slope beneath the trees and out of sight. Despite the command he tried to exert upon himself, his breath was shallow and his heart beat faster, his thoughts colliding with boiling images of nothing other than their recent encounters, her bold gaze and her hand on his cheek, the pulsing heat of her limbs close to his.

But she did not move and eventually, gradually, his body stilled in synchrony with the weight of puzzled disappointment. Around them the woodland was bathed in the dappled sunlight of late morning and a quiet had descended, the horses passive and drowsy, expecting in their assured way that no return trip was remotely imminent. Only the vine-larks warbled, soft, discreet, content. Even Adaim's disappointment passed, time and logic bringing grudging relief: after all, the consequences of anything further between them were too terrible to contemplate.

Then she spoke: "Come to me."

Her pale eyes were impossibly bright, her cheeks flushed. She guided his hand to her waist, to the opening of her fine silk dress, then trembling to her inner thigh. She kissed him and all restraint was lost. He moved his fingers, but gently, in obedience to her guiding hand, knowing he must bring her pleasure, and she drew him closer, moving her hips against his efforts, wet, urgent, demanding. Her rhythm was controlled, though she whimpered as her hand pressed his hand and she would not stop kissing him, feverishly, arm about his shoulders, fingers writhing in his cropped, peasant hair, trembling now and shuddering, and shuddering. Her back arched and she pulled away with a gasp, her knees together and his hand trapped between her thighs… He looked down at her. Her eyes were closed, lashes dark against the curve of cheeks, and for one guilty, astonishing instant he found himself free to stare at her face, to take in every detail, the red flush of her lips, the tiny droplet of moisture at the side of her mouth, the taut arc of the tendon down her neck. After some moments, as her gasping became a sigh, those eyes opened, as fixed and intent as an eagle's gaze. Of course, he looked away immediately, as stunned by what had just happened as anything that had yet touched his life.

"You are different," she breathed, and he could feel, without daring to look, the searing intensity of her regard, as if she were reading the most minute scintilla of who he was. "You are…" – and here she paused, searching for the right word – "clever." Her voice, normally so precise and controlled and pitched for the needs of command to servants and their like, lifted near imperceptibly on this choice of word, like a question or perhaps, Adaim reasoned, to express surprise. He felt in that heartbeat a flush of genuine delight.

Distantly, like the thrum of a thousand war-drums, he could detect the vibration of the waterfall a mile to the south. It was a warning, echoing off the rocky walls of the precipitous ravine that they needed to pass to reach this hidden sanctuary. It put him in mind of the handmaidens and he worried suddenly that they might return.

Then her hand found his cheek, a soft, cool caress against the thin stubble of his adolescent beard, newly shaved that morning. She turned his face up and, reluctantly, irresistibly, imprudently, he locked his gaze with hers.

"Adaim." She murmured his name, as if to try out its unfamiliar, peasant dimensions. His breath caught in his throat: he had been unaware she knew his name at all. He was unimportant, irrelevant to her life. To discover that she had taken the trouble, even the smallest of efforts, to determine his name, shocked him to his core.

And then, eyes hooded and implacable, she spoke again: "Fuck me."

CHAPTER 2

Youth I crave, yet wisdom more. Both are ephemeral.
Proverbs of Hatra.

*[…] the nanomedicine trials, successfully concluded in 2076 […] said to
[…] immortality in theory if not effect […] from gene manipulation […]
working at the cellular repair level.*
[…] indicates missing phrases.
Fragment of a larger document, purportedly a medical book, copied
and translated by a scribe, IYE 1047.

Nine hundred kems south-east from the sodden ground upon which
Skava quoted Shakespeare and Adaim bled out his life, the same sun rose a
handspan above the royal city of Chisua. Kellax, a printer by profession and
a spy – or intelligencer as he preferred, by secret association – walked the
winding curve at the top of the busy street known as the Higher Dirndorc.
Here he paused and, pushing through the noisy crowds, insinuated himself
between men, women and excited pointing children along the waist-high
wall overlooking the cliff face. Far below, monumental stone animals
wrought from single blocks of blue granite lined the causeway that crossed
the copper sheen of the estuary: camels, huge birds, horses and creatures
part-snake part-human, gazed out across the waters, distinctive even at
this distance. For two thousand paces in either direction from the halfway
point, where a small clot of robed figures and a white-curtained litter

edged slowly along the causeway, the hewn statues and the colonnade strode magnificently into the distant haze. Silently awaiting the party was another small knot of stick figures – this, as Kellax instantly surmised, the representatives and plenipotentiaries of the Council of supervisors. They faced towards the eastern end of the causeway where, crowded together on the tip of the narrow peninsular known as Cise Hook, were the temple buildings of the Archivists. The temple itself, constructed after the fashion of a stepped half pyramid, gleamed white as snow behind the black tide wall that ringed Cise Hook. The tide wall was old, older perhaps than the time of Echrexar, and accounted higher and deeper than the worst storm might overcome, built, it was said, in the Golden Age to stand against the worst that Echrexar might threaten.

Kellax watched, taking the time to convey to anyone who might be observing that he was merely the owner of printing shop about his business, but as distracted as everyone in this city on the day of the new king's accession, and excited to be witness to this rare event. Down on the colonnade, crawling from the temple, the white-curtained litter approached the tiny figures of the supervisors. From his high vantage, Kellax gazed across the broad expanse of the estuary and north towards the grassy slopes of the Chisuan gorge where, far below, the few landing quays and fishing boats were deserted. The waters of the Cise, normally brisk at this time of year, flowed sluggishly, undisturbed, under the arches of the causeway to join the calm, purple reach of ocean.

And so, as Kellax feigned for the sake of appearance a reluctance in his turning away and pushing a path back through the crowd, Council supervisors and Archivists met at a point precisely halfway between the city and temple, a point dictated by ritual and history and by the fine, acutely observed balance of power within the Realm.

Successfully back into the flow of pedestrians on the Higher Dirndorc, Kellax lengthened his stride. In the time he had taken to move through the crowd from the cliff face wall, he had scanned the people around him, searching always for the familiar face unexpectedly in attendance, or the movement of someone at odds with the inevitable rush of traffic – a momentary averting of gaze or the hunching of shoulders or rapid acceleration to match Kellax's own gait. These things he attended to with an automatic ease, and he was soon descending the Dirndorc towards the multi-coloured facades of the merchant houses on Becon-ni Way. His destination was Strad Place, a large open square at which seven streets converged and where he maintained his printshop and, more importantly, his pigeon loft. The first task of the day was to check for messages.

Almost a kem from the point where Becon-ni Way met the winding descent of the Dirndorc, the area known as Strad spread south to the towering walls overlooking the sea and east up to the ageing battlements of the Imperium. Strad itself was notable only for two things: the squalid poverty of Lower Town, known by its denizens as the 'Maze', and Strad Place. The former, a tortuous profusion of streets and blind alleys, on the more salubrious edge of which stood Kellax's narrow property, was populated by a polyglot community of traders, craftsmen and indentured peasants, and unofficially by all manner of footpad, swindler, thief and murderer. Strad Place, for its part, boasted more ale houses, theatres, distilleries, dens of entertainment and brothels than any other city quarter in Kiangsu, which made for a suitable blending in as far as Kellax was concerned, as well as a ready source of gossip, rumour and the occasional truth – all requisite tools of his shadowy trade. Strad's notorious existence, especially in such close proximity to the wealthy sensibilities of Monvar Hill and the seat of the Realm, almost directly above the towering cliff face, had not always been tolerated. In times past, the district had been partially cleared, but inevitably, owing to the acute shortage of space inside the walls of Chisua and the invariable attraction that such dark, twisted, narrow streets and blank-walled buildings always seem to have for the underworld of crowded cities, the corrupted and the corruptible returned.

Kellax entered Strad Place with a light heart. He had detected nothing untoward. Around him the world was as he expected. This morning there may well be messages to sift and perhaps even information to send on to his handler in the north. Yes, his heart was light. He was well paid for his intelligence. His printworks enjoyed a steady trade, and his apprentices were dedicated. At home, Kellax's wife had few complaints – although always more than he would like, in spite of the security of his income. He chortled to himself: if she only knew! But he was a dedicated intelligencer, well trained, and discreet. He had revealed nothing to her. He did not know the destination of his birds, yet he had few doubts that his work was important.

He began to make his way across the large open market forum, to his left the pillars of Strad temple, an ancient structure divinely spared from Echrexar and rebuilt many times, under whose portico an unusually long line of supplicants awaited their turn with the black-robed exarchs of the Faith: for a small blood sacrifice and a donation in copper, silver or gold, one might benefit from the Archivists' intercession with the gods for the interpretation of dreams. Today, following the death of Jamarin, the Peaceful King, and the accession of his son, citizens flocked to the temples with their dreams to understand what the future might hold at this most auspicious of moments, and to beg the gods to protect them from the return of Echrexar or the casual malice he might worm into their everyday lives: the betrayal of a husband or lover, injury and insult, theft and illness, the loss of home and hearth to debt. If the sacrifice was well done, a clean cut to the animal and its blood seen to be untainted in the copper bowl, and if the donation was acceptable and the dream told without embellishment or evasion, then the exarch of the temple, eyes closed, listening in silence to the dream, would become one with his dream wanderer, made flesh in the tiny finch in its copper cage near at hand and its whispered birdsong. The exarch would make his interpretation – a suggestion, a command, a warning, a foretelling – or say nothing if the bird was silent…this an ominous sign from the gods.

Kellax passed the temple, coughing a little on the smoke and the smell of the roasted flesh from a hundred sacrificed animals. Ahead lay the whitewashed shopfront of his printworks. He smiled and, in a moment of unconscious habit or whimsy, he turned to glance back across the expanse of Strad Place and the bustle of street vendors, carts, costermongers and traders – and saw a man turn away. A shock of recognition pulsed through Kellax. And yet he did not freeze. Instinctively he turned back. The shop front beckoned. His senior apprentice, alert to his master's arrival, opened the door. Kellax stepped inside and to his apprentice handed his cloak, a light tan garment, suited to Chisua's warm climate and current fashion, and then immediately glanced through the wide bay windows into the plaza outside. Whatever had alerted Kellax, the face, the familiar motion or shape or unusual attention, was gone.

"Good day, master," said Shen, unctuous and evidently pleased he had been in time to open the shop before his employer.

"Indeed," Kellax responded. "All is well?"

A slight hesitation from Shen, and Kellax knew instantly that his unconscious fears had spoken for him. He therefore followed with, "On this, the day of the new king's accession?"

"All is well," said Shen, his broad face breaking into a beaming smile.

And Kellax felt the overwhelming need to climb the stairs to the loft to find what messages might await.

***

The stairs to the loft were narrow. His elbows brushing the white-plastered timber walls, Kellax climbed at a pace he believed was normal: nothing should appear different. Shen was about his work. Shen and everyone else must continue to believe that Ke Kellax of Strad at Chisua was the printer, husband, and father of three children his life proclaimed him.

The warped door to the loft was latched. Kellax unhitched the rope and opened it. Dust motes played lazily in the broad beams of slanting sunlight that marked the eastern pop holes. The low cooing of the pigeons greeted him and in their partitioned roosts he counted the birds automatically: four new arrivals; four new messages. He retrieved them from the leg-ring pouches and filed each mentally according to the bird's known or probable point of departure. In the centre of the loft he had installed a small table built around the roof post. A stool waited nearby. He sat, laying out the tiny scrolls, left to right, on the table top. At once he recognized that two of the messages were correspondence from his factors in Kiangsu and Chulien, cities to the north – one a remittance for printing of pamphlets on behalf of the Council's regional administration, the other a request for funds. The remaining messages were in code, not obvious to the casual reader or, so Kellax trusted, to those who might take a deeper, professional interest.

He deciphered the first and checked it again, whilst the newly arrived pigeons cooed to him, blinking with white-rimmed red eyes that demanded the close attention he had neglected. The message in his hands confirmed only what he knew already: the Lord Shenri of Strath province was on the move with his retinue and heading south-west for Sohanyun in the neighbouring Lorang Province, there to take counsel with Lord Ordas. And so Kellax smoothed out the final scroll with the index finger on each hand, taking care to run the tips of his fingers across the top of the parchment to avoid smudging, should there be damp in the air or sweat on his hands. As the tiny words were revealed, he decoded them according to what he had recognized as cypher four – the highest of the secure codes he used.

Instantly, the blood drained from his face. His left finger slipped off the edge of the scroll and it rolled up. He cursed under his breath and flattened it once more. He had not been wrong. The message was shocking:

Shenri will be murdered. No survivors. Blame will be attached to northern nomads. Suspect Ordas as secondary mover. Yoiwa of Honam due here within days. Have identified new master intelligencer at work for Honam: Skava. My position now not secure.

Kellax sat back, his fingers still holding the scroll open on the table. His mind was racing. The number of items of import in the message was extraordinary. He considered the time sequence. Message three was from his source in Strath, undoubtedly some days old. No denying his spy there had deemed the news of Lord Shenri's departure for Lorang unremarkable and sent the bird some two, perhaps three, days after Shenri left. But that helped date the final message. Since both pigeons had arrived late last night, the news of Shenri's murder plot was no older than yesterday.

Lord Shenri of the Great Family of Strath was to be assassinated! But when? Imminent? Within weeks or months? What did the reference to Yoiwa mean? Who was Skava? Was there a link between Ordas, Lord of Lorang, and Yoiwa? Why was Ordas the 'secondary mover'? And, most crucially for Kellax: *My position now not secure.* What did this mean for his network? What had he noticed outside in the square?

Kellax collected the scrolls and stood up. For a moment he was indecisive. The news was so momentous, he knew an instant of disbelief… But his spy in Lorang was reliable. And whether he believed it or not, his course of action was certain: he must at once send a carrier to Morpheos, the name by which he knew the central node of his network. He moved to the roosts on the western side, these closed off behind a lattice-work with several internal pop-hole doors, and selected a bird that would deliver the message to Morpheos. Holding the pigeon firmly in his left hand he tightened the roll of the parchment in his right, then inserted the note securely in the small leg-ring leather pouch. At the southern pitch of the loft roof, he reached to open the release door, laying it flat to the outside as a platform for the bird…and then froze. A moment of alarm coursed through his veins: the memory of the half-seen observer in the square.

In his left hand the bird squirmed, eager to be off home. Kellax's eyes flicked beyond the platform and the sloping roof of the loft to the buildings opposite, then to his left, a cut-off triangular view of Strad Place, teeming with people in the frail yellow light of morning. Somewhere, his instincts told him, there waited a man, watching his printshop. Possibly several men. And, if he dared give substance to his unspoken fears, they would have a peregrine falcon or kestrel nearby, its handler at the alert, its target whichever bird was released from this loft.

Kellax closed the hatch, turned about and settled the pigeon back in its secure roost. For the briefest of moments he considered his options, matching them against what might be expected by Shen and the apprentices and his unwelcome watchers. Then, his mind made up, he went to the stairway.

"Shen!" he called down.

"Master!" came the instant response from the workshop below.

"Pen, ink and carrier parchment, if you please."

In moments, Shen emerged from the stairway with the items. Kellax was sitting now at the table, three scrolls in front of him, his expression the usual one of business and impatient bustle. "Remittances from Kiangsu and Chulien," he informed Shen as he laid down the writing materials. "And a probable commission, if we can satisfy the terms: a merchant in Ssu-Am. I shall be with you shortly."

Understanding this, correctly, to be a dismissal, Shen retreated down the stairs once more. Kellax picked up the specialised writing stylus, dipped in the pot for ink – high quality ink that would not smudge or run – and proceeded to duplicate the fourth message, still in code. Finished, he compared both notes and then glanced at the sealed roosts. The birds looked at him, expectant perhaps in their dim, loyal way. One of them would be killed this morning, snatched from its flight by crushing talons. The other, he hoped, would survive the thirty or so heartbeats it would take for it to be lost amidst the dozens of carrier pigeons taking wing across the city. He accepted that the message on the dead bird would be intercepted: the peregrine would return its prey to its master. But the code was secure. Logic told him so. In that he must show faith.

When he had both birds prepared, he carried them to the release door, placing one on the cane perch adjacent to the door. The other he held firmly, satisfied it would not be able to struggle prematurely from his grasp. Timing was everything. His heart beat rapidly now. He unlatched the door, both pigeons taking immediate interest. Kellax pushed down the hatch door, and the pigeon on the perch at once launched itself into the blue sky of Chisua. Kellax pulled the door back up and began to count: *One, two, three…*

He reached fifteen and opened the door again and released the second bird, gone in a flurry of feathers and the backbeat of the wings within the count to seventeen.

Eighteen, nineteen, twenty…

The buildings across the alley showed nothing. The grimy windows were closed. The rooftops gave no hint of trouble. But Kellax knew one of his birds was about to die.

***

On the top floor of an ageing tenement not forty paces from Kellax's printshop, a man known as Daved sat on a crude bench just inside the terrace doors overlooking the Street of Moths. Carefully he smoothed both hands over his dark hair, made the darker by the oil he habitually combed into it. With a neat twist he tightened the leather and gold braid that pulled his hair into a queue over his neckline. He looked up as the falcon master ducked inside. Having surrendered the bloody remains of the pigeon, the peregrine was enjoying its reward: in three jerky motions of its head it swallowed a proffered morsel and then submitted one claw to the corded leash its handler immediately attached.

Daved leaned forward and, as the falconer extended his hand, retrieved the leg-ring pouch from the rather sorry corpse of the pigeon, head flopping at a ridiculous angle. He extracted the parchment and read it. He grunted. Nothing obvious. A merchant's urgent missive: a commission that might be undertaken…perhaps nothing more than that. If it were code, it had no obvious pattern – and Daved was skilled in these things.

The falcon master coughed, then said, "Two birds."

Daved favoured the man with the intensity of his sea-blue eyes. "Two?"

"Th' second," the falconer explained in a matter-of-fact way, "twenty counts after this'un…" Here he gestured with the crushed corpse.

Daved smiled, merely a flat line of his lips. "Hmm," he responded. "Clever." He considered for long moments, his blue eyes still fixed on the falconer, who returned his gaze with the patience of a man much used to this behaviour. "Unusual for a merchant," persisted Daved, "would you say? Twenty counts between one and t'other?"

The falconer contemplated the mangled lump in his right hand, then the peregrine now comfortably perched on his padded leather glove. It blinked yellow eyes, in silent communion perhaps with its keeper, in a manner Daved believed was possible but could not himself penetrate. The Archivists of the Faith, after all, used finches for their dream-wandering. "Unusual," concluded the falconer, with his usual economy of speech, "but not unheard of."

Daved pocketed the parchment inside his brown leather jupon and wiped his hands together. A clot of blood had smeared itself on his knuckles. He rubbed it off, then smoothed his hair back once more. "If he released two," he mused aloud, "then he's onto us. Spotted something. Which is disappointing. I thought we were better than that."

The falconer shook his head sadly, as if he too shared the disappointment. His creased face, the same sun-weathered brown as his leather glove, gave no equivalent hint of sadness. He exuded only a coiled patience, at ease with the world, but calmly lethal, like a snake.

"I think…" said Daved slowly, his words matching his thought process, "that we need to change the boys. One of 'em got too close. We need a woman or some kids – careful, inconspicuous-like. I'll see what I can rustle up." He fixed the falconer with his sharp gaze again. "As for you and your mistress…" Here the falcon-master smiled fondly at the peregrine. "Stand her down. We don't want the Law taking an interest in a falcon let loose over Strad."

This was, of course, a crime in every town and city of the Realm. The falcon master made no response, perhaps thinking that the world might be a better place without the Law and without pigeons.

Daved made to rise, wistfully adding, "Then again, pity she couldn't snatch two out the sky."

"Aye," the falconer murmured, as if this were a challenge he and the peregrine might take up. "Two."

Daved stood up, fingers laced and inverted as he stretched his arms, knuckle joints cracking. "Well," he said, "we should send a bird north to Sklavin. I'll copy the printer's note. But we should send the original. Sklavin might know the style or the parchment itself, or the cypher…if there is one." Here he tapped his chin, which sported a short triangular beard. "What're the odds he's who he looks to be? A hard-working printer on the up, nice little woman at home and three demanding brats… What're the odds?"

"Nine in ten," came the instant reply. The falconer was chucking the peregrine under the cruel hook of her beak. She responded by nipping at his gloved finger, but with no malice, in the manner of a game she understood rather well or, Daved reflected with an arched eyebrow, like two adoring lovers.

"Oh, yes?" Daved enquired. "How so?"

"No missteps from 'im. No funny contacts. All sound as a drum, but…" And here he paused to look away from the peregrine and directly at Daved with those dark unblinking eyes. "Two birds."

Daved nodded slowly. "Mm," he agreed. "Nine in ten. He took one risk – a risk he gauged. Two birds had to go because he knew we'd get one. So the message is important – important enough to risk our closer attention."

The falconer was kneeling now to return the peregrine to a covered wicker cage. "Unless he's just a printer," he concluded without irony.

Daved laughed, a smooth, neat laugh, as smooth and neat as his oiled hair. "You are a card, Fortunas! For a fucking killer with a killer bird, you are a hoot – if you'll forgive the wordplay!"

Fortunas closed the wicker cage door and latched it, then stood up in a flowing motion. Dressed in a motley of different, tight-fitting dark leathers, his wiry frame looked remarkably serpentine. The black pebbles that were his eyes fixed blankly on Daved. "She's not a bird," he said, "she's a raptor."

Daved struggled to contain his mirth, then yielded. "Fucking card!" he chortled again, and headed for the door.

CHAPTER 3

And then it was that the peoples of the world were as the birds of the air – of a thousand forms – and each of the thousand spoke no single tongue. Until Echrexar, the eater of a million million souls. And Echrexar laid waste the land and the sea and darkened the skies until the people were nearly no more. But it was the Archivists of the Faith and the 10,000 Immortals who saved the people in their refuges and gave them the archives and the teachings.

The Book of the Dead, lines 1009-1014.

[…] is the sustainability of records, not so much in the immediate aftermath, as in the […] where the refuges must endure for decades, if not centuries, external conditions at least equivalent to the Toba stratospheric loading […]

Fragment of a larger document, copied by a scribe, IYE 1047.

***

For Adaim, there was the sun and there were the flies.

Once the mist and cloud had burned away, the yellow orb was merciless. Not its heat – Adaim's body offered only an agonized numbness insensate to the sun's fierce regard. It was its dazzling glare, unremitting, blinding to his single eye as if the light it poured onto the dreadful scene was never enough, and it must chase every remaining shadow from the world and throw its searching brightness under every open-mouthed corpse, between battered shield and broken armour, across curling fingers turned to purple claws. No detail of the twilight's murderous work was hidden from Adaim's flinching eye, not least the misshapen face of Lord Shenri, trailing bloody gore and still glaring at Adaim from near at hand. Too close, too close…

And then there were the flies. The morning sun had roused them, sluggish and hungry, to discover a banquet of blood that had driven them to a mad frenzy. In great black knots they gorged, tumbling, falling, weaving over one another, filling eye and ear and mouth and wound, for here was death and bounty in abundance. As for Adaim, and his twisted limbs, he was simply more carrion, another island of ruin for their insane landings as they skimmed from Lord Shenri's head to Adaim's body, with scant respect for the flicker of life yet pulsing in him. Only his eye they avoided – but there would be time soon for that…

A sudden flapping of dark, heavy wings startled the flies into drunken, rolling, buzzing annoyance. The arrival of crows, sharp-beaked and purposeful, would, Adaim realised, finish what his enemies in the twilight had failed to conclude.

***

Domita, a garrison in the southern steppes of Lorang Province, and more distant from Chisua and the concerns of Kellax, Daved and Fortunas than perhaps any place in Kiangsu, had been constructed on the brow of a low hill – the only natural elevation in the land as far as the eye could see. The engineering corps of the Army of Kiangsu, called the Ta-shih and fulfilling the role of a Realm-wide militia, had designed Domita fortress, as it had every other Ta-shih fortress, after the fashion of the original coastal strongholds of Kiang. Precisely circular, with concentric inner walls, these forts were raised using local labour and local stone. Where none of the former was available, soldiers were set to the task; and in the absence of suitable native stone, the resources of the Realm had been stretched to import what was necessary. In the days of Jamarin III and several of his successors, the threat of uprising in the Biljan Kingdoms had so preoccupied Kiangsu that currently two hundred such strongholds were dotted about the western and northern provinces, most of them abandoned or reduced to a skeleton garrison.

Apart from the diminished strength of the command, Domita had changed little in 250 years. The fort's location in the flat plains of the sparsely populated Lorang Steppes, once critical in the subjugation of the Biljan kings, now rendered it somewhat isolated, and it had taken on the role of a way-station in the heavily travelled routes of the Ta-shih and intrepid traders. Consequently, the garrison presently numbered fifty, a small contingent but adequate to the needs of the region. It fell under the authority of Company Commander Pillio, a silent and, one might say, morose man, not over-popular with his troops, nor indeed with his superiors, who considered him too independent and, if the truth be known, insubordinate. Yet, for three years Pillio had maintained the garrison at Domita with irreproachable effect.

From one of the four turrets of Domita, on a spring morning of clear blue skies and a fresh westerly breeze that had blown away the night's storm, Company Commander Pillio surveyed the familiar landscape, as was his wont at this hour of the day, just after the in-between time, the uncertain space flanked by twilight and dawn, the time for the nervous glance over shoulder, of troubling fears, of hastening indoors and not lingering on thresholds – only to feel relief when sunlight poured across distant horizons to drive silent shadows squealing from the wakeful world. Peasants, even soldiers, especially soldiers, made the sign of the sealing of the doors against the in-between time and the in-between places. Good people, educated, well-bred people of standing, stepped over the doorsill and not on it. Pillio had seen them do it, just as *he* would sometimes, and even make whispered prayers if they were outside in the twilight moments. They would not cease their ritual murmurings until they reached safety indoors. And though the exarchs, the black-robed Archivists, might bring order and alignment to Kiangsu in their dream wandering and the reassuring divination of the gods' intent, they too, from the humblest of their order to the most righteous of grandmasters, shunned the in-between. This also Pillio had seen. One did not tempt or insult the gods of road and river, of hearth and walls nor, worst of all, Echrexar, eater of uncounted souls and destroyer of the golden age. The in-between was where Echrexar still lived and might bleed into the world, unknown and unseen, breathing mischief, and tricks, and deceit, and terror, and horror. The exarchs said so.

But now it was full dawn. And Pillio was a less superstitious man when the sun caressed the world with life and light. So here he started his day, in a turret above Domita fortress, where he surveyed his world. Winding north-west away from the fort ran the paved road, one of the ancients' highways, double-width but only one narrower lane used now. The rest had crumbled to humped parallel lines in the earth, untended by anyone, here and there parts of its foundations removed by Ta-shih and peasants alike for the upkeep of sideroads, barracks or houses.

The road itself swept on towards Sohanyun, the walled town of Ordas, lord of Lorang Province. The journey was an easy hundred kems, or sixty miles, as distance was measured here in the north, and so had become the chief destination of Domita troops on furlough. Standing at the foot of the northern rim of the Alnaes, the mountainous spine of Kiangsu, which ran a jagged thousand miles through the centre of the Realm, Sohanyun offered to bored garrison soldiers not only the delights of shops, gambling and carnal excess, but also, in this otherwise flat and undistinguished part of the country, a breathtaking view of the snow-capped peaks dividing Kiangsu from the northern lands.

Pillio himself rarely left Domita. At thirty-eight he had resigned himself to a lonely and unpromising future in these far domains. The Ta-shih was shrinking. In a stable Realm with few prospects of active service, an officer's career could advance little. And Pillio had neither the cunning nor the hypocrisy to embroil himself in the political manoeuvrings of the Ta-shih general staff who might expedite his career.

As for wife and family, these things had passed him. He had loved, but been unlucky or, perhaps, as he reflected when a bleak mood took him, simply unsuited: too serious for smiling girls, too quiet to capture their interest for long, too awkward around women to attain anything more than the briefest of liaisons.

The sun by this time was several diameters above the distant haze of a sulphur yellow horizon. A bell rang and troops began to assemble in the paved yard behind Pillio. Morning parade would now begin: foot drill and squad manoeuvre with spears and sidearms. Shortly, the night patrol would return. Already, the jingle of armour and harness and the stamp of horses in the cobbled precincts of the fort signalled the preparations of the ten-man day patrol.

Behind him, Pillio's troopmaster stepped out of the stairwell into the wood-canopied turret and bowed smartly, then waited in silence. Without turning, Pillio nodded.

"Sir," reported the troopmaster, "the night patrol has been sighted."

"Very well. My compliments to the guardleader. Advise him to attend me in my quarters."

"Sir!" The troopmaster bowed again and left.

Pillio looked into the golden flame of the risen sun. The regularity of the day asserted itself. As he made for the stairwell, his deliberations returned to the mundane.

***

Pillio's quarters, comprising bedchamber, washroom and a large vaulted area which served as his office and study, were functional. His only concession to comfort was a red and black rug which covered the stone floor of his bedchamber. The cot and bedroll, the copper washbasin and jug, were no better and no worse than those of his troops. And the courtyard latrine block he shared with his men. Indeed, several of his non-commissioned officers, whose wives and children were accommodated on the other side of the fort, enjoyed a rather homelier environment.

On the wall behind a heavy wooden table and chair, a dozen swords, arranged crescent fashion over a blackened fireplace, dominated Pillio's study and, framed at their focal point, an archaic fire-weapon, long and black, its use and workings as obscure as its design. A rare piece, as most such artifacts had been broken for scrap or smelted for precious metals, it had been the gift of a merchant grateful for Pillio's assistance to his caravan in crossing a swollen river.

Iron-ribbed boxes, stacked neatly one on top of the other in a corner, contained Ta-shih despatches, regulations and records, and his own priceless collection of leather-bound books, some ten in all, treating of the wars with the Biljan Kingdoms, military tactics of the Ta-shih, and Hexil's *A History of the Civilized World*. Through the doorway and the two shuttered windows, Pillio's quarters faced onto the circular courtyard, latrine block and the stables. Beyond, the high stone walls and wooden platforms of Domita's defences rose with angular precision. Pillio's table and chair were so positioned that seated he could see the iron-studded fortress gates, eighty paces away. At that moment a single mounted trooper cantered his horse, followed by his remount on a tether, into the courtyard and was met by Pillio's troopmaster.

Pillio, expecting the full ten-man patrol, was surprised. Anomalies in the routine of garrison life were rare indeed. Restraining his curiosity as an officer must, Pillio awaited the report of the solitary rider.

The troopmaster appeared, rapped on the door, and announced from the opening: "Sir, a message from guardleader Kinei."

Pillio waved the man forward and the trooper, dust-covered and breathing hard, gave the requisite half bow and said, "Sir, I come from the guardleader."

"Make your report," Pillio responded.

"Sir, I have ridden from Estu, where the patrol waits, t'advise you of the destruction of Lord Shenri and his guard–"

"What?" Pillio started.

"Aye, sir. I regret."

Pillio, in his amazement, had half risen from his chair. He now rose immediately to his full height, glaring at the young trooper, whose face was flushed from the import of his news.

"Lord Shenri? Dead?" Pillio demanded.

"Yes, sir."

"And how many of his guard?"

"Twenty, sir."

"And the perpetrators?"

"We know little as yet, sir. Shafts in the bodies. Four or five Shur-Shur dead. Rest of th'armour and weapons is from Lord Shenri and his guard."

"You say 'as yet'. What do you mean?"

"A mile from the massacre, sir, we came upon men of Sohanyun, horsed and heavily armed – a detachment of Lord Ordas's guards. They says they attacked and captured a band of Shur-Shur" – he meant northerners from beyond the mountains, so called because of their language, which to southern ears sounded most often like Shur-Shur. "Great men, sir, of light skin and golden hair."

Pillio nodded. The northern barbarians occasionally wandered down off the mountains and into the plains to find grazing for their horse herds and trade with the locals. Usually, they were no trouble.

The soldier continued: "Guardleader Kinei then sends me with his message, sir."

Pillio strode from behind the table. "Kinei holds Ordas's men now?"

"So I believe, sir."

"In what strength are the Sohanyuni?"

"Twenty, sir."

Pillio cursed. "So our men are outnumbered!" He headed for the door, shouting for his troopmaster, "Sallan! Thirty men! Full chain harness! We leave on the instant!"

***

Pillio calmed his agitated horse and raised a hand to halt the Ta-shih troop. Behind him his thirty mounted soldiers reined in their horses and remounts. All of the horses, driven hard over twelve miles, were lathered in flecks and streaks of white sweat, and their eyes rolled in alarm as their riders sought to maintain two close files behind Pillio.

The men of Ordas's guard stood outside a large peasant cottage of rough-hewn limestone and reed thatch, the only building of substance in the tiny hamlet. The country hereabouts was as flat as anywhere on the Lorang Steppes, dotted with small meres and sloughs, reed-hidden waters sparkling as the sun climbed higher. The villagers, of course, had disappeared into the fields at first sight of the confrontation between Ta-shih and the Sohanyuni.

Pillio glanced at the night patrol and counted eight. Presumably one had been assigned to guard the remains of Lord Shenri. Five men of the patrol stood before several of the Ordas detachment, where clearly some negotiation had been in progress prior to Pillio's arrival. None, Pillio noticed with relief, had drawn a blade. Guardleader Kinei, sandalled feet spread immovably in front of one of the Ordas men, signalled to his fellows to withdraw, and all five stepped aside, never once however neglecting to face the men of Sohanyun.

The leader of the Ordas contingent, distinguished by a grey and yellow cloak attached to his steel corslet at the collar, now looked at Pillio. Pillio paid him no heed. Instead he took stock of the village, making a count of the Ordas men: nineteen, with six archers among them and, most interesting of all, roped to a tethering post near the cottage, a muscular giant of a man wearing an absurd concoction of armour and leather clothing, with deathly pale skin and golden hair braided like ropes and decorated with beads and silver amulets.

Though still on his feet, the man had clearly been beaten, and showed the evidence of several deep wounds to legs and arms, blood dried black against the pale skin. Near him, on hands and knees in the dust, was a woman.

Despite himself, Pillio stared for an unguarded moment, bitterly aware of the advantage this gave the Sohanyuni.

But a woman...also golden, and dressed much the same as the man. Her clothes, however, had been ripped from her torso to expose her breasts, and something in the drawn, anguished expression on her face silently enraged Pillio: she had been raped.

Pillio urged his horse closer to the leader of the Sohanyuni and met his eyes. An almost expressionless gaze was returned.

"Whom do I have the honour to address?" Pillio asked.

The Ordas man, clearly disliking the advantage owned by Pillio in being mounted, transferred his hand to the pommel of his sword, a bold move and one which occasioned a sharp hiss of indrawn breath from the nearest of Pillio's troop.

Pillio snapped, "You threaten me?"

The Ordas man, disregarding all politeness, sneered, and echoed the words: "*You threaten me*. What is your business here?"

"My business is the defence of the Realm and the punishment of transgressors." Pillio looked away. "I shall ignore your discourtesy. A lord of the Realm has been murdered. You hold suspects. You will hand them over."

"Under no circumstances!" The black-eyed gaze taunted Pillio. "We have apprehended these barbarians ourselves. We defend Lorang under the authority of Lord Ordas! He will punish these murderers!" He gestured beyond the village to a stand of juniper trees. "There," he declared, "if you seek the others, we found them and cornered them. They sought to flee and defied us. Take the bodies. You'll see: they have stripped Lord Shenri's camp. Swords, harness, some coin. We surprised 'em! Us, not your flat-foot dogs, arriving too late!"

He glared at Pillio, but in the black-eyed cast of his eyes there was a flash of cunning, which Pillio noted, but had no time to ponder. His insults Pillio ignored.

"Take the bodies and the goods," the Sohanyuni pressed. "All the evidence you need."

Pillio's horse backed up, still uneasy, agitated and thirsty and no doubt smelling the water nearby. Pillio squeezed with his knees and calmed the beast. He wanted to inspect the bodies, but something in the Sohanyuni's behaviour made him think he was being distracted. He raised his chin, exerting his authority in this sudden war of wills. "You mistake me," he snapped in his command voice. "I shall tell you one final time: hand over the northerners."

The Ordas man made no reply, merely flung his hands wide as if there was no reasoning with Pillio.

The position, so Pillio reflected, was finely balanced. He outnumbered the Sohanyuni detachment nearly two to one, and of his own troops' fighting ability he had no doubts: they were Ta-shih. The Sohanyuni were thugs, warrior thugs, capable with sword and bow, but thugs nevertheless, despite their swords and the impressive light mail and expensive steel corslets. This, however, was the physical disposition. Regrettably, these thugs also represented the lawful hand of Lord Ordas in Lorang Province. As such, they had legitimate power to maintain, as they saw fit, the Law of Kiangsu in Ordas's name. Any ill-considered and precipitate action by the Ta-shih would be a slight to Ordas. The repercussions of such an event did not bear thinking about. Tact and the appearance of courtesy, though superficial, must be applied here.

Pillio, pretending to take the other's silence as consent, said, "I thank you. You honour the Realm and your lord in releasing these individuals to my charge."

The Sohanuni officer threw up his hands again, apparently conceding the issue. "Very well!" he snorted. "Go see to the corpses yonder. We will untie this scum!"

He made a small circular motion with his hand, and two of his men moved towards the prisoners. Pillio half relaxed. It appeared that things would go smoothly. He glanced at the stand of juniper trees, and signalled a squad of his troopers towards the area, but had the presence of mind to turn back to look at the Sohanyuni, and watched the officer approaching the prisoners, right fist gripping his dagger hilt, the blade partway out of its sheath, ostensibly to cut the ropes on the giant northerner.

Pillio scanned his own troops and found that almost all had their eyes on the squad angling off to investigate the juniper stand. Quickly he looked back at the Sohanyuni officer whose blade was out, naked steel flashing crystal blue in the sun. The officer marched up to the prisoner, hacked at the rope bindings until they parted, and then jerked the huge man forward so that he stumbled. Instantly, Pillio surmised this was a trick. The officer, who pretended to be taken by surprise, yelled out, "Watch him!" and then skipped aside, blade swinging underarm to take the prisoner in the ribs. The big man, however, with an unforeseen turn of speed, twisted and rolled onto the hard-packed earth, yanking the rope out of the Sohanyuni officer's hand and narrowly avoiding the sweep of the blade.

"Hold!" screamed Pillio, heels to his mount. The mare surged forward in immediate response, as the officer darted towards the prisoner and three other Sohanyuni drew swords and tried to get at him. Pillio's horse made the short distance in mere heartbeats, shouldering between the Sohanyuni and the northerner. Pillio reined in. "Back!" he yelled, fighting the mare as she halted and strained at the bit, and then barked at his junior officer, "Sallan, the woman!"

Already on the move, mounted troopers surged around the prisoners to the steel hiss of drawn blades. An arrow buzzed past the mare's hindquarters, clearly intended for the woman. There was every danger now of a slaughter, but Pillio's instincts were to secure the prisoners. To his mind, the Sohanyuni wanted them dead. He pulled on the reins with his left hand, reached for his sword with his right and drew smoothly. In his loudest voice, he bellowed at the Sohanyuni officer: "Hold! Hold! Get your men back!"

"He tried to kill me!" screamed the officer. He too had drawn his sword, but Pillio could see the realisation on his face that things had plummeted out of his control and they were moments from a bloody battle that would see him dead.

"Withdraw!" he yelled. "Sohanyun! Withdraw!"

Pillio brought his mount back to order, turning a tight circle and gesturing his troops to get the prisoners to a safe distance.

The Sohanyuni officer, face darkening with rage, backed away from the barrel-chested horses threatening his survival. But still he screamed, "Give me that scum, you bastard! He tried to kill me! You saw it yourself!"

The troops had realigned themselves, the Sohanyuni in a ragged front near the farm buildings, Pillio's troops forming a wall of horseflesh opposite, the prisoners behind. Everyone had swords drawn. Pillio cast about for the Sohanyuni archers, who could flay his troops with a couple of volleys. In a moment he saw that all six were arrayed to the right of the cottage, bows drawn, arrows nocked. If they released, chaos would ensue. But, at that moment, the squad that had gone to investigate the barbarian corpses thundered up on the archers' flank, coming in close to force the archers to scramble back against the cottage walls. Good work!

Pillio made a mental note to thank the trooper whose quick thinking had closed down the threat.

He immediately pushed the mare forward, closing with the officer, slow enough to prevent bloodshed, bold enough to dominate from the height of his mount. "Enough, now!" bellowed Pillio.

The Sohanyuni had lost the advantage and the will to do battle now. Part surrounded, facing a wall of mounted troops and with their archers neutralised, they were looking to their officer to get them out of this alive.

Still he persisted. "Give me the nomads," he growled. "The gods will curse you for protecting murderers. Give them to me!"

Pillio snapped his gaze to the Ordas man and said with cold deliberation, "They are both connected to the murder of Lord Shenri. You have no claim and you release them both to my charge."

The Sohanyuni leader looked desperate now. "You desire this woman for yourself, Commander?" he shot back. "Aye, a delicious morsel of northern delight! What will my lord say when he hears that you and your men cheated the Law of the Realm for your own filthy pleasures! What? What will he say? And on his own land!"

At this, all the Sohanyuni muttered.

"Honour to your lord," retorted Pillio, observing the forms of hierarchy and nobility. "The Lord Ordas may approach me directly and, if he receives no satisfaction, then my superiors at Ingen fortress."

The Sonanyuni's eyes clouded with a dangerous hostility. Quietly he replied, "I shall have those prisoners. They are murderers—"

A moment of pure clarity of thought captured Pillio, the argument as plain in his mind as his next words. Advancing his mount to within several paces of the officer, he interrupted him: "You observe that this woman and this man had a hand in Lord Shenri's death?"

"I have said as much."

"Then it is clear that you know more of this incident than you have spoken."

The officer bristled, but his sword had dropped lower. Confused, he spluttered, "What do you imply?"

A hush had descended on the company.

Pillio spoke in icy, measured tones. "If you claim this woman was involved in the murder, then this confirms that you observed the incident – and you must then accompany us. In this case, you, your troops, and the nomads can help us with the truth of what happened. Thereafter, you will be free to make report to the Lord Ordas. If, alternatively, you yourself know nothing of the murder, we must needs take only the barbarians and your presence at Domita fortress is unnecessary... Now, what is your position? Perhaps you will clarify this?"

The man stared back, calculating but uncertain now. His own troops had all lowered their weapons and were looking again to their officer for a way out.

Taking advantage of his silence, Pillio said, "We will leave you to ponder the matter." And to Kinei, the Ta-shih guardleader: "Horses for the prisoners. Get them back to Domita at once."

When the barbarians and their ten-strong escort were cantering away to the east, Pillio turned his horse and, regarding the Sohanyuni leader over his shoulder, spoke gravely: "Will you accompany us?"

Trapped, the officer glowered. Eventually he sheathed his sword, ramming it home with a snap of irritation. "I will return to Sohanyun. You will hear more on this!"

Collecting his men, he strode off round to the other side of the cottage where their mounts were tethered. In moments the thunder of hooves had receded and Pillio was alone with his remaining troops, all still at readiness, Sallan having spread his small cavalry contingent across the paddock to minimise losses from any attempted arrow volley.

A fatigue born of the nearness of imminent conflict and the narrowness of having avoided bloodshed washed over him. He wanted to dismount, but there was much still to do, and the threat was yet alive in the fields surrounding them.

"Sallan!" he called. "Sentries to all points. Then water – men and horses. Form up thereafter. The Sohanyuni are still out there." He touched heels to the flanks of the mare. "Two troopers on me. We will see the barbarian corpses."

***

The crows had come back.

Some time ago, glutted and flapping in consternation, they had risen screeching into the air, disturbed by riders. Adaim, at first fearing the return of his enemies, had strained to see their approach. In time, shadows fell nearby, and a soldier's sandals appeared near Adaim's head. Voices called to one another in hushed tones, shock the overriding emotion. One of them drew closer to the piled corpses, peering in unconcealed horror, and Adaim recognized the uniform: Ta-shih.

He called to them, pleading, but his throat was a raw, useless thing, choked by blood, and a mere wheeze escaped his lips, drowned by the angry, bloated flies humming their displeasure at this latest interruption. Voices again, and instructions, and soldiers mounted up and the heavy beat of hooves took them away with urgent purpose. The flies settled to their task once more and the crows drew closer, hopping across the hardening mud, heads cocked, unblinkingly intent.

They see my eye, Adaim thought. *How perverse! To men, enemy or friend, I am a corpse. But the flies and the crows know.* Had it been possible, he would have laughed hysterically.

"Hah!"

The voice came from nearby. In response, the crows squawked and retreated, extending their wings but refusing to give up completely.

"Hah!"

A shadow fell across Adaim, and a soldier passed by him, brandishing his spear at the birds.

"Hah!" he challenged them again.

The crows flew off, landing almost at once beyond the edge of the camp, furious but undefeated. Their time would come.

Now the soldier stood still, his back to Adaim, spear grounded at his feet, perhaps in contemplation of the piled bodies, ignorant of the life bleeding out behind him. Adaim tried to move, to make a sound, to shout, to gasp even…but the torture of silence would go on, two sentries, in company of Lord Shenri, one cursing his luck to have drawn this grotesque duty, the other nine-tenths dead, condemned to be witness of his own failure.

Still the flies gorged. And the crows waited.

***

The barbarian corpses had been just that: a ghastly array of twisted flesh, men and women both, hewn down by arrow-storm and hacked to death in a bitter battle. Fourteen people, four children. No sign of Sohanyuni casualties, which Pillio found mystifying, an emotion which, on his angular, melancholic face, showed itself as a grimace. The whole suggested ambush, or brilliant tactics, and that gave him pause. After all, the Shur-Shur were well armed – lances, curved swords in the northern style and a dozen bows. After collecting the items stolen from Lord Shenri and handed over by the Sohanyuni, he had deployed a single small squad under orders to make a pyre for the dead. Then he had ridden at speed to the site of the murder itself.

At last Pillio dismounted. Despite hours in the saddle, he had dreaded this moment. But needs must: a report would be required and he could not expect his men to do work that he avoided, grisly as it was. Around him his men glanced furtively at him, uncertain, seeking leadership or perhaps…explanation. This brutality was beyond their experience, soldiers though they were. And the murder of a lord; well, their shock was evident.

The site revealed little. Lord Shenri's troopmaster had ostensibly chosen the place because it afforded some little protection from the storm of that night: a line of thick grey-green sage-brush grew twenty paces from the road, and it was here that the tents had stood. Either during the attack or immediately thereafter, the camp had been burned. Half-naked corpses were to be seen sprawled throughout the camp, and black flies rose buzzing in annoyance as the Ta-shih soldiers stepped carefully amongst the carnage.

Pillio moved over to Lord Shenri's baggage. Stained leather bindings of olive-green marked these boxes as the possessions of the Lord of

Strath. Only some of the caskets had been opened. Clothes and goblets, cutlery and a few coins had been scattered. The dead of the attackers, five northerners in crude armour, were sprawled on the edge of the camp. At first glance, this had been a well-planned ambush, with most of Lord Shenri's attendants cut down by accurate arrow volleys. The shafts of the arrows that had killed many of Lord Shenri's guard bore the same distinguishing fletching as the barbarians' arrows from the stand of juniper trees, where the band of nomads had met their end at the hands of the Sohanyuni. Pillio bent to inspect an arrow, attempting to ignore the man in which it was embedded. His stomach churned, but self-discipline prevailed.

Guardleader Kinei, examining the muddy tracks setting hard in the flaming midday sun, estimated a contingent of twenty on horseback. That tallied with the numbers of barbarians.

Whatever the case, the entire affair had moved beyond the jurisdiction of a single company commander, and Pillio had resigned himself to await instructions from his superior, the detachment commander in east Lorang. Nevertheless, standing in the centre of the blackened remains of Lord Shenri's camp, with the Sohanyuni cutthroats no more than a few miles away, Pillio's disquiet grew.

"Troopmaster Sallan!" he called out. "Once the inventory is complete, the bodies will need to be burned. Set some men to building a pyre."

Sallan started to call out names.

The sun, blazing down from a cloudless, white-blue sky, scorched his unprotected neck across the gap between the silver-crested helmet and the collar of his hauberk. At that moment, he nearly turned away, aching to be rid of the stench of death and the disgusting predations of the flies. But he paused for a heartbeat, dismissing the whispering urge to be gone, and instead removed his helmet to wipe the sweat from his forehead. In so doing he looked down and met the unwavering, one-eyed gaze of a soldier sprawled in the mud at his feet…alive.

Speechless, Pillio stared.

***

Skava, master intelligencer to Lord Yoiwa of Clan Ouine, the noble family of Honam, rode in the left-hand file, third rank. In a party of forty cavalry, this position meant she was close enough to Yoiwa to get his attention, but far enough back to excite no unwanted interest from members of her own trade. Today, like most days in the field, she was caparisoned as a trooper – a male trooper – known to all as Courier-sergeant Alin. She wore light mail, a small bronze helm, a lance gripped in right gloved fist and butt-rested in the harness trap of her stirrup. A short sword in a polished bronze scabbard was affixed to her saddle, and a dagger sheathed and clipped in the correct manner at her right side, poniard to the left, and of course a small arsenal of hidden weapons and poisons not usually carried by the elite troopers around her. As the entire column was approaching the capital of Lorang Province, the stone city of Sohanyun, on what amounted to an official engagement between nobles, she also wore the open cloak of red and gold, held with a gold clasp to better display both of the colours. Everyone was dressed to impress.

Skava rode with ease. She loathed horses but she was a superb horsewoman. In fact, in most things she was superb; and most especially in the business of spying and the exercise of power – real power, the power to move kingdoms and, she hoped yet again, the whole fucking world.

She had worked long and hard in the shadows to make all of this happen, to get Yoiwa to this point, to judge him good enough to help her shift the pieces on the board, to have confidence in his intelligence not to be too greedy and to play the game with patience, as it must be played, for the longer-term outcomes that would accrue. Also, to know, to really know, that he would not, would never, stumble because of some stupid petty vice like most of the vast horde of humanity: sloth, or some sexual perversion, or the demon drink or, god forbid, simple lack of ambition. Skava was forging something here. Yoiwa was good. Clan Ouine was tight-knit. Yoiwa's wife Mairu was a force to be reckoned with. Their son, Prince Mathed – every first son of every Great Family was a fucking prince – held promise. Even Jophan, Yoiwa's nephew, was capable, if a little fond of the spectacle of noble overstatement. She could see the game and the pieces, and she owned, in one way or another, nearly half the pieces across the Realm, if not beyond. The old king was dead, finally, and not even by her hand – that would have been too great a risk. But he was dead, the old fart, and his impatient son, Jeval, was a shiny new piece on the board. She could steer him with the right moves and counter-strokes, as young men were slow to learn, too distracted by the tackle between their legs and eager to prove themselves – especially princelings and monarchs – and fatally over-ambitious. And now Lord Shenri was dead too, precisely to plan, in a coordinated strategy that would bind Lorang Province to Honam and open the way for Strath Province to come under Yoiwa's sway. Yes, the plan had worked. During the grey in-between before dawn, together with Maki and Yan, she had arranged the ambush site just so…

But whilst she moved the big pieces around the board, she still had to ride across the godforsaken countryside, watching over Lord Yoiwa and controlling the fat moron, Ordas, who was taking his sweet time somewhere on the other side of the massive black-riveted gate ahead of her. This meeting was critical. The two would posture and make oblique threats and agreements, both real and symbolic, and meanwhile Skava would settle things in the background and the game could move forward.

At the head of the column, astride his snorting horse, Yoiwa, Lord and Master of Honam Province, was evidently impatient. With barely controlled irritation he searched the ramparts and towering gate of the walled town for signs of a response to his arrival. Nothing. The two guards atop the fortifications remained impassively still. The peasants and townsfolk on each side of the roadway stood with heads bowed, but nowhere, nowhere, was there the slightest evidence of protocol or any suggestion that a lord was expected in Sohanyun. *Patience, Yoiwa,* Skava cautioned him silently. *Patience.*

Yoiwa moved his horse forward. He sat the mount heavily, a thickset man, deep of chest and broad of shoulder, who habitually wore chainmail over a white jerkin, with ivory wool trousers and thick knee-length boots, disdaining at all times what he called "the ostentation" of any more elaborate apparel. Hard, uncompromising pale eyes and hair cropped short in a style favoured by peasants, and thoroughly unfashionable in

Kiangsu society, made him look dangerous. It was a look that Skava favoured. It distracted attention from her. His skin, swarthy like that of the Marshese from the northern coast, showed the lines of forty years in the extremes of climate of Honam Province.

Screwing up his eyes against the glare from the walls of Sohanyun, he scanned the town. Inside the ancient walls that ringed Ordas's capital, tiers of black-roofed limestone houses rose in a jumble of unplanned construction at whose centre stood the slab-sided monstrosity that was the citadel of Sohanyun. Built in ages past, before even Ordas's forbears, towers, courtyards and curtain walls had been cut into and mortared onto an enormous outcrop of rock, and even now it was said that none in Lorang knew the full extent of its dungeons and deepest passages, layered onto the ruin of the archaic city beneath. Legend said that the ancients had prepared a refuge here against Echrexar. Too fucking right.

The citadel, however, was far overshadowed by the soaring white peaks of the Alnaes to the north, west and east. A rolling green forest of pines reached up into the heights, clinging to the precarious slopes, here so often obscured by clouds, to dwindle at last against the leaden grey crags. The mountains at this point, and for three hundred miles west, were reckoned impassable. Twenty miles east brought the traveller to one of two tortuous but well-paved routes north into Strath and, if he was so disposed, to the barges of the Sav River, which coiled its way north into the Bay of Marshese.

To the impoverishment of Ordas, traders were disinclined to move their goods through the mountain passes when the trip into Kiangsu North was easily accomplished by travelling east around the Alnaes, and down the gentle wide waters of the Cise River to the insatiable, and profitable, markets of Kiang and the eastern provinces. Consequently, Lorang remained a land of peasant cattle farmers and fishermen, the Ordas family once powerful only because it had entered the alliance of Biljan kings four centuries ago.

The party moved up to the gates of Sohanyun. Yoiwa's nephew Jophan, first officer, issued orders, repeated by the booming voice of the guardleader, and the troop closed up neatly into four files, Skava directing her mount to the outer left file again, a position that she favoured, for all sorts of reasons. She checked the disposition of squads: first two ranks, the heavily armoured bodyguard, thick overlapping bronze-disk hauberks, double-blade swords strapped to saddles, wide coin-studded belts bearing light war axes useful in close combat, and round shields constructed of crossply with a central brass boss elevated from the rim so as to catch and turn the unwary attacker's blade or spear; third and fourth ranks – Skava's squad – equipped with lighter chainmail, shortswords, bows, two quivers of fifteen arrows apiece, lances but no shields – a squad used for covering fire and courier duty, vastly suiting Skava's needs; rear ranks, immediately behind her, medium cavalry, armed and armoured much like the bodyguard but carrying two heavy lances, lethal weapons for a shock charge to break the enemy. Each man's helmet spike was decorated with a short horse-hair crest in the gold and red of Honam Province, and the outer rider on the right of each line of four held a lance upright, the same gold and red in their fluttering pennons.

Skava was aware of the approaching rider at the same time as there was movement at the gate. The rider was moving fast from the rear; that meant a courier, and moving fast meant trouble. Bad news always travelled fast, in Skava's long experience. Whilst the hoofbeats tore closer, a single note of a gong sounded, accompanied immediately by muted cymbals, and the gates groaned slowly opened like a drunk grumbling at a rude awakening. A litter appeared, curtained entirely with mustard silk, and carried to the centre of the arched gateway by a dozen bearers in brightly coloured smocks of indigo and white.

At Skava's side, the rider skidded to a halt in a cloud of dust, pounding hooves and protesting horseflesh. Bad news, bad fucking news. The rider handed her a leather pouch, tied securely, then immediately swung his gelding and rode to the rear of the column where the remounts followed. Skava released her reins, the quicker to open the courier pouch, extracted the note and read it. It was in code, a simple cypher, and easy to make out. Under her breath, Skava gave vent to her feelings: "Oh, fuck!"

Ahead, the litter emerged from the shade of the gateway and was carried the ten paces to where Yoiwa waited. Several mounted guards accompanied the litter, all splendidly turned out in yellow and grey tunics, corslets of burnished bronze and, despite the warmth of the day, mustard yellow cloaks arranged to hang against the flanks of their horses. It was a splendid display – splendid and utterly bloody pointless. In the background, Skava's roving eye noted, two Archivists in their black robes watched.

She was painfully aware of the lack of time she now had to get this message to Yoiwa. If she left the column, she would draw attention – very dangerous in this city. Without the least doubt, there would be spies on the battlements or among the guards or in the streets. If she passed the courier bag forward through the ranks, it would be handed to Yoiwa as the litter arrived in front of him. Making her decision, she slipped the pouch into a saddle-bag and waited.

The litter bearers came to a standstill. From inside the curtains a bejewelled hand parted the material.

"Ke Ordas. Honour to you," grunted the Lord of Honam, observing the courtesies of equal rank.

Ordas flung the silk aside and bowed his head partway, the minimum required by protocol. "Ke Yoiwa, your visit fills me with pleasure. Honour to you."

Ordas was a fat, round-faced slug of a man, with the pale clear skin of a baby. Despite his corpulence, however, he moved with an economical grace, affecting the manners and accent of Chisua, where every princeling spent time as a child. Yoiwa had often remarked to Skava that he was reminded of an outsized, lubberly worm, squirming slowly and contemptibly in its nest. And yet, Skava cautioned him, the worm was more like a snake, meriting respect and watchfulness in equal measure.

With a curt rejoinder, Yoiwa responded to Ordas's punctilio: "The sun is no pleasure, Ke Ordas. You know my liking for courtly inanities."

Ordas half smiled, with teeth discoloured and black with caries. His eyes became almost invisible grey dots in his fleshy face as he said, "I know your likes and dislikes only too well, Ke Yoiwa. In addition to our lordly greeting, we have prepared for your refreshment a tasty collation in the palace. A light repast, so to speak. I enjoin you to partake of my hospitality this day. And then, perhaps, tomorrow we can talk of our mutual business." Ordas motioned ingenuously towards Yoiwa's mounted militia. "The needs of your troops have been foreseen. Magnificently arrayed, I might add, and in such strength..."

The Lord of Honam returned the smile. "A litter," he replied, with a nod of his head towards the large conveyance, "is too slow for the administration of a province."

Ordas laughed. "Indeed, Ke Yoiwa. An administrator as great as yourself must needs demand a sturdy mount to transport himself and his armour in the administration of his province, especially when he is well outside its borders!" Ordas gave a careless flourish. "But we waste time. The cool of the banqueting hall and royal entertainment await us. Ke Yoiwa, if you will permit me to lead the way..."

The bearers set off, turning the litter in the roadway with practised ceremony and heading back towards the gate. Once again the gong sounded and cymbals crashed as the procession entered Sohanyun, a small knot of musicians to the left of the massive wooden gate playing their instruments with sober concentration. The town's residents, lining the main street, bowed in silence as the two lords passed. Many of the townsfolk, following their lord's example, were dressed in a peculiar half-imitation of the Great Families and merchants of Chisua, but favoured the bold colours and patterns of the north. Thus, the men wore their dark chestnut hair collar-length, tied at the nape of the neck, and robed themselves in undertunics of light pastel shades, with mantles of blue fabric, collars stitched with silver filigree, and sandals strapped high on the calf. The women elected to wear ankle-length kirtles in bold red, white and purple, their hair long and intricately braided and set off by a fine headband. In the autumn and winter, of course, the fashions of temperate Chisua were discarded and replaced by the heavier garb more suited to the vagaries of this mountainous, storm-lashed region.

The procession entered the great courtyard before the citadel, the horses to be stabled and the troops taking their ease in the shade of canopies. As preparations were made to show Lord Yoiwa and his senior command to comfortable quarters to bathe and refresh, Yoiwa stood with his bodyguard loosely arrayed around him, Jophan at his shoulder. Skava marched up with her usual confidence. Tall enough to pass as a man, she had the muscle development that said *don't fuck with me*. Dressed as a courier-sergeant, her auburn hair tied back tight in a queue, the flat expression and dented broken nose that might have been a man's, and the gait and use of space that said to everyone she was a man, she had perfected this and a host of other devices to disguise herself. Rarely had she failed.

The bodyguard, serious-looking men who would remain in full armour with their arms to hand, eased aside for her. She noted that they were sweating heavily in full harness, but she could also see a number of them taking on liquid from water bottles, their own water bottles. Yoiwa's bodyguard took no water or food they did not directly control: there were no fools among this squad of killers.

Skava moved close to Yoiwa. He was squat and powerful, and so they were of a height. He regarded her with pale eyes, apparently relaxed, as if her approach was normal. Watchers would be everywhere – and not only spies in the employ of Lord Ordas – whatever precautions he took to root them out of his city.

"Sergeant," he acknowledged her.

"My lord." She would not pass the courier's message by hand: it would signal something important. This must be oral, the appearance of an update, a report on any number of tactical considerations familiar to any noble afield beyond his borders. "Your host," she began, her voice the voice of a man, honed by long experience and experimentation until it was as natural and identifiable as any man in Honam, the dialect pitched to eastern, as near to perfect as would fool the locals. "Your host has done the deed…but left two nomads alive." She let these words hang, then finished: "The Ta-shih have them. By now they will be inside Domita fortress."

Yoiwa did not even blink. He nodded. In this game, he too was practised. "This gives me leverage here in Sohanyun," he replied, "but would it present difficulties if they were to talk?" He had understood instantly and perfectly. Skava was pleased, despite the problems that two barbarian witnesses, still alive, in the hands of the fucking Ta-shih, posed for her and her network.

"I agree that it offers leverage," she said, toneless, with a nod for the hidden audience, as if this conversation were routine, when instead she needed to be gone from here, shovelling up the shit that Ordas and his idiot troops had left behind in their incompetent wake. "I shall deal with it," she promised. Then an idea shaped itself into sudden perspective in her mind. She added: "Of course, the barbarians being alive may help us…"

Yoiwa raised one eyebrow. He was accustomed to her thinking, her connecting ideas and fashioning advantage one way or another, and her unerring capacity to pinpoint the flaw or the angle that moved the game on.

"The protestations of the nomads," she explained, "may well be seen as the proof of their guilt. Had all twenty barbarians been slaughtered it might appear, perhaps, a little too convenient. Rest assured, Ordas will argue this: if nothing else, it digs him out of a hole."

Yoiwa stared at her with the kind of regard that spoke of both admiration and scepticism. He was used to her preparing a field that was rather less messy and, quite frankly, she agreed. She hated loose ends.

"I will deal with it," she said again, settling on a course of action even as she spoke.

Yoiwa merely nodded, as if it were already done. Skava saluted, the usual open-hand, forearm upright acknowledgement favoured in the small private militia of the provincial lords. She turned away, jerking her head at Maki and Yan, attentive nearby. Was she worried? She examined the problem and its implications. Coldly analytical, she reckoned she could handle this in a few days. On the other hand, intuitively, in the manner of thinking and calculating she had cultivated to a point of near absolute trust, she was more worried: loose ends of this sort had a horrible habit of unravelling. She had seen it too often. One damn thing led to another. She could have assassins in place for an ambush, covering as bandits, in no time. But that meant questions and unwanted attention which, even from the bumbling bureaucrats in the Ta-shih, could lead to suspicions, could trigger the jangling of alarms in the sensitive web of spy networks across the Realm. That the stupid Sohanyuni had cocked this up royally made her worried for the first time in a very, very long time.

And so she smiled, welcoming like an old friend the surge of nervous energy clenching her stomach. If you were worried, you were alive and you had purpose. She grunted at Maki and Yan as she walked abreast of them, "I need two birds for locations four and seven – sharpish – and somewhere private to get the parchments done."

"Problems, boss?" enquired Maki, tall and spare, with a face like a patient horse, long jaw, long nose, and flaring nostrils but liquid, trusting eyes. Not the eyes you might expect of an assassin of the first order.

"Ain't it always so, Maki?" she said through a grin. "Ain't it always?"

***

Yoiwa, dressed as before in a clean white jerkin and chainmail, stepped into the ancient hall with Jophan and three fellow officers, Skava, and four of his bodyguard, and was shown to a couch. His officers took seats to his left, and beside them and to Ordas's right members of the household and Sohanyuni guard. Yoiwa's bodyguard arranged themselves behind their master, Skava with them, her crossed arrow epaulettes and her presence here evidence for their hosts that she was the courier-sergeant, alert to her lord's need. Meanwhile, two birds were in flight and actions had been set in motion – contingencies to stay on top of Ordas's recent errors. Now she need only observe and play her role.

Lying sideways on soft white cushions, so that his bulk seemed less gross, Ordas raised his hand in a gesture of welcome to his guests. He regarded Yoiwa across the low table between them. "You are refreshed, Ke Yoiwa, after your journey?" he enquired, all smiles.

"Indeed, Ke Ordas."

"Good. Then we can begin."

Ordas snapped his fingers. Servants, bearing platters burdened with food, entered the hall from curtained doorways, and bent low before the guests to offer them their choice. The smell of roasted meats, sweet spices, absinth, lemon, pungent curries and heady wines filled the high chamber. The soft, reedy notes of a pipe lifted above the rustle of servants' gowns and the soughing of the wind through the balcony archways. A guitar joined in to strum out a popular tune, and across the smooth stone floor into the space between the couches and tables an acrobat cart-wheeled, leaping and prancing, oiled skin alive with the reflection of sunlight on rippling muscle. The music changed. To the beat of drums and bells dancers appeared, swirling diaphanous scarves across bodies dressed to tantalize and arouse, flesh redolent of a strong, musky civet. Skava took it all in, but her gaze went beyond, settling on other matters – not the possibilities of assassination or poison or any physical dangers; these were the duties of the bodyguard, trained and trained well, at Skava's own direction. No, she read the postures of the Sohanyuni officers, the close attendants, the way they stood or reclined, the mood reflected in facial expressions and the points of their attention. An officer intrigued her: he was flushed, though this could have been the wine, and his eyes flashed, the product of a restrained challenge…or embarrassment, perhaps even shame, emotions at odds with the occasion. Inwardly Skava smiled. This was the offending officer, the buffoon who had contrived to fuck up the ambush of the Shur-Shur. Doubtless he had made his report to Ordas and would suffer accordingly. Idiot. But his expression was not one of contrition. Skava's inner smile collapsed. Here was a man whose pride had been badly dented, his honour impugned, an officer who wanted to make things right, to redeem himself…or save himself. Being an idiot, he would compound the offence by doubling down. She sighed. A problem yet to transpire was not a problem she could resolve. But, as she said time and again, it always pays to know.

In the deeper shadows of the large hall, standing against a decorated pillar, Skava identified a servant who made an effort to appear busy, but spent too much time observing: a covert bodyguard or even an assassin. Among Ordas's retinue, a gentleman, dressed foppishly in high Chisuan fashion, affected an easy grace and chatted to his companions, except that his eyes roved every so often, fixing on Yoiwa's men, including Skava. Lorang's master-intelligencer? Or perhaps one of his apprentices and the spymaster himself was somewhere on the floor above, examining proceedings from hidden spyholes. It mattered little to Skava, who had perfected the insouciance of the bored soldier nevertheless rather pleased to be included in the inner circle of his lord, modestly ambitious in the way of peasants risen beyond their expectations and over keen to serve. It was a guise she had long found impenetrable to other spies and, to magnify the deception, she had arranged for one of Yoiwa's bodyguard to subtly exaggerate his role, as if he were a man playing the bodyguard, and doing it well, but leaking tiny clues that a journeyman intelligencer would eventually spot and draw the conclusion Skava wanted: re-directing attention away from her.

There was something about this hall though, the play of light maybe. Always focussed and attentive, she became, nevertheless, irresistibly distracted. Her thoughts strayed back to the night's work and the camp fire, the niggling memory and the avalanche of history it had triggered. Eslin. *Bury her*, said Skava. *Deep, as before. Where she is dead*, or was it *safe?* A flutter of tension pulled at her guts. This was not the anticipation of action or the churning excitement of grand strategy; it was uncomfortable, like a bleeding wound round the crucible that had been submerged deep enough to forget…but not still to *feel*, as she felt it now. Eslin. That woman was not her. Could not be her. It was a matter of control, meticulous and uncompromising. And yet Eslin was there, threatening… what? Memories and promises and anger. She had a voice, washed out by the slow creep of time, the voice of a little girl, but difficult to hear, like a distressed plea, teeming with emotion and incoherence. Waves of desolation rose in Skava, unstoppable, an ocean of tears she could drown in, big enough to drag her down into panic. *Get a grip*, she cursed herself. Intolerable.

With immense effort, Skava hauled herself back into the now, the sea of faces, and the sheen of perspiration on the dancers' bare limbs and reflected sunlight through the fluttering drapes and the unceasing thrum of music and conversation. The dislocation was like waking from a dream. Who were all these people? What had she missed? Had her face betrayed her? *You will get yourself killed*, said the voice that was Skava, or perhaps the cold disapproval of her mother. Would death be a blessing? Better than the despair and ennui. Oh, so much better. *Bury her.* And she did. Again.

The meal progressed. Yoiwa, discovering the fare too rich for his ascetic tastes, contented himself with good Strath fruit. On the entertainment he bestowed a coldly disdainful eye, outwardly indifferent. Behind him, standing with the bodyguard, Skava observed everything.

Ordas, studying his guest through slitted eyes, remarked above the music, "Our amusements are too tame, Ke Yoiwa? Perhaps something more enlivened?"

Yoiwa met his gaze. Ordas was renowned for perversions both outrageous and exquisitely tantalizing.

"No, indeed, Ke Ordas. Your dancers surpass themselves. But I think on other things."

"Ah. Do you care to unburden yourself, Ke Yoiwa?" And Ordas raised his eyebrows in the manner of one who fancies he knows what will be said but must, out of politeness, conceal this privity.

"Our work is done, Ke Ordas," said Yoiwa, without expression.

"In truth?" The bulging cheeks quivered in amusement. Gently, Ordas dabbed at his forehead. "This is good news, Ke Yoiwa."

"Aye. But there is more."

The grey eyes glittered. Ordas offered his smile of black, decayed teeth. Yoiwa glanced at the dancers: two, a man and a woman, swayed fluidly in front of Ordas, their limbs intertwined in the semblance of an erotic embrace.

"Events move fast, Ke Ordas," said Yoiwa. "Perhaps you are in need of a horse to improve your intelligence?"

Ordas's expression faltered not at all at the barb, then he replied, "Perhaps. But equally, perhaps I am in need of no such intelligence..."

Yoiwa raised his chin, the slightest of smiles playing on his lips. "When men die," he said, "wise men pay attention. When men who should have died, still live, wise men pay their dues."

Ordas's brow glistened. Rigid, he held his visitor's gaze, gauging the import of his words. Skava laughed inwardly. Ordas could not possibly have suspected that Yoiwa already knew of the Sohanyuni cock-up, as he himself would only just have heard.

"Men die or live," Ordas observed, selecting his words with care, "as the Shadow chooses. I pay no dues on that account."

Yoiwa snorted, a rasping, unpleasant sound, full of dismissive contempt.

"And in my province, Yoiwa," Ordas insisted, "no man tells me what dues I should pay. No man."

Now Yoiwa laughed, as always with his lips but not with his eyes. The dancers, understanding this to be an acclamation of their efforts, exerted themselves the more vigorously. The pipe, guitar and drums played louder, faster, and the audience, unable to hear the conversation of their lords and emboldened by cool wine, clapped in time to the music and cheered.

Yoiwa, meanwhile, returned to the conversation. "Our bargain was straightforward, Ordas. I had expected your officers would supervise the undertaking more closely than is their wont. There is a problem. You know there is a problem."

Ordas smiled a mocking smile, trying to obfuscate. "Yoiwa of Honam, is this concern? Is it fear? I had thought your hand steadier than this. As for me, see for yourself! Only the guilty and the fearful look over their shoulders."

Again Yoiwa laughed, though with an edge of threat which Ordas perhaps found unsettling.

"Ah, Ke Ordas!" the Lord of Honam exclaimed, and snatched a goblet from the table and raised it. "I drink a chalice to the guilty and the fearful, my lord!"

Seeing this action, those of the company nearest Yoiwa likewise raised their goblets and some cheered, thinking it a celebration of the bounty of Lord Ordas, and all turned back to the dancers, to gaze upon the cavorting frenzy of bodies.

Ordas, perplexed, and no doubt calculating the likely import of Yoiwa's behaviour, forced a smile. The Lord of Honam replaced his goblet on the low table. Frowning, despite himself, Ordas judged it inopportune to say anything until he had heard more. Meanwhile, the music and dancing, reaching a climax, ended abruptly. The audience applauded. On their knees, heads bowed, bodies soaked in perspiration, the dancers awaited their lord's release.

In the silence following the applause, Yoiwa said, "Ke Ordas, we must speak alone." And he held Ordas with a cool, unflinching gaze.

The Lord of Lorang delayed only a moment. Then he dismissed the dancers with a curt gesture and rose to his feet. Servants rushed immediately to his assistance. Composed now, he motioned them away and signalled the gathering to continue with the banquet. To Yoiwa he declared, "The north balcony will serve us adequately."

***

Skava watched them walk out. She could predict the conversation. Indeed she had briefed Lord Yoiwa to expect a primary scenario and how it might play. The Sohanyuni blunder in allowing the Ta-shih to take two of the nomads would come out. Ordas would pretend this was his plan — and indeed it had some merit. It largely augmented the case: the Ta-shih would have two living murderers rather than the corpses of suspected killers, all conveniently dead. Yoiwa would feign annoyance and concern about discovery, but ultimately would take the responsibility to deal with the problem. And, at one level, Ordas would be obligated.

What was more important was what was discussed next. Four hundred years previously, the alliance of the Biljan kingdoms in the north had come to bloody ruin against the power of Clan Ehri; this time, it would hold if other provinces of Kiangsu could be brought to allegiance. Lorang was nearly secure. Next would be Strath. Prince Mathed and the Lady Che Keleu were fond of each other. An alliance through marriage, after her father's untimely death, would be beneficial to Strath and could be made, in Council, to seem a path to peace and unity – who didn't want that? Upon peace and unity trade depended. And no one, neither high nor low, would jeopardise the lifeblood of trade, or its taxes. If Strath were linked to Honam by marriage, then Allpo in the north-east would be isolated and ripe for persuasion. Already Skava's informers and spies prepared the ground.

But today, Yoiwa must secure the public backing of Ordas to the marriage.

***

On the balcony, away from everyone, Ordas made a gesture of impatience. "And so it went. Shenri is dead. Nearby lie the culprits. Everything is satisfactory."

Lord Yoiwa turned him a hooded stare. "Not so. The Ta-shih stumbled on your men, Ordas. Two of your Shur-Shur live yet! Sloppy. Your fine soldiers allowed the Ta-shih to come upon them!"

"How do you know this?" demanded Ordas, turning pale. Inwardly he cursed the gods and his soldiers in equal measure.

Yoiwa snorted in disgust, ignoring the question. "For the great gains that you seek, Ordas, I asked only that Shenri's life be taken on Lorang's soil. I would spill the blood. All you must do is supply credible murderers." He sneered. "No difficult task in Sohanyun, with nomads crossing the mountains for grazing. In this you have failed."

Recovering rapidly, Ordas said, "You froth with anger, Yoiwa. Calm yourself. Think on this matter clearly. I concede the point. But…if two barbarians survive – what of it? Who will believe them? No one!"

Yoiwa narrowed his eyes. The argument was the expected one and Skava had prepared him for it. He tilted his head, as if given pause, then responded, "I like it not, Ordas. Your men are slipshod. A dead man's tongue does not wag. And the tale this golden-haired pair will tell may interest the Council more than you think."

Yoiwa turned his back, feigning deep calculation. He looked at the high crags of the Alnaes, snow in the upper reaches. A moment later he said, "Restrain your men, Ordas. Ensure their silence. I shall deal with the Shur-Shur."

"As you wish," said Ordas with hidden relief.

"And now to other matters. Lord Shenri's death is untimely," Yoiwa stated with heavy sarcasm. "I had not told you that in the summer his daughter Keleu was to be chosen…"

Ordas returned his sarcasm. "Indeed. Death is always untimely. Or so the poets tell us. Yoiwa, you display uncharacteristic evasiveness. Speak your mind."

"In truth, my lord, I do just that. Keleu will be chosen by my son this spring."

Ordas stood stock still. Yoiwa turned to face him.

"I suspected as much. But this spring?" Ordas echoed. "So soon?"

"Yes."

"And Shenri accepted this match?" Ordas curled his lip in disbelief.

Yoiwa laughed his cold laugh. "Lord Shenri, murdered by ferocious nomads, is in no position to reject this match."

"Your mirth is premature, Yoiwa. Shenri's family will greet your son and your ridiculous overtures with derision! If this is truly your intent, allow me the joy of witnessing the Choosing. The excitements of Sohanyun lack most seriously by comparison!"

Yoiwa still smiled. Softly he said, "Ah, Ordas. I have long believed an excess of excitements turns one's brain to water."

Ordas said nothing, though inwardly he boiled at Yoiwa's insults.

"Lord Shenri is dead," Yoiwa continued. "On his way to Chisua, however, before he died he accepted the right of my son to choose Keleu–"

"I do not believe it!"

"–and committed the same to paper under his seal, intending to submit this to the new king for his blessing. The document is amongst Shenri's personal effects. And his effects, removed by the dutiful Ta-shih commander at Domita, are soon to be locked within that fortress. The Ta-shih commander will make inventory of Shenri's baggage, the document will be discovered, and Shenri's family in Mamoba will be notified. They will demand the document. They will scrutinize the seal, doubtless with some functionary from the Council looking over their shoulders. The document will state Shenri's will that Mathed of Honam and Keleu of Strath be wed."

"They will suspect chicanery and deceit – and justly so!"

"Exactly. But relations between our families have been cordial for some time. I have extended friendship and ensured Strath's commercial gain these past two years. Shenri was to be my noble guest in a few days at Deka. What host would murder his honoured guests? Moreover, Shenri's daughter esteems my son – a fortunate circumstance. Only Shenri's own son, Prince Osir, will be suspicious. He is no friend of ours, but he dare not proclaim allegations of the kind you speak, at the time of the new king's accession, for fear of appearing to seek the favour of the king against Honam. Moreover, how can Shenri's family dishonour the name of Strath by doubting the veracity of the seal of Strath!"

"Which you, no doubt, have purloined–"

"I command loyalty where it is necessary, Ordas. Do not concern yourself with my means."

"Whatever your means, this scheme," Ordas broke in with a crafty look, "lacks in one particular."

Yoiwa smiled. "You anticipate me, Ordas."

"I anticipate a great deal, Yoiwa. You wish my open support in this 'match' with Keleu of Strath..."

"I do."

"And what of the king's blessing? Who will solicit this on your behalf? Shenri's son? Never. Isharri of Allpo? Not in a thousand years! So you honour *me* with this happy duty..."

"Aye, you, Ordas."

"Yoiwa, I find this honour somewhat bewildering. You are a blunt man, so I too will be blunt. Our plans these past months entailed only the removal of Shenri, who thwarts you in Council, in spite of your so-called 'cordiality'. I have assisted you in this great step. But our agreement ended there. All of it was – shall we say – undisclosed to polite inspection. No one suspects an arrangement between us. Now you seek to contrive an enforced alliance between Honam and Strath through your son's premature marriage. You have made criminal use of the seal of Strath and you wish me to sponsor your petition to the king – for me an entirely *public* undertaking..."

"You state the matter," said Yoiwa wryly, "with exactness."

"As always." Ordas, thinking furiously in an attempt to peel back the layers of Yoiwa's convoluted scheme, began to perceive traps laid out for his unwary entanglement. Otherwise why the haste, so soon after the murder, to secure the king's blessing? A sinking feeling in the pit of his stomach told him that somewhere, somehow he had already been snared. Why had his spies not gleaned something of this? Why was he always a day behind, a move too late? However, if this were so, best then to play Yoiwa's scheme out to his own advantage…if not to Yoiwa's detriment. As Ordas struggled with these considerations, a plot of his own began to hatch.

With a noncommittal expression he asked, "And how will my sponsorship benefit Lorang?"

"Ah, straight to the heart, Ordas." Yoiwa smiled. "Dedication to my cause is its own reward. And you have already gained much from Shenri's demise. He was never partial to you."

"And your manners were never urbane, Yoiwa. You speak in riddles. I have little time for intrigues that profit Lorang not even a bronze leol. Yes, Shenri's passing was to my taste…but, eventually, when your son is installed as master of Strath, I ask: how will Lorang's power wax with your own?" Ordas turned away, a look of cunning narrowing his eyes. Yoiwa's ambition was, he must concede, quite breath-taking. No, more than breath-taking: evidently he had planned this over years, each piece of the puzzle nudged and guided into place. And here, at last, all of it came together. Up until now Ordas had perceived in Yoiwa's intrigues only the immediate, short-term political manoeuvrings so common among the Great Families. Certainly, the Lord of Honam was more belligerent than most, and his murder of another nobleman a risk of dangerous proportions, but added together they suggested a scale, cleverness and ambition he could only admire. Ordas made a show of gazing out upon the roofs of Sohanyun to the pine forests climbing the slopes of the Alnaes before continuing, "I see your plans with clarity, Yoiwa, and they are bold. Between Honam, Lorang and Strath, a man could control the northern Realm…and if Allpo fell, such a man would be…well…master of the Northern Passage, the Bay of Marshese and the Biljan Sea – a tidy empire, as tidy as the Biljan Kingdoms once were…and under your fist alone…"

Yoiwa said with a veiled smile, "You talk of treason, Ordas."

And now Ordas laughed. "Aye, treason. Like the murder of a lord! But we'll say no more on that." He looked at Yoiwa over his shoulder and said, "You have much to gain, Lord Yoiwa…nothing less than the rebirth of the Biljan Kingdoms…and you as king."

Ordas turned squarely to face Yoiwa. It was time to hitch himself more securely to Yoiwa's aspirations, but not without substantive gains and promises in return. Confidently he declared: "I shall petition the new king, Yoiwa, on your son's behalf. I shall support you. In return, within one year of the consummation, Mathed will cede to Lorang all of Kacia in southern Strath up to the Sav River."

Yoiwa looked searchingly into Ordas's face for a moment, then replied, "So be it. The king will receive your petition within the month?"

"On my honour… Oh, and one more thing…" Ordas paused, choosing his words as carefully as he could, the necessary emphasis on loyalty, the right degree of threat. "I hope, as allies, that when your plans move towards complete fulfilment and the power of the northern Realm rises under your leadership, you will remember your friends, the assistance they have offered…and the *secrets* they have kept."

Yoiwa's expressionless look had altered by not so much as a flicker. In return he said, "Of course." Then he narrowed his eyes – a tiny movement but freighted with warning – and added, "So long as our allies' secrets remain secure within their citadels. I have reason to believe that some of my allies are careless – from time to time, you understand – and perhaps lack the necessary skills, or motivation, to flush spies out…"

Ordas regarded the Lord of Honam with genuine puzzlement. Was this a threat, a warning, wordplay? He could not be sure. At the same time, he worried perpetually about the security of his household, the possibility of informers close enough to his affairs to be a danger and innocuous enough to be invisible. Moreover, his own attempts to buy secret access to Yoiwa's inner circle had been impossible and, where he had placed spies, he had long suspected information was fed to them in some elaborate, coherent counter-ploy, suggestive of truth but always too late or inaccurate to be useful. Whatever the case, there was need for caution: his hand was weak and he was now embroiled in treason, with no easy way to back out.

He needed time, time to think this through, in an urgent and extended meeting with his spymaster. Perhaps Yoiwa was right. Perhaps events had moved so far and so fast he needed to review his intelligence gathering and the security of his province.

With the slightest inclination of his head, the better to suggest gracious acceptance of a friend's concern, Ordas replied, "I thank you. We must shield each other's backs…"

Yoiwa grunted, almost rudely. "Aye, but look to your own first… Honour to you, Ke Ordas."

"Honour to you," Ordas responded, but with a rising feeling of trepidation.

Yoiwa turned and left.

***

North of Spimarrin, some twenty miles from the rock citadel of Sohanyun. Maki and Yan were riding on the flanks, Skava in the middle some hundred and fifty paces back, forming a rough echelon they hoped would flush the spy. Skava's observers had spotted him leave the citadel in haste – as she had anticipated. But credit to him, this spy for a party unknown, to get so close to the Lord of Lorang, as the right-hand man of Ordas's spymaster. Clever. Well-paid. Unusual. And he knew he was in danger now. But with a single horse, he could not ride continuously. Skava's squad had their remounts and another four-man squad of regulars in signalling distance. They would bring him to ground.

Her spies near Sohanyun had tracked three carrier pigeons he released shortly before he fled. Intercepted by hawks, the messages delivered to Skava by a relay courier seemed sham – worthy, workmanlike efforts, to be sure, but not sufficient to fool her. He had probably sent a despatch earlier, by a hidden, more reliable route. And that would get through to whoever his master was. And she needed to know who.

The country here was mostly flat, with occasional copses of woodland and dotted meres, water sparkling in the afternoon sun. Sedge and tall grasses surrounded the meres. Human habitation was nowhere in sight. Some cover, then, but not much. Skava cantered down a gentle slope between tall juniper trees. They had followed his trail, indistinct marks here and there, but just enough to stay on his scent.

A tiny sound, almost like a small animal squeak, and long-honed reflexes made Skava duck and bend sideways into the flick of air as a bolt passed her shoulder. *Crossbow!* Already she was turning her mount and getting some speed, trying to work out the direction. *How had he hidden his horse?* She had checked the copse from different angles coming onto it. Then suddenly, in the distance near a wide sparkling mere, a horse and rider broke cover, riding at speed and away. *What?*

Two of them. He had linked up with someone else.

She hauled back on her reins, changing direction again, but was constrained by her remount, which was confused and jittery now, tugging back at the tether. In that instant she swung her leg out of the saddle and onto the ground in a practised move and stayed behind the flanks of both horses, frantically searching the hillock. He had to be close, maybe forty paces. Her mount whinnied in pain and stumbled, and a dark crossbow shaft had appeared in its shoulder. *Behind.*

At once she turned, left the panicked horses and ran towards the threat. Difficult to see in sunlight and the long shadows cast by the trees and drifting dust kicked up by hooves. There, behind a juniper trunk, a man in loose dun trousers and a doublet, crossbow raised and level. Skava dived into the earth, heard the snap of the string, then leapt back up and ran straight on, hand on her long-knife to draw it. Her attacker sprinted uphill, crossbow swinging on a lanyard at his hip.

Where were Maki and Yan when she needed them?

He dodged between the trees, not getting away, shortsword in hand now, a small weapon but lethal. Skava's was in a scabbard strapped to her mount. Balls.

This was all to delay her, Skava realized with certainty. The spy was gone, probably on a fresh horse. Now she hoped Maki and Yan did *not* come to her aid. They needed to stay on the spy.

The attacker rounded on her, feet planted, sword in guard position across his chest, point down and forward, foot-long poniard in left hand at hip height. A professional. Skava stopped, pulled out her own poniard.

Not quite evenly matched. *Oh well…*

He advanced, seemingly confident, and Skava did the same, trying to keep a tree on her left to prevent him swinging the sword, but he was wise to it and circled a bit and she was forced to play his game or go downhill and cede height. He was not tall, she decided. Wiry and probably very fast. Pale eyes held her own, a tight dark cap pushed down to his eyebrows, and there was a black rag across his nose and mouth, concealing his features. So he expected to get away. Confident, indeed.

His first strike was a lunge with the sword, right at her face, rather good and the expected follow-up with the poniard under her guard. She retreated smoothly out of range, shifting her long-knife in small up and down movements, working for distraction, but he wasn't having any of it. With the sword he had the greater reach. Another lunge, down this time, then a rapid twist of his wrist to shift the tip towards Skava's heart. She turned side-on, the strike missed, and she was able to parry the follow-up poniard towards her shoulder with her knife, then drive upwards with her own poniard into his sword arm. He grunted, peeled away, and backed up as Skava sought to take advantage, but she couldn't advance fast enough. He was bleeding, but the sword was still in his hand.

His eyes, though, were now worried. That bleeding was bad. He would weaken quickly.

"Enough," Skava offered. "We'll talk." Everyone wanted to live. Especially good spies, or paid assassins, or whatever he was.

Blood dripped vivid ruby into the dry dust and leaves. Skava watched his eyes. A tiny narrowing, an instant's intensity and he lunged again. She knew what he would do and she swayed, crouched then knocked his sword arm away with her fist and struck with her knife. It entered under his armpit. A pained cry, then he reeled away, tugging free of Skava's blade. Four steps, like a drunk striving to keep upright, but the bloom of red blood down the side of his tan doublet was too much. He dropped to his knees, the sword point slipping and raking a sharp line across the dust. Knelt there, he looked like he might get up at any moment, as if he was tired; but the blood drenched his torso now, spreading in a stain through his loose trousers.

Skava looked around her, alert for other dangers. If there was one assassin, there could always be two. No. Nothing. Except Maki, who was galloping up the slope to rein in nearby.

"Boss?" He calmed his mount, which was turning circles.

"All good," she muttered and glanced back at the attacker as he keeled over sideways, crossbow quiver spilling four shafts. "My mounts," she called out to Maki. "Get 'em, would you. One took a bolt. Probably no good now."

"Yes, boss. And Yan's still on the spy." And he was off, had no doubt already spotted the horses as he came in. Good man, Maki. Not stupid, even if he did look like a horse.

Skava stood there. She quivered from the adrenaline rush of lethal action, but the expected nervous release was the usual one of sadness and regret. Every time. She approached the body cautiously. Dead. Too much blood to be anything other than very dead. Pity. She bent, poniard extended to his neck, just in case, but he was gone. He wouldn't carry anything that would provide clues to identity, but it was worth a look, so she dragged down the black scarf round his mouth. Grey sightless eyes, olive skin, small lips. It was a woman. *Well, well. You're not alone.* Managing to avoid the sticky heavy covering of blood, she examined the matted clothing but, of course, aside from some coins, blades and crossbow, she had nothing on her. A waste, Skava thought again. These were the kinds of professionals she could use. Why did they have to try to kill her?

Can't delay. The spy's the real quarry.

Maki had returned, leading only her remount, expertly saddled. Bad news then for the horse with the crossbow shaft. Skava swung up and they headed out again.

***

He was smart. He got himself onto a cattle trail, a wide churned up roadway, frequently used, where his tracks disappeared. Still, Yan was confident when they rejoined him that the spy was not far ahead. The light, on the other hand, was not good news. Perhaps a cycle of a water clock remained.

Yan gestured over his mount's head. "In there," he announced, and avoided looking pleased with himself. 'There' was a slow, meandering herd of cattle, thousands strong, making for a wide, flat lake. These were the small breed short-horns, piebald black and white. If he was in amongst them, he was unquestionably lying flat to conceal his profile. Clever. Hide in the crowd until dark, then sneak out.

"Where," asked Skava, "is the squad?"

Yan kept his eyes on the herd, jerked his chin. "Working ahead. Should spot him if he tries to get through."

Skava stood up in her stirrups, then knelt on her saddle. It gave her quite a bit more vertical perspective. Except their quarry was invisible. She could see the lake, even through the dust raised by thousands of hooves, but details in among the cattle were hazy at best.

Skava came to a decision. "Right," she instructed them. "Spread out, same formation, work your way through the cattle. Use the whistles if you lay eyes on him. See if we can flush him if we get close."

And they did. A short time later, Yan blew a sharp single blast on his whistle. He was fifty horse lengths away from Skava, and Maki was further still, but she saw the spy's head come up from among the cattle as he urged his mount onward, cutting along the lakeside with all three of his pursuers behind. Pushing through the cows, however, was difficult. Their horses weren't bred for it, and they shied or tucked their heads and jogged sideways around the cattle, themselves unhappy with the riders in their midst and bellowing aggressively.

Three short blasts on the whistle: Yan's signal that the spy was breaking away. Skava cursed her way through the herd. Eventually, as she made her way round the sedge on the muddy shoreline, she broke through the cattle jostling each other for a drink and spotted her other squad converging with four more unidentified riders and galloping away to the north.

Her mount was tiring. She slowed to a canter and Maki rode up from her left. Pursing her lips, she said, "Squad'll get him. We'll come up on them at best pace." She glanced sharply at him. "Who's the other squad?"

Maki shook his head. "No colours" – he meant the clan colours – "but harness was Ouine."

Strange. A surprise. Skava didn't like surprises.

***

The spy was stripped and tied by his ankles to a low bough. Beneath him, and slowly, the better to draw things out and allow the mind's terrors to anticipate the horror to come, a fire had been built and stoked.

Skava and Maki rode into the secluded glade at sunset. Yan was apart, with his mounts, and her courier squad were standing sentry at the edge of the trees.

It was Jophan, Yoiwa's nephew. He greeted her with jovial heartiness. "Well done, spymaster. You pushed him onto us!"

"Ke Jophan," she intoned, observing the appropriate politesse. He was a noble, after all, and close to Yoiwa and...dangerous. Clever. Sceptical. Ruthless. Sometimes wantonly cruel. "May I ask," she enquired, "how you came to be here?"

He swigged back water from a flask, handed it to a trooper, then answered, "My Lord Yoiwa graciously asked me to attend you." A smile, full of sharp teeth, it seemed. "He wished to send a parting message to his host at Sohanyun."

It was all beginning to fall into place. Skava nodded at the spy. The fire was licking hungry and hot at the wood and soon his scalp would burn. "Ke Jophan," she said carefully, "I would prefer to deal with this spy in *my* way." It was a challenge, a demarcation of accountabilities, and as far as she dared go with a noble of Jophan's disposition and influence. "He will not talk. I think he serves not for gold, but for another purpose, loyalty perhaps. Knowing who his master is...would be worth something."

Jophan shrugged, as if the matter of the spy revealing secrets were irrelevant or beneath him. Fucking nobles. When they wanted whatever they chose was a thing beneath them, a subject they would not discuss. It made their lives more convenient and less troubled by matters that might touch uncomfortably on reputation and dignity. Skava did not like torture. It achieved little when a spy might be persuaded to turn, or even let loose to run and used to advantage. Worse yet, it sent ripples of menace to alert enemies to events from which intelligence might be drawn and countermeasures introduced and her whole fucking plan disrupted…

She tried another tack. "Ke Jophan," she asked politely, "what is the message that my Lord Yoiwa wishes sent?"

Jophan favoured her with another wolfish smile, sufficient to say *you shall see*. And, with no choice or recourse, she turned her back and helped Maki with the horses, currying coats and checking hooves. Her mount had thrown a shoe, so Yan got busy. All the while Jophan's squad applied themselves to the spy. Upside-down over the fire, his hair soon burned away in a hideous mass of red blisters and seeping blood. He jerked in spasms like a large fish strung up for gutting, but made no sound. A brave man. His bulging eyes managed at last to fix on Skava as she watched from a distance. She did not flinch, though it seemed he understood perfectly who she was. Jophan's guardleader ordered one eye put out, slowly. This done, the spy was revived by his tormentors, trickling water over his face and lips.

Jophan sauntered over to Skava. The dark evening was chilly and he had fastened his red and gold cloak about his shoulders. "Spymaster," he declared, "congratulations…again! He does not speak. You were right, as usual. Your shrewdness in these matters is gods-given." He folded his arms, eyes flashing in the firelight. "But tell me," he asked, "what do we know of him?"

A large question. A question of layers and complexity. She decided to tell him *most* of what she had concluded. "He has been placed in Sohanyun for years. Since we did not know he was a traitor to Lord Ordas until very recently, it tells us he has acted with great vigilance. He had an accomplice, to provide a fresh mount and to attack me. So, they were organized. I have reason to believe now that he has a contact in Kiangsu City, a merchant who in his turn is to report to an intelligencer in Chisua. Which faction of which body of the Realm takes an interest in our affairs, Ke Jophan, we cannot – and should not – surmise. These things, as you know, are kept in small cells, individuals who know only one other in their cell. It may be Archivists, lords of this province or that, even the new king… As to the spy's knowledge, the message we intercepted in Chisua lays bare our visit to Lord Ordas and suggests, with evidence, that his troops placed the barbarians in the vicinity of the murder as a convenient scapegoat, thus, that someone else – in other words, someone with influence – perpetrated the awful deed. The contiguity of our presence in Lorang and the murder are cause for speculation in his report, no more. However, the placement of this spy in Lord Ordas's household is more worrying. As I warned last week, he is…or was…the right-hand man to Lord Ordas's spymaster."

Ke Jophan received this report without emotion. He asked simply, "All of the spy's messages were intercepted?"

Skava knew they could not have been. This spy was good. Worse than that, he was dedicated. Dedicated men died for their cause. His escape had been, she realized, a deliberate ploy. He had made himself visible to her observers. Somehow another message had been sent. Still, she had no reason to tell Jophan everything. Instead, she replied, "Yes."

Jophan turned back to the fire and the swinging body above it. He called out with good humour, "How does he fare, the spy?"

The guardleader gave a half bow, his silhouette in front of the orange firelight a grotesque black hulk. "He sees with one eye, my lord," came the reply, "but begs no mercy."

Jophan made a gesture with his fingers, negligent but sufficient to confirm what he had already planned. "He sees too much," he concluded. "We shall return him to his master."

And there it was. The message to Lord Ordas. More theatre.

***

That evening, in contemplative mood, Lord Ordas dined alone in one of the high towers of the citadel. The stairs he ascended were constructed of a material, common in the ancient parts of his demesne, that seemed to defy age – not that he gave any attention to them, they had simply always just been. On the upper floor, he partook of what, for him, was a frugal meal of pheasant topped with damson cheese, washed down by a single chalice of clear Corcoran wine reputed to have aphrodisiac properties. Tonight's light dinner would enable him to better savour the sexual delights he had planned: at that very moment, Khead, Ordas's retainer, was ushering into an upstairs chamber two young girls, much favoured by their master not only for their beauty and extraordinary agility, but also for their erotic perversions.

Leaving the table to stand nearer the fireplace, for the day's warmth had brought cold winds with the sunset, Ordas gave himself over to an examination of the day's events, accompanied by much rubbing of his hands and pursing of his lips, actions which the servant, clearing the table, took to be anticipation for the night's pleasures. This was not, however, the case. Ordas thought only of Yoiwa.

Ordas grunted aloud at the memory of their meeting. The servant, unquestioning of his lord's behaviour, merely finished clearing the table and in silence withdrew.

Ordas rubbed his hands once more, twisting at his rings. From a bowl on a high table of intricate scrollwork, he took a handful of boiled sweets, eating one at a time in absent-minded enjoyment. Yoiwa's plans were shocking, certainly, but more than this, Ordas realized, they had a high probability of success. They had the powerful virtue of simplicity. One move led to another, with astonishingly large advantages, in the end, for the Lord of Honam. What had made the plan impenetrable until now was the timescale over which Yoiwa was working: the pattern could not be perceived. Neither Ta-shih, nor Council, nor indeed king would see what was happening. Until too late...

Except, perhaps, for the Archivists. Ordas gave his attention, momentarily, to this subject, and his instincts told him the Archivists would be alert to Yoiwa's machinations, perhaps even were part of them; but in his heart of hearts he knew, with a startling clarity, that their concentration would be distracted by their own factional disagreements and by their weakness in the north and west of the Realm. They would assume they knew more than they really did. Yoiwa would feed them palatable titbits to excite their interest in this or that Council matter. He would, in Ordas's estimation, divide and rule. *I would do the same, would I not?* came the thought.

And hard on the heels of that, there pressed the question: where lay the dangers or advantages in his secret alliance with Honam? The dangers first: informers, Ordas told himself with a hiss of irritation. Reliable information transmitted to Council? Not a likely problem – such a self-absorbed herd of functionaries obsessed with the petty tactics of immediate political advantage would, even with substantiation of treason of impeccable provenance, cavil and debate and delay, convincing themselves in the end of the impossibility of what they had heard, or rounding on those who proposed it with the bitter rivalry of school children. The king? A new king, an unknown, unproven individual, might he already have his spy network, or his father's, active in pursuit of new threats? Not impossible that one of his intelligencers would seek to impress his new monarch with astounding and secret news… Then what? And here, of course, were the advantages: the execution of Yoiwa and the confiscation of the province, lords loyal to the Realm rewarded, with one bold move Ordas demonstrating his loyalty to sovereign and realm and acquiring all of northern Honam…a wonderful dream.

Ordas laughed, ample shoulders heaving under his long, embroidered chiton. Ah, the exaltation! But less likely than Council taking decisive action. Where was the proof? To accuse a lord of Yoiwa's stature – painful as that was to admit – of treason would take a very bold king, never mind the youth about to ascend the throne. Even to act secretly on such intelligence would entail further delay, further investigations, the strengthening of spying operations, the testing and proving of loyalties among the Great Families and the other lords…all of which, Ordas concluded, Yoiwa would have anticipated. And what was his timescale, what ends did he expect, and how soon? What plans did he have for seizing Shenri's birthright in Strath? Did he seek to provoke outright confrontation with the new king or play himself into favour, becoming overlord across the north, the right-hand of the monarch?

He popped a last sweet into his mouth. Forgetful of the lamentable state of his teeth, he bit hard and pain lanced through his jaw. His physician had long warned him against sweet things.

Ordas sighed, all levity gone. He envied Yoiwa in too many ways, but especially in two specifics. First, his strategic cleverness, his grasp of the huge complexity of the Realm's power and how to shift it to his advantage. Second, his spymaster. The man was brilliant, quite simply a genius of the arts so vital to Kiangsu power and politics. Perhaps, to be sure, Yoiwa's advantage in the first grew directly from his superlative advantage in the second. *Skava.* That was the name that had been reported to Ordas, though no one was certain. His identity was hidden. He might have been one or any of Yoiwa's closest bodyguard, or a soldier or servant in close attendance, but anonymous, or not even travelling with his lord. Ordas had long attempted to uncover the truth of this, but had failed. Likely candidates had, enticingly, emerged and been dismissed, in time, as false. The resulting uncertainty – deliberately cultivated, Ordas was certain, by Skava himself – had discouraged further efforts. In the end Ordas had recalled his spies and put the gold to better use elsewhere. His own spymaster, by comparison, was middling, the best he could buy or cultivate. And were it possible for him to expend vast reserves of treasure on better, he knew, though it pained him, that none in the Realm could equal Skava.

All of which drew him to an inevitable conclusion: for good or ill, for the great glory of Lorang or its utter destruction, he was locked with Yoiwa in a complicated dance of moves he only part recognized or could anticipate. But Lord Ordas was nothing if not ambitious. He must work out the pattern of this dance. He must learn the moves.

By association of ideas Ordas was reminded of the girls awaiting him in his chambers and immediately made for the passage and stairs. His way was lit by ornate brass cressets, in which tiny flames were magnified by glass lenses. Along the high walls were long copper pipes, bringing water from the huge filtration tanks above the palace. Reaching the lower landing, with a newfound confidence and purpose, he brushed aside the heavy curtains across the doorway to his bedchamber and strode within. The two concubines, lovely girls dressed in gossamer fabrics that hid nothing of the smooth sheen of coppery skin, rose gracefully from piled cushions near the low bed and came to him. Ordas smiled at both in turn, heedless of the effect of his teeth, and reached for pendulous breasts. The girls showed effortless self-possession in ignoring his grin.

Pressing close and running her hands across his neck, one of the girls whispered, "Tonight we delight you with a hundred pleasures, my lord…"

"Yes, yes…" Ordas breathed, trembling with the thrill of anticipation. He thrust a fat arm around yielding flesh and bent his head to suck at the breast beneath the gauzy material.

The other girl took his free arm and drew him gently towards the bed. Disengaging himself from the first girl, Ordas watched as both stripped nude, casting aside their gauzy robes.

A discreet cough from outside his bedchamber brought a pause to proceedings. Ordas frowned. "Yes, Khead!" he snapped, though not unaware his chief retainer would have only good reason to interrupt.

"A package, my lord. From the Lord of Honam, bearing the seal of Clan Ouine."

Ordas drew a breath. Another move in the dance? The girls waited by the huge low bed, faces frozen in odd expressions halfway between seduction and startlement – comical, really. Their plans were forestalled, their purpose stripped away: *it is confusing, this dance, is it not?*

Ordas waved a hand and turned, the girls forgotten as they left the room in silence, dismissed. "Bring it," he ordered.

Khead parted the curtains and a servant carried into the bed-chamber an iron box, of a kind typically used for travel and the safeguarding of possessions of value, fine goblets perhaps, or coin for the payment of soldiers in the field. Placed carefully on a round table near the wall, and with the servant gone, the box sat, dull, grey, a gleaming gold and vermillion seal over the open clasp-lock, the mark of Clan Ouine, invitation or challenge to its recipient. In the half-light, Ordas stared at it and found himself tapping a finger absently against his thigh. *A gift from my new dance partner, something I must embrace…though I know it comes at a cost.*

To Khead he shrugged. "Break the seal," he sighed. "Tell me its contents."

Khead stepped close, bent over the box and, lifting the clasp, raised the lid. He stood back, turning to his master as a flicker of uncertainty passed for a moment across his habitually passive features.

"Well?" enquired Ordas. "What is my gift from the Lord of Honam?"

Erect and in a tone of calm restraint, Khead answered, "A head, my lord. It belongs to your spymaster's deputy. The eyes are gouged and the scalp burned. But it is he."

Ordas tapped his finger faster.

Ah, Yoiwa, thought Ordas, *that is what you meant at our parting. You are a master of this dance. But though you move more quickly than I, you lead it with more courtesy than I might have expected. And that…that shows me one thing, one critical thing: I am important to you. And thus the dance continues…*

CHAPTER 4

[…] In this I serve my king and the Realm. And swear upon my sacred honour and my life.
Conclusion to the Oath of Probity affirmed by Officers of the Ta-shih.

[…] genetic drift that changes the proportional distribution of an allele by chance […] due to the smaller size of the population bottleneck after the near extinction event […] probability of increasing the frequency of the fitter genes in the gene pool.
Fragment of a larger document, copied by a scribe, IYE 1047.

***

There was pain. What had been intermittent and remote had become persistent and, in surges and waves, pure agony. His limbs, for so long inert and useless, had been jolted and wrenched. His saviours, grim-faced soldiers in grey Ta-shih uniform, seemed intent on killing him with their attentions. They lifted his shoulders to cut the buckles of his armour and gifted him shooting pain through neck and arms. They pulled at his boots and blinding explosions of torment ripped through his spine and legs. They manhandled him onto a pallet, grunting ridiculous encouragement to each other to, "Take care!" and, "Gentle now…" whilst inflicting yet more pain. Even the cool wash of water on his face seared his left eye socket. And nothing, it seemed, would soothe the raw heat of his throat.

But there was the face of the officer – a serious face, under worried brows, a face of unhappy concern and deep suspicion, a face that deterred easy acquaintance. Yet it was a face that Adaim…trusted.

Under the assault of pain, all time, sequence and coherence cracked. Fragments of the outside world intruded like inexact clues to an impossible puzzle. Voices, perhaps the same, perhaps different, drifted into his consciousness: "Knife to the throat, Commander…Domita soon…not hopeful…regimental surgeon at Ingen would know best…" Jumbled images, unconnected to anything, flashed in broken pieces – the clear blue sky, the head of a horse at the edge of vision, a fire and bodies consumed in twisting flames – then blackness, perhaps night, and granite grey stone in the dawn light. Then his mother and his father, pale faces earnest and urging him to say something. *What?* he asked them. They implored him but, desperate as he was, he could not understand them. At their side, Lord Shenri, astride his mount…in dreams? Yes, in dreams. For in every waking moment there was only the nightmare of pain.

And then there was violence. He became aware of voices, the snap of commands:

"Hold him, hold him!"

"Aye, got him…"

Shock made way for terror. *What are you doing to me? What are you doing…*

Strong hands at his shoulders and a weight against his knees, then unbelievable burning coruscated through his neck and torso. His world imploded – bright white, yellow, then black.

In time, shards of lucid awareness cut through the heavy fog of pain and incomprehension. His shoulders and neck were immobilized. He was strapped to a pallet between two horses, and a small awning cut and expertly jury-rigged from a soldier's bedroll – a green Strath bedroll, he noted inconsequentially – shaded him from the sun. Nearby, if he peered with his good right eye, he could see the Ta-shih officer, crested helmet strapped to the saddle of the horse he rode, sword pommel and hardened leather scabbard at the man's hip, a worn but carefully oiled black leather belt over grey tunic. His face was stern, as if he disapproved of the world or was disappointed in it…or perhaps in himself. They had this in common then, the thought came to Adaim, and he wanted to say something, but managed only a pathetic wheezing accompanied by the coppery taste of blood. *What is it that I need to tell him?* Adaim was uncertain. Perhaps it was about the pain, he concluded. It must be about the pain, for it was all-consuming, a torture when the soldiers unfastened the pallet from the horses, lowering him to the ground and, clumsily gentle, tried to guide water down his throat and moved his limbs…and, to his shame, cleaned him where he had soiled himself.

"Easy now," came a voice.

Easy! He wanted to scream. He wanted to scream until death took him. Yet inevitable oblivion was followed by inevitable waking…darkness, sunlight, darkness, the overcast of grey cloud…and the pain.

But through it all there was the face of the officer…

***

Company Commander Pillio, together with the injured Strath soldier, the two golden-haired Shur-Shur, ten Ta-shih troopers, and all of the personal effects and appurtenances of Lord Shenri, had, on the day of King Jamarin V's funeral, started the journey to East Lorang from Domita fortress. Of course, the funeral of the late king was as distant to Pillio at this time as Chisua itself. Indeed, news of the exact date of the funeral had yet to reach these isolated regions. Thus, unmindful of the great events that moved the capital, Pillio ruminated on the crime which had become central to his life.

His men, sensing the preoccupation of their commander and deeply suspicious still of the two Shur-Shur, were quiet, even surly, and rode their mounts in two files with the barbarians between. Both nomads were bound at the wrist and tethered to the saddles, and the troopers spared them a frequent sidelong glance as if to reassure themselves that no magic was worked on the restraints.

Pillio rode next to the horses carrying the pallet and glanced occasionally at the ashen face of the soldier. He did not expect him to live. His own field surgeon at Domita was experienced in treating wounds, but rarely anything like this. Peace in the provinces produced, thankfully, little more than snake bites, accidental injuries and, rarely, a knifing between drunken soldiers. Butchery on the scale that Pillio and his men had witnessed was unknown. Still, the surgeon had washed and cleaned, cut and cauterized, and the poor soul still clung to this world.

So the odd little party made its way along the paved road in the flat Lorang Steppes until, on the fifth day, the hazy purple shadows in the distant north-east began to take on the definite form of mountains – this the narrow central spine of the high Alnaes, marking at its eastern-most point the common borders of four provinces: Lorang, Strath, Honam, and Kiangsu North. Ingen, the regional command of the Ta-shih, was in sight before sundown. The circular fortress, constructed to billet a thousand men, stood squat in the foreground of the small local town, itself at the edge of the robbed-out tumble of an ancient city, little more than irregular mounds now, like the cracked bleached teeth of a gigantic creature of fable. The sun played its weak, golden light against the town's drab stone walls and timber roofs. Over the road in an open field, Pillio's party passed two peasants who brought their plough horse to a standstill while they stared from under wide reed hats at the startling picture of the barbarians. Behind the two peasants a flock of birds wheeled in the air, diving down to the newly turned earth to pluck at worms.

Arriving saddle-sore at the gates of the fortress in the half-light, Pillio passed the injured man to the care of the regimental surgeon, whilst his squad were shown to quarters and the barbarians to guarded cells. Pillio's relief was immense: responsibility passed to someone else. He could return tomorrow to Domita and the excitement of the last few days would be gone. Eager to conclude matters, he reported directly to the detachment commander, a man several years Pillio's senior in age, of ruddy complexion and grim, hollow cheeks. He sat in the comfort of a large wooden armchair, hands steepled before him, boots near the radiant warmth of a fire, and listened with a deep frown upon his face to Pillio's report, the essence of which he had heard from Pillio's messenger a week earlier. Every now and then he gave utterance to staccato questions.

Refreshments were brought to the detachment commander's chambers, but Pillio ate sparingly of the roasted meats and rice. To his superior he handed a statement under the seal of Lord Ordas, detailing his understanding of the events, as well as a carefully prepared inventory of Lord Shenri's belongings. Then, searching for some reaction, he watched the flicker of shadows cast by the fire on the gaunt face. The detachment commander, holding the papers up to the light, read in silence, grunted now and again, then after a time returned the documents to the table-top and sipped thoughtfully at his goblet of wine.

The silence remained unbroken for several minutes. With the warmth of the fire and the food and wine he had taken, Pillio felt the tension begin to fall from him like a heavy burden. The darkness in the room seemed to cocoon him, so that there was only the beating brightness of the fire and the brooding features of the detachment commander, one half of his face hidden in shadow. Then, reaching a decision, the detachment commander replaced his goblet on the table, heaved himself to his feet, and directed Pillio to accompany him to the cell of the Shur-Shur. Jerking out of his languor, Pillio followed him out of the room down flights of steps and into a long, poorly lit corridor that brought them to a series of barred wooden doors. A soldier at the second of the doors came smartly to attention, grounding a polished staff next to his sandalled feet. The detachment commander gestured for the door to be opened, which was accomplished with a rattling of keys and the drawing of two foot-long bolts at top and bottom. The door swung open, and the soldier grasped a storm lantern from a nearby bracket and ducked under the stone lintel, again coming to attention just inside the doorway, lantern held aloft to illuminate the cell. Pillio entered behind the detachment commander.

On a large straw pallet lay the woman. She clutched a blanket around her body and had risen onto her elbow at the intrusion, her head twisted round over her shoulder. The wide, pale eyes stared from her face, framed by the shock of golden hair. Pillio was astonished at the ghostly vision that the flickering lantern produced. The detachment commander, standing in front of Pillio, remained motionless for the space of a dozen heartbeats, regarding the woman with a disbelieving scowl, then bestirred himself and enquired tersely of the whereabouts of the other Shur-Shur. The soldier replied that the "giant barbarian" was in the next cell.

During this brief interchange, Pillio watched the woman, who had not moved at all, and whose eyes were still fixed upon the detachment commander. A half-hidden fear lit her eyes and, behind it, a hopelessness that shamed Pillio momentarily.

"A curiosity, to be sure," muttered the detachment commander. "Does she not speak?"

"She does. But the Shur-Shur have many dialects and we have no one who can translate," responded Pillio. "My guardleader speaks a few words of Shur-Shur and she speaks a few words of Sanglix. Between them, enough to confuse each other…" He looked thoughtfully at the woman. "Though I suspect she hides something. Perhaps she knows what we say…"

But the detachment commander was no longer listening. Already he had swung on his heel to duck once more under the lintel. And Pillio, who lingered an instant longer than he should, and for reasons he could not fathom, met the haunted gaze before turning his back to leave the cell.

***

Dawn was bright and golden in the courtyard of Ingen fortress, but a chill wind moaned through the eaves of the stables, stirring the hay and swirling fine motes of dust that danced like jewels in the shafts of light between the dark wooden beams. Pillio, who had inspected the saddling of his squad's mounts before dawn, stood unmoving in the wide doorway. The straw dust speckled his boots and left a fine, almost invisible, coating on the thick grey twill of his trousers and tunic.

High overhead clouds scudded across the violet-blue sky, driven by the winds that still swept down from the Alnaes in the late spring. Carried on the wind were the scents and odours of the town: wood smoke and the thick tang of horses, and, from somewhere nearer at hand, the mouth-watering smell of grilled bacon.

Pillio hooked his thumbs into the broad leather belt at his waist, feeling the accustomed weight of the shortsword in the scabbard on his left hip and the officer's dagger sheathed at his right hip.

Iron-shod hooves clattered on the cobbles of Ingen's courtyard: the horses of Pillio's squad stamped and fretted and snorted steam into the cold air while their riders received orders from a guardleader. Today the men who had accompanied Pillio from Domita returned to their post in the Lorang Steppes. Pillio did not.

The detachment commander had summoned him in the grim, cold moments before dawn. "Your men will return to Domita," he had informed him, flint-eyed and abrupt, and immediately put the question: "Your troopmaster is a good man?" At Pillio's affirmative the detachment commander continued: "Then there will be no need for the moment for a replacement at Domita. I have no officers to spare, anyway. I shall have word sent to him that he is to take command in your absence. For you I have an assignment…"

Pillio was himself to escort the barbarians to Kiangsu City and make his report on the murder of Lord Shenri to the Cherson Regimental Command. The order had astounded Pillio, despite the detachment commander's careful assurances: *There is need of security in this. And your account is of greater value by far than any second-hand report or the words of a courier.* It was a circumstance, though logical, wholly unexpected, and Pillio, thinking the matter through after receiving into his care an authorization under the detachment commander's seal, experienced his first moment of annoyance. This was not a mission he had sought. He did not feel ready for it.

Into the brilliant sunshine casting long diagonal shadows across the furrowed fields, Pillio watched his men ride out of the fortress gates on their homeward journey to Domita without him. He frowned at his situation. His naturally suspicious cast of mind left him no comfort. It seemed that Ingen's detachment commander saw odium in this case which he knew he must carefully skirt. The man was politically astute; Pillio was not.

Brooding on the matter, Pillio struggled with his annoyance, finding himself despising the detachment commander and yet not wholly persuaded that he was not himself using this to excuse his own qualms. Was his duty not plain? He owed loyalty to the Ta-shih and the king. But it was the magnitude of the crime, and his equivalent responsibility in having to report it, that caused Pillio such trepidation. He realized only now how strong had been his conviction that by passing the burden on to higher authority, in the way of the Ta-shih, somewhere someone would have the answers and the power to take action, to restore the balance… to take the responsibility out of his hands. Instead, the problem remained his: a journey of over five hundred miles to the headquarters of the Ta-shih in the northern Realm. The onus on him seemed immense.

Pillio's men had gone, leaving the courtyard empty save for two sentries at the gate. He was alone. His world had changed. Preparations for the expedition must be made and he must meet his new guardleader and troops. Of the many things that worried him, he dreaded this moment: unfamiliar men, the need to win their confidence, to get to know them…

"Commander Pillio…"

Pillio turned. At the doorway to the officers' quarters stood the detachment commander.

Pillio made his way over and nodded. "Detachment Commander?"

His superior's face was blank and he stared unblinkingly at Pillio. "The injured man, Lord Shenri's trooper…"

Pillio waited, expecting a question or perhaps news on the man's deterioration overnight.

"It occurs to me," declared the detachment commander, "that the surgeons in Kiangsu may be better equipped to help him. Certainly we can do nothing more for him here. Moreover, if he survives, he is a witness… and the authorities in Kiang will want to hear his story." For the first time Pillio thought he detected a faltering in his superior's expression, an uncertain flicker, but quickly masked under military formality. "You are to take him with you. Your new squad's guardleader, Manei, he is quite competent as a field surgeon and will be invaluable."

Pillio, bewildered and indignant, began to protest. He was cut off by the detachment commander's curt nod. "Thank you, Commander Pillio.

Good luck." He turned on his heel in the doorway and was gone.

The sun, risen two diameters above the fortress walls, warmed Pillio's cheek but gave him no comfort as he made his way, stunned and sullen, to the barracks.

***

Skava had tied a dark leather flap as a flange to the end of the telescope to shade the lens. Precautionary: the sun was up and she wanted no one to know there was anyone out here watching Ingen fortress and the nearby town from the surrounding farmland. Next to her was Maki, also flat on his belly. A hundred paces further back were the horses with her other squaddie, Yan, behind a bank of sage-brush. The main gate to Ingen was open. If the detachment commander of Ingen fortress had done what her spies had paid him to do, she could execute the next phase of this sideshow, and get back to moving the big pieces on the board. Two days ago she had received a report from an informer in the fortress that not only were the two barbarians in the fortress, as expected, but that the fucking Ta-shih had found one of Shenri's bodyguard alive. Skava had been apoplectic. She'd had forty of Honam's finest all over Shenri's camp. Maki and Yan had made sure no one survived. Her planning had been meticulous. She had even accompanied them to be certain of the outcome, and still there was a survivor. So now she had two barbarians and a Strath trooper who could corroborate each other. It was bad. And it could have been a catastrophe, were it not for the placement of her informers.

Movement at the gates. Was this the Ta-shih troop on its way? Telescope to her eye, steadied on the back of her arm, deep breath, and she focused on the figures emerging from the fortress in the bright, misty light of dawn. The telescope lenses were grainy from age, but clear enough, and within two heartbeats she could see the lead man astride his horse – presumably the company commander, Pillio that would be, leading the troopers in two files. Barbarians on mounts between the third rank pair. Then two horses, yoked together by the look of it and bearing some load between them – the injured Strath trooper no doubt. Behind this, two more pairs of Ta-shih and the small baggage train: mules and a dozen remounts.

Skava counted them all, then counted again, and finally passed the telescope to Maki. "Check numbers," she instructed.

He took his time. Maki was orderly and methodical. She liked that. He grunted, raised his head and carefully laid the telescope in the crook of his arm. Without turning his head, he answered, "Company commander, ten troopers, one of 'em a guardleader I should think, a stretcher between mounts, two Shur-Shur, five mules and twelve spares. I'd reckon two crossbows among 'em and they're in half-mail for the march: he's not takin' no chances. Guessin' they've enough grain for the mounts for a week or so. If they resupply at a Ta-shih waypoint, that means another week and that means Nek Feddah cos that's where the barges go south."

Skava retrieved the telescope. "My thoughts exactly," she concurred, and scanned the party once more. Ten troopers. The two barbarians… count them as warriors. Company commander. Lucky thirteen. And then the Strath soldier.

It was warming up. The sun was hot on her cheek. Maki, at her side, was quiet. He knew she was thinking and he was no idiot to interrupt and talk aimlessly. She respected that.

Thirteen was a challenge. But hopefully the Ingen detachment commander had furnished a suitably poor squad of Ta-shih for Pillio: the dregs the Ingen commander didn't want. She sniffed. That was optimistic. Be careful, she warned herself. So, assume they were better than the average. She had to take them and get done with the barbarians and the Strath trooper – and the damned company commander, for all that, because he may well have extracted some intelligence from them all by now. And this whole thing was a fucking huge distraction she didn't need, what with Lord Yoiwa long gone and heading back to Honam and a thousand things she needed to be doing.

"Right," she said, hating the messiness and being unbalanced and in no position to bring this to an end yet, "we shadow them." She closed the telescope, pocketed the leather flange and wriggled back from the small ridge and down into a dry drainage gully. Maki followed her. Crouched over and invisible to both Ingen fortress and Pillio's column, they moved back to the horses, pushing through the sage-brush. Her other squaddie, Yan, was checking the remounts, patting a flank here and there and murmuring to the horses: he loved horses.

"Yan," she said, jerking her chin at the young man. "Keep them in sight. Maki and I will trail you by two miles. We reckon they want to make Nek Feddah for a barge south. With an injured man on a stretcher, they won't move fast, but I'm taking no chances. You stick to 'em like flies on shit, you get it?"

Yan ran his hand down the neck of his roan. "Nek Feddah," he echoed. "Keep 'em in sight. Slow. No chances."

"That's it. Report in nightly when they make camp. Maki will relieve you for first watch."

Yan prepared to mount up. He was moving light. His spare horse, which he would leave with Skava and Maki, carried slightly more than the usual in bags – each of them had stored most of their armour, the red and gold Ouine cloaks and any distinguishing kit. To anyone they met, they were now free guards returning to Nek Feddah to run another valuable shipment of gold or deeds of sale or whatever a rich merchant wanted couriered in safety. It meant they could still openly carry arms and courier pigeons.

Skava turned to Maki. "You got the messages from our man in Ingen?" She had activated a relay to this godforsaken fortress in the middle of nowhere. Messages from across her network to her base in Honam were now being sent on here by her hard-pressed birds, and Maki had picked up the despatches long before dawn. Transporting birds to every corner of her network, in spite of the gold and organisation devoted to it, was coming under strain.

"Yep," Maki confirmed, tapping his ribs where a pocket was looped and tied with leather thongs.

"Good." She glanced at Yan as he walked his mount off in slow pursuit of the Ta-shih squad. His remount he left with the others. "Let's have 'em. Correspondence, eh, Maki? Never a moment's peace."

He handed over a pouch and then went to check on the birds, four pigeons in a travelling coop with separate compartments. Satisfied, he set to examining each of the horses in turn, checking fetlock, hoof and shoe, tugging at harness and bending to critically examine ring buckles and signs of worn leather. The horses snickered and nosed him in their turn, enjoying the attention.

Skava squatted, laid out a folded bedroll in front of her on the stony ground to assemble her morning's correspondence. Seven messages, all in code, each marked secretly by her network so she could establish the point of origin. One was not her code – and her heart skipped a beat. For a moment she set it aside, and in the instant of scanning the other six she had a clear picture in her mind of what was happening across the Realm, what might affect her plans or need adjusting.

"Maki," she called. "Get rid of these." She handed the six parchments to him without looking up. He would burn them. They always burned them.

The seventh parchment was, at face value, a merchant note. But to Skava's eye it screamed complex code. There was a pattern – a good one – but she was the best in the fucking world at this and she would crack it in short order. Just needed time. And already she knew something about it. A tiny sigil on the pouch showed it had been intercepted in Chisua by Daved and Fortunas. It was from the printer they were watching. And they were watching him because he was new – or at least they had become aware of him in the last two months – and Skava got very worried when someone new started up and they didn't fit a modus operandi she recognized. It meant there was another player.

With an irritated sucking of teeth, she began to worry at the pattern, transposing letters and sequences rapidly, ignoring the numbers appearing as monetary amounts in several places, memorizing the known codes she was trying and excluding each time, moving on to the next combination, trying a different cipher method. She sucked her teeth yet again. Some of the words and quite possibly the amounts were names. But hypothesizing was not deciphering: the code remained obscure.

She took a breath to exert and re-establish discipline. In a heartbeat, she was calm. These setbacks and surprises were nothing new. However, a knot of tension resisted, a taut reminder in her gut that this cipher was too good. And that raised implications she was not ready to confront. She folded the bedroll tight to strap to her saddle. In her left glove, the parchment was curled up in a tiny roll, unchanged since its arrival. She moved it to a small pouch on her belt and clipped the flap shut.

"Maki," she said. "Let's go. We'll walk the beasts. No rush. And I need to think."

Maki was grinding the ashes of a tiny fire of the other parchments into the earth. If he had any thoughts on her recent flash of uncharacteristic irritation with the cipher, he knew her well enough not to share them.

***

The Cise River, whose enormous swelling length looped a sinuous thousand kems south through mountains and plains to flood at last into the Chisuan Reach, had its source in Honam Province in the eastern flanks of the Alnaes. Owing to the height of the mountains and the permanent snows capping the peaks, the main branch of the Cise in these parts was fed by innumerable spillways and cataracts that pounded the waters into a wide, muddy torrent. The gushing switchbacks were choked with the splintered limbs of trees. Huge boulders, recently swept from the precipitous scarps, lay at crooked angles like the insane architecture of a race of giants.

Cutting its way through the deep valleys of the Alnaes from the west, a road crossed the furious brown deluge that was the Cise by means of a high wooden bridge, built as a single arch to span the broken, choppy waters, its thick-timbered supporting limbs wide enough to avoid the seasonal flood occasioned by the spring thaw. It was here that Pillio found himself, twelve days later, accompanied by his ten-man troop and the two barbarians, all mounted, with three mules at the rear of the party burdened with additional supplies and two more to carry, slung between them, the pallet with the injured soldier. The remounts trailed behind the last pair of Pillio's column. Although they travelled light, with no more than their own armour and weapons, bedrolls, tents and sufficient hard-

133

tack for a two-week trip, they still needed oats for the horses as there was little grazing along this rocky route. And the heavy bags of feed meant the mules and horses had been loaded heavily at the outset. Things were easier now. The horses were lugging less and the mules did the hard work,

Pillio carried his own equipment and, wrapped carefully in leather in a saddlebag, the most valued of all his possessions, Hexil's *A History of the Civilized World.* He had packed the large volume in Domita, estimating that during the short trip to and from Ingen fortress he might profitably break the tedium of long hours on horseback by re-reading chapters of the great work. And now, on this unexpected journey whose duration he feared to guess, the book was of immeasurable solace to him in the cold evenings next to the campfire before full dark forced him to close the cover.

On several occasions, as the two files of horses plodded steadily up the rocky twists and turns of the road, Pillio would occupy himself by drawing his horse level with the barbarians who, by the Ingen detachment commander's orders, were manacled. He offered tentative words and phrases and was greeted at first with stony silence. Persisting, and by dint of vigorous hand signals and repetitions of his own name, while simultaneously maintaining a studied indifference to the raised eyebrows and broad grins of the soldiers, he discovered the man's name to be something like Kelukembrah and the woman Aneth – tongue-twisting pronunciations which Pillio approximated as best he could. Still the barbarians seemed chary of his advances, although at times he was convinced Aneth was on the verge of uttering some word or phrase he might understand. Not a sociable man anyway, and little given to smiling, Pillio wondered whether his manner imposed an impregnable barrier between them.

Again he caught the woman looking at him, the strange indigo eyes piercingly alien. Even the clothes that she had been given, a heavy green kirtle and a voluminous cloak she wore during the cold evenings, peculiarly accentuated her foreign looks.

As for the Strath soldier, Pillio paid close attention to his progress. Resentful as he was at having to take on this assignment, he felt a strengthening obligation to the man. He too had been doing his duty; he had suffered grievously, perhaps would never survive this absurd journey, but Pillio would do his best by him. In this he was aided by the new guardleader who, as the detachment commander had promised, knew more than the average field surgeon about the treatment of battle wounds. But suspicions clouded Pillio's mind about why this particular guardleader had been assigned. The word in the Ingen barracks, carefully garnered by Pillio whilst he prepared to leave, was less than flattering. This guardleader, Manei, was a trouble-maker, a man whose initiative strayed too frequently into stubborn insubordination and risky adventuring, a cast of mind that made him overly popular, in all the wrong ways, with the common soldiers and a problem for his officers. Pillio had yet to make up his mind. Thus far he could have few complaints: capable, unhurried, dispassionate, Manei kept good, if informal, order with the men and, critically, did not intrude on Pillio.

The party crossed the bridge over the churning Cise at mid-morning on a cloudless day. Sunlight slanted through gaps in the sheer crags above, turning the nearer slopes to looming shadows against the blue sky. The sonorous bellow of the river had been quite audible from a mile distant, and now the din had reached a drumming crescendo that made the very timbers of the bridge tremble. Gazing over the sturdy wooden parapet of the bridge, a structure erected a half-century earlier under the direction of engineers of the Ta-shih, Pillio admired the aerial view of the thundering waters beating against the rocks below: the dirty white deluge surged over underwater obstructions to bump and tumble half-submerged trees, their sodden branches dipping and rising from the waters like the limbs of a drowning man.

Succumbing to temptation, Pillio searched his pockets for something to drop into the torrent far below and, finding nothing more suitable than a bronze leol, he tossed the oblong coin over the parapet and leaned out of the saddle to watch it fall, its polished faces flickering in the sunlight before disappearing into the wash without even a splash. Somewhat disappointed at this result, Pillio steered his horse back to the centre of the bridge and acknowledged with a curt nod Guardleader Manei, who had ridden up alongside.

"Sir," this individual began, the rugged lines of his face creased in a stern look that whitened the dull scar running from cheek to jowl. "Ahead yonder, above the roadway, I saw movement. Only very brief."

Pillio raised an eyebrow. "And so?"

"These are remote parts, sir. I know 'em well, at least as well as anyone can know the mountains. There're bandits hereabouts."

Pillio raised the other eyebrow. "Bandits?"

"Aye, sir. Footpads. Not usual for 'em to trouble Ta-shih, so that's a puzzle, but…" Manei dipped his head meaningfully to the rear, "with the pack animals and the prisoners… 'Specially the woman…"

They were approaching the end of the bridge. The roar of the waters was muted here and the clunk of the horses' hooves on the wooden beams seemed suddenly and unnaturally loud. Pillio turned his attention to the rocky slopes two hundred paces ahead: fir trees clung to the mountainsides between outcrops of granite where grittle-weed and yellow spring flowers flourished side-by-side in tangled clumps. On its left-hand side the road passed under three natural buttresses, some twenty feet high, from where men with a mind to do so might launch a decisive attack upon the unwary traveler below. On the right, the ground fell away from the narrow road in a deep, rock-strewn ravine at the bottom of which coursed the angry rush of the Cise. Nowhere could Pillio see movement.

"Sir," grunted Manei in his battered voice. "If they've the urge to try us, I'm thinking there must be at least our number or more – I say more. They'll want a quick kill, with the odds heavy to their side. No stomach for a real fight, these bastards."

Pillio looked again at the rock face ahead. *I see nothing,* he thought. *And I do not know this guardleader. Does he mock me?* And yet, from nowhere, his strong instinct was to trust him.

Pillio raised his arm to signal a halt. "We'll stop here a moment, Guardleader Manei, with the look of enjoying the scenery. Pass the word along to the men. But they're not to slip the horses' bits. We must be ready to move quickly." He glanced at the guardleader. "And release the prisoners' manacles…"

Manei regarded him an instant with a bloodshot eye then, as if he had appraised the instruction and found it sensible, murmured, "Aye, sir." He turned his horse, and with leisurely gestures directed the men to dismount.

Pillio swung himself down from the saddle and stretched cramped muscles. With the reins in one hand he stepped over to the parapet and made a pretense of gazing down into the river. His horse nosed at his shoulder, unaccustomed to stopping in a place where there was no grass to nibble. Pillio lifted his shoulder to signal his irritation to the animal, then glanced back along the bridge to check the progress of Manei. All the soldiers had dismounted. Some leaned on the parapet; two appeared to be adjusting saddle belts – but these were the bowmen and would be loading their crossbows behind the flanks of their horses. Manei himself was already leading his horse back towards Pillio and, on the way, passed the two barbarians who stood hidden by their horses and in the company of two soldiers.

Pillio gave his guardleader an enquiring glance, to which he received in response an expression that, on Manei's tanned, wrinkled bulldog face, must amount to a grin.

"The prisoners? They understand, you think?" Pillio asked.

Manei merely shrugged, saying, it seemed to Pillio, in that one laconic gesture that the Shur-Shur were foreigners and thus beyond understanding. Perhaps, indeed, he was right.

"Very well…" breathed Pillio, and looked out over the vast expanse of the Alnaes while he gave his final orders. "We shall proceed as before. I shall lead. You will follow some short distance behind me with five men. Ensure that the rest of the party seems to straggle, effectively thereby forming two groups. Appoint one man to calm the mules for our injured friend and one to guard the safety of the prisoners, withdrawing them from the fray if necessary. He is to protect them with his life, Manei." Pillio turned and looked emphatically at the guardleader, who reacted not at all. "We shall proceed. Pray Dian looks kindly on our efforts."

Manei seemed to approve of this sentiment, Dian being the goddess of hunters and soldiers and luck.

Pillio moved away, patting the neck of his horse with one hand and feeling the warmth through the smooth hair. Then, involuntarily, he reached for the coiled steel and leather bindings of his sword grip. There was reassurance in both, in the living power of the animal and the cold steel of the weapon. Abruptly, his heart began to pound in his chest and, as he levered himself into the saddle, he felt light-headed. The world seemed brighter, colours startling: the deep blue of the sky and the nodding yellow of the spring flowers. The river raced beneath him and the timbers of the bridge quivered like the earth alive. His horse stepped onto the roadway. He was oblivious to everything but the road ahead and the buttresses of rock. Impossible that anything should be wrong. Impossible that there should be violence here. But his body flinched with the fear of an imminent arrow shaft, and he was breathlessly thankful for his own stubborn insistence that everyone in his troop, in spite of their muted grumbling, wear their mail shirts every day.

He neared the first buttress, his gaze travelling gradually up its sheer granite sides, and passed beneath. An unbearable tension was in him. He wanted to look behind, but must not. Manei was there. The squad was there. He must trust them…

A whisper of undergrowth and the rattle of stones from above and Pillio lashed his horse forward, snapping the sword from its scabbard as a figure plummeted down just behind him and rolled across the path of Manei. Pillio wheeled his horse, the beast whinnying in terror. A hairy, bedraggled man appeared on Pillio's left, wielding a fearsome cudgel. Pillio struck down at the creature with all his force and pain seared his whole arm as the blade bit deeply into something. Then he was past, kicking the horse into a gallop and heaving the sword up to his side. Manei was near the roadside, bending from the saddle and hacking at another of the attackers who ducked under a round shield and jabbed ineffectually with a pike at the legs of the horse. Several of the bandits, having hidden under the bridge until an opportune moment, were now pressing their attack against the rear of the party. Pillio was heartened to see four of his men controlling their horses in close formation, spears dipped to hold the bandits at bay while defending the prisoners, whose mounts had backed up against the shoulder of rock rising vertically from the roadway.

An arrow, loosed from behind Pillio, hissed past his neck. He dragged back on the reins and halted his horse, the poor beast staggering up onto its hind legs as Pillio attempted to turn. He glimpsed the archer no more than twenty paces away atop the first of the buttresses, already nocking another arrow.

"Bowmen!" Pillio bawled. "Bowmen!" And he waved his sword in the direction of the bandit.

A figure appeared beside his horse. Pillio leaned across his reins and swept the sword down, missing entirely. The bandit feinted, then thrust with a long pike that ripped along his chainmail and grazed the flesh on Pillio's ribs. Pillio urged his horse forward directly at the man and, at the last moment, pulled the reins aside and swung his blade underhand. A shriek and the bandit lurched to the dusty roadway, legs jerking in spasms.

And then it was over. The surviving bandits were scrambling down the steep ravine, weapons left behind in their haste, until Pillio could see only the dark bobbing heads amongst the jumble of rocks beside the Cise. One of the Ta-shih soldiers, having reloaded his crossbow, sent a bolt after the fleeing figures, but it shattered into fragments off the face of a boulder several paces behind them.

Pillio, breathing hard and in a condition of extreme excitation, hefted his sword, noting with a jolt of surprise the blood on it. Somehow the thick red gore did not seem connected to the recent violence. He laid it crosswise over his saddle and tried to control his agitation sufficiently to survey the scene.

Manei had dismounted and, sword at the ready, was kicking one of the corpses onto its back. Behind him two of the troopers were trying vainly to calm their mounts, but the animals' eyes rolled in their heads and they shied away from the misshapen bodies lying twisted in the roadway. The prisoners were nearer the bridge and a soldier had hold of the reins of the woman's horse. Halfway across the bridge waited the last soldier with the mules and the Strath trooper on the pallet. The remounts crowded the far end in a long, tethered column. Given the distress of their fellows ahead they were, thankfully, less agitated than Pillio had any right to expect.

"Manei!" Pillio called out. "Post sentries, if you please!"

The guardleader nodded. "Sir!" He called out names and troopers took up positions at the bridge and in the road ahead. Manei announced, "This one is still alive, sir..."

Pillio dismounted. His body trembled and his eyes would not keep from their wild darting. The sword was still in his hand. There was blood on his arm and he could not quiet the mad racing of his heart.

As Pillio came nearer, Manei knotted his fingers in the bandit's hair and, delivering the eloquent characterization, "A pretty rogue," heaved the fellow's head up from the road. Blood bubbled from the mouth. He was trying to speak. Pillio came to stand over him.

"This," Manei proceeded with his succinct commentary, "is the one you downed, I think, sir."

Pillio stared at the filthy, bleeding wretch. There was a deep wound between shoulder and neck and the man's clothes were drenched in blood: a pitiful sight.

"Dispatch him," said Pillio, and reached into the side pocket of his tunic to retrieve a cloth. He began to wipe the sword and paused momentarily as Manei, without hesitation, unclipped his dagger and slit the bandit's throat. More blood, a crimson cascade soaking into the dust. Pillio drew a deep breath and sheathed his sword. He looked up. The party waited in a tight knot some ten paces away, the horses pawing at the dirt. Half a dozen corpses sprawled in the roadway, and a soldier had piled an assortment of weapons to one side.

"Remove the bodies to the ravine," ordered Pillio. "And cast the weapons into the river."

Manei was staring at Pillio's torso. "Y're wounded, sir," he murmured.

Pillio looked down. A large patch of dark red stained his tunic at his hip. His chainmail had been scored deeply and rent below his armpit where the pike had gouged a hole. He dabbed tentatively at the injury but felt no pain.

"If we climb down to the river, sir," Manei went on, "I can clean and dress the wound."

Pillio frowned a protest, intoxicated even now by the frenzy of action.

"I think it best, sir," Manei insisted. "And," he added, lifting a full water skin from Pillio's saddle, "we'll 'ave a drink. Maybe some wine, sir?"

And Pillio, under the watchful eye of the guardleader, permitted himself to be escorted down the tumble of boulders to the bank of the river.

***

Skava knew it was Yan before she could see him: single rider, something in the beat of hooves, even though he was going too fast and it was midmorning and he wasn't supposed to be coming back until nightfall. An instant later, horse and rider appeared from the tall pine trees round the steep bend, raising dust and kicking stones. Skava and Maki drew up as he came alongside.

"And?" demanded Skava, sparing a glance up the road in case half the Ta-shih army were in hot pursuit.

Yan got control of his mount, impressively Skava had to concede, and then gave her a nod. Polite boy. "Bandits, boss," he said, calm, as she always expected of her squad. "Mebbe twenty. Under the bridge ahead and up in the crags. Had a crack at the column."

Skava's brain was working rapidly even as Yan completed his report: "Ta-shih sent 'em scramblin'. Counted six bandits down; mebbe one other up in the rocks – archer. Ta-shih were in good order. Shur-Shur still with 'em. Strath soldier still on his pallet."

Skava skewered Yan with a probing gaze. "Let me get this right," she snapped. "No one in the Ta-shih party injured or down?"

"Company commander," answered Yan, still calm. She'd selected him in part because of his temperament: calm, but quick-thinking. Perfect for this line of work. Oh, and he was a killer.

"What about him?" she insisted.

"Company commander. Wounded. Some blood. Still on his feet so not serious. Guardleader cleaned him up."

"And then what?"

"Bodies in the ravine under some rocks. Weapons in the river. Then they moved off. I headed back here."

Skava nodded. "Can you find the bodies again?" She wanted to inspect them. This was fucking mad. Were they bandits or paid killers? Was there someone else hunting Pillio? The last two weeks had turned into an insane sequence of unexpected cock-ups. An image came to her, the sullen face of the officer at the banquet in Sohanyun, the face of a man desperate for redemption. Arsehole.

"Yep," said Yan and turned his horse.

"Alright," she continued. "Sharpish then."

And they all set off. It made a change from torturing her brain on the sodding cipher that was burning a hole in her belt pouch.

***

She had sent Yan on to get his eyeballs back on Pillio, only taking the time to change horses. The last thing he needed was a blown mount and no way to catch up to the column. Meantime, Skava and Maki pulled rocks off the corpses. Looking down on them, she spat. They looked like fucking bandits. They smelled like fucking bandits. In fact, they smelled like shit. Wrinkling her nose, she even rifled through their pathetic scraps of clothing. Well, she'd done worse in her time…and it always pays to know.

Nothing. The rational answer was that they were indeed bandits, but paid by the Sohanyuni officer. It had not been an inadequate plan. Probably the previous night they got close enough in the darkness to scout the Ta-shih camp before setting the trap at the bridge. If there were twenty of them, as Yan reported, they doubtless got over-excited by the prospect of making a dent in the Ta-shih without taking too many of their own losses. Plan might have worked. The bridge was ideal for an ambush. So, either the Ta-shih were lucky – and Skava did not believe in luck, at least not in the way everyone else did – or the Ta-shih were rather better soldiers than she had first imagined. Soldiers who took no losses were disciplined and well-motivated. And disciplined and well-motivated soldiers were well-led soldiers. She was beginning to really dislike this Pillio, and his guardleader.

She wiped her hands on her leather trousers and jerked her chin at Maki, who was patiently waiting for her to decide what to do with the corpses. "Back in the rocks," she instructed, nodding at the crooked bloody limbs. "I need a piss. I need to wash. And then I need to think."

She did the first squatting in a gap between boulders. The other two she tackled together, stripping her boots off to stand in a calmer reach of water backing up in the lee of some huge black rocks away from where the drumming power of the river swept on nearby. The cold was delicious on her feet and calves. She bent to rinse her hands and splash her face and in that instant the cipher fell into place in her head. Standing stock still, water up to her knees, the warm sun above and verdant pine forest with its sweet citrus odour all around the ravine, she reviewed the elements with which she had wrestled for the last twelve days.

"Bollocks..." she murmured.

Shenri to be murdered. No survivors. Blame...something, something... *northern nomads. Suspect Ordas*...next bit fuzzy, possibly an actual number: *one, two, first* or *second...secondary...secondary* works...next word no idea. *Yoiwa of Honam here in days... Identified new master...* This bit made no sense. Something about Honam again. What is that word? *Master... Master* what? The transposition she had applied in the first half of the message wasn't quite working. A change in cipher mode in the same message? Possibly some random shift throughout the whole thing. Clever. And then there was context. Always critical to try to understand the context, which was now plain as the edge of tension in her belly. Someone in Sohanyun, someone close to Ordas, was very well informed. Quite probably the spy whose head Jophan had sent back to Ordas. She was at one and the same time pleased she had nailed him, and fucking furious that he had got wind of her plans before they had even implemented them. And if only, if only Jophan had given her the leeway to keep him alive, she might now have had a chance, slim perhaps, but a chance of tracing his master... Fucking nobles.

She tried again. And it cracked. *Master intelligencer at work for Honam: Skava. My position now not secure.*

Oh, great. Fucking great. Skava looked up. She noticed that her feet and calves were stiff and aching from the freezing water. How long had she been absorbed in the cipher? She stepped out and sat on the warm smooth rocks to wipe her legs dry. The leather trousers were soaked at the bottom where she had loosened the ties and rolled them up. Heedless, she got her boots on and fixed the leggings. The wet leather felt slimy, a most unpleasant sensation. She would need to change into linen.

She stood up and made her way back up the tumbled rocks of the ravine to Maki and the horses. "Ready, boss?" he asked.

Skava took the reins of her mare, having decided not to change her leggings, and mounted smoothly. "Ready," she replied and then muttered, "Double bollocks."

There was another player. A good one. And she had a horrible suspicion who it could be – disagreeable as that seemed. For the last time, she reached into her belt pouch and retrieved the tiny scroll. The message, deciphered, burned itself into her memory:

Shenri to be murdered. No survivors. Blame northern nomads. Suspect Ordas as second agent. Yoiwa of Honam here within days. Identified new master intelligencer working for Honam: Skava. My position now not secure.

She studied the parchment, held it up to the sunlight and squinted minutely at both sides, the edges, the type of paper; she even sniffed it, all so that she could recognize its equivalent again. Patterns. Habits. If she knew one thing about people, it was that they behaved in patterns and, no matter how hard they tried, they ended up slaves of habit. Finally satisfied with this examination, she steered her roan mare near to where Maki was standing and passed him the note. He knew what to do. He would use a flint-wheel lighter fixed to a small urn, a bit like a miniature brazier, and no bigger than two thumbs, to burn it. A few years back, when he first started to work with Skava, he had suggested eating the parchments when they didn't have a fire convenient. The look she gave him was not one he would forget. "Maki," she had asked him, with that odd but effective mixture of withering disdain and the patience you reserve for stupid children, "how long would you like to survive in this line of work? A day? A week? The scrolls can be poisoned. We handle them with gloves. We understand their smell. And we do as I fucking say.

And then we get to survive."

They *always* burned the scrolls. And he did so now, crumbling the ash between gloved fingers until nothing remained.

"We need to pass them," she said suddenly, meaning Pillio's troop, as Maki paused in the action of levering himself up into the saddle. Foot in the stirrup, he glanced sideways at her with a mild look of surprise.

"Of course," he concurred, and got settled on his remount. She hadn't noticed that he had changed both horses whilst she was in the river. Or maybe she had but didn't let on.

"We need to be in Nek Feddah before them, because we can't take 'em. They're too disciplined, and the risk is too high now they're on alert after those fuckers had a crack at them. Yan can stay on their tail in case they do something unexpected. But I think not. They'll take a galliot at Nek Feddah. And if they take a galliot, we can't stay with 'em. Too public. *And* we need to be going north. I need another plan and that means I need to call in some favours." She jabbed a thumb at the pigeon coop secured to one of the remounts. "Next stop, we send a message to Daved in Chisua. I need Fortunas moving north – fast. He should aim for Kiangsu City. That gives us options either on the river or, if we must, in the city itself when Pillio and the prisoners make port there." She urged her roan into a trot and Maki followed. Over her shoulder she flung the exclamation: "And change our damned cipher."

Maki raised one eyebrow at her back, but kept his thoughts to himself.

***

It was their final night on the road. They would reach Nek Feddah by mid-afternoon the next day.

Pillio was caught between two emotional states: on the one hand he looked forward to their arrival in the small river port and the next stage of this journey; on the other, he dreaded the impending severance of the link between himself and his life on the Lorang Steppes. He had never been further than Nek Feddah; it was the limit of his experience of the world. The break with his past seemed irrevocable, laden with the import of a disturbing, gods-sent dream.

Around him, the night had fallen to almost full dark. They had a fire burning and a slaughtered deer to feast on. One of his troopers was a fine bowman and a finer hunter and it pleased Pillio to see his squad in good spirits. After the usual evening arms drills, on foot and mounted, Guardleader Manei had supervised the preparations for the meal with his familiar ease of command, a prayer to Dian for the gift of the deer and the sacrifice of its life, a joke and brief word of guidance for the trooper setting the meat on stakes, ribald banter with the older squad members, stronger exhortation for others who were slow to make camp. The men would have wine tonight – watered, as usual, but welcome. Even the nomads shared the mood of optimism.

As the meat was passed round, a sentry near the eastern end of the roadway cried out, "'Ware, in the camp! Riders!"

Manei was standing and Pillio noted with surprise how quickly his sword appeared. Simultaneously, he snapped quiet orders to two of the troop, who at once armed themselves with crossbows. "How many?" he called back to the sentry.

"Two."

Manei retreated into the wooded darkness beyond the fire. Pillio, standing with dinner bowl in one hand, sword pommel cradled against the palm of the other, but blade still in its scabbard, watched the pair of riders emerge from the night into the warm ruby glow of the fire.

"Good evening," said the lead rider in a voice of rich accents, hard to pin down.

"Honour to you, sir," returned Pillio.

The rider began to dismount, which Pillio took as a sign of polite intent. "Sir," said the man, with a natural gentility, like a noble, but self-evidently without the entourage. "The road has been long. My muscles ache. My thighs are knots of hot needles. And it is now night. Might we trespass upon your hospitality?"

His tone, friendly and amusing, drew a half smile from Pillio. He strode closer, leading his horse, a very large beast, perhaps eighteen hands, into the dancing circle of firelight. Behind him, his companion dismounted, trailing three other fine horses on tethers.

Pillio nodded. "Of course. Be welcome. We have meat."

With a grin of white teeth, the gentleman made an apologetic gesture. "I confess, sir," he said, "I caught the smell of roasting from some distance. If I needed any persuasion to beg your hospitality, that aroma did it for me!" He grinned again and, closer now, Pillio saw him for the first time: he was clean-shaven and seemed almost boyish, despite his large frame and sonorous voice. "I shall, of course, be happy to pay my way."

Pillio would not hear of it. Hospitality on the road was a universal custom.

"I am Harbin," said the stranger and half bowed.

"Company Commander Pillio."

"And this," the newcomer announced and extended a large arm to his companion, "is Kesmet." Still holding his mount's reins, this individual also half bowed, then gathered the reins of Harbin's dun beast and began to move all five horses to a patch of grass across the road. Pillio guessed he was a servant. At that moment a large black dog padded silently into the firelight, sitting obediently at Harbin's feet, limbs neatly together like a canine sentinel, dark eyes reflecting the red of the flames. The stranger laughed affectionately and tugged at the animal's ear. "And, of course, Zuse," he said. "He likes company!"

And so they settled to eating, the dog at his master's side throughout, heavy muzzle resting on two large forepaws, Harbin's servant sitting away from the circle of men, on his own. Later, Pillio lay back on one elbow against his rolled bedding, easing muscles across his lower back taut from days in the saddle. He glanced at Harbin. He seemed relaxed and friendly, though perhaps not as talkative as Pillio had expected from initial acquaintance.

Feeling awkward at not being able to place the stranger's station in society, Pillio pressed a question, "Sir, your background or business, if I might?"

Harbin turned him a look, honey-blonde hair swinging in small curls across his forehead. "Banking," he answered. "I am from a family of bankers. The Honourable Bank of Royal Kemae – you've heard of it? – of the Kemae Islands."

Pillio nodded and Harbin met his gaze squarely. In the firelight, Pillio noticed for the first time that his eyes were a clear blue and intensely knowing, like the eyes of a much older man – certain, wise, amused almost. Eyes far too old for his face.

"You have travelled much, sir?" enquired Pillio, the question coming unbidden to his tongue. It seemed the obvious thing to ask, like a truth that merely required confirmation.

Harbin smiled, his eyes still fixed on Pillio as if reading something written there. "A little," he conceded. "I have seen a little of the world." And suddenly his expression changed, transforming him from charming young man to someone more intense and darker, as if a thousand crippling memories fought to release themselves upon his face, but were held in check by an immense counterweight of forbearance. The effect was unsettling. Pillio frowned, seeking to pose his next question, but the younger man turned his head and interrupted quietly, "There has been trouble in the west?"

Pillio was startled, not because of the question – any traveler encountered on the road at night might make the same enquiry – but because of the tone. The flicker of memories across Harbin's face from a moment before and his flat tone now chimed together like a cracked discordant warning gong in the darkness. It was a statement, not a question. And Pillio felt at once, ineffably, that Harbin expressed a deep understanding, deeper indeed than Pillio himself could muster, of the murder of Lord Shenri. In his rational mind, he admonished himself: such a thought was ridiculous… surely?

"There is often trouble," Harbin continued along this line, as if he had sensed Pillio's inner reaction, "in the west. And your trooper here…" – a gentle flick of his hand towards the still shape on the stretcher – "is lucky to be alive. His wounds are serious… a blade no doubt?"

"He…he is," Pillio started to say, then finished somewhat tartly in a way he had not intended: "He is hardly *lucky*. His wounds, as you perceive, are very serious. Perhaps he will not walk again and…" Pillio shrugged in an affronted manner, though he knew this Harbin had ill-deserved it. It was simply that he felt the need to defend the wounded trooper.

But Harbin seemed untroubled, merely sympathetic. His hound, Zuse, on the other hand, raised his large black head and stared directly at Pillio. "I have a palliative – a curative in fact – in my saddlebags," offered Harbin, "that would help him. Something we use in the Kemae Islands. It ensures sleep and recuperation. I've used it myself. May I give you a phial?"

"Well…"

Harbin laughed. "I shall leave it with you, but I understand your reservations. I hope you will use it but I will not be affronted if you choose not to."

Pillio nodded, then returned to his theme. "You ask about trouble in the west? What trouble do you mean?"

Harbin shrugged. "Rumours of violence. Disturbances in the peace of the northern and western Realm."

"And how do you know these things?"

Harbin laughed, a warm self-deprecating sound. "I am, as I said, a banker. I am not personally a very important member at the Kemae Bank, but it is part of my role to know where and when there is trouble. Banks like to know these things. When there is trouble, uncertainty arises. Banks dislike uncertainty, for the most part. Unless, it naturally follows, we can predict the cause and course of the uncertainty – in which case we welcome uncertainty like a fond friend returned! For then our clients are forewarned, we know whether this merchant or that market will rise or fall, if the noble lord of this province or that must borrow more, when the value of money itself is worth less or more than the gold and silver that backs it. And if we know that, we make more money! My job is to know these things."

Pillio nodded slowly, grasping the gist of the argument but lost in the economic detail. "Through informers?"

"Perhaps. Although that word has an unfavorable ring to it! We have interested parties across many parts of the Realm, and beyond. We like to be informed. Thus, we avidly collect information and particularly anything that suggests risk – and, yes, sometimes we pay for it."

At the edge of firelight, Kesmet, the banker's servant, appeared, stepping quietly past the troopers lying asleep in their bedrolls. Pillio realised that he had not seen him for some time. The man was bearded and his features swarthy. He bent at Harbin's side and talked in hushed tones. Harbin grunted and smiled and Kesmet withdrew.

Looking directly at Pillio, Harbin's smile remained fixed, as at some unusually good news that proved a point already made. "Company commander," he announced. "Do you know you are being tracked?"

Pillio's stomach gave a lurch. He frowned and flicked a glance at Manei, sitting across the fire. Manei narrowed his eyes, indicating perhaps that he was unaware or disbelieved the news.

"A single rider. An excellent scout. He has been observing the camp. No, I would take no action." He shook his head, as Manei started to rise. "By the time you began your search, he would be gone. And you would only alert him. And that, to be perfectly honest, would not be good for you…and would draw attention to me."

Pillio recovered his poise. "How can you be sure? That he is out there, I mean?"

Harbin smiled broader still. "Kesmet is sure. Your spy in the forest is, as I mentioned, an excellent scout, but Kesmet is better. I said earlier that I value information and this is one of the ways I gather it. To ensure my security…and the security of the bank."

Pillio could only nod. He felt distinctly out of his depth.

"Is there a reason he might be out there?" Harbin pressed.

Pillio struggled to answer. His natural instincts were to deny it, but this Harbin seemed to draw the truth from him. Instead he said nothing.

"Hmm," concluded Harbin. "Is it fair to say that you are surprised he is there, but it is not unexpected?"

Pillio nodded.

"One more item of information: this 'scout' has no remount, which probably means he has associates near. You follow my thinking?"

"I do…" breathed Pillio.

"It would be best if you do nothing – directly. But I urge you to be cautious, whatever your destination. Nothing will happen tonight: you have good men and I have Kesmet. But…be cautious."

After this, the sentries changed for the next watch and Pillio turned in. Harbin was already asleep, broad shoulders wrapped in a heavy cloak, and a comfortable padded bedroll under him. Kesmet had spoken quietly to Manei and, Pillio, his thoughts tumbling over one another, had fallen into troubled dreams.

When he awoke, before dawn, the strangers were gone.

***

"A decent man," said Harbin. "A dedicated soldier who knows his duty is to his principles first, and then the Realm. I liked him."

Harbin used his stirrups to half stand from his seat. Already, though the sun was barely risen and they had been riding for less than an hour, his buttocks were protesting. Why did he not keep up with his riding? A simple, regular discipline, which would in future prevent a week's agony. He knew the answer of course: he disliked riding. He was not built for it. His frame was too large and, yes, he was lazy…or at least he preferred his comforts.

"Still behind them, when we left," Kesmet announced. He was referring to the scout on Pillio's tail.

Harbin grunted. "Trouble," he conceded. "Let me draw the picture, Kesmet, if you'll indulge me. Feel free to paint your own strokes… The injured man is a Strath trooper, thus one of Lord Shenri's bodyguard. There are two northerners with the party, survivors from the apparently guilty party of nomads. So far, the message that Kellax forwarded from our man in Sohanyun is accurate in every respect. And we have learned something new: they are heading to Nek Feddah and presumably south. Why? Why are they not at Ingen, under the detachment commander's watchful eye? Why is the detachment commander not assiduously writing a report? Or, if he has written a report, why has he dispatched this Pillio to go in person? Caution? The army's mania for belt and braces, as the saying goes?"

Harbin lifted one buttock gingerly, then the other, in an alternating fashion that eased sore muscles but ultimately only served to remind him how much he disliked the tedious business of sitting on a horse. Possibly the horse disliked it as much. "I worry," he wondered aloud, "about our man in Sohanyun." Harbin preferred not to call his spies 'spies'. Other people had spies. "Nearly two weeks since that last missive. I am not hopeful. Are you hopeful, Kesmet?"

Kesmet gave no indication one way or the other.

The black hound, Zuse, appeared from the woodland onto the mountain path, loping to join their pace. "Well, Zuse," sighed Harbin, addressing the dog as if it might deliver a more fulfilling conversation than the one with the taciturn Kesmet. "We suspected there was more than the usual going on in the north. Murder of a lord *is* unusual. At least in these times. Spying is *not* unusual. But Honam's network is rather good. In other words, it is *better* than usual. What do we call something, Zuse, when it is better than usual, eh? That's right: we call it *unusual*."

The heavy-muscled beast swung his head to direct one eye at his master, sensing perhaps in Harbin's animation the imminence of a command. His long easy stride did not falter.

Harbin nodded. "Indeed, Zuse," he confirmed. "You may well give me that look. For here is another thing that intrigues me: the Lord of Honam's new spymaster. We have a name: Skava. Who is he? How has he escaped our notice these years? After all, you do not build a network overnight, am I right? And here's another thing, on which you, Kesmet, will certainly have an opinion: was there not a Sklavin of our acquaintance once? Is Sklavin not rather an echo of Skava?"

Kesmet, scanning the mountains on all sides and the rough stone roadway ahead, grunted a disagreement, "Uh-uh. Skava. Not Sklavin."

Harbin squinted as the full, blinding power of the sun shone on his face from between a gap in the trees. He reached down to unloop a large, broad-brimmed black felt hat from the saddle, settling it comfortably on his blond curls. The hat's band was wide and silver. Harbin preferred silver; it had a permanent quality without the showiness of gold. It perfectly matched his opinion of himself.

"Correct," he answered his companion. "But it could be Sklavin… What was it – ancient Germanix – Sklavin, I mean – for 'slave'?"

Kesmet declined to comment.

"Yes. Slave. And that, my dear friend," insisted Harbin with a flourish, "means that this Skava has a sense of humour. A self-obsessed, cruel, single-minded sense of humour, I admit, but a sense of humour. And of whom, I ask, does that remind you?"

Kesmet looked at Harbin for the first time, a long, hard stare with dark eyes under dark brows. "She's dead," he said with finality.

"That certainly seemed the case. But… Skava, Sklavin – slave. She once joked about being the slave of humanity, didn't she? A kind of droll fixation on her role in life. Ironic. She liked the irony: not the mover of worlds but the slave of worlds!" Harbin shrugged, a large movement of his large shoulders. "Or at any rate, this world."

"Dead," Kesmet repeated. He swung his horse, a gentle pull on the reins. He was an accomplished horseman, unlike Harbin. "We need to scout."

And he was gone, cantering into the trees to gain elevation and sightlines.

Harbin sighed again. Kesmet spoke little but always said a lot, usually without recourse to words. Zuse, meanwhile, said nothing. Where was a civilized man to find intelligent conversation on the road? Harbin let the trackway and his horse take them along the winding route to the north-west, as always trusting absently to his companions for his safe passage. Behind him, half forgotten, trailed the three tethered remounts, docile in company of the massive gelding that led them.

He contemplated the new pieces of the puzzle. They settled in a certain pattern, but it was incomplete. And he could not act decisively without certainty. This trip into the hinterland of the north, ostensibly on the business of the bank, would, he hoped, add pieces to the puzzle. Each town would provide gossip, rumour, threads of truth. Each of his people, carefully placed or selected in city, hamlet or garrison, would report his or her observations. He was nothing if not methodical. So, method first…but never forgetting to ask the big questions. He had always relied on the big questions, the interrogation of the facts that suddenly, unexpectedly, connected one thing to another. He liked questions. Even if his companions made plain their indifference.

And here was the biggest question of all: What if she was returned? Skava, Sklavin…Eslin? There: he had said her name. *Eslin.*

Now that really would be trouble.

Except she had died long ago.

CHAPTER 5

The Immortals are all gone. Or they are myth. Personally, I think they are a myth to explain uncomfortable realities. If your opinion differs, I ask those Immortals here present to step forth now. I see they are reluctant. Thus is it demonstrated: they are gone or never existed!

The Academician, Alanax, from a debate at the Roneca, IYE 1880.

[…] glass ejecta rained down […] widespread and complete destruction even in the early hours and days […] nothing next to the […] winter does not adequately describe the atmospheric conditions. […] cannot understand what it is to never see the sun. Never. It was near-dark, permanently dark, a ghastly in-between time that lasted years and people were terrified or simply gave up […]

The Diary of Giorgios Kellastis, assumed to be an Immortal, on the in-between time, copied by a scribe, IYE 1044.

***

Nek Feddah was the kind of town that could look very attractive, nestled close to the high peaks, the clean, cold headwaters of the Cise River underfoot, the steep pitched roofs and gaily painted beams of the buildings, even the spindly-legged wharves crouching over the river on massive piles to accommodate the seasonal floods. For Skava, standing on the balcony of a half-decent inn, it was just another place she needed to stop. The room was fine. It had a bed and, whilst it was a small comfort to sleep in it and have a roof over her head instead of the cold night sky and the stars, she was, as always, more concerned about whether it suited their cover: three guards-for-hire, Skava now calling herself Maeff, a woman, and Maki and Yan both slipping seamlessly into their aliases. The inn keeper, at any rate, had no objections to the silver they paid for lodging and decent stabling for the mounts. The horses had been used hard for a month. They needed proper feed and looking after. Skava had learned never to stint on this: to move fast, you looked after your horses. Luckily Yan loved his horses, any horses. And, being honest, with Maki looking like a horse, they were the ideal pair.

The usual packet of correspondence found its way to her, via a local merchant in her pay, the day they arrived under the midday sun, maybe four hours ahead of Pillio, and most of it was good news. She would think on it later. For now, as the dusk settled, she reviewed the afternoon's events. Her contact in Nek Feddah had set up a meeting with an exarch, one of the Zaggisa, the zealot hunters of heretics, with whom she had forged a working alliance, uncomfortable but aligned with Clan Ouine's interests. The Zaggisa hated the Ta-shih and wanted them reduced, and the Faith sought greater sway in the north and especially Honam, both of which goals Skava's grand strategy could abet. *War... Strange bedfellows and all that.* Arriving mounted, and by circuitous routes at the modest temple on the outskirts of the town, she made a small sacrifice of a goat, paid some coins and, legitimately or so it would seem to any watchers, took private counsel of the exarch. She presented herself as a scout, a nondescript young man, her face grimy from a long ride, and mentioned the name Skava. Exarch Hassin was a round-faced, smilingly unlikely scourge of heretics, but Skava had long ago appreciated that the doe-eyed meekest of creatures could often be the best spies. She had never worked with him, but knew his reputation and he seemed rather good, suitable to solve the little problem of Pillio and his party. He was that quirky combination of unfeasibly congenial, ardent in his religious mission – a mission that Skava had secretly fuelled for a very long time – and he struck her as decisive. He would do what was necessary and, hopefully, without managing to set alarm bells clanging all over the Realm. She found that she grudgingly admired him. And that was the only fly in the ointment: he was good enough to see something in her – not her disguise as a man, but perhaps her actual role as Yoiwa's master-intelligencer. He was one of those singular individuals who could read the most meagre of clues and grasp the correct deduction. Still, they parted with the requisite bow, on cordial terms, she with confidence he could do the business, he with an arch glitter in his eye.

Meanwhile, of course, Skava had the excellent Fortunas on his way from Chisua. He was the backstop; the guarantee she needed to avoid having to step in directly and be able to turn her back on this crotch-kicked mess. She needed to slide again into the shadows to concentrate on the critical moves required to manoeuvre the really big pieces across the board. Top of that list was preparing the ground in Strath, safeguarding the budding romance between those two love-birds Prince Mathed and Che Keleu. Her instincts, instincts she trusted implicitly, told her she needed to be in Strath sooner rather than later.

Skava took a last look around the town. It did not take long. Viewed from the first-floor balcony, she could see most of it in a single wide scan of rooftops, streets and wharves. Upriver were the stumps of the ancient bridge, one of the anchor blocks marooned well away from the current riverbank, a concrete colossus with no purpose, crumbling slowly with time and neglect. It was sunset. Everyone would move indoors to avoid dusk and the in-between times. Skava always did the same – in public. Odd behaviour would be noted. She had made a habit of blending in, superstitions and all. In any event, what she needed now was a drink. Good strong alcohol, and lots of it. And, she had to admit, a man. She needed a man. Or rather, she needed a fuck. The urge had been stirring inside her for days now. She invariably fought it; it could sometimes create complications. But she needed a man, and that was always tricky because Maki and Yan could not qualify: she did not mix business with pleasure. Ever.

The inn had running water, pumped into filtration tanks and through the kitchens by water wheels and cleverly engineered pipes from the fast-flowing spillways feeding the Cise River. She had washed and scrubbed and left what felt like half the road in the lukewarm water of a copper tub the pipes had filled. Dressed in a white linen shirt and twill trousers, she clumped through the bedroom, latching the door behind her, the position of every item of her kit in the room committed to memory. When it came to security, her habits and rituals were invariant. Downstairs, Maki and Yan were already propping up the taproom bar. She joined them – just another itinerant tough woman among a crowd of itinerant toughs. There were a couple of other women at the tables, hard-eyed, with tankards of ale, and long knives in sheaths at their belts, projecting confidence and animosity in equal measure. Skava recognised the play: I'm here to enjoy myself; don't mess with me, unless it's on my terms. They were with their crews, six or seven at a table, probably trader convoy guards laying up overnight between stints on the barges up and down river. Most wore the padded jupons in the colours of their trading house and hair tied back, shoulder length, men and women the same. Ta-shih shaved their heads to stubble, except the officers. The merchant house guards kept theirs long, shouting their hard-earned status.

Maki looked down at Skava, a half smile on his equine face. Yan was contemplating his ale. He looked half asleep or half drunk, but that was show. They had a rule in town: one of them was always stone-cold sober. "Buy you a drink, boss?" offered Maki.

"Too right," Skava replied. She put an elbow on the bar and, still fighting the urge, undid the two top buttons of her linen shirt. She didn't have a lot, but she had enough to get a man's attention. She also had her hair down, signalling she was off duty. Maki had seen this sequence before and he paid no heed, summoning the bar-keep and getting the ale lined up. Skava took a long sup: it wasn't half bad. On the Cise River, the inns could afford to serve the best in food and brew. The Cise was like an artery; it kept the Realm in rude health. Which was why Skava was seeking a way to control it – in time.

She took in the taproom. A typical crowd. No one set hackles rising. Still, she needed to check. "Yan," she enquired, with a thrust of her chin. He glanced up, feigning stupor. Fine actor, this boy. "Any interesting patrons?"

A slow shake of the head. "Nope," he said.

He would have scouted the whole the inn, including the stables. Maki usually did the streets, systematic and discreet, watching for the tell-tales she had taught them to spot, checking out access ways and exits from their room, should the worst happen. Tonight, Yan was on point. He would be awake through the small hours, weapons to hand, until second bell and then Maki would take over.

She downed half the ale and again surveyed the taproom, casual, a tough young woman looking for fun. One of the merchant crew was not shy. He was a big bull of a man, but square-jawed and attractive, and mostly clean-shaven like the merchant crews preferred. They pretended all sorts of standards, those lads. She returned the look, an eyebrow up. He might do.

"New bird in, boss," said Maki over a slurp of ale. "Our friend from Chisua is on 'is way." He meant Fortunas. That was good. She felt better about that. Fortunas was probably the best solo assassin she'd ever known. If he'd sent a bird, he was undoubtedly at Chulien already.

The clean-shaven merchant convoy lad had got up on his hind legs. He sauntered over, the familiar smirk Skava had seen all too often on a hundred other men plastered to his face. He really was a large lump, wide-shouldered and muscular and quite pleasing to the eye – and she couldn't blame the ale: she'd barely finished a single tankard.

"Honour," he announced, in the regular greeting, an eastern twang to his accent. "Desman. That's me." He inclined his head to Maki, who gave him a winning smile, all teeth like a braying donkey, and then a wink for Skava – taking the fucking piss, but playing it well. Just what crew mates would do. Yan kept staring at his ale, like he was looking for a fish in the depths. Skava had to grin, but directed it at the wide-shouldered lad.

"Maeff," she offered in exchange. "That's me." She jerked her tankard at Maki and Yan. "Don't suppose you care who these two are…" And laughed at her own joke.

Big lad Desman liked the humour. He laughed with her. It meant he wouldn't have to buy a round getting to know everyone and waste time if she wasn't interested. "South or north?" he asked, taking them for guards.

Skava wrinkled her broken nose in her cutest come-on. "Lay-over. Just come from the west." Always tell the truth when it doesn't matter. "You?"

"South," he said with a vague gesture of his tankard downriver. "Ung."

They chatted some more and Skava got to like him, and that was rare. Several ales later, amid the laughter and shouted conversation of a taproom in full swing, she found herself heading for the stairs with him. Maki gave her a last look, his protective *I'm-here-if-you-want-me* look, and then she felt Desman's arm around her back, and then her buttock, as they climbed the stairs. He wasn't going to waste time. She steered him to her room where Yan would know to find her, and Desman's hands were all over her body as they more or less fell through the door. But he was a strong boy and he lifted her up on her toes, his mouth finding hers while one hand banged the door shut. He had his thigh between her legs and she was as eager as he was, the animal in both of them taking over. Clothes came off, and then he was on her on the bed, and her fingers were gripping his rampant cock as he thrust and missed, until she steered him into the right place and she abandoned herself to the mad beating of her heart and the beast on top of her.

Later, she still liked him – and not only because of his stamina. He talked gently but not too much, and she made stuff up to play out the conversation. For some reason she cared. He stroked her hair and traced patterns on her breasts and belly and said nice things about her lean muscular tone. Maybe he said that to all the girls. Then questions about the scars, lots of scars, several lifetimes of scars, so she made more stuff up: accident on the river, bar-room brawls, jealous lovers.

"You've seen a lot o'fights," he concluded, not concealing a note of admiration while running a finger over her right forearm where a web of scars told the long history of her and blades.

"You should see the other bastards!" she joked, uncomfortable with the scrutiny.

He laughed and dropped the subject.

At one point Maki tapped quietly on the door and came into the darkness of the room.

"A'right, boss?" he whispered.

160

Desman tensed, uncomfortable at the intrusion, but she squeezed his arm and said softly, "Alright."

"Be in the stable," Maki concluded, pulling the door shut. By rights he should be sleeping in this room, but he was a clever sort and he knew when to stay away and when to give her a night off. Yan, she knew, would sit outside the door. And so she actually felt relaxed. Desman had his arms round her. She felt secure. A surge from deep in her belly through her chest and throat signified some longing or nostalgia…or just plain stupid emotional rundown. She felt like a little girl. Like Eslin. It really was stupid, but she felt it nevertheless. Her head was against his chest, one leg over his hairy, muscled thigh. She could hear his heart and then her own quietly seemed to pulse into synchrony. And she slept, deeply.

And woke screaming at the gigantic red sky-glow of superheated cloud and ejecta and the cataclysmic roaring and vibration through the very bones of the earth. She was throwing herself around like a mad woman, limbs flailing in pure terror at the imminence of her own searing yellow conflagration, until she realised that she was hitting someone and he was trying to get hold of her arms and dodge out of the way of her kicks. *What the fuck! What the fuck!*

The door burst open suddenly and, in the narrow vertical of moonlight, with Yan's silhouette framed perfectly in front, she got hold of herself and stopped kicking. Moonlight winked along a foot of thin steel in Yan's hand and Skava was instantly back in command.

"Hold up!" she snapped. And Yan froze, blade ready to thrust, Desman's life mere moments from ending. He still had hold of her wrists but his head was turned over his shoulder to take in the killer behind him next to the bed.

"It's fine," Skava choked out to the shadowed figure against the moonlight.

"Boss?" Yan needed certainty. He would kill Desman otherwise.

"All good," she breathed out, and Yan backed up to the doorway. Desman was breathing hard, like he'd run up ten flights of stairs. "Fucking gods-sent dream," she explained. "Just a dream."

Yan backed up again and the door shut.

"I'm sorry," she said then. She never apologized, but with this man it just came out.

He seemed to sag and let her wrists and his own huge sigh of relief go at the same time. To his great credit, he didn't start cursing her or complaining. He'd seen Yan and his steel poniard come through the door faster than a rat, but he'd done the right thing in staying still – as still as any man could with a raving bitch kicking him.

"I hurt you?" she asked.

"Nah." He swung his legs off the bed and just sat, took another breath and looked at her with his head on one side, like he'd just seen right into her. "Dreams in the night like that…" he ventured. "Dreams like that… well, you know who sends 'em."

Sitting on her knees, nude, she stared at him. Well, he was right, wasn't he? "Echrexar," she said tonelessly. "Too fucking right. Echrexar and his dogs, come to tear us to pieces again."

Even in the dark, she saw his face twitch, uncomfortable with her casual blasphemy. But she was angry now. She had *let go*. She had relaxed. And the whole fucking thing had come pouring back. What was *wrong* with her?

"You should get to the temple, see an exarch," he offered, hurt and not a little superstitious but trying gamely to help.

Inwardly she snorted. *I just saw a bloody exarch.*

"Make a sacrifice," Desman persisted. "Find out what it means. I'm guessing that ain't the first time…"

He was good. He could read her. And she had let him. Even when the warning voice was telling her to watch it, she had let the need take her. Nothing changed. Her biology was the same as his in every way… except one. Luckily he was solid. But another time, she could have been in trouble. Another time it might be someone much worse. Another time, Yan might not come through the door.

There mustn't be another time.

But the moment she thought it, she knew there would. However hard she tried, she was still a mass of churning urges like everyone else on the planet. It was only her rigid discipline that made the difference most of the time... And perhaps not even that, if she was honest. No, it was her *purpose*, burning as white hot as Echrexar's fires. No one, not a fucking single soul, had her purpose.

Desman was up and moving, feeling his way around the room, picking up and discarding bits of clothing.

"Open the shutters," suggested Skava. "Or you'll end up wearing my shirt on your dick..."

Clearly he was making a break for it. She didn't blame him. Beating a man up certainly ruins the mood. Who would want to settle down for the night with a crazy bitch who might kick the shit out of him at any moment?

He struggled into his trousers and she heard him buckle a belt. Then he did open the shutters and, with the moonlight, things proceeded a little faster. Finally, he stood near the door, looking down at her on the bed. She hadn't moved. "Well..." he started.

"Been fun," she finished for him.

"Mmm."

And he was gone.

***

The Prince's Way, linking Cise Hook to Chisua, was used exclusively for royal and religious ceremonies. Thus, entry to Cise Hook and the temple precincts was possible only, as a rule, via a circuitous route. The visitor, be he Archivist or acolyte, must turn east upon leaving the city, out of the busy traffic of the Higher Dirndorc and across the dizzying span of the Chisuan Gorge, over the Leol Bridge, so named on account of the toll – one leol. Across the bridge, looking back from the other side, one might pause and read the ancient inscription carved in huge archaic letters on the rock wall, with a shiver perhaps for its hallowed power against an ancient dormant peril:

The stars fell.
The oceans boiled and flooded the land,
A darkness descended.
ECHREXA! murdered our dreams.

From this point, obliged to negotiate the steep, winding cutbacks of the paved road that dropped away from the heights into wide stretches of uncultivated land, one arrived, perhaps a trifle daunted by the thought of the return journey, at the drawbridge and massive gates defending Cise Hook. Straddling the narrow isthmus was a convex fortified wall, rising eighty feet to its battlements and in whose shadow were huge iron-bound gates – the whole presenting an austere and intimidating face to the visitor. The gates were rarely opened. To gain admittance to the temple precincts, one ventured through a single postern door, this to the left of the main gates and wide enough for the passage of a cart. A dark vestibule or tunnel some ten paces in length, confirming the great thickness of the walls above, limited further access by means of a second gate, which could be closed instantly should the gatekeepers deem it prudent.

Here, from a small square aperture in the stonework above, certain questions were put to the visitor and the answers, if acceptable, allowed him ingress. These were the material defences of Cise Hook and they had stood, in the main, unmolested and impregnable for many centuries. But the dark walls and the melancholy aspect of the place was cloaked by a more forbidding, even terrifying, atmosphere. For this was the centre of the Faith. This was a place of obscurity and myth, as ancient as the ocean that surrounded it. At the gates and near the walls there was silence. From within there was silence. Only at night, and when the wind blew steadily from the north, were muted sounds carried outside the precincts: a slow, sad chanting said by common folk to be voices liberated from the tomb. None but Archivists and their servitors entered the gates, the servitors to remain within for the term of their earthly lives. What happened inside this place was a matter for conjecture. If the night's chanting was the voices of the dead, none but the Archivists knew. One might have been forgiven for believing that the silence and ghostly chanting of Cise Hook was indeed the whispering of the tomb; and yet there was life here, as bustling and incessant as the court of Ehri, directly across the estuary: the exarchs, the visible face of the Archivists, went to and from Cise Hook like black ants from a vast nest. Alone or in groups, from Chisua and from the farthest reaches of Kiangsu, they came and went again, shaven-headed men in black robes, imbued in every frowning line of face, in the tilt of head or narrowing of eye, with the power of the Faith, communion with the gods. And thus what was one to say of peasants' furtive tales of tombs and chants and silence? The sophisticated citizens of Chisua would cry "Superstition!" in one breath and "Truth!" in another. And whilst even a pilgrim to this place, seeking, as pilgrims do, the divine and the extraordinary, might shake his head in bewilderment, this paradox was as much a fact of the city's life as merchants in its markets or beggars on its streets. Indeed, our pilgrim might only appreciate this fact were he of sufficient devotion to attend one of four occasions during the year, when the flat grassy area extending east from the walls was filled by throngs of the faithful come to pay homage to the central icon of the Faith, on display for a single day: upon a raised dais a giant sculpture, three mets in diameter in the perfect form of three copper circles about a cube, the cube representing the hidden world of dreams, the surrounding circles the protections of the Faith against Echrexar.

The crowds would line up; long queues would snake past the holy icon. Here, you would think, there must be the drone of voices, the thrum of conversation, the laughter and shouts of children. But even at these times the nearness of the towering walls was an awesome, overwhelming presence, a reminder that this was a sacred place whose silence must not be profaned.

One evening, at about the time that Skava was surveying the rather limited streets and wharves of Nek Feddah from her balcony, as the westering sun cast long splinters of black shadow from the battlements across the roadway, an individual arrived at the gates by horse. The horse, though fresh but a cycle ago when mounted at the quayside of the Cise River docks, was labouring hard, having been mercilessly driven up the steep slopes of the gorge and then down the tortuous road to Cise

Hook. Both horse and rider hurriedly entered the vestibule and, after the usual whispered exchange, passed within the temple precincts. His horse taken by a young servitor, the individual made his way along neat chalk pathways past stables and squat stone buildings with barred facades that had once been armouries and now housed the gatekeepers. His route then took him between tall trees and so to a courtyard enclosed on three sides by columns and dark archways. These fronted a symmetrical, if architecturally uninspired, building of grey material, smooth to the touch though reputedly millennia old, and overrun by rambling vines. On closer inspection, evidence of strict tending could be discerned.

The Archivist, for this was what his bald pate and apparel declared him to be, entered one of the archways and, in the gloom therein, rapped at a door. A grille was scraped open. "I am Exarch Ataur," murmured the Archivist. "I seek Grandmaster Tam."

The voice behind the grille uttered a single word: "Wait."

Time passed. The sunlight touching the highest reaches of the walls that ringed Cise Hook turned ruby, gradually relinquishing the stonework to the climbing shadows. At the setting of the sun, the exarch, remaining stock still under the archways, made the sign of the shielding of the doors in a series of circular warding gestures with his right hand, until satisfied that twilight had ended. Soon the courtyard was plunged into night while, above, the evening sky remained a clear indigo-blue.

At the grille a bolt was drawn back and the door opened. An oil lamp flickering inside the room revealed a figure, strange enough to startle most men but not Exarch Ataur. A white-painted visage stared back at Ataur with unblinking eyes. This was the habit of a faction of the Archivists, the Zaggisa, or the 'Masks', as they were sometimes known, upholders of extreme orthodoxy in the Faith, the hunters of heretics and bitterly opposed to the power of the Ta-shih.

The darkness of the room made it seem that the face hovered, disembodied, on its own. But as Exarch Ataur stepped inside and the door closed behind him, he could make out the silhouette of black robes and the pale shape of a powerful hand. In this hand rested a small birdcage and, within it, though he could not see it, Exarch Ataur knew there was a tiny finch, the permanent companion, the silent dream wanderer of the grandmaster. The white-painted visage fixed upon Exarch Ataur.

"You have news," declared grandmaster Tam, neglecting even the coldest propriety and making this utterance in a voice that scraped like rough sand on stone.

"That is so, Grandmaster. From Lorang, by carrier pigeon. News not two days' old."

"Speak."

"The message begins: 'An investigation has begun into Lord Shenri's murder.'"

"Ah. And who leads this investigation?"

"A local Ta-shih commander—"

Tam interrupted: "The future unfolds with precision. And what of the master of Lorang, our impatient Lord Ordas?"

"He plots, Grandmaster. He believes Yoiwa to be alone in this. Certainly he knows nothing of our involvement. Perhaps, therefore, he is over-ambitious. Whatever his motives, Yoiwa restrains him."

"Just so."

"But there is a concern."

Grandmaster Tam made a small clucking sound of vexation. "And that is?"

"There are, in a manner of speaking, three witnesses to the assassination."

"'In a manner of speaking'?"

"Yes. Ordas kept his side of the bargain and produced the band of nomads —plausible, perhaps, to the Ta-shih and to Council, were it not for the fact that the Sohanyuni soldiers bungled and allowed two of the barbarians to live long enough to fall into Ta-shih hands."

Tam clucked again with annoyance. "This, I know."

Exarch Ataur bowed his head, acknowledging the rebuke. "But we have learned, Grandmaster," he pressed on, "that Yoiwa's assassins failed to…er, neutralize all of the Lord of Strath's bodyguard."

Tam, still staring with unblinking eyes at Exarch Ataur, considered this fact as if it lay plain before him like some object whose every facet could be viewed by simple scrutiny. Indeed, in his mind's eye an image from his dreams pressed urgently at his attention: a thick twine from which a single tiny thread depended. *Pull the thread, the twine began to unravel.*

"How many and who are they?"

"A single trooper, Grandmaster."

"Where is he?"

"With the Ta-shih. However, it appears that the Lord of Honam's spymaster exerted sufficient influence to have him moved with the Ta-shih and the nomad captives to Nek Feddah, *en route* to Kiangsu City."

Tam cleared his throat, in a manner suggestive of growing impatience. "Hmm," he grunted. "The master-intelligencer Skava, whose influence waxes most alarmingly with Yoiwa's own. A problem for another time. You have more to tell, it seems to me, Exarch Ataur. Pray tell it."

Ataur swallowed. "I do, Grandmaster. The spymaster requested our assistance in Nek Feddah to deal with the problem."

The thread unravelled faster.

"And you have done what?"

"We put Exarch Hassin at his disposal."

"A dedicated cleric. And?"

"They may already have made contact."

Grandmaster Tam changed tack abruptly. "Do we have influence amongst the Ta-shih in the north?"

"To say 'influence' would be to claim too much. The northern districts are the heartland of Ta-shih loyalists."

"Mmm. But the witnesses must be…silenced."

"To take their lives would be to risk unwelcome attention, Grandmaster."

"Entirely unwelcome. Violence is not our way, except *in extremis,* as the Faith demands when Echrexar threatens to break the walls of our defence against the in-between. We must find another path. Neither Ta-shih nor Council must be drawn to speculate. No hint of conspiracy must attach itself to the Zaggisa. The So-Chiyen watches. He is alert and he will thwart us if we give him good reason. Already he resists me."

After a silence occupied in careful contemplation, Tam said, "Ataur, you must contrive circumstances that relieve the Ta-shih of their new charges. You're a cunning fellow; surely you can see the potential in this? If you already have Hassin involved, you might even get him to throw suspicion on the Ta-shih themselves! Misfortune, sin, corruption – choose a good course!"

Grandmaster Tam laughed, then, with a sharp look full of meaning, added, "The Faith is under threat and is depending on you. When next," he continued, "we have contact with Skava, I want our spies to get close. Find him, stay close, and ensure he understands his obligations to the Faith. Honam grows too powerful with this intelligencer at Yoiwa's side. If he stands against us, his soul is forfeit. Skava is as much a heretic as the worst of Etil's followers."

"Grandmaster," Ataur interjected, his tone almost plaintive, "we have tried. Repeatedly. We have not succeeded."

Tam made a clicking sound with his tongue. "I was not talking of history, Exarch Ataur!" he snapped. "I was talking of the future. In the future, all things are possible. In the future, our past failures are our greatest assets. We who are worthy will have learned from those failures. Which is how we will succeed."

Ataur bowed his head. The heat of embarrassment suffused his face.

Tam grunted, as if at an unpleasant pang. "This Skava. He is too good. He has assisted Yoiwa more than we would like. One's allies' spies should not be better than our own. And what plans does he have that we do not know? My dream wanderer tells me he is a danger to the Faith. He is still in Nek Feddah?"

Ataur half nodded. "He was."

Tam turned the full mask of his face to the man before him. "The moment is opportune. Nek Feddah is isolated. He can be tracked?"

Again Ataur gave a half nod.

"Be discreet, Ataur. Let the spy Skava no longer trouble my dream wanderer."

The thread, severed from the twine, dropped into obscurity.

***

When Exarch Ataur had departed by the same door, Grandmaster Tam extinguished the oil lamp and then, in pitch darkness, made his way down a flight of steps and into an underground tunnel. The tunnel led to the temple and, one hand to the smooth wall, Tam followed its curving route, despite intersections and switchbacks, with the sureness and familiarity of a mole. Great steel doors, cold to the brush of his fingertips, passed. A long walk brought him to more stairs, upwards this time into the bowels of the temple, where the smooth material of the walls and floor became worked stone, crafted and mortared with precision but rougher and more recent than the deeper warrens. He emerged at a passage lit by oil lamps where he paused, glanced at the finch as it fluttered its wings, still mute in its copper cage, and headed down the right-hand branch of the passage. Two young Archivists drew near, inclining their heads in respect as they passed him. They did not look into his face.

More passages, more stairways. At last he reached his chamber and was unsurprised to see Serep, the So-Chiyen's adjuvant, waiting outside at the portiere. Serep, a man of middle years and dark liquid eyes of thoughtful intelligence, glanced up only long enough to assure himself that it was Tam, then resumed his repose.

Tam permitted himself a wry smile. *What does the So-Chiyen know? Is he off-balance with the boldness of events in the north? Does he fear such audacity?*

Knowing that Serep would remain outside, a living sign that the So-Chiyen was here, Tam pushed the portiere aside, stepped within.

Grandmaster Tam's chamber was situated on the highest tier of the western flank of the temple complex. Tall oblong windows overlooked the concentric curtain walls defending this northern point of the Cise isthmus. During the day one could see, immediately below these walls, the black line of the ancient tidewall that ran south hugging the rocky shore. It was known to some Archivists who had seen the surviving transcripts, Tam among them, that the tidewall had been constructed in the golden age along a cliff face, a hundred kems from the ocean, as a dam for the great river. Now the ocean smashed itself against the smooth black of its sloping, vertiginous defences.

Inside Tam's quarters, the windows were dark mirrors, reflecting a single shuttered lamp on the nearside wall. Directly opposite Tam a hooded figure occupied the centre of a divan that ran the length of two walls. Above the divan shelves supported the weight of hundreds of books and thin wooden tablets protecting the precious vellum pages inside.

Tam stopped in the centre of the room. "So-Chiyen," he said, with a bow, to open the exchange.

The figure remained unmoving. No face was visible. It was veiled inside the hood. Tam had known that face once, when he was younger. Now he struggled to recall its features: time had made the apotheosis complete; what had been a man was now the hidden face of the Faith, visible to the gods and no longer to the living. Features were unimportant. Here was the living shadow of the gods, the iconic defender of humanity against the return of Echrexar.

"You have hurried visitors," said the So-Chiyen, though the figure did not visibly move.

Tam placed the cage with its silent occupant upon a table. Then he faced the So-Chiyen again, his own mask of white paint nearly as impenetrable as the So-Chiyen's dark veil.

"Despatches," he part-lied, "on the activities of the Etil heretics occupy too much of my time. You will remember, So-Chiyen, that you yourself were pleased to set me this burden…"

The So-Chiyen laughed softly. "Yes. Tell me then, Grandmaster, how you fare?"

"The heretics die," replied Tam. "Even in the Hundred Islands the exarchs flush them with fire from their boltholes. One day we shall be rid of Etil."

"May Holy Eslo grant it is so. A happy thought. And this was the message that you received?"

"That and much else. Would you hear it all in detail, So-Chiyen?"

Again a soft laugh. "No."

"Perhaps," ventured Grandmaster Tam, "the So-Chiyen lacks faith in me? Perhaps I am not equal to the sacred mission you have entrusted me?"

"To the contrary," came the calm reply. "You set snares for heretics with unrivalled diligence. Who else might I choose?"

What does he really say, thought Tam. *There is a meaning within his words. Does he warn me or does he fear?*

The head lifted and Tam knew that hidden eyes watched him closely. "I think you plot," said the So-Chiyen as if, miraculously, he had read Tam's thoughts. "I ask myself what this plot might be. I ask myself what it is you seek… My dream wanderer shows me blood." Here the So-Chiyen moved his arm, and beneath a fold of his robes a cage was visible. "The Zaggisa always plot, but this time when I ask myself what the Zaggisa seek, my dream wanderer," he repeated, "shows me blood."

"You dream of heretics' blood, So-Chiyen."

"Do I? You read my dreams for me?"

Tam's macabre white face betrayed nothing. But he bowed his head. "I am corrected," he offered as apology. "No one reads the So-Chiyen's dreams, except the So-Chiyen and the gods." He was, however, intrigued. He had imagined his communications to be faster than any in the Realm. It occurred to him now that this might not be so. Perhaps he had miscalculated. Perhaps the So-Chiyen had himself already penetrated Yoiwa's network. Not impossible. But more likely it was bluff. He evidently feared some undetected new ploy. But Tam could weather this, as he had weathered many such storms. The power and flawless purity of his faith was proof.

"Heretics' blood," Tam repeated.

"Ah." The dark head moved, a nod perhaps. The So-Chiyen stood up, the copper bird cage gripped in white, bony fingers. "Tomorrow we meet in conclave," he said, as if their conversation had already been forgotten.

"Yes."

"What will the dream wanderers show us this night, I wonder?" The black figure moved past Tam, pushed aside the portiere and was gone.

Tam crossed slowly to the windows, a frown creasing his forehead, though release of tension coursed through his body like a drug.

***

The twelve grandmasters of the Faith stood unmoving in the centre courtyard of the temple. In this innermost of the sacred precincts of Cise Hook not even the ceaseless hiss and roar of the distant breakers against the tidewall could be heard in the night air. On every side of the courtyard rose the high walls of the temple, sheer to the inky black sky. A day of rain had long passed, but the soft chill of it remained in the wet stone and in the tiny beads of drizzling mist. From a shadowed archway, a servitor dressed in a long dark grey kirtle stopped and raised both hands, palms inward in a sign to the grandmasters, then stood aside, head bowed, as they filed in silence through the doorway. Dark voluminous cloaks swayed behind them like folded wings. At the end of a corridor a heavy door opened and golden light from within broke up the shadows to reveal the face of each man as he entered the inner chamber. Many were old; several carried themselves with shuffling difficulty; and all clutched the tiny copper cages in one hand, as inseparable as their souls. Like Grandmaster Tam, four had faces painted white, creating the impression of walking cadavers. They entered the chamber, lit on every side by oil lamps in round glass sconces. No natural light ever penetrated this room. The smooth material of the walls was bare of markings other than the black sockets of perfectly rectangular air shafts. The stone floor had been raised above the original to be covered by an intricate inlay in white marble of the icon of the Faith. Beyond this, down the centre of the chamber, ran an enormous low table of white wood decorated in a multiplicity of coloured parquetry, flowing with ancient and elaborate figures, the immortals in their ranks, standing with spears levelled against the towering figure of a yellow-eyed Echrexar and his iron dogs, their fearsome jaws flinging victims far and wide upon a nightmare landscape. A single calm presence dominated the centre of the table, Holy Eslo, in white robes, defender and martyr of the Faith. Here he held his hand aloft to protect the world from the dream murderer.

The servitor outside closed the door. All within preserved a solemn silence. At the head of the low table, hooded and seated cross-legged on crimson cushions, was the So-Chiyen. Quietly he said, "Join me."

The grandmasters took their places around the table.

"The Affirmation," said the So-Chiyen, "is complete. King Jamarin's death watch is ended. His soul has transformed from the corporeal to rest in the constellations of the gods. His ashes have been committed to the sacred protection of the four doors of the sealed earth. The Prebendaries have been summoned and have begun the meditation. We await only the pious observances of Council and the accession."

He paused, then intoned the words of ritual: "I have dreamed. And my dream wanderer tells of many things. It has flown beyond the edge of the world and its sight is dark. It brings me dismay – dismay for Chisua – and the Faith. And it whispers of darker things, of a host mightier and more vast than the oceans, and of demons that rise in blood against the Faith… My dream wanderer fled from such horror."

Following this, one of the grandmasters, bent and wizened, raised his head from his chest, but his eyes remained closed. Softly he spoke, cadaverous features impassive: "I too have dreamed of blood. I dreamed that between the death of King Jamarin and the succession of Prince Jeval, the ocean had changed. On the tide there was blood. And Jeval, now king, standing upon the shore, watched. He watched a pebble in the turning of the tides. The tide swept the pebble before it. He watched the pebble closely and the blood behind it. Did the pebble draw the red waters after it? My dream wanderer brought me to that place. And as the king watched I built a wall against the tides and, indeed, to my joy it began to hold back the waters, to channel their power, to shape the shoreline… until a great wave, as great as the ancient flood of floods, dashed my wall and swept aside my hopes. I tried in vain to stop the inundation…until it became plain that I could not see it. I was part of it. I could not stand outside it. And the blood was my own."

The effect of these words was to hold the conclave in reflective silence. Then Grandmaster Tam said slowly in his desiccated voice, "Three days ago my dream wanderer showed me the face of Prince Jeval of Clan Ehri in Mera, and though the boy spoke the ancient words of the Affirmation, in his heart and his thoughts he spurned the wisdom of the Archivists. In a secret place he laughed that we had blundered, that we had been complacent this ten-year. Two nights ago I dreamed of the old King Jamarin and the peace of his reign. Last night I dreamed of the king once more. In the frailty and compliance of his final years, he spoke to his son. He said: 'The Realm possesses inviolably one centre – the Archivists – one centre forever against Echrexar. They have witnessed no force against them, not even the Ta-shih, which grows ever weaker. In the north they have destroyed the Etil heretics. The Suhlin king has at last received their mission to his court. They have fulfilled the promise of the Faith... But in their vanity they have seen nothing of tomorrow. They have cast their attention so wide – to Suhl and the northern borders – that they overlook the power and the folly of Ehri Palace, here, under their feet. I tell you: they do not know you, Jeval! Woe to them! Mistakenly they have set Ehri free!'"

A deep silence followed. Tam, hunched within his heavy garments, nodded slowly to himself and the light from the lamps cast distorted shadow lines on the white-painted visage. Yet another of the group spoke: "My dream wanderer took me to a vine and the gardener who tended it. The gardener was a kindly, devoted exarch. For two millennia the vine burgeoned under his care. Then the vine was a throne and therein a king. The vine began to wither... I dreamed that I was blind in Ehri Palace, that I wandered great halls and heard only echoes of mocking laughter."

At once, one of the Zaggisa spoke. Within the white face his eyes stared fixedly, unblinking, like some predatory white owl. "In the whisper of my dream wanderer," he murmured, "I heard marching. Ten thousand warriors marched upon a plain as vast and dry as the Sea of Bones, crushed the white skulls of Archivists under iron boots, and profaned the Faith with their cursing and besported themselves in our temples. In Mera, in the Imperium, the new king cheered his regiments and the Council did nothing... My dream wanderer showed me an unfledged king and Echrexar's yellow gaze upon him. This king released the sword of Ehri and dismissed the Archivists who would ward him, and took his armies from the Imperium, forgetting the ancient prophecy that *the king who loses Mera is the king who loses the Realm*. This was the great nexus, the cleaving of worlds, as foretold in the Book of the Dead and in all the lesser faiths – the in-between time to end all time. This was the time of Echrexar again, when the power of the Ta-shih would be broken or would break the Archivists and the Faith."

Once more there was silence. In their cages the birds began to call to one another, faintly, gently, like the tinkling of crystal, and then lapsed into quiescence. At this signal, the So-Chiyen spoke: "The dream wanderers bring us wisdom from the gods. The future is theirs, and theirs alone to know. Though we understand Prince Jeval the boy, our dream wanderers tell us that Jeval the King we do *not* know. His soul is dark to us. The future has no pattern. Our dream wanderers see blood or turn back."

To this the gathering gave muttered approval.

"In the north," the So-Chiyen asserted, "a warrior host rises – whilst the Ta-shih wane. Are these warriors threat or succour to the Faith? We know not. The king," continued the So-Chiyen in the same heavy tone of ritual, "we must watch. We must not see vile design where only youthful folly speaks. But the king is also our future. Perhaps he brings us blood. We shall watch him. We shall communicate our will to our allies in the Council. We shall ensure that the eyes of this conclave are ever upon Jeval – within Council, within Ehri Palace, within the king's very chambers. And we shall watch."

The So-Chiyen rose. Then he said, "This is the Archivists' will."

A dozen voices answered to affirm: "This is the Archivists' will."

***

The next day, after the weekly assembly in the temple forecourt to make sacrifice of a pure white bull to celebrate the embodiment of the Faith, the So-Chiyen withdrew to the high balconies of the temple walls. The draw of the blade upon the bull's neck had been imperfectly made, or the bull had moved its head, and blood had sprayed beyond the wide copper libation bowl. The exarch who had made the cut was covered, chest and head, with blood – an inauspicious result. The exarchs holding the ropes to immobilize the bull's head through the iron rings upon the stone steps had flinched as the dark arterial blood spattered their legs. What this meant, no one could tell. Only the So-Chiyen could make pronouncement upon its portent.

With Serep always at a discreet distance, the hooded figure of the So-Chiyen gazed out across the heaving swell of ocean. A black overcast had turned the waves grey, and drizzle obscured the heights of Chisua. No more than the nearest columns of the Prince's Way were visible; the vast walls of Chisua and the great bastions of Mera and Ehri Palace had sunk into the gloom. Now, the first drops reached the temple and splashed off the stone balustrade. The So-Chiyen, however, was oblivious.

The rain fell harder, gathering in mirror-like pools and running in black rivulets off the age-worn stone. The wind too had strengthened, blowing the low cloud seaward and sweeping the rain with it. The vista across the Cise Estuary opened suddenly between roiling banks of cloud. Blue-black became abruptly crimson, then vivid ochre splendour as the sun burst upon the seas. A thin mist of rain fell, gilded rainbow colours alive everywhere. Light cast a dazzling sheen on the whitestone battlements of Chisua. Then, in the twinkling of an eye, the sunlight was gone again. The So-Chiyen lifted his arm, a summons to the watchful Serep.

"Grandmaster Tam," said the So-Chiyen when Serep stood nearby, "dreams of the Affirmation. He dreams of Prince Jeval and the father. He dreams that the Archivists have blundered. His dreams disturb the conclave. With the Zaggisa, his dreams divert us... Already the conclave wavers. And now the sacrifice..."

For a long time the So-Chiyen appeared to contemplate the dramatic seascape. Serep waited patiently.

"The gods are troubled," declared the So-Chiyen, giving voice once again to his thoughts, his communion with the gods themselves perhaps. "Echrexar is abroad upon the world. He has used the breach *in between* the death of Jamarin and the accession of his son to return. There has been a crack in our sacred vigilance; the omens and our dreams verify it. And so our concern now must be the new king."

Serep shuddered. Out there was Echrexar: the So-Chiyen had confirmed his worst fears. Echrexar. No longer quiescent, a mere shadow upon the threshold and bleeding into dreams, but active, menacing, *everywhere*. To strengthen his resolve, Serep spoke the ritual words, "As you say, so it is, So-Chiyen." Wind tugged at Serep's hood. He blinked fine droplets of rain from his eyelashes. Here on the open balcony they were completely exposed. Again he shuddered.

"How does the Council regard him?"

He referred to the new king, but Serep was uncertain if this question was rhetorical or real. He chose to respond: "In the main, they wait, So-Chiyen. They only know him as a wilful prince."

"Very well. Make no move against the Zaggisa. Let our people watch. Grandmaster Tam will expect it. He thinks I will strike against him." A soft laugh. "To the contrary, he is the gods' arrow; we shall help him find his mark!"

***

The Honourable Bank of Royal Kemae, in the city of Liphan on the very edge of the vastness of the Liphan Plains, occupied an imposing building on four floors whose barred windows started four mets, or twelve feet as the northerners preferred, above street level. This produced, side-by-side with neighbouring buildings of normal dimensions, an odd effect, as if the architect had forgotten the usual ground floor arrangements, offering only a single oversized doorway instead. This doorway had been furnished with monumental stone pillars and scrolled architrave, suggesting for obvious reasons that to enter here meant you were inside a place of immutable solidity, reassuring to investor, imposing to borrower. To Harbin, it had the look of a temple, but without the decoration. And, of course, if faith moved mountains, then mountains of money moved worlds.

Harbin had reached Liphan and repaired to this branch office of the bank a week or so after his encounter with the company commander and his assortment of companions. With Kesmet setting the pace, and spare mounts to assist, they had made good time. Only Harbin's buttocks and thighs had suffered. Fortunately, each branch maintained comfortable top-floor apartments for the senior partners of the bank. With the services of a local chef and a key to the small wine cellar near the vaults, Harbin had spent a delightful evening in his rooms, the balcony windows flung wide, the sights, smells and sounds of this small city of Honam Province stimulating his senses.

The following day he had tackled the essential correspondence, delegating banking decisions to the branch staff, receiving their news and generally pressing flesh and smiling at clients, important merchants and sharp-eyed provincial administrators. He was good at these things. They smiled back. They agreed to terms. They promised contacts and business. The work of the bank proceeded.

As the afternoon bell tolled its sonorous double note, triggered by the second discharge of the elaborate water clock on the grand red porphyry staircase, Kesmet was admitted to Harbin's apartment on the uppermost floor. He had not changed since arriving. Indeed he looked no different than he ever did: sleek, tall, dark of hair, brows and eyes; a trimmed beard and comfortable dark clothes with serviceable leather belts to secure items of importance, most notably a thin poniard and a broad hunting knife, one on each hip in black leather sheaths and, of course, a sword, suspended from a cross-strap and looped to his main belt.

"Kesmet." Harbin waved him to a seat on the other side of his writing desk, which he declined to take, preferring to stand. "Tea?" Harbin offered, extending the same hand to ceramic bowls and a covered pot. The set was ancient, from before Echrexar, and beautifully decorated with bucolic scenes picked out in white against a light blue glaze. It was, in a sense, more valuable than the rest of the contents of the bank. "The tradition of tea in the afternoon is one of the finest achievements of civilisation," Harbin pronounced. "We must uphold it."

Kesmet poured tea, sipped, and then regarded Harbin with lowered brows.

"The news is not good, then?" said Harbin. They were both awaiting messages from across their extensive network, at the centre of which was the fictional spymaster Morpheos. Kesmet had spent the morning sifting the particulars, weaving the threads together and constructing the tapestry of their intelligence.

"It is not."

Harbin steepled his fingers, leaned back. "Let me guess," he suggested.

"The Lord of Honam borrows against his name, or against some other collateral of which we are unaware. He does this through some shell arrangement, disassociated from Clan Ouine of Honam. I hypothesize an under-merchant…hmm…a small cartel probably in order to justify the scale of the amounts. You have received information proving certainty of this from our people. I speculate that a senior clerk at one of Kiangsu's larger banks spotted a letter of credit. How am I doing?"

"As you usually do."

Harbin flashed a smile. "Zuse!" he called out. The heavy black hunting dog padded over to the desk. "You need to pay attention, Zuse. Important events are being related to us by Kesmet." He patted the dog's head, its massive snout resting on the desk edge.

"So the question, Zuse," Harbin pressed on, "is what the Lord of Honam requires this line of credit for. I surmise, Kesmet, that he has been party to this arrangement for a while? A year perhaps?" A nod from Kesmet. "So he is building something, a thing that needs to be maintained perhaps. New farms? New industry? He has uncovered a gold hoard hidden in the breaker mines? Iron ore? Of course not. He is speculating in order to undermine the financial stability of his neighbours? Or the royal treasury? Possible. Unlikely. After all, the treasury can outspend him a hundred times. He would cripple Clan Ouine. To buy alliances with Lorang, with Allpo? More promising, but not probable. Not his way. He prefers leverage; sometimes threat; the imposition of power, the promise of…" Harbin waved his fingers to signal an amorphous set of motivations. "Of things, things of value."

At Harbin's elbow, Zuse turned his head to look at Kesmet. Harbin grunted, "If you insist, Zuse. I shall ask Kesmet what he has discovered. Kesmet?"

The tall scout had been waiting, silent and glowering. He rolled his shoulders, in the way he always did when preparing to draw a blade – or deliver a weighty conclusion. Harbin raised an eyebrow.

"Arms and an army," declared Kesmet.

Harbin raised both eyebrows. "Really?" He moved his hand from the dog's head, where he had been stroking the smooth black fur. "A secret army. Clever. And presumably deniable? Or how could he hope to escape notice?" Harbin narrowed his eyes, returning the scout's glower. Why was he glowering so much? "Do you know this or do you hypothesize?"

"We know it is arms and armour. In quantities ten-fold in excess of current deployment."

"Six thousand? Arms for six thousand? Where on earth would Yoiwa find another five thousand men?"

"In alliance with Lorang, and probably Strath."

"Not enough. A few levies, perhaps, here and there. And, more to the point, where would he hide them? King and Council would discover them instantly. No. He has another plan." Harbin looked sharply at Kesmet. "You have found something else. Have you not?"

"I have."

"Hmm. Stop looking pleased with yourself and tell me."

Kesmet's expression, far from looking pleased, had changed by not even a scintilla. He finished his tea, replaced the delicate ceramic bowl on the desk. "Prince Mathed and the Lady Che Keleu will wed."

Harbin raised his brows again. He decided to desist from humour, though Kesmet invited appropriate counterbalance with his stern, laconic cast of mind. Instead, his thoughts raced, items of the puzzle clicking into place like a steel machine.

"When?" he asked.

"Imminent. Ordas prepares to sponsor the Choosing now."

"And the Lord of Strath *wanted* this?" Harbin stated in a voice of rising incredulity. He knew it could not be so.

"That is how it appears," returned Kesmet. Letters under the seal of Strath, one among the possessions of the late Shenri, another in the hands of Lord Ordas as sponsor, a third I would guess on its way via Lord Yoiwa, with his official blessing, to Council. Very credible. Unimpeachable. Perhaps it is true. Perhaps Lord Shenri saw value in this match."

Harbin curled his lip, scepticism in every line of his expression. He tapped out his thoughts with a heavy finger: "So. Not only alliance with Strath. Mathed installed in Strath. Honam and Strath as one. Lorang under Yoiwa's thumb. And then...what, Kesmet? Allpo? Can Yoiwa suborn Isharri? That would be the *whole* of the north. Bigger than the Biljan kingdoms ever were."

Kesmet stared at him.

Harbin was struck that suddenly Kesmet had a lot to say. "You have more, do you not?" murmured Harbin. His optimistic mood had evaporated.

"Our man in Sohanyun."

Harbin made a face. "Ah, yes. Tell me the worst."

"A strongbox was delivered to Lord Ordas. Our man's head was inside. His eyes had been put out."

Harbin drew a breath, feeling the need to articulate something, a word or two to mark the sacrifice of a loyal servant. "He was a good…person," he offered lamely.

Kesmet responded with a ritual phrase they had used before: "We will remember him."

"Aye. We will." Harbin lowered his eyes then looked back sharply at the scout. "A head in a box. As a gift. Who would do that? Have you heard its like before?"

Kesmet stared at him, unblinking. Even Zuse was looking at him.

"You *have* heard its like, Kesmet. Perhaps not its exact form, but the theatrics of it. The *statement*. The twisted sense of humour. The irony. The hubris. The *signature*…"

Kesmet would not be drawn.

Harbin took a deep breath. They always sparred like this, the two of them. Kesmet taciturn and incisive in his challenge, demanding facts. Harbin prolix, making the argument, building the picture, linking the concepts, posing the theory and strategy. Even Zuse, the neutral caucus, had his part to play.

Harbin stood up. The partner's chair with its tall back, wide wings and padded green upholstery seemed diminutive next to him. "I fear," he sighed, "you have still more to tell me."

Kesmet put a hand loosely on the steel pommel of his hunting knife. "The Zaggisa are in play."

Harbin rubbed his chin, clean-shaven that morning. It was an absent-minded gesture, familiar to Kesmet, and in evidence only when Harbin was profoundly disturbed.

"There was some contact in Nek Feddah," Kesmet continued. "Exarch Hassin…we know him as a reclusive, though prolific, hunter of heretics."

Harbin shook his head, a sorrowful almost fearful motion not at all in keeping with his usual confident authority. "I see."

They had experience of the Zaggisa. Tragic experience. Their cruelty and persistence in upholding orthodoxy knew no bounds. In the Kemae Islands, where Harbin had made his home, the hunters of heretics were not welcome, but still they strove to bring low the followers of ancient Etil. The Faith permitted the hounding, but did not condone violence. The exarchs, of course, persuasive and stealthy, had many alternatives.

"And there is worse perhaps…" Kesmet paused and leaned both hands on the desktop, his eyes alight. "We understand…" – he never used vague words like *understand* – "we understand that Hassin met with someone at Nek Feddah. We do not know who. A rider, perhaps courier."

Harbin's heart was beating a little faster. "But…" he prompted.

"There is an odd tale, a circumstance really. It may or may not be connected."

Harbin had rarely seen Kesmet so tentative. He insisted on facts, on verifiable evidence. He was patient and meticulous to a fault in the pursuit of truth. "It is gossip," said Kesmet. "Taproom talk."

"And yet you present it to me."

Kesmet took a breath. "Our factor in Nek Feddah said it was probably nothing. He took a drink at an inn – one of his usual methods of acquiring and sifting news on the great river. He overheard a riverman or merchant guard. There was a woman…"

Harbin found he was holding his breath. "Yes?" he hissed.

"She was with two men – trained, good at their trade. Guards for hire or some such. You know the type. The riverman spent the night with her. She woke screaming from a dream, a terrible dream. He heard her words…she screamed of fire…and Echrexar."

Harbin stared at Kesmet. A clatter of links fell rapidly into place in his head. "The scout," he murmured, "the scout on Pillio's tail, observing from the woodland. Better than average, you said."

"I did."

"With others nearby, you said."

"I did."

"And a woman in Nek Feddah, who has nightmares." Harbin was breathing hard. "Kesmet, she was there. Right on top of us. Eslin… She was that close…"

Kesmet shook his head slowly. He was retreating to his role again, insisting on the empirical, decrying speculation. "Perhaps. Only perhaps. It may have been Skava, Yoiwa's spymaster. Most likely it was Skava. Or any guard for hire with cryptic nightmares…"

"Then why did you tell me about her? You know it is her."

"I do not." And yet he sounded uncertain.

Harbin moved. He stalked away to the windows, then returned, face inflamed with passionate intensity. "So much complexity, Kesmet. Complexity that is hard to see in its entirety. No one sees the whole! Not Council, not Ta-shih, certainly not king! *We* see only fragments, the tactics. But it is *huge*. And *that* is her way. She loves complexity. The whole of the northern realm under her palm, Yoiwa the spearhead that thrusts but distracts. The hunters of heretics brought into her plans. You know what that means: she has a route into Chisua and the Archivists. If she controls – no, not even controls – merely wields influence within the Faith, she can move in any direction she wants. With Yoiwa and the north she will push to sway policy in Council, abetted by sympathetic voices among the Archivists…" Harbin snapped his fingers at a sudden thought. "And with a secret army at her disposal!"

Kesmet moved his chin, a gesture that from him conveyed the significance of a shout. "Yet," he said quietly, "she makes mistakes."

Harbin sighed, closed his eyes. Eventually he answered: "True. True, Kesmet, my very dear, old friend. But she is certainly already fixing her mistakes. And, answer me this: are we too late?"

Kesmet looked away.

Harbin drew himself up. He seemed to have come to a decision. "Kesmet, we *are* late. It is like we have been asleep for years whilst she built her plans. It was only…" – and here Harbin's voice rose in anger – "only when she made her decisive move to murder a lord of the Realm that we had the slightest inkling! We erred in coming here rather than staying close to Pillio; but we could not have known she was *so close*, nor that his prisoners or the knowledge he has learned are so important to her that she trails him. Our choices are limited. With Eslin…" Kesmet gave him a hard look and Harbin waved at him impatiently. "Very well… *Skava*… With Skava loose, we must find her. Nothing else matters. Now we must hypothesize. Where is she? Heading south in pursuit of Pillio? Or elsewhere?"

Kesmet pursed his lips. "If Skava is heading south, what occurred between her and the Zaggisa exarch?"

"Indeed." Harbin shook his head. His mind was filled with a sense of gigantic consequences impending from just a few simple actions. The decision he and Kesmet made now would be profound – one way or the other. He regarded the black hound, now lying down, head between its forepaws. "So, Zuse," he asked with mock portentousness. "If you know the venomous snake has slithered right by and is behind you somewhere, whilst a pack of ravening wolves howl at you from the woods, what do you do, eh?"

Zuse opened his eyes and, from under wide wrinkled brows, returned his master's look.

"It's difficult, isn't it?" said Harbin. "Do you strike at the snake or scatter the wolves? Difficult. But we must choose."

***

Skava rode north. Their heading was Strath. And that meant a tricky journey of nearly a thousand kems, off the foothills of the Alnaes and north-east across rolling hills into the newly deceased Lord Shenri's lands. The main roads were good and they had been built on ancient routes and underpinned where they had fallen away, neatly surfaced and maintained with good slabs, not the cobbles that were used as poorer substitutes in villages and wrecked the wheels of wagons and carriages. Strath was wealthy. It was wealthy because of its exports in wine, grain and livestock to the voracious south. And that produced traffic. Lots of traffic. Thus, the roads must be good.

Unfortunately, Skava and her small squad could not travel the main routes. Her arrival and activities in Strath must be undisclosed. She had political ground to scout and preparations to make so that the nuptials of Mathed and Keleu might proceed without hitch. Securing Strath would enable her to turn her efforts to the recalcitrant Allpo, a more difficult challenge, but infinitely easier once Yoiwa controlled its neighbour.

Skava, Maki and Yan turned west long before the provincial border with its duty guards and customs officials exacting their taxes and tolls. This took them back to the lower slopes of the Alnaes, heading down into the Kacia Lowlands. The border to the east was well-populated, dotted by farms and villages, and invited a probability of scrutiny she could not allow. The lowlands by contrast were wet with the run-off from the mountains, and drainage was sluggish so insects thrived. No one lived on the routes Skava planned to take. But, of course, that made it uncomfortable for person and beast alike. Exposed skin must be smeared with ointment to keep the biting pests and bugs at bay. Horses must be inspected and curried more frequently. And, owing to the detour, they must haul more supplies. Skava had bought two more mares and so they had eight mounts to manage.

Winding down a rough trail amidst the scree of the mountain slopes, where few trees found easy purchase, Maki led their small group, Skava behind with the remounts, all untethered against the danger of a fall by one that might take the lot in a tumbling mass of broken horseflesh. It was a devilishly tricky business keeping the right pace on awkward ground where splintered rocks and glass slivers slipped under hooves, and the trailing horses wanted to shy from the dizzying drop. Yan was hindmost, ranging back and scouting, except if the remounts needed steadying. Ahead, when Skava dared to look up from the path she was picking downslope, there skulked the haze of the Kacia Lowlands, a vast expanse of swampy mist obscuring the distant low hills of Strath. Here, moving north, it felt like full summer, the sun's heat reflecting off the anvil of the mountains. They sweated. And they moved slowly, alert to the ever-present possibility of a fall by one of the horses and the nightmare of a broken leg or worse.

Maki made it to a more level outcrop wide enough to pause and collect the remounts as they stepped carefully down. He turned in the saddle and smiled uneasily at Skava. "You know this course, boss?" he ventured. She had confirmed she did, but he was rightly dubious. "All the way to the hills?"

It said something for his concern over the perils of this route that he had spoken up, in light of which Skava bit back a waspish retort and shrugged. "I do. I've done it a few times."

Maki nodded. Even with years working together, he and Yan were still occasionally in awe of her encyclopaedic knowledge of…well, just about everything. So she took a breath and, unusual for her, offered reassurance. "Not easy. This bit is bad, I concede. But it's dry. The lowlands…" – she pointed her chin at the distant bleached haze – "are flat but wet. Very wet. We're well kitted. We'll be fine."

Fine. The word echoed in her head. Not really fine. Her skin crawled. The lowlands were a long impact crater hard up against the mountains, but nearly as many kems wide as long, and shallower now with centuries of run-off and silt from the high escarpment. This was Echrexar's place, the bleeding wound of one of his dogs. Not that you would know. The melt-rock and shale glass shocked into instantaneous existence by that titanic blow were mostly cloaked now by the swamplands, except here, high on the rubble of the southern crags. But it felt to Skava like entering a vast sepulchre, a monument of menace and brooding malevolence. The crucible of her fear cracked open as if some bane worked misfortune on her. It seemed to have its own voice, a little girl's voice, squealing at her to turn around, to find another route, to avoid the calamity of this cursed scar on the landscape.

Yan pulled up on the outcrop, positioning his piebald to keep the remounts from wandering back upslope should their tiny, skittish brains persuade them to do something stupid. He understood them so well.

"All good?" she shot at him, welcoming the distraction. In her head the voice stopped protesting, silenced as the crucible snapped shut.

"All good," he said, cool as can be.

"Right then," she announced confidently, "we head on down. Getting easier…"

As if.

They worked their way along the switchbacks, scattering the occasional small rockslide, heart-stopping because of the clattering noise but not likely to start an avalanche. By mid-afternoon they were under the haze, still heading down but losing sight of the high mountains at their backs. Here they crossed spillways and edged around dwarf waterfalls and clear pools where they re-stocked on water and monitored the intake of the horses, lest they overdid it. Gods, they could be dumb. Then the rock scree gave way to a thick covering of moss, fern and burweed and the pace slowed. Before they lost firm footing on dry land, Skava called a halt and they spread out on some large hummocks between the listless waterways. Maki and Yan staked the picket lines and tethered the horses, and they all started with their brushes on currying flanks and necks and lifting and checking hooves. Apart from a few cuts and abrasions to hoof and fetlock, the mounts were in good order. Feed was next, nosebags, which the hungry creatures set to with some vigour. Only then, as the sun was westering through the green-tinged haze and the tall cattails on the water's edge, did they look to themselves, setting a fire with kindling they had carried down from the forests. Finally they sat, slurping through a good stew of lamb chunks and vegetables. Conversation, as usual on the trail, centred around the day just gone and the days ahead. Now and again they wandered into reminiscence about some small event in town or village, involving without fail the chance liaisons that interspersed their work and that gave cause for ribald comment at the expense of one of them.

After they had eaten, Yan drew a length of charred wood from the fire and dropped it outside the crude hearth, looked at Maki and asked him to listen to a dream. Skava surveyed them both, face blank, saying nothing whilst Maki examined the glowing red embers of the charred branch, seeking patterns, and Yan related his dream – the usual mix of the nonsensical logic of dreams and the primal terrors that surfaced in sleep.

She couldn't fault the two of them. Every soldier did this, and some were quite good at it, dispensing wisdom or advice to hopeful comrades. The Archivists tolerated it. Skava made no objections, but nor did she take part. "Not my thing," she would say. In another life, it *had* been her thing and probably would be again. After all, faith could move mountains.

Listening to the subdued, reverent exchange, she felt a twinge of anxiety. They were *here*, in Echrexar's boneyard. If they needed Maki and Yan's faith and a little of the good fortune of the gods anywhere, it was here. And she could not shake off the cloying apprehension, as much as she tried. It was stupid and irrational, but she dreaded being here. How would Maki and Yan feel if they knew what this place was? Insight came to her in a moment of clarity: no one lived here. No one had *ever* lived here after Echrexar. It was as if people *knew*. This was a cursed place.

And then, as if at a signal, the talk ceased and while her squad agreed the watch rota and checked the camp for night, Skava retreated into her head, planning, calculating, reviewing recent updates from her network. The latest of these, garnered in Nek Feddah, were satisfactory. The situation with Pillio and the Ta-shih troop would be handled. Ordas had fallen into line and was preparing to represent to King and Council, on behalf of Strath and Honam, his sponsorship of the marriage of Keleu and Mathed. Ahead of her in Strath, her spies reported on the household at Mamoba, the seat of the ruling family. At home, in Honam, there were the military considerations. The Law had long prohibited the building or recruitment of private armies in the provinces. The lords of the Great Families could each maintain a few hundred men-at-arms, with some leeway for the relative size of province and local conditions. Allpo in the far north-east, for example, could retain a fleet to scatter pirates from the Bay of Marshese. Kei, Sychomo and Biabaro, hard on the western border of their giant neighbour Kiang Province, of the king's clan Ehri, preserved contingents of no more than fifty soldiers each in their capital cities, preferring to rely on the Ta-shih for law and order. But Skava wanted Yoiwa to build an army in concealment, dispersed in small contingents but trained exactly to the same deployment and order of battle as the six hundred troops he was allowed under the Law. She wanted to field two thousand archers, a force unheard of in the Realm and big enough to shock but, perhaps, not yet outmatch a southern Ta-shih army, when that moment arrived. The news was good: the re-curve bows and new armour she had designed worked well, and some small numbers had been shipped and stockpiled in several locations. Only in Chisua, in the southern capital and political centre, did she worry at her plans, like a dog with a thorn in its paw. Even with Daved and his people installed in the capital, she had insufficient leverage where it mattered. The balance of power between Council, king and Archivists weakened her ability to make progress. Inevitably, therefore, she prepared Honam for war. *What did they call it*? she thought drily. *Diplomacy by other means?*

The night was uneventful, but she slept badly, plagued by dreams of fiery Echrexar in this mausoleum under the shadow of the mountainside. She stood the third watch in the pre-dawn, listening more than watching. No one could get near without making some noise in the waterways. The air was cool but would warm rapidly with the sun, so they packed and set off early, Skava directing the route with the aid of her pocket compass and Maki picking the exact footing. Mostly the trails they followed were above water, soft under the hooves but firm enough to make steady progress until they had to cross marsh or still ponds. Maki gestured at occasional patches of cowbane, tall plants carrying tiny white flowers on stalks, the roots deadly poisonous should the horses get near enough to try some. They steered carefully around them.

Mid-morning, with the insects swarming, Yan brought his piebald splashing up next to Skava. She gave him an enquiring look.

"Boss, we have company." Plain as you like. No expression. Reporting facts. She liked that, even if the news was fucking *astonishing*.

"Where? And how many?"

"Trailing us. A biggish party. I'm guessing ten."

"You seen 'em?"

"Nope. Can hear 'em. 'Bout a quarter back." He meant a quarter of a mile. Easy to stay invisible in these wetlands if you had a mind to stay hidden below the rushes and scrub.

Maki had paused and was turned in the saddle to listen to the news.

Everyone was silent for a moment, digesting the implications. No one wanted to ask the obvious, but Skava always insisted on it, so Maki piped up: "Not behind us by chance, then?"

Asking the obvious was a good way to face the truth fast.

Skava listed the reasons, raising a finger for each item. "This is not a trail. It's a big party behind us. No one lives here. Why would anyone *be* here?" Her apprehensions from the night before surfaced with new intensity. *A cursed place.* She blew out her cheeks, sending a fly buzzing away from her forehead, damp with perspiration from the humidity. Her shirt was stuck to her body like a bad second skin. "Yan?" she asked, not actually blaming him but showing her irritation. "How did they get so fucking close?"

Yan appraised her with a mild look. "Stayed back on the foothills…" – he meant the nightmare rock scree they had negotiated days before, where their attention had been rather more myopic than perhaps was wise – "and pushed hard in the wetlands. Maybe they know this place and can move better in the dark, when we was stopped…"

"Our options?"

He looked up at the sky and she knew he was calculating remaining light. "A quarter is a long way in this…" He stabbed a thumb at the wetlands. "They won't catch us but we can't move easy after dark. Might be they want the dark again to get close."

Skava made her own calculations. "Three days to clear the swamps," she decided aloud. "They *will* get close. On their terms. We need to thin them now – a lot."

Both men nodded agreement.

Skava felt the familiar tingle of energy through her gut, excitement and fear both. It never changed. "Echelon ambush, I reckon," she said. "Maki leads the full string of remounts, slow as possible, making a bit more noise. Yan goes east and waits. I go west and do the same. Bows, yes?" They would be faster than loading crossbows, sacrificing a little in accuracy. But since this was going to be close action, it made no odds. "Maki, you may be too far ahead to help when the shit hits, but get back soon as."

She looked at Yan. His youthful tanned face was calm. He was waiting for her to finish the plan. These boys were good. She was proud of them. "Can't synchronize first shots in this terrain," she explained, "so loose when you think it's right or if you hear me start. Same for me. Could do with one of 'em alive. Need some answers." She looked at both of them in turn. "All said?"

Maki pursed his lips, then said, "Armour, boss?"

"Fucking hot, but yes," she confirmed. They would roast. But it was right.

On an extended hummock, the lead horses having crushed the rushes flat, they dismounted and armed. Maki and Yan donned hauberks, with the overlapping oblong steel plates about the length of a finger that maximized protection. Skava had commissioned them and they had cost a small fortune, better by far than even their Ouine bronze scales. While they were buckling up, she changed her mind and hauled out the light chainmail for herself.

"Boss?" Maki challenged her.

"Too fucking hot," she muttered, hating the very idea of heavy scales on top of a padded undercoat and a sweat-soaked shirt. The squealing girl's voice started up a protest again about calamity and misfortune but she quelled it. "I can move quicker. Be alright. Help me."

Maki grunted, which was his way of making his objection known. He held the mail over her head and she got her arms in, settled the whole comfortably, or as comfortably as half a ton of metal could feel in this stinking humidity, and then allowed Maki to drape a tan raincloak over everything so the sunlight didn't reflect off the metal. They had both done the same. She rebuckled her belt, making sure she had easy access to shortsword and knife. They all checked their bows, lightweight recurve weapons, with more power. They got the gut strings on, which were perfectly dry from the pouches they kept them in…would have to watch out for moisture on those in this humid swamp.

They were ready. Maki led off with the remounts, slowly splashing through the shallows. Yan gave Skava a nod and she saw him murmur some prayer – "Dian be with us" she guessed, or some rot, though she never questioned their beliefs or their superstitions unless they got in the way. Then he turned his piebald and bent down in the saddle, staying below the high rushes as he guided her off east. Skava looked back the way they had come. Nothing. Yet. She eased her horse to the left, towards the sun, trying to move silently through the narrow waterways and up onto the hummocks, her head down, near the mane, minimizing her profile. At thirty paces, she pulled up the other side of a low island. Good cover on all sides, if she drew the horse in between the rushes, water above the fetlock.

She kept still and listened, head low down below the mane so she could use the neck to amplify sound. The insects murmured their lives away, a low drone that she excluded. No wind. Small splashes of tiny animals. But distant, and sure enough, the sound of moving horses, south of her position. She turned her head, bringing it down on the other side of the horse's neck, and there, north, the receding sound of Maki. Again she turned her head, manoeuvring to catch the occasional tell-tale suck and gurgle of hooves in the mud at water's edge. Her hands were trembling at the prospect of combat; familiar, necessary, her body gearing up for explosive action. She patted her roan's neck, a rhythmic calming to both of them. The animal stood stock still, just the occasional flick of her tail to disturb the insects. Skava wished *she* had a damned tail. The flies buzzed and landed on her head. The chainmail was heavy and she sweated like a rutting bullock.

Splashing nearer now. Unmistakably a group of riders.

Skava fingered her helmet, tied securely to the saddle and covered by a canvas flap. She couldn't wear it. She needed all round vision and it would restrict that and hearing. Her left-hand fingers strayed to the bowstring, gently testing the give. In her right hand she held bow and one shaft. The quiver was at her right knee, easy to reach, fifteen arrows.

The splashing approached and her heart rate climbed, a fast inner drumbeat. Now she raised her head, peering through the rushes. First, a lead scout, quite near Yan's location. He had his head up scanning ahead for trouble, glancing down now and again to check the trail. Soon there were glimpses of riders, a couple up front watching the scout. They were going carefully. Some were in half-chain, most in quilted leather, good enough to stop a glancing blade. And they were armed to the teeth: swords, lances, crossbows strapped to saddles, heavy axes. Serious men. Skava counted nine. Was that the lot? She moved her head cautiously, slowly, to take in the wetlands behind her and south of the party. Nothing more.

It was time. She transferred the bow to her left hand, raised it to pick the third rider, a big bearded bastard, and in that instant the man in front grunted loudly and fumbled at a shaft that had appeared in his chest. Yan. Fine strike. For long moments, no one reacted. It was almost comical. Skava pulled, fingers to cheek, taking the full draw weight, and released, the angle on Black Beard tight. The shaft took him in the back, but because he was side-on it penetrated shallowly – not a killing shot.

Now they started shouting, riders peeling off left and right in great sprays of water as the horses plunged and gained speed. Skava plucked another arrow, nocked and fired fluidly at the nearest man. Taken chest height, he keeled over backwards. She didn't see what happened to him. New shaft, nock, draw and release. This rider thrust his shield up, deflecting the arrow away. *Fuck!* He came at her, mount wading heavily in deeper water. Aim low. Draw, release. Shield up to protect his bare head, he tried to sway sideways to avoid it, took the shaft near his hip, screamed.

Skava kneed her mount forward, onto the higher ground. New shaft, picking a new target. Black Beard was heading her way, bellowing like a bear, every expletive under the sun, the blood-lust in him, heavy sword out, ready. His horse rushed towards her, spray showering to every side. Difficult shot. She released and there was a sound like a small axe on wet wood and he bellowed even louder. Skava threw her bow away onto the small island, right hand down to draw her shortsword, left fist pulling the reins to move right, out of the way of the massive horse bearing down on her, a clever manoeuvre she had used countless times to get her on the shield side of her enemy…harder for him to hack at her over the neck of his mount. But her roan struggled to move, lurching and stumbling like a drunk. Skava knew a moment of surging fear. His charging horse could flatten her mount. She looked down, frantically trying to work out why her horse wasn't doing what she expected: there was a crossbow quarrel embedded in the roan's shoulder. And then Black Beard's mount hit. The roan staggered and sagged, and Skava was nearly unhorsed. But she kept her eyes on the big blade swinging at her, left arm round the pommel of the saddle to keep her seat while she flattened herself against her mount's flank, almost falling into the water. The big sword swished overhead, clipped the roan's neck and then she was going down, the heavier enemy horse barrelling past. Water and mud exploded over her head as she twisted from the saddle and tried to get clear of the collapsing roan. She swallowed rank water, coughed it out, levered herself off her left arm and was on her knees in the bog. The roan was screaming a mad whinnying sound, thrashing in the shallows, blood spraying from its neck.

On your fucking feet!

She was up and Black Beard's horse was turning and the man himself was reeling in the saddle. Skava's arrow shaft stuck in his left shoulder. His face was red rage and he was still mouthing fury and fire as he drove his mount at her, swinging the sword down underarm. Big damned blade that, enough to cleave her one side from the other. Skava went right, just before the horse arrived, putting all the power of her thighs into the move.

Man and rider crashed past her in a welter of spray and curses, and she swung her blade across her chest and hard, cutting upwards for his unprotected thigh. She scored the mount's ribcage and sliced Black Beard's thigh in the same cut. Then she was spinning waist deep in the fetid slime to regain her stance and reckoning options whilst the big bastard tried to circle back, yanking the bit in the beast's foaming muzzle. His thigh was pouring blood. Bad. Main artery maybe. Killing wound that, she was pleased to note. He would bleed out. But not before he had a go at splitting Skava.

Back he came, leaning out to his right, looking like he might topple at any moment. Skava pulled her dagger and took a firm stance, not easy in muddy marsh up to her arse. The horse looked fucking gigantic, pounding straight at her with a wave-front breaking the green water, and this time she went left, away from the horse, but watching the four feet of steel that was dropping on her head. She pulled up, stopping the feint and swaying inside the blade, but too close to the damned horse and cutting up with the dagger to catch the bastard's hip; then she was hit by a hind leg and the world turned upside-down, swamp, mud and blood in her mouth like liquid shards of copper, and she was dragging herself up gasping into the light again. The horse was cantering to a stop beyond her dying roan. His left leg useless, Black Beard fell sideways, very slow, trying in a half-dead attempt to cling to his seat, and landing with a heavy squelch on crushed rushes and mire. He pushed himself up with his sword arm and was on his knees when Skava started splashing towards him, both blades levelled. Behind the hummock several riderless horses milled around. Maki had appeared, bow drawn, and was firing smoothly. Skava didn't see what he hit. She put her head down and waded out of the water, streaming filth from clothes, chainmail and hair. Her arse hurt like she'd been kicked by a horse, which was indeed the case. Back on the island, weighted down by half the wetland in her clothes, she got close to Black Beard, who glared at her with that fuzzy look they all had when too much blood was on the ground and not enough in their brain. He still waggled the thick sword, though. How was he still alive?

Sounds of fighting nearby. Swords rang together. Suddenly a horse and rider exploded out of the tall rushes, all battle scream, plunging hooves and curved blade. Ten paces away and Skava had almost no time to react. She pivoted and instinct and training were moving her legs to propel her out of the way of the charging beast. Another shriek – dead man riding now, maybe Maki's shooting, she reckoned in some part of her brain not preoccupied with survival. The horse pounded past and Skava was scrambling on her knees, and Black Beard was within arm's reach and she couldn't react quickly enough. His big blade was thrusting, and she felt like a stupid fool for a tiny instant until a tremendous blow to her hip and gut knocked the wind out of her. She lunged backward but swung a last weak parry, her sword connecting, crunching on something she couldn't see. Couldn't see because her face was in the island mud. Typical. And between the pain in her arse and the agony of not being able to breathe or move, she reckoned she was finished. Unbelievable. Finished.

Fool, fool, fool! The little girl's screeching had taken over her head in a torrent of animal fear and panic. *I warned you! This is Echrexar's place, the grave of billions. Why did you come here? Why? Why?*

Sounds of battle had abruptly gone. Bizarrely, she could feel the grip of her sword. Like that would help. But her brain was going into rapid survival mode. The shriek of the insistent, horrified little girl was drowning in her own dread and Skava was starting to think a little more clearly. So she tried to raise her head. It would be good to breathe. And important to know what was happening. Where was Black Beard? Fuzzy, white-spotted vision began to fade and there was Black Beard's knee and a lot of blood on his leggings and his head at a weird angle. More blood over the rest of his body. Dead at last. Balls-out, fearsome fucker. Had to respect that.

Squelching boots approaching and the splashing and sucking of hooves. Skava flinched. She twisted her head, at the same time weakly pushing at the wet earth to lever her torso off the ground. Pathetic. But she was a fighter and she would fight, even if it killed her.

"Boss," said Maki, alarm in his voice, though all she felt was the relief that it was him.

"Where the fuggin' rets?" she choked out, like someone had put rocks in her mouth.

"All down, boss. Yan's making sure. He's on point."

More relief. It would be alright. Maki and Yan: brilliant, both of them. The very rational part of her thinking was telling her they needed to get moving. Things to do. The terrified, kicked-to-shit emotional girl-animal in her was bawling to curl up and hide. She could understand both with absolute crystalline clarity. *Should never have taken this route,* said a disapproving voice in the impervious accusing tone of her mother, *not here in Echrexar's domain, not here where one of his dogs smashed the face of the earth to bloody pulp. A cursed necropolis.*

Maki's long face appeared. He was perspiring. Must be dying of heat in his hauberk. On his knees, he got hold of her, gently, and eased her over onto her back, his head down, looking for something. She was confused. What was he looking at?

"Yan," he called, enforced calm, but a decidedly panicky edge to his voice. "Secure?"

"Yep."

"Right. Fresh water. Bring the barrel. And the alcohol."

Sounds of creaking leather as Yan dismounted. He moved off fast, spattering muck and water.

Skava felt the pain in waves now, mainly her backside, but a cold seeping broken feeling in her guts and hip. Her mouth tasted of vomit and copper and putrid swamp, so she spat and managed to dribble blood and spittle down her chin and her cheek.

"Get me up," she gurgled.

Maki had a forearm under her shoulder and he was close, closer than he'd ever been. *Fucking getting fresh with me*, came the witty thought, kicked away instantly by the pure logic of her thinking.

"No, boss," he replied firmly. "Got a wound. Let's clean it up, eh?"

She coughed again, getting pink-flecked spittle on Maki's tan cloak. "Be fine," she croaked, but the blood in her throat said otherwise.

"No, boss." Firm. Like he was in charge. Fucking cheek.

It was quiet. After the frenzied action that was strange. Just the insects again and odd splashes and flies buzzing. A fine afternoon, here at the bottom of Echrexar's fucking crater. Yan came back and got hold of her shoulders so she was supported, and Maki stripped her belt off, then started lifting her cloak and chainmail and ripping her shirt open, and though he was gentle, pain burst inwards like fire.

"Got a horse knee'n m'arse," Skava burbled, feeling the need for some explanation. And, in a peculiar half apology, she blurted out: "Fuggin' chainmail, eh?" Maki's objection had been right. The steel links had parted like butter to Black Beard's heavy blade. Any other cut might have been turned, but a straight thrust…

Maki was squatting astride her legs – funny if he hadn't looked so damned serious – pouring water to clear the mud. He was working fast. Smell of alcohol; the purer stuff they kept for bad cuts, she knew. She found she was staring at Maki's face and he looked appalled, eyes widening before he snapped his expression back to flat. It was not good news, he had decided.

"Bad'un," she offered. "But be alright."

"Yes, boss," he said, quiet and calm like he was reassuring a dying woman.

But he was wrong. She could feel the mad surge of energy inside her, the redirecting of her body's defences, the insane crawl of the invisible stuff that healed and always seemed to be there like a frenzy of tingling and itching whenever this had happened before – and once, oh yes once, really bad that time. She was still staring at Maki's face, and he was having trouble meeting her eye. He thought it was all over. So she looked down at her midriff and saw the blood leaking out like a small river from a wide hole in her flesh that really shouldn't be there. That shit Black Beard had got her well and good. Be a fucking mess in her guts, and maybe her hip bone or pelvis. If he had nicked her intestines, she was in real trouble. Not going to walk it off. *Hah-hah.* Maybe she wouldn't make it this time. That was sobering, quashing the ridiculous optimism the frenetic emotional state was inducing at some deep biological sub-strata.

"Maki!" she snapped with some force. And her command voice worked. He stared straight at her, and she could see that behind his neutral expression, fixed on with the utmost discipline, there was horror in his eyes. "Get me clean'd up. Al'chol again. Stop th'fuggin' bleed. If it's a big vein, tie it off. Change dressin'ever'day. Be fine."

Almost certainly he thought she was losing it. He had seen bad wounds, inflicted them himself no few times on some luckless bastards, and this one was awful. As far as he could tell, she was a goner.

"Sure, boss." He looked up and gave Yan instructions and they did what she asked, cleaning and packing the hole with linen dressings, entry and exit wounds both. Black Beard's sword had gone through her and been yanked back out. Nasty. She was starting to shiver, but the clarity of thinking was still good. She knew it would not last. Things she needed to tell Maki.

"Maki. Lis'n up."

"Boss?" His horsey face was gaunt and spattered with her blood. But he was all attention. Last rites, maybe he was thinking. Yan towered above her, bow in hand, watching the swamp, taking no chances.

"Be alright," she repeated. "Heal fast. But–"

"Boss," he interjected, no attempt now to hide the horror on his face. "Boss, your eyes…"

Oh, fuck.

"Boss," he said, with rising alarm. "Your eyes. They're yellow."

And, too late, that was what she wanted to tell him.

Bollocks and double bollocks.

CHAPTER 6

The king directed Sa-Hwei, who was inebriated, to fetch the crystal chalice. But Sa-Hwei saw two chalices and returned to ask of the king, "Which shall I bring?" The king replied, "Cast one into the fire and bring the other." Sa-Hwei obeyed and both chalices disappeared.
The Book of the Dead – 'Dogmata', lines 2344-2349.

Below a certain level, resource constraints force different priorities. Our most significant challenge is food production. Priority has shifted in our refuge and, as we must hypothesize, for any other remaining refuges, to food production and storage and, reluctantly, away from archival storage, science and broader education. Agricultural yields in the year prior to the impact event were the highest on record but total food surplus for the refuge was two years. Our focus became, in a few short years more, animal husbandry and farming. Records of almost every other aspect of life were gradually forgotten or moved out of the secure archives to make way for necessities. We fervently hope that other refuges were not so single-minded.
Extract from a surviving document, ascribed to the Immortals, copied by a scribe, IYE 1047.

***

"The Mad Poet asks, 'What is the colour of the wind?' This is a question, we may safely say, not easily answered nor indeed, perhaps, worthy of response."

The speaker of these profundities paused and smiled benignly at Pillio in the manner that men adopt when the words that have emerged from their mouths seem unexpectedly to unite in both a pleasing and well-turned phrase. Pillio however, whose habitual gravity, he had always believed, led many to the conclusion that he was possessed of a good deal more wit and subtlety than was actually the case, greeted this conversational gem with nothing more than a polite nod.

Little daunted by the uncongenial nature of the Ta-shih officer, his companion smiled all the more broadly, so that what appeared as friendliness became, on this moon-shaped face, an expression of zest. The individual who wore the smile was a small man whose fleshy features and glittering, enthusiastic eyes perhaps deceived as to age. This vitality was a little offset by his sombre attire – black, formless robes – from which extended two slender, animated hands that seemed disembodied. Upon that very instant one of them strayed and found at its fingertips the Faith's talisman carved in polished red amber, suspended on a short copper chain that fastened to a leather belt tied at the waist. The fingers, having discovered the talisman, absently traced its intricate form.

Pillio's new acquaintance was indeed an Archivist. He had announced himself as Hassin, an exarch of the temple at Nek Feddah, this the northernmost mooring terminus of vessels plying the great Cise River and the highest point of navigable waters in the Kiangsu hinterland. Here Pillio would take passage to Kiangsu City aboard one of the fast galliots, the keel-less, flat-decked barges rowed by alternating crews of expert oarsmen who could accomplish the journey south in half the time it took to complete the trip overland.

Having secured passage on a vessel, the *Dust Devil,* and left the horses and mules at the local Ta-shih staging post where his party would spend the night, Pillio had repaired to a modest but comfortable inn for a drink and solitude. He had strolled out onto the sloping black timbers of the balcony over the inn's taproom and set himself at a table to watch the splendour of the orange sun sinking into the peaks of the Alnaes. It was at this time that Exarch Hassin had appeared, ostensibly to admire the slow sunset, and struck up a conversation with him. Truth to tell, the exchange was somewhat one-sided, perhaps because where Archivists were concerned Pillio was naturally suspicious – not on account of any impiety but only because he was a man of a rational and pragmatic cast of mind, whilst Archivists habitually dealt in the mystical and otherworldly matters of the soul. Moreover, the warnings of the stranger Harbin, the evening prior, still rang in his head. In time, however, encouraged by the magical properties of the rather pleasing ale he had sampled, the laconic company commander was drawn to speak more.

"Thus, speculation on the motives that drive men to take one course or another is wasted breath," asserted the exarch, thereby concluding a lengthy answer to Pillio's terse remarks concerning the attack of bandits on his troop. In truth, he was uncertain how they had come to land on the topic of the recent skirmish in the mountains. It was perhaps that the exarch was an easy companion.

Gingerly touching the bandage over his bruised ribs, Pillio felt moved to declare that, in his opinion, greed and stupidity were adequate reasons for so rash an act.

"Ah yes, greed!" said the exarch, warming to his subject once again. "But is not necessity an equally valid motive for the actions of these pitiful creatures?"

Pillio agreed that it might be.

"Or any number of a dozen motives! You see, Commander, it is not the motive but the act itself that is important. The Law of the Faith is explicit on this point. The robbery they attempt to commit is unlawful; you punish a number of them – with death! – for their crime. The balance is hereby redressed." Hassin's small hands smote the air with decisiveness. "There are no motives in this analysis. You need not bother your head with such detail. There is the Law and there is the hand of the Law, splendidly manifest in you and your fine men!" The hands turned outwards in a gesture of apology. "Forgive me, Commander. I am inclined to expatiate on these matters. But it concerns me, as it does my fellows, that in certain circles, and here I confess to some small prejudice as regards the modern teachings of the academies, that in certain circles students are actually exhorted to question the strict bounds of the Law – as if the Law itself, of ancient and unimpeachable provenance, were an issue of degree! Can you imagine where we might end up were the Law to become so diminished that the evil of Echrexar might bleed into the world again. The in-between places are not only physical and temporal, my good sir. They are the *cracks* that people, good people, people who should know better, unwittingly make in the edifice of the Law."

Pillio thought it judicious to nod but, in halfway accomplishing this act, paused, lest his response be misconstrued as approval for anything less than orthodoxy, and instead scratched at the stubble on his chin.

"You were injured in this grievous assault?" enquired the exarch. "I ask only because your movements seem stiff – those of a man whose limbs need recovery…"

Pillio touched his ribs again and winced. "A graze, Exarch Hassin. Nothing more. But, yes, I am tired from the exchange and the long ride. I thank the gods of earth, road and rock for the courage and discipline shown by my men."

At Pillio's casual invocation of three of the Faith's minor deities, the exarch touched the talisman then said, "With so excellent a leader, I wonder not at their inspiration!" Hassin steepled both hands on the table, gazing at Pillio with kindly eyes. "But tell me, Commander," he went on, "what of the others in your party? A fearful experience for them, no doubt?"

Pillio blinked at his companion. "Ah," he responded. "Yes. An unpleasant circumstance." And, since the whole town was doubtless gossiping about the presence of the Shur-Shur and some explanation seemed called-for, he added, "But they are…prisoners, Exarch Hassin."

"Prisoners?" came the surprised echo.

"Aye, prisoners. For transport…south."

The sun by this time had sunk behind the highest peaks, leaving distant clouds in the north suffused with a rose-pink luminosity. Below the balcony the smooth waters of the Cise, a lavender magenta hue in the dusk, churned past the worn balks that served as stilts to suspend the inn above seasonal floods. For five hundred paces along this bank of the

Cise, warehouses and lodgings alike were constructed in similar fashion, conveying to newcomers an impression of spindly precariousness that was far from the truth.

"This is *interesting*," said the exarch. "Is all your life so exciting, Commander? Escorting prisoners for trial, battling with fierce brigands in the mountains! I'm afraid we at Nek Feddah see nothing more thrilling than the embarrassing antics of inebriated rivermen and the prattling of the local fishwives! I am a parochial exarch in a dull parish."

"You flatter me," protested Pillio. "My life in the Lorang Steppes is humdrum. The peasant farmers are as blockish as their women are wrinkled. We are sixty miles from the nearest civilization. The land is flat, if not boring. And the single constant in the seasons is the harshness of the wind. My life, Exarch Hassin, consists of these essential facts."

Having declaimed, in what for him was so wordy a fashion, upon the nature of his existence, Pillio drew a breath and looked away quickly. At the entrance to the balcony the taproom potboy had stopped inside the doorway and was lingering on the expectation of some order from the two men but, in trepidation of the twilight and the accidental dangers of the in-between, was hesitant in approaching. The large balcony benefited from an awning, but its open aspect was one of those awkward challenges to the pragmatic superstitions of people: better to remain fully indoors than risk misfortune.

With relief at this distraction, Pillio summoned the boy, who overcame his fears on the promise of a tip and took instruction to bring a second large flagon of ale. The exarch politely declined any refreshment and explained, "Far be it from me to play the pietist. I thoroughly approve of good food and drink but, alas, the Faith forbids me. It is the time of the Dream of the White Peony and I must fast from sunrise until well after sundown."

Pillio gave a half bow of acceptance and, still embarrassed by his unaccustomed verbosity, turned away to feign interest in a large galliot that approached from the south, two lines of great oars rising above the flat deck with the tiny figures of passengers silhouetted against the failing light.

"Ah…" breathed the exarch, making the sign of the *shielding of the doors*, the usual four small circular gestures of warding against the in-between, for his own protection or that of the galliot Pillio could not guess. "The last vessel for the day. They make haste to dock before the twilight. Will they succeed, I wonder? Or will their tardiness bring misadventure?" He paused and Pillio felt compelled to face him again, whereupon the exarch enquired, "You take passage soon, Commander?"

Pillio cleared his throat. "Tomorrow."

"Your destination is Ung, perhaps? The Ta-shih garrison there?"

Pillio hesitated, again reminded of Harbin's admonition. But Exarch Hassin threw up his hands as if to ward off the answer, exclaiming in a self-reproving tone: "Forgive me, Commander! Forgive me! How vexatious for you to be pestered by so meddlesome an individual! I didn't mean to pry, I assure you! It is simply…and I say this without excusing my poor manners…it is simply that I shall myself be undertaking a trip south tomorrow!"

Pleased to have overcome this moment of awkwardness and genuinely warming to the courteous, unaffected geniality of the exarch, Pillio smiled an affable smile and declared, "I cannot accept your apology, Exarch Hassin, since neither insult nor taint upon my honour was intended. As to your question: Ung is indeed our first destination. We board the galliot dubbed *Dust Devil* tomorrow, one cycle after sunrise."

Exarch Hassin sat bolt upright and cried out, "*Dust Devil,* you say! *Dust Devil!* What happy coincidence! I too, Commander Pillio, shall be aboard that vessel tomorrow! Ah, the time of the Dream of the White Peony is a miraculous time! The wicked minions of the in-between-dreams sleep and the gods take pleasure in arranging circumstances in so delightful a scheme! Why, even the shocking events in the mountains, while unenviably taxing for you, I confess, show their own triumph: you and your men are spared from the evil of criminals and the perpetrators themselves are punished! Who would have thought that such rogues, who roam the footpaths and roads with arrogant disregard for the Law and make the high Alnaes their impregnable abode…who would have thought that half a dozen of their number would be brought to summary justice by so small a contingent, when the best organised forays of the Ta-shih have failed time and again in this very objective?"

Pillio conceded that none would have thought so.

At this juncture the potboy returned, having planned his timing to avoid sunset, and placed before Pillio a mug and a large double-handled flagon. "A full lit of Dark Gobble, sir," he announced and requested three leol. Pillio paid the coins into the boy's grubby palm, dismissing him with a nod, then poured himself a generous cup. He tasted the ale and found it again to his satisfaction, whereupon he once more gave his attention to the exarch.

In the now dim light, with the blackness of his robes against the backdrop of dark timbers, Exarch Hassin's pale face and hands had assumed an odd incorporeity. It was as if the remaining shape that was the Archivist might at any moment fade into the night.

Resuming his theme after successfully meeting his companion's eye, Hassin remarked, "Perhaps you are not convinced of the efforts of the divine in the examples I cite. In fact, it is plain that a man who must uphold the Law, who must face brigands and much worse when called upon, is a man who must remain unerringly pragmatic if not a trifle aloof from the world in order to see his duty with exact clarity. I do not dispute this. I fully endorse it. Commander Pillio, I pride myself in being able to detect in a person of short acquaintance his chief qualities; and in you, if you will indulge me but a moment more, I hazard the premise that your finest, your most important quality is the capacity to stand impartial until the facts present themselves to your uncluttered judgement. Thus, the intervention of the divine must show itself to you visibly and unclouded by the mumbo-jumbo that so often characterizes the Faith amongst peasants, and even some of the city dream-mystics, else you will hold yourself above it; and quite right too! Of course, I do not mean to impute that such impartiality – let us call it rather clear-headed reason – that such *reason* is in any way at odds with your unswerving *rectitude* in upholding the laws that are the pillars of our civilization. No indeed! Your duty is one thing. How you act upon such duty is quite another. It requires, does it not, prudence and forethought, the careful weighing of facts and opinion, then decisive action."

Pillio was favourably impressed by these sentiments, which, although he did not understand fully, seemed to strike at the heart of what he had been attempting to elucidate for himself in the irksome matter of responsibility that the detachment commander at Ingen had forced upon him. There was, in the exarch's words, a profound truth that seemed almost to excuse the annoyance, fear and guilt that afflicted Pillio.

And so, after one and three-quarters of a mug of Feddah's strong Dark Gobble, and feeling it incumbent on him to respond to the exarch in some intelligent manner, he said, "This would appear so, Exarch Hassin. However, I must bring to your recollection a particular you were at pains to affirm, namely – and I hope I repeat your words with exactness – that 'There is the Law and the hand of the Law'." Here Pillio paused, the ale perhaps fortifying him with more eloquence than usual. "Surely," he proceeded, "by this you mean to imply that my actions in defence of the Law should be as automatic as the prancing of a marionette when the strings are pulled? Where is prudence and forethought then?"

Exarch Hassin considered Pillio with a surprised smile, a flash of good white teeth in the darkness, then said, "You test me sorely, Commander! But I meant no such thing. I say only that the analysis of individual motives in the execution of the Law is singularly unimportant. Nevertheless, this still requires prudence and forethought in establishing what the crime and who the guilty. After all, not every unlawful act is as manifestly villainous as the ambush of your bandits."

In dismissal of the topic, Exarch Hassin's hands fluttered like large pale moths. He declared, "Enough of these intricacies, though. I have taken up an unforgivable excess of your time and I myself have preparations to make for tomorrow's trip."

The exarch stood up. The voluminous and all but invisible black robes made the man appear larger than Pillio had first imagined. Or perhaps it was a trick of the night and the flickering orange torchlight on the waters of the Cise.

"I wish you a pleasant evening, Commander Pillio," concluded Hassin. "And I must bid you goodnight. Honour to you. May the gods travel at your shoulder."

Pillio likewise had risen to his feet. Acknowledging the exarch with a half bow, he responded in the formal salute, "May the gods defend the Archivists."

Exarch Hassin departed. Pillio resumed his seat and drained the contents of his mug. He pondered on the conversation and the events of the last week, his thoughts flitting uncontrolled from one vivid tableau to another: the wretched bandit brandishing a club and the sensation of numbing pain as his sword cut into flesh and bone; the twisted corpses of Lord Shenri and his guard with the black flies buzzing under a withering sun; the staring, imploring eye of the half-dead Strath trooper; Harbin, the itinerant banker and his mysterious companion; the exarch, a pale image in the blackness of the evening; and always, stabbing into Pillio's consciousness like some persistent nightmare, the unfathomable blue of the nomad woman's eyes, ice in the winter sun.

Aneth. Pillio repeated her name to himself, and then softly, as if by speaking the syllables aloud he might grasp at a dim understanding just beyond his reach, he cast the name out loud into the night. Instantly he felt he had committed some sacrilege, and involuntarily looked over his shoulder to see if the exarch still lingered; then, equally quickly, he berated himself for stupid superstition. But the comfort and self-forgetfulness he had enjoyed with the exarch and the ale had evaporated, and the press of responsibility again weighed heavily on him.

***

Exarch Hassin came aboard the galliot the following morning in the company of two young acolytes, likewise shaven-headed and robed in black. There had been some quarrel on the pier prior to the Archivists' embarkation, to which Pillio paid little heed. He was occupied with settling the Strath soldier on his pallet, as well as the prisoners and his men in seats under the vessel's deck canopy whilst stowing all their kit in the hold. It was perhaps for this reason that Pillio failed to notice the sharp look of calculation cast in his direction by Exarch Hassin as he arrived and, indeed, the assertion with which he approached the angry, purple-faced under-merchant. The quarrel, between this worthy merchant and the master of *Dust Devil*, was a dispute which, had he observed the world about him more closely, Pillio would have discovered concerned the legitimacy of the merchant's passage aboard the galliot, a fact with regard to which the riverman had some objection. Exarch Hassin and his party came to a halt in front of the merchant. The Archivist spoke in earnest tones, evidently persuading the under-merchant to accept a later passage. Impressed by the force of the Archivist's words, this gentleman at once acquiesced. Both men bowed. The quarrel was resolved.

Beaming as brightly as the sun upon the sparkling waters of the Cise, Exarch Hassin stepped aboard. The red amber talisman swung upon its copper chain from his waist. The exarch's hands were clasped behind his back. Then one appeared at his brow, shading the brilliant sunlight from his eyes as he surveyed the vessel and its passengers. He approached Pillio.

"A fine, beautiful morning, Commander Pillio!" he exclaimed by way of a greeting.

"Aye. It is," agreed Pillio, and took the trouble for a moment to appreciate the new day. A gentle breeze had cleared the usual dawn mist so that the quayside and buildings, which had looked so dull and grey in the hour before sunrise, were now awash with colour: nearby, the mustard yellow of timber walls with a vertical slash of red for the sturdy uprights of merchant warehouses; and the distant inn, black balcony and whitewashed shutters, standing half in the river and half upon the grassy bank like an overburdened peasant on tottering brown legs. Upriver, the massive crumbling stumps, all that remained of the archaic bridge, pointed mutely to the heavens, while behind them the green foothills of the Alnaes rolled away towards the vast plains of Kiangsu North, leaving behind their giant cousins, the jagged, immutable towers of the high Alnaes. And at the centre of all this the passengers and crew of the galliot seemed flushed with a singular light, so that the chequered white and green mismatched smocks sported by the rivermen and even the grey twill of the Ta-shih uniforms exhibited a startling lustre.

"A fine morning," Pillio echoed, picking up the mood of the Archivist, who smiled, if it were possible, more broadly still at Pillio's response, in the way of tacitly confirming that his role in life was to point out to all men the vivid detail of existence that they so sadly missed.

"And the journey begins," observed Hassin, and glanced past Pillio to the two ranks of soldiers taking their places on the raised wooden planks that served as seating for passengers on the cheaper fares. "The prisoners are secure?" enquired Hassin further. He peered at the foreigners. Without waiting for Pillio's reply, Hassin declared in hushed tones, "I am astonished, Commander. I confess to having heard some of the gossip yesterday evening about your captives – this from the locals, you understand – but the reality truly amazes me. Golden creatures. And the fetishes they wear. Foreign marvels. Never do we see nomads here in Nek Feddah."

Pillio frowned in embarrassment, the exarch's expressions of wonder reminding him acutely of the focus of attention that his small world had become. He straightened his shoulders as if to deflect the stares of the crew and the beetle-browed goggling of a huddle of peasants squatting in the sun at the bows of the galliot. Surprising even himself, Pillio turned abruptly away from the exarch and strode to the gunwale. The master of the *Dust Devil* stood near the gangplank supervising the efforts of a clerk of the port, who was counting off large bales of tea for stowage below deck. Spying him, Pillio snapped, "We are late, it seems to me, shipmaster!"

At this interruption, the bull-necked riverman raised an impassive face in the manner of one upon whose mellow temperament the vicissitudes of life, whether the battering of storms or the inexplicable pique of morose Ta-shih officers, made not the slightest impression. "Aye, sir," he rumbled in a courteous bass. "Away 'fore tha' knows it!" And he returned his attention to the clerk.

"And none too soon!" retorted Pillio after a moment. He debated with himself rapidly and in silence the merits of pressing the matter further but, puzzled by his own impatience, and galled by it, instead he spun on his heel, intent on engaging the exarch in conversation on some trivial matter. He was greeted by the peasants' curious stares, and withered them with a terrible look until they desisted.

Before long, the shipmaster took up his position. Seating himself upon a well-worn wooden throne next to the massive tiller in the stern, he cried a series of uninterpretable commands in the singsong vernacular of the rivermen, and, as a result, mooring ropes were cast off, the crew thumped oars into iron rowlocks and raised them aloft, and then with a perfectly synchronized dip and thrust the heavy-laden galliot was swung away from the quayside. The powerful current of the Cise seized the vessel, thrumming under the hull. The ten-man crew, at a single barked command from the shipmaster, swept their oars down into the water until, like a bloated crab, the *Dust Devil* pulled herself from the clutches of the current and with every heave of the oars surged towards the centre of the great river.

"Superbly handled," asserted the exarch, having joined Pillio at the railing, well out of the way of the oarsmen.

Always a man to give credit where it was due, Pillio admitted that the speed of the vessel was impressive, the skill of the crew undoubted.

"I did not know," continued the exarch with an enquiring look full of concern and sympathy, "that one of your men was wounded in your battle in the mountains..." Here, the exarch glanced towards the pallet, set under the deck canopy, where the Strath trooper lay.

Pillio frowned, feeling awkward, as if he had failed to pass on an essential fact to the exarch, who waited patiently and silently. "Ah, no," Pillio responded and then rather pointlessly, in an attempt at deflection, added, "It was not really a battle, exarch. A skirmish. Hardly a battle..."

The exarch's eyebrows rose and he exclaimed, "A skirmish! But this man is very seriously wounded. I am right, I believe, in thinking his injuries life-threatening!"

"Indeed." By now Pillio could not help but feel an obligation to explain, in spite of Harbin's warnings and his strong inclination to maintain the strictest confidence about Lord Shenri's murder. For here was a compassionate man, a man of the Faith, genuinely concerned for all people, who offered his sympathy and his help freely. Pillio frowned again and said, "He is a soldier...well...from Strath. Er...from Lord Shenri's household guard."

There he intended to stop, but Exarch Hassin, leaning forward with interest, pressed him: "But how was he brought to this terrible condition? More bandits? Was he alone or did he accompany you?" The exarch abruptly paused, holding up a hand, then apologized. "Again, Commander, I must beg your forgiveness. You are an important personage, on a critical mission, pestered by a lowly provincial exarch. Ignore me! Send me to the stern or belowdecks! Exile me!"

Pillio assured the exarch that he would do no such thing, and then proffered the explanation: "He accompanies us south. He has recovered somewhat, although I feared at first that he could not escape the Shae's iron grip. Day by day he takes more sustenance and has even been able to sit up, with assistance. We do our best for him and my guardleader deserves the credit for his steady improvement."

The exarch, a picture of studied empathy and benevolence, laid his hand on Pillio's forearm. "And his name, this poor man?"

Pillio hesitated yet again, this time in some confusion. "W-well…" he stumbled, "we do not know. He cannot yet speak… A knife wound to the throat, you understand…"

The exarch compressed his lips, to convey understanding. "I see, I see…" he breathed, and nodded slowly to himself several times, during which the sweep of his glance encompassed the Strath soldier, Pillio's men and Pillio himself, and alighted finally on the barbarians again.

Exarch Hassin's left hand pointed open-palmed at the peasants, some fifteen in all, who squatted on their haunches and chattered amongst themselves, now not once sparing a glance for the barbarians. In their simple way they had accepted the reality of the two foreigners just as they accepted the material fact of the timbers beneath their bare feet, or the swell of the great river. "I have promised a short extolment," proceeded the exarch in explanation of his gesture, "in supplication of Sadon's benevolence. We pray that the river god may grant fair passage. These men travel south for the spring Hiring at Ung. They must secure employment within a seven-day or be sent back without a leol to support their families in the Feddah hills." Hassin paused and regarded Pillio with a smile. "You have witnessed the Hirings?"

"I have sometimes been the officer in charge," Pillio confirmed. "But only on a small scale, in Spimarrin in Lorang Province."

Spring, summer, and autumn gatherings were held in towns like Ung and Spimarrin every year to supply labour for farming and trade, and the manual work required by the unwieldy bureaucracy of the Kiangsu provincial administrations. Pillio had watched peasants flock to these gatherings in their hundreds and, doubtless in the larger towns in their thousands, to stand in long queues awaiting the critical eye of tenant farmers, under-merchants, artisans, and clerks who selected their seasonal quota. The peasant successful in working three seasons usually returned home with sufficient wages to see his family through an entire year, before the process began all over again. Those failing to secure employment returned home to eke out an existence in the poor fields granted them through the munificence of their landlords.

Exarch Hassin was talking: "Perhaps you would care to join us and I might include the injured soldier?"

"Ah," said Pillio, who was not a man given to public displays of piety. "I thank you, Exarch. I fear my presence would be a distraction. But for him…" Pillio indicated the occupant of the pallet. "Of course…"

"Very well. I thank you and I shall not press you personally." The Archivist glanced towards the Ta-shih soldiers. "Perhaps your men…?"

To this Pillio gave ready assent.

After the exarch's acolytes had circled amongst the passengers and crew to direct those who wished to take part in the extolment to the open deck forward of the canopy, Hassin spread out a holy mat upon the deck timbers and stood within its tasselled fringes. He raised his arms above his head, closed his eyes, then turned until the sun, no great distance above the eastern horizon, shone full upon his uplifted face. He maintained this attitude for some time, while the peasants and Ta-shih troopers stood in absolute silence in two groups, a little apart, near the bows.

Pillio watched from under the canopy. At his side, Guardleader Manei was methodically slicing a core of liquorice sank-root preparatory to exercising his jaws upon it. His blade, which Pillio chanced to notice was the same one that the guardleader had wielded so skilfully upon the throat of one of the bandits, moved back and forth, back and forth, against the calloused brown thumb, making a flick-flick sound that alternated with the creaking groan of the oars.

The Archivist began to chant, intoning prayers in the ancient language of the Faith. This orison continued unabated while the galliot made rapid progress downriver and Pillio, tiring of the ritual, let his attention wander to the scenery that passed. To their right the mighty Alnaes reared grey and white above the green walls of the valley. Here the valley dropped in a vast sweep of woodland to the water's edge. Bowed trees stooped over the rushing Cise, exposing twisted roots to the wash. Now the wide river divided around a verdant island, thick with lime-green shrubs and the angled boughs of fallen trees, like a bemilered fortress bristling with pikes and staves. The galliot surged close by, oars dipping and rising in silvery arcs of spray, then gained the open water once more. On the left, the margin of the river was host to the same woodland, but a quarter mile beyond this the trees thinned out on the rolling landscape and gave way to a lush grassland only occasionally visible on the remote high ground. Much nearer, a hundred paces from the galliot, a white heron perched on the upended bole of a tree. With high-stretched neck it bestowed the same attention on Pillio as he on it, and the two regarded each other in this fashion until *Dust Devil* plied inexorably towards a bend in the river and the overhanging foliage prevented them from further mutual inspection.

Exarch Hassin had completed his introduction and was proceeding apace with that part of the extolment in which the prayers of those present were individually represented to the deity. The Archivist's acolytes moved among the congregation and placed their hands upon each man's head, and the exarch for his part exhorted each in turn to name his labour or skill.

The first responded: "Cartage-work, Holiness, and tree-felling…"

And the second: "Holiness, 'tis ploughing and tree-felling when ordered."

The third: "Holiness, I do roofing, thatch or tile."

And so each of the peasants made known his expertise. The Ta-shih soldiers, standing in two ranks slightly apart from the peasants as befitted their station, need not respond: they served the Realm. This was understood. The ritual ended with the exarch's heartfelt invocation to Sadon, of the great river, to look favourably on the peasants' intent, and the two groups chanted in unison the well-known allocution of the Dream of the White Peony.

Some short time later, the soldiers returned to their bench and the peasants, having donned wide straw hats, to the bows to wait patiently on their haunches in the hot sun. Exarch Hassin retreated from the heat of the day under the canopy and occupied himself with a frowning study of several thick parchments, although, notwithstanding the apparent weightiness of the subject matter, the corners of his mouth still turned up in an irrepressible smile.

Pillio, whose mouth exhibited an equal slant at the corners but of precisely the opposite tendency, made several attempts to concentrate on Hexil's great work of history, balanced heavy upon his knees. But, distracted by the beauty of his surroundings and the constant display of birds and, more rarely, deer and other animals at the water's edge, he thrust the book back into a satchel and leaned against one of the canopy's stanchions to enjoy the journey.

**

His world had changed. In spite of the pain that resulted, there was a small degree of comfort in the physical movements he was able to make, the relief at shifting his muscles by degrees, the tiny sense of control he could exercise over his life. The worst injury, he had discovered, was to his shoulder – broken bones, no doubt, and muscles sliced and mutilated beyond healing. Something in the initial damage had paralyzed his body for days. His left arm was still limp and sensation stubbornly absent, beyond the numb tingling between spasms of pain. But his right arm he could flex, using it to lever himself up and scratch – utter bliss! – and even feed himself, though his throat could tolerate nothing other than cold soups and thin porridges. He knew he needed to eat more, to fuel his body's recovery. In this he was fortunate: the Ta-shih guardleader, Manei, seemed to anticipate his needs and pushed him to try more and to move his limbs when his body screamed that it was impossible. Gradually, with this help, he had embraced both a fierce determination to survive and an iron discipline to exercise wasted muscles and ligaments as much as his limited strength would allow.

The Ta-shih spoke to him, of course, but he could not answer, beyond what nods and gestures might communicate. The officer had even asked him if he could read or write; but literacy amongst the soldier class in the provinces was rare, and he had shaken his head. The passing of information between them, therefore, remained limited.

His left eye was gone, the wound cauterized. The healing skin itched, feeling taut and unpleasant as if covered by an invisible spider-web. With his good eye he observed his new companions, the habits and quirks of the Ta-shih; the way they cared for their kit and mended sandals, oiled and polished their weapons and armour, cooked their meals, exercised daily in arms and wrestling and rubbed along together. He envied them their comradeship, and the simple fact of their daily routines and the disciplined, no-nonsense attentiveness of their guardleader – a sharp-eyed veteran with a fine economy of words and movement, seemingly at rest, indifferent and at ease, until required, when he was abruptly all action. Adaim, with his soldier's point of view, could see how this nonchalance might infuriate an officer but delight the troopers, who were kept sharp, and did what was needed, but were never put to wasted effort and the mindless duties that so characterized the lot of soldiers. These men, Adaim was certain, would sacrifice a good deal for their guardleader.

Of their commander, the men were less sure, and Adaim could see why. He preferred distance and solitude. He had none of the small talk or comfort with their world that might make him well-liked and, though he was a man of decisive action, it seemed he was displeased or unhappy – and that gave soldiers pause: they wished, in their straightforward way, for an optimistic leader who would get them through and here, instead, was one who appeared, at least on short acquaintance, to transmit worry, perhaps self-doubt. A soldier could get himself killed on a commander's self-doubt.

And then, of course, the Archivists had arrived. On his pallet, bandaged, still and silent, Adaim was easy to overlook, and that gave him an advantage, he had realized. He observed more than people thought. He saw the small things unnoticed by others engaged in the busy diligence of their day, or the careless assumptions they made about what they looked *at* rather than what they *saw*. He observed the altercation between under-merchant and shipmaster; he noted the Archivists on the quayside and the manner in which the exarch conversed with the merchant; he discerned the outcome and he deduced the linkage Pillio had missed. In itself, this was not cause for suspicion: Archivists were known to assert, from time to time, their privilege in the name of the Faith, and if that required passage aboard ship to the frustration of an under-merchant, so be it. No, Adaim saw something more. He saw the intent of the exarch, the momentary lapse of concealing good nature that betrayed the focus of his mind – not the under-merchant, not securing passage aboard the galliot: it was Pillio. And that made no sense…

Perhaps the murder of Lord Shenri, the fracturing of the order of his world and his own near-death had heightened his vigilance, made him especially sensitive to threat. His failure and the failure of his fellow bodyguards that night had been catastrophic. If there was peril, he would see it. Mute and motionless on his pallet, he watched.

***

The voyage south proceeded without incident for three days. Every evening, before sunset, the shipmaster berthed the vessel at a staging point, typically no more than a sturdy pier and a nearby thatched inn where passengers might spend the night in some comfort, depending on the weight of their purses. The peasants preferred the hard timbers of the pier; Pillio and his men made use of their blankets and packs and, next to Adaim, settled themselves on board *Dust Devil* under the canopy, with a strict rota of sentries; the crew joined the shipmaster below decks in cramped quarters amongst the cargo of tea bales, fruit, and furs; and Exarch Hassin retired to the inn or small temple if conveniently located.

In the evening of the fourth day, however, the galliot pulled into a pleasant cove where a dozen huts and larger wooden abodes rose immediately behind the long pier in a series of terraces, at the summit of which was the blank verticality of temple walls, entirely whitewashed except where the facade was regularly broken by the dark oblong shapes of windows. A complex articulation of red-painted beams, overhanging a number of finials carved to represent the divine symbols of the Shadow Lord, the hunter and warrior goddess Dian, gods of earth, river and farming, and every other, supported a black ridged roof fifty strides in length. As the galliot neared the pier, Pillio, who was studying the edifice with interest, could make out a stairway zig-zagging its way up to the gates of the temple.

A voice at Pillio's shoulder declared, "A fascinating structure, is it not?" This was Exarch Hassin, smiling his broad smile. "The foundations were laid by Eslo, generations ago, when he faced the power of the Etil heretics in Kiangsu North and drew the local people to the Faith. A triumph of architecture, this! A monument to a man of the Faith!"

Pillio nodded slowly and lifted his elbows from the railing. "Hmm…" he murmured with an air of thoughtfulness. "If memory serves me, Eslo was murdered by one of the Biljan kings…"

Exarch Hassin turned to him, and in the half-light his eyes twinkled brighter. "Commander! You are a man of depth!" The Archivist laughed. "I presume to educate you, and you pre-empt me!" Both men turned back to the sight of the temple whose character and position atop the brow of the hill rendered it the chief focus of almost everyone aboard *Dust Devil*, in particular the peasants who, as they endeavoured to see past the heads of their fellows, rocked from side to side, lifting half up from their haunches in a variety of odd jerks and hops.

"Perhaps," continued the exarch in the tone of having abruptly reached a decision, "you will do me the great honour, Commander, of permitting me to show you the interior and grounds of the temple? They are not to be missed! The inner chambers are, of course, sacred. But my brothers and I will be privileged to share the evening meal with you in the magnificence of the temple. Indeed, ten centuries speak from those walls! Ten centuries!"

A little taken aback by the vehemence and excitement of the exarch's invitation, Pillio simply blinked, but the intensity of the Archivist's expression and the glitter of his eyes in the gloom roused him. He acquiesced.

"Excellent…" breathed Hassin, and started to move away, then added over his shoulder, "Bring your good second, the guardleader! I insist! I insist!" And in a swirl of black robes and flashing smiles he went to supervise the packing of his baggage.

With the *Dust Devil* berthed, and his men and the Strath soldier installed once more for the night under the canopy, Pillio issued final instructions and then climbed the ladder to the high pier with Guardleader Manei, chewing speculatively on a sizeable portion of sank-root, in tow behind. Together they started the steep ascent through the village, passing the bustle of street vendors in high-pitched exchange with the crew of the galliot who had coin to spend. In front of a poor tavern the peasants who had disembarked squatted round a stone firepit, scooping mouthfuls of rice and fish pieces from earthenware bowls and chattering amongst themselves about the prospects of work in the south. A gaggle of children, chasing each other around the stone firepit in a game of tag, shrieked and cried out and drew the attention of the peasants, who mostly smiled, reminded it might be of their own families back in the Feddah hills.

Darkness had fallen completely. The village, in the lee as it were of the hillside and the looming summit defined by the temple's mass above, was enveloped in a night of black heavens and golden stars that pulsed and faded through the tendrils of smoke rising from mud-brick chimneys. Soft orange firelight streamed through the cracks of window shutters and made irregular shadow patterns on the path that Pillio and Manei trod. The smooth river pebbles that neatly covered the way between the houses crunched under their boots and, as they negotiated the first of the narrow stairways switching back and forth up the higher terraces, the comfortable warmth and sounds of the village were left behind. Here, away from the sheltering walls and roofs below the heights, the night air was cooler, clearer. Overhead the dim expanse of white walls crouched like a gigantic mythical beast whose cavernous insect eyes, the black depths of windows, gazed out insensibly over the coiling headwaters of the Cise.

The two Ta-shih climbed the second of the stairways, and the third and fourth, to arrive at a high portico in the centre of the outer wall. Adjusting his uniform and the sword belt at his waist, Pillio, a little out of breath, glanced at his companion, who by contrast appeared entirely unaffected by the long climb and still worked his jaws upon sank-root. Pillio frowned and Manei, apprehending his meaning instantly, leaned towards the parapet and with practiced ease spat the sank-root core into the night.

Pillio gave his attention to the portico and the massive doors within. Neither the individual columns, these rectangular and unadorned, nor the roof supported by the colonnade were of an impressive size so that this diminution of the visual importance of the entrance had the simultaneous effect of drawing the observer's eyes towards the doors. Pillio found himself staring at a colossal face, crafted into what, reason argued, must be two doors; but sight told him was the lifelike visage of a god, stern, unforgiving, graceful, with a woman's delicate beauty in lips and cheekbones and an otherworldly omnipotence in the single terrible white eye. It was hard at that moment for Pillio to see anything other than the face, hard for him to believe that he did not, for that brief instant, stand alone against the incarnation of Dian.

Then the face split, the white eye torn apart and collapsing in on itself so that brittle yellow light poured out upon Pillio and Manei like the reflection of the moon off shattered glass. A whispered gasp of cold air crossed the threshold to accompany the opening of the doors. Exarch Hassin waited inside. Apparelled in his customary black, he also wore a white mantilla over head and shoulders, giving him an appearance of solemnity that was quite uncharacteristic. With him were his two acolytes, similarly dressed. Behind them oil sconces illuminated a hallway whose stone flag floor evinced the smooth hollows produced by the tread of men over years beyond imagining, a shallow gully like the remains of some stream long since run dry. Discernible upon the walls in the shifting glow of the oil lamps was an intricate network of cursive script, in thick scarlet paint badly faded with age, covering every part of the stone up to the arched roof.

"Commander Pillio! Guardleader Manei!" exclaimed Hassin, and signalled both men to enter. "A thousand welcomes! I have advised Exarch Vedex of your arrival and he wishes me to pass on his welcome. We shall meet him in person shortly." Hassin ushered them along the corridor, and as Pillio glanced behind he glimpsed the peculiar half-visage of the goddess, one immense unblinking half eye that flung Pillio's gaze back at him even while the acolytes heaved the doors closed.

With Exarch Hassin in the lead, they walked the ancient passages and steps, and when the Archivist fell silent Pillio found he could hear nothing save the dry swish of robes and scrape of boots. They might have been in the deepest recesses of the earth: no windows betrayed the existence of any world other than this, the heavy stone and the unfathomable writing upon it.

At a spiral stairway in the corridor Exarch Hassin turned to the Ta-shih men and produced from his robes a white mantilla for both, explaining that they must pass by the inner chambers and could not remain bareheaded. They moved on, thus attired, and followed the stairs to another passage, which here gave onto black doors at intervals to right and left, until their journey ended at a high archway. Within was a spacious, columned hall lit by the ruddy glow of a log fire hidden from Pillio's sight by half a dozen Archivists who stood together behind a long trestle table. Exarch Hassin politely retrieved the mantillas from Pillio and Manei, removed his own to lay them all across his left arm, and made a sign of invocation with his right hand: thumb bent, four fingers erect. The waiting group made the same sign. Exarch Hassin began the introductions.

And so the two Ta-shih partook of the evening temple meal. After the usual awkwardness attendant upon formal occasions, in that period when etiquette must rule and wine has yet to open hearts and loosen tongues, Exarch Hassin aided proceedings by telling something of what had passed between Pillio and himself during their journey, and slowly each one of the company joined the conversation. Only Manei seemed oblivious to the ebb and flow of verbal exchange, and did not speak except to utter monosyllabic answers to the Archivists' polite interrogatives. Instead he occupied himself with the serious business of eating, bringing a remarkable adroitness to the task of consuming crab's claws, stuffed fish and an array of simple but delicious dishes. By contrast Pillio was, in stages, tense, suspicious, annoyed by Manei, and finally, after a sufficiency of wine had passed his lips, as sanguine and hearty as was possible for a man of his nature. He spoke at length with Exarch Hassin and laughed at jokes; he listened attentively to Exarch Vedex, on occasions staring into the polished table top as if the subject of their discussions were before him and could, the more deeply, be grasped by this inspection; he chatted of his life at Domita Fortress, his ill-luck in never finding a wife and regret at having no children; he told stories from the history of the Ta-shih and, in return, heard one of the legends of the Archivists, of a time after Echrexar, the in-between time of darkness and ritual and the immanence of the gods in the affairs of men.

Now quite animated, Pillio leaned forward with elbows on the table, the Archivists clustered about him, dim silhouettes against the dying glow of the fire. All the pettiness and distrust that so largely defined the relationship between Ta-shih and Archivists was nowhere on Pillio's horizons. He conversed as with the closest of friends, finding in these men the warm-heartedness and tolerance of Exarch Hassin, multiplied by each of their number. Starved of such companionable understanding in his wearisome existence at Domita, the effect was as intoxicating as the good wine he drank.

And so, by degrees, he found himself unexpectedly speaking of the prisoners and the murder of Lord Shenri, unsure of how the words had come to spill from his lips.

"Ah," said Exarch Vedex, "it is a sorry burden…"

Pillio nodded.

"You must let us help you…"

"Help me?" Pillio felt lulled by the voice.

Exarch Vedex proffered a bowl of fine red tea. "Indeed. Exarch Hassin will help you…"

Again Pillio nodded. What assistance had he accepted? The alcohol dazed him. He returned the Archivist's ready smile.

"Perhaps," said Exarch Vedex, "you might care to view the temple grounds?"

Pillio gave immediate assent, and rose from his seat with the exaggerated steadiness of a man who is keenly aware of his befuddled condition but is resolved that his fellows must notice nothing of it. He found Manei close by his side, the square, scarred face composed and alert.

"Lead on, Exarch Vedex!" exclaimed Pillio. "Lead on!"

At this juncture, Hassin smilingly excused himself with the declaration that temple matters required a moment of his attention. Pillio returned a lopsided grin.

They left the columned hall and retraced their steps partway along the corridor to take a doorway that gave upon a narrow spiral stairwell. Down they climbed and entered another passage, curving out of sight ahead of them. They strode on and Pillio glanced now and then at the spidery lines of crimson script that covered the walls. He felt obliged to ask Exarch Vedex: "The writing – what is its purpose?"

"Ah…" breathed the Archivist, "forgive me for not explaining earlier. It is, to us, such a commonplace that we neglect the edification of our guests. The writing is an ancient form of Sanglix and one that the Faith has preserved. So much for its character. As to its purpose…" Exarch Vedex reached out to touch the nearest letters, but his fingers stopped short. "Upon these walls Eslo inscribed many of the teachings contained in the Book of Life, especially those appertaining to the foundation of the Faith and, of course, the dire threat of the heretics."

"Etil…" Pillio breathed the name.

The Archivist shook his head, a warning and an entreaty. "We do not use that name here." Then he gave a wry smile. "You see, to Eslo it was marvellously germane that the words that tell of the building of the Faith and its defence against heresy should, in symbol and in fact, invest the very structure of the temple that he raised for the Faith! A remarkable man, Eslo. He lived a very long time, blessed, it seems, by the gods' favour." The exarch made a gesture, open-handed, in the direction behind Pillio. "It is recorded that the face of Dian upon the doors is of a semblance with Eslo. A gentle man, of both feminine and masculine qualities."

They had reached an outer door which stood open upon the terraced grounds at the rear of the temple. Pillio and Vedex stepped outside, followed by Manei and the Archivists. In the grounds, here atop the hill upon which the temple resided, the air was cold and Pillio's breath sent out rolling tendrils of opaque, spectral mist. Overhead, the familiar river of stars blazed in the blackest of night skies.

The grounds which Pillio had been brought to see were bounded on three sides by high walls, indistinct in the darkness but clearly of such a height that their external aspect must discourage intruders, were any so reckless as to brave the sanctity of a temple. Within this precinct, the ground dropped by four levels of paths traversing the square limits of the entire courtyard, the inner of each several spans below its neighbour so that the centre-most path was directly opposite the temple door from which Pillio had just emerged. In the middle of these neat chalk pathways stood a circular shrine, no larger than twelve paces in circumference, constructed entirely of what appeared to be pink marble, a rare stone, and one to which the Archivists attributed profound and mystical properties. The base of the shrine was difficult to see in the darkness, but a little above, the light of the waning moon, now rising over the pitched roof of the temple at Pillio's back, illuminated the edifice so that the stone seemed translucent, alive. The writhing forms of serpents and grotesque winged creatures, half bird half insect, had been worked into the solid marble of six columns; the feet of the nethermost beasts clutched the plinths beneath them in a lifelike animation, and the tops of the columns each displayed the visage of a different creature: one was the open maw of a striking serpent, another the triple heads of a scorpion, and the razor fangs of a bird, and more that Pillio could not see. Supported on these shocking figures, as if its weight must crush them at any moment, was a pyramidal block of marble, of such unembellished starkness next to the ornamentation of the columns that the two together bespoke a kind of architectural violence. Pillio might have believed the block had been dropped onto the columns only moments before were it not for the soft green lichen that marked the deepest crevices of the stone and, more than this, the inscrutable brooding atmosphere that imbued the shrine with a palpable antiquity. The whole structure, from massive circular pedestal right up to the point of the pyramid, far overreached the chalk pathways and the walls above them, but with its position on the hill, the mass of the temple and the high walls on every side, the shrine was doubtless invisible to anyone outside.

Pillio stared at the strange monument, which with the passage of the moon was now fully flooded with silvery light, and discovered that his mood had undergone a complete reversal, swinging from heartiness to a grim despondency. Despite the clever symmetry of form and the impressive stonework, the ancient, sepulchral character of the place was unsettling. Realization dawned on Pillio. He turned to Exarch Vedex.

"This is Eslo's tomb…" he ventured.

Exarch Vedex stood amongst the Archivists, a pale face in the night. He answered, "Eslo's tomb, yes. Eslo's shrine. A holy place, Commander Pillio. It may not be viewed except in darkness, under the eye of Dian and the Shadow Lord." Vedex regarded the shrine, then added with whispered reverence, "It is a wondrous thing…"

But for Pillio the spell had been broken. The passion and veneration of the Archivists was no part of his world. He trespassed here.

He glanced at Manei and, though wearied by the wine, saw as for the first time the rough grey uniform and studded leather sword belt weighed down by the heavy blade, the soldier's boots, and the soldier's face and hands: this was something he understood.

"Exarch Vedex," declared Pillio bluntly. "We must leave you."

Faces turned to him. For an instant the Archivists' dimly perceived features betrayed consternation, or anger, and Pillio feared he had given offence.

"You have been kind and hospitable," said Pillio, frowning at the lameness of his words. "This," he gestured at the shrine, "has been a privilege. We are obliged to you. But we must return…"

Exarch Vedex took a step forward. "Commander, there is no hurry. You are welcome amongst us."

"Thank you. Thank you. We are obliged to you. But I regret we must take our leave."

A look passed across the exarch's face, like a ripple on the surface of a pond, barely discernible, then he inclined his head. "Just as you will, Commander Pillio. We have enjoyed your company, but we cannot detain you. We shall escort you out. Honour to you."

Pillio responded appropriately and they departed the still, cold aura of the shrine. Returning the way they had come, but with some delays as the Archivists insisted on small rituals of leaving, after a time Pillio and Manei walked out onto the portico alone.

***

Voices woke Adaim. In the darkness he did not recognize them, but they were joined by those he did – the Ta-shih, evidently delighted by an unexpected delivery of drinks and food from the tavern. Adaim raised his head stiffly to see a man, the tavern-keeper he guessed, stepping back onto the pier, two potboys in tow as they passed the lone Ta-shih sentry standing nearby. The oil lanterns on the galliot showed Adaim the Ta-shih soldiers close at hand, some standing, some sitting, arranged around a game of sticks. They called the odds, laid their bets and, to much cheering, someone tossed the small wooden rods. The newly arrived pitcher was passed around and the game proceeded.

Towards the bows of the galliot, on a bench together in the flickering lantern light, sat the Shur-Shur, watching the antics of the soldiers with that look of half-smiling curiosity that people have when they see others enjoying themselves but cannot take part. Adaim joined them in that smile, in the honest appreciation of the soldiers' delight. In time, settled by the rhythmic to and fro of their banter and by the slow, deep burble of the river under the hull, his thoughts glided back to memories of the Lady Che Keleu, delicious, hot and guilty. Helplessly he imagined every stolen, sunlit moment with her, the exquisite softness of her body, the silk of her inner thigh, the musky tantalizing scent of her. But guilt at last overburdened him. The faces of butchered comrades gawped at him, and Lord Shenri's decapitated head scowled disapproval and betrayal. He silently spoke the words of a prayer, desperate for inner peace, and repeated them again and again until sleep took him into the salvation of dreams.

He awoke to silence and a deep unease. Then, above the murmur of the river, he heard snatches of conversation from the pier. Straining to raise himself, Adaim pushed with his good right arm and managed to move his legs to lever his body until he was half sitting against one of the benches. Under a single guttering torch stood a Ta-shih sentry, close to the end of the pier, near the village pathway. He seemed to be in two minds: he had been giving his attention to the pale, round visage of Exarch Hassin, smiling up at him. Now he glanced back at the galliot, then, evidently reaching a conclusion, shrugged and marched back down the pier to reboard the barge, all the while muttering under his breath and cursing his fellow soldiers. Adaim searched for the other Ta-shih and, in the gloom, made out the sleeping forms of men where they had been playing sticks.

Meanwhile the sentry had found the barbarians and was urging them towards the pier, signalling with half-hearted gestures in the direction of the temple on the hillside. "C'mon now," he instructed them. "Company commander wants you up at temple an' he won't brook no waiting, our fine leader… Up you get."

The barbarians, still manacled, took his meaning and preceded him up the short ladder to the pier, the sentry giving vent to further complaint concerning the luck of some soldiers in drinking themselves into oblivion and leaving the hard work to their comrades.

This is wrong… the thought came to Adaim. *Wrong.* If he could have shouted at the sentry, told him not to leave, he would have done so, but clumping over the wooden planks and accompanied by the smiling exarch, the threesome disappeared into the night.

Again there was silence. Adaim stared into the village, struggling to make out more than a jumble of walls and roofs, lit here and there by the vertical slits where orange light marked out windows or the angular gaps of ill-fitting doors. His unease had not abated. Mere paces away, the Ta-shih slept and, Adaim noted suddenly, without the orderly night-time arrangements that normally characterized them: men lay curled up on the deck or slumped against each other. *Dead?* No. He knew death with ghastly intimacy now. They were not dead, but nothing would wake them. Dead-drunk perhaps, but that was unlikely, as at least two of them would be assigned for guard duty, to take over from the sentry at second or third watch in the small hours of the night. *Poisoned then, or drugged, and insensible to the world.* A horrible feeling of dread made him sit up higher, again staring fixedly towards the pier. Without knowing precisely what he was doing, he began to drag himself away from the pallet, away from the ladder and the feeble light of the single torch, pushing with frantic strength against the smooth deck, his legs weak and almost useless, but all pain forgotten.

On each side of the galliot were the raised walking boards, a handspan above the deck, where the oarsmen worked. The deck itself between walking board and the central benches provided a clear corridor, four feet wide at this point of the barge on both quarters, for the crew to move unhindered. Along this corridor Adaim heaved himself, slowly, encumbered by his failing legs, until he found himself near the stern, the bulk of the huge tiller and shipmaster's throne rising above him, black against the black night. Here he paused, breath coming in ragged gasps as he struggled to peer again onto the quayside.

Where is the sentry now? He tried to reckon. *Nearing the temple? No, not more than halfway up the switchback pathways. Perhaps only just leaving the village.* He would not return for some time. *And what of the crew? In the tavern,* he seemed to recall.

On the pier, shadows moved. Adaim's heart began to pound and involuntarily he held his breath. Though he strained with the utmost will to see, he could make out nothing distinct on the pier – only the solitary torch, burning low now, casting imprecise light over a short length of the rough timber pier. In his growing distress, he suddenly seized upon an idea. Why hadn't he thought of it? The shipmaster! He must be below decks, in his usual bed for the night, amongst the tea bales and other cargo. If Adaim could alert him…

In the instant of raising his fist to bang on the deck, Adaim stopped. What if he were ashore? Making any sound would be equally certain to attract the attentions of whoever was out there on the pier, directing them straight to Adaim. He lowered his fist and then, casting around for a place of concealment, dragged himself in panic closer to the shipmaster's throne, until his head knocked against one of the sturdy timber feet. The sound seemed deafening and once again he froze, eye fixed on the only section of the pier illuminated by the torchlight. Two figures in black clothes, faces covered, flitted quickly into view, crossed in front of the torch on its pole and approached the galliot.

Sheer terror took possession of Adaim. He was rooted to the spot, transfixed by the insubstantial ghostly shadows nearing the ladder down onto the galliot. The first reached the edge of the pier, turned and began to climb down. Spurred to action, Adaim shrank back, pulling his body closer to the shipmaster's throne. The second shadowy figure began the descent onto the deck. At that moment, Adaim's good right arm slipped and he fell sideways so that he was completely prone, his terror multiplying. He flailed with his forearm, seeking a purchase on the deck, a way to haul his body away from the men who crouched now, silent and still, a mere twenty strides away at the bottom of the ladder. As luck would have it, his hand fell between the back of the throne and the stern transom. Here there was a small gap between the throne and the heavy transverse beams supporting the pivot of the tiller. If he could squeeze in there…

With the urgency of a hunted animal, he pulled his head and shoulders into the gap and then hauled helplessly at his legs, stabbing pain ignored in his desperation to conceal himself in the pitch darkness of the cavity. After agonizing moments, he was in. He could see nothing except a triangular patch of shadows that was the starboard decking, and a coil of what he thought must be rope, close up against the throne, perhaps employed by the crew to lash the tiller overnight. He drew breath, anxious to calm his racing heart, and bent all his energy to listening. Silence. Then a tiny sound reached him, the sound, he told himself, of bare feet moving slowly, cautiously, on the deck. A pause. The feet moved again. Silence again. He pictured the two men moving gradually towards the stern, assuredly one on each side of the galliot, searching with quiet efficiency, until they reached the throne – a moment more, then powerful hands would have him, hauling him out…

A whispering voice near at hand jolted him like a physical blow: "Where could he go?"

"Somewhere near," came the hushed reply.

"The village?"

"Not likely. We'd have seen him. Anyway, how far can a cripple crawl?"

Adaim, at an extreme of agitation, nearly gasped at these words. Perhaps, deep down, he had stupidly believed that they had come for someone else, that he was not the target of their murderous intent. His last vestige of hope fled.

"You checked the Ta-shih?"

"I checked 'em. Not there."

"He said," whispered the first voice, pitched higher as with a growing sense of urgency, "to do the business now. Time is passing. Sentry'll be back afore long."

"Can't throw him overboard if we can't find him," came the muttered response.

Adaim's blood ran cold. He squeezed his body tighter, crushing his legs against his chest as if he could disappear into the solid timber of the galliot.

"Below decks?"

"What? With the shipmaster?"

"Nowhere else, is there?"

"Right. Have to ease that hatch full open so I can get in – dead quiet. Don't want the riverman coming at us with an axe…"

"Leave it to me."

Silence descended again. The deep murmur that was the voice of the Cise, unceasing, hid further sound. Adaim waited. Perhaps they had gone? An irresistible urge to flee came over him. *Get out now. Get out now. The village – in the village there was safety!* With a supreme effort of self-control, he resisted. Like a hunted deer, safety now lay in utter stillness and concealing night. Neither flies, nor crows, nor assassins would have him, he concluded, and this grim humour settled his panic. Once again, he began to imagine the two men creeping silently in the cramped quarters below the deck, stepping carefully around the shipmaster asleep in his cot, then, discovering nothing, returning up the companionway to the ladder and onto the pier. Adaim's breathing came easier now, his heart had stopped its mad racing. The sentry must be close by…

The unmistakable silhouette of a foot and dark leggings appeared within an arm's length of Adaim's face, closer than the coiled rope next to the tiller. His shock was enormous. His head jerked back, although his body was too tightly confined for him to move much at all. This, no doubt, saved his life. In the instant of his reflexive flinching away from the threat, his soldier's discipline reasserted itself. *Steady, steady!* He stayed stock still, breathing in and out in tiny increments as if he were part of the steady pulse of the river.

The silhouette remained as before. Then a whisper reached Adaim: "Nothing…I was sure I heard something…"

"Hmm… He ain't aboard. Time to go. Sentry's got to be close."

"Yes," came the voice, reluctant, then: "The Shae's curse on him. May Sadon swallow him down to the depths."

The silhouette moved back. Adaim was alone once more. Exhaustion, pain and fear engulfed him.

***

The amber lights of the village lay below at the foot of the steep zig-zag path. Against the pier were moored the brown hulks of vessels, the galliot at right, a dense shadow on the river that oozed past like molten lead. With Manei a step behind, Pillio began the descent. He did not look back. And even when he remembered that he had not seen Exarch Hassin to thank him and bid him goodnight, he hesitated only a moment before continuing.

The village was quiet. In the heavens the constellation of Besanal, the wounded deer, was lying at an acute angle to the pole star and from this

Pillio determined that it must be near to midnight. He walked through the village at a measured pace and inhaled deeply to clear his head of the lingering effects of the wine. At the edge of the village, a dozen prone shapes under a fisherman's awning marked where the peasants had made their beds for the night. At the end of the pier, the galliot rode her moorings with a dull creaking.

Suddenly Pillio's heart went cold. Something was wrong. He started forward. Manei, likewise alarmed, ran ahead and, disdaining the ladder, leapt down to the deck before him. The guardleader yelled, "Wake up, damn you!"

Pillio climbed down the ladder, taking in the scene while surges of rage and fear raced through him. The huddled forms of the soldiers moved slowly. Manei kicked at inert bodies, cursing in the vilest language. Abruptly, he swung towards Pillio. "The prisoners, sir! Gone!"

Pillio went completely cold. He strode to the slumped bodies of his men. "Are they injured?" he asked breathlessly.

"Dead-drunk, more like," growled Manei. "Fools!"

From the bows the Ta-shih sentry arrived, concern written all over his face.

"What happened here?" Pillio demanded.

The young soldier blinked. "Sir?"

"The prisoners!" cried Pillio.

A moment of panic and confusion bereft the soldier of words. Then he stammered, "W-with you, sir! A-at the temple!"

"How can this be?"

"I escorted 'em there at the start of my watch. On your orders…"

Pillio was left stupefied. "My…my orders?"

"Aye, sir. T'bring the prisoners. And not to let 'em out of my sight afore they're safe inside the temple. The exarch brought word, sir."

The below decks hatch creaked open. Manei crouched and the heavy sword hissed from his belt. It was the dark bulk of the shipmaster.

"Eh?" he growled and, barefoot and tousle-haired, lumbered forward. "What's the damned noise about?" He recognised Pillio. "Ah, Commander! Back from t'revelry?"

Pillio cried, "What happened here? What happened? My men are drunk! The prisoners are gone!"

The shipmaster was now close enough to peer at the dark shapes struggling to their knees under the canopy. He pursed his lips and volunteered the cheerful opinion: "A good night's drinking, seems t'me – "

"You saw the prisoners taken?" Pillio interjected, leaning towards the man and grasping at a brawny forearm.

The shipmaster seemed not a bit surprised by Pillio's urgency, which he took to be simply another manifestation of the Ta-shih officer's quarrelsome disposition. "No. No. I bin below decks…"

"Commander!" Manei, prowling the rest of the galliot, had found Adaim, having crawled out from his hiding place in the stern.

Pillio strode over as Manei was lifting the man bodily to carry him back to his pallet. "What happened?" Pillio demanded, then checked himself: the man was mute. Even so, fear and relief both were evident in his bruised face. As Manei laid him gently on the pallet, the single eye implored Pillio but could tell him nothing.

Manei moved back to his men and, on his haunches, began sniffing at a flagon of ale. He glanced at Pillio and said, "Strong stuff, sir. More'n a noggin or two in their gut, I'll wager, but my boys don't have the coin t'buy these quantities of ale."

"Aye," murmured Pillio, and felt suspicion growing upon a hot rage. "But Archivists have gold, do they not?" He directed a question at the sentry once again: "Who brought the ale?"

The broad, flat features of the soldier registered incomprehension.

"The Archivist?"

"No, sir. 'E said you'd arranged some ale from the inn, but the sentries not to touch none till the prisoners was up at the temple." The soldier, now thoroughly uncomfortable, added as a pathetic defence: "I didn't touch none, sir. I was the last watch."

"So it was the innkeeper…" Pillio looked up at the shipmaster. "You know this innkeeper?"

"I know him…" admitted the huge man slowly.

"And where shall we find him now?"

The shipmaster extended a large arm from his side like the branch of a tree and pointed towards the tavern. "E'll be indoors."

"Where are your crew?" Pillio demanded.

"Long-room at tavern." Again the extended arm.

Pillio made for the ladder, with Manei and the sentry at his back. "Secure the ship," shouted Pillio over his shoulder. "Under no circumstances let anyone aboard!"

The shipmaster was left muttering to himself.

At the tavern door, latched from inside, Manei applied himself to the rough planks with a boot and the door crashed open. Someone began to scream, a woman's voice, and nearby a dog set up a furious barking. Pillio entered the darkness of the tavern, the guardleader already ahead of him in a narrow corridor and engaged in the business of opening doors in the same manner as before. Pillio waited near the entrance, fist on the pommel of his sword. The fury that possessed him had brought his body to near-trembling. It was as much as he could do to remain still, to hold in check the fierce press for action.

Barely visible in the darkness, pale faces appeared at doorways. Manei demanded in a terrible voice the whereabouts of the innkeeper. Half a dozen voices answered at once. A nude figure darted from a room at the end of the corridor and made a pathetic attempt to dodge past Manei, who jabbed his leg out and tripped the unfortunate individual. To prevent further flight the guardleader placed his boot upon the man's neck. Behind him, wailing in the most ardent manner, came a woman. To her breast she clutched a blanket which, sadly, failed to cover those parts of her person distinguished by large quantities of tremulous flesh. Pillio strode forward. He instructed the nearest of the tavern's guests, one of the oarsmen from the galliot as it happened, to fetch light, then approached the innkeeper.

"You have plied my men with liquor…soldiers of the Ta-shih."

The fat woman gave vent to a series of stertorous whimpers. Manei stepped off the innkeeper's neck and raised the back of his hand to the woman. The whimpering ceased. Meanwhile, despite the removal of the boot from his neck, the innkeeper hugged the floor.

Pillio said ominously, "You conspire against the Ta-shih!"

"Conspire! I did nothing, lord!" came the gasped reply. Manei bent and jerked the innkeeper's head up by his hair.

"Speak truth, friend," he snarled. "The officer is angry!"

"Have Archivists spoken to you this night?" Pillio demanded.

"Aye, lord!" screeched the wretch.

A man returned with a bright oil lamp and hovered uncertainly behind Pillio. The lamp cast quivering coppery light and made a distorted mask of the innkeeper's open mouth and wrinkled, tormented expression.

"Tonight," breathed Pillio, "you brought food and drink for my men. Perhaps the drink was laced. Who shall I hold responsible? Who shall I execute?"

"Oh! No! No! Lord, the Archivists brought word that I was t'serve my best and strongest ale, and coin t'pay with too! They said, 'Tis from the Ta-shih officer,' they did! 'E's 'avin' a fine time up at temple,' they said! 'Give the lads yer best, an' on the officer!' they said! I weren't t'know no diff'rent, was I! 'Give the lads yer best!' they said!" The innkeeper choked into silence.

Pillio eyed the others present, the wide-eyed woman and a few frightened faces peering around the doorframes. "The prisoners of the Ta-shih. Who has seen them?"

A terrified voice quavered: "Went up t'temple, lord, t'join you... Soldier took 'em..."

Pillio cursed explosively. Someone must pay for this! Amongst the villagers there was utter silence. Eyes were downcast.

Barely audible, Pillio said, "Manei. Bring the innkeeper."

They left the tavern, the innkeeper on all fours, pale bare buttocks prodded from behind by Manei's boot. The tavern guests shuffled in a herd out into the street where the chinks of orange light from windows signified a wider audience in the village.

"Here," ordered Pillio, and the innkeeper scrambled into a kneeling position at Pillio's feet. "Guardleader," Pillio cried in a loud voice. "We must execute this man!"

Manei gave a grin, the product of which was a wolf-like display of incisors and a most unpleasant elevation of the long white scar on his face. With a flourish he drew his sword, holding the weapon at an angle in the guard position, and advanced towards the anguished innkeeper, who shrieked at once, "Lords! Mercy! I beg of you!" and at Manei's further preparations, laying the edge of the blade against the unfortunate's neck, gabbled at extraordinary speed, "Save me lords! Save me! Take my money!"

Struggling with the icy rage that gripped him, Pillio motioned with his hand and Manei paused, but left his sword in attendance upon the innkeeper's backbone.

"An uncommonly generous innkeeper, to give his strongest ale to soldiers!" said Pillio.

"I…I am generous, lord, I am honest. The Archivist gave his blessing!"

"His blessing!" Pillio reflected a moment, then said, "I understand. I understand all too well! And what was the value of his blessing? Is your purse heavy this night?"

The innkeeper began to tremble.

Pillio waited. He felt calmer now, though the rage still quickened his blood.

The innkeeper said nothing. His trembling grew worse. The blade upon his neck rested steady as a rock.

"Justice," remarked Pillio, after what to the innkeeper must have seemed a lifetime, "must be served. You conspired, albeit unknowingly, against the Ta-shih! You accepted bribes to do Archivists' bidding. However, we will spare you, miserable man, but only so that you may be punished less honourably." Pillio jabbed his finger at a villager. "You! Bring rope. Bind this creature's hands then secure him to the pier, only his head above water, you understand. I declare that he must remain there fully three days. Whether the waters rise or fall, we shall leave him to the mercy of the Cise and Sadon!"

A groan went up from the assembled folk. The river god could be a vengeful god. The villager ran to do the bidding of the Ta-shih. Pillio gestured to Manei and the sentry and set off towards the pathway to the temple, leaving a cluster of people at the quayside and a slowly swelling chatter of agitated voices. Halfway up the steep incline between the village huts a shape detached itself from the deep shadow of a timber wall and stood motionless in their path.

"Hsst!" rasped Manei. "Out of the way!"

The shape, which Pillio now perceived to be a woman, whose white-knuckled hands held a shawl close about her face, shrank back at Manei's unwavering advance. As Pillio came abreast of her, believing her to be simply a curious villager irresistibly drawn to the spectacle at the river, she blurted out urgently, "Sir, you will not find 'em at the temple!"

Pillio stopped in his tracks. Manei, in a swift movement calculated to prevent the woman's possible flight, reached out to clamp her wrist in a cruel grip. She did not resist and the guardleader drew her close. Pillio looked down into her face and was surprised to see a sensuous, if coarse, beauty in the features, and, to his greater disconcertment, a bold angry stare exceptional amongst the common classes.

"I know where they took 'em, sir," she whispered, and darted her eyes towards the crowd at the river as if afraid this admission might be overheard.

"What do you know?" enquired Pillio, at once both cautious and eager.

"I know enough!"

Manei jerked her wrist in harsh reprimand, and she dipped her head to cower, but made use of the action to try to writhe from his hand. The attempt met with no success.

"I came of my own will!" she hissed. "If I meant t'run I would never ha'come!"

Manei smiled and drew her close again.

"Tell me your secret, woman," said Pillio. "I tire of games."

"Archivists have 'em, your demons. I said so. I know where they went."

"So do I. They went to the temple."

"No! Not there!"

Pillio's heart beat faster. With great self-mastery he replied evenly, "Then say."

"Promise me justice first!"

"What justice? Speak sense, woman."

The flashing eyes fixed upon Pillio. There was expressed in them; a kind of contracted desperation as of a person who has chosen some irredeemable, self-destructive course. At last she found her tongue: "Kill the Archivist…"

Pillio drew a shallow breath. "You profane the Faith, woman. Are you mad?"

"Aye, mad!" she snapped. "I have been ill-used by Archivists. Kill them all and be damned! Let the Shae take me! I'll drown in Hell forever and be torn to pieces by Echrexar's iron dogs… It will be worth it if you kill the Archivist."

Pillio held up a hand. "There is no justice in killing Archivists. What harm have they caused you that you—"

"What harm!" the woman spat. "That Hassin made a whore of me! That monster Hassin! Now I carry a child and they cast me aside and they'll pay me nothing! He says I am beyond the Faith now. Me! Kill them all!"

"Enough of killing! Tell me what you know."

She fell silent, and in the breathless moment between them a screeching wail from the quayside split the night and set dogs barking again. The sound seemed to rouse the woman. "First, give me money…" she whispered, "for the child."

"Only if your information is sound," retorted Pillio coldly. "If not, my good guardleader will take you to join the innkeeper!"

Licking her lips the woman glanced from Pillio to Manei and back again.

Pillio placed his hand suggestively on his belt-purse.

"They've gone south by boat," she said. "I watched 'em. Two Archivists and servants. They set off downriver with your demons." She uttered a laugh, the humour in her tone as bizarre as her demand for justice. "Such demons!"

Pillio interrupted, "How can they travel the river by night?"

She laughed again. "You know Archivists not at all. No riverman'll stand against an exarch's curse! The black river's the dream murderer's nightmare, gone in the morning light. An exarch's curse is perdition, in this life and the next!"

Pillio stared a final time into the wide-eyed face of the woman, pity and an urgency to take action at war in his heart, then tossed coins at her feet, swung on his heel and hastened down the path. Manei and the sentry followed.

"What of me?" hissed the woman behind them. "If you let him live, he'll damn me for sure! Justice, hear! Ta-shih justice! Kill Hassin!"

Once again at the quayside, Pillio pushed past the assembled villagers, who shuffled from his path like frightened sheep. At the end of the quay, the innkeeper's wife, who by now had succeeded in covering her ample person within the bounds of respectability, leaned her head against a timber bollard and sobbed piteously above the moonlit waters of the Cise where, hard up against the lower column of the same bollard, a bedraggled head jutted. Pillio, having bestowed a single glance on this scene, made for the galliot and climbed down to the deck.

"Shipmaster!" he said, addressing that individual who stood in the bows, fingers and thumb astride his chin in frank contemplation of the misfortune of the innkeeper. "Shipmaster, make ready for an instant departure!"

Transferring his frowning gaze to Pillio, the shipmaster replied as patiently as if the directive were the misguided nagging of a child, "Sir, th'darkness prevents it. We'll away at first light–"

"No!" snapped Pillio. "Now!" He approached the towering riverman and looked up into his face. "This vessel is now under the orders of the Ta-shih. We pursue criminals, men who have acted against the Law. At this moment they run from us, south to Ung."

"In the pitch night? On th'river?" The man was incredulous.

Pillio's fury only amplified his authority. "Yes!"

"What of the labourers?" retorted the shipmaster, with a glance at the quayside. "They've paid their passage…"

Pillio offered a sickly grin, his meaning clear. "They are welcome to join us…in the night…on the river…"

The shipmaster regarded Pillio a moment, then his features settled into an expression of fateful acceptance and he gave breath to a sigh which conveyed more than a hundred rancorous protestations might have. Signalling to his crew, gathering wide-eyed on the quay, he started preparations to get *Dust Devil* underway with a subdued haste.

CHAPTER 7

Peace or war, you're still damned poor.
They drive you hard and shave your head,
So close the doors and roll your whores
'Cause time is short and then you're dead!
Soldier's Marching Ditty.

[…] heating of near 10 degrees […] resulting de-glaciation and meltwater
pulses from the poles […] refuges critical for their archival collections were
lost to the great flood and […] some, even later, to the gradual re-glaciation
[…]
Extract from a surviving document, copied by a scribe, IYE 1047.

***

A ruddy dawn obscured by heavy clouds lit the water streaming down *Dust Devil*'s oars. Their every rise and fall released an arc of bronze spray that spattered into the swell of the great river. The rivermen, stripped to the waist and sweating from their exertions, walked back and forth, back and forth, in a familiar rhythm. In the bows, two soldiers leaned out over the gunwale to keep watch for snags and submerged obstacles. Their fellows were asleep under the canopy – this by order of Pillio, who wanted them ready for daylight. Manei stood aft of the canopy, his boots planted shoulder-width apart to counter the yawing of the galliot in these channels of the Cise where dozens of rocky islets disturbed the smooth currents and produced dangerous eddies and vortices. The shipmaster, enthroned as usual in his place at the tiller, gazed out upon the cloudy dawn with an easy confidence that must have been fortified – though from his expression it was impossible to tell – by his triumph in negotiating the hazards of the river in the dark and now by the strengthening light and visibility.

Pillio sat on a bench. Shoulders slumped, his hands hanging limply over his knees, he was exhausted. In the several hours before dawn he had taken no rest. The rush of pursuit and the necessity of assisting the crew while they plied the shapeless realms of the Cise in the pitch night had provided him a tangible purpose, but the grey half-light of the in-between time preceding dawn, when the world was yet faint and indistinct, had leached hope from the attainment of that goal. With his head dropping on his breast he felt futility oppress him: the Archivists must be far ahead; they would reach Ung hours before their pursuers and would doubtless find sanctuary in the temple there. And then, of course, perhaps the prisoners were still at the Temple of Eslo; perhaps Pillio had been roundly deceived at every turn… It did not bear thinking about, but think about it Pillio did, endlessly, and with the growing certainty that this entire business had long ago achieved a complexity and import way beyond his capacity to perceive.

Had he in some way agreed to this? Had the Archivists mistaken his intentions? Pillio flung these tortured questions at his reason as he might pebbles into a dark well, hearing only a babble of misleading echoes in response. Like any man under the extremes of pressure and perplexity, Pillio imagined a hundred different errors he might have made – a gesture misunderstood, a word misplaced, an ill-considered phrase – and with the full force of hindsight, events over the last week that had seemed innocuous became the subjects of his intense, regretful scrutiny. Harbin had warned him. Yet he had allowed himself to fall under the spell of Exarch Hassin. Then again, how was he to trust the words of a stranger met on the road? Had he been duped all along? It required only a short mental step for Pillio, in his current emotional state, to suspect treachery where before this day he would never have supposed it. Yet, in the same instant, he dismissed such thoughts as absurd.

He returned, however, from each bout of ponderous rumination to a single theme: these events, every step, seemed to move in circles of political power as remote from a lowly Ta-shih officer as the heavens from the earth, and as incomprehensible…

The old fears returned: was he good enough to be an officer in the Ta-shih? Perhaps he shirked his oath? If all of his comrades in the Army of Kiangsu quailed, as he did now, how could the Ta-shih fulfil its allegiance? how could it stand against corruption and apathy? To question his duty was to place himself above it. And that was anathema.

Pillio shook his head, drawing back from questions which, though he understood it only poorly, he sensed tore at the foundations of his existence.

His misery was little helped by his abortive attempts to understand from the Strath soldier what had transpired. By means of gestures and stumbling questions they had communicated. Two men, it seemed, had come aboard in the night. "*Why?*" Pillio had asked.

The soldier had pointed at himself and appeared to gesture over the side of the galliot.

"To take you?"

A shake of the head, then an awkward one-handed gesture of throwing.

"To throw you into the water?" Pillio had considered a moment, then said, "And in your current weakened state, drown you…"

A nod.

"But who were they? Archivists?"

A nod, but accompanied by a half shrug, implied he could not be certain.

Pillio had surveyed the Strath trooper's face for long moments. At last he had murmured, "So what then is it that you know?"

The sun was higher now, a squashed marigold orange behind sluggish banks of clouds; it disappeared, then rolled into view again to touch Pillio's tunic with watery golden light. Nothing was certain. He needed help, a senior officer to make sense of it all, to tell him what to do. He began to feel a desperate need for sleep, and rose to his feet with an arm outstretched against the canopy stanchion to support himself. By force of will he squared his shoulders and signalled Manei.

"I must rest," he said to the guardleader, and could not prevent the words from sounding like an apology.

Manei, in the act of nodding, was interrupted by the shipmaster, who addressed Pillio with the honorific, "Commander…" and then paused with the air of a judge about to pronounce judgement. Too weary to respond, Pillio simply stared at the man. "Commander," said the shipmaster once more and then in his laconic manner: "My men must rest."

Pillio was instantly irritated by this parroting of his own words and snapped, "No! In one hour your men will train mine. When they are proficient, your men can rest! This vessel will move all day and all night if necessary."

The shipmaster, looking for all the world like a surprised mountain bear that has been struck on the snout by some invisible object, digested the import of this speech then remonstrated against Pillio's directive with the reminder, "Faith in the gods! Tis not th'way of the rivermen. Tis skilled work this…"

"Indeed! Indeed!" said Pillio with vehemence. "And my troops are skilled too! Your men will teach them. They will learn. They are Ta-shih!"

And the delivery of this fundamental truth silenced the shipmaster's protests.

Pillio retired to his bedroll under the canopy.

***

Not even bad dreams could wake Pillio, though he tossed in his sleep and cried out more than once. Manei, who had supervised the instruction of the soldiers in the rivermen's skill at the oars, gave one eye to the diligent efforts of his troops and the other to the restless form of his company commander. The disturbances in Pillio's sleep concerned him little: experience had taught him that if a man dreamed, though his dream wanderer led him terrible places, he rested. So Manei watched and was at ease.

The soldiers, after a period of fixed concentration and a dedication, Manei knew, in proportion to their shame at their conduct last night, settled into the rhythm of rowing. Manei had instructed them to aim for precision rather than haste, reasoning that experience would teach them pace in due course. Meanwhile, the shipmaster sat his throne above the deck. And the result of these two facts was that the galliot made best speed ahead of the current. Manei found time to doze under the canopy, but came alert at even the slightest change in the regularity of the vessel's sound and motion. Several times they passed small fishing boats and Manei inspected their crews, who showed nothing more than the blank indifference of peasants. *Dust Devil* swept by without check.

The landscape changed, though the grey overcast did not. Gradually, under the stern immeasurable heights of the Alnaes and the undulating woods that clothed the shoulders of the great mountains, more and more habitation became apparent. On the banks of the Cise, wooden jetties thrust out from the fringes of the forest; solitary huts told of their presence with thin columns of woodsmoke; the tiny figures of men appeared on the shore and, less common now, deer stalked the shallow waters of coves and rocky inlets. On the eastern bank, a small village took shape, a huddle of huts around a central courtyard; outlying fields were ploughed in precise lines. Nearby, half a dozen fishing boats rode the tug of the Cise. Their crews, lithe men clad only in red loincloths, and balanced precariously in the cockleshell vessels, cast great lengths of hemp netting suspended on dried bull-reeds. In places rents in the green roof of the forest marked where trees had been felled and, far ahead, a jagged brown line rising up the flanks of low mountains against the horizon suggested the more extensive labour of men. Manei enquired upon this point to the shipmaster, who peered at the distant scar through red-rimmed eyes and pronounced it to be the breaker-mines at Chanee.

"What do they mine, the breakers?" asked Manei, who knew little of the world this far south.

"Iron, great lengths of steel," came the response.

"In what quantities?"

The shipmaster's lips creased into a smile, exposing two huge yellow teeth, hitherto concealed from public view, in the top of his jaw. Manei was reminded of two parallel standing stones. "Big mines, guardleader," asserted the riverman and, perhaps owing to the honest interest shown by Manei, proceeded at length: "Four hun'red year 'r more the tunnel rats bin breakin' the hills and diggin' the old city beneath. Iron ever'where. Good steel they break from the ancients' walls an' their tunnels. Strange engines. An' coins too. Hoards o' coins in great vaults." He jerked a thumb at Manei's belt. "Coins like those on y'r belt; some bigger. Hard, like… harder'n a bronze leol. Look ahead, then," and the shipmaster levelled a spar-like arm towards the brown slash that was the breaker-mine workings. "Cise runs west o' that range, where th'old city lies beneath the forest. Shot through it is with pickings, though they must go deeper ev'r' year." The shipmaster drew a sighing breath, as if in sympathy with the efforts of the miners, or more probably in anticipation of a question from his audience. "But the Cise runs west o'it," he said again.

Manei obliged with what seemed the appropriate question, "West, eh?"

The shipmaster nodded, slowly, deliberately, as if Manei had struck upon some vital clue to a secret to which only the riverman held answer. "Aye, west. And what d'ye think lies west o' th'river?"

"The high peaks," observed Manei, casting a narrowed eye in that direction.

"Aye, aye. And what more?"

Manei gave the issue a moment's thought and, being a man to speak his mind rather than cudgel it, the moment was a short one. He replied, "Honam Province lies west of the river."

The yellow standing stones were again given an airing, this time to the sound of a rumbled laugh. "Honam, aye. And the breaker-mines lie east of the Cise. So the iron and the coins and the gold the breaker-rats pull out goes to Kiangsu and not to the Lord of Honam – all by the whim of the river. May Sadon be forever wise!" The shipmaster made a ritualistic sign of the snake to accompany these words.

Manei smiled to show his appreciation of this rare joke so cunningly played by the river god. "Then you believe," he interrogated the shipmaster further, "that mighty Sadon offers no favour to the Lord of Honam?"

The riverman shook his head, in the languid manner of a bull. "Honam," he pronounced with gravity, "is the caged beast. Ever fretful. Honam tests the gods."

Manei responded with a nod. It seemed right, what the shipmaster had to say. He glanced back at the workings which, with the passage of some miles, now revealed more of their character. The tall ranks of trees ceased abruptly on the edge of a vast tumble of shattered rocks and huge concrete blocks, flint grey under an identical sky, that seemed to have poured like a solid waterfall from the precipitous heights. Three such wounds had been cut all the way to the gentle slopes two miles below, so that the scattered scree lay exposed within the green pelt of trees like the twisted intestines of the gigantic eviscerated city beneath. At this distance, fine detail was impossible to make out, but Manei could see the dark shadows marking the entrances to tunnels and the angular frames of a profusion of steel and timber hoists. The old city must have been vast.

"The iron and steel," said Manei. "They transport it to Kiangsu?"

"Aye," rumbled the shipmaster. "To the mills and forges."

"In barges, I'll wager."

"Aye."

"So there are many vessels up and down these parts?"

"Aye."

"Our Archivists might board another vessel here, then?"

"Aye. Aye."

"The we'd best berth here awhile and discover as much…"

The shipmaster frowned and bestowed upon the inert shape of Pillio a glance full of meaning. Manei adjusted his swordbelt, resting a calloused hand on the smooth steel pommel of the sword. "I'll wake the commander in good time," he murmured. "Now he can rest."

***

"That one!" cried Pillio, pointing at a square-rigged sailing vessel two miles ahead. The river here flowed straight as an arrow shaft, with no islands to obstruct the view, though a score of barges and other vessels claimed their place on these waters. Pillio and Manei leaned over the bows of *Dust Devil* and stared hard at the distant brown sail.

"Aye, that one," Manei concurred. The Archivists had boarded the ship at Chanee, according to the report the guardleader had received from dockworkers, information he had procured through the persuasive powers of five silver ru. And they had departed without haste, presuming themselves secure from immediate pursuit. Half a day's hard rowing had taken *Dust Devil* away from the clutter of piers and steel-laden barges under the huge scars of the Chanee breaker-mines and within sight of Pillio's quarry.

The clouds remained and the light, as a consequence, would fail sooner this evening. Already some barges had tied up on the riverbanks for the night. But *Dust Devil* plunged onward, oar spars rolling overhead to slice the blades back down into the waters with a sibilant hiss. They gained on the vessel with every stroke of the oars, but the landscape around them crumbled into attenuated shadows that quickly blurred. Soon the world became only the mirror-like sheen of the river and the charcoal cloud above. Nothing sundered heaven from earth. Ahead the dark sail billowed and flapped like a black wing over the waters.

Pillio turned from the bows and called out to his men: "Arm!" And the Ta-shih troops made haste to unpack and buckle on harnesses of segmented plate armour to protect chest and shoulders. With Manei's help, Pillio himself shrugged into a mail hauberk and refastened his swordbelt over it. Next he fitted his silver-crested helmet over his head and tied it fast. Manei, attired now in chest armour and helmet, stepped up to Pillio.

"Dispositions, sir?"

Pillio looked towards the dark sail ahead, so much nearer at every oarstroke. "We shall close from their right and secure the vessel. Inform the shipmaster. Also, place two archers, one in the stern, another in the bows. You and I and two men will board the ship."

"Sir!" Manei turned smartly and set about issuing orders.

The dusk lingered no great time and abruptly, as if in response to some cosmic signal, it became night. The rivermen muttered prayers of thanks for deliverance safely through the in-between time and to beg the gods for their safety in the darkness. If his troops did the same, Pillio did not hear.

Distances were foreshortened so that the flapping sail across the waters seemed nearer, though *Dust Devil's* progress was no more rapid than before. To Pillio, their movement had the character of a dream where, despite every strenuous effort, the object that one pursues grows only marginally closer, tantalizingly out of reach. He half expected that at any instant the dark sail might vanish completely.

"Guardleader!" Pillio shouted. "Bring light!"

In due course Manei arranged lanterns over the gunwales, and lurid pools of amber light spilled onto the dark waters and shattered in the splash of the oars. The effect, of course, of this illumination was to throw the vessel ahead further into the shadows of the night until lanterns were similarly struck by the master of that ship, tongues of flame whose reflections trailed over the water towards *Dust Devil* like writhing silvery snakes.

Suddenly they were close. The shipmaster of *Dust Devil* bawled instructions to his oarsmen. All but the two stern oars were shipped.

A voice from the square-rigger cried out across the intervening wedge of water, "Beware! Sadon's balls, you're too close! Beware!"

Manei returned the cry: "Hold there! An officer of the Ta-shih will board! Lower your sail! Hold there!"

"Are y'mad?" came the irate bellow. "Board? On the river? Tis black as the Shae's arsehole this night! Stand off! Stand off! Ye'll sink us both!"

The shipmaster of *Dust Devil* rumbled, "Th'river god's own truth, Commander. Better to make for the shore and tie up."

In the jumping torchlight Pillio shook his head. "No. We board them now!"

The distance between the vessels had halved; they were no more than ten paces away. *Dust Devil* started to slew as they lost way and were carried by the current. The oarsmen plunged their oars down and *Dust Devil* righted. Holding a timber post against the lunging of the deck, Manei placed a boot upon the gunwale in readiness to board the ship, and gestured his troops forward with coils of rope. Coppery light from the lanterns multiplied on dull armour like *Dust Devil's* own display of lightning.

Figures on the square-rigger ran under the lanterns. The curved hull heaved against the swell of the river like an intractable bullock. At the wheel the shipmaster raised a fist and cursed, "Damn you! Stand off, you mad fuck! Stand off, I say! Sadon help us all!"

"Bring her round!" cried Pillio to the shipmaster of *Dust Devil.*

Unexpectedly a face appeared on the deck in front of the Ta-shih: Exarch Hassin, stern with condemnation. Perhaps the oarsmen hesitated at the sight of this Archivist and his terrible visage, or perhaps a sudden swell caught the galliot, but the two vessels surged apart ten paces and the soldiers gazed at the Archivist with superstitious awe, reckoning some cause and effect in the arrival of the exarch and the abrupt retreat of the galliot.

Pillio roared at the shipmaster: "Again! Close on the ship!"

Then Exarch Hassin cried out, "Why do you molest us? What madness is this? We dock at Kiangsu in a few days!"

He wants to escape! thought Pillio. *Just as we catch him!*

A passionate sense of the rightness of his cause made him deaf to the cautions of the Archivist. He swept his arm over his head, signalling the shipmaster to approach again. The galliot heeled, then righted. The nearside oarsman flipped his oar neatly from the water and swung it upright from the rowlocks. The vessels struck with a booming thud, grinding together along the painted timbers. The shipmaster of *Dust Devil* was shouting something to his crew.

Manei was first aboard, leaping up to the greater height of the square-rigger and immediately securing rope to cleats along the gunwale. Pillio followed, scrambling onto the deck as the hulls parted then crunched together with a splintering of wood. The two soldiers came behind, uncertain and afraid.

A dark form pressed close. Exarch Hassin was transformed: flashing eyes stabbed; the lineaments of his face were drawn taut and skull-like; the palms of his hands stood outstretched before him, a formidable threat. Pillio stared down at him and his heart raced in his breast. This was the culmination. This act was the embodiment of his duty.

"Manei! The prisoners!" he said in a voice that was startling in its passionate intensity.

"You have risked our lives with this madness!" hissed Hassin, but Manei passed him with the two soldiers close behind, and only Pillio remained, a figure of glittering steel, seemingly grown in stature and authority as the spirit in him swelled with triumph.

"You deceived me once, Archivist," he remonstrated. "I take back what you have stolen from the Ta-shih."

"Stolen?" cried Hassin. "We agreed! You passed the prisoners to my care!" The Archivist's tone became distraught: "I do not understand!"

"What agreement is this?" Pillio protested. "There is no such thing, Archivist! I owe allegiance to the Ta-shih and my duty is clear."

At this juncture Manei returned with the prisoners, and the Archivist was interrupted before he might answer. The two Shur-Shur stood under the soft gleam of a lantern and their pale alien eyes fixed upon Pillio with a mixture of relief and trepidation. Beside them the soldiers waited, rigid, refusing to look at the Archivist.

Only dimly conscious of the atmosphere of fear pervading the world around him, Pillio snapped an arm out to direct the prisoners to *Dust Devil*, then turned on Hassin with a jubilant gaze. A shadow thrust itself between them. Pillio, in a state of feverish elation, believed this to be an attack upon the prisoners. He reacted instantaneously. His sword was in his hand; the shadow was close to the woman; her eyes were wide with shock. Pillio thrust downwards and a man collapsed at his feet. Even in the poor light the red blood upon his blade and on the deck was obvious. Pillio stood motionless with burning cheeks in the terrible silence that followed. In all the world there seemed only this brutal event and the horrified witnesses and the shame that seared him.

Then Exarch Hassin gasped, "Oh, by all the gods! You have killed him!" He knelt at the corpse and his hand came away with the gleam of blood, scarlet against his pale fingers. "You have murdered one who serves the Faith, an Archivist!" came the accusing cry. "I curse you! I curse you for this most horrible of crimes, for this bloody act against the Faith!

Remember this, all of you!" Hassin swept his frantic gaze across everyone on the deck. "Remember that the Archivists curse this man!"

Shock and anguish had stripped Pillio of the capacity to properly comprehend the events that had just transpired. Nevertheless, the incident had doused the emotional agitation that had lately shrouded the order and clarity of his reason. The exultation of regaining the prisoners was gone, and it was a characteristic of his temperament, perhaps to his credit, that he was better able to deal with the harsh and unanticipated blows of life than with its transitory bounties. A part of his consciousness rose above the paralysis and roused him to action. He moved and saw the staring, spellbound faces and everything around him with the most striking acuity, heard his own voice, cracked and unfamiliar, as if someone else spoke loudly through the tight constriction of his throat.

"Guardleader! Secure the prisoners on board!"

Manei acted at once, and the moment of stillness and amazement was ended. The soldiers hurried to the gunwale and climbed shaking to the deck of *Dust Devil*, assisting the prisoners down from above.

Pillio began to turn, his gaze riveted by the corpse, and in tearing his eyes from the arc of blood that stained the deck he was confronted by the Archivist who stood now, immobile, like an appalling icon, the incarnation of Pillio's conscience. *"Kill the Archivist!"* came the sickening memory of the strange, ardent woman at the temple. *"Kill Hassin!"* Pillio moved aside, grasped the worn timber of the gunwale with his left hand and climbed aboard *Dust Devil*. Manei released the cleats and leapt to the deck as the two vessels, with a curiously animal vigour, jerked apart, the ropes that had held the hulls together snapping back against *Dust Devil's* planks.

Pillio, bloody sword in hand, looked over his shoulder. The Archivist stood under the swaying lanterns with both arms raised aloft, one extended palm dark with the evidence of murder. His words, cleaving the stunned silence like the vengeful whisper of a blade, an echoing reply to the woman's imploring demand, cut at Pillio: "We claim your life!"

And then Pillio bowed his head from the spectral figure in the lantern glow and from the terrified expressions of the soldiers and crew of *Dust Devil.*

***

For a day Pillio said nothing to anyone. He drew apart, ashen and haggard of expression, frequently to be seen staring into the middle distance, but it was clear to all that his gaze was turned inward to the deepest recesses. Like a man in profound sleep, the emotions passing across his face told of the painful drama repeated time after time in his mind's eye. Though he was silent, the mood that was on him touched his troops and the entire crew so that a brooding oppressive disquiet hung over *Dust Devil*, as virulent as a disease.

The shipmaster, exhausted from his long vigil at the tiller, had ordered the galliot to the riverbank, where they berthed for the first night, but not without some initial difficulty in negotiating the shallows and mudflats. The following day, near mid-afternoon, *Dust Devil* put into the walled city of Ung, passing the ancient fortified breakwater with its crenelated walls and towers, before tying up at the busy pier. Accosted almost at once by an official who demanded a docking levy, the shipmaster paid over the coins wordlessly and then set his crew to unloading the merchant cargo. The rivermen worked diligently, heaving the bales of tea from one to the other with the necessary speed but with the same air of unease that hushed the troops and made them wary of meeting their fellows' eyes. It seemed that the dockers and the scores of rivermen chattering and calling out all along the swarming length of the stone wharf must notice this pocket of fear and uncertainty, but the city of Ung was too big, too absorbed in its own incoherent, restless vitality to pause for even a moment of curiosity.

That evening the crew were paid their wages, and with a hasty awkwardness took their leave of *Dust Devil*. As was customary, an alternate crew would board in the morning.

Towards nightfall Pillio seemed to struggle hard to master his depression, rising from his anguished self-contemplation with a bizarre obstinacy to complete an inspection of the Ta-shih squad. Immediately thereafter, his face a studied mask of martial discipline, he passed on orders to Manei that the men were permitted a two-hour furlough in the city. The soldiers departed. In the darkness *Dust Devil* rode her moorings with a gentle bump-bump against the heavy coir mats hung along the dock. The shipmaster, having retired below decks, regaled himself on several demi-lits of dark wine, and was to be heard giving voice to mournful ditties interspersed, as his mood and the wine took him, with pieces of a more indelicate composition. As lanterns sparked into life along the length of the dock, illuminating beneath their flickering orange light the shifting population of the warehouses and harbour-side taverns, the volume of the shipmaster's refrains attracted the attention of three streetwalkers, with painted faces and red lips, who came to stand at the edge of the dock, ringing their wrist-bells and calling down to *Dust Devil*.

Pillio, under the canopy, watched them with hooded eyes. Manei did likewise, but smiled at their antics as the shipmaster, who had heard the tell-tale bells as he had doubtless heard them on countless occasions, staggered up onto the deck, demi-lit in hand, and drank their good health. The three women laughed, teasing the shipmaster with good-natured taunts, and tossed their skirts with a practised skill.

"Need help with your rigging, sailor?" one called out. "I'll get your oar up. Three ru, that's all." One thigh exposed where she had hitched up her skirt, she smiled down on the shipmaster.

"Three ru!" he challenged, with mock indignation.

"Just for you, sailor."

The shipmaster drained half the contents of the demi-lit, spilling a goodly amount upon his barrel chest, and then addressed the woman again, "For three ru I'll have a wine-merchant's daughter!"

"A wine-merchant's daughter wouldn't know one end of an oar from t'other! Two ru, then!" she cried. "For a night's comfort. You'll make me poor!"

Perceiving that the shipmaster's choice had been made, the woman's companions began to leave.

The shipmaster roared out a thunderous laugh, then swung the demi-lit over his head. "After this day I need thrice a night's comfort! Four ru and I'll have the three of you!"

Greeted with calculating glances between the women, the proposal was at last accepted, and *Dust Devil* played host to garish costumes and shrill laughter while the shipmaster encircled all three whores with his impressive arms and steered them towards the hatch.

Sometime later, after the shipmaster's bellows from below decks had subsided, Manei approached his commander at the gunwale, where Pillio looked out over the harbour. The tiny flames of a myriad lanterns upon the old battlements ringed the harbour, reflections dancing in the ripples so that the scene before the Ta-shih was like a thousand bright stars at their feet.

"Sir," said Manei in his forthright way. "The prisoners are secure. I'll watch until the men return. Maybe you'd wish to turn in…"

Pillio, apparently following some complex line of thinking which had led him coincidentally to the topic of the prisoners, murmured, "Did I agree to hand them over to the exarch?"

Although Pillio had not turned towards the guardleader in saying this, Manei could see the expression on his face: never had he seen him look so grave and intense.

"No, sir," Manei replied.

Pillio said nothing more. The troops returned just after the harbour bell struck the appointed hour, reaching *Dust Devil* together in a tight knot as if the awful knowledge they shared set them physically apart from the revellers in the city. Manei saw them bedded down for the night and posted sentries. Meanwhile, Pillio stood alone in the bows. Irregular black masses of shadow from the dock hoists created in the tense outline of his form a gaunt, sinister shape. Nearby, sitting on a bench, legs awkwardly tucked to one side, was the Strath soldier. He too seemed on edge, unable to sleep and watchful. Seated close together under the canopy, the prisoners stirred, and unfamiliar words passed between them. Immediately Pillio's outline shifted and Manei imagined he could see the haunted gaze of his commander fix upon the foreigners like an animal terrified by sudden movement.

Later, when the dockside had cleared and a hush settled over the city, leaving only the battlements, streets and buildings with their twinkling pinpoints of light mysteriously, silently alive, Pillio moved away from the bows, where all this time he had stalked the timbers with a caged restlessness. He settled himself on his bedroll. From the shadows a figure crossed the deck. Manei tensed, but it was the barbarian woman. She knelt in front of Pillio, and Manei was close enough to see her face. The strange, outlandish features conveyed a fierce intensity. She made a series of gestures, and spoke in hesitant, accented words, searching Pillio's expression for signs of comprehension.

"Pillio," she said in her odd dialect, hesitating again as if his name needed to be mastered before she said more. "Dead…lord…"

Manei saw Pillio tense. He grasped the woman's shoulders. There was moment of silence, broken by Pillio: "The lord, yes! Lord Shenri!"

The woman lifted her hand, opened it to reveal a scrap of cloth. She pointed at the scrap, then at Pillio, as if willing him to understand its fragile meaning.

The cloth was two colours, side by side: red and gold.

The woman gestured again, this time in a stabbing motion, unmistakable to her audience, then pointed once more at the cloth.

Behind him there was a hiss, and Pillio turned to see the Strath soldier leaning forward, right arm outstretched, suddenly animated. He was pointing at the cloth, then slowly, deliberately nodded.

"Red and gold…" breathed Pillio. "Ouine Clan. Honam." He took the cloth from the woman, nodding and muttering to himself, "Is it possible?" whilst she returned to her place, swallowed by the darkness.

Much later, when Pillio had turned in and his huddled form had become still, Manei, head pillowed on the soft bulge of his pack and fingers interlaced across his chest, waited until satisfied that the sighing exhalations from his commander signified the onset of sleep. Then, with a final glance at the erect form of the sentry on the dock, he allowed himself to drift into vivid dreams.

∗∗∗

Adaim had felt almost liberated. And with the feeling had come a physical transformation. This might be a miracle – in the way that he understood such things were conferred by the gods – for he thrilled to the profound improvement in his body's strength, the relief at last from more-or-less permanent pain. Hesitantly, he had started to look to the future, believing that one might exist.

The Ta-shih officer *knew* now. *Red and gold. Ouine. Honam.* A secret, guarded by voiceless silence and, he dared to admit, the shame of his failure, had been abruptly, unexpectedly released. He was no longer alone – profoundly, desperately alone – and he would live, would see Mamoba and Strath again, and could serve Lord Shenri's memory, at least in the overthrow of his murderers…

That wonderful sense of liberation, however, was tempered – no, *strangled* – by the slaying of the Archivist. What horrible consequences had that set in motion? Adaim had a peasant's respect and fear for Archivists. In spite of his elevation to the ranks of a soldier in Lord Shenri's household, and the modest authority that brought, he perceived that Archivists moved in the world like a force of nature – the wind, say, or the rain. You did not seek to understand the motives of the wind, or stand against its ancient power; it blew where it would and, sometimes, perhaps in response to the gods' plans or the Shae's whim, you were in the way at its fiercest. And when that happened, who could guess what the consequences might be? And yet this officer, this Pillio, seemed to comprehend, dared to question, dared even to stand against Archivists and their incalculable power, as if it were even possible…or indeed were his duty.

Such a man could not be easily measured, but might easily be underestimated. He was too remote, too disconnected from what was normal or expected. He appeared to doubt; yet beneath the doubt Adaim discerned an inner reserve of certainty – utter certainty – that most missed. Where all this might end, Adaim did not know, but his assumptions about the world had cracked, and the single remaining point of stability was the certainty he saw in the company commander.

Yes, he trusted him…

***

"Kiangsu, sir," Manei reported.

Pillio nodded, "Very well," and strode to the bows.

The city lay before them, four miles to the south-west on the furthest visible reach of the river, a dusty white smudge of structures that rose suddenly above the flat plains of Kiang, west of the Enlun Basin. In every direction, as far as the eye could see, villages and tilled pastures divided the land into neat symmetrical lines; fences and pathways stretched the perspective to limits deceptively distant. Huge nodding fields of luminous green hemp, cultivated for rope, stable bedding and medicines, encompassed foreshore and the furthest reaches. Further downriver, smoke curled from forge, factory and timber yard. On the riverbanks, separated here by a mile and more, jetties thrust out across the waters, black fishing nets strung from towering frames with the tiny figures of men labouring along their length like industrious spiders. Cargo vessels, roped together six at a time and loaded so heavily that their rotund hulls were almost completely submerged, coasted sluggishly down and upriver. Lethargic crews dipped their oars in the sunlit mirror of the Cise and paused to chat and gesticulate to their fellows across the water as the laden barges passed one another.

Pillio called Manei over to him. "Guardleader," he began, his tone carefully neutral. "Exarch Hassin will be waiting here. He will have soldiers with him, I have no doubt." His look became haunted and he added, "After all, justice must be done. He will take the prisoners…but the Strath soldier…" Pillio trailed off, awkward, as if he were about to suggest something inappropriate, another betrayal.

"…is at risk," Manei finished for him. "Aye, sir. I'm thinking the same. The galliot'll be watched when we dock. Best to get 'im off separate-like. Leave it to me." He looked directly at Pillio, then said with emphasis, "If we get asked, sir, in the city there" – a nod towards the port – "then it must be said, sir, that the poor Strath soldier died of 'is wounds. A day after Eslo's tomb, that would be. We put in to th'riverbank to see his soul delivered from the pyre. Right sad it was to lose 'im, right sad. The shipmaster – 'e'll confirm it as such. I *know* 'e will."

A shadow lifted momentarily from Pillio's face and he gave the guardleader a grateful look, then turned back to the bows. The shipmaster's new crew, innocent of the vessel's terrible secret, made good time, and it was not long before *Dust Devil* took its place in the queue of river craft jostling for entry to the new harbour. Finally, after some impressive handling by the shipmaster, *Dust Devil* tied up at one of the many wharves, overlooked to the south by the slate-grey high walls and towers of old Kiangsu, where bright blue and gold pennons fluttered in the breeze along the battlements, and to the north across the busy harbour by row upon row of taverns, flophouses, stables, and tall residential mews, many built upon the broken, re-used walls of the old city that stood here before Echrexar and obedient to the ghostlines of the age-old street plan. Painted as if their owners vied with one another for the brightest and most attractive facades, the waterfront buildings curved round the circumference of the harbour like an untidy rainbow. Reds, blues, greens and yellows made a startling backdrop to the hundreds of peasants, merchants, rivermen, officials, and soldiers constantly moving in the foreground.

The Ta-shih squad stood to attention in two lines on the open deck, in glittering drill order, between them the prisoners, both contemplating the variegated noisy world of Kiangsu with frank admiration. Manei spoke low words to the shipmaster, who leaned against his throne in the stern, an unreadable expression on his stalwart giant's face; but after a moment he nodded ponderously, even reluctantly, and the two shook hands. Turning away, the guardleader issued commands with trumpet-tongued decisiveness, and the soldiers busied themselves with unloading their kit, rucksacks for each man and a couple of large oil-skin duffel bags for cooking utensils and the like, manhandled onto the dock by a couple of troopers and then straight onto a four-wheeled handcart, pushed up close by a porter quicker than his rivals the moment *Dust Devil* had arrived. With handcart behind, piled with bags and bundled spears, the squad marched towards the city gate. *Dust Devil* was left behind in the bustle of harbour life.

The crowds parted for the Ta-shih. Those closest stared at the prisoners, bending their heads to comment to one another about the alien looks and braided golden hair. Pillio made his way to the front of the squad, Manei beside him. And abruptly there were soldiers in front of them, a squad of ten men in full armour, their officer bearing Sadon's trident insignia on his helmet of the elite Cherson Regiment of the Ta-shih headquartered here in the old city of Kiangsu.

The officer raised a hand to halt Pillio's troop. The crowds pressed close on all sides, sensing tension in the air. Beside the officer appeared the moon-face of Exarch Hassin, a visage of unyielding triumph and exultance. The world about Pillio blurred hotly, and he felt the weight of his armour like a terrible burden, and the resolution and conviction which had carried him through the last week collapsed.

The officer's voice was carefully weighted, "Company Commander Pillio?"

Pillio nodded dumbly.

"Commander Pillio, I am Detachment Commander Hanrab of the Cherson Regiment responsible for Kiangsu. I must ask you to surrender your weapons and your prisoners and accompany me. You are charged with the wilful slaying of an Archivist."

At these words a collective gasp broke from the crowd. Two soldiers moved towards Pillio. Instantly Manei stepped in front of his commander, fist on the pommel of his sword. The soldiers stopped.

Manei growled, "I beg the officer's pardon, but it may be the officer has only half the truth…"

Roused from his stupor, Pillio placed a restraining hand on the guardleader's arm. "I shall accompany Commander Hanrab." As Pillio moved around Manei he looked at him over his shoulder, his face hidden from the Cherson soldiers, and whispered with desperate urgency, "Do not involve yourself! Look to your safety and your men!" Then he tore his eyes from Manei, took four paces to the waiting soldiers, and unbuckled his swordbelt to hand it to them.

The prisoners, wide-eyed and tense, were ushered forward, staring nervously at Pillio and the black-robed Archivist. The officer gave his attention to Manei, displeasure in every frowning line of his face, and snapped, "Billet your men at the Cherson barracks in the city, then await instructions!"

Manei drew himself up with dignity. "Aye, sir."

Exarch Hassin meanwhile jerked from one foot to another, peering at the squad. "Wait!" he commanded. "There is another prisoner – a soldier, injured – from Strath. Where is he?"

Pillio, his face sombre, said at once, "He died."

Eyes narrowed, Hassin barked, "Hah!"

Manei interjected, "A day downriver from Eslo's tomb. We set a pyre at the riverbank, gave 'is soul to the heavens and not to Sadon's dark waters."

Hassin's features twitched. He moved again from foot to foot, then glared at the Cherson officer. "Send men," he snapped. "Search the vessel. *Dust Devil.* Quickly now. *Dust Devil*, down the dockside somewhere."

The officer frowned, gave orders to dispatch four men, who trotted off through the curious crowds. The remaining Cherson soldiers stood watching Pillio and his troops with suspicion, then, as time passed, boredom. The sun was hot. The gabbling onlookers began to drift away. Life resumed.

Finally, with Hassin still peering anxiously along the dockside, the soldiers returned. A conference was hastily begun between the troops, the officer and Hassin. At last, the officer, his expression having altered by degrees from brow-furrowed scepticism to nodding acceptance, turned to Hassin and half shrugged with the words, "Shipmaster confirms it."

Hassin's face twitched once more. He glared at officer, Pillio and soldiers alike, then appeared to conquer his agitation. "Very well," he declared, a thin smile compressing his lips before vanishing. "We shall see. Go on, go on."

The officer shrugged again, signalled his sergeant and, as his men closed ranks around the prisoners, orders were yelled, and the party set off towards the high walls of the city. Manei stood unmoving on the wharf and watched the tall, diminishing figure of Pillio for a long time, until the shifting murmurous crowds slowly flooded across his line of sight like the rolling waters of the Cise.

***

Fortunas watched this scene from behind the shoulder-high wheel of a wagon. He was dressed as a dockworker, black leather skull-cap over loose, hanging hair and wearing a waterproof cloak, ideal for the concealment of weapons and as common a sight in this city as to make him invisible. Between the press of gawping bystanders he watched the regimental commander make the arrest, listened when Pillio revealed the death of the Strath trooper, and observed the actions of the guardleader. As the Cherson guards and their prisoner moved off, Fortunas did not follow.

Meanwhile, the wagon, laden with stacked wine barrels, rumbled away, drawn by two oxen. Fortunas found a tall crate and leaned one buttock and leg upon it, as he had seen sailors hereabouts doing, took a short flensing knife from his belt and worked off a small core of sank-root, which he popped into his mouth to chew. All the while, he followed the activities of the Ta-shih.

Ten troops. Nine and the guardleader. The correct number. Normal Ta-shih deployment. Fortunas looked more closely as the squad hefted rucksacks in preparation for a second departure after the arrest of the officer. The porter, squat and affable, made some remark to the guardleader, a joke perhaps, before putting his weight onto the handcart. Then squad and handcart ambled along the curving dock. Fortunas nodded. "Ten," he murmured to himself. "But no Strath soldier."

A puzzle. Perhaps he *had* died. He scrutinised the squad more closely. The numbers were right. So, he asked himself, what was wrong? What was unusual? His eye was drawn to the handcart. The two heavy duffel bags. The spears, bundled, their sharp points wrapped. The party moved slowly past him, pressing between the crush of people.

Now he began to take an interest in the wider group of onlookers, dispersing after the arrest of the company commander. Fortunas was possessed of an exceptional gift for remembering faces. Like numbers. He admired the symmetry of numbers and tallied them with the same facility as he recalled the lineaments of someone's head: the overall shape of skull, jaw, bone structure, muscle, the tics and shifts of expression and, most important of all, the movement. People moved their heads and their limbs like a signature: erect, stiff, loose, tilted, afraid, cowed, wary and so on. Fortunas could recognize a signature instantly. When he did so, he would then detect the other features and their context and rapidly he would know when and where he had last seen the signature.

Scanning the milling crowds, he soon marked four individuals of interest. Three had been here, on the harbourside, this morning and the day before. One was a woman, selling sweetmeats from a cart. The others were men: an exarch, newly arrived, not hiding, merely watching from a distance; and two fellows working together, solid, professional types, concealing poniards and cudgels under their coats, probably hirelings of the exarch, muscle to execute the veiled policies of the Faith.

Satisfied, Fortunas moved away from his crate, stepping around the ox droppings and sauntering down the quay towards the city. Ahead of him the handcart moved more quickly, two soldiers pushing while the owner pulled the hitching bar, shouting at the crowds to get clear, and so steered through the traffic. The wide stone pillars and archway of the port gates with their scroll-work and decoration came and went, Fortunas blending into the crowd, pausing now and again to slice more sank-root and, at a public fountain, to scoop a drink of water from the trough. He had removed his skull-cap and his cloak, both now residing in a shoulder bag. He tied back his hair in rapid, fluid movements. He wore no sword – they were prohibited inside the city walls to all but Ta-shih – but he carried several hidden weapons, more than enough to end any hostile encounter. From behind the stone centre-piece of the fountain spout, fashioned as a sea monster, he looked back as he drank water, eyes picking up the faces and their unique movement. Of the exarch, there was no sign. The muscle were tracking the Ta-shih, the two men walking separately, doing an adequate job of not being noticed by the soldiers. Sweetmeats, however, was better. She had left her cart and her general concealment was good. Fortunas used the fountain as cover to turn away again and preceded the odd party along Stonemason Street. He knew the city quite well. His work took him to all the cities of the Realm. In this case, he could predict the course the Ta-shih would keep in order to reach the Cherson barracks, so he walked some thirty paces in front, doing what he mostly tried to do when following someone: stay ahead where they usually failed to check.

But he also hypothesized a stop somewhere. The odds were very good, allowing for the haphazard emotions of people and the random events that might always scupper or change…everything.

Sure enough, the Ta-shih stopped outside an inn, after a short detour down side streets, which had caused Fortunas to adjust his movements, hanging back to let the squad and the three spies pass him. He remained fifty paces away, with a corner in between – a break in the horizons of the eyeline that people naturally did not look beyond. A number of the squad went inside – four to be exact, Fortunas noted – and then a couple of the troopers emerged bearing cups of ale and the others filtered in and out in an apparently random manner, taking a drink inside or standing around the trestle tables in front of the tavern. In short, to anyone watching, there was a good deal of milling about, sufficient to hold the eye. The handcart porter accepted a drink with good humour, toasting the guardleader. A moment later the guardleader appeared to notice that the bulky handcart was in the way and directed a couple of his lads to move it around the corner into a side alley. Meantime, he put a hand on the porter's shoulder, steering him to a trestle table near the door, where they took their ease. After a time, the two soldiers returned from the alley and the guardleader sauntered inside.

Sweetmeats and the muscle stayed back, discreetly trying to blend in here where the crowds were thinner than on the high streets. In something under half a cycle, the guardleader reappeared from inside the inn and the squad downed the last of their ale, straightened themselves out and marched off with the handcart and the bags. But, as Fortunas was both particular about details and methodical in their analysis, he perceived that something had changed. At the handcart the soldiers pushing it had removed their rucksacks and loaded them aboard. But one of the duffel bags looked wrong. It had been moved. The spear bundle rested awry and the bag was a different shape.

Fortunas smiled. He had found the Strath soldier. The guardleader was canny.

Under the shade of a low awning outside a wheelwright on the street corner, Fortunas watched them go, the three observers in tow. They had missed their quarry. Once out of sight, he sauntered towards the inn. He mused on the ingenuity of the guardleader as he observed the front of the inn, absorbing every feature: a single entrance, double front door, the position of the windows, night shutters, the outside storm lamp, upper dormers and shingled roof. A single side alley, where the handcart had been moved, travelled to the rear of the inn. There were no other routes in or out. He ambled past a trestle table and four patrons sitting in desultory communion over their ale, and turned down the alley as if it were perfectly normal to be there. The alley ended in a high wall. To his right was an iron gate, fitted snug within the frame of the wall. Through the gate was the cobbled yard at the back of the inn, some timber storerooms, a glimpse of the solid wooden stable doors that secured the rear of the property.

Fortunas lingered, cut some more sank root, savouring the liquorice hit on his tongue, then strolled back up the alley and round to the porch, ignoring and ignored by the foursome at their drinking. He stepped inside the darkness of the taproom. The place was half full. Shafts of low afternoon sunlight cut the large saloon into quarters, dividing the patrons into haloed or shadowed denizens. Fortunas found himself a place in the bay window, back to the sun, his face indiscernible except from close by. A teenage potboy came over and bobbed his head as Fortunas set down his satchel on the bench beside him.

"Your best cider," he smiled at the lad. "A flask."

As he moved off, Fortunas extracted a small leather-bound book from his jupon. He undid the ties and opened it and, never once looking up, positioned it on the table to make the best of the light. It was a work entitled *Falconidae* and devoted to falconry. He leaned forward, elbows on the table, and appeared to read. He was, however, scanning the room, head unmoving. Methodically, he checked every person, those seated, the few standing, the bar-keep, the tavern owner supervising the opening of casks, the two servants at work and the potboy, returning now with a flask and a pewter cup. At the bar, a woman appeared, the tavern owner's wife, Fortunas surmised. Some particulars in the lineaments of the face suggested a family resemblance with the teenager. Father, mother, son, then.

A single patron sat alone at a table, towards the rear doors. An older man, it seemed, careful in his movements. He hunched over a cup, watching the room, glancing occasionally at the tavern owner with one eye, long fringe of hair covering the other. Something in the looks he gave the proprietor was anomalous. A suggestion of dependency, then? Was the innkeeper to help him? Why had the guardleader spent time indoors?

Fortunas paid the potboy, poured himself cider and sipped. All options were on, but each was dependent on timing and circumstances. Poison was preferable inside the tavern. Outside, well…

Fortunas pretended to read. But he watched the lone individual with an intense regard, studying his movements, understanding him. Clearly he was seriously injured, but in being seated carried himself in a way that might mask it. And the long fringe of hair, hanging over one eye…a wound? Evidently, Fortunas could discern with his close scrutiny, the effort to merely sit up cost him. Even in the dimness of the shadows, he had detected that it was actually a young man, but exhausted. Another option formed itself: if he could get the boy alone, in a back room or unobserved in the lanes, he could have the business done by hand. A crushed windpipe. Silent.

Fortunas contemplated these arrangements with dispassion, like the ordering of furniture in a room – by effect, function, position, suitability and ease. Meanwhile, he drank the cider, appeared to read his book and assessed the room. After some time, he closed the book and fastened the ties, slipped it back into a pocket and stood up. Then he headed for the door and stepped out into the late sunshine.

The Strath boy could have been a corpse by now. But Daved had been explicit about Sklavin's directive: stay close; watch; minimize our risk; do not intervene in the exarch's work; do the business if the exarch fails or the youth leaves the city. In his judgement, on the balance of the odds, the exarch had not yet failed – his assassins had merely lost the quarry. The youth had not departed Kiangsu. Was the exarch deceived? Would they return to the tavern? Unlikely. So now, Fortunas needed to place his assistants, three young street urchins and their adult handler, to observe and report. They had worked for him in the past. All was in order.

He allowed a rare smile. He could return to *Falconidae* and spend time with his peregrine. Her name was Peri. She would be hungry.

CHAPTER 8

Such is the reputation of the Clan Ehri, and such the strength of the Council at Chisua, that the cohesion of the Realm is guaranteed. It is a tribute to the dignity and wisdom of the supervisors.
First Supervisor Ke Geverti's address from the 'The Great Debates'.

The greatest danger is utter reversion, the abandonment of progress, of science, of striving. How can we replace what is lost if [...]
Fragment of a vellum document, dated by scholars to the century after Echrexar. The document itself is thought by some to have been deliberately burned.

***

It was summer in Chisua. The great city sweated under a humid miasma of smoke and light sea fog, with no breeze to clear the pall. Only on the heights of Monvar Hill, where the clan families and the wealthy merchants kept their homes in the capital, did the smallest of zephyrs stir the fountains and waterways, taunting lord and servant alike with the promise of a cooler night. Across the estuary, at Cise Hook, barely discernible through the heat haze, the pyramidal structure of the temple shimmered. Things were different underground. In the tunnels below the peninsular and in pitch darkness, it was quite cool. Grandmaster Tam, right hand to the smooth wall, left hand carrying the copper cage of his dream wanderer, marched through the chill of the underground maze to another meeting with Exarch Ataur. The two men met regularly in the dark chambers close to the gate of Cise Hook, in the place reserved to Tam, the scourge of heretics, for his use. Knowing that the So-Chiyen's eyes followed his moves, Tam maintained the usual security of keeping his cohort of spies from seeing or knowing one another or indeed knowing their master. As far as they were concerned, they served the Faith and the legitimate obligations of the Archivists and, sometimes, the Zaggisa, were the two in concert or unlikely to compromise the former. In any event, the public position of the Zaggisa was no secret, aggressive in pursuit of heretics and set firmly against the Ta-shih, and thus aligned with those 'reformist' factions in Council demanding a reduction in the taxes that funded the army. Latterly their influence was indeed supported in some quarters of the Council, where it coincided with the interests of provincial lords and noblemen of particular ambition. In all of this Grandmaster Tam had been assiduous. Thus, from Ataur he received his reports and through Ataur he executed his secret bidding.

On this occasion, as the oppressive heat of summer tested even the dark cool of the convening house near the massive gates of Cise Hook, Tam listened carefully to the information his intelligencers fed through Ataur.

"And what of Lord Shenri's daughter, the beautiful princess Keleu?" Tam demanded.

Exarch Ataur replied unhurriedly: "The Lady Che Keleu left here to return to Mamoba. By fast galliot it is a journey of five or six weeks. I am told she is nearing Kiang, halfway."

"And her mood?"

"She observed the mourning of both king and her father. Chisuan society rallied round in this time of shock and loss. She was well supported and behaved with dignity."

Tam grunted. He had not seen Che Keleu. He had not stepped beyond Cise Hook in fifteen years. But he had insisted on having portraits brought to him: she was exquisite. Magnificent. Hard for any man to resist. "What of Ordas?" he asked. "Has the legate set the appointed time for the petition of Choosing?"

"No. The new king knows. But the legate has yet to formally announce it in Council. The contiguity between Shenri's death and the petition may be somewhat awkward. Already there has been rumour and speculation concerning Lord Shenri's death. Chisua will feed off such scandal."

Tam waved his hand. "Use our influence to encourage him to announce it. Let Chisua seize upon the outrage. It is so crass and ill-timed a Choosing that people must believe it entirely innocent. Even so, for lack of better entertainment they will create such a fine rash of gossip that no one will be the wiser – including, perhaps, the So-Chiyen."

"As you wish, Grandmaster."

Tam lifted the copper bird cage close to his white face, gazing at the finch with unblinking eyes. The bird fluttered, disconcerted by movement and voices in this otherwise darkened room. Tam continued: "It is, of course, essential that the Council approve the marriage. You will need to plant that seed firmly in the heads of those supervisors loyal to us."

"We risk uncomfortable scrutiny if factions sympathetic to the Zaggisa are seen to espouse the marriage *en bloc*."

Tam nodded. Ataur made a good point, as he so often did. "Then let them be seen to be even-handed," Tam stated. "Ensure a motion is proposed by a reformist that the marriage cannot be approved unless it is agreed that a supervisor of impeccable reputation be despatched to Strath to officiate at the wedding. In this way, Council itself will believe it has acted wisely. The *more* Council embroils itself in scrutinizing the marriage, the *less* it will be able to oppose it. As for the supervisors, can you think of one that is suitable?"

"There are several such supervisors."

"They are bound to elect a senior."

"Then the choice is clear: he is a dull individual, but as yet incorruptible."

"The perfect choice. Who is it?"

"The senior Ke Beyil."

"Excellent. I know him. He will be deemed unprejudiced. Let's see if we can move Council to insist that he departs for Mamoba at once. With his reputation, the marriage will seem untainted and legitimate, even desirable for the stability of the Realm."

Ataur seemed only half convinced. "It will not be enough, Grandmaster.

We will still be exposed."

"I agree," said Tam with a haughty self-satisfaction. "I so value your caution, Exarch! It is a spur to our ingenuity. You must also unsettle the Council and the So-Chiyen's spies with excitements worthy of their attention! Arrange for a supervisor or two to address the Council, charging malfeasance or dissimulation, or even simple advantage in the matter of the murder. I have in mind accusations against Isharri of Allpo and against Ke-Wai Clan. That should raise some temperatures!"

Reflecting on this, Tam was unable to restrain a laugh. He added, "Of course such charges will come to nothing, but the efforts of the legates to dismiss them will stimulate enough suspicion to confuse the king's advisors and the sharper members of Council. *And* the So-Chiyen – and so divert him."

Exarch Ataur nodded, but only after a moment of hesitation in which Tam, at once divining incertitude, glanced at him sharply. Ataur at last started to speak, but was interrupted by the grandmaster's complaint: "You have not told me of the witnesses and Exarch Hassin's efforts."

Ataur resisted the temptation to play only on the good news. Tam demanded facts. He would make his own interpretations. Therefore he answered with candour: "Although the exarch has secured the two nomads and has contrived the arraignment of the Ta-shih company commander for murder of an acolyte…"

Tam raised a white eyebrow in admiration. "That speaks well of Hassin," he said.

"Yes…" Ataur hesitated again. "However, the Strath soldier, one of Shenri's bodyguard, is missing, somewhere between the Tomb of Holy Eslo and the city of Kiangsu."

Tam sucked his cheeks in. "When last we spoke," breathed the grandmaster, "Hassin had planned to help the soldier drown in the Cise, overcome by grief and guilt for his lord's death."

Ataur nodded. "At the village under the Tomb of Eslo."

"Well, that could hardly have been more auspicious. And yet he failed."

"He did, Grandmaster. The soldier was not aboard. Or…they did not find him."

"Perhaps the spirit of Holy Eslo was testing Exarch Hassin. Perhaps Hassin is wanting in his faith." Tam dropped his chin, glowering at Ataur as if to fill him with the zeal that Eslo might demand.

"Of course, Grandmaster," Ataur conceded. The prospect of the spirit of Eslo manifest in the world made him tremble with devotion.

Tam closed his eyes and opened them again, like an albino woodland owl. "And what of Yoiwa's master-intelligencer, Skava? Have we better news on his demise?"

"We do not know yet, Grandmaster. You recall the meeting with Exarch Hassin at Nek Feddah…with a man purporting to represent Skava. It is most probable that it *was* Skava and he soon after left the town. We have men working on his whereabouts. They have not failed before."

"Hmm. I am convinced that Yoiwa's master-intelligencer enacts a longer, more protracted, more veiled plan." Tam looked at the copper bird cage. He spoke, as if to the bird within: "In Conclave, our dream wanderers brought us blood. Across the land. From sea to sea and even *upon* the seas. The next day, at the embodiment of the Faith, the signs were not good. The animal did not die well. The blood of the sacrifice touched all three exarchs, an unheard-of event. Later, the So-Chiyen pronounced that this was more than augury, that it was a foreshadowing. What do the gods tell us, do you think?"

Ataur made a warding sign, right palm covering the back of his left hand. It was profanity for him to interpret such omens.

Tam held up his own hand, acknowledging the exarch's distress. "Forgive me, Ataur. I should not have voiced that question. But, you see, I fear the presentiments. For the Zaggisa, the Faith itself and, conceivably, the *world*. Echrexar cannot be allowed to return."

Again Ataur made the warding sign.

A grotesque rictus formed by Tam's white mouth indicated that he smiled. "Ah, my dear exarch! Bring me better news next time. We are equal to the task. Go forth. Go forth. We shall succeed."

***

Presently, at the Imperium and even in Ehri Palace, Ataur's spies and exarchs loyal to the Zaggisa went about their work, with the result that the great engine that was the Kiangsu civil authority lumbered a fraction further along the course contrived by Grandmaster Tam.

Meanwhile, within the high chambers of the temple at Cise Hook, the So-Chiyen received his adjuvant's reports.

"It is rumoured," explained Serep, "that Council will reach a decision on both murder and Choosing within the week."

The So-Chiyen, standing with his back to the tall windows overlooking the Cise Estuary, was a tall featureless silhouette, black against the daylight. "So soon?" he responded drily. "Such uncharacteristic swiftness!"

"Indeed. And yet the debate in the seniors' booths has been fierce. Ke Funir spoke for five hours, Ke Xehavi for three. Legates from Allpo, demonstrating a notable lack of discretion, addressed the Council at greater length than Ke Xehavi and were jeered by seniors and juniors alike. Only Clan Ke-Wai stood aloof from the clamour, and this because the Lord Racusal was present and would not permit his legates to answer the accusations. In the end, when tempers were cooler, he sought an apology…and received it."

"What of Council's decision? In which direction does the sentiment move?"

"That we await."

"Hmm. But they cannot fail to approve the marriage. Anything less would be seen to be partial, a lax and illogical slight against Lorang and Clan Ouine – and the wishes of the late Lord of Strath…"

"Whose votes in abolishing the mining levy the reformists in Council are keen to solicit…"

"Precisely. They would approve the marriage…" The So-Chiyen stepped away from the windows. "Were it not for Shenri's murder. The legates will fret over that and so will the supervisors. It cannot be ignored: that would be a miscarriage of the Council's justice."

The black hood turned, fixing on the adjuvant like a gigantic dark, insect eye. Serep endured this inspection without quailing.

"Given these circumstances, and given the nature of that species known as 'supervisors', it seems to me," said the So-Chiyen, "that Council will do that at which it excels. It will procrastinate. It will point no fingers. It will accuse no one. It will 'investigate' the murder, and on that pretext it can approve the marriage in the interim."

The So-Chiyen appeared to sigh. "And somewhere," he said, now thinking aloud, "somewhere in this, Grandmaster Tam gains advantage for the Zaggisa."

"I fear he does, So-Chiyen," Serep agreed cautiously.

"Of course. But the advantage will be temporary – the advancement of the Zaggisa's interests in this province or that, perhaps the discomfiture of the Ta-shih, or the subornation of half a dozen more supervisors to the reformist cause, perhaps even all of these things. But Tam's thinking is limited. He is driven by ancient hatreds and by fears of the Ta-shih. I know his soul: I underestimate him and the grandmasters by nothing so much as a single hair! Their dream wanderers whisper truth to them in the darkness, but like Tam they are flawed and look no further than the hatred or the love that binds them. Alas, that is the nature of balance – even for the Faith. They are necessary."

"Grandmaster Tam and the Zaggisa may become dangerous, So-Chiyen," Serep insisted.

The So-Chiyen had raised his hand, instant authority. Quietly he said, "Perhaps. But they are still instruments of the Faith."

***

Evidently, it was a crude hut. Dry reed bundles for the thatch; mudbrick walls with bits of reed sticking out. There was a pervasive rank smell of rotting straw and urine. Above, a black and red insect, maybe a flying beetle, was crawling slowly across the thatch, so slowly that its entire day must have been devoted to the task. From time to time it stopped, seeming to check its whereabouts, lost no doubt on this vast upside-down landscape – an insignificant spark of life even in the bounds of the hut, never mind the rest of the world outside. Skava could empathize. The little bastard was a microcosm of her own life. Except that he could actually move. Lost he might be, but he could make decisions: go left, go right, turn around, start again. Yes, fucking start again. That was the idea. Brilliant.

Every part of her ached. No, that wasn't true. Some parts hurt so insanely badly that it was like bits of her were trying to part company from each other. And she was thirsty. Not the thirst of the woman who has neglected to take a drink because she was too busy. No. The thirst of the woman who has not had a drop for a month, whose throat is raw, whose tongue is stuck to her palate and her teeth because there is no moisture to be had anywhere. And she was cold. The blankets laid across her were utterly inadequate, like someone had played a sick joke on a freezing woman. "Here, take this blanket. It won't make any damned difference, but wrap up well." She hated the world and everyone in it. She wanted to kill something or, better yet, *someone*. That would help. Definitely.

But first she needed a fucking drink.

"Muh-i," said her voice. She had tried *Maki*, but a stupid mumble emerged. Fabulous. She couldn't even speak. "Tyun," she tried next, thinking that *Yan* would be easier but discovering that her tongue had other ideas.

"Boss?" Maki, appearing at what passed for a low doorway and an impression of sunlight at his back.

"Fuddun dink," she got out with a combination of fury and concentration.

To his great credit, he had come prepared, and he pushed a wooden bowl onto her chin and tilted it to get a flow between her lips. When she could part her lips, she lapped at it like a dog, but without the same competence. Still, something wet was in her mouth. Maki had another go and they got a crude system going that delivered water to her throat. Maki was careful. He was avoiding giving her too much when all she wanted was to swallow a lake.

After a while, and no little retching, she worked her mouth and managed to produce something approaching human speech: "How long?"

Maki blinked horsey eyes and long lashes. "A seven-day," he replied.

"Balls," she said. Then, "I'm freezing."

"Sorry, boss. You were sweating buckets earlier." He found another blanket nearby and covered her.

"How am I?" Stupid question, given the impossibility of physical movement, the pain everywhere and her total obsession with drinking.

Maki gave a small shrug as if to say 'haven't a clue' but knew he needed to be somewhat more comprehensive. "Bleedin' stopped days ago. Wound front and back looked pretty bad, maybe infected, thought it would spread…from the look…uh…of the flesh." He meant a discharge of pus, no doubt. "Cleaned it up. It's raw, but I'd say the infection is down. Inside…"

He stumbled to a halt. Yes, inside – damned mess. It *felt* like a mess.

She held his eye. "Does the wound smell?" she demanded.

"Nope. Not now."

Well, there was good news. Even if she stank of piss and sweat like a sack of cats had been living under the blankets for days.

"Eyes?" The topic had to be broached.

He looked down, like he was party to a guilty secret and worrying about gods and demons. Couldn't blame him. "Uh…" he started. "Fine now." It took him some courage to say that, squirming as he was with the blasphemy of it – superstition or otherwise. And, face it, Maki was not the most pious of men.

"Sure?" she persisted.

"Sure," he acknowledged. "Maybe a tinge of…"

"Yellow," she said, to spare him, and to get it out there. Needed to be handled. If you spoke it, it had less power. "It happens," she explained, "when I get a bad injury. It's normal. Nothing sinister." Then she started lying: "Parents were the same. Healed fast as well. Lucky, I guess."

He looked slightly more comforted, like a little boy waking from a nightmare and being shown that no monsters were under the bed. She decided to go one step further: "I mean, Maki, do I look like fucking Echrexar?"

That got a smile. And a twitch of his face, the joke landing like she'd intended, unwinding the skein of credulous fears that lurked at the irrational core of who Maki was, who most people were. And so she moved the conversation on: "How are we fixed?" Safer ground. Back to business.

Maki visibly relaxed, even squatting as he was on haunches next to her. "Lost two mounts," he began to report. "Your roan" – she remembered the poor beast going down to a crossbow quarrel and Black Beard's sword – "and one of the other mares. But we picked up five of the mounts from the ambush."

"Mm. Any survivors?"

"Yep. Yan winged one and we had a chat."

"So who the fuck were they?"

"The one we chatted to swore blind they were down on their luck. Found out about the new mounts we bought and got an idea we was carrying a couple boxes of gold and silver. Ten hard men on three of us: very good odds."

Skava put on her unconvinced face. "We sure about that?" In her line of work, it was rather more likely they had had a paymaster directing things.

"We're not sure." Maki had his old mood back and he looked confident. "Yan recognized a couple of 'em from Nek Feddah. That much is true. But the one we took down squealed plenty. Kept sayin' only the boss man knew anything."

An uncomfortable memory made her guts twinge. "Black Beard?"

Maki compressed his lips and nodded.

"If they were a crew down on their luck, then how did they track us without Yan knowing?"

"'Cause they're good, boss. Four were locals, like the lad we squeezed. Know these parts, even the Kacia swamps, pretty well. Born trackers. No need to get close. Threw in their lot with the guard crew for easy pickings."

Maybe that was true. If not, no more to be done about it, however. "Is he still with us?" she asked, meaning the lad Yan had winged.

Maki pursed his lips. "In the swamp, boss. Wasn't goin' t'make it."

"Fair enough," she concluded. Though not for the bastard growing water weeds out of his skull. She looked hard at Maki. He wasn't quite telling everything. "Out with it," she demanded.

He winced. "Could be true," he shrugged. "But their kit was top-notch. Right weapons for a hard fight, or an ambush, or a long pursuit… And some coin. Plenty of silver – expenses an' such, I reckon." He was worried. No one liked assassins who were better than half good getting so close.

"So…" she breathed. "Let me get this right. Six assassins, well-kitted. Four local boys to swing the odds and do the tracking. And coin."

"Could be…" He looked miserable, like talking this out had made it true.

Her brain was starting to work properly again. Who had known she was in Nek Feddah? Big boy Desman she spent the night with and that Exarch Hassin. But with Hassin she had played a man and claimed to be Skava's courier. Fucking Archivists. Was she on their hit list now? Or was it just chance?

She grasped at an idea. "Any messages?"

"Not out *here*, boss."

The slow progress of the red and black beetle caught her eye again. "And just where is 'here'?"

"Out of the wetlands. Foothills. Crofter's hut. Abandoned. Maybe ten days south of Eloy."

Foothills, the thought landed. Out of the crater, away from misfortune and the wailing of that shrieking little girl.

"We're behind schedule," she complained and Maki nodded – the 'no kidding' nod people give when you've stated the fucking obvious. "Food going to last?"

"Our's will. The guard crew had plenty. Mounts are alright. Low on feed but grazing's fine."

Skava was now feeling too warm. She tried to lift her arm to adjust the blankets and every muscle in her arm, chest and torso screamed agonizing protests. She gasped and Maki looked concerned again. Panting, she subsided. "Need food, Maki," she managed to say. "Broth. Chicken, if you can find one. At any rate, meat." He was nodding. "And I have to move…"

"Boss…" He looked in pain himself. "Movin' you…" And he shook his head, a gesture of perfect eloquence.

"No!" she snapped. "Not *move* out of here. Get the limbs moving. I'm wasting. Need exercise. Slow but sure, every day."

Understanding now, Maki looked happier. "Right. But careful-like, boss. Don't wanna open the wounds. Or…anything."

"Yes, yes. I get it. And, Maki," she said, fixing his eye. "I need to get cleaned up."

Now he was unhappy again. Men…

***

It took another two weeks. Two weeks of agony, sweat and stiffness, her muscles and tendons contracting overnight only to go through the damnable stretching and flexing and pain the next morning. But she ate more and drank plenty. The range of her movement gradually extended. Her head was clear and she was thinking. The result was that twenty-one days after she went down to Black Beard's blade, she was shuffling around upright, Maki or Yan with an arm round her waist as she grunted and groaned with each tiny step. The fucking black and red beetle had long gone, the bastard. He had probably got sick of the sight of her.

Her left hip was painful. Her pelvis felt bruised or broken – maybe the sword had notched the bone. She had been pissing blood for a week, but now liver and kidneys were in working order, just slow. Weight loss had stopped. Maki said she had colour in her face – and not in her eyes. But she knew the rapid healing was costing her elsewhere – in pain, energy and a desire to sleep all the time. So she ordered Maki to wake her on a strict schedule in order to flex and stand and walk and go through all the same fun without fail every two hours, except overnight.

Meanwhile, Yan built timber steps, high enough to walk onto a saddled horse. Skava watched him from the doorway, her legs trembling like an old woman, as he hammered and cut and worked out how to assemble and disassemble them so they could be carried on the mounts. Somehow, she had to get on a damned horse. Maki jury-rigged a saddle on a fallen log, so she could practice getting astride it and sitting. First time, she nearly fainted. Maki had her firm anyway under the armpits, but they abandoned the idea because of the pain and reluctantly she agreed to try side-saddle on kit Maki had cobbled together from the other mounts, stripping harness and pommel and changing stirrups. That worked. It protected her left hip better but she felt like a damned fool princess sitting sideways on her new saddle on top of a log in the middle of a stony field. Maybe she'd never open her legs again. That would be a lesson, alright.

And all the time she burned with the intensity and frustration of a caged wild animal. Since leaving Nek Feddah, they had passed into mid-summer and she had been twenty-seven days blind. No messages coming in, none going out. That was too long. Tomorrow she would send a bird to Yoiwa, something straightforward, update on events, nothing to frighten the horses. In Eloy her people would have an established loft and she could get the birds moving both ways to check the important parts of the whole network, like what the exarch had achieved in regard to Pillio, the nomads and the Strath guard. Unfinished business. But first she had to get on a horse.

So she tried the next morning. Yan had his steps assembled and was holding the bridle, whispering calming nonsense in the ear of the most docile of the mares. Skava got to the top, grunting with the effort of lifting her feet, until her hips were level with the saddle. Here she turned around, getting her arse side-on and letting Maki guide her onto her seat. The mare stamped but stayed steady, and when Maki had helped her get boots into stirrups, she was set. A triumph. Here she was, the woman who was still trying to shift the whole fucking world, and she was celebrating the victory of getting her backside onto a horse. She could have wept. But instead she got the beast in motion, walking her to get used to the newness of having both legs stuck on one flank and the need to learn new ways to command and steer. She was astonished at how much the squeeze of her knees, one side or the other, in tandem with subtle bridle movements made the difference between riding well and riding badly. This was like starting again. And starting again gave her frequent flashbacks to when she was Eslin, learning to ride a horse, and discovering with some considerable surprise that the fabulous creatures from the posters on the wall in Svalbard that she had ached to ride were stupid fucking creatures that needed hours of care and would jump at their own shadow. Even though they seemed from a time before time itself, she couldn't shake the memories – clear as crystal, like they happened yesterday. She cursed them. She banished them. She hated that she had no control. So instead she concentrated fiercely on riding again, persevering through the sunny daylight hours, changing horses and clambering up the damned steps, until she had good control. The ache in her hips was bearable. The scabbing wounds were closed, livid purple scars healing up.

As the riding became easier, she had time to think. By rights, she should be dead. Anyone else would have died in delirious, gibbering agony. Well, *nearly* anyone else. But that was an imponderable, not worth worrying about now. What if she had died? She dismissed the thought. She had not. She'd been in this position before – worse, in fact. She had come through it. Eventually. More important was what she learned from this. There had been a string of cock-ups since taking out Lord Shenri. In a sense, she accepted the inevitability of unintended consequences, the small random errors that splintered off, spiralling out in different directions with their own momentum, because the scale of the effort to kill a lord and the public nature of it was bound to generate uncontrolled repercussions. No point trying to control that. What mattered now was to wrest control back: a degree more caution in everyday work, maybe pick up a couple more of her people from Honam so she could operate with more muscle, accepting the trade-off that working with a larger squad was safer but more visible; and also stand back from the driving need to intervene in critical things herself. Was that hubris? Did she believe no one else could do the job? Not always. Only the big things. But everything at the moment was big. They were poised, as they had been long ago. And she had learned then and in other circumstances, mighty difficult circumstances, that she had to have maximum control of the levers that mattered – especially now, when she had pushed to accelerate events, when she no longer had time and anonymity to plan, manoeuvre, adjust or simply wait for affairs to produce the right outcomes.

She worried too, in a corner of her mind, about Maki and Yan and what they had seen of her miraculous facility for recuperation and the change in eye colour, on top of her encyclopaedic knowledge. Possibly they suspected, as she was never short of gold, that she had hidden sources of wealth that were not owned by the Lord of Honam. Possibly. Would they reach that tipping point of greed or fear that would put her in jeopardy? It had happened before. But then she had been careless, afire with self-righteous zeal. And she'd had enemies, powerful enemies who had known who she was and where to find her and a bloody determination to end things. These days, for years now, she had been assiduous at fitting in, actually *being* the master spy, bending the knee to Yoiwa, constructing the shadowy false history that convinced those who sought to poke under rocks and dig among the worms that she was indeed the clever young peasant made good, toughened by poverty, family death and ruthless survival and utterly committed to the cause of Honam and the triumph of Clan Ouine.

She trusted Maki and Yan. She even liked them. And, on balance, since most things in life had to be fucking balanced, she believed they were loyal and would not falter – less because of her, though their steadfastness was substantial, but mostly because of their own allegiance to Honam. They believed in the cause – the cause she had engineered as the rightful inheritance of Clan Ouine. Still, all being said, she would not flinch from removing them from the field, should it come to that.

So she gritted her teeth against the pain and practised riding the damned horses, and then she told Maki and Yan they would move off the following morning.

***

"She has disappeared. Possibly gone to ground." Kesmet looked unhappy as he said this. Or rather, he looked more unhappy. Kesmet was never happy.

"Or simply changed identities," Harbin ventured. "She was always adept in that regard. And her role as a master-intelligencer plays beautifully to her skills."

Kesmet frowned. "Skava *is* a master-intelligencer," he insisted, refusing still to let go of his principles.

"Skava, Sklavin, Eslin, it is all one. You know it is."

"I do not."

Harbin sighed. He knew better than to bait his friend. "Very well. Skava." He turned to look across the wide reach of the river. Here in Ung they had built in stone and brick and ancient concrete: the fortified breakwater, the towers at the harbour entrance, the squat quayside and, above it, the battlements and loopholes of the castle and surrounding town, sturdy walls to every side. Stone, brick and concrete blocks were plentiful. The Chanee mines were north of here, and the spoil the breakers hauled from the ground had been and still was a ready source of material, conveyed by the barge-load on the back of the ceaseless river.

Harbin wore his black broad-brimmed felt hat with the silver band, a black and grey town coat and a scarf in the same colours, with a silver stallion rampant, emblem of the Kemae Bank, picked out in filigree and repeated in a pattern. Kesmet as usual wore his dark clothes, whose colours seemed to defy description: browns and perhaps greens in diagonals might be the dominant forms, separated by his leather belts and the arrangements of hunting knife and sword in scabbard. A dark cloak hung from one shoulder. Economical. Kesmet was economical, in clothes, physiognomy and speech. He blended. Or dominated.

They stood together, both men, overlooking the wharves, a gentle breeze tugging at Harbin's hat, rippling the brim. Zuse sat erect and powerful next to Harbin, head still but eyes roving. It was late afternoon and the rest day of the week, with a minimum of traffic and activity down here. Inside the town, things were different. Families strolled. Itinerant actors performed. Stallkeepers sold their grub. The city square would be full. Life was there to be lived. Wages to be spent.

"Tell me again," said Harbin, "of the last reliable news."

"A gang of ruffians," Kesmet answered mechanically, "persuaded to trail her by four locals. Word is they thought she had gold and was easy meat."

"But no information on the direction they took?"

"No. And none of them has returned."

"So she turned the tables…"

"Or they got rich and are living well in another town."

Harbin gave Kesmet one of his looks: arch scepticism.

"I know," Kesmet conceded. "Unlikely. We would have heard. The locals, at least, would have come back to Nek Feddah."

Harbin resumed his survey of the Cise River beyond the massive stone mole of the breakwater. It was a pleasant vista. The air was mild, almost sweet smelling, like fresh pine. A few high cirrus clouds were painted gold and orange to herald day's end. To the river, if not his companions, he said aloud, "What does she want?"

Neither Kesmet nor Zuse gave answer.

It was approaching sunset and the in-between time would soon see people heading for doorways. Harbin put his back to the river and all three repaired to the inn they had occupied a week gone. It was a fine establishment, quite to Harbin's tastes, a solid structure with good sized rooms overlooked on one side by the high concrete and granite walls of the castle, and on the other by the main square, itself a pleasant greensward with plane trees bordering the neat paved pathways, a parade of shops to either verge. Harbin watched the sunset from his room. He enjoyed sunsets. But he enjoyed dinner even more and, this accomplished in the company of Kesmet and Zuse in a private dining room, he again asked the question, "What does she want?"

This time, it was apparent to Kesmet, he wanted an answer. They had played the game before. Somehow it helped Harbin to make sense of complexity. Kesmet did not see how. It was too conceptual for him, a caper with shadows and ghosts. But he had learned to go with it, for inevitably Harbin reached some insight or decision. And then their course was reset. He could have few complaints on that score.

"What she always wants," he answered, in time-honoured fashion.

Harbin waved his wine goblet side to side to register his disagreement – and his delight that Kesmet was willing to engage. "Which is what, exactly?" he challenged.

Kesmet leaned back. The chair was comfortable. The wine they had taken was excellent. His sword in its scabbard rested tip to floor and crossguard against the table edge, within easy reach. The windows were closed but still offered the ruby glow of sunset. He was relaxed. The contest could proceed.

"Power," he said, knowing that this would not satisfy Harbin.

"No," came the immediate riposte. "Power is a mechanism for her. She uses power. Her motivation is much deeper. We are all similar…you, me, Eslin–"

"I think not."

Harbin raised his left hand, seeking to be humoured. His right still held the goblet. "We *are* similar. Perhaps not you. Who knows what drives you?" This, with the arch of an eyebrow.

Kesmet kept his face blank.

"But Eslin and I…" Harbin insisted, "well, we *are* similar. We want a route back to…" Harbin paused, thoughtful. Then he finished: "A route back or a route forward to…I was going to say 'what was'. We have always believed in regaining what we lost. But that is vanity. That is the vanity of people. Do you remember? When things settled, we had dreams – hah, a poor word, these days! We had aspirations, honest hopes. With the hindsight of so much time, so much reflection, it is still attractive to imagine rebuilding that world, especially after…what happened…what was lost."

Harbin took some wine. Tonight his youthful features were set more grimly. He was maudlin. No, not that. Intense. Searching for truth. Kesmet was intrigued. The game had gone beyond a game.

"But I was talking," Harbin pressed on, "of vanity. My vanity – and Eslin's even more so – was to build again what we had. Oh, not exactly the same, but as much the same as we remember – chiefly the essence of what was good. And so much was good." His expression became both troubled and wistful as he continued: "Perhaps we have…forgotten, Kesmet, what mattered so much. You know as well as I that when you are long-lived, very long-lived, and you have got past the terrible weariness, the imminent death of your soul, and you have determined that you wish to go on living – no easy decision, eh? – and when you have decided to go on, and so much time has passed, your head is filled with the fact of the world as it has *become* and your choices are both thinner and more varied."

Kesmet frowned.

Harbin pressed on: "Thinner, because eventually you recognize you cannot *go back*. More varied, because you can experiment. You can try things. As Eslin has tried things and keeps trying. If it is her, if this Skava is Eslin, *if* it is her – and I am gracious enough to respect your sensibilities in this – then she has taken her time and used it well. And *we* have been asleep. She has made sure to command resources and people at depth… But I repeat myself. I was talking of motivation. I was talking of vanity."

Harbin leaned forward, an imposing man when passion or imagination fired him. "Here's the thing, Kesmet," he said, as if it were a legal stipulation. "We are different, Eslin and I, in one thing. Her vanity is that she will shrink from nothing to make real her idea of a return to what was. Nothing. She was not always so. But now…well…" He frowned, before changing tack: "For her part, she would call me an idealist and perhaps that is *my* vanity. I would call her a tyrant. Is that the right word? Tyrants were welcomed in the ancient world, were they not? Elected, even. I think so. Some at least. But tyrant is not the right word. She wants what was lost. There is good in that."

"Not at any cost."

"Agreed. But we all wanted something good…still want something good. How, then, did we become enemies?"

Kesmet shook his head. This was a new direction. He spoke coldly: "She made herself our enemy by hunting us. By killing our friends. She wanted us excised from the world."

"That is true. We were in the way. We *stood* in her way. We tried to prevent her, remember. We made the choice. But still she wanted what was right for humanity."

"She murdered. Have you forgotten already? And not a month gone, in Sohanyun, our man was tortured and his head returned to Lord Ordas." Kesmet blinked once slowly, then added, "*If* it is her. I still doubt it–"

But Harbin had seemingly not heard. "It goes to the point," he mused.

"Our aims are aligned. We believe in the same things – mostly: the value of knowledge, science, progress, although perhaps not at the same pace. Eslin was always in a hurry."

"And yet she caused the hunters of heretics to be forged. When you created Etil–"

It was Kesmet's turn to be interrupted. "I did not create Etil," Harbin countered quietly.

"We had reason to encourage him. Our influence at times is more direct than you care to think."

Harbin looked hurt, genuinely hurt. Kesmet knew that this was painful. Even when Kesmet used the word 'we', Harbin was not fooled. He had, on occasion, acted unequivocally, powerfully, to move events, to start things. Kesmet had helped, but he was only ever an actor, never the author.

"I try not to intervene. I have tried to do the right thing," Harbin said. It sounded like an apology.

"You have. *We* have. But she had no such restraint…"

Harbin put down his goblet. He reached out with his right hand below the chair's arm and immediately Zuse's head came up. Harbin patted the hound, a light touch full of affection, perfectly understood by the dog. "Is that the difference, then?" he asked, his voice still subdued.

"For me it is," Kesmet confirmed. "She will kill, slice, maim her way across this Realm, or anywhere for that matter, in pursuit of her ideal – rebuilding 'what was' I recollect you called it. I still think she loves the power. It always struck me that she had convinced herself, or been convinced in some way, that she was…I don't know…a god." This seemed to trigger a thought, which he put to Harbin in a cautious query: "You don't think she is searching for weapons?"

Harbin looked at him under his brows. They both knew what he meant. "Unlikely," he countered. "Those that survived are all long gone, lost, buried, displayed in museums, broken for scrap, destroyed by flood and fire."

"But it's possible."

Harbin exhaled. "It's not *impossible*. But I think we would know. After all, nothing has been found for many decades. Nothing useful. And the Faith proscribes the concealment of such artifacts, as you are aware."

"We don't know everything. There are places still buried, perhaps still intact, uncontaminated…"

Harbin shook his head, but conceded enough to say, "I shall think on it."

"Hmm." Kesmet played with his wine goblet, turning it so the liquid swirled. "As for the woman we discuss, *if* she still walks among us, I say she wants to control everything. She gives nothing."

Harbin looked at him, a pain in his eyes that Kesmet had not witnessed for what seemed like a lifetime.

"Perhaps she *gives everything*," Harbin breathed, a faraway look crossing his features like a cloud before the sun. "Perhaps she always has – the slave of humanity, the sacrificial god. She gives everything, and we do not. She intervenes directly, uninhibited. We stand back. We move in and out of the world." A sigh. "And that is my contention, my dear friend," Harbin stated with some emotion. "Would it not be better if we stood aside?"

Kesmet stared at him. He was surprised, actually surprised. The fact of who they were and what they did was so fixed, so much a part of his existence, that Kesmet was forced to confront himself to accommodate this new perspective. But the words that formed on his lips were protest: "She has killed our friends, Harbin! She created the Zaggisa. She is…" He hesitated.

"Evil?" Harbin finished the sentence, with some emotion. "You know better. Leave that to the Faiths. And as for murder, have we not blood on our hands?"

Kesmet flicked an arm, a gesture of dismissal. "Not murder, but yes, blood. Her worst lieutenants. She forced the choice we made. I would do the same again."

"And Eslin herself…"

"Aye, Eslin. And I thought we had succeeded." Kesmet tapped the table top with his fingers, like a curse he would not voice. "Or perhaps we did. And this woman is just Skava, Yoiwa's master-intelligencer, brilliant, gifted, ambitious and homicidal. But Skava. And in time, she will be gone."

Harbin smiled, but not with any pleasure. "Refusing to name her does not make her go away. You know it is Eslin."

Kesmet gave silent demur. Instead he drank wine. It no longer seemed excellent. "So," he asked, knowing it would nettle Harbin but equally that they needed to be unambiguous. "Will we stand aside?"

But Harbin was cleverer than that. "I know *you* will not," he said. And Kesmet understood that to be true, even if he had not properly considered it. "As for me, you have helped me see deeper. My fear is that Eslin is our enemy *only because she is our enemy.* Maybe we helped make her that. But our aims have always been the same. If that were all, we should stand aside. But our methods are different. And I have begun to articulate what I think I have known for some time now. In the end, her obsession with rebuilding what was lost leads her to ventures that are wrong, that warp the world, that make a kind of scaffolding in society to oppress and undermine the harmony of civilization, its striving and its necessary conflicts too."

Kesmet interjected, "Is this not what I moments ago conveyed? That she seeks only control, at any cost?"

"It is. You are cleverer than you pretend. You are a philosopher at heart."

"No, I am not."

"Well, you have helped me. I see it clearer now. It is means and ends. Our ends are the same. The means are different and–"

"Hers will not help deliver the ends," Kesmet concluded.

Harbin sat back, a smile playing on his lips. "There. You are indeed the philosopher!"

Kesmet grunted. A happier conclusion had been reached. But what was unsaid was not happy. They both knew it. They never spoke of it…until now. How could they speak of their purpose without destroying it? Eslin's purpose had not wavered: it kept her moving, committed, ruthless… alive. And Harbin and Kesmet's purpose was to stop her. If not, they had no purpose.

Would it not be better if we stood aside? Harbin had asked the dreaded question. And they had skirted it.

***

Two days later, at the ornate writing desk in his room, Harbin settled himself in the wide leather chair. He faced the windows and the view across Castle Square. It was morning, and sunshine streamed through the open sash, like bright inspiration. The air was fresh and cool; mountain air from the north where the Alnaes soared skyward, black, grey and white. He was alone. Kesmet had gone out the day before, with Zuse – *scouting*. They both needed to run, to be in the world, to be part of it. Where the countryside or the streets of the city were Kesmet's habitat, Harbin's was inside his head. He was entirely comfortable there. It was ordered and clear, and he had learned the disciplines to understand and control his emotions. And yet, he was not cold, nor aloof. He knew this. People warmed to him because he could be emotional. He could touch people with enjoyment, with humour and optimism. Sometimes with sorrow.

Today, he needed calm and distance. He needed the flat expanse of the desk, the open sash windows and brilliant sunshine. Upon the desktop was a large sheet of heavy paper. Upon the sheet was a finely crafted black lacquer and silver fountain pen. It was ancient and heavy. The specially cut nib had been replaced many times, as had the piston filling system. Harbin kept spares, acquired from craftsmen closely copying the originals at great expense, in the offices of the Kemae Bank in locations across the Realm. But it was the silver and resin barrel that was the marvel, embellished with representations of the Long Wall and ships of old Venito.

He picked it up, unscrewing the pen, the nib gleaming like a fine sword point. In the centre of the paper he inscribed 'Eslin', and then across the top of the page a sketched map of Honam, Lorang, Strath and Allpo. He marked each province that had fallen or might fall under her sway. He drew an outline of the Cise River down the centre of the page, culminating in Chisua and Cise Hook towards the bottom. He wrote 'Zaggisa' next to Cise Hook, then above Chisua he added a triangle, with 'Council', 'Archivists' and 'Ta-shih' at each corner. He paused and inserted 'King' in the centre of the triangle.

He sat back. He stared at the triangle and imagined the removal of one of the names. When he looked at 'Ta-shih' he nodded. Expensive, weakened, bureaucratic, corrupt in its upper echelons, it was under attack from Council reformists and noble clans. He pondered the world as he imagined Eslin would. He circled Ta-shih, scratched a neat line through the circle, sat back and took in the whole picture. Then he stood up and, bending across the emerging landscape, began to fill in the surrounding provinces, noting their current allegiances, their reformist leanings, their known or probable military strengths, mostly negligible except for Kiang of Clan Ehri, the king's royal family.

An idea struck him. He looked out of the windows, closed his eyes, opened them, and jotted down black circles in four sites to represent the known refuges from before Echrexar. Dissatisfied, he raised his head to stare out at Castle Square again. The morning traffic moved noisily around the perimeter. Citizens walked the greensward. It was a place of normality and peace. However, the worm of a thought worried at the edge of consciousness. He noted it, unformed as it was, then looked at the limits of the page and added with flourishes of his gleaming pen the broader world, scattered, broken, beyond the Realm – the tribes and thriving nomadic peoples, the struggling communities and uncertain trade routes. He had seen them all, to the north over the landbridge and across the oceans. They mattered, but the Realm mattered more. Because Skava/Eslin was here. This was the board upon which she moved the pieces written in Harbin's flowing script, items of her accounting, debits and credits to her name, enlarged or struck through like a balance-sheet of power.

Harbin read the pattern and a knot of fear lodged like a creature of writhing tentacles in his gut. She would move these pieces, some of them, to deceive him. And with Eslin, anything was possible. She was never predictable. She was brilliantly creative... But there was a pattern, intricate, conceptual, organic.

He had learned two things. One emerged from the page: the black circles of the refuges. As yet it had no meaning, only possibilities. The other came from the view outside: the busy tranquillity of Castle Square. She would hate it. It was both substance and symbolism. In this alone, he could predict her. But even the vagueness of that predictability made the tentacles of the creature in his gut squirm.

She would want to provoke and agitate and control. But how – and why?

***

At last the network was responding. Birds were coming in and going out. After two weeks on the road and a week in old Eloy, Skava had some control. Yoiwa had returned to his capital, Deka. The Choosing had been formally announced. Approval would be automatic, once the Council's appointee, Senior Supervisor Ke Beyil, reached Mamoba and satisfied himself of the legitimacy of the late Lord of Strath's intent and the dispositions of the various parties. Yoiwa and Mathed would journey to Strath for the wedding ceremonies in the autumn, and Skava would rejoin them then, becoming Courier-sergeant Alin once more, and therefore *inside* Mamoba, with access to the Council supervisor and both Prince Osir and the Lady Che Keleu.

Down south, Exarch Hassin had got the Ta-shih commander arrested – an outcome of remarkable manoeuvring. Skava was impressed, even if the exarch had lost the Strath trooper. It amused her that, by contrast, Fortunas had picked him up in the city so early. All in all, that threat seemed neutralised, if delicate. She could not have Fortunas act against the trooper yet: it might signal there was more to Lord Shenri's murder than the greed of nomads; and might therefore prevent the union of the clans of Honam and Strath. If Pillio was tried and found guilty, he would be executed – an end to things. Fortunas merely needed to keep the trooper in sight.

If it were not for assassins trying to kill her, paid for it seemed by her own allies among the Archivists, she might revel in a period of satisfaction, content that even without her hand constantly at the helm, her fleet navigated difficult waters, as she had planned. That had to count for something. She had leverage across the Realm. Her people acted as she intended. She could afford to step back, to think beyond the immediate campaign and concentrate a substantive effort on Allpo. And find out who the fuck was spending gold to see her dead…

Meanwhile, Maki and Yan slipped into the life of the walled town of Eloy with practised ease. Their subterfuge was a familiar one: guards for a merchant house distributing fish oil from the west coast of Honam. Under that guise they could lodge at the small barracks adjoining the sprawling depository, where four of the regular guards were part of Skava's dispersed squad anyway – not the best, but solid. Maki and Yan exercised in the yard, alone or paired up, wrestled in the gymnasium and took long runs around the perimeter walls of the merchant warehouse. Such was their discipline that they were not daunted by the especially pungent smell from a nearby tannery at the northern end of their route.

Skava limped. She knew she was healing, but it was slow. Proof, she acknowledged, that the wound had been awful – fatal to anyone else. She was fitter and could sit a horse without having to climb Yan's damnable steps or sit side-saddle, god forbid. She walked a lot, practised arms with Maki and Yan, and even did some drill with the other squad members. It was not clever to spar only with fighters you knew. That bred bad habits and smug complacency. Thus, they had at each other with staves and wooden swords, heavy enough to take the breath away and bring up a nasty bruise and, critically, teach anew the muscles and reflexes that had been neglected. The exercise, sweat-soaked and strenuous, was what they all needed.

Information about the household at Mamoba filtered in. Skava ran two spies on the estate, paid informers so not ideal. Maki drew the strands together and one evening reported to her in an upstairs office of the depository.

"Prince Osir," Maki was saying, "is a hothead. Not stupid. Young and educated and been in Chisua for long spells. Prefers Strath."

Skava paced the floor rhythmically, across one blank wall and back. Two things to accomplish: get the fucking hips working again and absorb every detail of the characters and life at Mamoba. Maki sat, forearms on knees, watching her route. He had taken his jupon off and wore a loose smock, so that the braided leather necklace sporting a large pearl in a silver setting was visible – the talisman he wore to impress the ladies. God knows he needed something to distract them from his equine muzzle. Three storm lanterns cast enough light to make the timber-walled room almost cosy. A heavy table, unadorned, occupied the space under a wide window, now shuttered, that looked out onto the inner courtyard. On the table was a large glass flask and two goblets, as yet untouched. Juniper berry brandy. For serious drinking. But first, they needed to work.

"Younger than the princess by a couple years. Mother taken in childbirth. Lord of Strath took no second wife. A few local women over the years…like most nobles…hush-hush. No bastard offspring. Osir hates Honam. Didn't always see eye-to-eye with his father – and we know Shenri opposed Honam in most Council votes but he was smart…in a political way. Wanted Clan Ouine on side–"

"Hmm," Skava interrupted. "Know all that. What of the girl?"

Maki took a breath. "She's a beauty. And clever. Spent time in Chisua. A thinker. Educated. Seems won over by Prince Mathed. Bit like her old man: political. And would never go against him. The letters we wrote under Strath's seal seem to have done the trick…"

People want to believe what suits them. Skava had laid short odds on that – on many an occasion. Clever the girl may be, but she was a young woman. She wanted her Prince Mathed. She would convince herself it was her father's actual wish. "She and her brother – close?" she asked.

"Close. But he's no friend of Honam, as I said. Polite to Mathed, but curses our Lord Yoiwa."

Skava grunted again. "Do we have anyone close enough to either of 'em?" She meant to gain some influence.

"Nope."

Skava stopped pacing and stared at him. "Find out who her women are – ladies in waiting, maids, that sort of thing. Osir is our problem. He can make trouble with the supervisor. I don't want slip-ups. If we get close to Keleu, we control the marriage. If we work things right with Osir, we get him isolated."

A series of ideas clattered together in her head. She resumed her limping, trying to take a little more weight on her left hip, driving her body to discipline while she ordered her thoughts.

"How many troops can Strath field?"

Maki was taken by surprise at the change of course, but answered briskly: "The household is down eighteen from the ambush, including the spymaster. Sixty available at the keep."

"And if they muster?" She was worried about Osir whipping up sentiment against the marriage, calling in favours across the province from nobles loyal to their dead lord.

Maki shook his head. "Good fighters? A hundred. With sheep herders and farmers, another ten score." Without intending to, he had sounded scornful.

Skava, of course, missed nothing. Again she stopped, turned to face him. "Sheep herders and farmers," she said acidly, "can stick you with a spear same as any fucker with a history of killing as a long as your arm. This is about numbers, Maki. If Osir has the brains to work it out, he can raise numbers to swamp the few we'll be able to bring into Strath legitimately without shouting to king and fucking Council that Honam is conspiring against the Realm! We need the gorgeous Che Keleu to fall into the arms of our handsome Prince Mathed and convince Osir to keep quiet or fuck off. We need to know who the nobles are who'll swing Osir's way. We need to know how many they could muster, and we need to know what sort of weapon stocks they hold."

Maki was sitting up. "Aye, boss."

Skava gave him a sidelong look, half relenting. "Important, Maki," she told him, without the spark of anger that had just singed his pride. "We get it *all* right this time. We nail the advantages and we stack the odds. So I need detail…but–"

"Without drawing attention," Maki finished, keen to bury the last little conversation.

"Exactly so."

They talked further. She built a picture of Mamoba, its family, its servants, its soldiers, the economy, possible debts and who the bankers were. She pondered its history as Maki gave his views. Her plans were sound, but she tweaked some and laid foundations for contingencies. A long time later, maybe a cycle or so before midnight, she broke the seal on the bottle and poured the brandy, high quality alcohol from around Eloy – but lethal stuff. It sent fire through her chest and abdomen, but a good fire, a welcome heat that did the job of taking her tension down several notches and allowing the two of them to blow away the madness of the past six weeks – especially Black Beard's last act with a sword and the agony of her recovery. Drinking the brandy felt like an ending, closing the chapter on a tricky passage. She was oddly pleased. No one had killed her yet, even if they seemed to be queueing up again. If she hadn't been such a sceptic, she might have believed in fate or some shit-faced gods standing at her shoulder. Maki did.

Thunder rumbled overhead and a heavy rain fell. The storm lanterns cast their yellow glow and the brandy worked its timeless magic on body and brain. They talked of stupid inconsequential things and those of slightly more import, like how they set the ambush for Black Beard and his crew and what had worked and what went wrong. Unlike most fighters or soldiers of Skava's experience, her squad didn't exaggerate the skirmishes or their role in personal combat. Professionals.

"Was one back," Maki opined, not slurring but maybe half cut. "Scout up front an' one back. Maybe thirty paces. Should've known."

"He the one that charged me?"

"Aye."

"Would've had Black Beard otherwise. Nine-tenths dead anyway. I got him across the thigh. Femoral artery. How did the fucker stick me? How'd he have the strength?" She was genuinely intrigued, in an angry sort of way.

"You fell towards 'im. Blade up, 'e couldn't miss. Near dead men're like snakes. Fuckin' dangerous."

"My experience, they bawl a lot – usually for their mothers."

"Some jus' want to take you with 'em. Like snakes, hissing and biting."

"We got 'em all, though."

"Did. Close though."

"Close," she agreed, and poured more brandy for both of them.

Maki looked at her like a horse weighing up a high fence – not keen on making the leap. Uh-oh: Skava knew he wanted to say something difficult. That was fine. It was why they drank, in part anyway. "Boss…" he started. "You got lucky. Damned lucky. Never seen the like." He took a gulp – not a clever trick with brandy like this. Rolled the liquid in his mouth and managed to get it down. Tough, was Maki. She wanted to laugh. "So, boss…" he came around to his point. "You gonna step back?"

She gave him a level stare, not yet too pissed to manage that. "Some," she conceded.

He looked uncomfortable still.

"You think I'm slowing up," she challenged him. Not a question.

"Boss…"

"Sure," she said, calm. "We fucked up. A few times. In my experience these things come in threes. We've had our three, Maki." Threes, fours, whole fucking battalions of cock-ups. They did seem to run together.

But, from his expression, that wasn't the point.

"What?" she demanded.

A look at his goblet, a glance at her. "Next time…"

"Huh," she grunted, understanding percolating through the brandy fumes. "You think my luck's out? Dian turned her back on me? Maybe half the gods? All the gods? Shae got me in his sights?"

Maki flinched. It was real for him. He was no devout believer, but even trained killers have their crude convictions. Dragging a little luck your way was a no-brainer. She immediately pulled back. "Sorry," she offered through her teeth. Maybe it wouldn't propitiate the gods, but it might soothe Maki.

"Just saying," he muttered.

"I know. But hear me, Maki. This is too important. More than you can know. I don't do this for me. Not for me–"

"I get it, boss…"

She shot a sharp look at him. "You have no idea."

He looked like she had struck him in the face. No matter. Her fury was up. "It's not enough, Maki," she growled. "It's not enough to do your best. Life or death for you or me or anyone else simply does not matter. We came too close, Maki. Far too fucking close. And now we're sleepwalking and pretending that dreams can guide us. It's all taken too long. And we seem to be going backwards. I thought I could turn it around. What if we're going backwards? What then? It wouldn't take much." She was rambling, and the part of her brain that was fighting the alcohol told her so. "We were nearly gone – the lot of us," she added, as if that would explain everything.

"Yes, boss. We lost that war. But we'll–"

"Not the war, you idiot! Long before! What if Echrexar is coming back?"

Maki jerked his head away. A voice in Skava's head was yelling *careful!* She wanted to scream that she was sick of being careful, and that these pricks around her needed to wake up. Maybe with pure unadulterated rage she could shatter illusions and fears and…and…what? With the utmost effort she tamped down on her fury, stood up, swaying some. She turned to the shutters, unlatched and swung them open. The smell of rain and cool air and ozone flooded over her in a great wash of a thousand thousand memories. Abruptly the blackness outside ripped open with silver threads and a crackling detonation as lightning blasted across the night. She flinched, and she was Eslin and fearful. Then it was black again and blown rain made a sheen of fine droplets on her face whilst the thunder boomed and echoed through the town.

"*When shall we three meet again…*" she muttered to the night, "*in thunder, lightning, or in rain? When the hurly-burly's done, when the battle's lost and won.*"

When she turned, Maki was blinking at her like he'd learned something new but wasn't sure what. What could she tell him? She had tried in the past – with others. It just made her a threat. People envied the gods and feared them. They were terrified of what they couldn't understand and generally they killed it or, worse yet, *worshipped* it until some other fucker killed what was worshipped. It was impossible to be a living god – impossible and a curse. A curse of unique horrors. She could not tell anyone. She could not trust anyone. *Gilgamesh.* Accept your fate. The gods will not help you, even if you are two-thirds god yourself. Perhaps that was what her mother had meant in Svalbard – on a day in an age long vanished, but as clear and as undeniable as yesterday.

Slowly she closed the shutters, a drawing down of her fury and her impotence against the black and argent blast of the world outside. Encompassed by the timber walls of the room and the familiar cocoon of the yellow storm lamps and the startled, unhappy face of Maki, Skava was calm again. Here she could exert control. Here she could make a difference. Embrace the complexity, move in stages, in increments, as slow as you dare. More haste, less fucking speed.

It would be on her tombstone.

CHAPTER 9

There is a madness in love,
As destructive as a thousand swords...
'Prince Reu's Daughter – A Drama'.

But the day of the Lord will come as a thief in the night, in which the
heavens will pass away with a great noise, and the elements will melt with
fervent heat; both the earth and the works that are in it will be burned up.
Surviving fragments of the book of Petra from the great Biblos of
Kristum, the old religion of the north and west, now supplanted by the
true Faith. One of many prophecies of Echrexar. Copied by a scribe,
IYE 1067.

***

The following month in Strath Province, on the chalk track that led east
from the late Lord Shenri's estate, Mamoba, two peasants removed their
hats and bowed deeply as a lone horseman, neither slowing his speed nor
acknowledging their tardy courtesy, thundered past. He continued out
of their sight, disappearing through the trees that ringed the nearby hills.
Moments later, had the peasants chanced to look back, they would have
seen horse and rider, black against the morning sky, plunge furiously up
a ridge that formed a natural access from the lower slopes to the hilltops.

Along the highest part of the ridge the horseman spurred his mount,
ignoring stands of blackthorn that snagged his gabardine breeches and

caused the roan to twist, though she pounded up the slope at a near gallop in an erratic course around the tallest of the bristling thorn bushes. Reaching the grassy hilltop, he halted the panting beast, allowing her to shake her mane in belated protest at the arduous climb and the stinging punctures of the blackthorn. Twice more she flicked her mane, turning her head and an aggrieved eye on her master so that the reins pulled in his left hand. But his gaze was locked on the far distance, and his thoughts too, and after fretting at the reins one last time the roan stood unmoving.

The horseman was Prince Osir of Strath.

Below him he looked out on a panorama whose familiarity in no way diminished the passion he felt for its beauty. He had first climbed this vantage as a boy, fifteen years ago, when all that had been different from today was the dappled pony he rode and the boyish excitement of stealing out without permission. The land was the same rolling green vista of valleys and hills, unmarked by cultivation except in the farthest west, where the vineyards of Mamoba, suffused with the warm summer sun, were a hazy dreamworld, and only a keen eye might discern the red towers of the ancestral home of the Lord of Strath. Even the sky was the same: a clear blue wider almost than the horizons would allow. The scene was as dear to Prince Osir as his life, a landscape of precious memories, made keener and more achingly beautiful by the circumstances of his visit here this day.

In the spring, news of his father's death had reached Mamoba, and a shocked household had composed itself for mourning. Within a week, the ashes of Lord Shenri were borne into the Great Hall where he had so long presided, the great urn carried by soldiers of Strath and the procession attended by officers of the Ta-shih and local exarchs of the Faith. "It is Dian's blessing," some whispered, "that Osir's mother is not alive to witness such tragedy…" She had died giving birth to Osir, and so now responsibility for the funeral and the management of the affairs of Strath fell to the young prince.

His sister, the Lady Che Keleu, returned to Mamoba several weeks thereafter. She was distraught and Osir, hot-blooded and solitary, was small comfort.

And then the supervisor, Ke Beyil, arrived with his retinue.

The emotional strain caused by his father's brutal murder had ill-prepared Osir for the news which he brought. The very suggestion of a marriage between Honam and Strath sent Osir into an explosive rage. He stormed about the estate like a berserk dog, the servants, and Ke Beyil, in terror of his violence. Keleu, who was always clearheaded and phlegmatic where her brother was proud and intense, understood the pain of his loss and reasoned with him patiently and in the face of his fury.

And so, in the weeks after Ke Beyil's formal announcement of the Choosing, Osir came with difficulty to accept the inevitable. Though every circumstance of his father's death and the abrupt Choosing of his sister had marked upon it the treacherous hand of Yoiwa of Honam, Osir was powerless against the will of the Council. And, of course, there was the petition, in his father's own hand and under the seal of Strath. This document, so Ke Beyil avouched, had been handed to him by Ta-shih officers, who discovered it amongst Shenri's personal effects, and was identical to one delivered to the Council by Lorang's legate in Chisua and another to Clan Ouine and Yoiwa himself.

"Surely," protested Ke Beyil in one of his more fiery encounters with the young prince, "this is irrefutable proof of your father's intention!"

Such words were as torture to Osir. What to believe? Perhaps his father had indeed wished this marriage, perhaps had purposed to keep it from both son and daughter until approved by Council or King. And there was logic in such a course: the union would strengthen the cordial ties Yoiwa had initiated in recent years. It would bind Honam as a powerful ally in the complex politics of the Council. And maintaining a veil over his intent, concealing the matter even from his son, even this, painful as it was for Osir to admit, was credible. Since the untimely death of his wife, Shenri had entrusted his confidences warily, even amongst his family.

And yet…and yet…

The notion that his father might not have trusted him in this…

Osir jerked his head down as if to ward off a blow. The torment of his contemplations brought tears to his eyes. He gripped the reins until the pressure hurt his fingers. *Had he so little faith in me?* he thought.

Had he so little faith in his son and, his own guilty voice derided him, *perhaps especially in so quarrelsome a son?*

It seemed as if the gods had forsaken him. They had measured him and found him wanting. Was this their punishment? Or was it a test? A flutter of reverent fear choked his throat. He felt deserted, the certainty of his destiny undermined.

Gathering up the reins, he turned the roan and urged her back down the slope at reckless speed, fury and humiliation at war in his heart.

***

The seat of Strath, the home of the lord of Mamoba Province, had been built on a grand scale by Osir's ancestors, in a style that defied simple categories. The additions and modifications had been executed by successive generations, beginning with austere, moving through half a dozen different variations of the elaborate and ornate, and culminating in the last generation with something of the functional. The overall effect, however, was not, as one might expect, a confused mishmash of conflicting architectural tastes stamped with the identity of each lord. Mamoba was somehow larger than this; there was, rather, more of a sense of serene antiquity – as if the stone and red brick of its construction had been infused not with the particular character of individual lords but with the ageless, elemental spirit of the brooding hills of Strath, a place of small changes and enduring permanence.

Set in a valley between low hills to the north and east, and a wide sweep of hills to the south, the lower slopes of which had been given over to neat vineyards as far as the eye could see, Mamoba Estate, as it had come to be known, presented this aspect: a mansion, built square around a spacious central courtyard and large beyond all need, rose four stories to a red pitched roof, the whole dominated on either side by two towers, twice the height of the mansion, which were overgrown by a tapestry of bluevine right up to the very turrets. At intervals along the mansion's rambling facade, standing the height of a man above the gutters, three whitestone statues whose last traces of paint had long disappeared, depicted God in each of the old religion's forms – father, mother, son. The portico, whose arch above the main doors was adorned with sculpted figures in bas relief, engaged in the various stages of wine-making, stood at the end of a colonnade roofed with bluevine, thereby creating a long pergola which led away from the mansion to the hardwood gates. These had not been closed in living memory and slouched now from their iron fixtures with a kind of listless immobility. The high pillars supporting the gates, like old men obliged to stand to attention too long, similarly displayed a noticeable slant from the perpendicular, thereby causing some crumbling of the stone walls framing the entrance. The damage had been repaired on repeated occasions, but this partial flaw in the symmetry of Mamoba Estate added a rustic charm to its dramatic grandeur. Within the walls there flourished magnificent flower gardens, formal, precise, but with a little wildness in the meadow blooms of the borders. Outside the walls and to the east were several large outbuildings – stables, a granary, the old winepresses – and a short walk down the dusty road, a small circular temple supervised by the local exarch. To the west, a quarter mile from the mansion, a circular keep housed the incumbent lord's personal soldiery, in Shenri's time no more than a hundred men-at-arms, though a hundred more were quartered in small contingents elsewhere in the province to assist in law enforcement and tax collection. The town of Mamoba lay four miles west, an industrious centre of several thousand folk kept busy by the steady, heavy-laden traffic from the rich farmlands and vineyards of northern Strath.

It was a quirk of history, in keeping with the wistful tranquillity of Mamoba Estate, that the walls of the mansion and the sturdy battlements of the nearby keep had never endured the destructive blows of war visited upon so many of the towns and citadels of what had been the Biljan kingdoms. Though Strath, because of blood ties to the Ouine Clan of Honam, had joined the alliance of the Biljan kings against Jamarin III, and though war had raged across this land, Mamoba Estate had been spared. After the war, Strath gave allegiance to Jamarin, for who could resist this remarkable man, and the then Lord of Strath vowed publicly to break the kinship that bound his people to the Ouine Clan, and that had swept Strath into the bloodiest and most crushing of wars. Since that time, Strath had prospered, and with it Mamoba Estate.

A little under half of Osir's youth had been spent in Mamoba, the balance being devoted to his education in the south at the academies of Chisua; but he had, unlike many of his princely peers from other provinces, a deep and abiding love of his lands and his home. The excitement and sophistication of the southern cities and the political intrigues of Chisua occupied a place of second or third importance to him. And he had observed in his father a gruff ambivalence about this preference for Strath, as if Shenri approved of his loyalty but wished his son had developed the political shrewdness that might secure Strath advantages in Council. At times, alone with his sister and father in the comforting ease of the Great Hall at formal dinner, he would argue with Shenri about the balance of power in Kiangsu, the vote against the mining levy and the Ta-shih. He would make his case with passionate intensity, and see from the enthusiastic gleam in his father's eye that this was the son he wanted. But though Osir understood the issues of his time and held fervently to Strath's cause, still he had no stomach for the deception and perfidy that, for him, epitomized Chisuan society. There were occasions when he asked himself in all candour whether it was want of subtlety or maturity in himself – and in this he envied his sister her tolerance and discernment. Always it had seemed to him that the single year's difference in their ages was a gulf of experience and understanding that he could never bridge.

He came home to Mamoba Estate this sunny afternoon at a slower pace than he had left in the morning. Still, the roan was streaked white with sweat and the stable boy gasped at the blackthorn cuts on the animal's flanks. Osir, dismounting, noticed the lacerations for the first time and, with concern for the horse and self-reproach in equal measure, bid the boy tend to her. Then, head down, he walked the chalk gravel to the gates and met, coming out, Ke Beyil.

An average example of his kind, and possessed of few qualities other than his stolid patience, that might excite an acquaintance, he was an individual remarkable only in one or two particulars of physiognomy and presence. Taller than most men, if not taller, he carried around his midriff irrefutable evidence of his participation in the essential luxuries of life. Of his hair little could be said, although his eyebrows, as grey and lowering as storm clouds on high mountain crags, expressed a stern reserve, oft-times amplified by the sardonic curl of his lip. Of his nature, Ke Beyil himself, had he been pressed to self-reflection, would have chosen the epithets 'placid' and 'sagacious', whilst younger men in the Council might have contended, and in secret frequently did, that Ke Beyil was 'pompous' and a 'bore'. But younger men in the Council were few and, in occupying the juniors' booths in that great and civilized institution, their scurrilous remarks were as dust beneath Ke Beyil's exalted feet.

Reluctantly, Osir stopped in his tracks. A greeting was required. Their relationship, since the first stormy days of Ke Beyil's arrival, had seen a minor improvement. Osir tolerated the supervisor. Ke Beyil, with crude diplomacy, remained smilingly aloof.

Ke Beyil dispensed upon Osir a smile now that conveyed the same, and touched his tricorne riding hat by way of greeting. "Prince Osir. Good day."

Osir nodded, observing the necessary forms, to return the salutation. "Ke Beyil. Good day."

"I have not seen you this morning," Ke Beyil continued, now stating the obvious: "But you have been riding…"

"Yes."

"A lovely day for it. I have not your stamina for early morning exertion, but this afternoon I intend to remedy matters. I believe a steed has been saddled?"

Osir nodded absently. "I think I saw the groom so occupied."

"Good, good. My aides are less inclined to exercise and I have left them in the library. We shall have your company at dinner tonight?"

Osir nodded again – "Of course…" – but failed to keep a sigh from his response. He forced a smile. "Until dinner then, Ke Beyil."

The older man inclined his head with perfect grace. "Until then, Prince Osir."

They parted company, Osir with an impatient, distracted air, and Ke Beyil with a ponderous elegance brought about by the awkwardness of his equestrian attire.

Inside the mansion Osir asked after his sister and was directed to the library by one of the servants. He had hoped to find her alone, but was disappointed. She sat with Ke Beyil's aides, foppish and stiff in their formal Chisuan dress, but clearly enjoying her company. Nearby sat her lady-in-waiting, Che Peri, her companion from a lesser noble house of Strath. Osir stopped in the doorway, and for several moments his presence went unnoticed. It was rare that he had the opportunity to see his sister as others saw her, but here with strangers in their home, in the familiar surroundings of Mamoba, he looked on her with different eyes. She was enchanting, having the good fortune to possess both the glowing beauty of a girl and the sober thoughtfulness of a mature woman, delicate of features yet firmly expressive. There was in her face the same vibrancy, usually restrained, that had characterized their father. And, of course, she was tantalizingly desirable: dark hair, pale eyes, smilingly playful.

Keleu glanced up and saw Osir, her face breaking into a wider smile as she beckoned him. "Osir. You've been out so long. Favul said you left at first light."

Ke Ivik and Ke Lavi had risen, executing the requisite bows with studied precision, but with a stiffness that said they had rather he had not interrupted this exquisite time with his sister. Osir exchanged courtesies with Che Peri and then the Chisuans. To Keleu he replied, "I was riding. Up along the south-east ridge, towards the cataract." He flopped carelessly into a chair, where the soft afternoon sun poured in through the high windows. His sister's expression had changed: she knew he rode up that way to be alone. Half embarrassed, he concluded in a toneless voice, "It's a steep climb…"

"And your clothes, Osir," she chided him gently. "They're pulled and torn."

He fingered a rent in his shirt and commented, "Blackthorn. There's a lot this year."

Ke Lavi said with the merest hint of alarm, "I trust Ke Beyil will avoid the thorns…"

Osir snorted. He wondered idly whether the supervisor had even managed to get into the saddle. "None round here. Only on the high slopes. I imagine Ke Beyil will stay near the estate."

"Of course."

Che Peri enquired further about his ride and, in answering, Osir glanced at Ke Ivik, sitting to his right, and caught his eyes guiltily roving from Che Keleu's face to her neck and breasts. Abruptly Osir stood up, occasioning the same reaction from the aides. He remarked to Keleu, "I have something to show you in the gardens. Will you come?"

Keleu smiled in surprise and agreed. Excusing herself and Osir, she waved to Che Peri to remain and accompanied her brother from the library. Osir led her down wide hallways covered in beautiful frescoes of bucolic scenes and out into the gardens by a side door. For some time neither spoke. There was only the high song of a lapwing and the half-heard buzz of a distant hive of bees. After a while, as they wandered slowly under an ornamental tree and between the flowerbeds, Keleu, who had hold of Osir's hand, placed her other hand upon his and asked, "What did you mean to show me?"

"Oh, nothing," he responded. "I tire of Chisuan manners and the reek of Chisuan perfume."

Keleu laughed. "They're not so bad!"

Osir did not match her mood. As if he had not heard her he went on, "Always they are here. We are never alone."

"We're alone now."

Osir said bitterly, "And for how long? Before you know it the Ouine horde will arrive and Mathed will rule Strath!"

Keleu grasped his hand tightly. "We shall rule Strath together."

Osir looked into her face. "Who? You and I?"

"Please, Osir. Don't set this between us. Mathed is a good man. He will not interfere in Strath. He respects you..."

"Me?" Osir withdrew his hand from hers. "No, sister. He respects *you*. He loves *you*. He has always loved you. I wonder only at his great good fortune in securing control of Strath through your Choosing, and by the timely *murder* of our father!"

"We have argued this before, Osir," Keleu said, more firmly now.

"Father is dead. We cannot change that. We cannot change the tragedy of his death. But we must respect his final wishes and the wishes of Council."

"It is such an unnatural haste!"

"I know it seems so. But Father wanted the marriage this year, in the year of the new king's accession. And I say again: Mathed is a good man. The marriage is in Strath's interests–"

Osir interrupted. "So you say. But it is all too convenient. I tell you, I see Yoiwa's hand in this! Your good Mathed is his puppet of a son!" Clenching his fist Osir hissed under his breath with a terrible savagery, "Our father's blood is on Yoiwa's hands! I know it! I know it!"

Keleu gasped. "Osir! Faith in the gods, what are you saying? You mustn't think such things!"

Her brother, beside himself with this feverish rush of accusation, would not be stopped. "You think Mathed will rule Strath with you! Oh, my poor naive sister! Yoiwa will rule Strath! Yoiwa! Only Yoiwa!"

And as abruptly as the passion had come upon him, so with the most strenuous of efforts he quelled it. Osir looked at his sister, the pale frightened expression on her dear face, and in himself felt the beating anger and humiliation like a physical pain through his limbs.

Keleu pressed close to him, speaking with the grief they shared, but this time also with a poorly concealed fear, "We loved him, Osir! We loved him dearly! But he is gone. Nothing is served by these terrible words. You frighten me. Promise me you won't repeat them. Promise me!"

Sorrow welled up in Osir and stung his eyes, sorrow for Keleu and for their loss. He embraced her, holding her close while he blinked back the tears. When they parted, neither could find words to speak. In silence they returned to the mansion.

***

Lord Yoiwa sat at the table, the Lady Che Mairu, his wife, to his right, Jophan to his left, Vedarahava, lieutenant of his bodyguard, hulking behind in full armour and weapons harness. *The inner circle.* Skava sat opposite, arms on the table top. She had eyed each one in turn, playing the role, indeed the role within the role. They were sharp, the lot of them, and ruthless. Prince Mathed was not here. He was *not* ruthless. He did not know of the ambush and the murder of his future father-in-law. His time would come. He held promise.

Yoiwa drank tea, left to cool, from a pewter cup. He was abstemious to a fault. His hands were on his lap, under the table. He looked relaxed, square face untroubled, eyes half hooded under black eyebrows and the greying stubble of his skull. He listened, but looked only at Skava while Jophan asked questions.

"What of their spymaster?" was the latest.

Skava, dressed as Courier-sergeant Alin but dispensing with the guise in front of these people, answered simply, "Dead. In the ambush, as we planned."

"I meant," Jophan corrected her, "the new man."

She had of course known this, but playing down your skills was essential in the small ways that made others feel comfortable you were not a threat. "An underling of his deceased master, a journeyman, Ke Jophan," she replied. "He reports to the Lady Che Keleu and her brother once a day… and in private to Prince Osir at night."

"What does the prince suspect?" This from the Lady Che Mairu, a handsome woman of deep-set eyes and high cheekbones, dark curly hair, long but tied and ornamented with sparkling precious stones in the northern style. She was matronly, erect of bearing, haughty or charming as need demanded, but as tough a warrior as Yoiwa, even if she didn't wield a blade. Instead, she controlled Clan Ouine's treasury and the bankers and merchants upon whom Honam's wealth was multiplied.

"Everything, my lady. He is one of those hot-blooded young men who intuitively draws the right conclusions from the wrong information – even though we feed his spies, where we can, news to ease their concerns."

Jophan drew breath, a small polite signal of noble protocol to entreat of his betters that he might proceed with the questions. Mairu allowed this by raising a hand from her lap. "What action," said Jophan, "might he contemplate?"

Skava lifted a corner of her mouth, not exactly a smile, more an acknowledgement that she had thought this through in some detail. She leaned back in her chair, the very same chair in the very same room in the depository where weeks ago she had consumed a bottle of juniper brandy with Maki and nearly said too much. The shutters were closed again: this conversation would go no further than the timber walls.

"Prince Osir has choices," she began, lifting a finger to indicate the first of several options. "First, he may accept his sister's position and the planned arrangements for the nuptials. Not impossible: he loves her. Perhaps a little too much–"

Jophan, a sharp thinker and therefore always at Yoiwa's side, interjected, "Meaning?"

Skava lifted one eyebrow. "They seem quite close, physically." She raised a hand to forestall the next question, amused in a distant way that Mathed would be squirming at this revelation, were he ever to discover it. "But there is no scandal, and we cannot get near enough in such a tight-knit household to find out more. Nevertheless, they are close. Close in age, close in love for Strath, for their father and each other. After all, she was the mother he never had… The difference is their temperaments. You know their temperaments. I need not detail them again. Except in one particular: whilst he loves his sister and would see her happy and ensure the stability of Strath, he is envious of her. Possibly she is cleverer than him. Perhaps merely older and calmer. These facts are irrelevant. The effects, however, are important. That is, he feels that he was not good enough for his father, that he is inadequate. Now, stepping into his majority, enforced by the death of Lord Shenri, it means–"

"He has something to prove," Yoiwa concluded for Skava.

She inclined her head, observing the forms. "My lord. Indeed. He has a *lot* to prove. Which leads me to Osir's second choice: he will not be content to be quiet or passive. He will accept the marriage but protest it. Already we know he has argued loudly with the Council supervisor. He has become enraged at times – actions forgiven by the supervisor as the anguished fury of a youth in mourning. In this instance, I expect that he will make the choice to do the same when we arrive, privately…and publicly."

Jophan took another breath, and received the smallest of nods from Yoiwa to proceed. "Why publicly?" Jophan argued. "That would breach decorum. He would be dishonoured and…" – he coughed delicately as a buffer to Mairu's sensibilities – "bring the same to the Lady of Strath."

Skava shrugged. "Indeed, Ke Jophan. But in the balance of things, he would have taken steps to demonstrate to everyone that he had done something to voice his dissent and, more importantly, to prove himself – to the shade of his father, if no one else."

Jophan blinked, an indication he was taking this on faith and Skava's reputation, not on any conviction that he believed it. Openly dishonourable behaviour was never countenanced among the nobles, even these whose ambitions were far from modest. Screwing over rivals in secret, however, was a fucking pastime.

"Very well." Jophan rubbed both sides of his chin. He was close-shaven. Lord Yoiwa insisted on this, a long-standing tradition of the warrior cult of Honam. "And so to your third choice for Prince Osir…"

"Yes. The third. He will persuade his countrymen, the nobles of Strath to muster and take up arms against us."

Even Yoiwa reacted to this: a tightening of his jaw. Jophan was about to protest. The Lady Che Mairu interrupted before him: "Against the will of Council? Against the approval of the king? Against his sister?" Instead of outrage, her tone was curious.

Put like that, Skava decided, it did sound mad. But she could see it. She could always see these things as they might develop, the linear and the parallel possibilities and the resulting certainty, because she was completely unencumbered by the cloying idiocy of human prejudices, superstitions and social mores. People seemed utterly unable to escape their cultural chains.

Mairu had not finished. "He could not succeed," she explained, as if to a dim child. "He would be raising his hand against us, his brother-in-law and the Lady Che Keleu, against Mamoba and Strath itself. He would defy the Law of the Realm." She stated these things as self-evident truths, without high emotion.

Skava smiled inwardly. Here was an opportunity for them all to see the world as it could be, not as they wanted it. She pressed on, face blank. "Not so," she said.

That brought another reaction. Even Vedarahava, standing like an armoured statue behind Yoiwa, looked directly at her. This was, Skava thought, a moment of shock for them all. Necessary. Necessary that they faced the truth of what might happen.

Jophan looked insulted. He believed the world worked a certain way and being a noble and outraged ought to get him his way. It usually did. He knew better, of course, but here, in Strath, within weeks of their taking possession of the new prize, he was offended that the way his head had ordered things was being turned upside-down and he was told it by a commoner, Honam's master-intelligencer, but still no more than a commoner. Skava looked at him, awaiting the inevitable outburst.

To his credit, he regained some self-control, and in an icy tone said, "Why is it 'not so'?"

Skava put both hands flat on the table, owning it and the conversation. "These are the reasons. Osir is well-liked. He is passionate and can lead – though he is young. Aye, Ke Jophan," she added when he looked sceptical, "it is not what you wish to hear, but it is true. Second, if the noble families of Strath are persuaded, they can raise four or five hundred men-at-arms, perhaps two hundred mounted. I have confirmed this. No, they are not our equal, Ke Jophan, but they outnumber us eight to one. My Lord Yoiwa cannot intervene in this, with additional troops, even were he to order them now from far Deka. Think of the reaction in Chisua: King, Council and Archivists. Thus, the small contingent my Prince Mathed is permitted here in Strath will be all he may have: sixty at best of Clan Ouine's warriors."

Jophan took a breath and Skava was pleased to see he was now thinking, coldly, as Yoiwa would do – Yoiwa sitting next to him, expressionless, watchful, waiting. "But Skava," said Jophan, "he cannot legitimately raise arms without just cause. We will not give him cause."

"Indeed," she conceded. "we will not."

"Then this option is not one he can choose."

"Regrettably, it is."

Jophan remained quiet. Now he was listening.

Skava continued: "There is a law, an ancient law of the Realm…the Law of Constructive Trust. It is a formula that has not been invoked in three hundred years or more. The great Jamarin's peace has seen to that. Yet it remains on the books of decree."

Jophan coughed and was given leave to say, "I have not heard of this. What does it mean?"

Skava reached into her belt pouch and withdrew a page. "Ke Jophan, it is a legal remedy…" And she started to read aloud: "'*Available to a relative of any of the clan families who has been wrongfully deprived of rights due to another either obtaining or holding a legal property right which they should not possess through unjust enrichment or interference.*'"

Skava looked up. "This 'wrongful deprivation' can be challenged," she explained, "within forty days and forty nights – usually through the offices of a plenipotentiary of the monarch."

Jophan clicked his tongue in irritation. "The Council supervisor…"

"Just so," Skava said.

"Then we have the same right, were Osir to bring this…this complaint, to refute his accusations. It is all one."

"It is," Skava agreed, "except that within the forty days, he may prosecute this 'complaint', as you call it, by honourable force of arms."

There was silence in the room. Now, they understood. Skava looked at them, each in turn. And they looked at her.

Yoiwa leaned forward. "Which option," he murmured, speaking quietly in that way that commanded instant attention, "will he choose?"

Skava paused. Everything about Prince Osir made her concerned. His intensity, his emotional imbalance, his need to prove himself. Guessing what he would do, even with as much evidence as she thought she had, was nigh on impossible. She was, however, always decisive.

"He is unlikely to raise arms," Skava answered. "Even if the nobles mustered at his request, his sister is all that remains of his family. He will, I think, want to protect her. And she, for her part, will urge him to caution. My prince…" – and Skava gestured as if to the absent Mathed – "will play an invaluable part in this: he must guide her hand, encourage reasonable action and, most important, befriend Osir, make him like a brother. In this case, Osir will start by being polite. He will want, at some level, to accept the new order and support his sister... But then he will over-react – probably at a perceived slight, an insult – and so he will show his anger, argue with us, embarrass himself and his family, and..." A conflicting set of thoughts caused Skava to hesitate.

Yoiwa spoke into the silence: "And leave. He will not remain for the consequences. Dishonour, he will find, is harder to bear than the death of his father."

Skava nodded slowly. That was how aristocrats viewed their world. Yoiwa echoed her thoughts. It sounded right. Probably.

Yoiwa stared hard at her. "It would be better," he added, his voice cold, "in those circumstances that you describe, spymaster, circumstances of public scrutiny and disrepute, if the Prince Osir were to exile himself... and never return."

Once more Skava nodded. There was a neat symmetry to this. Yoiwa had understood it clearly. They did not need a hostile prince free to cause trouble in the future. However, it would need to be handled with care – his self-imposed exile and his disappearance. And rushing it would produce what it always did: unintended consequences. What was it that niggled? There was something in Yoiwa's manner that gave her pause.

"My lord," she replied. Separately she was thinking of the 'circumstances' that she might engineer. She would need to be at the estate, in the house; and she would need leverage, a way to get close to Che Keleu and perhaps the prince.

She glanced back at Yoiwa, now in a hushed conversation aside to his wife. Skava wanted to test this idea with Yoiwa, but she would have to wait until lord and lady had completed their private by-play. In this room, Yoiwa was master. Skava must adhere to her role, without exception.

Yoiwa had finished. He turned his attention back to her and, with an air of pronouncing judgement, said, "Mathed must be the sole lord of Strath, with his wife. There is no room for the prince. You have said he is a hot-blooded youth. You have said he will perceive insult on the smallest provocation. The means are unimportant, but his disgrace, his discredit, before a senior member of Council and, most preferably, some of the nobles of Strath, is very desirable to me. I foresee his exile and his disappearance. The gods are not kind."

Skava listened, with a needle of worry pricking at her. Osir's discomfiture and exile she could manufacture, but this was starting to feel like a personal thing between Yoiwa and the youth. Fucking nobles. Always there was some slight, some slur or affront that occupied their energies, perhaps generations old. She had missed it. But there it was. Somehow, in enumerating what Osir was likely to do, she had confirmed the affront and, worse, laid out the stratagem for redress – as far as Yoiwa and Mairu were concerned. Silently she cursed herself: too fucking clever by half! She should have simply told them what needed to happen, but what she knew about Osir troubled her. He was unpredictable, in odd ways the vast majority of his noble peers did not understand. Anyway, doubtless the insult went back a long way. Yoiwa may well have insisted on this course of action, regardless. She was stuck now. What Yoiwa had just said was not an opinion or hope; it was a command, in the form that nobles sometimes issued them, with oblique references to dreams in words like 'foresee' and by invoking the gods to specify outcomes whose attainment could not be questioned.

Intuitively she saw the dangers. She had only one card to play, so she played it. "My lord," she began, an overt acceptance of his decision. "This I will accomplish. The timing is important." Hooded, implacable eyes watched her. "It cannot be rushed. Provoking Osir to precipitate action may lead to unpredictable outcomes."

"When?" A single question, the bastard. She had to give an answer.

"My lord. I need to be inside Mamoba. I need to get close to the Lady Che Keleu and Prince Osir."

"We shall be there at the end of summer." Meaning that she, Skava, as Courier-sergeant Alin would be part of the Ouine retinue for the nuptials.

"I mean, my lord," she persisted, "that I arrive as a servant, a female servant, provided by a thoughtful Prince Mathed for the use of the bride."

She was pushing it now. Lord Yoiwa did not sully his hands with this level of detail. It was beneath any noble to discuss servants, and it was equally an irritation to him to engage in the finer points of the filthy business of espionage. Idiots.

Yoiwa's face had not changed. "You cannot," he declared without hesitation, "be both. No." He meant she could not be servant and Courier-sergeant Alin at the same time. For whatever reason, he needed her there as the latter. And that was it. Not ideal. But not impossible.

She inclined her head. "My lord."

"Spymaster." Jophan again, an eyebrow up and showing his sharp teeth. What did *he* want?

"Ke Jophan."

"Your injuries? They are healed?"

Some prick had been talking. Probably Maki. She was furious. Then again, if Jophan, Yoiwa's cousin, posed questions of a man as lowly as Maki, what choice did he have but to answer them? She instantly forgave Maki and cursed the arsehole in front of her. Silently. And in the same instant, gave an unspoken grudging compliment to the three nobles on the other side of the table: they were clever, no denying it. She would have been asking questions, in their shoes. And they had put her, by this simple expedient, very firmly in her place.

"Completely, Ke Jophan," she replied with breezy confidence. Her hip still hurt and sitting with a horse between her legs was no fun – a worrying thought, for all sorts of reasons.

He didn't even blink. "Very good. Thank you, spymaster."

And she was dismissed.

∗∗∗

In two weeks Mamoba Estate was host to small parties of nobles from the districts of Strath, men and women well known to Osir both for their friendship to the family and their loyalty to Lord Shenri. They offered formal commiserations to Keleu and Osir and, in private, pledged fealty to them – this they could do without difficulty, until Mathed became Che Keleu's husband and Lord of Strath. Osir's spirits were lifted by the presence of familiar faces and the warmth of his kinsmen's support. The wildness and unpredictability that had characterized his moods of late dwindled and Keleu, though preparations for the wedding absorbed her attention entirely, showed a noticeable relief. The mansion had had until this time a feeling of emptiness about it. Despite the joyless atmosphere induced by the tragedy of Shenri's death, and the loss of his entire bodyguard and some of his closest advisors, the presence of those who had always known him brought to Mamoba an immediate diminution of the anguish, perhaps because the burden was more widely shared. Osir was even moved to humour, remarking to his friends, "Now at least the kinsmen of Strath outnumber the Chisuan contingent!"

Ke Beyil and his aides, too, seemed to find the company stimulating. Conversation over dinner became less solemn and more relaxed, even though the Chisuans' attire did not. Each day the household was treated to at least three changes of clothes. Morning wear was light in colour, usually tan corded breeches, buckled shoes with narrow heels and a mirror-like polish, a white silk shirt with high embroidered collars, and a short mantle of the finest tailoring, with higher collars than the shirt so that the individual thus caparisoned was compelled to keep his chin up. Even in the dullest of men this established an appearance of sublime haughtiness. Afternoon wear was less casual, requiring darker colours of blue, grey, or green, where the brightest flash of colour was restricted to neck scarves traced with gold and silver, and finally, of endless fascination to the northerners, stylish riding boots utterly unsuited to riding. All of this was removed for the panoply of evening, when there was revealed a splendid combination of heeled shoes, baggy trousers (these dark blue with the finest silver skein to pattern the fabric), a white silk shirt of the highest collars imaginable, a short topcoat of the same material as the trousers and cut in such a style that the Chisuans might display magnificent yellow sashes tied around their waists; and to complete the uniform, a square blue cap at the front of which was affixed a tiny silver emblem, the triple swords of the Council.

This exhibition was greeted by the nobles, whose contact with Chisuan personages was limited, with startlement, disbelief, amusement, and finally admiration. More impressive than the astonishing parade of clothes was the ease with which the three gentlemen carried it off. And after only a few days there was, Osir noted, a distinct mood amongst his kinsmen of grudging respect, evident not in any obsequious flattery but in their readiness to listen, to defer, and to seek the opinion of the Chisuans when Osir found them only affected and conceited. Frequently, over meals or on those occasions when all of the household were gathered together and conversation had passed away from him, Osir would observe Ke Beyil and his aides, scrutinizing their attire and their manners, as well as the subjects of their intercourse. In contemplation, he would attempt to comprehend this effect upon his fellows. It was neither fashion, nor gentility, nor yet intellect that distinguished these three men. It could not be simple ostentation, since uncountable numbers of functionaries and merchants in Strath and elsewhere comported themselves with fashion and elegance. So what was it? Snobbishness, Osir reasoned, high-mindedness, an overbearing arrogance? But this was inaccurate and frankly unfair: Ke Beyil was grace and charm itself. So what then? And gradually Osir admitted to himself that, unpalatable as it might be, the three gentlemen carried with them that rare quality of being at the centre of the world, in Chisua, where the glorious events that moved the Realm and power were as palpable as the giant walls of the city that nourished it.

Osir understood this well. He had been part of that power for six years. As an outsider, he had felt the thrill of participating in the great debates of Kiangsu, of mixing with the brightest young men of every province of the Realm, and showing off to the gorgeous daughters of the same Great Families.

Issues such as 'the Ta-shih's oppression', 'provincial oligarchy' and even 'rights of the peasants' had been his serious preoccupation during countless heated arguments in the galleries of the Roneca. On Monvar Hill he had met men of the Council and been lovelorn for the most beautiful girls of clan and rich trader alike. He had watched processions of the Archivists with their black robes and uncompromising expressions as they trod the grey cobblestones of Temple Way and held aloft the icons of the Faith. And more often than he cared to remember, in the gaudy streets of Strad he and his wealthy companions had caroused with women, not all of them prostitutes. Throughout all of this he had observed in those native to Chisua, from the highest to the lowest, that singular quality – as if their proximity to the seat of power had endowed them, though they were only obscurely aware of it, with a conspicuous prestige, an easy confidence of always being right. And it was the Chisuans' ready acceptance of this prestige as a natural condition of their lives that so bewitched the northerners.

Osir looked upon his kinsmen with friendly amusement during these discourses, and when questioned about the smile that played at the corners of his mouth he would respond in all truth: "Ah, I was thinking only of the times I spent in Chisua!"

One night whilst Osir sipped thoughtfully at the clear golden wine remaining in his goblet, and the company sat replete after an excellent meal in the friendly orange glow of the glass oil lamps, the conversation turned to the matter of shifting political power in Council. Ke Androc, a heavy-set choleric nobleman of Eloy in south-east Strath, had challenged Ke Beyil with the assertion that the new king would be inclined to favour the continuation of the mining levy.

Ke Beyil smiled in that maddening way that said, *I forgive you your bucolic ignorance and I shall be pleased to edify you,* and responded, "Ah. I believe not, Ke Androc. Council moves towards unity in this matter. Before his death, Jamarin V – glory to his name – had already agreed in principle to the abolition of the levy, in addition to the tithe reduction of the treasury's funding of the Ta-shih decreed in his name this past ten-year. All that remains in this burdensome matter is for the supervisors to design a state mechanism appropriate for the maintenance of the Ta-shih – a Ta-shih considerably reduced in size and appetite, I might add!"

"And how far," enquired Osir, "have the supervisors progressed this issue, Ke Beyil?"

Ke Beyil lifted his chin higher than usual above his silk collars. "I may speak with some authority in this regard, Ke Osir. Fortunately, my aide Ke Ivik…" – and here the king's representative opened his hand, palm upward, in a gesture that brought his companion into the dialogue – "has been charged with the task of studying the problem." Beyil inclined his head in the correct form, the senior to the junior, to convey as it were the topic into the hands of the young man. "Ke Ivik, perhaps you might care to elaborate?"

"Of course, Ke Beyil." Ivik addressed Osir: "Prince Osir, it is plain that the lords of the provinces have secured for themselves adequate personal forces for the control of their lands and for upholding the Law of the Realm. Where this does not pertain, the Ta-shih act as constables: I note Kei, Biabaro, Sychomo and Atho, lands close to Kiang. The lords themselves, in the main, seek the abolition of the mining levy and a reduction in the garrisons. Ke Beyil and distinguished supervisors of the Council support this view–"

"I am aware of these facts, Ke Ivik," Osir interrupted with easy charm.

"Ah! Forgive me." Ivik cleared his throat and had the grace to look chastened. "I spoke merely as preamble. I shall come to the point. We, that is the supervisors, recommend a three-quarter reduction in the active manpower of the Ta-shih. This will be achieved over a three-year period. Remaining forces will be stationed strategically to protect the interests and power of the Realm: Ladore, where Suhl's intentions are never clear; Lorang, where the north intrudes and…er…where terrible deeds have been done. My apologies, Prince Osir, for this awkward reference. Pray, allow me to continue. The lords of the provinces will be invested with the authority of the king in the disposition of their personal forces, which will be limited according to need and the general agreement of all provincial lords. Council will act on matters pertaining to the interests of the Realm, but otherwise will not interfere in the provinces' affairs. Responsibility for funding the Ta-shih will fall entirely to the treasury, thus relieving the provinces of any and all obligation for the levy."

There was a pause after Ivik had delivered this report. Then Osir, gazing at the young man over the top of his goblet, remarked, "I think we are impressed, Ke Ivik. These proposals are radical. They are entirely adequate to address the problem. I ask only one question: where will the treasury seek the gold to support what remains of the Ta-shih? Though its forces will be a quarter their present size, I have difficulty in seeing how the treasury can undertake to pay a quarter of the levy to which all the provinces now contribute. The proposed sum is still vast."

Osir sipped from his goblet and glanced down the table at his kinsmen, Androc, Dykal, Kesiden, and Kesiden's wife Tensi. Opposite them, Keleu watched him with a bright-eyed expression that hovered halfway between anticipation for what Osir was on the verge of saying next, and an eagerness to break into the conversation herself. Osir looked back at Ke Ivik and declared, "I forget the exact details of the accounts, but from memory the Ta-shih requires – what? – a tax on the income of the order of three hundred mines to support it. And only the breaker mines, of course, where the old cities beneath still have treasures in the ruins."

Ke Ivik nodded, as much as his collars would allow. "More or less. More or less. Very true, Ke Osir. A good point. Our response is straightforward: the breaker mines are largely robbed out. The steel, the machines, the engines, the coin are mostly gone. The breakers go deeper and endure greater dangers, at higher costs, but the earnings are poorer. Eventually, and certainly within our lifetimes, the breaker mines will be quarried out, whole and entire. The treasury must direct its attention to trade, to the under-merchants who presently enjoy, I think it fair to say, more than their fair share of commercial profit and, in disparate arrangements, favourable duties and tariffs. As you are doubtless aware, it has been the supervisors' steadfast contention that the merchants have been protected under the Great Jamarin's decree for too long…"

Ke Androc grunted. "Interesting proposition, Ke Ivik. I wager you'll have riots if you interfere with the merchants!"

Ke Ivik flushed at the directness of the northerner's observation. With a thrust of his chin he responded, "Ah, no, no…I beg to differ–"

And was interrupted by Osir, who spoke in dismissal of Androc's point: "The merchants have had their taxes increased progressively over a century. The amounts have not been crippling. Nonetheless, are you saying, Ke Ivik, that one more increment of the rather large magnitude you have outlined will be accepted by them?"

Ivik collected himself and looked down a pointed nose at Osir, knowing but not disrespectful. "The merchants can be persuaded of the necessity to revise taxation policy. They themselves will benefit from the consolidation of the Ta-shih. The move will, in itself, create new markets in the provinces: the new provincial militia will need to be equipped and maintained…therefore, buildings, weapons, fabrics, victuals." Ke Ivik, having regained not only his composure but the attention of the entire company in addition, proceeded with some confidence, his head angled and his eyes surveying the velvet hangings of the hall so that he appeared to be addressing a wider audience than the one assembled here: "It is our belief that the reconstitution of the Ta-shih and the new taxes on the merchant houses will not only relieve the onerous burden of the mining levy endured by the provinces, but will, moreover, ease the proclivities amongst the provinces and the Great Families to secure advantage in Council. And that, I think you must concede, will be welcome to us all!"

Here Ke Ivik paused to allow his own chuckle to lead the smiling agreement of the company.

Keleu, who had sat quietly through the conversation when it had turned to politics, leaned forward and spoke to the group at large: "I think, Ke Ivik, that your proposals are very clever. I admire your insight, and we are privileged to hear it expressed with such eloquence." Keleu smiled, a lingering quirk of sensuous lips, and Ivik inclined his head in polite acceptance of the compliment and delight in the attention of what was, in truth, the secret object of his deepest affection. Keleu went on, "There is one question, though, that I would wish answered. Forgive my ignorance, Ke Ivik. You have studied this matter. I know less than I should."

"By no means, Che Keleu," smiled Ivik, flattered. "If it is within my poor capacity, I shall venture to answer your question."

"Thank you, Ke Ivik. It is only these two observations: first, should the changes the supervisors propose become reality, will not some thirty-eight thousand men, men of arms and – let us be candid – trained violence, be released into the Realm over three years? Where will they find occupation? I hazard they will return, as most such soldiers do, to their provinces, to seek position as soldiers in one or another of our noble militias…but this time in their tens of thousands. Or worse yet, they might cross our borders into other lands, into Suhl or the Kemae Islands, to enlarge *their* armies and share our military secrets and strengths? Or join with bandits in the rough country and swell their ruffian ranks? For ourselves – and here I arrive at my second tentative question:" – a dazzling smile, and a series of blinks in return – "will not the Realm be in the same position it was two centuries ago, with the provincial lords claiming hegemony in their *kingdoms*, using their own personal armies against each other instead of in defence of the Realm's stability? My study of history tells me, as I think we might all agree, that standing armies, even those of modest dimension, are a great temptation to great lords – at the very least to settle honourable differences with their neighbours; at the worst, to expand their influence and even territories. In other words, Ke Ivik, I ask: does your proposal not fly in the face of the Great Jamarin's very intent in establishing the Ta-shih – as a force to unite the Realm?"

Ke Ivik, who had listened intently to Keleu's questions and whose frown had deepened with every word, now opened his mouth partway, hesitated, and then spoke in a series of short sentences imperfectly devised: "Ah. The Realm as it was… Yes, Che Keleu. The lords will claim hegemony… But, but…does the Ta-shih unite the Realm?"

Ke Androc, disdaining all appropriate social restraint, burst out laughing. "She has you, Ke Ivik! Gods, she has you!"

To his own great disconcertment, the gentleman who was the object of this remark flushed hotly in red patches above his white collars. More unfortunate still was the readiness of most of the company to join Ke Androc in an explosion of laughter. Only Ke Beyil, who furrowed his brows and regarded Androc with a black look, and Keleu, who offered a smile to the poor Ivik more akin to sympathy than to jest, refrained from mirth.

Recovering himself, Ke Androc apologized. "I beg your pardon, Ke Ivik. I do no dishonour, I hope? But this fine woman is a keen adversary, is she not?"

These words had the happy effect of steering the company delicately through the awkwardness of the situation and relieving Ke Ivik of the necessity to deal with his predicament himself.

After an unsuccessful attempt by Ke Beyil to revive discussions where they had ended and thus to reverse a reversal, as it were, the conversation hereafter drifted to topics more cordial. As was customary in the north, people withdrew to the adjacent chamber to stand at tall ornately carved tables and partake of warm sweet wine and sugared fruits, and the chatter became as varied as the small groups that had formed. Osir, by chance, found himself engaged by Ke Ivik in a peculiar and one-sided discussion about an estate owned by Strath in The Corant, that most beautiful of coastal tracts some distance to the south of Chisua. Ivik, it transpired, had had occasion to spend a few days on the estate and, evidently searching for some way of burying the humiliating memory of his recent discomfiture, spoke rapidly and at length about the estate's charm.

Osir, for his part, paid the young supervisor scant attention. He was absorbed in thoughts of his own, and his gaze followed his sister. She spoke with Ke Beyil, his placid self again, doubtless about their short acquaintance in Chisua, and on some topic which caused Keleu to smile and laugh and her companion to rub his hands with the satisfaction of having entertained so lovely a woman. *She is so compelling*, thought Osir. *She sees matters so clearly. The rest of us beat about the issues like cattle floundering in mud, while she, with one thought, one single argument, cuts to the heart of it and shows up our limited vision. This is what father saw: Keleu, the real power in Strath, the future of Strath. And for me…*

Osir felt again the growing gulf between them, and the envy that so shamed him – envy for her intellect and her charm and their father's favour…mostly their father's favour. In this state of agitation he could no longer endure the inconsequential prattling of Ke Ivik. With as much grace as he could summon, he made his excuses and his apologies and withdrew.

***

The Lady Che Keleu anticipated her coming nuptials with excitement. Certainly her friends, if they could be called that, young women from the minor noble families of Strath who visited more frequently now, were excited and told her that she must be *very* excited. The wedding would be spectacular. Everyone who was *anyone* in Strath and Honam would be there. And Mathed was handsome. He was *noble*. He was muscular of leg and arm. Keleu's friends were wont to sigh and smile when they spoke of him. It was what they thought she expected from them – and she herself found no cause to criticize. Politesse forbade it.

But she discovered, even in their company, that her thoughts drifted from Mathed, and there was another man in the way, whose strong lithe masculine body seemed to become Mathed, so that she could not disentangle them. It was Adaim, her soldier, her dead soldier, but in her mind's eye captured always at his best, a hot physical presence in her memory and in her feelings. It made her flush and drew titters and knowing comment from her friends. They chattered about her prince and so, they observed, Keleu blushed. It was expected. But it was silly. A part of her was amused: her secret was all the more delicious for the young women's ignorance. It was like having an illicit liaison in this very room without them suspecting.

At times, there was guilt. She wondered how it had happened, and marvelled at the ease with which her feelings refused to bend to her conscience. She believed she loved Mathed. She had always *liked* him. He was sophisticated and optimistic and charming…but not…not deep. And she could foresee their marriage in the same way you could foresee the flow of a river: its course was inevitable. But perhaps it was not love. That seemed wrong, but there it was. And her mother was not alive to tell her anything different. She could not broach these things with her father, and talking to Osir was like arguing with the wind: calm one moment, a storm the next. She had learned to rely on herself, her own judgement and feelings. And her feelings drew her thoughts back to Adaim, beguiled by the sweet memories of a summer of rides into the hills, picnics near the deep waterfall where the gorge fell away, and he was there, next to her, with his young man's intensity, uncultured but intelligent, his hands on her hips, the sweet salt flavour of him on her tongue. She remembered him, the first time, in the gardens of the mansion, the young sentry in his smart olive-green surcoat and light chainmail, tall against the red-brick wall. He was beautiful, perhaps seventeen, and he tried to look straight ahead but his eyes betrayed him, following her for an instant with a startled glance full of meaning. That was the first time she had been surprised, for anyone below the Lady Che Keleu's station to make such an error should have been impossible. For her to meet this with anything other than disapproval was astonishing. And yet there it was. A frisson of delight had sparked through her body as if the youth had actually touched her. She did not, of course, look at him. That would not have been seemly. But she had been suddenly, decisively aware of her body and of his regard, his eyes on her, and the sensual pleasure that filled her. She had lingered in the gardens, when her intention right before that moment had been to walk indoors. His mere attention, the hungry stolen looks, infused her with an energy that was immodest. Yet it felt…enthralling and right.

Her thoughts cluttered when she remembered. And always there was the sensation, deep in her belly, that she could not name or describe but was good and exciting – guilt and all. It was as if Prince Mathed, her love, her intended, was not quite authentic; like a beautiful, desirable ornament, a thing you had always wanted, but when within reach, in your possession, lost its lustre and you knew that it was disappointingly both what you wanted and did not want – or rather it was what a part of you expected and everyone else expected, but it was not, in the end, what you really sought.

If this was a shock to her, and she supposed that it should be, it did not register like that. Deep down, she *felt* the materiality of Adaim: he was of the world, real, the thrilling source of the sensations she could not control. But, of course, he was gone. He was a corpse – no, mere ashes, scattered from a funeral pyre in the empty fields of Lorang. Unlike her father's ashes, his had not been returned to Strath. She did not understand the sense of loss. After all, she had hardly known him. The spring and summer of assignations had been brief, but the memories were powerful, undimmed, like the recent vivid dreams that woke her, shuddering, wet and elated.

One of her ladies was speaking to her. Her focus snapped back and the flush on her cheeks was obvious. Her friends laughed. Keleu smiled, and she was the virgin bride of their presumptions and she played her role again once more.

***

Harbin walked Castle Square in the wan light of early morning. The air was cool, with perhaps a touch of winter blown down from the north where autumn threatened an early cold snap. Around the greensward, along the parade, shopkeepers opened their doors. A dozen young men played at bats, scampering after the ball with good natured ragging of one of their number who had slipped on damp grass. A few optimistic folk sat on benches near the lines of plane trees, watching the game and enjoying a basket of breakfast before, presumably, heading off to employment of some description. They did not look like people of wealth and leisure.

Harbin walked the greensward perimeter every morning. He had instilled this discipline upon himself. Or rather, Zuse had instilled it. Zuse wanted to be out with the dawn, but since no person moved outside in the in-between time, they had compromised on this lovely period after sunrise, with its silver river mists, cool air and relative quietude. Harbin convinced himself that he enjoyed it. He was depressingly aware, however, that the autumn would be more bracing. And winter, well…

After a third circuit of the park, as the game reached a conclusion, and with his thoughts deliciously turning towards the prospect of breakfast, footsteps approached from behind. Zuse, striding at his master's side, turned his great black head, ears up then back again: Kesmet.

Harbin spoke brightly, without looking, "Good morning, Kesmet," as the scout drew alongside. He was not a scout – or not *only*; he was many things, but he preferred that sobriquet. And Harbin thought of him in those terms, in the broadest possible sense.

"Morning," came the reply. Brusque. He had news.

"Have you broken your fast?"

"I have."

Of course. Indeed, most mornings began with those words. It was a ritual, old, unfailing, perhaps begun as a stab of good humour once; Harbin could not recall. "You have news, my friend?" he asked.

"Birds in, last night. After you retired."

A worm of tension returned to Harbin's gut. "Ah-ha!" he exclaimed with a pretence at buoyant assurance.

"The wedding retinue of Clan Ouine is in Eloy," Kesmet reported. "And therefore Skava will be in Eloy. Word is that they head on for Mamoba within days."

Harbin digested this. It was entirely expected, but Kesmet was merely saying this as preamble to some other announcement of moment. He enquired carefully: "How large is the party?"

"Lord, lady, Prince, Jophan, Yoiwa's nephew, a minimum of attendants, his bodyguard and a hundred troopers, in the usual proportions: light, heavy and archers. Yoiwa has enough…" – and here Kesmet paused to dwell on the word – "to leave sixty in Strath and still return in safety to Deka."

"Hmph," Harbin grunted. "And who would dare to trouble the Lord of Honam on the king's roads?" He waved away the question and, Zuse, ever alert, perceived an imminent command. "No, Zuse," he corrected the animal, "heel," then directed his comments back to Kesmet: "It is all show, I know. The right numbers to convey the right aristocratic significance."

"Just so." An arch look. "And to consolidate sufficient strength in Mamoba."

They walked some more, Harbin's dawn constitutional being extended by every stride. Kesmet was silent, awaiting the inevitable question. Eventually, surrendering to curiosity, Harbin insisted peevishly, "Speak your mind." Kesmet had won this game of patience. Didn't he always?

"If you insist." Kesmet's bizarre humour – indeed, the only humour he indulged – was always at Harbin's expense. It kept them honest, humble, grounded…something like that. "Skava will accompany them," Kesmet explained. "She will be in the confines of the great house at Mamoba. We have one informer, and not even in the house. We need to be closer."

"Why?"

Kesmet turned his head and Harbin caught his look, one of sardonic disapproval.

"Very well," Harbin conceded. The time for playful diversions this morning was over. "We could travel to Mamoba town, close to the estate. There we would be well positioned to act quickly–"

"No."

Harbin looked at his companion in surprise. Quickly, with an arched eyebrow, he said, "You have been indulging that most dangerous of occupations: thinking."

Kesmet ignored the gibe. "Skava's network will be well established in the towns. If you, a senior partner in the Bank of Royal Kemae, go suddenly to Mamoba, it will be noticed."

Harbin admitted to himself that this was very probable.

"But the bank…" Kesmet proceeded, "has dealings with Strath and the estate directly."

"Indeed." Harbin drew up and faced Kesmet, whilst Zuse pressed on, only stopping to turn his head with a look that plainly signalled his discontent at this interruption of the morning's routine. "We could," Harbin finished the thought, "arrange for a partner in the branch at Moba to be…shall we say, available to attend the happy occasion…"

"Exactly. Good form. Suitably boring. Your typical banker."

Harbin acknowledged the taunt with a small nod. They walked further, and Harbin found that he was completing one additional lap of the greensward than was his habit or his preference. Zuse seemed pleased, in his canine way. And it did, Harbin discovered, add a tantalizing piquancy to the prospect of breakfast. He was also abruptly aware that this extra walking meant Kesmet had more to say. He decided to be haughty.

"And?" he demanded.

Kesmet favoured him with a long look, and with startling abruptness everything about him seemed to be concentrated on something utterly important: the intensity of his dark eyes under a frown, the way his beard made him look more gaunt this morning, even the focus of his gaze, unyielding and direct – like a hunter. Harbin did not want to stop walking. Ridiculous. But that was how he felt.

Kesmet gave voice to his intensity: "Skava will be there, Harbin. In the estate, at the mansion. Right there."

Harbin could see it. Skava, Sklavin, Eslin, whatever name she went by. She would be there. He breathed out, a long exhalation of mercurial vapour that caught both cold air and sunlight together. The worm of tension had become fear. He expressed it instantly: "She will be there in force. Her own people, capable men, the same men we learned of at Nek Feddah. And Yoiwa's bodyguard. And his elite troopers." He left the rest unsaid.

"All true," came the reply. "But she will be there."

They were heading now towards the inn and breakfast. But Harbin found that he needed to keep walking. He was surprised when he realized he did not want this conversation. He was trying to delay it. And that was stupid. Kesmet, he knew, was already committed to a course of action. He was merely informing him.

As they neared the roadway, Harbin asked, "What will you do?"

"Get close. Understand what is happening. Do what is required." Kesmet's voice was husky with his own tension. Harbin had not heard him sound this way in a very long time.

"On your own?" This thought alarmed Harbin. It was Eslin, after all.

"I shall be careful. Cautious, even."

"We were that *before*," Harbin remonstrated. "And we had numbers. Yet still, it seems, she survived…"

Kesmet drew breath, exhaled. "Quite so. On my own, this time, I might have greater fortune."

They stopped at the road, on the excuse that there was traffic, when of course it was still scarce here in the centre of the town at this time of day. Harbin found he was facing his old friend. Zuse was between them, like a solid barrier of living flesh.

"Will you need Zuse?" he asked, his voice a little choked.

"Yes." Kesmet looked pained, like this all hurt. Of course, it did.

Harbin's gut was wrapped in coils of fear now. "She is very dangerous," he blurted, pointlessly.

"Aye." Kesmet raised his chin, a motion that announced an impending request. "Harbin," he said. "Will you think on any manner that may assist the young prince…?"

Harbin realized at once that, in his need to see the whole picture, he had failed to spot the obvious and immediate. "Osir," he breathed. "She will want him out of the way."

"I fear so."

"I see. I will." Harbin was breathless. Still he had the presence of mind to ask, "When will you leave?"

Kesmet looked up towards the sun, and seemed to appraise its position above the horizon as if this provided a cosmic answer. He turned foresquare, his hand reaching out to grasp Harbin's shoulder with iron reassurance. "*Now*, my friend," he answered, his voice strong and resolute. "Now is a good time."

Harbin was bereft of words. Kesmet glanced at Zuse, who appeared to understand completely what had transpired, and now prepared to follow the scout. Both strode away, heading for the docks.

At long last, Harbin rediscovered his power of speech. "Send birds!" he called out.

Kesmet raised a hand, laconic as ever.

CHAPTER 10

The first and most obvious fact to be observed about the alliance of the Biljan kings and the war that embroiled Kiangsu for nearly two decades, is the centrality of the Ouine Clan. It is entirely insufficient to view the conflict as either a logical outcome of the frontier pressures between those clans loyal to Ehri (in the south and east) and the military aristocracy of the Biljan kingdoms (in the north and west), or indeed simply as the result of the ambition and conquering spirit of Jamarin III, remarkable as this was. Ouine Clan is perhaps the most ancient of the Great Families; it had dominated the northern regions for centuries; it had long resisted the missions of the Archivists to its courts, and persuaded the other Biljan kings to do likewise, with surprising success; and more than this it sought to extend its power south into Ssu-Am against its old enemy, Ke-Wai Clan. To maintain its dominion over all the northern lands it must unite the Biljan kingdoms around it… The alliance was not mutual. It served Ouine Clan. Hexil – 'The War with the Biljan Kings' in 'A History of the Civilized World', pages 4356-4357.

They despaired. They could see no end and no purpose. The others, in small groups, argued and disputed angrily or drew away. In time only a handful remained. Unknown author, from the Time of the Immortals, modern scholars arguing that this fragment of text refers to the War of Asunder, when the Immortals joined battle one against the other and were no more.

***

On a day cold and blustery, with heavy bruise-blue thunderclouds tumbling in from the Bay of Marshese, Yoiwa, Lord of Honam, arrived at Mamoba. The rain had held off, though the wind bent back the trees, and their boughs, clothed in the full green of summer foliage, whipped to and fro like giant flapping birds in an extremity of distress. Leaves raced each other across the dusty roadway and gathered in drifts against walls and fences, while more and more of their fellows leapt from the branches above. Dust from the dry ground moved like a mist over the land, so that the nearest hills were an indefinite verdigris bulk and the horizon a copper continuation of the lowering clouds. It was still early afternoon, but the light was poor and this together with the imminent storm had turned the peaceful landscape into one of wildness and extremes. It was a day to be indoors, cocooned against the mighty whims of the lesser gods of nature by stone and shutters.

The entire household of Mamoba Estate, however, was outside. In the gardens and along the colonnade leading from the main gates to the portico there were a dozen servants and, looking stern and awkward in their best clothes, twice as many of the tenant foremen who worked the vineyards hereabouts. Fifty men-at-arms lined each side of the colonnade, in smart olive-green surcoats and polished armour, wooden-faced and immobile, as if the worst ragings of wind and storm might never stir them. Nearer the mansion stood the nobles of Strath and their kin, dressed in the richest of attire, heads held staunchly high despite the gusting of the wind. Opposite them, the three Chisuans, with as much solemnity as they could muster, grimaced against the dust that assaulted their eyes. Twisting the tailored folds of their robes, the wind threatened at any moment to remove their tall, beribboned hats, clamped in place in each instance by the left hand of each gentleman. At their side were three Archivists, indistinguishable either by expression or vesture, like solemn black night birds that had mistaken the half-light for the onset of evening. And finally, there was Prince Osir, who had elected on this day to wear armour and who rested his gloved hand on the pommel of the magnificent sword that had been his father's. He stood flanked by the most senior officer of Strath, also fully armoured in bronze hauberk, ceremonial helmet held under his right arm. Only Keleu was not present; she would be introduced at a ceremony the same night.

Through the gates at the end of the colonnade Osir could see the winding road as it passed the stables and the granaries and, further still, the circular turret of the family temple, its normally vivid red and white roof tiles rendered a uniform grey by the dust and penumbral light. Yoiwa approached. That was certain. His arrival had been heralded in customary fashion by one of the officers of Honam, who had at once returned to his master, and indeed details of the Honam contingent and its progress had been passed to Osir, first by his spymaster, and then by his scouts several days earlier. Nevertheless, as yet, the Lord of Honam was not in sight.

The days of waiting, once the certainty of Yoiwa's arrival was evident, had disturbed Osir not at all. He had surprised himself with his own detached calm, and his kinsmen had followed his lead, to the palpable relief of Keleu. For days she had tried to gauge the mood of the northerners, and even now remained apprehensive of tension between hardliners like Ke Androc and men in the Honam party who might return an equal measure of distrust.

And so they waited, and the storm threatened. And then, above the groaning and soughing of the wind, Osir thought he detected the rhythmic beat of drums, deep, sonorous, unmistakable when he listened hard. His lip curled in a sneer. *He comes as conqueror*, Osir thought, and all the bitterness returned.

The drums were quite audible now and, hearing them, the assembled company shifted distractedly, and then with the same abruptness fell still once more, the better perhaps to judge the proximity of the drums as they neared the estate. Osir, from his vantage on the highest step of the portico, frowned into the gloom and there, distinct against the wild dancing of the trees around the temple, were the horses and the fluttering red and gold pennons, the glint of armour and the dark shapes of the riders and carriages. The thud-thud of the drums filled the air. The double ranks of horses and a carriage reached the gates of Mamoba Estate and halted.

The drums ceased.

The lead rider dismounted and behind him half a dozen of his armoured company. Without hesitation the small party came forward and passed inside the gates.

The Lady Che Mairu at his side, the Lord of Honam had entered Mamoba.

***

So there he was. The Lord of Strath – for not very much longer. Prince Osir. Any more miserable and he would collapse in tears. Skava marched forward, in the second rank of four behind Yoiwa and his wife, together with Mathed, who walked two steps behind his parents, in strict order of noble standing. Skava took in the mansion, her first time inside the garden walls – though she had scrutinised its every facet from the hills through her telescope. It was big, old, and downplayed its wealth, a gentle power, hinting at clever politics and patrician graciousness. The family had endured for hundreds of years…until now.

As they crunched the chalk gravel driveway, Skava noted the three supervisors of the Council. She knew everything about each of them, in detail; what to feed to Yoiwa, Mairu and Mathed, even his officers, to flatter and persuade in casual conversation, over drinks, dinner and breakfast. Small things that would encourage warmth and a favourable disposition for Clan Ouine. She examined the Archivists, important in their own way as observers. None, her investigations told her, was a spy. As they walked, they passed the assembled household, the lowest ranked land-foremen at the beginning of the colonnade, then the servants of the house and the officers of Strath, among them the new spymaster, pretending anonymity and, finally, arrayed on the steps of the portico, the provincial nobles and Osir himself. He was armoured: a polished bronze cuirass with beautiful decoration across the breastplate. His hand rested provocatively on his sword pommel – a very large sword for a youth. Skava smiled inwardly. So keen to be a man.

Much depended now on how Yoiwa chose to behave. And how

courageous or angry this youth was.

***

He had not changed. He was just as Osir remembered him, though the passage of time must be a decade. He wore his habitual white jerkin over heavy chainmail, together with ivory wool trousers and knee-length boots. Buckled to his belt was a dagger with a simple coiled steel handle. The belt was studded with archaic silver coins in two rows. As always he carried no sword, though, as Osir noted wryly, his officers bore a veritable arsenal of blades. As a boy Osir had always been impressed by the supreme conceit of this man, expressed in a face both handsome and coldly impersonal and in the unchanging, unfashionable attire that, in itself, announced as much self-assurance as the tilt of head and the rake of glittering eyes. His wife, Che Mairu, was no less a figure: regal of bearing, head erect, dark hair visible under a waist-length heavy shawl to defend against the wind. Her attire was rather more colourful: the inevitable red ankle-length chiton and a gold strap worn around the neck, under the armpits and waist and crossed at her back. Both of them stopped, imposing and impressive, at the foot of the steps.

Yoiwa addressed Osir: "Honour to you, Prince Osir! Honour to your family. We bring our son, Prince Mathed, who chooses your sister, the Lady Che Keleu, princess of Strath, by election of your late father, the noble Lord Shenri, by sponsorship of Lord Ordas of Lorang and the highest approbation of King and Council. Prince Osir, we seek your response."

At the mention of Mathed, Osir looked at the young man. He stood to the right and slightly behind Yoiwa. Osir's contemporary in more than just age, they had become acquainted in Chisua where they were students at the Roneca, and though their relationship had always been cordial, Osir had maintained a distance, in part because of his distrust of Honam and in part because he saw too much of the father in the muscular figure. Today Mathed was dressed in light chainmail, a fighting sword at his waist – the educated youth Osir had once known, equipped for war and here in Mamoba to claim a wife and all of Strath.

Osir looked at Yoiwa and, in a monotone, recited the words he must say, "Honour to you, Lord Yoiwa. Honour to the Lady Che Mairu and your family. I welcome you, I welcome Prince Mathed to Mamoba…" – and despite the obvious breach of protocol, he added, "the seat of my father's lands."

In the periphery of his vision he saw the supervisors shift uncomfortably and could imagine the sudden attention of the Archivists. Yoiwa, however, seemed unmoved. His pale eyes were impenetrable, his face an impassive mask over unreadable calculation.

Osir continued in the same toneless voice: "Mathed chooses Che Keleu of Strath. Lord Ordas of Lorang sponsors the match. King and Council approve. I say: so be it."

And the deed is done. I forsake my lands and forswear all claim to Strath by those words. Mathed takes my sister, willing as she is, and Yoiwa takes Strath. So be it. Would my father have handed Strath to Honam with as much ease? Keleu would have it so. The Council approves; they send the supervisors. The Archivists approve. They see some advantage for the Faith and the Realm in this. And my father mocks me with the approval of his dead hand and the seal of Strath. But he is gone, victim of a treachery that is both too brutal and too subtle for me. And do I too fall victim to the same treachery? Is there treachery? Gods! I feel it as keenly as I see this murderer before me!

The assembly awaited Osir. He stared at Yoiwa, but the mask was unchanged. Mathed smiled, as sincere as his father was cunning.

With a heavy heart Osir made the gesture of welcome, hands wide, palms up, that opened the home of his forefathers to Ouine Clan.

***

Keleu was beautiful and Mathed, so everyone agreed, was stricken. Though the young man tried hard to maintain the composure and dignity that protocol demanded, even so his ingenuous gaze wandered towards the daughter of Shenri and, as often as not, lingered there. Those in his company who found themselves without Mathed's attention whilst they conversed with him, were unoffended. He was well liked; there was a youthful honesty about him, and he smiled as if nothing mattered to him but the obvious love he had for Keleu. And what man or woman can fail to warm to the sight of two young people so enraptured?

On those rare occasions when Osir spoke to Mathed he felt guilty for his suspicions. Thus he kept an iron grip on his bitterness in front of Mathed, for he caught his sister's eye on more than one occasion and was pained each time by the pleading he read there. *She is dazzled by the integrity of Mathed*, Osir thought, *and sees nothing of the shadow of Yoiwa. 'Let me love him,' she cries silently and thinks me a reckless firebrand resentful of the favour she had from our father…and the power she now wields in Strath… And perhaps she is right.*

Mamoba Estate was now full of people. The halls and chambers echoed to the conversations of Archivists, supervisors, the two noble families, and officers of Honam and Strath. Their separate and ancient loyalties kept the officers apart during the day, but the presence of the supervisors and the Archivists mixing freely amongst them forced polite contact. Indeed, after the first day it seemed to Osir that Yoiwa had instructed his men to throw off their reserve, so that some awkwardness was apparent in the abruptly cordial demeanour of Honam's po-faced, unfashionably clean-shaven officers. As a result, the revelry expected of the occasion was achieved, but with something of a wrench.

What was wanting in the spirit of the event was fortunately abundant in the decoration of the mansion, which had been spectacularly made over for the celebration of the nuptials. Garlands of early autumn flowers decorated the stairways; over every doorway was a knot of wild romantic reesp with its bright pink blossoms; the hallways and reception rooms boasted freshly cut adips and gold water petals; and for three days preceding the wedding the women of the household wore circlets of tiny flowers in their hair. Che Keleu loved flowers.

Elsewhere, the olive-green colours of Strath and the gold and red of Honam were in evidence in the pennons that had been hung from the beams of the Great Hall and in the banners outside that snapped and tugged at their guy ropes atop the two red-roofed towers. Wagons had been trundling daily into the rear courtyard with great quantities of food. In the fire-bright warmth of the kitchen, cook could be heard bemoaning the late arrival of some delicacies and roundly cursing the kitchen boys for sluggards.

The weather had improved only to the extent that the wind had eased. From leaden skies a steady grey mist of rain turned the steps of the portico into puddles and the magnificent flowers and colourful beds of the garden into slouching bundles, despite the best efforts of the gardeners. And with the rain had come the cold, unseasonably early, so that Osir, peering out his upstairs windows at the dreary scene, imagined that had he been superstitious he might almost have believed Yoiwa's arrival to be responsible for the weather.

At dinner on the eve of the wedding, a different atmosphere pervaded the Great Hall. Forty guests sat the high-backed chairs at the long table. Keleu and Mathed occupied seats opposite each other. Osir sat at Keleu's side, Yoiwa at his son's. Jophan and Vedarahava, the commander of his personal guard, were close by, together with six other officers. Osir's officers were also present, good men, genial now but wary of those who wore the gold and red of Ouine Clan. The supervisors and the Archivists entertained each other further along the table. Osir's kinfolk were at the end, with several of the local merchants and their wives. At the two entrances to the Great Hall pairs of soldiers stood guard, framing the open doors, men of Strath and Honam in immaculate uniform, staring straight ahead, swords sheathed. Servants came and went in silence, attentive and unobtrusive. Goblets were filled and refilled with the best of Mamoba's wine, the finest in all Kiangsu. Course after course appeared, each one vying with the others in the splendour and skill of its presentation, and were greeted from different quarters of the table by applause and amazement.

***

Skava stood at the south entrance of the Great Hall. A Strath sergeant, immaculate in olive-green, stood four paces to her right, the other side of the huge double doors. They had acknowledged each other earlier as they assembled for duty, but no more. Skava herself looked resplendent in Ouine red and gold, she had decided: a magnificent specimen of manly trooper. Her location afforded her uninterrupted views of the entire room. The guard roster throughout the mansion had been arranged by both parties of duty officers, but Skava had ensured that she was in the room for the dinner itself.

Everyone was enjoying the splendid occasion. Even Skava. For there was the Lady Che Keleu, the gorgeous Siren and breaker of men's hearts. Dark hair, lush lips, almond eyes, brilliant smile. Marvellous tits. She had it all. Oh, and intellect too. She would need shepherding after the wedding: perhaps Che Mairu might surround her with suitable companions, ensuring she moved neatly in lock-step with her new husband and Honam's imperatives – clever women learned to control their husbands, and noble society was entirely comfortable with the arrangement. Skava watched her and, intermittently, the others in the hall, including guards and servants. The guest list had excited no concerns; simply the nobles of Strath, a few notable merchants and their wives, the local Ta-shih regional commander, even a junior partner of the Bank of Royal Kemae. All had reason to be here.

If there was a conductor of this grand affair, a fulcrum on which the equilibrium of this diverse attendance must be steadied, it was the Lady Che Mairu, flanked by Yoiwa and their son Prince Mathed. The matriarch worked the table in her immediate vicinity with the skill of a general marshalling and contending with the forces arrayed on both fronts – Che Keleu and Strath to one side, Clan Ouine to the other. For Keleu she had smiles and warmth, jokes at the men's expense and openly 'secret' conversations with her future daughter-in-law. Che Keleu seemed to delight in her company. An impressive performance.

Prince Osir, Skava noted, was not impressed. His expression was closed. He spoke mechanically, answering Yoiwa's questions with stiff courtesy. And he drank wine. A lot of wine. He was, Skava decided, withdrawing from the festivities like a hound retreating to a corner. Cowed. Trapped. Dangerous.

Skava began to worry.

***

The buzz of conversation rose steadily through the evening in direct proportion to the volume of wine consumed. Yoiwa, dividing his attention equally between Keleu, Mathed and Osir, smiled his joyless smile and to Osir spoke politely of the beauty of Strath and the coastline along the Bay of Marshese, which he knew well. Near the end of the meal, he rose from his seat and around the table immediate silence fell. He was one of those men whose natural authority commanded instantly. Yoiwa looked down on Keleu, and although it was clear he addressed the entire company, his words seemed directed only at her.

"My Lady Che Keleu, first and most beautiful daughter of Strath. Just to see you is to bring exultation to my son's heart, and joy to mine. Every Choosing is a political necessity amongst the Great Families. By this means we maintain the peace and stability of the provinces. No Choosing is motivated first by love though from the bond love may grow. But here…" And the Lord of Honam smiled on Keleu and Mathed in turn. "Here there *is* love first. And the Choosing is a good one. Honam and Strath are bound in unity and draw strength from it."

Yoiwa raised his hand and at once, from the doorway, between the Strath and the Honam guardsmen, a young man came forward. He was dressed in the light-blue garb of a poet and carried a twelve-string guitar slung across his shoulder. He stopped at the head of the long table and, without further ceremony, started to play. The harmony of the strings lifted to the high vault above, a theme repeated in a melodic pattern of gentle climax and cadence. Softly he played, and gazed at Keleu with an unreadable expression. And she, smiling in wonderment and pleasure, was rapt. The young man began to sing:

"New dreams awake like the moon on a lake,
Shiver, cold, fade and are old
In a moment.

But you are here and the gods are near,
And beauty speaks, forever seeks
Eternal love.
New dreams die, fade on a golden sigh;
A jewel's gleam, briefly seen
For a moment.
But time is yours and passion soars
Through darkling skies, heartfelt sighs
Of love…"

The final phrase lingered. The young man bowed his head. His fingers were unmoving. The song was over.

Keleu, whose eyes betrayed glistening tears of joy, looked at Yoiwa. And he, with great tenderness, said, "Che Keleu, love this man, my son, Mathed of Honam, of Clan Ouine. Ke Mathed, love this woman, Keleu, daughter of Shenri, Lord of Strath. Bring power to these northern lands and hold the peace of the Realm."

In the Great Hall there was absolute silence. Yoiwa raised his goblet high. Reflected light from the oil lamps winked red and gold from the steel wristband on his upraised arm. In a loud voice he cried, "To the lady, Che Keleu and Prince Mathed of Strath!"

And three dozen voices chorused the same, so that the Great Hall was suddenly filled with the vocal echo of Yoiwa's tribute. People smiled with excitement. There was celebration in faces, in every animated gesture.

Ke Beyil leapt to his feet, bright-eyed and with his square blue evening cap askew. He tugged at his topcoat to free it from the chair arm upon which it had snagged, spilling his wine in the process. He raised his goblet. "Princes, my lords, my ladies, nobles of Kiangsu," he called out above the buzz of conversation. Partway between dignity and abandon, for the wine had been very good this evening, he waved in front of him the goblet, which fortunately had little wine left to escape, by this means contriving to secure the attention of the company. Succeeding at last in his intent, he repeated the honorifics, "Nobles of Kiangsu!" and then proceeded in a voice with only the merest slur: "I beg, my Lord Yoiwa, a moment of this distinguished company. A pledge! To Jeval Ehri, our new king, Lord of the Realm!"

Goblets were thrust into the air. Men called the name of the king. Ke Beyil, his face flushed by wine and emotion, found his seat again with the assistance of Ke Ivik. Someone called for the poet to play more, "A rousing tune this time!" And the young man obliged while several of the officers of Honam and Strath clapped in time and added their voices to the popular refrain. Soon almost everyone had joined in. The poet played louder. Two of Yoiwa's officers danced a jig, to the delight and applause of the company.

Osir, through all of this, had watched proceedings with a face of stone, unable to smile and not trusting himself to meet Keleu's eye. He ordered more wine and drank heavily on top of the quantities he had already consumed, his gaze drawn irresistibly to Yoiwa – the handsome, lean countenance and controlled, capable air; the smile that to Osir was as cunning as a wolf's but which to the company about him was so winning. Every action of this man smacked of manipulation, for those who only had eyes to see! And here was his sister – so clever and so favoured! – leaping to Yoiwa's whim like some ridiculous puppy!

Osir reached for his goblet and knocked it over, soaking the white table linen with a dark stain. He snapped fingers at a servant and more wine was fetched. Around him the festivities continued, as if he and his objections were invisible.

But across the table Yoiwa was watching him. Osir glared back with a bold challenge fortified as much by liquor as by resentment. He hitched himself forward, and through the heat and fervour that suffused his face growled loud enough for only Yoiwa to hear: "You are content, my lord?"

Yoiwa's expressionless face changed not even minutely. He replied, "Aye. I am content."

"It seems," Osir went on, "that your minstrel's fine words tug at my sister's heart."

"Aye. They are fine words."

Osir threw back half a goblet of wine, wiped at his chin with the back of his hand. "Even Ke Beyil and the supervisors have succumbed to fine words. Perhaps I shall be next!"

Yoiwa said nothing, only watched him.

"It seems also," Osir pressed, though he knew Yoiwa's impassivity was like a trap under coiled tension ready to spring shut, "that you already lay claim to Mamoba and Strath."

Yoiwa smiled, predatory.

Through his teeth Osir hissed, "My sister, my lands, my father's life!"

Yoiwa's smile widened, derisive and wolf-like.

***

Something was passing between them. Skava had watched it unfold. The trading of words, just a few words, and the resultant and visible tremor of tension in the youth. The dog was cornered. The dog had no options. She had foreseen this. She had said he would at first stay quiet and then react – emotional, uncontrolled. He would cause a scene and dishonour himself.

She could read the angry prince of Strath, but she could read Yoiwa even better. He had listened carefully to Skava and what she had to say about the prince. He had planned something, but not told her. He was baiting the boy. He was seeking the fucking confrontation. And he knew just how to beat this particular dog until it attacked.

***

It was more than Osir could stand. He could see only the grinning visage of this brute. A rage boiled up in him. His limbs tensed. His fist clamped on the handle of the poniard at his waist, coldest steel in his fevered grip. Yoiwa was unmoving. Osir leapt. The chair toppled behind him. Goblets, dishes, food scattered over the table. His arm lifted, the poniard directed underhand in a thrust to Yoiwa's neck that could not fail to strike its mark. Elation surged through him. It was as if he had killed the brute already. Despite the effects of the wine, Osir's cat-like pounce was lightning fast. His strength carried him across the width of the table. The tip of the poniard drove up towards Yoiwa. At the last possible moment, Yoiwa moved. Already he was on his feet, his shoulder turned towards the weapon. His arm shot out. A vice-like grip fastened on Osir's forearm. With a twist of his body Yoiwa pitched Osir over table, the chair and onto the floor.

The Ouine officers reacted instantaneously. Two of them fell upon Osir and pinioned his arms. Jophan unsheathed his ceremonial dagger and bellowed, "Dishonour! He has attempted the life of a lord! I claim *his* life!"

He thrust the raised dagger at Osir's throat. Keleu screamed.

Yoiwa's voice rang out: "Hold!"

Jophan cried, "It is our right!"

"Hold!" Yoiwa repeated and pushed the chair aside to come forward. His back deliberately to Osir, he faced the shocked faces of the company. All were caught in attitudes of direst alarm, like so many open-mouthed statues.

"Ke Beyil, supervisors of the Council," Yoiwa said. "You have witnessed an attack upon my person. What is my right?"

Ke Beyil swallowed hard and rose unsteadily to his feet. He blinked at Yoiwa, momentarily incapable of speech. With an effort he gasped, "You…you may claim Ke…you may claim Prince Osir's life. I…"

Yoiwa nodded. He motioned to Jophan, dagger still poised. "Jophan, release him."

His nephew made to protest. Yoiwa silenced him with a look. "Release him. I would not spill blood at a Choosing. I will not spill blood at my own son's Choosing. And I fear Che Keleu has been much distressed by this incident." He faced Osir, whose wild eyes darted from face to face. "Ke Osir," Yoiwa said. "I lay no claim to your life, neither now nor in the future. You are at liberty. Only keep yourself from my sight…"

Tears of rage and shame stinging his eyes, Osir tore himself from the grasp of the Ouine officers and hurried from the Great Hall.

***

Skava had not reacted at all. One part of her had worked out that it was impossible for her to get close enough to make a difference. Staying still was more important than intervening – chiefly because doing so might draw attention. Another part of her was spitting fucking mad. Yoiwa had taken a risk, had not told her and had succeeded, which vindicated his highborn notions that the damned nobles did stuff that had nothing to do with anyone who wasn't highborn, and that they could do this and it was right. But it wasn't right. It was going to scupper longer-term plans, when she'd tried to educate him over the years that the old ways were not going to work.

Yet another part of her was working out what might happen now. The boy had gone. But how far? If they had learned anything, it was that he overreacted. Yoiwa had predicted his response, had used it to achieve what he wanted. Now Skava would have to clear up the consequent mess. What was it Yoiwa had said, back in Eloy? *His disgrace, his discredit, before a senior member of Council and, most preferably, some of the nobles of Strath, is very desirable to me. I foresee his exile and his disappearance.*

He had said it and he meant it. She had thought him to be ordering her to contrive something, but he had simply foretold his own action. And had executed it perfectly.

Unless the little bastard Prince Osir surprised everyone and went and raised an army... Now that would be a total fucking disaster.

Nobles!

***

The general mood of celebration which the guests at Mamoba had contrived, with some difficulty, to achieve in the days preceding the wedding now evaporated entirely. The shock of Osir's deranged attack seemed to strip the household of life. The servants spoke in whispers, with the same uncertain expressions as they had worn when news of Shenri's death had been announced. The officers of Strath, taut and frowning, kept to themselves, having summoned as much dignity as could be salvaged from the ignominy of their circumstances. By contrast their counterparts, the men of Yoiwa's guard, made no effort to conceal their contempt and suspicion. Indeed, Jophan and his officers kept hands to sword pommels in a deliberate insult.

In the grey half-light of morning, news of Che Keleu's condition was brought by Che Mairu and one of the noblewomen of Strath, who had been attending her, in the form of an announcement that the wedding would proceed in the early evening as planned. A rumour at once circulated amongst the servants that the Lady Che Mairu and Lord Yoiwa had exerted their considerable persuasive powers upon the bride in this regard. And despite the best efforts of Favul, the housekeeper, to quash it, at times with the aid of a rod about the servants' backs, the rumour persisted.

The day dragged by. The servants came and went. Mamoba's guests assembled in dour groups in the library and the reception rooms. Che Mairu and Yoiwa joined the company for lunch and appeared unaffected by the terrible events of the previous night. Ke Beyil felt moved to comment on both the courage and magnanimity of the Lord of Honam, sentiments which Yoiwa dismissed with a selfless shake of the head understood by the company to be wholly in character and wholly indicative of a nobility and generosity of spirit far beyond even Ke Beyil's compliment.

Of Osir there was no sign. A stable boy reported that a horse had gone during the night. But no more was heard.

In the late afternoon the Archivists called for the start of the nuptials. The Great Hall, transformed from the feast the previous night, now contained a circular shrine, erected in wood and painted in the red and white colours of the temple that stood beyond the walls of Mamoba. Garlands of flowers encircled the columns that supported the dome. In the centre of the shrine a white silk shroud, translucent, hung over a giant head, though the features were indiscernible. Behind the material a candle burned, casting a soft amber light and imbuing the giant head with a quality at once vital and spectral.

The Ouine Clan assembled. In full and glittering armour, Yoiwa's officers escorted Mathed to the entrance of the shrine where he knelt, head bowed in the silence that followed. The three Archivists, with attendants, appeared from a doorway. Shaven-headed, faces painted in a macabre emulation of stern sagacity, like unblinking owls, the three men brushed past Mathed in a swirl of black robes, placing the icons of the Faith behind the shroud before turning to face the assembly.

"Present in this shrine," murmured one, "is the visage of the So-Chiyen. Because of him, the dream murderer is banished from here. Because of him, no evil dream-spell may threaten bride or groom. Through him the gods see all. Let no man stand here faithless or with malice in his heart – lest Dian choose to cast her terrible white eye upon him!"

And then the three began to chant, joined in unison by the attendants and, at a signal from the Archivists, by the whole assembly.

***

The ceremony proceeded.

With the devotions and the contemplation complete, Mathed and the Archivists repaired to the temple beyond the walls. The Ouine Clan, the household and the officers of Strath formed a long procession in the gardens as darkness fell, and walked the distance to the temple with a measured step. In front, a group of players sang hymns to honour the manifestation of the gods of marriage and procreation joined in union with the other selves: the fertile, the wise, the merciful and compassionate. Behind the procession the mansion was left empty, except for Keleu and her servants, and the bearers of the litter that would carry her to the temple.

Osir, standing in the shadows of a large ornamental tree in the gardens, watched the procession leave. He had wandered the countryside all night, in spite of the rain, and had stayed clear of the estate until that evening. He had eaten nothing, his clothes were still damp, and he shivered now in the cool twilight, though the tremor in his limbs owed as much to anguish as to his physical condition.

Keleu would leave soon for the temple. He must see her before then. This was his chance, though the dishonour and disgrace of the previous night made the blood pound in his head and sucked dry his courage.

With a low cry he grasped at the trunk of the tree with one hand, terrified he might turn and run at any moment.

How can I face her? It is too much! Her hatred will kill me!

***

Skava watched the youth. Astonishing good fortune, if she were one to give credence to such things: he had climbed over the estate wall and, in all the wide gardens, crept close to her. He was oblivious to her presence, perhaps eight paces from the deep shadows of the circuit wall buttress where she had taken up her vantage. She had swapped ceremonial uniform for dark colours, the better to blend into the night. In a belt at her right hip she had clipped a standard hunting knife; in the small of her back a thin, short poniard; and in a pouch two vials – the sticky fluid in one inducing immediate paralysis, the other death in a matter of days. Her blades were tipped with each of the poisons – hunting knife slow-acting, the poniard fast. Both were secured in special sheaths.

Stationed at shadowed points elsewhere were Maki and Yan. They were covering the front entrance and the kitchen doors to the inner courtyard. But he had come over the wall near Skava. She had guessed he would return. Keleu was in the mansion, accompanied, but not yet the wife of Mathed. He wanted to see her. It had to be now.

He was quiet, agile, and moved as smoothly as a cat. This was of course his home. He knew it intimately, and with the familiarity of the boy who had evidently climbed these walls and concealed himself from tutors and guardians during his boyhood. Skava needed him dead. Yoiwa had contrived his disgrace, but he was now very dangerous, a rallying point for disgruntled Strath nobles.

Osir was holding onto a tree, head down. He seemed to shiver, but it was hard to tell in the night. Skava crouched, preparing to move up on him. This needed to be done well. A messy scene, onlookers, any taint attaching to Clan Ouine would be catastrophic. He must simply disappear – an ignoble prince, dishonoured, to all appearances fleeing into anonymity or distant, shameful demise. She took three steps, still crouched low, poniard tipped with fast-acting poison in her right hand, close to her thigh. Osir looked up, straight at the silvery light of the broad windows on the second floor where Che Keleu's chambers were. He was utterly absorbed. He would know nothing about the threat behind him until the knife entered his neck below the skull.

Another step. She knew the ground. She had studied it minutely that evening. Eyes only on Osir, she took another pace, onto her left foot. A fluid approach from behind and he would be dead. She could see his dark hair, the loose curling strands where they had come away from the roughly tied queue, just where she needed to sink the poniard. His shirt was wrinkled and stained. He was still looking up. She took the weight on her left leg – and her injured hip collapsed. Not enough to fall, but enough to cause her to immediately pivot onto her right, her balance gone, the killing movement abandoned.

And then the little shit slipped away from the tree.

***

Osir steeled himself. The fear of facing his sister nearly unmanned him. But he moved toward the mansion nonetheless, staring with trepidation at the silvery light pouring from the high windows, his legs unsteady under him, and a pain that threatened to burst his chest. The garden entrance portal loomed, the sculpted figures on the arches glared down on him like the spirit incarnate of his father. He pushed the door and stepped within, enveloped suddenly in the bright orange glow of the oil lamps, an intruder in this place so familiar and so dear.

The hallways were empty. He pushed at a disguised door, climbed the servants' stairway, found his sister's chambers, but hesitated at the sound of voices from within. In that briefest of moments before he entered, he imagined the look upon her face – the horror and the betrayal, the same look his father might have bestowed him.

Without further delay he opened the door.

There was a subdued gasp from the women present. At first Osir could not see his sister, and was startled by his own reflection staring back at him from a glass across the room: his dark hair awry, fine clothes soiled and torn, and his eyes as wild as a hunted animal. Then he recognized Keleu. She stood to his left, dressed in the formal ochre of the bride, as radiant and beautiful a woman as ever he had seen. He could say nothing, only look at her.

After a space, Keleu gestured to her attendants, and with a soft rustling of skirts they left the room. Sister and brother were alone.

"Osir…" Keleu murmured. In her face there was great sorrow, and it shamed Osir more than had she shown how much she despised him. He looked away, fighting the emotion that swelled in his throat.

He choked out an excuse, "I had to come…I had to wish you well. I have brought Strath dishonour. I hope I do not bring you unhappiness and ill luck as well…"

She came to him and embraced him, though he flinched away. "Osir," she whispered, "I love you!"

He held her gently at arm's length. With a hoarse whisper he remonstrated, "Don't say that. It's more than I can stand! I would rather you hated me! If you hate me you allow me at least the excuse to hate Yoiwa for bringing this between us!"

Again she embraced him, her eyes brimming with tears. "I love you, Osir! I shall never hate you!"

"You must!" Osir hissed, struggling with the violence that threatened to break from him. "I cannot abide his gloating! He has murdered our father! I tell you he has!"

Keleu, pale and shocked, shook her head in dismay. "This must end, Osir! You try Lord Yoiwa's patience. Think on what you have done! Think on it!"

"On what I have *not* done, sister! By this much I missed his throat! The Shae grant me a steadier hand next time!"

Vexed beyond the limit of tears, Keleu stepped back from him. She feared the profanity and the turmoil of this man, her brother, the ungovernable rage that fired his eyes. He paced across her room now, as incongruous and terrible a sight amongst the beautiful feminine things of her bedchamber as a ravening beast. Abruptly he rounded on her.

"You cannot accept Mathed! Tell them you must postpone the ceremony!"

"Osir! Stop it!" she pleaded.

"Stop?" He laughed, a horrible sound, with lips drawn back in a grimace. "I dream terrible dreams now. Blood and the murder of my father and my own failures to protect him. He is cut down in my dreams and I am feeble. I can do nothing except stand fixed, my legs sunk in mire. And in front of my eyes he is cut down by that monster Yoiwa!" Osir gasped a ragged cry of pain, then shouted, "These dreams are sent by Echrexar! He torments me with my failures! I dishonour Mamoba and my sister in my bungling attempt to execute a murderer, and in accepting my sister's Choosing I dishonour Shenri and Strath! I cannot stop. Twice damned, Che Keleu, betrothed of Mathed of the Clan Ouine! But I shall salvage at least a flimsy shred of honour if I rend Yoiwa! On my oath I shall!"

Keleu had backed up against her bed. Osir seemed suddenly to notice her. Shame softened the features of his face and he became her brother again. He held out his hands in half plea, half apology. "I think of father, Keleu," he said in a voice of breathless, aching despair. "I think of him and of Strath and I…I feel the loss so greatly."

He hung his head, arms limp at his sides. Keleu, hesitant, searching his face for a sign that the riot of emotion had passed, said quietly, "We share the loss, Osir. And while we share it, do we not make the pain a little less?"

"Aye…" And he stood silent and still for long moments, a figure alone under bright yellow light, and there was no sound at all.

Then, distant and barely audible, came the muted ripple of chorusing voices, the chant of hymns carried from the temple on the wind. Osir lifted his head as if at some alarm. He went to Keleu. Forlorn hope lit his eyes, twisted his face.

"You will not go to him…? You'll reject Mathed? I beg of you, Keleu–"

"Osir, please–"

"You must not! Say you will not!"

He grasped at her arm. Frightened, she pulled back. "He is a murderer!" Osir cried in frustration.

Keleu moved away. She gasped, "Osir! Leave me, please! Think on what you have done! Please!"

"Enough then!" he bellowed. "Enough! Share this murderer's bed! Be his whore! You have my blessing, sister! But then you are my enemy, hear?"

"Osir!"

But the young man stormed from her room and was gone.

***

Skava cursed in every language she knew. It had happened absurdly fast. One moment he was within range, the next he was across the pathways and into the house. Standing next to the tree where Osir had been waiting, she worked her hip, rubbing at the bone and muscles to banish the cramp. Waiting in the cold autumnal night air had been fatal. Her body was not yet recovered. Good enough for most things – walking, riding, even hard training – but not the real thing, not standing stock still for too long in the cold and then shifting abruptly into attack. It was a tiny physical slip, but sufficient to create kicked-in-the-balls failure.

In silence she watched the garden doors where they had closed only moments before. The mansion was quiet. Above, on the second floor, the silver light spilled out of the curtained bay windows of Che Keleu's chambers. Skava cursed again. She was stuck. He was inside, come what may, and she could do nothing. She considered going around the house to link up with Maki or Yan, but that would leave the garden doors unattended. Instead, she maintained her concealment under the tree, massaging her hip, working the muscles with small, regular movements.

Raised voice: Osir's voice. Shit. What if he attacked Keleu?

Again she considered moving. Maybe get inside. No. Disaster if she was spotted. She took a deep breath, waited. Quiet now. No sound from within. She forced herself to look away from the doors, to survey the whole length of the house, checking carefully in the darkness for movement. There were seven entrances, all of them visible, from their respective vantages, to Maki, Yan or her, but innumerable windows at ground floor level. She looked at the garden doors again. Closed. Looked back to the clumped shadows that were the plants and borders. A silent dark figure dashed across the pathways towards the walls. *Where the fuck did he come from?*

Skava reacted immediately, crouching again, closing on her quarry from an acute angle. The figure reached the wall. Definitely Osir: she could read the physical dimensions, the way he moved. He swarmed up the vertical brickwork at the buttress where she had first concealed herself. He knew the walls from boyhood, clearly. In moments he was swinging himself onto the top and was gone. Skava had already sheathed her poniard, taking a moment with her gloved hands to make sure none of the poison was misplaced. Then she felt for handholds on the wall, started to climb on the uneven mortar, bracing herself between buttress and masonry. She made the top, swung her leg up in some discomfort and flattened herself on the mossy broad capstones crowning the length of the wall.

Thirty paces away, even in the darkness, she could see Prince Osir was mounting a horse.

Oh, for fuck's sake!

In moments he had become one with the impenetrable gloom.

CHAPTER 11

Keleu of Strath was the most beautiful and the most tragic of women. Though she dearly loved her brother, how could she betray her husband, Mathed of Honam? Though Osir had committed the most dishonourable of crimes against her father-in-law, how could she condemn him? Thus was she torn. And the household at Mamoba pitied her.
Ke Ivik – 'Diaries'.

We had the records and the knowledge but not the energy sources. Our ambition exceeded the basic fundamentals. Ultimately, this is what caused the breakdown and what some have called the reversion.
The Diary of Giorgios Kellastis, assumed to be an Immortal, on the in-between time, copied by a scribe, IYE 1044.

***

The two weeks following the nuptials brought Mamoba fully to autumn. Though the skies were clearest blue and the sun was warm during the day, the leaves that fell from the trees were russet, brick-red and yellow, and the neat gardens and chalk pathways of the estate became blanketed with their fragile, curling forms. The gardeners set to with rakes each day and frowned when the wind got up, as it did mid-afternoon with the golden sun hovering, uncertain, above the blue-grey hills, and the leaves plucked one by one from the tall, ever more skeletal trees.

Nights were cold. The chill air made the lake of stars above electric, and the moon, waxing, silvered the rolling landscape. The hills, hunched black masses under the stars, seemed to close around Mamoba like giants stirring in sleep. The mansion itself was shuttered against the cold. Pinpoints of orange light streamed from embrasures or winked and were gone at the opening and closing of a door.

One bitter night in the courtyard at the back of the mansion, the figure of a man, hunched against the cold and swathed in dirty woollen scarves, crossed the cobbles and, at the kitchen door, paused to stamp his boots upon the first step, in the manner of one who performs the action more as a perfunctory gesture of habit than of forethought. This done, he entered the homely rush of warm air and ruddy light that greeted his opening of the door.

A voice from inside cried out, "By the Shae's bony arse, Iken! Close the damned door!"

And the fellow so named made haste to seal the door behind him, grumbling into his beard, "T'is but a moment, ye miserable lout! I been down th'stables an'back – and in this cold!"

The individual identified as a miserable lout was sitting with his back to the large double doors, which gave onto the kitchen courtyard. At the end of his legs, thrust out towards the blaze of a fire in a huge stone hearth, were two hairy, calloused feet, which flexed and turned, their owner evidently occupied with the exquisite pleasure of thawing his extremities. The rest of this individual was portly but otherwise unremarkable, save for a large potato nose whose scarlet tincture made no secret of the alcoholic inclinations of its wearer.

Iken, shuddering, as people do, at the sudden warmth of the kitchen, squeezed past his companion's feet and stood with his nether portions to the fire, his hands spread wide at his sides in a peculiar emulation of the movements of the aforementioned feet. Neither man said anything for a moment. The fire snapped and spat. A warm smell of wet wool and horse filled the space around the great fire as Iken, who had been riding up and down on his toes the better to distribute the radiant warmth against his buttocks, now drew slightly away and, unwinding the scarves that encircled his neck and shoulders like the coils of a somnolent snake, turned to toast his front. In a conversational tone he observed, "Lord Yoiwa's horses are snugger than we are… So's the boy. Snoring like old Gexa, the little brat! I give 'im a smart clout round the ear! Teach 'im."

"By th'iron dogs' bollocks, leave 'im be, ye rag-eared bastard. And fetch the cider. I've warmed it agin."

Iken sniffed, and with a reluctant shuffle moved away from the fire. Gingerly he picked up the cider, steaming in a large copper pot, this suspended over the red embers remaining in the vast circular stone oven that dominated the centre of the kitchen. Pouring not quite equal volumes into two tankards, Iken selected the larger and, with a carefully neutral expression, proffered the other to his recumbent partner.

"There ye are, Ovska," he grunted.

Ovska, appraising Iken with a suspicious eye, ignored the proffered tankard and, to Iken's chagrin, thrust out a hand to take the other.

"Ye mean bastard!" Ovska berated his crestfallen companion. "Steal mother's milk, ye would!" And he consumed a quarter of the contents of the tankard in a noisy gulp, progressing with admirable vigour to an even noisier belch. Then, returning to the topic that had dominated the household for days preceding, Ovska asked, "E's gone at first light, then, is 'e?"

Iken, staring into the fire like a mesmerised hound, responded lethargically, "Aye…first light." Then with more energy, "An' good riddance, I say, 'e an'is mob! Bah! A more 'igh an' mighty lot I don't wish t'see agin. How they gloat over our Prince Osir's misfortune!"

"Aye, aye," Ovska concurred. "And our lady don't wear 'er brother's troubles well neither. That's a bad thing, a woman new married like that an' all. Ill luck or a dream spell. Sad, it is. Sad. Sad."

"But our Lord Mathed is alright, ain't 'e?" observed Iken.

Ovska grunted. "Mebbe. But 'e's 'is father's son, eh? And them Ouine Clan's all the same. Right arrogant."

Iken pulled a face to mean he remained unconvinced but, receiving no further comment from Ovska, returned to his contemplation of the fire, occasionally dipping his face into the tankard of steaming cider. Ovska, one arm crooked upon a table to support his head and with the tankard balanced in his lap, sank into a reverie. His eyes began to close. His chin rested on his chest. Only the tiny glint of firelight reflected in one eye suggested that he had not joined the deceased in his long slumbering.

This repose was abruptly curtailed by the clatter of a horse's bronze-shod hooves on the cobbles outside, and the thud, as the unknown individual dismounted and headed towards the kitchen door, of what Ovska instantly recognised as a soldier's boots.

Iken turned wide eyes to his companion and stared at the door. Ovska struggled to his feet, hopping on one foot as he tried to insert the other into his boot.

A thunderous knocking followed. Ovska, with his boot half on, frantically gestured Iken to the door.

"The spyhole! See who it is!"

"Open up!" came the cry from outside.

Iken reached the double doors and snapped back the spyhole, pressed his face to it, then quickly glanced over his shoulder at Ovska to whisper, "An Ouine trooper!"

Ovska, dancing around once again in a hopeless attempt to pull his boot on, complained bitterly, "Open the door, then, you old sow or 'e'll 'ave our ears!"

The door was hurriedly opened. The Ouine trooper swept in with a blast of freezing air and billowing red cloak and fixed Ovska with a fierce eye. "My Lord Yoiwa! I have an urgent message for him!"

Ovska, bent double with one hand on his boot, jabbed a finger upwards, by this gesture intimating that Yoiwa was in the upper chambers of the mansion.

"Where?" demanded the trooper.

And at this moment an officer, on duty within the mansion and alerted by the commotion, marched in to investigate.

Both men departed the kitchen, the new arrival calling over his shoulder for his horse to be stabled. Iken and Ovska were left staring at each other. The icy air stirred the coals in the oven and made the fire leap and sputter. Ovska narrowed his eyes and bestowed upon Iken his most meaningful look, as if between them they had suddenly become privy to the most secret of information.

"Better see t' the nag…" Ovska gestured to the courtyard.

"Damn me!" came the response. "I bin out already! It's your turn, ye lout!"

"Without boots! Lookit m'feet!"

"Oh no! It's your turn…"

Ovska threw both hands in the air and gestured with his head towards the door. "We'll both go!"

Iken, recognizing in this statement as much of a compromise as he was likely to attain, acquiesced. And when Ovska had succeeded in pulling on his boots and his coat, both men hurried into the courtyard, their imaginations filled with the riot of possibilities that this night's messenger had brought.

***

Lord Yoiwa had received the intelligence from Skava, via one of her couriers, in the early hours of the morning, and had at once delayed his scheduled dawn departure, an act which, like dry tinder upon an already fiercely raging fire, sent the household servants into a frenzy of hushed speculation. Ovska and Iken, happily foregoing sleep for the slack-jawed amazement bestowed on them by their fellows, and especially several pretty maids whose habitual coldness towards the two had undergone a remarkable thaw, entertained everyone with suitably embellished accounts of the night's events.

A party of Ouine officers had thundered into the courtyard, so the story went, and the two servants, arming themselves with stout cudgels – for who would be calling at such an hour? – had sallied forth to defend the mansion. This part of the tale typically raised at least a gasp from a wide-eyed audience. Identifying the officers' colours, the brave gentlemen had rushed to assist, for many of their number, a detail never disclosed, appeared bloody and dishevelled as if from battle! A question at this point would receive a tight, knowing smile from Ovska, encouraging in the audience the conclusion that the location and objective of the skirmish, like all matters military, were secret, imparted only to the privileged. *And the message? What of the content of the message?* Aha! would come the response, in tandem with lowered brows and the sagacious nodding of Ovska's unlovely head. Like every accomplished gossip, he perceived, in his own dull way, the extent to which the limits of truth should be pressed. Thus, allowing exaggeration to touch only looks and mannerisms, he would conclude in a slow speech accordant with the gravity of the subject, that he and his fellow were sworn to absolute silence, but that he could reveal – and here the audience would, without exception, lean tensely forward – that the message appertained to the Lord Yoiwa himself – himself, no less! – and our good Prince Osir!

Of course, in passing on the gossip in their turn the other servants, with no great advantage to be gained by adhering to this particular rendition of the story, added both detail and colour and, where Ovska had instinctively left the ending obscure, they obliged with explications to rival the greatest playwrights of Kiangsu. As a result, by the time the story returned from its rapid journey through the surrounding tenant farms and villages, like the ripples produced by a stone in a pond which swell over each other and disturb the initial ordered pattern, not only the details but the characters inhabiting the story had become alarmingly distorted. To his abiding annoyance, Ovska, in hearing the tale from a local merchant's factotum later that same morning, was astonished to learn that his own name appeared nowhere, and that the courage he had displayed in the cold hours of the night had been ascribed to some nameless Strath officer of epic stature. Since this mythical stalwart had no likeness to the corpulent, ill-dressed villain that stood before the merchant's factotum, this same individual was moved to gales of laughter at Ovska's emphatic insistence that the hero of the night was none other than himself.

Lord Yoiwa was aware of the rumours. Like all men of cunning he made no attempt to quash the talk, recognising the value of feeding the rumour appropriately to his own advantage when the time came. Nevertheless, the true import of the message had worried him sufficiently to put off his return to Honam. Skava had sent the courier and was still out in the countryside, picking up intelligence on Osir's movements. She was on her way back, but Yoiwa could not wait.

On receipt of the news he had dismissed his officers, dressed himself in his usual attire, and then summoned Mathed to meet him in the library downstairs. It was still dark when Mathed joined his father there amongst the orderly rows of books and vellum manuscripts that filled the shelves around them. Oil lamps cast cold yellow light and made the darkness beyond an unshuttered window inky black and impenetrable. No fire had been lit yet in the fireplace and the room felt cold and unfriendly to Mathed. His father stood behind a writing table, hands locked behind his back, dark eyes brittle. It was the father he knew well – as distant and severe as any man can be. From his earliest years Mathed had learned to fear him as greatly as he loved him, and in all his life, in the fortress city of Deka which was his home and in the Court of Chisua amongst the Legations, he had witnessed no man who was not cowed by the extraordinary authority of the Lord of Honam. Though he stood taller than his father, Mathed still felt diminished and vulnerable in his presence. He felt that way now, sensed the force of will that was both familiar and frightening.

"I have had word," began Yoiwa, "from outside Eloy where Osir has taken up with Ke Androc. Apparently, the noble Androc sympathises with your displaced brother-in-law. In itself this fact is immaterial: the company Osir chooses for himself is of no interest to me. However…" Yoiwa paused and came round the table, close to Mathed. "However, young Osir has had contact with other nobles in Strath. In two short weeks he has been busily engaged, his fervour and his hatred for me undiminished by the dishonour of his attempt on my life. Some might say, in this one regard, that I miscalculated, that I was too generous. Had I permitted Jophan to take the young fool's head, we might have dispensed with his interference immediately. But that would not have endeared me to your wife, nor to the king's representatives, nor to the great noble families of the Realm. It is important that you see this. We must think further than these temporary irritations."

Yoiwa paced away again to stand at the dark fireplace. He regarded his son sidelong. "The news is this: Osir incites the nobles of Strath against you."

Mathed exclaimed, "In arms? But surely not! He cannot turn on his own sister!"

Yoiwa smiled and shrugged. "He is a hothead. Think of him on the eve of the wedding, like a rabid dog! Accusing me of Shenri's murder!"

Hesitant, Mathed ventured, "You had no hand in that…" He had meant it as a question, for he needed to believe it could not be so, but under his father's stern regard it was neither one thing nor the other.

Yoiwa lifted his chin the merest fraction, profound disapproval in this smallest of gestures. "And if it were?" he challenged. "Would it change your duty?"

Mathed blinked. It was not a response he had anticipated and yet the word 'duty' hung in the air, its sound, its feel, its implications as familiar as the beating of his heart. Always there had been duty, at every juncture of his life – duty to his beloved Ouine Clan, to Honam, to its vast history, to the restitution of its betrayals and ancient enmities, to the cause of nobility itself, and most of all to his father. There was no answer other than the one he gave:

"No."

Yoiwa pressed on, as if this interlude in their discussions had never happened. "Osir should not be taken lightly. Skava warned us that he might attempt this. He has the legal right I discussed with you. He has chosen to prosecute the issue by force of arms. He has the passion that will fire men and the words to whip them to war. In any event, we need not debate the point. I have it from our people in Eloy that already Androc and others have sworn to levy two companies."

Mathed, recovering quickly from his dismay, observed, "And we cannot rely on the soldiery here at Mamoba, at least five score…"

"Precisely. They will never fight their own on Honam's behalf."

"And the Ta-shih?"

"They may not intervene. And when they are permitted, here in the north their numbers are pitiful. What, a hundred troops scattered over twice as many miles? The largest garrison is in Woel or at Desdang Fortress. Meanwhile they must remain neutral to arbitrate any legitimate challenge to control over Strath. They will not interfere until the fortieth day. By then Osir will have butchered us, and doubtless his sister too… and will reclaim Strath."

Mathed stared hard at his father, who returned his look with a narrowing of the eyes as if to say, *Come, Mathed, what will you do? This is your province, my gift to you. What will you do? Will you have it stolen from you? Here I test you, Mathed…again. Do not disappoint me. What will you do?*

But Mathed was accustomed to such tests. He had learned to think quickly, to determine strategy and tactics and then set priorities. Earnestly he said, "We must secure the Council's support, above all. The king's representative is disposed towards us. If we guarantee his safety he will surely give his blessing and his authority to our striking at Osir first."

"You have fifty men…against his hundreds."

"Indeed. We shall strike at once. Skirmishes to delay him, to keep him from Mamoba. Ouine troops are twice the soldiers of these northern yokels!"

Yoiwa glowered. "Do not underestimate their zeal. They will fight as Osir fights. They see us as invaders. Worse yet…" – and here Yoiwa fixed his son with an intense, penetrating stare – "they see us as the murderers of Shenri. Do not forget it."

"No. No, I will not."

"And what of your wife? She is your ally. And she is persuasive…"

"But she could never dissuade Osir from force."

"She might delay him."

Mathed nodded. "Aye, aye. She might at that." He looked at his father once again, abruptly aware of the pace of events. Here they held council in the dark of night and spoke calmly of war. There was a remorseless inevitability about all of this, as if each word that passed their lips set in motion a dozen other events, each one drawing them closer to conflict. Mathed half expected that violence might explode about them this very instant. Quietly he said, "I shall speak to Keleu…"

Yoiwa delayed a moment, as if out of respect for Mathed's feelings, then he said, "She is strong. Men will follow her."

And he meant the men of Strath, whose loyalty Mathed might no more command than the insensate trees of Mamoba. He felt suddenly alone: something in his father's expression, a remote finality in the accent of the eye, made his heart sink within his breast.

"You're still leaving…" he breathed.

Yoiwa nodded. "Aye. I shall begin the journey back tomorrow. I cannot be seen to be embroiled. We must encourage the opinion that Osir attacks his own sister and brother-in-law – not the Lord of Honam, whose motives might be construed as imperial ambition."

Yoiwa came forward, grasped his son by the shoulders, and his touch made Mathed inexpressibly happy, for pride, for honour, for duty.

"You will not face the challenge alone," his father said, calmly, deliberately. "I have instructed Skava and her squad to remain here. Listen to her. Learn from her. But make your own decisions. Command her. It is a hard thing to go to war alone. But I know you and I have faith in you. Moreover, Vedarahava will be your commander, and his troops are Honam's best. Hold Strath against the usurper. Hold it for Ouine Clan."

Mathed, smiling, bowed his head. A fire lighted his eye. It seemed to him that a new and irresistible meaning had burst in upon his life. He looked at his father and, through choking emotion, hoarsely whispered, "I shall hold Strath. Strath is ours."

***

Lord Yoiwa completed his affairs that day and ordered provisioning for forty of the Ouine troops, the closest of his elite personal guard, and Jophan. It was announced that he and his wife would depart Mamoba the following day. That night, however, in the cold hour after midnight, Ovska, nursing the blow to his esteem inflicted by the wild distortions of his escapade the night before, was interrupted in his deliberations over a steaming pot of cider by urgent news brought by the stableboy. Shivering in the frosty air, for Ovska had kept the lad standing on the doorstep, he reported that the Lady Che Mairu's carriage and forty cavalry bearing the Ouine red and gold had left only moments ago and, may the Shadow Lord send iron dogs from the deepest waters to tear him limb from limb if it wasn't the truth, he had recognised one of their number as the great Lord of Honam himself!

This was, of course, so. Ovska, unfortunately, was unable to profit from gossiping about this news since, with the dawn, word came from Lord Mathed himself that Prince Osir had taken up arms against Mamoba. The household was shocked. At breakfast Ke Beyil and his aides expressed their horror and publicly gave their support to Mathed. Reluctantly, Mathed admitted that he had advised his father to depart Mamoba in the dead of night as a precaution against assassination. The supervisors were appalled. Ke Beyil lauded Mathed's forethought and was moved to a not inconsiderable anger at the ignoble circumstances forced upon Strath by Prince Osir. Mathed, rising to the occasion as his father might have done, begged Ke Beyil to maintain his neutrality – "for the sake of Strath and the Realm."

That same morning, a message arrived for Ke Beyil under the seal of Ke Androc but signed by Prince Osir, setting out his legal challenge. Mathed and Che Keleu listened in silence to its reading. In short order Mathed drafted, under the seal of Strath, a document guaranteeing the safety of the three supervisors. Consequently, Ke Beyil, in spite of his aides' alarm and their advice to the contrary, refused to budge from Mamoba and enthusiastically elected to remain until the fortieth day, dramatically declaiming, "Though swords and missiles threaten my very life!"

And so Mamoba armed for war. Strath's soldiery, housed at the keep west of the mansion, Mathed ordered disbanded. He addressed them personally.

"You owe me no loyalty, no allegiance," he said to them. "I must earn that from you. Whilst this legal challenge by arms endures, I free you from obligation of service so that you may choose your lord. I, like you, serve only Strath. And my love for Che Keleu is a measure of my love for Strath."

The sentries of Strath left, and men in Ouine red and gold took their places on the sturdy walls of the grey stone keep, at the gates of the mansion, and on the winding roads under the green hills of Mamoba. Small squads of mounted soldiers, heavy with armour, rode out on patrol from the estate in the sun-bright autumn days, while folk in the neat fields and vineyards stood to watch in awe, thrilled by the sight of bright armour, the wash of sunlight on lance and sword, and the slash of crimson cloaks against the ochre and earthy brown of the season.

Rumour of war swept the land like swelling currents in the ocean, gathering force this way, and then sweeping back that way, so that truth became as elusive as the myriad leaves flung swirling by the afternoon winds.

Half of Strath's soldiery, perhaps sixty in number and including many of the officers, pledged allegiance to Mathed. Some smaller number were known to have joined Osir, and the rest had apparently remained undecided, withdrawing to the nearby villages. This unexpected and significant addition to his forces pleased Mathed. It promised a groundswell of support he had not believed existed, though he knew it to be less on account of any personal esteem for this new master of Strath, than of the great love accorded Che Keleu.

But no matter: Keleu was his wife and was at one with his cause.

***

Skava slipped back into her role as Courier-sergeant Alin. It afforded her legitimate access to Mathed and therefore time with him and Vedarahava to plan their campaign. Osir had been canny. He had moved frequently in the early days after eluding her in the garden. Once amongst his kinsmen, it was impossible for her to get close. With conflict in the air, strangers excited suspicion. Informers refused to be bought off. The options were narrowing. They faced a set of decisive battles as Osir sought to take Mamoba: he would force submission or kill Mathed.

That presented Skava with two unwelcome challenges: she must keep the new Lord Mathed of Strath alive, and she must support him in taking the field against Osir. He could not be secured behind the walls of Mamoba. That would be seen as cowardice and, in any event, Mathed would never agree to it. He must lead and be seen to lead.

"Vedarahava is your commander and his squad will be your bodyguard, my lord," she informed Mathed one morning. They stood near the shadow of the keep, the rolling hills and the vineyards in the distance. Grey skies threatened rain. It was dismal. Not the best weather for war. But maybe that was to their advantage: a smaller force, on difficult ground, was more mobile.

"Yes," said the young man.

"His squad will not leave your side, my lord. There may be assassins…"

Mathed raised his chin in distaste. Vedarahava, wisely, voiced his agreement, "The threat is real, my lord."

"Yes," he said again.

Skava glanced towards the hills. Two hundred paces away, in an outbuilding, was Yan, watching the southern approaches. Down the road, to the east, was Maki, holding six mounts among a stand of oak trees. Sentinels walked the keep tower, men of Honam and Strath.

"I need to track Osir, my lord. I need to know his numbers and strength."

Mathed turned to her. His eyes were red-rimmed, but alert. He was tired but rising steadily to the demands of leadership in war. "Of course," he acknowledged. "We rely on you, Alin."

It was supposed to be encouragement, a show of faith. It amused Skava. But she applauded the intent.

"One more suggestion, my lord," she said.

He lifted both eyebrows. He did listen to her. Mostly. What worried her was the moment he chose to stand his ground and ignore her advice. It was coming.

"If I may propose," she advised him politely, "that my lord change the uniforms of our troops. If they wear the colours of Strath it will bind the men of Strath to our cause, and it will still the suspicions the people might have for their new lord."

Mathed pursed his lips. Vedarahava nodded: he was loyal to Clan Ouine alone but he was a killer and he was pragmatic. "It would be best, my lord," he agreed. "The green of Strath and perhaps another colour, white, I think, to make our new livery stand out from the enemy."

Skava looked at the tall bodyguard with new eyes. A clever idea. She could rely on him.

"Sound advice," said Mathed. "It will be done."

Skava turned to the bodyguard, armoured as always, and nearby two of his men, carrying shields at all times. "Commander," she began, using the title that denoted his new role. "In the estate, in the mansion especially, I urge that we maintain twenty troopers at all times, always in pairs, but working with the loyal men of Strath." She jerked her chin at the squat stone fortress towering over them. "The keep is no use to us, if Osir takes the mansion. The mansion is the seat of Strath in law. I recommend you garrison the keep with Strath soldiers." She held his gaze, searching for the tell-tale resentment that would doom their efforts. To her relief, there was none: Vedarahava nodded approval. She nodded back, one professional to another. Who would have fucking thought?

"In three days," she added, "please assemble forty of our most able. Equipped as heavy cavalry. I have scouted the old winery, south of here some four miles – you know it?" Vedarahava nodded. "It is abandoned, but large. Send the troops out as small patrols, in the usual pattern. At the winery keep them and twice that number of remounts hidden. Eyes will be watching. If they are even half alert they will discover our intent, but not immediately. Give me four days."

A note of excitement in his voice, Mathed said, "With that number of remounts, we will strike and run, rapidly…" He spoke as a statement, projecting his leadership, but Skava knew he wanted assurance. After all, he had not been tested yet. The next forty days would make him or break him. Or kill him.

"Indeed, my lord," Skava confirmed. "We shall be fast, do him damage, move on. We have secured resupply, mostly for the horses, in secret locations. They will be our rally points. If he suffers a reverse – once, twice, three times – his men will lose heart."

Mathed's excitement was now evident. Good. He *believed*. He would need that belief. Skava recognized, as no doubt did Vedarahava, that every hit they made would cost them as well. Sixty troopers would soon become forty. In winter, the cold and illness might steal another ten. With thirty, they would have run out of alternatives. And Skava's plans would have to change. A wholly unwelcome outcome.

She smiled at the youth, a confident, winning smile. "My lord," she finished, "by your leave…"

He returned her smile. And with his nod, she turned and left.

***

Five men. Two stood apart, oblong blood-red shields resting upright at their feet: these would be the close bodyguards. The remaining three stood together, in conference. The tallest might have been Mathed. But he was equipped like another bodyguard, caparisoned in a heavy bronze hauberk, and his attitude was wrong: he faced the central figure, who surely was the new Lord of Strath. And so the last man, left of Mathed and nearest the keep, might be a lieutenant or the commander of the Ouine forces, limited as they were. He wore chainmail and a dun field uniform, not Ouine red and gold, which meant he was preparing for an excursion, probably scouting.

Kesmet adjusted his telescope, newly engineered by craftsmen in the Kemae Islands, the lenses finer and more powerful, the image sharper. On one knee, up on the slopes amongst the dormant vines with their leaves mostly gone, he rested one arm on his other knee to steady the image. Zuse lay flat at his side. Nobody would get close without the hunting dog alerting him. One of the distant figures moved away, the man with the field uniform, walking steadily but not urgently, and disappeared behind an outhouse and then reappeared. He was walking back towards the mansion walls. Kesmet carefully lowered the telescope, taking in the whole perspective. He remained stock still, only his eyes in motion. Nearer, from the outhouse, a double storey barn or warehouse, there was movement. Kesmet watched closely as another man, likewise in dun-coloured uniform, left the barn. A lookout, astutely placed. Kesmet had not spotted him.

Up with the telescope, in slow, fluid increments to avoid catching the eye of practised observers. The image showed a gait that was familiar; the easy movement of a young man. Kesmet studied him as he walked directly away, towards the first figure. It was the set of shoulders, the hitch of his right arm – his sword arm, that would be – that was most familiar. He had seen all his before, near Nek Feddah, a hidden scout in the woods, overlooking commander Pillio and his prisoners.

Kesmet found that his mouth was dry. As rapidly as he dared, he moved the telescope to pick up the first individual again. He was nearing a stand of oak trees, and visibility was poor against the background of yellow leaves and tangled branches. The figure stopped, turned towards his approaching companion. A pale face. Words between them, perhaps. They moved off side-by-side, virtually invisible among the trees. Kesmet made fine adjustments with his fingers to sharpen the focus, and the black outline of horses materialized. More than four. There was further movement, a change in the profile of the horses. The men were mounting. They emerged from the trees, three horsemen, three tethered remounts, heading south-east, along the road. In the time it took for the small party to canter a quarter mile, Kesmet had noted as much detail as he needed: the set of harness, the way the equipment and bags were packed and attached, and the manner in which each of the riders sat and controlled his mount. He would recognize them again.

His heart was thumping in an unaccustomed manner. The pale face of the distant figure was burned into his mind's eye, an image he knew he would not easily forget. He could, from some buried memory, add its features, the detailed lineaments of the jaw, cheeks and eyes, but he was loath to do so. Instead he watched the retreating riders through the telescope, and an insistent voice in his head was urging him to follow. The same voice was telling him that this was the group of riders from the forests near Nek Feddah, the central rider the woman from the inn who had woken from a nightmare: Skava. He thought of Harbin and could hear his voice. *Eslin*, he would be saying. *It is her. You know it is her.*

The small party turned off the road, taking a narrow, unpaved access lane between the vineyards. Soon they would be gone. They were experienced riders, assuredly killers, and very good scouts. Eslin, if it was her, would surround herself with the very best – and then train them to be better. The challenge was daunting. But Kesmet was unhurried. He retracted the telescope, slipped it into a leather side bag, tied firm at his right hip, then looked back at the estate. The four remaining men were walking towards the circular keep, a small affair by most standards, an anachronism really, but adequate to remind any visitors that this place was the seat of the Lord of Strath. It might hold for a few days against a resolute assault, a week perhaps. But its purpose was more like that of a strong-point, a bastion from which to sally and divide an enemy force. Kesmet could visualize its effective use, the shock deployment of a concealed troop and the concentration of heavy weapons on its high platforms. He had seen its equivalent before. He had seen most everything before. On its battlements, Kesmet could spot two sentinels. They were unaware of him.

He turned, satisfied that he was unobserved from any quarter and, patting Zuse once on the flank with a gloved hand, ducked through the vines, crouching low to ascend the cultivated hills. Zuse loped along behind him, testing the air with his snout. Over the top of the ridge was a tumble of blackthorn and misshapen scrawny trees, their autumnal brown-gold leaves damp with morning mist. Here his large black gelding waited, invisible in the gloom of the limp foliage.

Kesmet rubbed the beast's nose. "It's time, Gexa," he murmured, leading the horse by his reins and walking him down the reverse slope towards the fringes of a dense forest a mile or so across the rows of vines.

***

There was heat and ecstasy in their love-making. Mathed's strong, muscular limbs twined about hers and she wanted more of him. She wanted his hands on her hips and her breasts, to feel his strength and power and the shuddering boyish vulnerability of him when he came inside her. He would caress her face, tracing a line down her cheek and neck, telling her she was more beautiful than he could believe, a gift from the gods of marriage and love. She smiled at these words. He adored her and she loved the feeling of it and, if he was not an accomplished lover, he was a good lover. She had expected that. She had anticipated that much and desired much more, with an urgent, almost painful hunger.

Because there was a lack. Privately she remonstrated with herself, but the memory of Adaim, *her soldier*, as she preferred to think of him, had returned. The feel of him, the need for him had never left her, but she had banished him from her consciousness, like a guilty secret that could not be contemplated beyond her dreams. Now…now she ached for him, for the sensuous, stealthy thrill of his insistent, sword-calloused hands on her inner thigh and the curve of her belly, the modesty of his stolen glances and the mad press of his hard body against her, in her…

She fought the recollections of stolen sunlit moments in the hills, her handmaidens despatched on an errand to collect flowers, her soldier in attendance, the tension in him, in his snatched looks and culpable silence…and his rough responsiveness, his knowing calculation, his sheer handsome physicality. She could still smell him, his male otherness, a musky scent that was Adaim, and only Adaim, when the man on top of her, between her legs was the man she loved, the man she ought to love.

But she could not feel shame. It did not touch her, though she willed that it were so. She convinced herself that she needed Mathed and hoped that her womb would quicken, and that pregnancy would be the right thing, in every way – for Mathed, for her and for Strath. She did not *feel* it, though. Her emotions and her memories made her a liar. An unashamed liar, here in the night, turned on her side against Mathed's back, in her marital bed, the sheets twisted, her body slick with perspiration and the stickiness of lust. If there was a scintilla of regret, it was, she realized, the regret of her soldier's death in Lorang. A young man of no social consequence, who should have been invisible to a woman of her standing, yet it seemed impossible to believe that such a vital presence should be gone, utterly gone from life, from her life. It was wrong.

And that made other things wrong.

If the love for Mathed she had earnestly hoped for and expected felt diminished by an illicit intimacy she could not justify, and for which she could not feel shame, she had equally lost faith in other certainties. And she desperately needed certainty.

She put her hand on Mathed's shoulder and he stirred in his sleep, like a boy deep in dreams, needing the comfort of her protection. At once it caused her to think of her brother, Osir, and a flutter of fear and anxiety coursed through her body. This was the certainty she had to have: Mathed and Osir safe. The two men left alive that she loved.

**

In the eyes of the household, news of the impending conflict disturbed Keleu very greatly. She was quiet at breakfast and became distraught at first mention of Mathed's martial preparations, a topic that now dominated the men's conversation. The latest reports, the disposition of forces, the reinforcement of the keep or some merchants' prattling that excited speculation by Ke Beyil about Osir's movements – which were always wrong, though Mathed chose not to correct them – were details that provoked a seemingly endless fascination amongst the men. Unfortunately, in spite of Ke Beyil's honest attempts, in Keleu's company, to embrace subjects outside the usual ambit, few of the officers had the presence of mind to extend discussions to topics of greater refinement, certainly not the hulking armoured Vedarahava and other bodyguards who were constantly at Mathed's side. Consequently, at the long table at mealtimes there were deep silences broken only by Ke Beyil's civil enquiries of Keleu and her female companions, and that lady's equally civil answers. Che Keleu endured these occasions with her usual, if somewhat strained, charm, and Ke Beyil, observing both her distress and Mathed's sorrow for his wife, was quite moved. He gave Keleu what solace he could, well aware that an excessive solicitude in this matter would only compound her suffering: she was too proud, and too selfless, to be in willing receipt of pity.

Che Keleu for her part, though she had pressed Ke Beyil and his aides, for their safety, to depart Mamoba, seemed exceedingly glad of their company. Overnight the estate had been transformed from the tranquil home of a thousand warm and precious memories of her childhood, to the frightening place of cold steel, strange armoured men, and the nightmare events that had torn from her those she loved most dearly. Thus, she responded to Ke Beyil's kindly attentions as she might have done to her father's, seeking his company alone away from the Ouine officers in their unfamiliar new uniforms of green and white and with their deep western accents. And all the while she tried to put the horror of her circumstances out of her mind.

One morning she was sitting with the king's representative in the sunlit warmth of the parlour, overlooking the gardens. The mansion was quiet: many of the servants were at market, and Lord Mathed and his officers had left early on what frightful business Keleu dared not ask after. She sat stiffly upright in one of the high-backed, cushioned chairs near the windows, her hands clasped in her lap, and the sunlight falling directly on her head and shoulders. From Ke Beyil's chair opposite, her fine hair was alive with an auburn lustre, and the cream fabric of her dress reflected the light against her complexion so that her being seemed suffused with its own special energy. Upon glancing up, Ke Beyil, who had been reading aloud to her from Undan's *Discourses of the Felicities*, was distracted from his task by the beauty of the tableau. He stopped his reading abruptly and gazed upon Che Keleu, whose head was turned toward the windows, her eyes fixed distantly upon what Ke Beyil guessed was some object of her imagination. He was gripped, and his own thoughts tumbled uncontrolled and, suddenly afflicted by a surge of longing for what he had failed to secure in his own life, for a mad moment he saw her as his wife. *A woman as erudite and sensuous as this lady – what might have been, had I made different choices?* For that instant Ke Beyil's life in Chisua, his devoted service to the Realm and his stature in the halls of power, seemed irredeemably wasted. And so he stared at her, lost, bereft, wondering.

So deep were Che Keleu's meditations that it was several moments before she took note of his protracted silence and faced him, the return of her attention to the here-and-now signalled by the flicker of eyelids.

"Ke Beyil," she said. "I'm sorry. Have you finished the chapter?"

"No, no," the councilman replied, stirring himself from his bemusement and casting about for some tactful excuse. "I was distracted," he said truthfully.

"By my dreaming, no doubt," Keleu observed, perceiving the facts with a startling, if unintended, exactness. "I'm sorry, Ke Beyil. I have wasted your valuable time, not to mention your good voice. I should not be insulted if you wished yourself secluded somewhere away from me."

Ke Beyil shook his head with vehemence, an action which caused his collars to flutter in a manner not unlike an exotic Oriole shaking its plumage. "Not at all!" he protested. "Not at all, my dear!" This endearment had slipped into usage over the past several days and Che Keleu had not reproved him for it; indeed, secretly she was delighted by his gentle familiarity.

"Do go on," Keleu pressed him.

"Ah, no, my dear." Ke Beyil closed Undan's *Felicities* with a decisive thud. "An incident springs to mind which I feel I must relate, as it bears on your present mood. I hope you will indulge me...?"

At Keleu's smile and nod, Ke Beyil proceeded. "Some years ago, in my capacity as a junior supervisor of the Council, it fell to me to look out for the edification – I shall not say education – of the junior-most officials appointed to the Court at Mera, a post to which every young student passing from the academies most earnestly aspires but rarely attains. One young nobleman, I forget his home province now...but one young nobleman was assigned to my charge, together with several others, all bright, all enthusiastic. This individual, one Ishseu, applied himself with admirable zeal to his work amongst the Legations and in the organisation of the records – a tedious duty, I might add. And he was fastidious in every other demand made upon him. But one day – I think it was in the month of the Great Harbour Fire – I chanced to notice him during the debates of the Grand Council. Now you will of course appreciate that the debates are a thrilling event for any aspirant young supervisor. The tension! The presence of men and women of legendary stature! The statesmen! The nobles! The Archivists and Ta-shih! The overwhelming sense of enormous powers at work! And what of my young man? Well! By chance I am distracted – as I was just now – and glance to my left to the juniors' booths. What do I see? I see Ishseu staring blankly ahead. And this at a time when Supervisor Geing is lambasting General Onoma for the outrageous financial demands of the Ta-shih in Kei Province! However, do not be deceived into believing that my young charge is bored and dreaming. No, no! I suspect deeper concerns here. Consequently, after the debate I investigate. Lo and behold! At my insistent prodding, Ishseu reveals that he is lovelorn! And naturally it follows that, in such a condition, he is useless to me. I offer my assistance in securing a meeting with the enchanting creature of whom he is enamoured. He meets her; they are together at last; they find each other boring; the love affair is at an end; Ishseu returns to his duties with redoubled vigour and dedication!"

Keleu, who had listened to the tale with a frown and then a knowing smile, now laughed appreciatively. "You are on the verge of pointing out a significant moral to this story!"

"Ah, yes. Though in no wise do I seek to compare my friend Ishseu to your gracious self – in no wise, please understand – though I make no comparison, I do indeed glean from your air of distraction a mood not unlike the young gentleman's. And it proclaims a soul in some, shall I say, unhappiness…" Ke Beyil leaned forward and said in a soft voice, "I understand that this matter is private, of course, yet I wonder if it would not ease you to speak of your troubles. While I confess to being powerless to intervene further than I already have in this business, I have a good ear, so to speak, and should be glad to listen."

The laughter that had brightened Keleu's face was gone. She looked away out of the windows once more, and her face in profile seemed to Ke Beyil to be worn and fragile. He waited, expecting some response, but Keleu said nothing.

Finally, Ke Beyil ventured to say, "I am sure that it will not come to war, my dear. I have seen the posturing of young men so many times; they argue and threaten and stir up the blood of other men…but nothing comes of it."

This roused Che Keleu. She glanced sharply at Ke Beyil and demanded, "But these are not just young men, are they? They are the eldest sons of Strath and Honam! Terrible pride and bitterness boils under the surface of the posturing that you have observed. Forgive me, Ke Beyil, but there is so much that you, as an outsider, cannot know. We who were once tied in blood to Ouine Clan broke our alliance with them after the Biljan Wars. Our forefathers feared the ambition of Honam that could lead us again to war. So for four centuries there has been a gulf between Strath and Honam…and only Lord Yoiwa and my father have sought to heal it. But still Osir sees treachery. And he is not alone. Ke Androc, Ke Kesiden, and others, they fear Honam. And who can blame them? This fear breeds still more fear. Now my own Mathed fears Strath. He arms more and more men. They plan a first strike – to destroy the enemy, my countrymen! While Osir does likewise! Oh, Ke Beyil! Can you not see? This business spirals ever faster!"

Ke Beyil, surprised by the young woman's heat and logic, made no reply. There could be no reply. She was right, utter and complete. The two sat in silence for several moments; then Keleu, as if her constant ruminations had made her desperate, rose quickly from her chair and, with a swish of her skirts, knelt at Ke Beyil's side to clasp his arm. "Is there nothing you can do?" she cried. "There will be war, Ke Beyil! They will kill each other!"

Completely taken aback by Keleu's sudden entreaty, Ke Beyil, wide-eyed and in an agony of ineffectuality, bade her return to her seat, which she refused.

"Why will the Ta-shih not intervene?" she begged of him.

"They cannot, my l-lady," Ke Beyil stammered. "The Law forbids them until the fortieth day. Only the king may command the Ta-shih to hold the peace – and he will not, even if he knew; it is not the way…"

Keleu fell silent again, but for long moments she searched Ke Beyil's face as though for some answer he held secreted there.

Abruptly she said, "And what if I went to him? To Osir?"

Ke Beyil felt himself go instantly cold, and for the briefest time misunderstood this to be some ghastly threat to abandon her husband, until he perceived in her expression the cool, clear reasoning that informed her question.

"Che Keleu!" he protested, and held her shoulders with a gentle grasp as if to ward off the Shadow Lord himself. "Please! It is dangerous to contemplate such things! I will not hear it!"

But Keleu, with a calm that shocked Ke Beyil still more, insisted, "But what of it? I could go to him, persuade him to stand aside. He loves me.

He might stop this madness."

His protests mute and his convictions beclouded by nameless feelings, Ke Beyil blinked at her.

"If I could convince him, he might be reconciled with Mathed. He might find some role," Keleu pressed him, determinedly. "He might find a role with us in the cause of Strath and Honam. Wouldn't that be wonderful?"

Ke Beyil shook his head, in an unexpected conflict of hope and a sick feeling in his stomach, and minded once more of the utter powerlessness he had felt throughout this conversation. "Yes, my dear Lady Che Keleu," he murmured. "It would. But…at the same time, think on Prince Osir's…um…conduct, his, his contempt for the Lord of Honam and his dreadful actions that night. And now he has challenged Lord Mathed for Constructive Trust by force of arms. It will be resolved by force of arms. The only honourable course."

He remained seated and unmoving even as Keleu slipped from his clasp and returned to her seat. He hated himself suddenly for the harshness and the plain-speaking reality of his answer. If there were anyone across the wide world he wanted to help, to offer kindness, then it was the delightful woman whose slender shoulders he had just released. In moments all was as before – the sunlight upon her, the chestnut flame of her hair, and the elegant contour of her limbs – just as if their conversation had never happened.

Che Keleu asked him to continue his reading of Undan's *Felicities*. And Ke Beyil, with every reason but without the courage to do otherwise, yielded.

CHAPTER 12

War is, by and large, imperfectly executed,
its objectives obscure, and its consequences unexpected.
General Arrudhin, 'Military Tactics of the Ta-shih', page 131.

We expected unity. After all, we had common cause. Near extinction is a
fantastic incentive. But they fell out and competed and then fought.
The Journal of the Lost, assumed to be an Immortal, copied by a scribe,
IYE 1040.

***

They moved quickly, south for the most part, with some zig-zag to confuse
chance observers. Always they kept to the shadows and concealment of the
forests, unless forced to cross open ground, where they wound through
the low valleys and sunken ditches, seeking cover. On two occasions they
were met by a solitary rider and then the pace picked up: these were the
other scouts she had out, stationed ahead and running relays to save time
as they shadowed Osir's muster and reported his numbers and strength
of arms.

Kesmet studied the group. Over two days he had learned their patterns
and their habits. One of their number regularly hung back, angling away
from their trail, seeking concealment to establish if they were being
followed, then hurrying forward to catch up. Kesmet observed carefully.
Always the same man, the younger one from the forests at Nek Feddah.

For his part, Kesmet stayed well away during the daylight hours, mostly following them by their tracks. In this he was lucky: one of them, with the smallest boots, walked with a distinctive gait, betrayed in the mud, as a small scuffmark on the left boot print, possibly where the individual was favouring that leg. The mark appeared when they were walking the mounts through difficult terrain and Kesmet surmised that it was an injury, aggravated during extended hiking.

On the two evenings gone, they camped together, no fire, taking the watches in turn, well-drilled and efficient. At these times, Kesmet had worked his way closer, leaving Gexa, his great black gelding, and Zuse far back in a secluded spot. On the third evening, as they stopped in a dell to set camp, with the utmost care he took up a position eighty paces away on one knee and used his telescope to look at the figures. The tallest was seeing to the horses; the youngest was on lookout, slowly making a circuit of the area; the third was handling a pigeon coop, untying it from one of the mounts – presumably a message was about to go to Mathed at Mamoba.

Risky as it was with one of them on lookout, Kesmet wanted to see the faces. And he was running out of daylight, having used the early evening to work his way close on foot. He rested the barrel of the telescope on a low tree branch, still directed at an angle to the ground so he did not cause a reflection of the wan light. The lookout was moving away towards the far side. The tall man was currying the horses. The central figure was turned partially away, wide hat still covering half the face. Kesmet raised the telescope and focussed the lenses, using his other eye to confirm direction. The face leapt into view, side-on: the nose was blunt, maybe broken, a strong jaw and cheekbones, clenched as if with an intensity of inner concentration. The image moved, swam out of focus and was gone. Kesmet lowered the glass, covering the lens with a gloved hand and folding it away slowly, quietly.

He discovered that his hands were shaking. His heart was beating loudly. Even after all this time, he knew it was her. It seemed both impossible and utterly familiar, as if he had gone back in time or simply excised the gulf of life's passage between their last encounter and this one. She had been *gone*; definitely, irreversibly *gone*. And now she was here, a returning shade from another existence. He felt unbalanced. Imperilled. He needed to recover his certainty, to act.

Without shifting his body or head, he checked for the two men. The tall one was still with the six mounts, ducking between them, checking tethers, fixing small abrasions, busy with a smart efficacy. Of the sentry, there was no sign.

Kesmet breathed deep of the evening forest air. These small endeavours to reassert discipline and habit brought a measure of calmness back to him.

He remained stock still, shoulder hard against a thick pine tree trunk. They would see only the single shape if they chanced to look directly this way and if he stayed kneeling motionless. He knew this with complete certainty. His clothes were perfectly blended to the woodland. He was distant enough to be invisible. Of moderate concern was the sentry. Kesmet could not lay eyes on him, but he was confident of his route: they had just made camp, so he would stay close, within thirty or forty paces, to warn of dangers, then later move off in a much wider circuit to make his checks. More alarming was the wind veering. It had been directly in Kesmet's face, as he had planned, for him to get close downwind. Now, with nightfall, it was blowing gently from his left quarter. If it backed more and if they were good – and he knew they were – either their mounts or one of them would catch his scent, a small shift but sufficient to alert them to a *difference*: the gelding's smell on his clothes or the oil on his crossbow…or Zuse.

The young scout appeared, crouching, moving crablike under tree branches, pausing, still for moments at a time, stepping behind a tree. Kesmet watched him and watched the camp. A pigeon flew up suddenly, released by Skava, flapping in that noisy launch they always had until it gained speed and altitude and was gone. Instructions for her new master, Lord Mathed of Strath, to bring up his forces or attempt some diversion… it mattered not. Kesmet must focus only on the three individuals in his line of sight. He had options, but not good options. A quarrel through the neck and she'd be down – maybe. It would be an extraordinary shot, through woodland, using the small crossbow he had brought. The bow, of his own design, could be loaded with two bolts. That gave him an advantage. If he missed, well… No, he needed to be close. Effective range was eighty paces for a probable hit; thirty for certainty. Even with a good hit, this time it had to be certain. And he was concerned, in a corner of his thoughts, that he was too preoccupied with Skava…Eslin. He might well put her down, but the other two were *good*. Like as not, one of them would get him. They had worked together closely for a long time, by the look of it. They would coordinate with automatic understanding, improving their odds.

He did not like his own state of mind: it was wrong. She had this effect. She stole attention, pulled on emotions, fascinated, inspired and distracted. He *was* distracted. He was no longer coldly objective. Harbin would laugh…but he would *know*. It was why she was so dangerous. Better to wait until they turned in: a single individual on watch; but, on the other hand, pitch-dark, with all the attendant challenges. Also it would be very difficult to move close enough without alerting either horse or man…or woman.

And the damned wind was shifting. Alarmingly.

The young scout was completely still, fifty paces away, difficult to spot, but Kesmet had seen him take up position between saplings. Small movements in the camp, although they were mostly silent, professional. It was near full dark, merely a deep mauve through the trees overhead to show that the evening sky was clear.

The best option was to take them on the trail, soon after breaking camp, in daylight, from ambush, then close in. Of prime importance, Kesmet told himself, was to allow time. Time to be careful. It was her. He could follow now without losing her. Or until she rejoined Mathed's main force, if that was the plan.

Someone was taking a piss, the unmistakeable spattering on leaves and pine needles from near the scout's position. In the tangled shadows to the right of the camp a figure detached itself from the trees and moved towards the scout.

"Yan," came a hushed voice, easy to hear in the forest tranquillity. "Into camp." It was the tall one.

"Yep," came the reply.

"All good?"

"Good."

More movement. Kesmet saw the two figures return to camp. They were preparing a cold dinner. Now the light was gone it was very difficult to see much. Kesmet slowly moved up from his kneeling position into a crouch. Three of them, tight in the centre of the camp. Horses close at hand, making the sounds they made, which might hide his approach, were he to commit now. The opportunity gripped him like a physical need. His heart rate accelerated again.

She is dangerous. Harbin's voice, in his head, bringing him back to cool reason. Now was not a good time. He needed clarity, detachment and opportunity.

He prepared to pull back and stepped slowly to his left, covered now by the pine tree bole, turned, made his way five paces along a route he had confirmed as clear earlier, turned about again and checked behind, towards the camp. A black silhouette flickered in and out of view, heading to the right of his position. He froze, part-crouched, hand feeling for his hip knife, a foot-long hunting blade, optimal in this woodland where there were obstructions everywhere to swinging a sword. If he looked hard enough, he could convince himself that the figure was wearing a wide hat: Eslin. Again his heart rate climbed. If it was her, he had the perfect opportunity…except that he was stuck in an open position. The moment he moved, she would see the change in the contour of the woodland shadows. He held his ground, frozen but consciously relaxing his upper body and limbs, prepared for instant action.

The shape sank out of sight, about thirty paces away. A familiar and urgent voice was insisting in Kesmet's head that he was about to be attacked, demanding that he act. His body was involuntarily tensing for the blow that would be a crossbow bolt. He had, however, been through all this before, and he ignored the familiar physical and emotional pressure to flee. His body remained still, only his eyes roving methodically over the snarled and twisted gloom between himself, the camp and Eslin's last location. Nothing. The breeze was shifting once more, back round from its previous direction and, on it, the distinctive smell of human urine. She was relieving herself.

Kesmet reached slowly round to the small of his back where the crossbow was strung from a diagonal lanyard over his shoulders. He eased it to his hip, gripped the handle and brought the weapon horizontal. With his left hand he felt for the small bag on the same lanyard, pulled open the ties and slipped a bolt out, fed it onto the lower flight groove, did the same with a second bolt for the upper groove. The weapon was already cranked. He pushed down the safety lock. It was ready to fire. He eased the lanyard strap to give more play, extended his arm and lined up on the shape he thought was Eslin.

Chance and opportunity. It seemed extraordinary, but he knew it was simple probability. If you persist, you need only seize the moment.

A shadow lifted directly on Kesmet's sight line. His finger tightened on the upper trigger. There was a shuffling, trousers being pulled up. She was utterly vulnerable. His arm was level and unwavering.

"Boss?" came a low hiss from Kesmet's left.

In spite of every instinct, Kesmet did not move at all, but his eyes flicked at once to the sound: a tall black outline close to a tree, cut through by a mass of low branches.

"Fuck's sake," came her quiet curse.

"All good?"

"Breeches round my fucking arse. What?"

"Checking…"

And she went quiet, as if this single word were a signal.

Kesmet glanced back again in the direction of his raised arm. The shape was gone. He released a shallow breath he now realized he had been holding too long, a slow, steady exhalation, inaudible. There was no light, so no visible vapour from his breath. But he was now in some difficulty. The two killers were in a V-shape angled ninety degrees, the tall one to his left, Eslin low down to his right, both about thirty paces away. If the youngster, Yan, was working a wide circuit, he would be behind Kesmet in short order: an immaculate, if fortuitous, piece of work, surrounding him on three sides. He needed to make a decision, fast.

He began to drop lower in the crouch he already held, in tiny increments, slower than the human eye could perceive, left thigh burning until he was on one knee. Meanwhile he had pulled his aiming arm in and hunched his shoulders so that his body made a very small profile. He listened, mouth slightly open, as this minutely improved hearing. What he picked up now would make the difference between life and death.

Small sounds reached him. To his left and some way behind him there was an intermittent series of barely audible scuffles, boots on small twigs, legs brushing past plants. Yan was closing at a range of no more than twenty-five paces, presumably shifting right as he did so. Kesmet was blind to him. He could only pinpoint his position from the sounds he made. Ahead, he could see just the variegated black hues of night-time woodland, except where he thought he could make out part of the silhouette of the tall man, who had stayed upright, ostensibly to maximise his vantage.

Kesmet decided to risk a slow rotation of his head to the left, hoping to spot Yan. As he waited, he heard the almost inaudible pressure of a boot on wet leaves and pine needles and saw a matching slow, fluid rearrangement of the shadows: Yan, stepping over something, working his way sideways. Then he stopped.

Kesmet calculated his options. He knew where two of them were and he had a double-loaded crossbow. If they came at him, he could deal with them. But not Eslin. She might or might not be where he had last seen her. It was entirely possible she had used Yan's approach to cover her own movements. But she would not have got far, perhaps merely two or three paces. Kesmet considered the problem from their point of view. They were alert to an intruder – a probable intruder – and they needed certainty about whether it was an animal, a single scout, several or nothing at all. They were well armed. But they would be cautious. Since Yan was moving, he was the one designated to flush out the threat. He must take the greatest risk, revealing his position in order to trigger a response. Assume that the tall one was ready with a crossbow, Yan likewise, possibly Eslin: would they fire at shadows? Unlikely, as they risked hitting each other…unless their agreed protocol in these circumstances was to press for certainty, to keep Yan moving until they had confirmation one way or the other.

So Kesmet did nothing. He kept his head turned to the left, eyes tracking the lump of darkness that was Yan as he gradually eased through the pine trees and undergrowth. Kesmet's limbs were in a good position for waiting, one knee down, his left hand free to draw the hunting blade, his right hand curled round the crossbow stock. Yan was now directly behind him, twenty paces away, still moving, so that Kesmet could no longer see him. Then there was silence. This was the time of maximum danger. The temptation to take a look over his shoulder was irresistible. Yet he did not.

The moment drew out, long and full of menace.

Then there was a soft bird-like click-click sound from Yan, an answering series of clicks from the tall scout. Silence again.

Finally, the sounds of Yan moving along his circuit, edging to the right of Kesmet. In forty heartbeats he was as many paces away, nearer Eslin, and Kesmet could risk the slow rotation of his head back towards the camp.

***

Lying in my own piss, for fuck's sake. Her leather breeches were still half down, stuck round her arse, the wet ground against her lower belly. She had her head up, but she was in a dip, selected earlier for the best of reasons when one needed to squat in the middle of the damned wilderness.

Still, caution first. Maki had noticed something, probably a scent picked up in that horse-like conk he called a nose. She had dropped flat at his signal and decided not to move. Maki was not the nervy sort. So here she was, forty strides from the camp, flat on her tits, soaking up her own piss, with a poniard in hand and no crossbow. Yan was doing the right thing, making enough noise to flush anyone out and give Maki the best chance to spot them. Unless it was a deer or a fox, or some nocturnal bird, in which case it would go to ground or bolt.

She scanned her immediate vicinity – a brief task, given that she was in a dip. Even with her head up she could make out very little. If she backed away, she would simply expose her pale arse as a wonderful target to whoever was out there; and if she went forward, she risked showing her face for the same reason. As both alternatives had little to recommend them, she decided to take her hat off and slowly lift it sideways to her left as if she were taking a look. It might trigger a reaction and might therefore help Yan or Maki, who had the best view. She held the hat up for as long as her arm would take the effort, then lowered her elbow to the ground, still with her hat exposed. Whoever or whatever was out there was not taking the bait.

She listened. Yan was still doing his sweep. Maki would be scanning. How long to persist? She waited, for what seemed a long time. Eventually, Yan returned, closer now, to her and to the camp. Eight paces away, he set himself where she could just make out his head and gave a single click, tongue on palate: signal for her to back up under his cover. She wriggled backwards, not worrying about her breeches, and emerged from the dip, still on her belly. She chanced a look, knowing her pale face was a target, but could pick up only convoluted shadows. Enough.

She got to hands and knees, moving sideways and back like a crab, until she had cover behind a tree. Three clicks from Maki: clear so far. She took a moment to pull her breeches up and lace them, helpfully sealing pine needles and soil in her crotch. The evening was not getting any better. Yan was twenty paces to her left, an irregular lump, with the vague outline of his arm out, hand-held crossbow levelled. She took some comfort from that, raised herself behind the tree bole and swung her head the other side to expose one eye and take a good look: the same black mass of humps, knotted shadows and staggered array of dark trees. How much time had passed? A full cycle? Probably.

Something moved, fast, scattering pine needles and leaves, heading left. Yan's crossbow made a *thwunk* sound as he released. Skava realized she had followed the sound towards Yan and snapped her eyes back to the ground directly in front of her, searching for tell-tale movement, a sudden attack with the diversion.

Nothing.

She looked right, towards Maki, and could see him, upright, fifteen paces off, good position between three close pine trees. Trying to read his silhouette, she thought he had his crossbow levelled.

Skava was beginning to doubt there was anything but an animal around – and it had bolted. Either that or the best assassin in the world was patiently outwaiting them and the animal scuttling away had been a coincidence. They were getting nowhere. Their rehearsed procedure in these circumstances was to stay together, to cover each other. Separating meant being picked off. She made a decision, gave five rapid clicks and got the double-click acknowledgements. Then they all started to withdraw towards the camp. As she was in the centre, she did the rearward check, ensuring they weren't stumbling into a trap behind them.

Back in the camp, behind a couple of old fallen trees, she asked Maki, "What do you think?"

Maki was a dark shape at her side, watching the surrounding woodland. "Damned odd, boss," he whispered. "Scent was a dog."

Skava screwed up her face. That was a surprise. "Dog?" she echoed.

"Not strong, but…dog."

"And it bolted?"

"Yan didn't hit anything. So, yes."

"What the fuck is a dog doing out here? You sure?" This was sounding utterly bizarre.

"Tracker hound?"

"Hmm." She was rooting through the possibilities. "But you're not sure? Why not?" He was usually very sure.

"Well, boss. The…uh…piss."

Skava exhaled slowly. Fucking great. Her own piss, all over her clothes, was interfering with Maki's sense of smell. She grunted. Talking about it had reminded her how badly she needed to strip off and clean up.

"Yan," she said. "You got anything? See anything?"

"Nope. We can check tracks in the morning."

Indeed. Dog. Whatever next?

***

Forty miles north of Eloy, in the pine forests that stretched sixty miles further to the Bay of Marshese, Osir had made his camp. He had chosen high ground in a part of the forests which gave easy access to streams and nearby villages where provisions were being secured. For a week, dozens of men had been arriving, and the low hill had changed from a peaceful glade to a site of campfires and canvas, where horses stamped and fretted at the inactivity, and soldiers tramped the paths between the tents until the ground was pitted with the muddy impressions of armoured boots. Every day patrols rode out through the rough palisade of sharpened stakes, into the forest and returned at night to the leaping red flames of a score of fires scattered through the camp. Beside them the armourers' grindstones creaked and hissed incessantly as point and edge of swords, lances and pikes were honed.

It was a bright morning, golden and coldly clear after a night of rain, when two riders approached the camp. They were accompanied by a single woodsman on foot, seemingly a guide, and two sentries from the watch, who picked their way across the muddy ground towards the centre of the concentric rings of tents, past faces of men looking up from what they were about to stare in surprise at the riders. Steam rose from the flanks of the horses and they snorted rolling coils of vapour from nostrils flared after a long ride. Near the crest of the hill the sentries stopped. An officer, in olive-green tunic and silver epaulettes, ducked out from behind a tent flap. He glanced up at the nearest rider, clearly not expecting what he saw.

"My lady!" he exclaimed, and immediately bowed, then hurried forward to assist her to dismount.

Che Keleu accepted the officer's hand and gracefully stepped down.

"My brother…Prince Osir. Is he here?" she asked, dropping the hood of her cloak so that her dark auburn hair tumbled free over the green mantle.

The effect of this simple action on the soldiers in the immediate vicinity was instant. Some few of them, to whom the officer's cry, 'My lady!' was not in itself meaningful, nonetheless recognised the beautiful face revealed as the hood was thrown back. The curious hush which had endured since the riders entered the camp was replaced by whispers and calls. "It's our Lady Che Keleu!"

"Che Keleu of Strath…the princess!"

Within moments, the fact of Keleu's presence was communicated throughout the camp and produced in scores of soldiers the same reaction – the stir of excitement and a need to get closer. As a knot of onlookers assembled, one man shouted to his fellows, "A cheer for our lady! A cheer for the Lady Che Keleu!"

A multitude of voices raised a ragged cheer, and then another. Che Keleu, startled to hear her name in the clamour, looked about her at the men, at smiling faces amidst the dull silver sheen of steel, the yellow and green of shields, corselets of brown leather, and a dozen other of the trappings of war. She blinked in surprise and, her first question both unanswered and forgotten in the tumult, she asked of the officer: "Why do they shout my name?"

The officer grinned and replied, "For joining them here, my lady. They cheer you for lending weight to their cause – Prince Osir's cause."

Che Keleu stared out at the ranks of men, suddenly and helplessly aware of the impression she had created. Meanwhile, from his horse, Ke Beyil was descending rather inelegantly. In gratitude he handed his reins to a young soldier, who had steadied his mount, and stepped gingerly across the mud towards Che Keleu. She turned back to the officer and, breathless, entreated him to lead her to her brother.

All smiles now and unconscious of Keleu's discomfort, the young officer shrugged, "Prince Osir is not here, my lady. Oh, but he will be pleased to see you when he returns! No more than a cycle or two and he'll be back." And then, mindful of his manners, the officer gestured toward the largest of the tents. "But come inside, come inside, you and your companion both! It's warmer and drier."

This accomplished, the officer offered hot refreshments to Keleu and Ke Beyil and strove gallantly to entertain them with stories of the prince's martial preparations. The young man's excited gabbling had quite the opposite of the desired effect and Keleu became agitated, asking suddenly if he did not hear horses, his lord's return perhaps, hoping by this device to persuade him to take up his station outside the tent and leave her alone.

"Ah, no," rejoined the officer, impervious to her hints, "the sentries will announce the prince's return, never fear! The men adore him, my lady. They cheer him. They would ride into the blackest waters of hell for him! He is remarkable. His plans, his attention to detail is extraordinary. He has the best blacksmiths with us here, and thus we have the finest weapons and armour, and readily mended. Supplies are regular – a matter easily forgotten by even good soldiers on the march. Our scouts are superior to any in the land: they know the woodland and river, valley and hill. After all, they were born here and grew up here and make their living off the wild places. The gods of rock and river are with us. Even the old clansmen Ke Androc and Ke Chaaggar, noblemen in their own right, defer to him – and one so young. He has found his path, my lady: he is a great general! He will overcome the Ouine invaders!"

Che Keleu, seated on a cushioned stool, had listened in some astonishment, but now leaned forward. With steel in her voice she asked, "Why are they invaders?" The officer glanced at her in surprise.

"My lady?"

"My husband, the Lord Mathed, why is he an invader? Was he not invited to Mamoba by the will of my father, *your Lord*? Did not Osir accept the Choosing?"

"It is said so…" The youth's expression had altered to frowning bewilderment.

Che Keleu persisted: "Why then are the Ouine Clan invaders?"

The officer hesitated. Keleu had transfixed him with her gaze and would not let him go. He felt her invisible grip on him through the glitter of her eyes like the thrust of a spear. Though he searched for answers to her question, certain of a vindication that was too obscure to put to words, finally he could only protest: "If you heard Prince Osir! If only you heard the prince! He is the orator that I am not! He can tell you why!"

"You insult me with such a remark," declaimed Keleu with a scorn which, although uncharacteristic, was expressed eloquently in the arch of eyebrows and the tilt of her head. "The prince is my brother. Who knows him better? As to the facts: they are incontrovertible; yet you gush meaningless objections. Have you no opinions of your own? Have you not the wit to tell orator from spellbinder?"

The officer was exasperated. In open-mouthed amazement he stared at Keleu. Then he drew himself rigidly to attention and pronounced, "My lady, we are at war with your husband, the Lord Mathed. There is nothing more to say." He began to withdraw from the tent, pausing to add with cold primness, "I shall be outside, should you require my services."

To Ke Beyil, who stood in silent attendance nearby like an immovable oak, Keleu exclaimed, "Why do men always plead 'war' as their only excuse when common sense has deserted them, as if war were its own just cause?"

Ke Beyil's heavy silence was her only response.

***

He was much changed.

In the face of her brother there had always been worry, a look of tormented resentment and dissatisfaction both, which she had understood and which she tried hard with their father to remedy in the years when his disappointment in his son became more evident. But now…now the careworn face was leaner, the jaw muscles knotted, mouth closely compressed, and his eyes were as granite, cold and obdurate. In his stance too, in the strong athletic limbs and the cant of head, there was a difference, unnoticed perhaps by others but starkly obvious to Keleu: here was purpose and certainty.

He had been wearing a helmet so that his hair, which was habitually tied in a knot at the nape of the neck, fell loose about his cheeks and brushed his shoulders. It was the only sign of the wilful disorder which had so stamped his youth. All else now was grimness and reserve, and with it a chilling sense of menace like the threat of a killer dog.

It was, Keleu told herself without serious conviction, perhaps the armour he wore that had altered him. These steel plates and bands of iron that made him larger than life; and the great sword at his side, his father's sword; and the mud and dirt on his boots and on the tarnished steel greaves – all this was so real. It was not the polished panoply of fine armour she had seen her father and her brother wear at a hundred ceremonies, so civilized and now so empty of meaning. This was real. This was war. And Keleu was frightened.

But her own resolve was enormous and she commanded herself well, even though she could barely find a voice sufficient to challenge the antipathy of the figure that filled the entrance to the tent.

"Are you well?" she breathed.

"I am as you see me," was the response, as icy and unbreakable as the message in his eyes. "Why have you come?" he asked then, but did not wait for her answer. Instead he exchanged a look with Ke Beyil, one filled with umbrage.

Keleu cast a glance full of pleading at Ke Beyil. In the days of their journey to this place he had vowed to remain with her, and voiced his protests anew when she had begged him to stay behind with their small party of servants, to be absent from this meeting. But now, alone with brother and sister, he sensed he could do no good. "I shall be outside," he told Keleu and, gathering his fur-lined cloak about him, he left the tent.

"Your officer greeted me," Keleu said then. "And your men cheered me. Have you no welcome?"

Osir grunted and moved for the first time since entering the tent. At a table he poured wine for himself and drank half a goblet, all the while regarding his sister with hooded eyes. "Soldiers," he intoned with a kind of dread sarcasm, "will make fools of themselves for a beautiful face. They will get miserable and love-sick. They will babble poetry. They will forget themselves and become like monkeys, gibbering at some novelty… You flatter yourself if you believe my men think any more of you than…"

Osir did not finish. He raised the goblet in gauntleted fingers, chainmail scraping on pewter.

Keleu looked at him quietly and clearly, and pressed him to finish. "*Think any more of me than* – what?" she asked.

Osir glanced away. With a jerk of his head he said, "Than what you are – a woman. You have no place here."

Keleu, bruised as she was by his stony indifference and by the callousness of his words, nevertheless checked her emotions. In spite of her knowledge of Osir's intractability and her memory of the acrimony of their previous encounter, she had nurtured, over the preceding days of her journey here, earnest hopes that Osir would have in his heart at least a spark of love. She knew that the merest hint of emotion in him would show his willingness to bend. And so she searched his face, refusing to acknowledge that the impassive visage of this man could betray nothing but pitiless rejection and the promise of violence.

"Why have you come?" he demanded, again in a tone he might have used with a servant or a foot soldier.

"You know why, Osir," she remonstrated gently, though his expression gave her no encouragement. "Are you so hardened by…by all of this…" – and she gestured about her to encompass the men-at-arms and the weapons beyond the tent walls – "that you would shame your sister with such taunts?"

"What sister is this?" came his retort, as cruel a blow as yet he had delivered.

Hurt beyond bearing, Keleu could only stare at him. The entreaties that she had planned, so carefully constructed in the logic and order of her thinking, were scattered like the pages of an open book at a sudden gust. The force of Osir's words lay in their brutal, calculated dispassion, as alien to Keleu's understanding of him as the sinister accoutrements of his armour.

Unperturbed by her distress, Osir said, "I had a sister once. But now she is the wife of my enemy."

At last, realizing the pass to which they had come, Keleu fired up. "You are wrong, Osir!" she cried. "Deny me if you will! But you are wrong! You will resolve nothing with this headstrong action. Think of the misery you will bring to Strath with your war. It is so futile!"

"Nevertheless, it is begun."

"But why? What can you possibly gain? If you engage Mathed's force, if you storm Mamoba, even if you kill Mathed, what then? Lord Yoiwa will not accept your authority in Strath. He will strike against you. Think on it! All of Honam's power against Strath! The Council would be bound to order the Ta-shih to remove you for fear of such a war. You would lose everything."

Keleu stood up and moved closer. Osir remained still. In a softer voice she said, "With Mathed you could rule Strath. This union with Honam must advantage us. And though you distrust Lord Yoiwa, you cannot say the same of Mathed. I know him…"

The silence played out between them, a long time it seemed to Keleu in the intensity of her present emotional state. Her brother was, she began to think, given pause by her reckoning. Perhaps he saw another way. Perhaps he could envisage the political ramifications that she saw so clearly. Perhaps, she fervently hoped, he would relent…

Osir was unmoving and unchanged. He held her gaze and she his as if this were a contest of wills and the world around them waited silent for the conclusion. *I cannot read his face now,* she thought, *he is lost to me. But then why does he hesitate?*

Thus, grasping at this most tenuous thread of hope, she begged him, "If all of this is so – what then? What then can you gain from these dreadful preparations?"

Her words seemed to move him suddenly to a conclusion: "My birthright," he said simply. "Strath is mine now. My sister is dead."

And all her resolve collapsed. It was as if, for the very first time in their lives, he knew and exercised the means of her humiliation with the precision of a blade.

"Oh, Osir," she whispered, in physical pain at this torment.

"I am committed," he continued in a matter-of-fact tone. "By your husband, as it happens. He is moving a force of sixty men not twenty miles from here. And you will be pleased to learn that he is with them… Or perhaps you knew that already. It is of little consequence. This morning we strike camp. You would not be in time to warn him or pass him information on our strength. It's back to Mamoba for you – or, better yet, Honam. In a little while there will be no place for you in Strath."

Osir set down the goblet on a map table. "And so I must bid you goodbye. Leave these parts instantly: it is a dangerous world of late…"

Her eyes reflecting the misery of failure and a broken spirit, Che Keleu looked imploringly one more time at her brother, to be greeted by the unrelenting enmity set in every aspect of his armoured figure. Then, all dignity forgotten, she flung herself at his feet and grasped his hand, weeping piteously and begging him to desist from the course he had chosen. "In the name of our father!" she cried, reaching an extremity of torment. "In Shenri's name!"

These words had a terrible effect on Osir. From the cold haughtiness of his previous disposition he was carried swiftly and unnaturally to a violent, ungovernable rage. "Get out!" he stormed at her, tearing his hand away and beating at the air with his mailed fist. "Were I any other man I would strike you for such irreverence! Get out!"

Summoned by the noise and fearing for the safety of Keleu, Ke Beyil swept into the tent. On her knees, her heavy skirts and green cloak spread around her on the canvas floor of the tent, Keleu wept, her hands to her eyes and the magnificent fall of chestnut hair covering her shoulders and face. Osir stood over her, as much a contrast from the young woman as dark from light. Violence distorted his features, made his eyes start from his skull; his limbs seemed to be frozen in self-mastery of the most savage of emotions.

Ke Beyil, who had checked himself on beholding this appalling scene, now hurried forward and drew Keleu gently to her feet. Weak and insensible of events about her, Keleu had to be supported on Ke Beyil's arm.

Then together they left the tent.

***

Two more troopers had joined her squad, soon after daybreak, and stayed with them. That changed the odds significantly. Meanwhile, as they pressed on, other riders came in and departed, messengers for Lord Mathed. It was getting crowded, here in the pine forests and hills of Strath.

Kesmet knew he had missed an opportunity. Reviewing the night's action, he could pinpoint moments when he might have taken the risk, pulled the trigger on the crossbow and succeeded. Yet he also understood that her squad were very good. They had been alert to threats, had anticipated and countered the likely permutations of an attack and had prevented his succeeding. It was not the first time he had missed an opportunity.

He walked Gexa, his reins loose in one hand, as they crested yet another valley, this one sparsely wooded. Zuse ranged ahead, tasting the air, tracking the squad and stopping when they stopped, dropping to his belly as a signal to Kesmet.

Foiled in his early endeavour, Kesmet was unconcerned. He knew now it was her. He knew she was central to events in Strath and that she could not go to ground and disappear. He knew her alias. He had studied her tactics and her squad. He was learning everything about them. Even though he expected her to make contact with Mathed's force in short order, which would make a strike at her impossible, he could track her easily.

Likewise, he accepted that in the daylight she would have scoured the area around her camp for tracks. She would find his marks – that much was inevitable. She would suspect a scout from Osir's growing army, but no more. The increasing activity of two small armies in the field, with all the attendant scouts, baggage trains and local villagers in motion, afforded Kesmet greater cover than before.

It was just a matter of time. And time had never been his enemy.

***

The late morning sun was quite warm, and made the day pleasant after the dismal cold of the past week. Skava sat her roan and looked quizzically at Yan, who had been out to her scouts near Osir's camp and then back again. His horse was breathing hard as they trotted side by side down into a glade.

"The wife?" she repeated. "Che fucking Keleu?"

Yan nodded. "Her ladyship…" he breathed. He seemed to rather like her, but the use of her honorific was, Skava thought, not out of respect but intended to wind Skava up, even though he kept a straight face. Yan had hidden depths, the young prick.

"Into the camp?" she persisted.

"Aye. With the councilman."

"The supervisor? Which one?"

"The tall bastard."

"Ke Beyil. Well, well…" She gave it some thought, fixed Yan with a sidelong look and asked, "How long were they in camp?"

"Scouts said mebbe two cycles. Left on the same mounts. Heading for her servants, 'bout a mile out, small camp and tents – an' a carriage."

Very civilized. Even on a desperate mission to her brother, she knew how to travel in style. Skava shook her head. What exactly had she been doing there? It needed more thought and more intelligence.

"The woodcutter…" she said abruptly. "Our man in Osir's camp – can we get him to tell us more?"

Yan looked sceptical.

Skava bridled. "I need to know, Yan. I don't care if you have to flay someone's arse or pay a year's fucking wages in bribes to the bastard, get me more on what happened between Osir and her fucking *ladyship*."

Yan looked chastened. "Boss," he acknowledged.

"Get on with it, then," she urged. And he put heels to his horse. Maki was drawing back on his reins to pull level with her as Yan took off. He made a motion of his head towards the north and reported, "Lord Mathed is ten miles away. With all the remounts. Near Lug Hill."

Skava grunted. It was as they had planned. "Fine. Get a messenger back and tell Vedarahava to split out our remounts and corral them nearby." She made a face. "Osir's scouts?"

"We scattered a couple squads," he replied, "but there're plenty more. Good woodsmen. Know the land well."

"Yes," she said, matter-of-fact. "We're up against the whole blasted province. But that's not a problem. We *want* 'em reporting. Tell Vedarahava to keep a third of our troopers in reserve, tight in amongst the trees somewhere east of Lug Hill. They need to stay hidden. And everyone to equip as heavy cavalry, but cover up – light capes, like we said. I want Osir's scouts to report a force that has divided, harnessed for fast riding, strike and run. If he buys that, he'll keep his army together. Lord Mathed's main force to head slowly west from Lug Hill. We'll pick 'em up there and make our move when we know where Osir is aiming."

Maki nodded and beckoned a messenger to issue the orders.

She wanted Osir to see an opportunity, a smaller force, fatally divided, lightly armoured. Then she needed the hill and sixty heavy cavalry.

***

They came upon Mathed suddenly, sooner than Osir's scouts had contended they would, and on ground that favoured neither side. The morning sunshine was gone. Clouds rolled in, turning the sky to a grim washed-out uniformity. The vanguard of Osir's force was strung out on an incline, one-third the way up a grassy hillside which breached the green blanket of the forests hereabouts like the humped back of a sea monster bursting from the waves. The slopes were bare of trees or brush, and afforded cover only in the sodden gullies, thick with grittle-weed, that zig-zagged, cutting gradually deeper as they neared the base of the hill.

The scouts reported to Osir that Mathed had split his force and was seeking to reach this promontory amidst the forests with the motivation of the desperate: the advantage of the high ground and the open terrain which allowed him to use his cavalry to greatest effect. Perhaps twenty troopers were missing. The scouts suggested they had peeled away to head south, and Osir expected an attack on his flanks. Coming upon Mathed so soon, perhaps half a day ahead, thrilled him. It confirmed that he had anticipated Mathed and surprised him.

The Quine men, riding in from the north-east, were visible to Osir's outriders when the main forces were yet three miles apart. They appeared to be moving fast in order to make up time. Orderlies galloped back across the uneven ground to Osir to report that the enemy, all cavalry, were light-armed, the better to move quickly. They had immediately turned towards the summit of the hill, clearly in a bid to secure the highest ground. Ke Chaaggar, one of the nobles of western Strath, at once sought orders from

Osir to wheel their troops and head directly to the summit.

Osir refused. Ke Chaaggar, dragging at his reins to control the excitement of his horse, gesticulated wildly towards the distant line of cavalry, green and white pennons flying stiffly in the bitter winter wind. "Prince!" he protested. "They are flying our own fucking colours! Or some bastardized mix! Let me chase 'em off the hill!"

Osir looked at the noble with a smile. "Aye, so we shall!" he laughed, turning his face into the wind so that the mist of rain that had begun to fall wet his long hair and plastered it to his forehead. "Let them think so!" he continued. "Ke Chaaggar. Send skirmishers towards the top at a run. Let the enemy think we are desperate to beat him to the summit. Then wheel the main force, but slowly. Give the impression that we are encumbered because of our heavy cavalry and foot soldiers. Slowly, hear?" Osir jerked his fist towards the rear. "I shall take a third of our cavalry and flank the bastard! But give me time, Chaaggar! The usurper will strike hard and flee – he has not the strength to waste men in one decisive engagement. But we must have him this time! Dian has given us the open hill. It must be here! In the forests he will harry us and deplete our numbers. It must be here!"

Osir leaned from the saddle and clamped Chaaggar's forearm with his gauntlet. His armour, stained by the long, hurried march, was covered by the first fine droplets of rain so that the afternoon light upon the steel made his body seem almost incandescent. In his eyes there was the same fire, as passionate and furious as Chaaggar had yet seen in him.

"Slowly, hear?" Osir whispered vehemently. "Hold him." Then he wrenched his horse round and galloped back along the column.

Tension eating at his stomach, Ke Chaaggar watched him go. Behind him, over his shoulder and below the enemy's view, on the lower slopes of the hill, horsemen began to peel away from the main body and raced to catch up with the lead rider. Within minutes Osir's troop had been swallowed up in the murky half-light at the edge of the forests.

"May Dian grant us her favour," Chaaggar muttered to himself. Then he looked up the slope into the drifting rain and urged his horse forward. "Troopmaster!" he bellowed, and when his man came running, "Forty skirmishers, immediately! Make your best pace to the top. If the enemy strikes, stand your ground behind your shields. We shall be with you forthwith."

The troopmaster, staring at his commander with that startled look that accompanies the onset of action, bowed, gathered up his shield and halberd, and set off across the soft turf.

Ke Androc, joining Ke Chaaggar on his fine black warhorse ahead of the main body of troops, called out to him, "Your eyes are younger than mine, Chaaggar. Tell me: are those Strath colours only?"

Ke Chaaggar peered into the rain. A hundred paces in front of them the skirmishers struggled up the slope in two lines. Beyond, nearly a mile away, Mathed's horsemen were nearing the summit. Green and white pennons fluttered in the wind. Chaaggar could see no other colours.

"Green and white, the bastard," he responded, outraged. "By the Shae's bony arse, he's stolen our colours!"

Androc nodded slowly, scowling in his characteristic manner. "So are they Ouine Clan or men of Strath? And who guards Mamoba?" he said.

"*Our* countrymen," Chaaggar grunted on reflection and with a bitterness he had not intended.

"Perhaps today, then, we shall only kill Ouine men…"

"Aye, we'll kill some Ouine men today. But then there's tomorrow. Mamoba must be taken. And there's many a countryman of ours who'll stand behind Che Keleu in defence of Mamoba."

Chaaggar raised his arm and signalled the turn. He looked at Androc. "The prince requests that we advance at our slowest pace. If you would be so good as to lead our left flank?"

"To be sure. But answer me this: the skirmishers – they will engage the enemy far ahead of us…at our pace they will be left completely exposed… so what is their role?"

Ke Chaaggar drew a deep breath and picked up his helmet from its hook on the saddle. He buckled it on, then gazed at Androc from the eye-slits. "They are to fix the enemy," he replied finally, "until the prince has flanked him."

Ke Androc's face broke into an evil smile. "Aha!" he exclaimed. "They will fix him! Oh, excellent!" Then he laughed and, turning his mount away towards the left, could be heard to remark, "A noble sacrifice!"

The entire body of troops and cavalry began to turn, the van slowing to no more than half pace, while the rear echelons moved forward more briskly to take up triple ranks on the left flank, where Ke Androc's horse, tossing its black mane, cantered sideways ahead of the field. As the gap between the main force and the skirmishers widened to some four hundred paces, Chaaggar's cavalry lingered behind the advancing troops to allow them to spread out in their three ranks over a front of more than two hundred paces. Trudging up the difficult slope, boots sinking in the soft grass and mud, groups of soldiers soon fell behind, especially where the gullies made it impossible to move at the same speed. The line started to take on a ragged disorder. Troopmasters roared expletives and hastened the men forward. Behind them the cavalry horses skittered nervously, impatient with the excruciating slowness of the advance.

"We've got a fucking rabble on foot," Chaaggar muttered under his breath, though he took care not to appear anything less than confident before the young officers around him. The awkwardness of the terrain worried him. The impending difficulty of getting his cavalry to manoeuvre in and out of the gullies would militate against the successful repulse of any lightning attack on his flanks. His men would be tired soon. And there was the rain, beating down harder, turning the slope into a treacherous mire.

Ahead, against the grey backdrop of the autumn sky, the skirmishers were breaking up into several knots, despite the best efforts of their troopmaster.

Fools! Chaaggar thought. *Stay as a unit or you'll be butchered quicker than a wink*!

On the summit the green and white pennons showed that the Ouine force had stopped. Chaaggar could make out individual figures. Most of the men had dismounted to rest the horses. He started to count them, but they were walking to and fro to disguise their true numbers. That suggested a ruse, possibly a small expedition hidden behind the hill or back in the forest for a flank attack. No, it was too far to launch an attack from the trees…

Ah well, he sighed, *we have our own plan and we must abide by it*. But the more he thought about these matters the more an infinite number of potential disasters occurred to him. What if the prince were delayed – or came too soon? Given the former, Mathed would annihilate the skirmishers and round on Chaaggar's flank, then retire swiftly. In the latter case, the Ouine cavalry would spot Osir from their vantage and engage him away from Chaaggar's reinforcements. In both instances, the prince would suffer losses. Ke Chaaggar pulled at the chinstrap of his helmet and rubbed his beard, striving hard to throw off the feeling that this sudden onset of gloom made him conspicuous to his own men. He fixed a mad grin to his lips and glanced to right and left. The officers close by rode their mounts stiffly, hands resting on sword pommels, eyes facing directly to the front. Behind them along the coiling lines of the foot soldiers, faces were grim and, Chaaggar earnestly hoped, determined. Shield slung across his back, each man carried his halberd in both hands, using the shaft butt as a staff to help him over the most treacherous of the undulating tract.

The skirmishers were within arrow-shot of the enemy. Now they were bunching, plainly dismayed by the proximity of the armoured cavalry at the crest of the hill and, in contrast, by the distance between themselves and the security of their own force.

Mathed's troop was remounting. The skirmishers loosed a few arrows to mark the range. The troopmaster has some sense, Chaaggar decided – a career soldier, not one of the inexperienced volunteer levies they had been training for two weeks on the march. But they were quailing now under the threat of Honam armour and Honam blades. The enemy could ride down on them in moments…

Alarmed by these first ominous movements of the Ouine force, and by pressing qualms for the outcome of this battle, Chaaggar cried out to his drummer, "Take up the pace!" And, with a jolt of misgiving for disobeying the prince's command, he urged his horse to a trot.

Around him, on both sides, the soldiers seemed to take heart and surged forward out of control, thereby breaking the line. To the shouts and curses of the troopmasters, discipline and order were at once restored. However, at the flanks, where the mounted officers were furthest away, the men were edging forward again and, in so doing, extending the line into a crescent.

Still the rain hissed in the cold air. Drops of water splashed from Chaaggar's nose-plate onto his lips and he licked at it, discovering to his surprise that his mouth was bone dry.

A prolonged cheer marked the Ouine force's charge.

Chaaggar looked up. The skirmishers stood their ground – all honour to them! – and loosed a flight of arrows, which seemed to have no effect whatsoever on the thunderous downhill attack. Then they swung their halberds up and grounded the butts, forming a bristling wall of steel points behind their shields.

Heart hammering with excitement, and helplessly intent on the onslaught up ahead, Chaaggar allowed his horse to draw away and with him went the nearest ranks, bulging out in an effort to keep up. By the time he had checked himself, Chaaggar noticed that the whole line had broken and the troopmasters, likewise rapt by the imminent action in front, were doing nothing to rectify the situation.

"Close ranks, you fucking scum!" he fulminated, waving his right arm in a gesture meant to draw the troops back into line.

"Ke Chaaggar!" burst out the officer to his right. "The enemy! They're not stopping!"

Chaaggar turned startled eyes to the charge of the Ouine cavalry. In two streams they were heading around the half-circle of skirmishers, leaving them unmolested. Nearer now, with their cloaks flung back, he also saw that they were heavy cavalry, wearing knee-length hauberks, round shields up, steel-tipped lances lowering fast. Instantly perceiving their objective, Chaaggar began to shout: "Regroup! Stand your ground! Stand your ground!"

But his troops, moments before a disciplined formation and now a scattered mob, darted about in different directions, some heeding the orders of their troopmasters to stand firm, others floundering backward in huddles or retreating to the safety of gullies. Ke Chaaggar was appalled.

Within the space of two dozen heartbeats the Ouine cavalry would be among them. Horrified by the inevitable disaster, he lashed his horse along the remnants of the line nearest him, bawling to the men to kneel and ground their halberds. Elsewhere, encouraged by his example, others did the same. But by then colours of green and white were everywhere. Cries and screams lifted above the ring of steel. A horseman flashed by Chaaggar and, as he raised his sword instinctively, a tremendous blow to his shoulder flung him sideways in the saddle, leaving him desperately attempting to recover his balance or fall. The horse under him stumbled, then recovered. Chaaggar's left side was paralysed, and what seemed to be a stream of warm water was soaking his arm and back. Righting himself in the saddle, he raised the sword again, utterly disoriented, expecting his troops to be behind him, but discovering the serried ranks of olive-green tunics immediately to his right. The men were casting about with their halberds on all sides, backing up against each other in a defensive knot. None of the enemy was in view. With some difficulty, for he could not use his left arm, Chaaggar turned his horse, laying the sword across the pommel and his thigh in order to grasp the reins in his right hand.

The battle resolved itself in Chaaggar's mind as he took in the scene on the left flank of his battered force. Lances were pinned in the earth or in the corpses of a score of foot soldiers. The Ouine cavalry, having shattered the weak left flank with their lances, were harrying small groups of soldiers, weaving in and out of the disintegrating lines and slashing all about them with their heavy swords. Blades glinted. The bronze hauberks of the Ouine men could be seen everywhere. Further down the hill, Chaaggar's own cavalry was wheeling in disarray under the first shock of the headlong rush. Taken thoroughly by surprise and overwhelmed by the speed and force of the attacking horsemen, only a few had been able to come to the assistance of the panic-stricken foot soldiers. Owing to the enemy's concentration on the left, Chaaggar's right flank and centre were intact.

All of this Chaaggar discerned in a moment. But in that time the bronze hauberks were already beginning to regroup. *Act at once!* came the thought.

***

Skava had seen Osir break away and make for Mathed's flank up the crest of Lug Hill. She had twenty lancers, dismounted, holding their horses in a deep gully, now six hundred paces behind the advancing formation of Osir's main contingent. All of the cavalry troopers had draped their cloaks over the heads of the horses to calm them and stop any whinnying that could alert the enemy. Timing had to be right. She needed concealment until Mathed started his charge downhill into the left flank. Through her telescope she could follow the Ouine cavalry at the summit mounting up. Now.

She stepped back from the gully edge, snapped, "Lead out! Form line, quarter closed-up."

The troopers moved quickly and, in better order than she had hoped, were soon formed fifty paces wide. Between her and the rear of Osir's contingent she had scouted the ground and it was clear of trenches and obstacles. They had a clear gently uphill run until the final hundred paces where it steepened.

"On me!" she cried out loud enough for the line-closers to hear. And she was off at a canter, heavy lance still butt-sheathed in the stirrup cushion, and covering the ground fast even at this initial pace. No need now for orders: the troop would follow her lead.

Halfway and she hitched up, then canted the heavy lance to a comfortable forty-five-degree angle, ready to be levelled. She tightened her grip on the round shield, lowered her head so that the steel of her helmet was in place if someone was alert enough to get off arrows, then kicked her dun gelding into a gallop. The effect was instant, as the beast exploded into the full power of its stride and the distance closed unbelievably rapidly, even as they began to drive up the hillside.

Left flank of Osir's main contingent was in disarray. Mathed and his cavalry were among the soldiers. Then it was too late to see more. Her lance came down, couched firm under her armpit. The straggling lines ahead were swinging. They were trying to wheel, spear points and halberds clattering together overhead to defend the sudden onslaught from behind. She aimed her lance at a mounted officer ahead of the foot soldiers, braced, and the massive weight of her own horse blasted through three men, the lance took the officer in the side as he tried to turn, shattered in her grip and she let go at once, thundering uphill until she wheeled right as they had planned, gratified to see most of the rest of her troop doing the same.

A trampled heap of corpses and dying men fifty paces wide on this far right flank of the Strath formation littered the hillside. Exhilaration and bloodlust coursed through her veins like a victory song. She unsheathed her heavy cavalry blade, but there were no enemies nearby and already her thoughts were turning to the dangers of a counter-punch from Strath cavalry or the archers up the slope.

Where was that bastard Osir?

***

"Turn!" Chaaggar yelled. "Face left!"

The troops moved, running in frantic droves to take up positions. But from his far right there was a stupendous thunder of hooves and reverberating crashes, and suddenly another enemy cavalry troop had flattened a hundred foot soldiers on his flank. He was appalled. His centre was still intact and had mostly swung to face the original threat from the left; now they were hesitant, dozens of soldiers turning away to defend against the new danger uphill. Chaaggar had only heartbeats to make a decision before his formation fell apart.

While his centre ranks were still forming, Chaaggar cried, "Charge!"

The drummer beat the order, and his troops poured forward at the retreating Ouine force downhill. He held his own mare back, straining over his shoulder to see what was happening behind him. Some two dozen of his foot soldiers had grounded their pikes in self-preservation and were presenting a bristling steel wall to the small cavalry squadron up the slope. By pure luck his formation had created a defence of his rear. Then he kicked heels and his horse was galloping toward the action below, and all around him his own cavalry was pouring across the slopes. From the higher ground came Prince Osir and a tight formation of thirty horsemen. Their mounts were lathering, but had picked up considerable speed on the downslope and passed ahead of Chaaggar, ensuring that, as Mathed's cavalry, already disengaged, retired diagonally across the gradient of the hill, it was the prince's detachment that was closest to them.

Osir reached the hindmost horseman, struck out with his sword and the man toppled sideways with peculiar slowness, sliding from the saddle to hit the ground and tumble over and over. Then Chaaggar himself was past the inert form and all he could see was his own cavalry in front of him. The pain in his shoulder and the helplessness which had gripped him were replaced instantly by the eager excitement of the chase, the euphoria of being here amongst his fellows to rout the enemy.

All at once the horses directly ahead were swerving to right and left to avoid a deep gully. Chaaggar began to slow. Again there was chaos. The depth of the gully frightened the horses and they shied and whinnied. Riders were unhorsed. Officers bawled instructions, which were unintelligible amidst the thunder of hooves and the shrill protests of the animals. Half-buried in the mud at the bottom of the gully by the weight of his armour, a man groaned piteously. His horse, the first victim of the treacherous depression, lay broken and unmoving at his side.

The shortest route around the gully required a sharp turn back uphill, where more of Chaaggar's cavalry was arriving. Chaaggar sheathed his sword with his good arm, reckoning that he would have no immediate need of it. Cursing roundly, he forced a way through the press of horsemen and at last gained the shallow part of the gully where he might cross. Reaching the other side, he could see Mathed's force, now merging with the smaller troop that had smashed his right flank. Both were six hundred paces away, approaching the trees at the tenebrous fringes of the forests. The detachment of Prince Osir's horses, exhausted by the cruel ride that had been necessary to the success of his strategy, had fallen behind and were slowing. Only the prince himself and three of Chaaggar's men, who had passed the gully by another route, were still close enough to attack the rearguard of the Ouine force.

***

Skava wanted to laugh. A mad grin was plastered to her face as they thundered across the broken turf towards the woods. Maki and Yan were either side of her, both with blades drawn. The mounts were tiring, but were fresher than the enemy's. The forests would afford cover and the remounts were not far off. She had a moment to reflect on the battle. Both flanks of Osir's main force had been shattered beyond her expectations; a third of his cavalry had been drawn away in the abortive flanking manoeuvre; the rest had been clumped in the centre and left and had been mauled but largely survived. In sheer brutal numbers, Skava knew her plan had trimmed more than two hundred of Osir's foot soldiers, who now lay in shattered heaps along the slopes. Better yet, the survivors' spirit would be broken. They would know, would understand and feel at the deepest level, that they had been defeated, their friends and comrades killed and maimed, and that it could happen again. In a single skirmish, she had achieved what she had planned for a whole campaign.

Yan was craning round to look behind where some of their troopers were lagging, their horses fatigued and making heavy going on the soft turf.

"Boss!" he yelled. And Skava was twisting in the saddle to check what was happening.

A knot of Prince Osir's cavalry, lashing their horses to a last-ditch effort that would inevitably kill them, was drawing closer, the lead rider, fully armoured and without a shield, extending a lance.

Dammit!

Skava peeled away right, Yan following. She hoped Maki would go the other way to split the pursuers. She dragged at her reins, slowing, attempting to turn the tightest circle and get inside the lance. As she did so, the three straggling Ouine riders burst between her and the lead attackers to make good their lumbering escape. Then the lance was swinging towards her, deadly and sharp, and she could see the wild grimace of the face under the helmet in the moment that his weapon would run her through. Except that she stepped her mount neatly in towards his line of attack and, helped considerably by the exhaustion of his horse, was able to deflect the lance with a swinging smack of her shield. He was an accomplished rider though, and used his mount's momentum to get around her, gaining time to drop the lance and draw his sword for close quarters. They immediately traded blows, low then high, and Skava thought she could get him because he had no shield, except that she spotted Mathed was involved in the fray, making his own cuts to one of the Strath cavalrymen.

Oh for fuck's sake! What misplaced notion of leadership or nobility had persuaded him to come back?

Now she needed to extract everyone before the young fool got himself killed. She ducked a blow, giving up on her own combat to spur her mount forward, and deliberately collided with the Strath horse, knocking the rider back. Then she yelled in her loudest command voice, "Off! Withdraw!" and gestured firmly with her sword towards the forest, saw Maki disengage and pretty much barge Mathed's horse away from the action, before she was swaying again to avoid a lethal thrust from her first adversary, madly backing her mount as a second uppercut glanced off her hauberk's shoulder pauldron and missed her helmet by a finger's width.

Jabbing heels to flanks, she was away again, the gelding finding his stride in moments. Bent low to minimize the target she made, she took the reins in her sword hand, swung the round shield behind her back and urged the horse to best speed. Mathed was a short length in front, sitting too upright for her liking, and his mount beginning to falter from the long run. She was catching him and the forest was getting closer, and the exhilaration of the battle and the success was still roaring through her veins.

***

In anger and despair Chaaggar spurred his horse forward. He knew that it was too late. They had failed. *Does Dian withdraw her favour?* he demanded of himself. *Did my own loss of nerve cause this? Why did I not hold back, true to the prince's orders? 'Slowly, hear?' the prince had said.* So much had gone wrong. So many of their troops must litter the field, lifeless and wasted. If there was victory here it belonged squarely to Mathed.

Three or four of the bronze hauberks hung back, deliberately it seemed to Chaaggar. A lance and swords flashed as the prince and his men drew abreast. Chaaggar whipped his horse, but the animal could give no more speed, stumbling now in exhaustion.

The melee broke up. Chaaggar could make out the prince, whose horse, shambling at no more than a canter, was evidently near to collapse. The Ouine men moved off, with neither side having suffered any loss. As Chaaggar neared them, Osir flung his sword, point first, into the turf, then reached across to the young soldier who had brought his horse up close to the prince.

"Your bow, fool!" he shouted. "Give me your crossbow!" Their horses were now virtually at a standstill. Osir seized the heavy crossbow, already cranked before the battle, took and laid the proffered bolt with practised ease and immediately fired. His target was Mathed, with whom Osir had only just traded sword blows, and who had delayed to ensure the safety of his slower riders.

At fifty paces, the range was doubtful. Mathed and his men were already under the towering black boughs of the forest. The bolt, however, perhaps by luck, ran true. Its needle head sliced between both the heavy plate disks and mail of the hauberk and lodged in Mathed's back. Chaaggar saw him jolt, his sword fall from his grip as his right arm flailed behind him in a reflexive attempt to pluck at the bolt. Then he slid forward, and would have fallen had not another rider swerved in to support him.

And abruptly it was over. Mathed and his men disappeared into the great black maw of the forest. The Ouine force was gone.

In agony now from what he guessed must be the wound caused by an Ouine lance, Chaaggar clasped his hand to his side. Crimson blood coursed from the broken armour. He pulled off his helmet and let it drop to the ground where his horse stood. His head drooped on his chest. A moment of the worst exhaustion and black depression made him want to sob.

Ten paces away, Prince Osir stared into the forest, the crossbow in his hands. A baleful look, partway between rage and elation, burned in his eyes.

CHAPTER 13

Evil to him who evil intends.
Motto from the banner of the coat of arms of the Honourable Bank of Royal Kemae.

[…] Echrexar and his dogs in the shorthand parlance. Since the records were lost, we had no real idea whether it was Echrexar that caused the obliteration or one or more of the dogs. A particularly vocal group insisted there were archives showing that Echrexar would return, with or without his dogs. I am agnostic. My single observation is that Echrexar has become a byword for evil…and who can say otherwise?
Fragment of a vellum document, dated by scholars to the century after Echrexar. The document itself is thought by some to have been deliberately burned.

***

"Copper-bottomed?" Harbin enquired, one large hand fastened to the poop deck rail as the sloop kissed the crest of a wave and the distant islands appeared as brown smudges again in the grey dawn.

"Aye, sir," came the response from the skipper, his eye on the horizon, the helmsman and the mainsail all at once. "All five vessels now. Much faster. Less time in drydock."

He referred to the bank's small fleet, a necessity in the Kemae Islands and an advantage if one needed to travel fast. The copper plates sheathing the entire hull below the waterline were expensive, requiring tons per ship, but mightily effective, killing shipworm and the growth of weeds which on wooden-hulled vessels, even those with the best tar coating, caused handling problems and significant drag. Harbin had discovered the technique in the copy of a book, itself badly damaged by age and therefore incomplete, in the bank's archive, persuading his senior partners to experiment. One of the secrets of the technique he had deduced was to use a copper alloy bolt, not the usual iron bolts, to fix the sheathing to the hull. Otherwise, the iron and copper produced together an electrolytic reaction that destroyed the iron.

If that experiment, like many of his initiatives over the years, had met with an initial scepticism from his fellow partners, his latest proposal would be dismissed as proof of his headlong slide into insanity. The snake that was Eslin needed sustenance to grow her army of snakes, and if Harbin could control the source of that sustenance and ultimately choke it off... Well, she needed capital, loans, huge quantities of it. Harbin understood these things better than anyone and he had discovered the most recent source. He could see his own plan with clarity. It might work, if he could redirect the considerable assets of the bank to his venture. The challenge was the need to proceed at pace...and win over the cautious, soon-to-be incredulous, Partner Oversight Committee, that most senior, august and austere of the Honourable Bank's governance bodies.

The sloop, dubbed *Sadon's Luck* by her crew, and carved in silver-painted script on bows and stern below the vessel's more proper name, *Bank of Kemae III*, plunged into the next trough, and a scatter of spume speckled Harbin's heavy cloak and his face. He did not mind. Whilst he and horses had never been the best of friends – he was too large and ungainly – ships were another matter. He loved them and had sailed everywhere. It was the only physical thing in which he outmatched Kesmet, and a source of considerable good-natured ragging when they put to sea together.

To cut weeks from his journey, he had been tempted to take a fast Royal Post carriage from Ung through Strath and on to the coast at Moba, but he knew he would be noticed, if not by Skava's spies then those of competing banks and the merchant guilds; and they would talk, and talk would be passed on to spies. Neither was welcome, at this time of uncertainty and brewing…what? Trouble. Threat. He had heeded Kesmet's advice, and so travelled east by the bank's fastest carriages to Sero and Run, embarking from the port there to sail north across the Bour Ocean around Wisib Point and the rugged coast of the Northern Passage. Here, the autumn storms were yet to rise, and they made good time in three weeks by hugging the cliffs and coves until putting in at Uvaol. There Harbin looked in on Lord Isharri of Allpo, whose family had long been a client of the Kemae Bank, and they spent a pleasant evening in the high palace of Uvaol Castle, in the smaller wood-panelled dining hall. Amidst the sumptuous black and white wall hangings and banners of Allpo's colours, before the huge mullioned windows overlooking the crashing sea far below, the two men exchanged news. It was, of course, more than a fine dinner between a lord and his banker: they knew each other well, and Harbin was able to gently introduce the topic of Prince Mathed's marriage to the Lady Che Keleu and the cloud of Lord Shenri's untimely death. Isharri, however, was already well informed. He spoke of war in Strath and the tensions at his western border, and Harbin, pretending to be starved of intelligence because of his time at sea, expressed astonishment and dismay. His thoughts, of course, privately turned to Kesmet, and the tentacles of fear gripped at his innards once more.

"Ke Harbin," Lord Isharri exclaimed in good humour, when the first course was done, "you look as young as ever! Perhaps it is the burden of four children, but I feel older than ever whilst you never seem to age! What is your secret?"

Harbin smiled broadly at this compliment and rejoined, "No children, my lord. And good wine. That's the secret!"

Towards the end of the meal, he was left alone for a short time while Isharri received a message in an ante-room. Upon his return, over cheese and a fine straw-yellow dessert wine of Strath's late harvest, Harbin ventured, "The Lord of Honam is said to have the services of a very effective master-intelligencer. Do you see his hand anywhere in Allpo?"

Isharri gave him a look. He was a man of middle years and quiet intelligence, steel eyes and greying shoulder-length dark hair and beard.

"Hmm," he grunted. "And what do you know of this master-intelligencer?"

Harbin shrugged. "Only what my sources in Honam report," he offered in return. "A man of talent, and different faces, sometimes a man, oft times a woman, employing many names, chief among them Sklavin – and Eslin." These names, Harbin knew, would be passed directly to Isharri's spymaster, if he were not already listening behind some panel in the hall. "A person of fierce ambition," he added, "…for his lord."

Isharri was watching Harbin closely. He raised his goblet, a clear crystal of fine design and workmanship, and contemplated his guest over the rim. He had understood at once, Harbin concluded, that this was not a casual reference, and perhaps he knew more than he revealed. Much as he trusted this man, Harbin needed to tread carefully, whilst conveying enough to bring Isharri's own spy network to high alert and be ready to counter Skava's moves.

"Ke Harbin, my friend," declared Isharri. "I am well aware of Yoiwa's ambitions. But it seems to me you know something more of this spymaster…" He trailed off, his silence inviting comment.

Harbin returned the other's gaze. "I do, my lord. Part knowledge, part speculation. I believe his goal is to unite Honam, Lorang and Strath–"

"Lord Yoiwa…"

"Indeed, Yoiwa." Harbin had meant Skava, but the nobility could not readily comprehend how anyone other than a noble could be the motive force for anything – and least of all a commoner, and especially a woman who was a commoner. He held up both hands to emphasize his next remark: "But this Skava, the spymaster, is clever, my lord. I beg you to have a care. In the course of the bank's dealings in Honam and Lorang, we have had reason to learn much that alarms us."

Isharri grunted again, as much to say there was little that could alarm him. "I am listening," he replied with pursed lips, "Ke Harbin. I have no cause to doubt you. But what can I do? My fleet is prepared. The coast is secure. My army, small as it is, patrols the border. My own spymaster reports to me daily."

There was an undercurrent of impatience to Lord Isharri's remarks. Harbin understood it. Broaching such matters was, to aristocrats, a private affair: it touched uncomfortably on the abrasion of honour. The master of Allpo tolerated this only because of his regard for the Kemae Bank – and the consistency of the bank's support in loans and trade for five generations.

"Moreover, my friend, as I told you earlier," Isharri went on, warming to his theme and perhaps equipped with the latest news from the recent message he had received, "Prince Osir has raised the province against the new Lord of Strath. Lord Yoiwa has returned to Honam, with nearly half of his troops. Mathed must hold the seat of Strath against the legal challenge of Shenri's son." He laughed. "Constructive Trust! Who would know such a thing? I confess, I did not."

Harbin nodded. He did know it. He had ensured this knowledge was passed conveniently to Ke Androc through a junior supervisor of the Council at Chisua. Ke Androc, canny if parochial, would not have wasted time in edifying Prince Osir. In fulfilling his promise to Kesmet, it had been Harbin's attempt to protect Prince Osir. He was not at all certain it would be sufficient.

"The war proceeds," Isharri pressed him, "in a manner more favourable to Prince Osir than perhaps you have heard." He allowed a half smile of condescension to crease his face, then became serious. "Lord Mathed is gravely injured – taken, it seems, by a crossbow bolt."

Harbin was now astounded. This was news indeed, delivered, he surmised, in the last few minutes by Isharri's spymaster.

"A bolt," Isharri concluded, "shot at the new Lord of Strath by Prince Osir himself, or so it is said."

Harbin stared at his dinner companion in startlement.

"You can imagine," declared Isharri with a half smile, "the effect upon those fellows loyal to Prince Osir. He is like an Immortal now! He has struck against the occupying Ouine Clan and in a single skirmish has cast down the Lord Mathed. How can it be other than the will of the gods? Dian walks at Prince Osir's shoulder, together with every hedgerow god and sprite, and his army swells now with any under-merchant that can field a horse and his own cobbled armour and half the able-bodied farmers and commoners in hill and dale!" Isharri threw back the contents of his goblet then, with a shake of the head, added, "Fortune and misfortune are often intimate companions. In the battle itself, it seems Mathed's contingent badly mauled Osir's regiments. But a shaft in Lord Mathed and everyone has forgotten the scores of trampled corpses." He stabbed at a triangle of soft cheese, contemplating the tiny blade as if it were the crossbow shaft, then shrugged and concluded, "I feel, of course, for the young Mathed… and his new bride. What will become of her? A tragedy. But the politics suit Allpo, do they not? Clan Ouine will be thrust from Strath, Yoiwa bested and humbled, Osir upon the seat of his father once more."

He had secured the cheese titbit on his knife and now popped the morsel in his mouth. Harbin drew a breath, sighed. Isharri grew serious again, stroked fingers through his trimmed beard in contemplation of some inner thought, then said, "You are not convinced."

Isharri was shrewd. Harbin raised an eyebrow. Yes, the news was astonishing. It appeared that Skava had suffered a major reverse. And yet…

He fixed Isharri with a look of resignation. "This spymaster, Skava, is not to be underestimated, my lord," he intoned. "He is more powerful and more dangerous than you may believe. It is likely, sir, I contend, that Lord Shenri was murdered by this Skava. The disconcertment of Lord Yoiwa in Strath need not deter his master-intelligencer from pursuing his aims here in Allpo."

Now he had Isharri's complete attention. If one lord could be assassinated, so could another. The man nodded once. He would not ask for proof. It was enough that Harbin had voiced it, because it was a distinct probability he had certainly discussed with his own spymaster. Harbin lifted his goblet, turning the glass to catch the yellow glow of the many lamps holding back the night.

Finally he said, "As for events in Strath and Prince Osir's imminent triumph, you may call me a pessimist, but you will know the old saying, my lord: there's many a slip 'twixt cup and lip."

**

The Partner Oversight Committee of the Honourable Bank of Royal Kemae always convened in the senior partners' room of the headquarters of that venerable institution. The senior partners' room was whitewashed stone and ancient scrollwork depicting on each of the four walls the patrons of the bank: the merchants, the trade fleets, the farmers, artisans and engineers and, of course, the noble families. The depictions were elaborate and colourful, ships and cargo, deals struck at a handshake, bucolic scenes of crops and animals, engineers working with ruler and protractor, great machines for construction, weavers at banks of looms and, naturally, the rainbow of clan shields, of Kiangsu and the lands beyond – all of this running below the cornice and along the entirety of the entablature and framing at the head of the room the Honourable Bank's enormous coat of arms, a steed rampant, in jet and silver. Eight windows, three to both of the facing sides and two at the end opposite the coat of arms, gave views onto the town down the steep hill the bank headquarters occupied. Kemae town was modest in size, but still the largest of the four ports on the largest island of the Hundred Islands, as the Kemaes were also known. For their part, the Islanders were distinctly people of commerce and opportunity, independent of spirit and shrewd in business, running large trading fleets and fishing flotillas and, of course, the institutions that financed and insured them. The Kemae Bank was, in its understated way, the centre of this northern world that sat like a chain of a hundred silver links across the Bay of Marshese, never part of Kiangsu Realm but essential to it. Indeed, the Islanders had defended their freedom more than once.

And thus the twenty senior partners of the Honourable Bank sat in their high-backed black leather chairs at the enormous table, surrounded by the icons of their practical world, with an air of confidence and coolness.

Harbin liked them. He smiled at them and they smiled back, for the moment.

The chairman of the Oversight Committee sat opposite Harbin, and Harbin sat with his back to the great double windows that framed both him and the vast Bay of Marshese. Sunshine blessed the day and poured through the glass over his shoulder. It was a wonderful day for new things. Harbin felt *alive*, his entire being quivering with the thrill of an excitement he had not known for far too long. Even the remote, pained acknowledgement in the back of his mind that the proximate cause of his excitement was Eslin, back in the world as his enemy, could not dampen his spirits.

The chairman, Ke Kezenov, squinted at Harbin. Without preamble he declared, "We are quorate. We can begin this extraordinary meeting of the Partner Oversight Committee, requested by our fellow partner, Harbin" – merely his name, no honorifics were used between partners – "for the tabling of a proposal…" – Kezenov tilted his head to indicate, it seemed, a gentle rebuke – "where no papers have been submitted in advance."

Eighteen heads swivelled from their regard of the chairman to scrutiny of Harbin. Yes, they were indeed intrigued. Harbin smiled a broader smile and replied brightly, "Thank you, chairman. And my profound thanks to the men and women of the Partner Oversight Committee for their indulgence."

The men and women stared back at him, with a curiosity as plain and equally shared as the black tailcoats and silver-striped waistcoats they all wore. Fashion in the Hundred Islands changed slowly, and slowest of all in the Honourable Bank. A uniform identity was one of the principles of the institution. It suggested to clients that nothing here was untoward, or risky, or incautious. If not exactly trust, it proclaimed sturdy reliability.

Kezenov tilted his head again, this time with an air of polite acknowledgement of the right form of words. It always paid to be gracious.

"Your roving brief, Harbin," Kezenov said, "takes you across the breadth of Kiangsu Realm. You will have seen first-hand the troubles of our neighbours. Moreover, a new king has ascended the throne in Chisua, and in Strath there is war – actual war. Do you judge this war to be a matter of small moment…or is it the harbinger of more serious import?"

A very good question. Harbin took his smile down a notch. "It is both, Kezenov. But, of course, it is impossible to speculate on how it will turn. Like the honourable partners, I seek only to serve our clients and protect the interests of this venerable institution."

They all heard the word 'protect': an ominous word for bankers, ringing with the clamour of disruption and losses.

Harbin dived straight in: "With this perilous backdrop in mind, I believe, my fellow partners, that the Honourable Bank needs to better balance its overall risk."

A hand was raised: a woman with hair as silver as the stripes of her waistcoat. "Chairman, the Risk Committee has only this quarter determined that our position is satisfactory. Losses arising from the Chanee mining accident and the collapse of the Bellast horse-breeding merchant house are offset by buoyant profits for the fleet investments and adequate returns across the portfolio. We have agreed to draw down our exposures in mining. Horse-breeding, by contrast, is always good business."

Harbin waved a hand. "Of course. For the moment. But not for the future. I speak of the medium-term future. There is a rising threat in the northern and western Realm, possibly a more widespread war. The old certainties will be tested, if not overthrown. The Zaggisa…" – he drew out the word – "are invigorated and move among our Islands, clandestinely but no less lethal in their purpose. Clan Ouine grows in influence, whatever may be the outcome in Strath–"

Another hand. "The indications," declared a partner, clean-shaven like all the men here, "are that Prince Osir will regain Mamoba."

Harbin gave him a mild look, suggesting in the arch of one brow that he was missing the point. "Perhaps. If so, Clan Ouine may turn their attention to the Hundred Islands instead. Lord Yoiwa is close to Lord Ordas, and Lorang sits behind me on the far side of the Bay. Their ambition is dominion and control."

There followed a silence.

Harbin pressed his case: "There is, additionally, and directly appertaining to my imminent proposal, the matter of Honam's substantial investment in a secret army."

The silence was, if anything, deeper still.

Kezenov broke in, tonelessly neutral, "Do we know what scale this 'army' might be? The provinces have long disputed this way and then that the merits of expanding their militia. A doubling? A tripling? If so, it may be the Lord of Honam is merely *anticipating* a vote in Council, applying to all the clans, to the same effect."

Harbin looked straight at the chairman. "Ten-fold – at least."

And that got everyone talking at once, including a vociferous demand for evidence. Harbin opened the leather folder on the table under his large hands. He withdrew a thin sheaf of documents and held them up as a lawyer might in a dispute. "The Bank of Kiangsu City," he intoned, "has committed in loans a *million* gold leol to six merchant houses – shell arrangements crafted by Honam's master-intelligencer, I believe – for the purchase of iron, bronze, old steel and other materials and the building of new furnaces…secret furnaces of a new design. The output of these industrial efforts will be arms and armour for six thousand. A staggering number."

He held up the other hand to forestall interjections. "Permit me, please. I seek no vote today. Merely the description of the landscape we occupy in these changing times and the proposal I submit for our defence…and, I hope, future success."

The partners allowed him the floor and he continued, "I propose, my fellow partners, that we take a controlling stake in the Bank of Kiangsu City."

Uproar.

***

Two days later, the senior partners met again, this time to cast their vote, for or against, and counted by the proportion of their partner shares. The intervening time had been occupied in discussions and side-bar conversations and queries, to which Harbin gave answer as best he could. The acquisition of a stake in the rival bank was difficult, but legally and financially workable. Nonetheless, since his proposal was unprecedented and his vision for what might be achieved impossible to assess in any actuarial sense, it might result in astounding returns or ruinous losses. He expected dissent.

And was not disappointed.

The senior partners voted, aye or nay, for Harbin's proposal, in order around the table, with few meeting his eye. The proposal perplexed and terrified most of them. At the end, when Kezenov paused in his minuting of the procedure to put down his fountain pen and declare his own vote, "Nay," only three partners had joined Harbin. Carefully formal, the chairman consulted his notes and his calculations.

"The 'ayes': thirty-seven preferential shares." A low murmur of approval around the table, as the outcome was anticipated. "The 'nays': forty-three."

Harbin looked squarely at each partner in turn.

Kezenov cleared his throat. "The vote appears to run against your proposal, Harbin. It appears the 'nays' have it…"

Harbin opened his leather folder again, drew forth a silver-edged certificate, held it high in his hand and turned it to show the assembled partners the black seal of the Honourable Bank. "Chairman, fellow partners," he said carefully, seriously. "I do not, as you know, bring proposals to this committee very often. And even then, as is right and proper, I trust the judgement of my estimable partners in the judicious governance of this institution – as has my family for generations. On this one occasion, at this juncture of what I earnestly perceive as the most profound hazard to us and our Islands, I am using this proxy, sealed before the bank's highest committee and granting me, Harbin, the right to vote this partner's shares. On his behalf, I say 'aye.'"

Kezenov closed his eyes once, then opened them. He understood. The other partners, as one, looked stunned.

"Who is this partner?" came the question from one of them, looking around the table as if for an empty seat. "Who is missing?"

Harbin felt for them. Their world, cautious, ordered and unchanging, was no longer immune. He looked straight at Kezenov.

The chairman took a deep breath and spoke: "You will not know him, but his name is on the list. He holds twenty preferential partner shares, as the proxy states. His name is Kesmet. The 'ayes' have it. Fifty-seven to forty-three. The vote is carried."

Uproar, again.

***

Fortunas received the reports from his assistants every day: three boys, perhaps ten years old, street-wise, scruffy and invisible to both authorities and the objects of their scrutiny. Their handler, a nondescript man of several guises, seemed to treat them well but with discipline and they worked hard, fulfilling Fortunas's requirements exactly.

Twice more, Fortunas himself visited the inn where the young Strath soldier now worked and where he kept to the back of the establishment, cleaning dishes and handling the collection of jars, bottles and casks that rolled endlessly in and out of the taproom. Fortunas would sit in his accustomed spot in the bay window, cider to one hand, book to the other, observing, studying and learning. The rules of the inn were simply numbers: bottles, jars, dishes, cutlery, the exchange of money, the provision of meals, the cleaning of the taproom and accommodations upstairs, all repeated in cycles during the day, once, twice, three times, four times, or weekly, or monthly. From these rhythms Fortunas could predict the actions of the owners, the servants – and the young soldier. They called him Patris – an assumed name, Fortunas realized, because in the early days he had not always responded to it without prompting. He worked hard, as his injuries recovered, fitting in nicely to the patterns of the inn, but ever in the background, ever wary.

Streets away from the target of his observation, alone in a garret room of the apartment he occupied, Fortunas picked up the occasional message from Sklavin. His orders remained the same and he sent no message in return: there was no need. Instead he looked after Peri, and once a week took her outside the old city to the open countryside where he released her to hunt and to exercise, swooping between the tree-cloaked valleys and diving in a spectacular plunge upon unwary pigeons or other birds. While she hunted and his mount grazed nearby, he drilled with sword, knife and axe, slowly at first then with intensity, practising foot placement, an advance, a diagonal, fading back and lunging. He used tree stumps and branches set upright as targets for throwing knives, rehearsing the draw from different body angles, imagining the defence and openings that unique positions offered.

Afterwards, warm and sweat-soaked, he would work through his stretching, surveying the valleys and smiling when the falcon raced across the skies. Patient, he waited for her return to the fist as he lifted his arm in the familiar signal. Then it was back to the city once more, a pleasant ride through the tawny apple red of fallen autumnal leaves with Peri on his armoured leather glove until it was time to secure her in a covered wicker pen: the authorities did not look favourably on raptors, the scourge of messenger pigeons.

One day, as the evenings began to draw in, a cycle after sunset, he stopped on a street corner near the old timber quays running out over the riverbank mudflats into the copper expanse of the great Cise. It was busy. People were finishing their work, having come outdoors again after the in-between time. Along the stretches of the quays, most lit by storm lanterns hanging from tall uprights, children ran up and down, screaming in that way that children do, all joy, excitement and in-the-moment elation before they were summoned to bed. Fortunas paid for some chicken skewers from a kiosk and planted himself next to a doorway in the gathering shadows. He studied the crowds, the movement and patterns, children, adults, a couple of Cherson guardsmen in polished bronze helmets and breastplates, making their rounds, a clot of workmen in black leather aprons, raising tankards to one another outside a packed inn, and a young boy, weaving his way through the press towards Fortunas.

He arrived at the doorway and Fortunas handed over a skewer, which the youngster nibbled at delicately, a gourmand now that he ate with the same regularity as his handler: steady work was a welcome habit.

"Hey," said the boy, by way of greeting, when he had consumed his dinner and finished licking each of his fingers in turn.

Fortunas kept watching the crowds.

"E's still in the fortress dungeon." He referred to Pillio, the subject of tonight's report. "The notaries 'ave bin gatherin' the evidence. Provost interviewed the Ta-shih and took the riverman's testimony before 'e headed back to Nek Feddah. 'Pointment of judge tomorra."

Fortunas nodded once. "The trial?"

Mothers were beginning to call for the scampering children to return. As usual, they ignored the call.

"Lists're packed," replied the boy. "Two months mebbe…"

Fortunas reflected. Two months until the trial got underway, a week or two for the trial itself, he guessed. They would be thorough: it was a Ta-shih officer, after all, and the murder of an acolyte of the Faith. All the forms would be observed.

"The guardleader?" he asked.

"Troop confined to barracks, excep' one day a week," the boy rattled off the details with professional ease. "Guardleader's name is Manei. 'E has leave to come an' go. Duties in the barracks an' the fortress."

Fortunas handed another skewer to the boy, who accepted it between two fingers, turning it and making an examination with a connoisseur's regard.

"Have you a copy of the Provost's register of witnesses?" Fortunas enquired.

"Nah."

"Seen it?"

"Nah. Want it?"

"Yes. Discreet – yes?"

The boy glanced up at him and, if Fortunas had bothered to check, he knew he would have seen a derisive look. Not that he cared. He would need to follow the proceedings carefully. It might be that Sklavin would not want the Strath trooper to be called to testify. It might be he would need to disappear before that. Fortunas was puzzled by the guardleader, Manei: he did not fit patterns. He was difficult to predict. And yet, in Fortunas's experience, soldiers were easy to predict.

"Where does he go?" he asked of the boy.

"'Oo?"

"The guardleader."

"This 'n' that… The barracks, an inn, wanderin' the city – aimless like…"

But not back to visit the Strath trooper, not even in secret. No pattern. Aimless, the boy said. Fortunas was intrigued and disturbed. This Manei might well be aware of his spies, or even *other* spies, which showed he was a thinker or exercised simple animal cunning – both of which Fortunas respected. He felt a need to be on his guard.

He glanced down at the urchin, who was finishing the second skewer, slowly, savouring each mouthful. "The Provost's register," Fortunas said.

"Aye. I'll get it," replied the boy through much licking and smacking of lips.

"Scratch that," Fortunas instructed. Alert to a remote prickle of danger, he had changed his mind. "Bad timing."

The boy stopped eating, looked up at the assassin with an offended expression. His professional qualifications had been questioned. "I c'n git it," he objected.

Fortunas returned the look with one of his own: coldly murderous.

The boy, no stranger to violent men, ducked his head in apology. "Done," he murmured.

"Don't try to impress me by showing off," growled Fortunas. "The guardleader is on to you. He'll know if you try for the register."

"Didn't do nothin' wrong. Shae's bony arse, I ain't fucked up."

"And mind your mouth." Fortunas disapproved of foul language. "That doesn't impress me, either."

The boy lapsed into silence, two wooden skewers held in one hand like ineffectual weapons.

"Go," said Fortunas. "And take a different route."

With a sniff, the boy discarded his skewer sticks in the gutter and then moved off through the crowds. It was full dark. Fortunas scanned the river of people, the shifting currents this way and that, the still backwaters of clots of companions in conversation at stall and inn, the shopfronts spilling people and yellow light onto the cobbles. He could sense the shift, with the instinct of the hunter losing the scent, the confusion of tracks and the imminence of ambush.

He needed to move.

Winding his way along the shopfronts, he walked into and out of pools of light, not his preference, but an advantage to spot incongruities or threats. Despite his confidence, he felt the insistent prickling at the nape of his neck, but could spot nothing untoward either ahead or behind. Soon, he turned right, heading directly away from the black, unstoppable wash of the river, down quieter streets and blank-walled alleys. To flush out the hunters necessitated open ground in quiet byways. Kiangsu city sprawled, above ground and under it, perhaps the most ancient of the Realm's largest settlements. He knew it well, but was under no illusions that whoever followed him would have learned its maze of routes with even greater intimacy.

And then there they were: three men in coats striding into view not fifty paces away, at a narrow crossroads. Likewise, behind him, he could hear footfalls, and he glanced back to see a couple of shadowy figures some thirty paces to the rear. The alleyway was deserted. Their tactics were impeccable. Three ahead and two behind. He let his hands hang limply; there was no need to rush to weapons. He could draw his shortsword instantly, strapped under his coat at his back, the pommel and grip hidden below the thick high collar over his right shoulder. Three knives rested in sheaths at hip, high on his thigh and on his calf inside the top of his left boot, all adapted and weighted for throwing or tight work. A light, single-bladed axe was secured to his belt in the small of his back. He had a moment to admire the synchrony of the numbers: five assassins and Fortunas carried five weapons, not counting his hands. Five and five.

He stood still, taking a position sideways against the wall of the alley, able to watch with only a turn of the head the approach of both groups of killers. He recognized their kind: capable, silent, sharing a mutual understanding of tactics without having to talk. This would not be easy. He needed to know if any of them carried a crossbow, as that would be his priority. The pair behind stopped. Fortunas spent five heartbeats assessing them, as they were nearest. One was a woman – not obvious, but he could detect a signature in her build and walk. The other was favouring, or more likely hiding, his right arm under a half-cloak: a crossbow, Fortunas concluded.

In the street ahead, they came up in an arrowhead arrangement, one forward and two back. That was odd. It was either a ruse or they wanted to talk.

They wanted to talk. The lead man touched his hat, a wide brimmed affair, and stopped five paces away – a good distance that favoured his people, especially crossbow man, who was further back but in deadly range.

"Good evenin'," he said. Southern accent, rounder vowels, undoubtedly Chisua. He sounded calm, hinting at insouciance, like this was a chance meeting to transact some business that wouldn't take any time at all. Fortunas knew that these things were in inverse proportion: the more politeness that killers were willing to show, the more likely they intended to break limbs to make their point.

"Mm," said Fortunas.

"Might we 'ave a moment of your time, sir?"

Fortunas flicked a glance back at the two behind, obeying the discipline of combat rather than the temptation to join the personable conversation and focus his attention where they wanted it. They had not moved, but the hidden hand was ready: still, a crossbow was heavy and, Fortunas reckoned, his arm would tire. That was good. His speed and accuracy would be impaired. The woman probably had throwing knives and would be faster: she was the first priority.

"My time is yours," Fortunas replied in a flat tone, "until it is no longer yours."

A moment of silence followed as the lead man digested the meaning, recognizing a challenge and calculating the import. "I see," he said, although evidently he did not. "We have a request, y'understand."

Fortunas examined each of the three to his front: the two on each side had concealed swords, badly covered by the bulk of long coats, and probably other weapons. They were big men and would have heavy gear: a cudgel or two between them for non-lethal persuasion; daggers for close work. They would not be slow, but had distance to cover and needed to be close. They were the lowest in priority.

"We are tryin' to reach someone," said big hat. "Someone you know."

Fortunas looked back at the couple behind, turned his head to a position to keep all five individuals in his eyeline, those behind in the periphery but enough to pick up the slightest movement. He studied big hat. Smoother lines to his clothes, a slim coat, fashionably unbuttoned, possibly knives inside the wide lapels; a man who did the talking and gave the orders, fastidious about his appearance and reluctant, himself, to spill blood. Fortunas had known his type before: one whose leadership had allowed him to step up a rung and avoid getting his hands dirty, but still a killer. He was the third priority, after knife woman and crossbow man.

"We have a polite thing to ask," big hat went on in his reasonable tone. "Polite." That word again. They would make an example, send an uncompromising signal, marked in violence that could not be ignored. It was their way and they expected it to work, as sure as wild dogs expected to run down and eat the sheep. Fortunas understood predators better than most. He knew what they would do and so he was ready.

"We want you to tell us about someone. His name is Skava. You know 'im?"

Fortunas flexed his right hand inside the soft black leather glove. "No," he responded truthfully.

A low laugh. "Sure y'do. The master-intelligencer. Lord Yoiwa's man. Skava."

"I know no Skava."

"Well," big hat continued in his reasonable voice, "we know you do an' we need to get a message to 'im. We tried to talk to 'im up north, but... well, happens 'e declined our chat. Will you take 'im a message, sir?" A smile in the voice. Very polite.

They were mere moments from violence. The muscle behind big hat would do the business – cudgels probably. But they would expect him to defend himself, so a crossbow bolt to bring him down was probable, low, at his legs, then the muscle would begin their work – a careful beating, broken bones, messed up face, a hand cut off...and the message.

It was time to distract them. Fortunas gently moved his right hand, with a tiny shift in posture to take more weight on his right leg, suggesting he would draw a hidden sword. His left hand meanwhile was still, but ready to move to the small of his back for the axe. Without seeing it, he knew they would be focussed on the imminent move to bring his sword to bear.

Crossbow man was freeing his right arm from his cape. Knife woman had altered her stance: she would have a throwing weapon in her fingers.

Fortunas ducked, got hold of his hip throwing knife to ready it, then rolled head over heels, levering off forearm and shoulder, towards crossbow man. A flash of steel as a knife from the woman ricocheted off the wall where he had been standing, and he was on both feet again, right hand up to flip the weighted blade hard at the woman, the distance now only five strides: she staggered backward with a gurgling howl, the blade embedded in her cheek, arms wind-milling. And Fortunas was side-stepping fast, hand to axe, ripping it clear of the padded flap behind his back, closing in as the crossbow fired, quarrel missing him by a handspan, before he was inside the man's guard and the axe blade in his left hand gouged meat from throat in a fluid arc. Hot blood spattered Fortunas's forehead as he spun behind the collapsing corpse to see the two muscle advancing, big sword blades glinting, one two-handed, in the soft guard position, blade behind his right shoulder, ready to swing, the other with a wide stabbing knife in his left hand, sword in right. They were accomplished, used to working together, not getting in each other's way.

"For fuck's sake!" bawled big hat. His plan was unravelling.

The muscle came on, fighting stance, heads forward, instinct and training taking over from rational thought. Fortunas reached over his head, gripped his short sword under his coat and released it smoothly from its quilted scabbard tight against his back. The axe was ready in his left hand, hanging at his side, difficult to see in the darkness. He moved the sword in a small side-to-side motion, attracting the peripheral vision of even these trained killers, who would be watching his face, searching for the first indications of attack or feint – a tiny advantage.

Big hat had pulled two thin poniards from his coat at the moment Fortunas lunged forward to put his weight into an underarm lob with the small axe. It spun end-over-end with astonishing speed to strike big hat in the chest, sternum probably, blade not buried but its flat steel poll hitting hard enough to floor him, dropping with flailing arms, and to leave him gasping like a stranded fish. The muscle were good. They didn't get distracted. Simply came on fast, the man to the left swinging his sword in a feint and following with a straight stab with his dagger; the one to Fortunas's right went diagonally from high to low – a clever strike to cut through his lower leg, a blow to end the fight once Fortunas was crippled. But he danced back, lightly stepping between the bodies behind him. And now the muscle had a problem, with two bloody corpses to step over and Fortunas perfectly balanced for a killing hit.

The man at left took the initiative, planted a boot over the body of the woman and took a defensive guard with his sword hilt at his ear, blade forward at head height and dagger over his left knee. Fortunas dropped lower, made a show of an attack with his shortsword and simultaneously pulled the second knife from his thigh sheath. He flicked it underhand at the killer's throat where it got tangled in his greatcoat collars, nicked his cheek but did no damage. An attack now came from his right, the other one swinging low again, but Fortunas was skipping sideways back over the corpse, using the involuntary backward flinch prompted by his thrown knife to swing his blade up, low to high, to score a finger-deep cut from belly to chest in the first adversary. The killer stumbled backwards from the injury and was now between Fortunas and the second assailant, fouling his space. Fortunas dropped low and swung his blade down in a forty-five-degree arc at full extension, taking him at the ankle and completely severing his foot. He went over at once, like a large tree, screaming and dropping his knife to clutch at his shin. Fortunas stayed back: even on the floor, he could still swing a blade.

The last man was now wary, sword in right hand, left hand out for balance, all his mates down, a total reversal of expectations in the space of a hundred heartbeats.

A groan and cursing from big hat. He was trying to get up, gasping from being both winded and what was probably a broken rib or two. He would be on his feet soon and he might cause problems. Fortunas circled back to his right, around the downed muscle still clutching his ankle and calling on the gods, but not letting go of his sword, knowing that he had little hope but desperate not to give up while his partner was nearby.

It occurred to Fortunas that no one had bolted. Even with four of them down, the brute with the sword had not taken to his heels. Coin did not keep people like this facing death and in reach of the Shae's soul-stealing. Only honour to a cause or fear could do that. Fortunas guessed fear: therefore the Faith, and exarchs. And coin.

He reached the right-hand wall, two corpses behind him, the whimpering lump of the third attacker flopping around to his left now, the final assailant steadying himself, maybe fancying he had an opening with Fortunas's sword arm close to the wall and no room to swing or defend properly. Fortunas faded back a pace, dropped to a crouch, left arm down, a feint to make him think he was going for another throwing knife. His opponent jerked back and sideways, off balance, and that was when Fortunas leapt forward and made a series of rapid cuts, back and forth to bring the man's blade into a defensive posture, opening his wrist to danger – and Fortunas swung down, then up, his shortsword slicing deep into the flesh and bone of his forearm. The big sword clattered onto the cobbles, Fortunas thrust and stabbed him side-on under the armpit as he tried to get out of the way: a fatal cut, possibly heart, certainly major arteries. He staggered back against the wall, right arm pouring black blood in the uncertain light, left hand pressing at the killing wound. He was muttering, praying by the sound of it, as sure of his fate as his partner on the floor was desperate to avoid his.

Fortunas stepped nimbly back to his left, skirting the killer with his hand gripped around his severed ankle. Big hat was up, backing away, keeping his eyes on Fortunas, his poniards held before him, but awkward now, broken ribs curtailing proper movement. Pausing as he advanced, Fortunas stooped to retrieve his axe, slipped it under his coat and back into its place in the small of his back.

Big hat decided it was time to talk. "Wait," he choked out, an animal sound of terror. "Wait!"

Fortunas walked to his left, the better to keep the killer who was lacking a foot in sight: he might decide to throw his sword or crawl for the crossbow.

"Who?" Fortunas asked, devoid of emotion. He made no threats. Threats were elaborate and unnecessary; games for those who enjoyed the pain of others or whose souls were twisted.

Big hat, who had lost his hat when he fell, began to tremble. "E…" he breathed, a stertorous exhalation of both fear and the agony of crushed ribs.

Fortunas angled his head to the side, a motion of expectancy he knew would induce terror beyond the power of mere words.

"Exarch," gasped big hat. The poniards were drooping lower, hope abandoned. Transfixed by the imminence of his doom, he would not even run now.

"Name?"

"H-Hassin, of…the Zaggisa."

"And the message?"

"'W-where is the Strath t-trooper?'"

"That's all?"

A strangled cough, "A-and… 'g-give 'im to us'."

Fortunas let his eyes glide over the crossroads behind big hat, along the walls on either side, over the corpses to his rear, the long dark alleyway. Nothing. No one. Further questions were wasted breath. He stepped close, thrust the sword into big hat's throat, grasped his coat as he collapsed so he could more readily slide the blade clear, then walked back to the big brute with no foot. The bleed-out from the arteries of his leg had been bad, a huge pool across the cobbles in the middle of which was his boot, pale bone from the diagonal cut gleaming around gristle and flesh, but still he lived, wide white eyes following Fortunas, knowing what was coming. Fortunas considered for a moment letting him bleed out, but at once dismissed the idea. He checked the man's sword arm, but he was too weak to do more than flick the blade from side to side until Fortunas placed his boot on it to prevent any silliness. Again, Fortunas thrust into his throat and spine, withdrew the sword with a sucking sound, and then cleaned it thoroughly in the folds of the dead man's coat. Satisfied, he inserted it carefully over his shoulder into the padded scabbard between his shoulder blades.

Near at hand was his own throwing knife, which he retrieved, cleaned, noted the rough nick on the edge, damaged from hitting the cobbles, and slid it back into its sheath on his thigh. The other was sticking out of the woman's cheek, below the eye, and she appeared to have choked to death on blood from her tongue. Crimson gore leaked still from her mouth and nose, covering her face. He squatted over her, extracted, cleaned and sheathed the knife, and took a moment to wipe the blood from his face with his leather glove. The result was inadequate but good enough for now; he would clean up at a drinking fountain.

As he stood up, he took five deep breaths, calming the surge of energy that still fired his body for combat. He moved to the alley wall, leaned his back against it, feeling the shape of the shortsword against his spine. He knew what to expect and it came, as if the Shae stood close by and drained the vitality from his soul. He was tired and thirsty and felt the onset of despair, but it would pass. When you killed, you paid the Shae its tithe – in energy and capitulation to black thoughts.

For long moments he waited. Then he looked at each of the corpses in turn. Five. He had used four of his weapons. The odds had been more favourable than he had expected.

Turning towards the crossroads, he began to walk. His thoughts assembled themselves into orderly lines. He believed they had found him through the boy, tonight and not before, but the high garret apartment where he lived might be watched – and Peri was there, his mount stabled in the same neighbourhood. He would need to arrange for someone to move both. Not difficult, merely delicate, and inconvenient. It could be done tonight.

But before then he must send a message, to Sklavin, whose other alias, he had learned, was Skava, master-intelligencer to Yoiwa of Honam. He cared little, either way. His habit was to avoid the complexity of these things. They obtruded and disturbed him. In his head, he composed the message, refining the sentences to deliver the clearest meaning for the fewest words – facts, events, names, numbers, no more.

Then he walked on, imagining his peregrine falcon soaring across a clear blue sky.

***

Skava was exhausted. She pinched the bridge of her nose between finger and thumb as if that might ward off the heavy press of sleep. A moment to close her eyes, she told herself. Then she would be fine. The draw of oblivion was so compelling, she forced herself to stand.

Maki, squatting on a fallen tree branch at the edge of their camp, turned his head at her movement. It was false dawn, the in-between time. Only Yan slept, curled up on the ground in an oilskin and blanket, his head covered, dead to the world. They were out here alone, the three of them, still tracking Prince Osir's growing army. Mathed was back in Mamoba, barely alive, attended by doctors, guarded by Vedarahava. Their army, if you could call it that, was down by eight, miraculously light losses, but significant when Osir's ranks were swelling with volunteers. Fifty Ouine cavalry launched carefully prepared hit-and-run attacks on Osir when he drew up in column to march. But he had learned how to counter these, his foot soldiers drilling and learning to use their spears and halberds to present a bristling wall against cavalry, his wagons and baggage train kept secure and tight between the ranks of marching men, and his own cavalry ranging wide in blocks of thirty troopers, readily redeployed and able to assist other blocks.

"Sleep, boss," Maki suggested. He had just taken the watch, so she should be asleep, but she had a problem to solve. She had ten thousand fucking problems to solve. But this particular one was like a rash: it needed scratching. Or it was telling her something. And she was too damned tired to work it out.

"Can't," she lied. She could have slept standing up, or standing on her head, for that matter. She decided to talk instead. Maybe that would work. "The woodcutter in Osir's camp," she reminded Maki.

"Hmm," he grunted, knowing the part he needed to play to help her think.

"The report last night. Che Keleu went to plead with her brother. He received her. Raised voices. He shouted. She wept. Ke Beyil took her away. What the fuck does it tell you?"

Maki shifted position, scanning the barely visible landscape. The light had dropped again, as if the sun was reluctant to rise. "She wanted to stop it all – the fightin' and such…" Maki spoke into the damp air, keeping his voice low, aware of the dangers of sound carrying.

"Mmm," she murmured, with a weary nod, stepping her own circuit to watch the surroundings: if you were awake, the habit was involuntary. "They talked. They argued. She loves him. He…loves her. Does he love her? Does he hate her? He hates Mathed. We know that. But does he hate her too now?"

She was making no sense. Even in her sleep-deprived, befuddled state, she recognized that.

Maki hunched his shoulders deeper into his cape. This time of the morning you always felt cold. "Both, boss," he answered. "He loves her. Flesh an' blood, y'know? But he's got an army t'lead. An' he's good at it."

That made sense.

"Got a lot to lose," Maki persisted.

Skava stood still. The inescapable urge to sleep had abruptly lifted, like someone had thrown cold water on her head. "What?" she demanded, rather stupidly.

"Said 'lot to lose'. Already lost his honour. *Still* a lot to lose, boss. His lands, his family home, his sister. The war."

"Yes," she said.

"I'm no noble, boss. Can't pretend to know. But no one wants to lose too much."

"Fuck, no." Skava could understand that all too well. She resumed her pacing, a circular route of six steps, past Yan's sleeping form, behind Maki and back round again.

"What if you were faced with losing one of those things?" she asked Maki, and herself.

"You got the south, boss?" Maki interrupted the conversation. He wanted to know if, since she was up and moving, she was going to watch the southern quarter while he concentrated his attention elsewhere. It was sensible and good thinking.

"Got it," she confirmed. She admired Maki, sometimes, more than just…professionally.

"If I'm goin' to lose somethin' I love," he resumed, "I'm goin' to stop it happening."

"Yes. I know," she grumbled. "But given a choice?"

"How do you mean?"

"Two things you love. A difficult choice, maybe an impossible choice."

He went silent. For him, this was real: he had his own pain, somewhere back in the scabbed bits of his life he didn't show. She paced, quiet, instincts telling her not to push him. She was on the cusp of something.

"You make a bad choice," concluded Maki finally.

She knew what he meant, but she asked anyway: "Bad? Why?"

"Because you might lose both ways. And you're certain to lose if you do nothin'."

And it made sense. "If we can force him to make a bad choice…" she said, halfway to asking a question but without doing so.

"He loses something," Maki finished for her.

She looked up, sensing the dawn, calculating when they would have light enough to get going.

"Maki," she said, feeling a warmth towards him, doubtless brought on by lack of sleep. "Thanks." Then: "We got good parchment?"

Entirely accustomed to her bizarre changes of tack, Maki replied, "Message?" He wanted clarity about why she wanted good parchment for a scroll sent by bird.

"No. A letter."

"Don't think so."

"Doesn't matter. Mamoba, then." She knew what she needed to do and was working out the requirements. She stopped pacing. "Maki, I need to get back to Mamoba."

He nodded. She could see his head moving, so it was getting lighter. "We can leave," he responded, "once the mounts are ready."

"No," she stated flatly. "Just me. You got the watch?"

He stood up. "I have."

She immediately started packing – a rapid endeavour, given their usual preparedness in the field. Disturbed by the change in routine, Yan sat up, yawning and stretching, sandy hair sticking out in all directions. When her mount was saddled, she spoke to Maki. "Listen up," she said. "You track the army. Take no chances. Report if he looks to be moving fast. Tell Ucat" – their cavalry commander now that Vedarahava was back with Mathed at Mamoba Estate – "his orders are, first and foremost, to slow Osir. Time is what matters. We will not defeat Osir in the field. I want no heroic charges. Delay him. We need to last twenty-three days."

"Slow up Osir, boss," Maki confirmed. "No heroics."

Skava looked up again. The sky was a dirty salmon colour. She pulled out her compass, attached by a leather thong to a belt pouch, satisfied herself of her route, then mounted up.

"I'm leaving the remount," she announced, and glanced down at Maki and Yan. "And no fucking heroics from either of *you*. Plenty of work to do, even if this all goes to shit."

A nod from each. She jerked her chin, grunted, pretending by that gesture that she thought they couldn't be trusted to put their boots on the right feet without her, then kicked her dun mare into a canter.

***

Osir's old rooms were divided into bed chamber, washroom and study. Gaining access was as simple as opening a door. Che Keleu occupied rooms well away in the southern wing, where Lord Mathed had been installed near to her in a room set aside for him, frequented by doctors – and his wife. It was as if the homely corridors leading to Osir's chambers were cursed; no one came this way, except servants, and then infrequently.

Skava had cleaned up. She had changed, dressed again as Courier-sergeant Alin, and carrying the appropriate light weapons. Rushing to this task might otherwise have been noticed. The spymaster of Strath still occupied his post, ostensibly working for the new Lord of Strath, though this was sham, a gesture to avoid offending Che Keleu.

The bedroom was darker on this northern range of the old house, away from the bleak sunlight, but Skava could pick her way easily around the wide bed towards the interleading doorway. She pressed a hand to the door to deaden sound, turned the heavy brass doorknob and, with a click, eased it open. His writing room, or study, untouched since he had departed in dishonourable exile, presented itself: a wide polished desk in front of the double windows, low-backed chair against them, the better to catch light over the shoulder; two high-backed upholstered reading chairs, cushions, a footstool, three walls of heavy wooden shelves, decorated with fluted columns and beautifully wrought carpentry in the style of hanging grapevines for the capitals. Upon the shelves there were ornaments, knick-knacks and statuettes from other provinces, mementoes of his travels or distant friendships, an array of books, neatly arranged, a few on their sides, hastily tossed back. On one shelf, in pride of place, was a glass bottle, of elaborate design, like a series of rings one atop the other. The once clear glass had become smoky, but Skava recognised its like: it was ancient and valuable. In the corner was a pair of falconry gloves, discarded upon an occasional table, scattered playing cards underneath, two on the floor. It was a room that no one cleaned, private, and understood to be treated so by the servants. It was Prince Osir's space.

Skava went to the desk, alert to the possibility that she might be seen through the wide windows. She crouched, moved around to the chair, satisfied she could not be seen. On the desk were three diminutive swords, each a different length, letter openers, as beautiful and well-crafted as the real thing, with blade, grip, hilt and silver pommel. The gleaming blade on all of them even had the correctly grooved fuller running to the tip. They sat in a rack, imitating a sword rack in a drill yard. Papers were stacked to the left, letters from acquaintances, probably of no importance. A heavy bronze ornament representing two men, stripped to shorts and wrestling, muscles straining, legs extended, held down the papers. It was fashioned from an ancient original that Skava had seen before – very ancient indeed. For an instant it gave her pause.

She found the first of the items she was looking for: a pen, in a stand, both elaborately decorated with tiny animals, a hunting scene perhaps. Next to them another pen, a fountain pen, plain and workmanlike, for everyday use, a glazed pot of ink, stained blue where the prince had spilled repeatedly, dipping and writing over the years. She examined the desk drawers, gently slid them open. There: a small stack of writing paper and envelopes, good quality, the sort the nobles used for their informal correspondence. The envelopes were creased by design, ready for use but left open and flat to encompass a standard letter of multiple pages folded in half, awaiting only a wax seal. Skava removed a dozen sheets and four envelopes, putting them inside the doublet of her uniform.

She lifted the bronze paperweight of the wrestlers, leafed through the letters, all of them unsigned papers or correspondence to Osir. Disappointed, she replaced the weight. She looked in the drawers again, feeling around. Some coins, discarded money pouches, nothing else, save the writing paper and envelopes. Her eyes scanned the bookcases. A polished wooden box caught her eye. She walked in a crouch away from the windows, reached for the box and put it on the floor. It was locked, secured simply but lacking the key. She stood up, reaching out with her right hand, determining what she could touch on the shelves nearby, as if she were Osir himself, impetuous, always in haste. Running her fingers along three adjacent rows of books, she found nothing. On tiptoes she could feel the boards along the ornate molding above the highest shelf. There: a key, in the place an impatient youth hides something he wants within reach.

She inserted the small key, turned the lock, and opened the box. Papers, of varying sizes, letters, printed pages, an envelope with a blue seal, carefully broken so that its shape was largely intact, a love letter perhaps from a devoted girl; a bookmark, stitched in gold and silver thread, depicting a house, with bunches of grapes to either side. This Skava studied, drinking in its details. There was also a brooch, expensive, recognizably a masculine ornament to be worn by a boy to pin upon a lapel or embellish a riding hat. It was a horse, carved from a garnet stone, blood red and brilliant even in the failing afternoon light, about the length of a thumb and set in heavy silver to amplify the shape of the horse at full gallop. Skava knew instantly what it was and who had most likely given it to him. It was a woman's gift to a boy. An instant of excitement thrilled Skava. She held up the object, turned it to catch the light, examined every facet and angle, then replaced it.

Next she took out a few selected handwritten pages. She compared them, closely inspecting the script. On one of them, on a final back page, it was signed 'Osir, Prince of Strath' with a flourish, somewhat inelegant, the work of a boy. She set it aside, took out other pages, devoting equal care to their examination. Going back to the desk, she leafed through the correspondence once more, found a letter whose script matched the handwriting of the signed paper from the box. This one looked recent, the style rapid and informal, an incomplete missive in Osir's hand, a complaint to Council via the offices of Ke Beyil to void the Choosing of Che Keleu, to call a halt to her betrothal. He had never finished the piece and therefore had not signed it, which was a pity, but Skava was content now. She could replicate the script, and she could manage a good approximation of his signature by using the signed page of the boy prince, and the mature writing of the angry son and heir. She kept both documents, putting them away inside her doublet, then replaced the box and its key. A last look round the room: everything as it was.

Quietly, she left.

CHAPTER 14

Understand that Echrexar murders dreams in both a real and a metaphorical way. He may deny our hopes by planting fears and suspicions: how often have you woken from the dream when the faces you see move in and out of one another, a father who becomes the husband, the son who is also a neighbour, the lover who is your enemy or your best friend? You recognize them but they are not who they seem. We know this to be self-evident. And Echrexar works even in subtler ways. The unseen menace chases you in your dream; you run but cannot escape; your feet are like stones; he is near! You awake to nameless fears: Echrexar has stolen your confidence or your trust. Beware!

Catechisms of the Exarchs.

One by one we declined. Some were murdered. Some suffered accidents. Others chose to end things by their own hand. Dispersed across the vast face of the earth, many simply disappeared. I think they had lost purpose or meaning. Ennui. It is a hard thing to keep going, even for those with the wildest hope. We had been called immortals and hated the name, the irony of it. It was a malediction.

Unknown author, from the Time of the Immortals, in a modern collection of fragmentary text treating of the War of Asunder, when the Immortals lost their faith, joined battle one against the other and were no more.

***

It was the courier-sergeant, the clean-cut youngish man who said little, but was sometimes in evidence about the estate, rushing quickly to and from the Ouine force in the field. His wide cheekbones never showed a smile and, were it not for his broken nose, dented rather than misshapen, and the uncompromising cast of his mien, he might have been accounted handsome. He stood before her now in his smart uniform with the crimson crossed-arrow epaulettes, a trifle awkward, looking at the floor, as servants and commoners always did, but perhaps more uncomfortable that he had stopped her here in the hallway, a breach of decorum in normal times. But these were hardly normal times.

He held a letter, sealed in the green wax of Strath, which Che Keleu had seen at once, but politesse forbade she should overtly notice. So they stood facing each other, in the wide hallway of her home, with the bright yellow blades of morning sunlight cutting down through the right-hand range of windows.

"My lady…" he began, gauche but observing the forms.

It was an interruption to her day. She had been in the autumnal cold of the gardens after the sun rose, walking the pathways and communing with the world of her past, trying to draw strength from what had been strong, in the permanence of the old trees and the immutability of the red-brick walls, before she returned to her vigil at Mathed's bedside. But she gave the trooper her attention, feeling sorry for him, even in the anguish of her own fears.

"Yes," she said, searching for a name, but unable to place one on him. "Sergeant?"

"A letter, my lady." He looked decidedly uncomfortable, reluctant even.

"I see."

He did not hand it over.

"Who is it to?"

Now he glanced at her, embarrassed it seemed. "My lady," he murmured. "It is for you…"

She showed no confusion, but she felt it. In her world, such things did not happen: servants smoothed the daily transactions of life at the estate and, indeed, had Ke Beyil or one of his aides been present, they would have intervened. They were more accustomed to dealing with soldiers, she presumed.

The courier-sergeant turned the letter in both hands, its face towards her, the handwriting clear on the cream paper of the folded envelope. A jolt of shock coursed through her. She recognized the hand instantly – her brother's. Her heart was beating faster, and the cold from the gardens that had chilled her cheeks and hands was abruptly gone in the heat of this realization. She found that her palm was open, as if to take the letter, but the soldier made no attempt to give it to her.

"My lady," he said, more confident now and in the strong dialect of north-eastern Honam. "It is for you. But we intercepted the messenger who thought to bring it to the gates. He said, you see…" A long pause. "He said it was from your…the Prince Osir."

She had recovered her poise. She stood in front of the soldier, hands folded at her waist, ready to command, peremptory words springing to her lips.

Instead, he anticipated her, spoke rapidly, apologetically: "My lady. It is my duty to give this to my Lord Mathed. You understand? We are at war. Though it bears your name, it is my duty to do so…"

Keleu was crestfallen. Again the heat rose in her face, a growing sense of powerlessness. The words she was about to speak fell away, forgotten. She felt utterly wretched. A part of her wanted to plead, but the discipline of propriety took over.

The soldier looked directly at her and his tough features seemed, genuinely seemed, to soften. "My Lord Mathed," he pronounced, "is gravely ill."

It was a fact. It shocked her to her core. No one had spoken those words in her hearing, preferring euphemism and hope in misguided respect for her misery. Now it was as though a god had ripped apart a veil of make-believe to utter a foretelling. The hot sting of tears blurred her vision and she blinked, utterly bereft, close to sobbing in front of this soldier, this man that she did not know. It was her lowest point and she was alone.

"My lady," came the trooper's voice again. Through swimming tears she looked at him, incapable of words. "My lord will not be able to read this letter," he went on.

She shook her head, the smallest of motions, the best she could manage. It was true. Mathed was barely conscious, the gaunt shadow of the man she had married.

Beyond her tears she found that the trooper was closer to her, the letter extended in one hand. "Perhaps," he whispered kindly, "you would take it. Perhaps you will read it…for him."

Che Keleu's heart swelled with irresistible gratitude. She brushed tears from her cheek, wet and hot and foolish, and the sergeant's hard, hazel eyes offered comfort. Then the letter was in her hand, and she did not hear what he said as he bowed and stepped past her and she was alone in the hallways of her home.

***

An atmosphere of despair had settled over Mamoba Estate as heavily as the thick overcast that, like cold ashes, had driven the glittering sunshine of the morning from the land and lingered now on the surrounding hills. The rain came in fits, spattering against the windows, then dying away, as if fretful spirits were clawing at the panes. Inside the deepest part of the mansion, even the mountainous log fire blazing in the hearth of the Great Hall seemed only to accentuate the general mood: the firelight threw the space beyond the long table into dim obscurity; at the movement of one or another of the men seated around the table, their heavy shadows would make the vague shapes depicted in the wall hangings attain an abrupt and spectral life so that one might almost believe the insubstantial legions of the Shadow Lord lurked just out of reach.

It was a very different Great Hall from the one decorated and festooned with bridal flowers in which Skava had stood sentinel and Osir had made his ill-fated attempt on Lord Yoiwa's life. Skava, standing near the long table, listened to the trickle of discussion among the men. None was of a disposition to speak more than necessity demanded. Six in all, clad in armour that told a tale, in every stain and cut, of desperate battles, on every face there was the gaunt exhaustion that only the most extreme and prolonged of physical effort might induce. But, more than these material manifestations, there was the unmistakable and overwhelming air of defeat which marked everything about them.

Skava could hardly blame them. Their options were diminishing by the day. Vedarahava sat at the centre of his men, arms splayed wide on the table where maps and despatches lay discarded. It had taken all of his iron discipline to keep the despair from his voice and yet, even so, Skava could see that he knew he had failed. The evidence of his failure and his men's impending defeat lay in the downcast eyes and sagging shoulders of these, his officers. It showed itself in the vacant, far-off looks of the troops…and in the gaps in their ranks.

But Skava also recognized that their collapse in morale had more to do with Mathed's being struck down than any reverses in the field. Their fate was bound up through noble duty to Clan Ouine with the survival of their lord. If he recovered, they would fight with a spirit that could only be overwhelmed by sheer weight of enemy numbers. If he died, they would throw their lives away in some rash assault that, in their definition of duty, brought glorious death in battle. She had seen it before and she needed them to avoid it, so she had spoken to Vedarahava so that he could play his part in turning their despair into shame and shame into purposeful action. She needed them to try something different, to employ the darkness of probable disaster as a tool to surprise and shock Osir.

She could see that even Vedarahava had lost his purpose. Lord Mathed lay dying. Despite their cleaning and treating of the wound, he would not live, the physicians reported. And so the onset of each bitter night carried them all closer to that awful, inevitable moment when their lord would be no more, when the eldest son of Honam would be dead. For Vedarahava that fact was unbearable. It signified betrayal of the worst kind – unthinkable in his world. He had failed to protect the boy. In every waking moment he would be imagining the expression of Lord Yoiwa… and how he might redeem himself through some stupid inglorious death in battle. It was fucking pathetic. So she had spoken to him, and he had listened, and she had watched the small flame of a different kind of hope kindle in him.

At the head of the table he straightened up and composed himself to receive the worst of the news from the field. They all needed to face the facts.

"Ucat," he said and, because his voice broke the silence like a whip crack, the officer addressed jerked his head up as if under attack.

"Commander Vedarahava!" he responded.

"Your report."

"Aye. Sir, I must report that Prince Osir has split his forces. We engaged one brigade some twenty miles from here…but they have learned from their mistakes. I hoped to bolt the enemy's pack animals and inflict sufficient losses on Osir's troops to assure him of our strength. Owing to my ambition in this objective, I confess that I committed my men to the action longer than was safe. Their troops were ready. They have learned. We did no more than slow their progress."

"By how much did you slow him?"

Ucat looked demoralized. "Half a day."

"His losses?"

Ucat hesitated, then breathed, "None, sir."

"Our losses?"

"Four…"

Skava could barely restrain a curse. Pricks. She had been at Mamoba five days and already they were making mistakes in the field.

Vedarahava acknowledged this report without visible emotion. He turned his head towards another officer. "Leher?"

"Sir," said this individual, "we are certain that we saw the prince himself no more than thirty miles to the east, with maybe two hundred and eighty foot soldiers and fifty horse. Another contingent was sighted within signalling distance – their strength about the same. They continue to deploy in cavalry blocks and signal quickly when we are sighted. In short order they can combine to twice or three times our strength. In accord with your directive, I could not risk two dozen cavalry against such odds…" Leher trailed off. He dropped his eyes away from his commander's gaze. "Sir, I beg you," he whispered without looking up, "permit me to lead an attack against the prince. We gain no honour by these tactics. We have slain a hundred of them, yet daily the prince's strength grows while we decline."

"It is so, sir," Ucat agreed, though he slid a glance towards Skava, perhaps anticipating a biting rebuke. Her status among these men was a source of awkwardness She lived in the shadows but was impossible to ignore. They knew at least something of the breadth of her activities, were sworn to secrecy through duty to Yoiwa, but had become increasingly uncomfortable since Vedarahava had returned to Mamoba to accompany Mathed, with her directing military strategy.

"And I have heard talk amongst the locals," Ucat complained in a loud voice, stupidly resorting to bluster, "that the prince is twice blessed – with the eye of Dian and the hand of the Shadow Lord. 'How else,' they say, 'could he have struck down the Lord Mathed?'" Ucat clenched his fist in fierce determination. "We are dishonoured by the peasants of Strath! Let us strike back at Osir! We are soldiers. Let us die like soldiers!"

Skava said nothing. Giving Ucat command in the field had been an error. He was a superb cavalryman, but a poor tactician. Under pressure, he was at war with himself – all glory, honour and bombast. But who then could lead? In this, Honam's first serious warlike skirmishes for generations, Ouine's officer class had been found wanting. But that was a problem for another day – if they survived the next eighteen.

Vedarahava looked from face to face. He would not join their sabre-rattling and the mad tumble from wretchedness to glittering-eyed suicidal bluster. Such was their plight. This was the moment for him to speak well. On cue, rising to his feet, his back to the fire, Vedarahava stared down upon them all with a mighty disdain and Skava was pleased.

"Ucat, Leher," he growled. "You shame yourselves with these uncivil grievances. You beg me release you to do honour for yourselves, full knowing the strength Osir mounts against us. What would you attain? Two score of the prince's troops for the lives of all your men? Is this the total of your honour? A bad bargain? Are you merchants? Shopkeepers? Hah!" Vedarahava scoffed, the sound as dry and as far from humour as a howl of despair. "I tell you," he continued then with a ferocious intensity. "I have no honour for myself! I renounce it! My honour is the honour of my Lord Mathed! And while he lives, Ouine lives and commands me, body and soul!"

He turned completely away, reproaching them with the indifference of his back. Skava wanted to applaud. It was a masterful performance and she had newfound respect for the man. He had understood their predicament with exactness and, crucially, had placed his trust in Skava.

"Let me hear no more of your honour," he said in a voice barely audible. "We defend our Lord Mathed and the Lady Keleu."

Now she watched the faces around the table. They looked down. They had been shamed. They would feel the burning humiliation of their self-pity. Now they would be compliant and it was time for hope.

Skava spoke up: "Commander," she said. "With your permission…"

Vedarahava lifted a hand in mute acknowledgement, swung round to face the group and allowed her the floor.

"I have some options in play," she began and they all looked at her with that peculiar expression with which she was so familiar, of hope mixed with suspicion and dislike. Since they were soldiers and men of honour, they found her world distasteful if necessary. At the same time, they knew her value, understood all too clearly how close, at Lug Hill, they had come as a unit to snuffing out Osir's challenge with tactics devised by Skava, and were equally embarrassed by their failure to protect Mathed.

"I cannot tell you about all of our plans, but I have a stratagem which I know our troops can execute. Your Commander and I…" – she nodded to Vedarahava – "believe that this will not only give the usurper a bloody nose and force him to regroup but, together with our other plans, may cause him anguish and doubts. If he doubts," she said quietly, forcing them to lean forward to hear her, "we can destroy his troops' morale. If we do that, for a second time, remember, enough of his men will flee, aghast at the cost. And that will even the odds."

They were alert now, sitting up, intent. She stepped nearer the table and noticed Vedarahava came closer as well – a good move, a physical statement of unity and purpose. "We are all agreed, I hope," she went on in a tone of unbending steel, "that our primary objective is to cause the usurper a loss of time he cannot afford. We are all agreed, I hope, that Commander Vedarahava's commitment of honour, not to himself nor to vainglorious recklessness, but to our Lord Mathed and the Lady Che Keleu, is paramount." They were now trapped by their own code of honour, the stupid fuckers. Skava glared at them, pretending that she and Vedarahava alone shared this true commitment, reminding them of their shame. "If we agree all this," she argued, "then you and your men will also agree that our tactics must adjust as the enemy adjusts his."

Grudging nods.

"Good then," she concluded with a broad smile. "Then we will shock him. And we will win."

They nodded again, this time with a growing confidence. They had something to believe in.

She began to lay out the plans she had made.

***

The letter was with her constantly. During the day, she concealed it inside her bodice and she could feel it, hard-edged, against her skin. At night, she kept it under her pillow, afraid one of the servants or her handmaidens might see it and wonder and set tongues wagging. In her chambers, alone, with the door closed and locked, she held it before her and drank in the liquid, cursive script of her name, inscribed by her brother, by his hand. With her forefinger, she gently touched the seal, a green wax oblong along the opening, and stroked it as if it might give up its secrets. There were pale discolorations across one corner of the envelope, water marks it seemed, stained during its handling by the messenger or – a secret, unadmitted part of her hoped foolishly – by the tears of her brother, weeping when he sealed the letter.

It terrified her.

She could not open it. She dreaded what it might contain. And she felt an awful guilt that it should so occupy her attention when Mathed lay immobile, in pain, dying, only two doors away. And yet she could not stop herself. She sat in her bedroom, this feminine world of her youth, where she had played and dreamed and hoped, while the grim light of a collapsing wintry day lit the letter in her hands with an uncertain glow. She looked outside, through the windows, but her gaze soon returned, fixing again on the writing, a single word, her name, Keleu, and she heard it as he would have said it – in kinder times.

Then her imagination ran to wild optimism. He would have relented. He sought a way out and begged her to forgive his vehemence and the bitterness of his last words to her, there under canvas, in the horrifying camp of soldiers and sharpened stakes and steel. Forgiveness. It brought the hot sting of tears again and with it the insistent rational voice that told her the letter was something else entirely. For what other possible reason might he send a letter when his army still marched upon Mamoba? To repeat in writing the harshness of his threats? To warn her to leave? To offer terms?

The agony of conflicting thoughts and feelings was too much. She found she was holding the letter tight in both hands, her fingers and nails making marks, like she had unconsciously determined to rip it in half and then to shreds. She wanted to. And she realized that *that* was who Osir was: he had always been the ardent force in her structured life; the impassioned intruder between the studied calm of their father and her quick-witted argument, so that, too often, when she was honest with herself, she saw herself too clever by half next to his fiery objections and impetuous energy, even if he infuriated those around him.

And therefore Osir's letter lay in her hands, a promise and a threat, and she dare not open it.

***

Ke Beyil was in a constant state of worry and anxiety. Thoroughly off balance for the first time in his life, he watched the beautiful woman with whom he had become acquainted struggle with her own anguish and despair. The Lady Che Keleu was with Mathed most hours of the day. The physicians attended him with the same regularity they had exercised when his inert, bloody form had first been carried into the hallways of Mamoba. But now the grim-faced encouragement they had offered had run out and they shuffled quietly to and from the chamber with barely a word to the young woman who sat at the bedside and had eyes only for its pale occupant.

Ke Beyil was often here, alone with Keleu and her husband. His visage betraying the hollows and lines brought on by weeks of tension and worry, the Chisuan still spoke words of comfort to Keleu as if he did not see the slow, pitiful deterioration of Mathed and with it Keleu's growing desolation. She responded infrequently now to his sympathy. Perhaps she did not hear him or feel the gentle touch of his hand on her shoulder; she had drawn further in upon herself with every heartbeat.

The physicians whispered amongst themselves outside the door, each day becoming more alarmed that Che Keleu too would weaken like her husband. Nonetheless, bereft of any treatment that might surpass the ministrations of Ke Beyil, they were powerless to help the young woman.

And still Prince Osir and his army advanced. For Ke Beyil and everyone else in the household news of his progress came most reliably from Commander Vedarahava. His riders would thunder up to the front gate, whereupon hushed discussions took place amongst the residents at Mamoba. *The prince is come! He encamps just beyond the hills. His forces prepare to launch an attack from the east! The west!* And at last Vedarahava, showing some little of the irritation he felt in having to fulfil this most irksome of duties, would assemble the three Archivists, the Chisuans, Keleu's loyal kinswomen, and the servants to announce what knowledge he had gleaned. Inevitably, the servants received intelligence via additional sources and the subsequent circulation of wild rumours had the long-expected effect: several servants disappeared one night and Favul, brandishing his rod the following morning, promised severe punishments for the 'deserters' and equally dire consequences for any others contemplating similar action.

In one particular the rumours were correct: the prince's force had been augmented by locals to nearly four times its original complement. Ke Beyil could tell that Vedarahava held a poor opinion of the fighting prowess of this new mob, which comprised a motley company of Strath soldiers, traders and under-merchants, farmers and probably no few adventurers, experienced with a blade but loyal only to the coin the nobles of Strath were paying, but he recognized the damaging effect the news might have on the morale of his men. It was as if they faced a demon whose limbs, once hacked off, grew more stoutly than before. And there were deserters too from the Strath troops who had pledged loyalty to Mathed. Everyone sensed victory – victory for Prince Osir…

And yet there was, Ke Beyil detected, an indefinable air of self-belief among the Ouine troopers. They did not look beaten. They went about their tasks with something of a newfound purpose, with much coming and going and knowing nods or banter between them – hardly jolly, more akin to gallows humour, but resolute.

At last, fifteen days before the fortieth, when the prince was so near that it was dangerous to remain at the mansion, Vedarahava sought out Che Keleu and Ke Beyil and made clear his concerns. He wished to order the household to the keep. Only there could they hold out and it would gain them time. Even a day was vital.

"Mathed cannot be moved," said Keleu with absolute finality. "It will kill him."

Vedarahava begged her. The mansion was vulnerable. Its walls were weak and he had not the men to cover the perimeter with anything like a proper defence. But Keleu refused his appeals and bade him save the rest of the household. Ke Beyil, who only a week ago might have interceded in the matter, stayed mute, his bowed head declaring eloquently the hopelessness of any further petition.

Two days later Vedarahava, with misgiving and a heavy heart, ordered the gates of Mamoba shut, although troopers still came and went from the postern. The green and white pennons flew high over the mansion while Mamoba Estate awaited the approach of Prince Osir and his army.

**

This same day Che Keleu apprehended a change in Mathed, the faintest of colour that touched his paper-white cheek. As she was accustomed to do, her fingers rested upon his hand which was spread limply on the bedcovers. Abruptly she understood that he would live – though his still motionless body gave no more clue than the one she had perceived.

"Thank you," was all she said, softly, almost inaudibly. Ke Beyil, who sat in an armchair in the window bay, looked over his shoulder. He could see her face in profile and a glistening tear that clung to her eyelash. Her pale fingers clasped her husband's hand. And she smiled.

For a moment Ke Beyil remained unable to comprehend this unexpected sight. He sat looking at her, then gave a long sigh fraught with the most profound emotion. He would have spoken, but joy swelled in his throat, overburdening him. He was close to tears himself.

For a time neither Keleu nor Ke Beyil stirred. Through her tears Keleu watched Mathed, alert to the proclamation of life in each breath, each tiny flicker of muscles under the pallid skin. And Ke Beyil watched Keleu, a smile of sadness, love and unction on his face. He had witnessed, he was certain, the invisible hand of a god this day.

***

The fluttering joy of hope lifted Che Keleu. When the physicians attended Mathed, they too were encouraged. The wound was healing, the infection abating. Their constant efforts in medicine and prayer were beginning to tell.

She withdrew to her chambers, waving her handmaidens away. As she leaned on the door to close it, her face pressed to the smooth white-painted wood, she turned the key and it creaked then locked to the sound of a final click. With trembling fingers she unlaced the front of her bodice, drew forth the letter and stared again at the writing. She turned the envelope. The green wax seal had cracked during the days of concealment tight against her warm flesh. Without further thought, she broke the seal, scattering small emerald fragments across the pale rug on the floor. As she opened the folded letter, her heart began to race, pounding against her breast as if she were a hunted animal, cornered, terrified.

It was his writing, neat but hurried in places, small ink blots at the end of sentences where he had paused, struggling, she could readily imagine, with his thoughts and the turmoil of his feelings, reluctant to commit them to the permanence of paper. It was Osir.

Keleu

It is a hard thing to write to you. I could not ever have conjured the circumstances of our present fate. It is horrible. I wish it gone. I wake each morning believing it is gone and live an instant of joy and hope. You are first in my mind when I wake. And I dream of you. You must know, of course you do, that I bitterly regret my harsh words that morning when you came to me. I lead an army. The nobles of Strath have rallied to me and rest their hopes upon my shoulders. I am caught in the trap of doing what is right against doing what I love. It is no easy thing. You face the same despicable choice, so you understand all too well. Forgive me if I could not govern my feelings when last we spoke. But you know my fervid nature.

Do you remember the red garnet horse? It has been in my mind of late. I know not why. Perhaps because it has always been precious to me and I always kept it close and it holds so many dear memories. I think on it now and it gives me comfort. My dear Keleu, if there were some way to stop this, I would. I regret the harm I have done Mathed. He is not my enemy, though events have made us stand on opposite sides. If only you could have stepped away from him. If only you could leave his side, forever, he and I would have no just cause to persist in this deadly enterprise. Foolish words! You will laugh at me. There is no cure. We are all three doomed to our ignoble fates.

I love you, Keleu.

Goodbye

Osir

Che Keleu wept uncontrollably. Osir's words had tugged at her so deeply that she could no longer think, only feel her own raw desolation and the imminence of tragedy. The image of the garnet horse, pinned to Osir's lapel when first he learned to ride, a wonderful posthumous gift from their mother, filled her mind's eye – memories of empty joy, drained by the oppression of her misery. The exultation at Mathed's recovery was swamped in the wretchedness of the truth of Osir's letter. She walked, trembling to the bed, set the open letter upon it with the utmost care and then lay next to it, her face close enough to smell the paper and the burnt wax and what she imagined was the smell of Osir. She cried, quietly, even through the gentle knocking and concerned enquiries at her door, until she could give nothing more, only to sleep and beg for dreams.

***

Here. Twenty miles from Mamoba in open farmland, with isolated small stands of oak for cover and this two-storey cottage and a scattering of barns and fenced paddocks: it would work well enough, Skava decided. Forty cavalry troopers were concealed here. They waited in the barns, stroking the horses, calming them, calming each other. This was new to these elite Ouine soldiers. They had trained over six days, well away from the estate, in secret. They learned fast; but it was training, not the real thing. Still, Skava gave it good odds they could inflict damage on Osir, a shocking reversal, so alarming that he would be forced to rethink, to rally the waverers, to lick his wounds and take up time. Twelve days until the fortieth. Too long.

Skava clicked her tongue in vexation as she swung up into the saddle of the fast mare she was using. The beast got the wrong idea from her clicking and wanted to be off before Skava was ready, so she spent moments turning circles and looking like a bloody amateur while Ucat glowered up at her from the barn doorway. He had buckled down, she was pleased to see: somehow he had found a way to bend his noble honour to the needs of pragmatism and even envisage some glory in what, for him, was an inglorious ruse, a subterfuge only spies and thugs would employ. Well, he could go fuck himself. Vedarahava had fallen in foresquare to her plan because the alternative was too shameful to contemplate, and he had allowed his officers no room to do otherwise or bring eternal dishonour to their lord.

It would work.

She got the mare under control. "Lieutenant Ucat," she said. "We shall lead them onto you. Remember the timing. And the signal for the second phase. Your mounts will be faster and fresher. Afterwards, rally at the agreed point for your remounts." She paused and then added, "To avenge Lord Mathed. For his honour."

Ucat nodded. "Aye," he grunted. He looked hungry for blood. Revenge was a good incentive to throw off your noble pretensions. But he still hated her: she could see it in his eyes.

She nodded as well and then was away, the mare eager to use her power.

***

Maki greeted her on the tree line of a copse, a mile from the farm house.

"Boss." He looked tense.

"All set," she said and they cantered back inside the trees. Yan was there, walking along the column of horses as they whickered and snorted, doing his own whickering. It was a ridiculous sight. On all thirty-five of the mounts was a dummy, fully caparisoned in the green cloth of Strath, with helm, breastplate borrowed from the Mamoba armoury and long sticks strapped upright from the saddles to emulate heavy lances. A red and gold pennon was fixed to every 'lance': Skava wanted to incense her enemy, to draw him out in mindless fury against the hated red and gold of the Ouine invader.

But the dummies looked fucking stupid. They didn't even have legs. All of the effort had gone into making sure the damned wickerwork frames stayed upright and didn't break apart when they got up to a gallop. Tying them securely had been the priority. It would not do to have arms and heads falling off her heavy cavalry. A flash of doubt crossed her mind. Then she closed her eyes and opened them and, for that instant, seen as a mass, they looked like the real thing. That was all she required. If Osir's mounted squadrons got no nearer than two or three hundred paces, it would work. Probably. Unless some bastard had a telescope.

She dismissed her doubts, dismounted and walked up to Yan. He flicked her a glance, neutral, like this was a normal outing in the countryside. "All good?" she asked, in her usual way.

"Good," he said.

"Nine each?"

"Aye. Nine."

Maki, Yan and two other troopers would each lead a column of nine horses and their dummies. They had tested the tethers and the horses had been selected for their submissive nature. They should follow the one in front, and if things went to shit in the chase, Skava hoped it wouldn't matter if they got disordered. Panicked troopers did that. It was all about how it *looked*. If she was right, the Strath cavalry would be more intent on sticking a lance in their backs.

She flexed her hips, thought suddenly about the sword cut she took from Black Beard, months ago, in the spring. She had vowed to back up a step or two, to extract herself from immediate danger and let others do the work, out in the foul weather and at the point of a blade. So what the fuck was she doing here again?

She shook her head, as much apology to herself as she was willing to make, then took a deep breath. "Maki!" she snapped, harsher than she intended, as nervous as any soldier on the edge of action but with a whole lot more to lose. "Let's go hang our arses out for the pretty Strath cavalry!"

To her surprise, that brought a ribald laugh from the troopers and a snort from Maki. Who'd have thought?

Mounted up, they moved out of the trees and round the back of the coppice, in a thick column, four abreast, then cut away east up a ridge. At the top, Skava leading by twenty horse lengths, the only one not tethered to other mounts, she saw, eight hundred paces away, Prince Osir's army – or at least the half they wanted to bait. Osir had decided to stick with his marching tactic of moving his army in two brigades, both now boasting some four hundred troops, perhaps a third cavalry. The mounted regiments were doing their regular sweeps, in blocks of twenty, two on each side of the vanguard of marching foot soldiers interspersed with the wagons and stores, two manoeuvring at the rear and then a block on each flank, perhaps a good three hundred strides from the main column.

Skava drew up, some way down the ridge, her lance up, the red and gold pennon stiff and fluttering in the cold wind. Already she had their attention, the nearest of the van cavalry slowing and wheeling. Horns sounded off. She cantered parallel to the main body and, because her own column was hidden behind the ridge, she appeared as a single rider as far as Osir's officers were concerned – like a big fucking middle finger, festooned with red and gold, taunting them from a distance.

After some stop-start wheeling, the cavalry block resumed position and the large column continued its march, not rising to the bait, demonstrating admirable discipline – and exactly as Skava had predicted. She continued with her parallel line, glancing to her left where the ridge was flattening out and where Maki and Yan and the dummy brigade would soon come into view. Ahead she could just see the farmstead buildings. That was good.

The 'lance' pennons started to appear along the ridge to her left, and then the 'troopers'. Skava, only twenty horse lengths way, snorted with grudging admiration. They looked the part. They looked like the full Ouine force, ready to commit to some final desperate heavy cavalry attack, precisely as any noble would expect, to toss their lives away for honour in a glorious charge. They were fully in view now, a solid mass of horseflesh and armour, proudly flying the red and gold pennons. It would work. The pennons were what drew the eye: forty of them, a blazing contrast against the green and fallow mud colours of the Strath fields. A tumble of nervous excitement spilled through Skava's veins. Time to break some heads.

She urged her mare forward, closing up with her column as the Strath horns sounded off their brassy warnings. "Deploy!" she bawled.

They moved slowly, portraying a cumbersome organization of heavily armoured riders, moving into a long line at least two hundred paces end-to-end. The animals jostled and did not keep station as a mounted horse under the control of its rider would; but it didn't matter, because the plan was to keep moving, so the tethered mounts followed tamely and the spectacle, from six hundred paces away where the Strath cavalry blocks were being drawn forward, was of a mass of red and gold lancers positioning for a brave but suicidal attack.

Skava pulled up, slipped her telescope out of its saddle pocket, snapped it open and swept the magnified view along the Strath contingents. The van was assembling, both blocks coming together. Further back, the flank escorts were cantering forward. Messengers were galloping between the main column and the cavalry. The whole column slowed and came to a stop. Halberds and spears were being swung down in the usual defensive wall of bristling points. She could see someone standing on a lead wagon, an officer in command of the brigade perhaps, straining for a good view of the field, suspicious of another ambush or deception. Towards the rear, the cavalry blocks were holding station, under orders to ensure no attacks came from behind. Skava smiled. They had learned. They were cautious. They would make sure. And that would be their undoing. Because once they were sure, they would commit.

She put the telescope away, squeezed knees to her mare and caught up with the long file of dummies. It was extraordinary. It felt like she was rejoining a real cavalry troop, so compelling was the impression created by the whole tableau of the walking horses, the glitter of armour and helmets and, of course, the red and gold pennons. Passing one of the troopers, she grinned at him and he smiled back, nervous, but excited. Halfway along the file, she slowed up, playing the part of the commander for her distant audience, as though waiting for the right moment to wheel her column and form line for their final, destructive act.

The horns blew signals again and she watched the van manoeuvring, while behind them the far off rumble of the rest of the cavalry blocks told her they had taken the bait. As far as the Strath commander was concerned, ahead of them was the entire remaining Ouine force. The country here was flat and wide. Their scouts had surveyed the ground. It was ideal for cavalry. There was no possibility of ambush. This was the moment: here they could crush the Ouine threat once and for all. And then Mamoba would be open…

Twelve days, came the thought. Could she delay Osir maybe six days this time? Four? It needed to be a bloody slaughter. It needed to frighten his officers with the high cost. It needed to make the merchants and the tradesmen and the rest petrified to move. She shook her head, for the second time in an hour. If they could not succeed here, she had other options – less good, more reliant on hope than planning, but options.

There was the letter. She did not know what Keleu's reaction might be, but it was there – another trick, another loaded die, already cast. It might get Keleu to ride out to Osir again, and then who knew what might eventuate?

And if all of it failed, and Osir stormed into Mamoba and Mathed died and Yoiwa's dreams with him, well then, she would have to regroup, go to ground and disappear, adjust her plans. Painful, but nothing she hadn't done before.

The horns blasted out a long signal.

Skava pulled up, took in the changing formation in a glance and shouted at her squad, "Ready!"

The Strath cavalry were all moving forward, four blocks edging together in the centre facing towards Skava. They were making a mess of it, inexperienced riders being pushed into position by the officers but, even so, they presented a formidable wall of armour and lances, eighty strong. And on their flanks the remaining blocks of mounted troopers were cantering forward to swing into the wings of the formation, intended by whoever was in command to create an envelopment, cutting into the Ouine force from the sides. They anticipated a decisive and bloody end.

A clatter and banging of lances on shields rung out now as the assembled cavalry got themselves worked up, thumping into a synchronised rhythm which stuttered to a halt as another horn blasted out a series of notes. And they started forward, holding together for a while at a canter, one hundred and twenty armed men, the very earth beginning to tremble with the weight of horseflesh accelerating across the open ground.

Six hundred paces.

Skava raised her voice in a bellow: "Halt!"

The red and gold cavalry to her left looked diminished now against the oncoming rush of the wide mass of Strath cavalry. But they came to a halt, some of the horses skittish and nervous now, jumping sideways, backing up, nipping at each other, edgy and ready to bolt without riders to control them.

Five hundred paces.

A rumbling thunder rolled forward with the packed Strath contingents.

At a canter, they were holding together so far, a glittering wedge of lance points and sparkling helmets and flashing bronze armour, seemingly impossible to stand against.

Four hundred.

Another braying of the horn. Three simple, clear notes. The lead ranks erupted with a surge of power, moving immediately to the gallop and the entire mass of cavalry raced towards Skava.

"Now!" she bellowed, for an instant doubting that she would even be heard above the bass rumble of the enemy horde.

Maki and Yan at once led off, heels to their mounts to turn and leap to best speed as fast as possible. Even from a few horse lengths' away the effect seemed like a collapse of nerve among a section of the Ouine force, and the immediate disintegration of the rest into headlong flight. The other two troopers followed and Skava was behind, trailing the wild retreat of her imaginary force, her head low, marvelling at the mad bobbing and jerking of the wicker dummies as the mounts raced away, and the spatter of mud and clods thrown up by their hooves. She could not see the farmstead, and had to trust that Maki and Yan were heading straight there.

She risked a look behind.

Three hundred paces and gaining. Good enough.

Ahead, one of the dummies lost a helmet. A 'lance' with red and gold pennon tumbled from its fastenings and snapped under the stampede of horses. Then a whole dummy broke apart. No matter: the cavalry behind, fixed on their frenzied pursuit, would notice nothing but churned mud and discarded bits of armour as they hurtled over the ground.

Suddenly they were slowing, and the high sides of a barn appeared, then another, the stables and the stone farm house behind them. The horses ahead bolted left and right between the buildings, turning, skidding to a halt, dancing sideways as Maki and Yan and the troopers pulled up behind the buildings. It was chaos. But it was what Skava had planned.

She rode through, dodging in between rolling-eyed beasts, and saw the four men cutting their tethers with knives so that the mounts and their dummies, though still tied one to another, were no longer being led, and backed up against one another, confused and alarmed.

"Right, right, right!" yelled Skava, and the four troopers followed her just as the first ranks of the pursuing cavalry pounded into the farmstead, shunted from behind by the mass of mounted troops to their rear. The whole boiling mob had lost all coherence when they reached the buildings. Lances went up to avoid injuring one another. Officers were screaming invective, and a dozen or so in the lead were running down the dummies, driving lances into unyielding wicker and empty surcoats and shouting to their fellows in bewilderment.

And that was when the slaughter began.

The forty Ouine troopers began to rain crossbow bolts into the heaving mass of Strath cavalry, from windows, doors, the roofs. Skava had stripped the Mamoba armoury of crossbows, quarrels, bows and shafts. Every man had a quiver of twenty, with orders to use the entire stock. In nearly the same amount of time it had taken to gallop back to the farmstead, four hundred shafts were fired into the Strath cavalry. As man and horse fell screaming, the more tangled the entire wedge of packed troopers became. The range was never more than twenty paces. For the Ouine soldiers, unaccustomed to the use of crossbows and with only six days' practice, it was still impossible to miss. It was point and fire, and for the crossbows rapid cranking of the string to draw the weight, by far the slowest part of the process, and fire again. For the Strath cavalry, where the more experienced troopers got their shields up, the layout of the buildings meant that there were Ouine archers behind or to the side. They were flayed.

On the right perimeter of the farm buildings, Skava and her small troop, all proficient archers with recurve bows, rode around the flank and behind the Strath cavalry, shooting into unprotected backs, taking a terrible toll and running down any troopers trying to make their escape.

With eight hundred shafts fired, the farmstead was littered with the dead and dying, man and beast crushed next to one another. With it came a hideous cacophony of screams, cries and pleas, made worse by the piteous shrieking of the wounded horses. Furthest through the buildings, the other side of the stone house, a few clots of troopers made good their escape, heading north, away from the carnage, away from their own column, their only thought to get clear.

A shrill whistle cut through the charnel-house noise of butchery. Skava was forty paces away from the nearest barn, waving her bow above her head in a circular motion. Maki was at her side, the whistle in his mouth, bow in hand, eyes jumping from corpse to flopping body, searching for danger amidst the murder, a wounded cavalryman with a lance or a soldier with a blade. But the massacre had been overwhelming. Those who yet survived had no fight left.

Now that the whistle had sounded, the Ouine troopers were emerging from the buildings and climbing down ladders from the roofs. Smartly, to a pre-arranged plan, they led their own big mounts from the stables, stepping gingerly between the tumble of dead and dying, no few trying to avoid looking at the bloody bodies, feathered shafts everywhere: the merchants' sons, the farmers, the shopkeepers with glory in mind, and the trained fighters, loyal to their notion of Strath or in the confident belief they had enlisted on the winning side; all the same, blood-spattered, brought low in moments by a storm of heavy shafts. Beyond the mud and the black gore of the fallen, the Ouine cavalry mounted up, each man with a heavy lance and a light javelin, full harness of hauberk, helmet, greaves and armoured boots, shields over left arm, sabres sheathed at their sides. Skava rode close and Ucat looked at her between the narrow eye gap of his helm.

"It's done," he growled, speaking as if he were vomiting. It had been butchery and he didn't like it one bit. "The rout you promised."

Skava did not require high praise. She nodded, pretending she took his words at face value. "More to be done," she growled back. "Stick to the plan. The remounts will be at the rally point. Then back to Mamoba keep."

He said no more, merely waved a bronze-clad arm, and the forty heavy cavalry troopers headed out behind him at a canter in two files.

Skava licked her lips. She was parched and she needed some water. And the screaming of the horses and the groans and curses of wounded men were getting on her nerves. "Yan!" she barked.

He was behind her, water bottle in one hand, wiping his mouth with his sleeve. "Boss."

"Get your boys and do the necessary. And I want as many shafts back as we can manage."

He gave her a look, one that said she was pushing it, without actually saying no.

She was tired, but she gave him the courtesy of an explanation: "I know it's a bloody business, but we need those shafts. Not finished yet. Osir is out there with four hundred troops." She relented a little. Hacking arrows and bolts out of bodies was an awful job and probably too time-consuming. "Just the shafts that are easy, hear?"

He gave a nod, securing his bottle and sliding neatly to the ground. The two troopers did the same, and the slaughter began again.

Skava took a long swig of water from her own bottle. The stench of blood and ordure was almost too much to bear. It never got better. Best that could be said was that it was getting quieter, as the boys did their thing with dagger and sword blade.

"Maki," she said.

"Yep." He was still on his mount. Wise: high enough to spot trouble.

"I'll take the watch. Get the cart in harness. Couple of horses. We need to collect the crossbows, the other horses, and anything else we can use."

He dismounted and went off to make it happen. Skava climbed a ladder, bow in hand, got up onto the shingle of the main barn, with good views to all sides, and sat down on the gentle slope of a roof beam. She worried a little, if she was honest, about the Strath cavalry that had escaped – perhaps thirty or so. They might circle back, *if* they had a good officer with them. They could make mincemeat of the five of them here, *if* they had the stomach for it. While Maki and Yan and the other two worked among the corpses and the wounded below, she scanned the countryside, and from time to time did a body count in sections around the farm. She made ninety-four. A rout, alright.

Now, if Ucat did what she'd planned…

***

Ke Androc stood on the lead wagon and stared into the distance ahead. He could hear fighting. The sound of screams and the ringing of metal, he had learned on this campaign, travelled far. Anxious to close up with his cavalry, he had ordered the column to march again. Around him the foot soldiers slogged forward with confidence. All were carrying shields, all with halberds on their shoulders. Long spears and wide spiked timber frames were carried in each of the wagons, ready to be deployed as a defensive wall against the Ouine mounted troops. But no one expected an attack now. The entirety of the red and gold cavalry was somewhere ahead near a range of buildings, vastly outnumbered and likely surrounded, if they still survived at all.

The young lad next to him, holding on to the wagon front bench as it rumbled and jerked over the ground, suddenly pointed and cried out, "They're coming back!"

Not the most martial of announcements, Ke Androc decided, but the youngster was from a good family in the south, he recalled, land owners near Eloy and, like most of the rest of the soldiers slogging forward, this was his first experience of war. He could not suppress a grin. As expected, their own cavalry was returning. His eyes were not the best, so he asked, "How do they look?"

"Erm…" said the lad, peering ahead. "Three groups, at a canter, I think. Can't see any flags…"

"They've used their lances up."

The leading foot soldiers had seen them too and a cheer went up, repeated in waves along the column as word spread.

Androc spotted the lumps of cavalry in the distance. "Are they in good order?" he asked. He was concerned that they might have taken a mauling. The Ouine heavy troopers were not to be trifled with.

"Well!" said the young man, excited now at the prospect of tall tales of battle about to be delivered to his commander. "Straggling a little."

"How many?"

"Oh, fifty or sixty," came the happy reply.

Androc frowned. Perhaps half the original complement. Where were the others? Destroyed? Surely not. Pursuing the Ouine survivors? He looked over to his troop captain, one of the few mounted men remaining with the column. "Ke Tanzim!" he shouted.

"My lord!" said Tanzim, with a smile.

"I think we should have water ready for the cavalry and the horses. Call a halt and we'll rest up while we get their reports."

"Aye, my lord."

Orders were bellowed. The column stopped. Foot soldiers stood their shields on their boots to keep them out of the mud, leaned on their halberds and watched the approaching cavalry. Tanzim was supervising the unloading of water barrels and troughs for the mounts.

Androc glanced at the young man in his too big chainmail and helmet, a fine sword strung in a loop under his arm. "Lad," he growled. "Keep a lookout on *all* sides. Y'never know!"

The youth grinned and did as bid, but his gaze wandered back again to the cavalry and Androc could hardly fault him. It was victory. Prince Osir would be ecstatic.

"Forming up," said the lad.

Androc looked ahead. He could see it too. They were three hundred paces off and they were trotting into two squads, neat as you like.

"They *have* got lances," the young man informed him, delighted to be the bearer of news.

"What?"

"Lances. Low down, in the saddle wallets, I would guess. I can see them sticking out…"

"Dian!" Androc cursed. "Tanzim!" The man was afoot, thirty paces back, but running now. "Spear defence!" Androc roared, his voice cracking.

And by the time he turned back, the cavalry had exploded into a gallop and they were racing over the ground impossibly quickly, two files, maybe twenty each, flowing into single parallel lines, the left heading for the column's western flank, the right hand swerving across the vanguard and down the column's eastern flank, heavy lances already levelled.

Androc's men were not ready, but they did their best. Shields came up, halberds swung, although there was no defensive cover of grounded spears.

A few of the more experienced crouched on one knee, shield covering their bodies, halberd butt dug into the soft earth, a smaller target even for determined attackers. The left hand file of Ouine cavalry streamed down the flank, lances lowered, plucking at soldiers as they passed and, when their lances broke or were used up, they swung away, pulling their lighter javelins from the saddle wallets, turned and charged back. Javelins thrown at any target along the column, they veered away and galloped off singly and in small clusters.

Ke Androc, standing aghast on the wagon bench, sword useless in his hand, stared at them. It had happened with such speed, he could hardly believe it. He noticed abruptly that the young man was no longer at his side, then saw his body in the bed of the wagon, a spear through his chest, the look of astonishment at the moment of death still fixed upon his inert features. That spear had almost certainly been aimed at Androc. He shook himself into motion, glaring angrily down the length of the column.

"Spear defence!" he bellowed. "Get the fucking spears and frames out if you want to live!"

And suddenly soldiers were in motion, performing as they had drilled – just too damned late. Down each flank, Ouine spears and lances were sticking up out of the earth and the wagons. Lifeless bodies lay here and there, scattered like a fatal wind had blown them over. In a few heartbeats he had a sense of the losses, fewer than feared, more than he ever wanted. How in Dian's name had the Ouine heavy cavalry survived as a coherent unit and come back at the column? It made no sense. He had seen the red and gold pennons, watched them appear on a parallel course and manoeuvre to his front – then lose their nerve when his own cavalry assembled into an overpowering mass. They had fled the field! They had been chased down. How had they survived, intact, to mount an attack?

"Tanzim!" he roared. "Tanzim, get the fuck over here!" He cast about, glaring down the column as the foot soldiers finished the erection of the shielding spears and the frames of sharpened stakes. Twenty paces away he spotted Tanzim in his distinctive decorated cuirass, but he was being supported by two soldiers, a spear through his thigh, bright crimson blood pouring down his leggings. Their troop physician was fixing a tourniquet, but Tanzim's face was already a waxy grey colour. Eventually the two soldiers got him lying on his side, so they could work on the spear, but by then Androc had turned away, murder in his heart.

How had they done it? Androc's mouth worked, as if he could not properly articulate the right question, so bizarre were the circumstances. Reinforcements? Another troop, hidden from view? He stared at the distant brown lumps of the farm, but his eyes were not young enough for the task. A more troubling thought began to wrap cold fingers around his anger and anxiety: *The Ouine troop had come directly from the farm.* That was the chief reason he and everyone in the column had believed it to be their own returning cavalry. He had heard the screams and the fighting from that location. Now he urgently needed to get there, to find out what had happened. But without any of his own mounted troops, his foot soldiers on the march were vulnerable to another Ouine attack. After all, he could not see a single Ouine casualty in all the field of battle.

Androc unbuckled his old warhelm, ran fingers through his greasy grey hair – he had not washed properly in days – and he felt sick to his stomach…this entire business smelled like a disaster. His men would now be looking to him for leadership. They must have confidence. A night alone out here, jumping at shadows, with no news of his cavalry, and the daylight hours would show gaps where whole squads had deserted to seek safety. He knew he needed to act.

He stood up straight, climbed onto the driver's bench and bawled, "Troopmaster!" He had forgotten the names. Tanzim knew them and was a good staff officer for that reason.

"M'lord," came a rasping reply, and a burly soldier appeared at the wagon wheel, his bearded face half familiar.

Androc fixed an expression of decisiveness to his face, then said, "Troopmaster…?"

"Ah…Petra, m'lord."

"Petra. Yes. I remember. Excellent. Congratulations, Troopmaster Petra, you have been awarded a battlefield promotion. You are now my troop captain, in Tanzim's absence."

The man gulped and looked astonished.

Androc lifted an arm and pointed at the farm. "We need to make best speed to that farm. Without our mounted support, we must have solid defence with halberd and spear in a tight formation around the wagons until we get there. I propose we bring the wagons in close to form a box, with the infantry as the outer perimeter. Get the wounded aboard fast. And get some fucking archers on the wagons with plenty of shafts. What in the Shae's name were they doing when Mathed's cavalry arrived?"

Petra blinked. To that he had no answer and ventured no opinion. Androc relented. Blaming would inspire no confidence. "Good man," he said. "Go to it!"

And they did.

***

Ke Androc stood watching from a short distance. He was staring at the back of Prince Osir, in the full panoply of his armour. Discarded at his feet was his helmet. He had tossed it there when he walked up to the mounds of corpses. He glowered at the scene before him. For a long time he had not moved. His hands were fists. Only his eyes roved again and again over the appalling carnage throughout the farmyard.

With the arrival of Osir's brigade and the bulk of the army, they now surrounded the entire farm. Sharpened stakes had been set up as a defensive abatis. Foot soldiers patrolled the boundary. The cavalry blocks were scouting at agreed compass points. And the rest of the troops waited in silent groups, not even muttering, simply alarmed and fearful. Androc could see it. Their shock and superstitious awe at the brutal successes of the Ouine cavalry had demoralised the whole army.

Androc's remaining mounted troopers had done the right thing. The twenty-five survivors had regrouped and made for Osir's brigade, two miles away, to relay the horrible news and he had immediately marched to the farm. Androc had seen to it that the troopers change horses and then sent them out again on patrol. None would meet his eye. They needed to be busy, and to be away from here, from the horror and the guilt. Even so, the day had been a catastrophe. He did not know how they could stiffen the army against this bitter blow. As the afternoon sun westered and the in-between time approached, his own self-belief had waned. From deep down, the doubts were surfacing. Again.

He looked now beyond the prince at the corpses, the bulky rumps and barrel-round flanks of the dead horses and, between them, the limbs of the slain, his troops: a booted foot, an arm thrust skyward like a last signal for help, but stiff and motionless, repeated and repeated. The only movement came from the flies and hungry insects attracted by the intense, gagging stench of death. They were like a black, insubstantial shroud. Ke Androc had never seen so much death in so small a space.

"Lord Androc." Osir spoke but did not cease his vigil.

"Aye, Prince Osir." He stepped forward, reluctant to draw closer to the massacre.

When he reached the prince's side, Osir asked, "How many Ouine dead?"

Androc closed his eyes. "None, my lord," he answered. Extraordinary, but true. The guilt would live with him forever, he knew.

Osir had not ceased his slow inspection of the butchery. Flatly he stated, "There are not many shafts." His voice was cold. Perhaps it was the only way he could hold on to his emotion.

Surprised at this observation, Androc took a breath, trying to keep his hand from his mouth and nose, in a small, barely conscious, gesture of respect for the dead. "True, my prince. There are few weapons anywhere. I would say they were stripped of all the useful arms."

"But the arrow shafts?" Osir insisted.

"Crossbows, I think…"

"So where are the shafts?"

Androc licked his lips. He could taste salt and blood. "It seems that they cut many of them out…"

He had said it. It was true. He had examined the corpses earlier, punishing himself by getting close to look down at the faces of the dead – his men. Foolish, gullible men and boys, playing at war. The undamaged crossbow bolts had been cut from the bodies, a wanton but very pragmatic act.

Prince Osir was not finished. "How many wounded?"

Androc's jaw worked. He took a moment to speak. "None, my prince."

"How can that be?" The same cold tone. They might have been talking about the sale of timber, or grain, but they were not.

"No one was alive when we got here. The wounded had been despatched. Cleanly. Under the jaw, into the brain." Androc found that once he began speaking like this, it was simple. You reported what you had seen, and the words had meaning but were empty of emotion. You merely felt dead inside.

Abruptly the prince turned to him. His eyes were fierce, in stark contrast to his tone. "My Lord Androc. I shall speak to the army. Be so good as to assemble them. What I say, you and your officers will support. No one will gainsay me. I will tell them the truth, as it needs to be told. Do you understand my words?"

Ke Androc blinked. "Yes, my prince."

He could think of no other answer.

***

Skava was sitting on the cart bench when the rider came up. Her arse ached. The bench had no padding, just solid timber, but she was resting her mount, tethered behind the cart, and it made a change from living in a damned saddle all day. At least the sun was out, a watery white fireball struggling to free itself from the distant tree-lined hills.

The rider was one of her courier squad, straight from Mamoba. Swinging alongside, he pulled a salute, hand up, then passed a leather pouch to her. Skava grunted an acknowledgement and busied herself with the correspondence – three items, two in simple code: update on dispositions and defences at the mansion from Vedarahava, and a second message from Yoiwa demanding an account of her plans should Osir invest the mansion. And what was she supposed to say? *We'll fucking scarper and hide in a hole? We'll use a damned dragon to fly your precious son and his new wife to Deka and leave the ruins of Mamoba to Prince Osir?* With a sigh, she sketched a message in her head, simple and reassuring for the Lord of Honam and his wife, then committed it to parchment using a pencil, again in code, and rolled it for the leather pouch, ready for the return bird.

The third message was from Kiangsu City – Fortunas. It was longer than usual: trouble. Skava took a deep breath, controlled her features to project flat calm and read it.

> *Exarch Hassin, of the Zaggisa, sent a question for Skava. He wants to know: Where is the Strath trooper? And: Give him to us. There were five messengers. They were told to make a point. All five are dead. All good, here. Send instructions. F*

Skava felt a heat in her face. This was not good. What in all the wide fucking world were the Zaggisa up to? She was certain – almost certain – Black Beard had been sent by the Zaggisa to kill her. Now they knew Fortunas worked for her. And they had decided to make a statement. But why? Because they knew she had survived? Was this a warning? She had been explicit with Fortunas: keep the Strath trooper observed and leave him to the exarch, unless he tried to leave the city. Why would Hassin send the heavies after her man? And what was the message the Zaggisa were conveying to her? *Get into line. Do not mess with us.* Fucking religious zealots.

Bit unfair, another part of her reasoned. *After all, you created the Zaggisa.* In another lifetime, she argued in return. And I can't control what they have become. Bastards.

One of the two horses Yan had hitched to pull the cart was stretching its neck and trying to bite its more docile companion. A perfect bloody metaphor. Skava eyed the beasts with a sour expression. It began to dawn on her that her erstwhile allies had decided she was a threat. The five corpses Fortunas had left in some street in Kiangsu City would not do anything to contradict that impression. She could make a concession and give the Strath trooper to Hassin. Or maybe not. If they wanted her dead, a realignment of interests had already occurred. She needed to change tack. Something plucked at her subconscious and she knew she needed to think, to sit on the problem for a time.

The grey gelding was nipping at its mate in harness again. The scout holding the reins clucked at it like a father chiding an unruly child. The gelding desisted, and the cart rumbled along the rough trackway with its heavy weight of arms, armour and crossbows. Mamoba was several miles away but they would arrive before dark.

Skava glanced at the courier, a young trooper but battle-hardened and tough, with a curving pale scar across his cheekbone. He saw something in her face – probably the murder in her eye – and he looked away.

"Bird to Deka," she snapped, thrusting the pouch back at him. Yoiwa would get his answer tonight. "Nothing more."

He took the pouch, secured it in his jerkin and cantered away, mud kicked up by his mount's hooves. Skava watched him go. Her thoughts converged as quickly as his horse's rump disappeared over the next low hill. She was worrying about Hassin and the Zaggisa and the complication of bloody plots. Too many extraneous factors. Getting Hassin involved had seemed like a good idea at the time. The Zaggisa, up to their necks in this, had as much to gain from the waxing of Honam and the waning of the Ta-shih as Yoiwa. Medium-term. But…long-term they would want to clip Yoiwa's wings, and what better way to do that than to demand a blood-price from him for their support…

She narrowed her eyes, as if the focus helped her seize the future and drag it close. What better price to exact than the head of Clan Ouine's master-intelligencer? Had the business with Fortunas been a follow-up threat or warning, hard on the heels of the first, nearly successful attempt by Black Beard to take her out? And to whom was the threat addressed? Her? Or Yoiwa himself? Would Yoiwa bite? Did Skava and Ouine Clan need the Zaggisa? Yes, if she were to get some control over the temple at Cise Hook…

Skava lifted her head, took her broad-brimmed hat off and smoothed a hand over her hair, adjusting the leather thong tying the queue in place to hang down over her coat collar.

It was complicated. Ever since she decided to take out Lord Shenri, it had become increasingly fraught. Her goals were unchanging but her plans were constantly being tested. Maybe, if she managed to keep Strath

for Clan Ouine, maybe things would improve…
As if.

CHAPTER 15

I drink to the peace of she that has gone.
Though the Shadow Lord's mark lies plain on her cheek,
I drink to the joy that she gave us to speak.
I drink to the peace of she that has gone.
Oh Shae! Oh Shae! Get thee from here!
Grant one more moment for one held so dear!
I drink to the peace of she that has gone.
Funeral Dirge.

Communities organize themselves according to the environment they inhabit. They quickly forget. Survival trumps education. Illiteracy is everywhere evident, in spite of oral tradition and the archives that remain. Some of the communities I have visited in my travels have vested the Archivists with religious authority. It seems to work. They teach morals and obedience to their gods, certainly, but also sanitation, medicine, the rule of law and much besides.
The traveller, Kerl Adressi, from his book The Wanderer, at the end of the first millennium, surviving in a modern translation.

***

There were two days of conflicting rumours about Lord Mathed. As one might have expected, those closest to him, out of deference to Keleu and for fear of tempting the whim of the Shadow Lord, claimed no more than that he was again conscious of the world. The troops and the servants, however, seized upon the news with relish, the consequence of which was a tremulous ebb and flow of joy at Mathed's recovery, and confused dismay at the refusal of their betters to confirm the report.

It was dawn on a day that might have been like any other were it not for the special designation of the culminating day everywhere called, and by everyone at Mamoba Estate, 'the fortieth'. The result of this was that each day was referred to by a number and today was the 'eighth' and tomorrow would be the 'seventh' and so on.

High on the wall of the estate a sentry swept up his arm and pointed directly towards the old wine press. But his gaze was fixed on a point far beyond the sagging corbelled roof. In that direction, where against the hidden sunrise the sky was a mottled cerise that melted smoothly into the purple and black of the high clouds, a couple of riders had appeared, scouts for Prince Osir's army.

Vedarahava nodded an acknowledgement to the sentry. He placed a hand on the top of the old wall, feeling even through the mail of his gauntlet the pliant moss that thrived here out of reach of the gardeners. He surveyed his defences. All along the wall his men had erected wooden platforms from which to beat back attackers. However, on the outside the wall was no higher than the height of three men. And moreover, Vedarahava had thirty-five able-bodied troops to Osir's hundreds. He knew that Osir would ring the estate and begin the assault from all sides. The Ouine soldiers would not be able to resist for long. On his command they would withdraw to the mansion itself to protect Mathed and Keleu. Beyond that moment, Vedarahava had made no arrangements.

He turned now and looked at Skava, who watched the distant scouts with a brooding glower.

"He is close," Vedarahava said needlessly.

Skava sniffed. Perhaps, she thought, Vedarahava wanted reassurance, or the god-given promise of a miracle.

"Ucat tells me," Vedarahava added, "you inflicted great slaughter upon his army. The whole of one cavalry wing wiped out. Ucat's mounted attack destroyed some thirty or forty foot soldiers."

"True." She could guess what was coming.

"Yet still he advances. He has not slowed at all – except to commit his dead to the flames."

"Also true."

Now she returned his stare. He was not accusing, simply seeking explanation. His eyes were tired, as though all the strategy, military planning and deceptions were too much for him to manage. They probably were. He was a straightforward man, Vedarahava, a bodyguard who could command other guards. He could do it in his sleep and would be right as rain. But this…this constant pressure of complexity and planning, trying to outguess a clever foe, to ponder their motivations and their tactics, to inspire his exhausted troops and lead them, day after day, this was bleeding him dry.

"You said the shock would slow him. To lose so many men…"

"I did. He lost heavily in that ambush, twice. He lost heavily at Lug Hill. But he is smart." Skava took a deep breath, released it slowly. "My Lord Yoiwa saw it, as you know. He wanted Osir…out of the picture. In this we have failed. If you are asking why he still comes at us, despite his losses, my answer is that he is able to inspire the mob of farm boys and nobles in ways we have not comprehended."

Vedarahava looked away, his eyes unfocussed, seeing something only in his mind's eye – his fate, perhaps. "We defend the estate, then?"

"Yes," she said. "While I work through my other plans. After all, we have a surfeit of crossbow bolts and much else besides to repel his assaults. A wall the height of three men is not a high wall, but it is still a difficult wall to scale when someone is trying to kill you."

He nodded gravely. This was something he understood well.

A shout from the mansion made them both turn. In the morning half-light that inflamed the red towers of the mansion he could see two figures on the steps under the portico. One of the figures wore armour, the other a smock, startling white against the dark doors just behind. A moment of shock and exultation both, superseded instantly by concern, made Vedarahava stand stock-still.

"Lord Mathed!" he cried.

A glorious cheer went up from the soldiers to echo the shout of the man who had seen Mathed first. Vedarahava leapt down from the platform with a wild enthusiasm, and raced across the gardens towards his Lord. Skava followed, discreetly, at a distance.

With the assistance of an officer, Mathed stood on the top step. He had dressed in a loose smock and breeches and knee-high boots. Around his waist was his belt and sheathed sword. His handsome face was thin and ghastly pale from the effort it must have cost him to dress and make the journey downstairs; but his eye was lit with a passionate defiance and he smiled at Vedarahava as though at a brother.

Vedarahava fell to one knee. "My lord!" he cried. His adoration was plain to see.

"We shall have this bastard, eh?" said Mathed, and in speaking these words to Vedarahava made all things possible again. He was unafraid of death, but now, Skava perceived, no sacrifice would be too much.

"Aye, my lord!"

"Vedarahava, do we have time to occupy the keep?"

"We do, my lord. Though the enemy is close."

Skava had moved to within a couple paces. She coughed, at once attracting Mathed's attention. "Courier-sergeant?" he said.

"My lord. It is a good thing that you are with us." He nodded an acknowledgment and she pressed on: "The keep, however, is best used as a decoy, a distraction. Mamoba Estate, the mansion, is the seat of Strath. Not the keep."

Her point was not lost on him. If the mansion fell to Osir, Mathed's claim fell with it. He nodded again, then his gaze took in the defences, the platforms with their lances and spears piled in readiness, the crossbows on their wooden stands, the dull bronze armour of the men, and the white and green pennons that fluttered bravely along the walls.

"You are well prepared, Vedarahava," Mathed observed. "Tell me: what is our strength?"

"Thirty-five men, my lord."

"Ouine men?"

"Aye, lord.

Mathed was silent for a space. Skava supposed he was thinking of those who had died. Almost to himself he said, "It has cost us much…" Then, "And what of our Strath brothers-in-arms, who gave us cause to praise their loyalty?"

"Some dozen remain. They hold the keep. I did not think it wise to have them here at our backs…"

"Wise, indeed. And how does the enemy approach?"

"By all appearances in one column from the east, my lord. Several hundreds. They have outriders and small detachments elsewhere and some one hundred and fifty cavalry"

"But you have thinned their ranks?" He sounded hopeful.

Vedarahava gave a grim look. "Aye, my lord. Hundreds. But still he comes."

Mathed slipped a glance in Skava's direction. She knew what he was contemplating. He spoke to Vedarahava: "But there is one large column, you say. Vedarahava, Osir thinks to terrify us with this show of strength. But perhaps we may wound him yet. Prepare twenty horse. I shall ride with you."

Vedarahava protested, "My lord! You cannot do this! The ride will be too much…"

"I must. He thinks he has killed me already. His army thinks the same. That is why their ranks are so swollen. Cowards and faithless villains have flocked to his banner, doubtless on the expectation of favours or quick plunder. The good prince will learn how many stand by him when they discover a real battle awaits them!"

Skava listened. This was not bluster. Mathed believed it and no one could doubt his courage. While it was dangerous, it might help. After all, they had underestimated Osir.

"My lord," she said, realising that both of them would follow her lead. They had no ideas left. "Showing him and his troops that you live is a good move. But attacking him is not. Again, we must make him hesitate. To take the estate, defended by Commander Vedarahava, will be a bloody business and, most importantly, a destructive one. He will be reluctant to wreck the seat of his family."

"What do you propose?" asked Mathed warily.

"Ride out, my lord, with a good bodyguard. At least twenty. His scouts will see you. With those numbers, he may well assume we have more troops than we do – if you are seen to be protected well. Make a pretence of examining the lands around the estate, as though you were contemplating ambush or a set-piece cavalry assault. His men will be alarmed that you live and doubly frightened of another trick. We have cost them dear by such means. They have each and every one lost comrades from their ranks."

Mathed nodded, tacitly giving assent.

"It will force him to move cautiously," Skava concluded, "spending days. The longer he does this, the more opportunities we have to frighten his troops."

Vedarahava, standing protectively at Mathed's shoulder with the other officer, let the scepticism show on his face. "He has eight days to invest the estate. More than enough time to reduce us."

Skava shook her head. "Remember, Commander Vedarahava," she said pointedly, "Osir had *forty* days. Still he is not here. We have given him pause, inflicted losses. Eight days remain. Another three days…and who knows?"

Mathed was breathing uncomfortably, a man struggling through pain. "Very well," he gasped. "But what else can you do?"

There was desperation in that question.

Skava tilted her head, made her expression flat, and answered, "My squad and I will try for Osir himself." She did not elaborate. It was a stupid idea and a last resort. She had no wish to expend the lives of Maki and Yan in suicidal assassinations, though it might come to that. And if it did, she was beginning to think it might be time to disappear. "If we cannot succeed," she intoned, "then we must determine the best manner to move you and the Lady Che Keleu to safety–"

Mathed made the smallest of motions: a shake of the head. "Never! I will not yield. Strath is mine."

"My lord…" she protested, knowing full well that she was wasting her time.

Mathed drew breath, leaning heavily on the officer who supported him. Perspiration stood out on his brow. It was clear that even the small effort of talking exhausted him. With a weak motion of his hand he declared, "Go now, Vedarahava. I must prepare."

He returned within. Vedarahava strode back to the walls whilst Skava lingered, outside the door, as the officer brought Mathed to a chair in the hallway where he sank down, gasping raggedly, his face twisted by pain. Even so, he pulled at the officer's tunic and hissed earnest instructions in a series of stertorous utterances: "You must show only the bravest face when we ride from here. And get more of the physicians' remedy for the pain. I must take it. The men will think me well enough. Do not show your fears. Only keep me in the saddle. I rely on you."

"Aye, my lord." The officer made as if to speak again, hesitated in confusion, then said, "My lord, the Lady Che Keleu…"

Mathed raised his head with difficulty. "What of Che Keleu?"

He followed the line of the officer's gaze. Keleu, immaculate and beautiful in a foulard dress the colour of magnolia, stood motionless nearby, at the foot of the wide staircase. Just as Mathed had gradually recovered and the strength had returned to his limbs during the past days, so Keleu's complexion had resumed its characteristic glow and a vital light been rekindled in her eye. But now something – doubt or uncertainty – clouded her expression and spoiled the tableau for Mathed. Instantly he knew that she had overheard his instructions to the officer.

"Keleu," he said, and was conscious of how like an excuse it sounded. "I am much recovered." And from somewhere he found the strength to stand. But when he faced her he could not say anything more: her look was not so much accusing as simply incredulous.

"You're going to seek him out," she said.

Mathed moved his head in a gesture communicating both apology and resolve, as if he had tacitly denied that his determination to ride out against Osir was his wish and he was, instead, compelled inexorably by some noble obligation.

Keleu was beautiful. He looked on her with an acute longing and with all the desires and aspirations that made him wretched at the hurt he did to her. But time pressed, Osir drew nearer.

"Go," he commanded the young officer and, when the youth had gone, dashing from the hall and holding his sword firmly to his thigh, Mathed focussed all his strength on the need to remain on his feet at this moment and to say the right thing to Keleu. A dozen phrases suggested themselves, to be dismissed in Mathed's mind as quickly as they were conceived. The directness of Keleu's look was more challenge than mere words could confute. Again he found himself at a loss.

"You're going to seek him out," Keleu repeated.

"I must," said Mathed quietly, but did not repeat Skava's caution to avoid an engagement with Osir. It seemed to him to be undignified and, in this moment, he did not want Keleu to see him as weak.

"You cannot hope to hold Mamoba," she whispered.

"No."

"Will you return to Honam?" she asked, with an eager hope, and covered the few steps between them, though she held back from touching him.

"No."

At last he reached out to take her slender shoulders, and steeled himself to say what he must. "Keleu, I love you dearly, perhaps more dearly than I should, for if I were bound only by my own inclination I would leave here with you…go to Deka, happy with you, even in defeat, even in my own dishonour…"

Keleu began to speak. Mathed held his hand up to forestall her. White-lipped he went on, "But the honour of Ouine is greater than me. It commands me, Keleu."

She stared at him and his love for her remained an irresistible, passionate force which moved him in a moment to self-abandonment. He clasped her body to him and pressed his lips against the hollow of her neck. Breathlessly he whispered, "I must go. I must go, my love." But he did not break away from her. He could not.

After many moments, when all that existed in the world for him was the warmth and life of her body, and on his chest the damp of her tears through his smock, Keleu lifted her face to him. He was shocked: her skin was transparently white and it seemed that she suffered from a hidden wound, so tormented was her expression.

"Honour," she said softly and with an obvious effort to regain her self-possession, "has cost me dearly…"

Mathed could not know what terrible emotional privations Keleu had endured in the past weeks. He had, before he was wounded, understood something of her anxiety, but in all truth it had been of secondary importance against the conduct of the war with Osir. Now, though he perceived clearly enough the depths of her despair, it was a condition he felt powerless to mend, and knew well that the comfort of promises that might give another woman hope would, to Keleu, remain only the most negligent of empty words.

And so he was silent, bereft of alternatives, and fixed irrevocably on a course that admitted no ignoble act. He looked at Keleu with an unbearable unhappiness, seeing in her face the tenderness and feeling he knew so well and, with it, the agony of understanding that wrenched at her.

And then she appeared to win the struggle with her emotions and compose herself. Though her eyes were still bright with tears, she said in a voice as steady as her look, and with a percipience that startled Mathed and made him think she had read his thoughts, "Men are bound by honour – or what they like to call honour. My brother called his rage honour. For you honour is the obligation you owe your father." Keleu smiled sadly. "You are more alike, you and Osir, than ever I realized."

She pressed his hands. "Mathed," she said simply, but with impassioned feeling, "I love you."

***

A powerful black warhorse was brought to the main entrance of the mansion. There, Mathed, in light chainmail and olive-green surcoat, mounted. He rode stiffly, pretending a strength he could not possibly feel, along the chalk driveway to the main gates with Vedarahava walking beside him. Che Keleu watched from an upstairs window as the gates opened, the spiked abatis was pulled aside from the entrance, and he was joined by a squad of twenty heavily armed lancers near the stables. Soon they were gone, cantering into the winter landscape.

Che Keleu returned to her chambers. She had dismissed her handmaidens and was alone. Standing in the centre of her bedroom she felt that she *should* be crying, but could not. She knew now with a certainty and clarity that she had passed a point of no return, and the only thing beyond her desolation was a welcome oblivion. Somehow this made perfect sense. And therefore the tears did not come.

After a while, during which time the light in the room waxed and waned with the rolling cloud cover beyond the windows, she took out Osir's folded letter from her bodice, but did not open it. She merely held it, her fingers roving over the fabric of the paper as though it might communicate something to her that was not in the curling, flowing script. Soon she moved to the window and stared into the world with sightless eyes. She did not see the sentries on the walls, nor the weapons piled in readiness, nor the green and white pennons flying from spear point and keep. If she felt anything, it was that she felt paralysed, her consciousness awash with tangled images and flashing memories that added up to nothing: she was unable to think or decide.

Then a movement in the gardens caught her eye. Perhaps her attention had at last regained a focus, or perhaps it was the dimmest recognition of familiarity and a kind of immanence. Whatever it was, somehow it mattered. Walking through the gardens she could see the courier-sergeant, lithe and swift. She remembered his uniform and the purposeful cant of his head. For a moment she was struck by his certainty. No one in the mansion seemed quite so certain. Then an idea began to shape itself in the chaos of her thoughts, and the promise of it was so compelling that she embraced it; it was like a rock on which she could cling whilst the rest of her thoughts were submerged, drowned in the gathering flood of her emotions.

She walked to her door, opened it and summoned a handmaid. "My writing box," she instructed. "Lay out paper and pens."

The maid gave the requisite bow. "At the small writing desk in the library, my lady?"

Che Keleu looked at the woman for the first time. "No," she replied. "Here."

If she was surprised, the handmaid kept her faced closed.

***

Kesmet had settled on a hide three kems from the mansion. A broken tumble of walls, some head high, were what remained of an old croft. It occupied a dip on the side of a steep wooded hill, overgrown by blackthorn and invisible from the approaches. It looked to have been unused in decades, the undergrowth thick and impassable. With careful cutting of a path and flattening the scrub, he was able to stable Gexa under a jury-rigged oil skin roof, covered by cut blackthorn. A fire was out of the question during the day because the smoke might attract unwanted military visitors, but at night he had sufficient cover to make and use a small fire for cooking, at least for short periods. In any case, Gexa seemed happy enough – certainly until Kesmet's oat sacks were depleted.

Away from the hide, at selected high points overlooking the valley and the distant mansion, for some days now Kesmet had observed the estate. After the slaughter of Strath cavalry, he had tracked Skava and seen her return with her squad, the cart piled high with weapons poking from the tarpaulin. Recently, he had spotted her out and about near the mansion and the stables, but she had never ventured any further on her own. Still, he was patient. Something would draw her out, either alone or otherwise vulnerable. And he would be ready.

Meanwhile, through his telescope he watched the son of Yoiwa, the new Lord of Strath, ride from Mamoba on his black warhorse, surrounded on all sides by his bodyguard. Their actions were odd. They seemed to be surveying the landscape, loitering in places that might suit ambush, pointing here and there, setting distance markers for the archers and generally doing things that an army might do on the eve of battle. Except, as Kesmet well knew, they had no army. More than half the entire muster of Ouine troops had ridden out – twenty, Kesmet had counted.

About fifteen remained. Clearly, it was a ruse. Skava up to some trick. Like her trick to lure the Strath cavalry to their doom. A decisive strike. But still Prince Osir marched on his home. Somehow he had galvanized his ragtag army. That was impressive. What would Skava do next? Time was running out.

Kesmet had long pondered the probable course of action she might take. He did not think like Harbin, in all his glorious complexity, but he felt certain that if Mamoba fell and Mathed were killed, she would try to disappear, seeking out her next opportunity or pursuing a dozen other avenues already prepared. Here one moment, gone the next. If that came to pass, Kesmet knew, with absolute assurance, he would not easily find her again. It made his stomach coil with tension. She was close. She had been *very* close, in the pine woods, close enough to see her face, close enough to hear her voice, close enough to kill. And yet she lived. It was unsurprising. The normal rules twisted when it came to Eslin. She bent circumstance to her side. She prepared meticulously, even in the hour-to-hour precautions of getting through another boring day. Disciplined habits, training, thoughtfulness and the loyalty of the people around her – these were her protections. She used them like a shield. And thus the odds fell in her favour, more times than she deserved; a gambler who had devised the near-perfect response to the stakes of the game, at every turn.

Kesmet eased his position. He had been kneeling for some while, training his telescope now and then on horsemen in the vineyards, scouts working in pairs, and the occasional traffic along the main road to the stables. In amongst a sparse treeline, he overlooked the estate two thousand paces away, and could see the surrounding terrain on all sides. Behind him, further along between the meadows and whisper trees, he could hear a distant cataract, the volume of water producing from its precipitous fall a reverberation at the edge of hearing. These hills and hidden valleys would be beautiful in the spring and summer, carpeted with flowers and the verdant green of the leaves. Even the blackthorn would be festooned with white spiky blooms, whilst now they were stark and sharply forbidding, their wrinkled sloe berries a sad reminder of autumn.

Zuse seemed content. He was leaner from days constantly running, his coat like sleek black oil, his deep brown eyes attentive and knowing. This was his habitat. He fitted into it and owned it. He hunted with startling ease, but was never far, a sentinel that would sleep but was always alert. He lay now, four paces away, head up, black nostrils twitching, ears pricked to hear the landscape hidden to Kesmet. The scout allowed himself an inner smile: if he had learned one thing in his long life it was the value of true companionship, the unspoken understanding between two beings. It was the bond that drew Kesmet back from the shadowed depths of self-reflection, places that at times could seem both terrible and seductive.

Zuse shifted his head forward, a sudden focussing of energy and concentration. Kesmet noted it from the corner of his eye. Twenty heartbeats later, down the slopes below them, two horsemen crested a rise, attempting to keep cover between them and the estate – Osir's scouts, dressed in dun colours and deerskin. They were no more than four hundred paces away. There they paused, their horses pawing at the ground, looking for grass to crop and not finding any. One of the mounts whickered suddenly, shying and shaking its head. It had turned towards Kesmet and Zuse, undoubtedly picking up the dog's scent. The rider pulled back on the reins to regain control, concerned about attracting attention from the defenders at the mansion.

"Down," said Kesmet, very quietly, and Zuse dropped his head, flat to the earth.

The riders meanwhile were casting around for danger, surprised by the horses' unease and fearing ambush. Kesmet stayed still. It was unlikely they would spot him, and the blackthorn hereabouts was impenetrable. He had ensured that it remain that way when he picked out a route some days before, so he could move from vantage to vantage and back to the hide.

Abruptly, they moved off, returning down the crest and out of sight. Kesmet kept glancing back to Zuse until the dog's tension passed. It was a reliable indicator that they had gone.

Towards the estate, there was movement at the main gate. Kesmet swung up the telescope. Emerging from the postern were two figures, one in uniform, the other in darker colours suitable for a scout. The magnification of the lenses showed them clearly, although it was impossible to see the detail of faces. Kesmet knew them both. Eslin and the tall one from the pine forests. They walked towards the stables, disappeared from view behind walls and roofs, and Kesmet lowered the telescope. Presently two horsemen rode off south and only Eslin returned, walking rapidly to the postern gate. Then she was gone.

Kesmet was still undecided on his next move. No opportunity had yet presented itself. Patiently, he waited.

***

The letter was finished. Keleu had closed it in neat folds and affixed the green wax with her seal. She turned it in her hands. On its face it bore, in her immaculate cursive hand, Ke Beyil's name, no more than that – an address that was not formal but rather partway to familiar, insisting, she hoped, on its treatment as confidential, a matter of trust. Now she stood, uncertain, next to her reading table in her bedroom, the writing paper and pens forgotten while she looked at the bed with vacant eyes.

Before long, she came to a decision…or perhaps the time for action was incontestable. She smoothed her hands over her heavy winter dress, a velvet emerald green like spring leaves, and this seemed to satisfy her. On one of her occasional chairs was her cloak, the same velvet emerald but with a golden yellow lining to the hood. She rarely wore it, preferring her other cloaks for riding and country walking, but it seemed appropriate now, so she draped it over her arm. As she did so, her right hand strayed to her side where she could feel Osir's letter against her skin, low down above her hip. The envelope for Ke Beyil was in her left hand. Then she opened the door and walked downstairs. Her handmaiden saw her go and noted the chamber door left open, which she took as the usual unspoken instruction to tidy things away.

Che Keleu reached the wide hallway with its beautiful hangings and mirrors. She could smell food. Cook was preparing lunch and no doubt Ke Beyil and his assistants would be in the library before the call came to take their meal. Mathed and most of his troops were out near the surrounding hills. They would return very late.

Keleu hesitated. She looked at the high table near the bottom of the stairs, with the silver platter where correspondence was arranged by the servants before being passed to the household. It was empty, and she began to cross to it, intending to leave the letter there; but then the main door swung open and inside stepped the courier-sergeant. He saw her and stopped and they both stared for a moment. Then he dropped his eyes, remembering his station, and said clearly, "My lady."

Che Keleu turned away from the table and a small emotion of what might have been relief touched her. "Sergeant," she breathed, "if you please. Come with me to the stables."

His hazel eyes were unblinking, calculating even, but she noticed nothing of this. "Of course, my lady," he replied, and they walked outside, down the steps and through the gardens along the main drive. At the gates, heavily barred now, the sentry acknowledged her and the courier-sergeant with a nod, then opened the postern door. Together, in silence, they stepped through the gap in the abatis and paced the chalk road to the stables where no one stood guard and only two stable boys looked up in surprise from their work mending tack. At the wide folding doors, Che Keleu came to a stop whilst the boys scrambled to their feet and bowed. She was uncertain how to proceed. Normally servants from the house would convey her instructions to prepare a horse. Fortunately, the courier-sergeant intervened.

"A mount, my lady?" he enquired, although he spoke the words as a command, and both boys instantly bolted for the stalls. Only a handful of horses remained, two of them Keleu's. A saddle was fetched, and harness, and preparations were rapidly made.

Keleu shrugged into her cloak, the letter still clutched in her left hand. She faced the courier-sergeant and his carefully neutral expression.

"Sergeant," she said.

"My lady."

"You were…very kind…the other day. The letter, you understand?" She found that her breathing was laboured. She was unaccustomed to this, and did not know how to express her gratitude. But, once more, he seemed to apprehend what to say.

"Of course," he stated, and his hazel eyes held her gaze, as if their encounter in the hallway only days before had altered all the normal rules of propriety.

She nodded and smiled weakly. "I would like you to…" she began, and faltered, then started again more firmly, "I would like you to take this letter."

He did not extend his hand, merely asked, "For my Lord Mathed?"

"No," she countered at once. "For the Council supervisor, Ke Beyil. You know him?"

"I do, my lady."

Her horse, a fast piebald mare that she loved, was being led from a stall, saddled. She looked over and the boy was uncertain, seemingly torn between bringing the horse to the open doors near the mansion, or the closed doors at the opposite end where anyone might normally ride out to the hills were these normal times and not times of war. A sharp hand signal from the courier-sergeant bade the boy turn the mare and head towards the far doors. Keleu was grateful.

"This is the letter," she ventured needlessly and proffered it.

The sergeant frowned, his eyes sliding to the second stable boy who waited nearby, head down in contemplation of his feet, clearly uncomfortable. "For Ke Beyil, my lady?" the courier-sergeant said, echoing her words. Then, to the boy, "Help with the doors." And the lad scuttled off.

"Yes…please." She was still holding the letter out and, finally, he took it, not once glancing down to it. "But, sergeant," she insisted, "I ask you to deliver it to Ke Beyil this afternoon, when I have…when I have gone."

"Gone, my lady?"

She flushed, but recovered at once. "Riding," she responded. "I need to ride. I shall not be long."

The hazel eyes were unflinching, and in any other circumstance his assurance might have seemed untoward, but here it gave her comfort. Or rather it saved her from shame. At the far end of the stables, one of the heavy doors creaked open, stealing Keleu's attention. She began walking towards her horse, held by the stable boy where wooden steps had been placed for her convenience.

Behind her, the courier-sergeant called out, "My lady. You do not require a guard?"

She wanted to stop. It was right to stop. But it seemed unclear whether he had asked her a question or simply confirmed a matter of fact. She instead made no response and mounted the piebald, arranging her skirts and cloak decorously with practised ease, before urging the mare out of the stables and towards the hills. A quarter-mile along the road, there was a secondary trail. She knew it well. There she turned off and a smile touched the corner of her mouth. The trail led gradually upwards to the distant slopes, and the blackthorn and the scattered whisper trees and her memories of her soldier, Adaim…

***

Kesmet saw the lone rider long before Zuse. His eyes were better, after all. He raised the telescope, but horse and rider had cut away along a covered trail, taking a route that he knew headed up into the hills and towards his current position. If the rider held his course, he would come out thirty paces below Kesmet's vantage. The trail wound its way up to the high meadows and, he recollected, went no further than the cataract. There was no route beyond that.

It was a puzzle. One of the reasons Kesmet had selected this high ground was because there was no reason for anyone to come this way. To go around the ravine and the rushing waters, one would have to turn back and take the lower road, where a stone bridge linked the two banks in the flat pastures of the river valley. A rider's only purpose on this trail was to visit the waterfall.

More movement caught his eye. Back at the stables a second rider had emerged and, as Kesmet raised his telescope again, intrigued, a shock coursed through him. It was Eslin. She wore her uniform, but no armour, and carried no shield, not even saddlebags – only a sword.

Zuse had pricked up his ears. He had heard the first rider, the scatter of pebbles on the steepening trail and the clop of a horseshoe on stone.

Kesmet knew there was a long gap in the scrub that secluded the trail, so he trained his glass on it and, sure enough, the rider came into view: a woman, dressed all in green, with a flare of yellow lining where her hood hung down, like a frame for the dark tumble of her hair. Kesmet stared. She was without doubt a noblewoman. Her dress, her bearing, everything about her told him so. The trail dipped, winding aslant and away, and she was gone from view.

Kesmet swung the telescope back to the main road, in time to see Eslin turning off, following at a slow canter, a pace that would bring her near to the woman but not quickly, as if she had no intention to catch up.

Zuse was now looking directly towards the sounds of the woman's approach. Kesmet took a deep breath. None of it made sense. He looked back to where Eslin had last appeared and then to the stables. They were quiet. The estate was quiet. He moved back behind a tree, stood up and reached into the leather bag that contained his crossbow, pulled it out, cranked it for both bow arms and loaded two quarrels. Eslin would pass no more than thirty paces from him as the trail swung up through the blackthorn. He had already checked the range as part of his regular precautions. It would be a simple shot. And with two quarrels fired in quick succession, he was very confident that he could put her down. In the event she survived, wounded, Zuse could do the rest, hauling her to ground for Kesmet to finish the job.

His patience had been rewarded. It was extraordinary luck. She was alone, unarmoured, on a narrow trail with nowhere to run, and a long way from help. Kesmet prepared himself, folding the telescope and securing it, tightening and cinching belts, checking his stabbing sword and knives. In front of him, upright in the damp earth he stood four more crossbow bolts: he might need the additional quarrels to bring down her horse.

Then he waited, eyes inspecting the terrain, without neglecting the road from the stables in case Eslin's squad were following or someone else stumbled onto him. But it was quiet. Only the approaching horse with the noblewoman broke the silence of the hills. Soon she rode into view, moving directly towards him before the trail switched back and she was side-on. He was momentarily taken aback. She was beautiful, vibrant, an incongruous tableau amidst the harsh skeletal limbs of bare trees and spiny blackthorn. Why was she here? And the truth dawned on him: she was Mathed's wife, the Lady Che Keleu. And behind her, following on the trail, was Eslin.

Puzzlement and an abrupt fear made him tentative. He stared at the retreating horse and rider, the emerald green of her velvet cloak and the black and white of the piebald. They were now passing up the slope above him to his right, submerged in the undergrowth, only torn slashes of the yellow lining of her hood visible, and then gone. An agony of indecision locked his gaze on where she had gone. He believed he should follow. The truth of it was overpowering. He lowered the crossbow, halfway to departing, but caught sight of Zuse, whose large head had turned back downslope, ears forward to track the approaching second rider. His muzzle twitched and he showed incisors and canines in a deep growl.

Kesmet's attention snapped back. "Down," he whispered. Zuse lowered his head, slowly, unhappy with this turn of events. He had sensed the imminence of a hunt from Kesmet's preparations and he recognized the approaching scent: he had been stalking it for weeks.

Kesmet positioned himself against the bole of the tree, concealed from the trail, and composed himself for the explosive onset of action. The sounds drew nearer. Then stopped. Peering around the tree trunk, Kesmet could see the head of a horse down the trail at the point where it straightened, seventy paces away. The horse tossed its head but did not move forward. Eslin had spotted something, or the horse had got a scent, or she was just cautious, or she did not want to get too close to her quarry. Any number of reasons might be true. Whatever her motives, she had stopped. He would have to wait. And the wait, for Kesmet, in this unusual state of agitation, felt interminable. The rational part of him insisted on patience and warned of the extreme risk of precipitate action. But the tableau of the woman on her journey up the slope to the cataract tugged at him with a frenetic, remorseless logic. It was wrong. And Eslin was part of it, and that made it worse than wrong.

With a silent curse, he knelt, removed the quarrels from the bow, secured the spares and packed everything. Then he turned, ducking under the cover of blackthorn and low tree branches to follow the path he had made back through the undergrowth up the hillside, concealed from the lower slopes, but slow, zig-zagging. He knew his destination with certainty and he moved fast, powering through the climb with Zuse obediently at his heels, pleased no doubt that the hunt had begun in earnest, if in an unexpected direction. By the time they reached the more open meadows, with the scattered whisper trees, Kesmet was breathing hard. No one was in sight. Keleu had gone ahead, towards the falls and, if Eslin had decided to press on, she might be near. Kesmet stopped, behind a tree, listened and heard the hooves of her horse. Almost at once she appeared, some sixty paces away, cresting the trail between stands of trees. She was alert, her head moving to check the broad field all around her; then she cantered forward, accelerating past Kesmet's position and up towards the gorge and the muted thunder of the cataract.

Kesmet began to run. He must stay off the trail, for if Eslin stopped she would hear him. That meant he needed to pick his way along some parallel route and get past her if he could. By now Eslin was gone, hidden by trees and long grasses and the tangled scrub along the trail. Fortunately for Kesmet, the blackthorn was scarce up here, so he could move quickly and soon he was crossing the stony chalk bed of the trail. There he stopped, listening, attempting to get his bearings on the waterfall. The trail curved away to his right, rising gradually, and he made a guess, from the pummelling sound of the water, that the path would veer left again around the steeper rocky heights directly above. Intuitively he made his decision, searched for the best route and set out to cut over the summit. It was more like climbing than walking. He used his gloved hands to grip rocks and saplings and pull himself up, driving hard with his legs, slipping on occasion and scraping his shin but always moving upwards until, breathing heavily and perspiring despite the cold air, he scrambled over the top of the hill to level ground and, between the trees, glimpsed the white tumble of the cataract some distance below. Here the noise was thunderous and the impression of the plunging cascade simply majestic. The river on the far side of the gorge split into a dozen spillways around granite outcrops carved by the ceaseless power of the water, then sluiced down, falling forty paces to the unseen torrent beneath. He ran on. No sign of Che Keleu or Eslin and, worryingly, soon the ground in front of him dropped away in a vertical cliff of exposed rock and chalk, snarled trees, roots and clumps of blackthorn overhanging the edge. It was at least the height of eight men to the lower meadow, that extended in a broad swathe of grass and the yellow rust of a carpet of leaves. If he had had time, it would have been perfectly possible to pick a route down, but he did not. There, to his right was Eslin, mounted, two hundred paces away, stationary amid the trees off the trail. She was perfectly still, watching the scene unfold at the edge of the gorge.

And there was the woman in green velvet, her piebald horse nearby, reins trailing on the grass. She was facing the cataract and the immense drumming power of the torrent. She stood utterly absorbed on the brink of the chasm, while the water opposite plummeted endlessly, and Kesmet was trapped fifty paces away on the summit above. He could barely catch his breath, so strenuous had been his mad scramble to get here. Now, a deep horror seized him. He knew what was about to happen and he was powerless to prevent it.

Despite the great roar of the cataract, and the danger from Eslin, he decided to shout, to call at the top of his voice but, in the same instant, Che Keleu simply stepped off the edge and was gone.

"God!" he gasped.

The field at the lip of the gorge was empty. Kesmet could scarcely believe it. He stood, fixed to the spot in shock. Then he began to run, Zuse bounding behind him, away from the cataract and downstream along the precipitous scarp of the gorge.

***

The Ouine troop had circuited the estate all morning, the scouts reported. It brought a fluttering tension to Androc's stomach that had not been there before the slaughter of his cavalry at the farm. Here, on the hillside, with Mamoba a distant outline of towers, the dozen officers of Osir's command held council. Some fidgeted. Others looked stern, determined to overcome nerves with steel-eyed gravity. One or two, it seemed to Androc, were frankly petrified and could not hide it. They were for delaying, scouting the land for trap and ambush, when of course Osir's woodsmen and spies had already done this. The bloody reversal at Lug Hill and the twin attacks on his column had made his men fearful. The manoeuvring of Mathed's lancers had convinced them the same fate was imminent. Their tension had not been allayed by the sightings of Mathed in the saddle – reliable reports, from the best of Osir's scouts. Some took this as a sign from the gods, and no few of the common soldiers were already grumbling to each other, swapping dreams from the night before and seeking interpretation from the older men who might know a thing or two. The exarch accompanying the army had accepted the sacrifice of a cow that morning, but his reading of the signs was ambiguous: an end to fighting, which pleased the soldiers, but no assurance of victory. For their part, the men examined the cold burned branches of their fires and agreed on this meaning or that in the pattern of the charcoal cracks.

It was only days since Osir had overcome, by the most extraordinary feats of oratory, the despair brought on by the ambush and defeat. Where everyone in the army had seen only the devastation of being tricked and overcome, Osir assembled every man and woman and pointed to the horrific piles of corpses, told them to look and look well. For this, he told them, was how Honam ruled Strath. Not a man had been spared. Each of the Strath wounded had been killed when they were defenceless, their throats slashed, crossbow bolts cut from their still-warm bodies.

Prince Osir had walked along the lines of his brigades, facing them, eye-to-eye, and pointed with outstretched arm at this man or that youth, brothers and cousins to them all, lying in grotesque twisted disorder, naming them. Farmers and tanners, shopkeepers and nobles, he had cried out. These were their people. This was Honam's rule.

And, to Androc's astonishment, he had witnessed the army begin to murmur, to growl in indignation and then fury. They had drummed defiance on their shields and roared their anger at the afternoon skies – and Osir *had* them again, a coherent army, united by grief and vengeance, ready to advance once more and kill the Ouine usurpers. They spared a night and a day for the dead, building pyres so that the souls of the fallen could be swept into eternity with the spiralling columns of smoke from a dozen blazing fires. And finally, they marched, in one great army, near seven hundred-strong, without a single individual having deserted.

In Osir's deep gaze there was, it appeared to Androc, who watched the prince closely from near at hand, something that was almost enchantment. Since the last encounter with Mathed, the prince had without difficulty maintained a public face of strict order and purpose which had served to bind the forces under him. His calm, and especially his confidence, had been crucial in persuading soldiers overwhelmed by the ferocity and success of the Ouine attacks that Mathed's cavalry, impressive though they undoubtedly were, nevertheless had lost their leader and were no longer to be feared. Such confidence, such utter commitment, was infectious. A day after the battle, men whose comrades had fallen in whole ranks under the fierce discipline of Honam lance and sword were as eager to hurl themselves at the enemy as their young prince. It was remarkable.

But now, waiting on this hillside, with Mamoba so close, and Mathed riding among his lancers with all the confidence of a victor, the mood was slipping. When officers lost faith, Androc knew, when just a few betrayed their fear or showed reluctance, the loss of morale spread rapidly.

With the army at battle order along the slopes, the prince was standing in the centre of a ring of officers. He had sensed the alteration in mood. And he did not like it.

"Ke Robax," he said, addressing one of the officers who had already expressed his reservations.

"My prince," came the reply. Robax looked uncomfortable at being singled out, but his tension was palpable. He had been one of the surviving officers from the last ambush.

"You have told us you have reservations."

A number of his fellows looked at their feet.

"I have, my prince. Their cavalry may be stronger than we think. Mathed is alive. He rides out with his bodyguard inspecting traps and devising stratagems. It is said that one of his officers is a master of battle tactics."

Osir listened, then replied, "And yet, Ke Robax, we are here, seven hundred-strong, and Mamoba is there…" – he pointed – "and Mathed has not prevented us."

The man looked away. "I seek only to ensure we are successful, my prince. Another trap would be a disaster."

"What is your advice, then, Ke Robax?"

The lieutenant of cavalry looked back at Osir, the hope of reprieve lighting his face. "Set up a strong camp here, my prince. Probe the mansion's defences."

Osir nodded. He looked appraisingly at his other officers. "Who agrees with Ke Robax?"

No one ventured support.

"It may be sensible," Osir allowed. "But what are the risks?"

Chaaggar, his arm in a sling over bronze breastplate, growled, "We postpone the inevitable. We should not bear delays. The usurper fights only to delay. He cannot win."

Osir smiled. "Indeed, my Lord Chaaggar," he said, swinging around to encompass the ranks of his army arrayed in a great square around them on the hill. "And what else?"

A younger officer spoke up. He was a contemporary of Robax in not only age and rank but his leadership of a cavalry squadron that had distinguished itself in turning back the Ouine lancers on two occasions. "The effect on our men, my prince," he asserted with confidence. "If we dig entrenchments and protect ourselves with spikes and palisades this near to Mamoba, they will have good cause to believe we can be beaten. Then they will hesitate when they should be strong, and the weaker among them will run. We *are* strong. Why hesitate and throw advantage to the enemy?"

Robax flushed and, embarrassment nearly overcoming fear, he bridled, "You were not there, Ke Phelep! Whole squadrons were annihilated by the Ouine troops. They massed sixty archers in the buildings and then fifty lancers near at hand to attack the column! By that counting, they can defend Mamoba with a much larger force than we imagined."

Phelep shook his head. Androc was pleased to see that he showed no arrogance – merely disagreement.

Robax was not finished. "Sixty archers!" He spread his hands, an appeal to reason for all the officers. "Imagine sixty archers on the walls of the mansion! Or hidden somewhere out there, with fifty heavy cavalry on our flanks and–"

Osir cut him off. "You have made your case, Ke Robax," he said sharply. "I note your concern and your advice. My decision is that we march on – and quickly. Everyone will commit fully to the advance and adhere to the battle order I have proposed when we are outside the walls." He eyed Robax with an arched brow. "I take it, Ke Robax, you will lead your squadron with distinction?"

A nice turn of phrase, Androc thought. To back out now would be dishonour. Osir had skirted the danger.

Perhaps the angry brush with Phelep had steadied his nerves, or perhaps he had indeed discovered there was a prospect worse than death, but Robax acquiesced with a part-bow. "My prince…" he breathed.

"Then we are ready!" Osir called out, flashing a broad smile, as much for the nearby troops as the waverers among his officers.

***

Chaaggar's arm hurt. It ached at night and it healed slowly. At least the physician assured him there was no rot. He had, he supposed, taken an Ouine lance at Lug Hill, deflected by his armour. His recollection was blurred, for it had happened so fast. That had been a shock. The aftermath of battle had left him depressed, close to giving up. But Osir, half his age, had rallied him, had whipped them all to greater effort for love of Strath. Now he noticed in Osir, underneath the dispassionate exterior and despite his strenuous efforts to quell it, a growing tension, an excitement which had nothing at all to do with the imminence of battle. *He can taste victory,* was Chaaggar's thought. *It has become the reason for his existence. Victory, vindication, honour – it is all one to him.* Chaaggar looked away, his reflections producing within him an unexpected disquiet. He preferred the prince's icy resolve. It had inspired Strath and frustrated the Ouine forces at their every attack since Mathed had fallen – except for Androc's failure at the farm, when the prince split his army into the two brigades. A nasty business, that. The bloody ruin of Androc's cavalry was proof of that, seared into the mind of every soldier who stood witness.

This new mood of the prince, so starkly evident now that they were but a mile and a half from Mamoba, was the other side of the coin: the inexperienced youth, capricious and impulsive, gleeful even. But then, Chaaggar must concede, how could any man know the need that drove the boy: the loss of his father, the huge expectation on him to uphold, as he viewed it, the pride of Strath, and respond to the enmity he self-evidently felt for Honam?

"Ke Chaaggar!" came the prince's call, startling Chaaggar from his doleful reverie.

"My prince!" Chaaggar urged his horse closer. Steam rose from the animals' flanks like a mist upon the cold air of the afternoon.

Prince Osir, his hair wild upon his cheeks and curling over the steel neckplates of his cuirass, fixed his eye on Chaaggar. "Now's the time, Ke Chaaggar!" he cried. "Strath's mine now!"

And he touched his horse and cantered forward briskly, with the army at his back, seven hundred-strong. Olive-green pennons snapped and fluttered from lances. Drummers beat out the advance. All around was the jingle of harness and the rapid tramp of troops.

Its brilliant orb released suddenly from amidst the rim of clouds poised on the horizon, the western sun turned the red towers of Mamoba to fire. Underneath, all along the dark walls of the estate, steel glittered like defiant stars. Unexpectedly, Chaaggar saw a lone horseman emerge from the gap on the road between Mamoba Estate and the old wine presses. The figure moved slowly, unaccountably so, as if war were unheard of here, and headed through the brown, fallow fields towards the oncoming mass of Osir's army.

With a laugh, and an expression of boyish amusement, Osir announced, "Another stratagem! Chaaggar, how shall we cope with this?"

Chaaggar found himself drawn into the laughter this joke occasioned amongst the nearby officers. It was a good joke. It was at the enemy's expense. And when he laughed his unease was gone. It was easy to slip into the prince's mood. War was a thing of madness: death and destruction one moment; hope, elation and glory the next. The prince suited it perfectly. He looked across at Osir and answered in a booming voice for everyone around him to hear: "Single combat, perhaps, my lord!"

This produced great mirth, more uproarious than before.

Ke Androc, who was farther away, commanding the right wing, but had heard the merriment, rode closer. He wanted to be part of this, more than most probably. He concealed his guilt well, but Chaaggar could read it, as only a veteran leader could. Veteran! His combat had involved being very nearly run through by an Ouine lance. He had not even seen the man who wielded the lance, merely the blur of horse and armoured rider. Not once in a month of this campaign had he used his sword. He shook his head. Androc drew closer.

Helmet in hand, his characteristically scowling, beet-red face creased by jollity, Androc grumbled, "My lord, you've deceived us! You said there were at least two of 'em left!"

The prince took this as very funny, and slapped his thigh. He was now in his element. Standing up in the stirrups, he gesticulated grandly at the lone rider and shouted with sardonic delight, "I think they've propped Mathed up in the saddle with a lance up his arse!"

Chaaggar winced. That seemed perilously like a slap in the face of Dian. Chaaggar was hardly a pious man, but war made any man sensitive to ill fortune: one did not tempt the gods to prove the error of hubris.

Nonetheless, Osir had again tapped into the feeling of his army. "Then we had better retreat now, m'lord!" cried a voice amidst the laughter.

Chaaggar smiled ruefully. It had become 'm'lord' now. Everyone believed.

The bravura of the officers affected the men and they marched the more briskly. Some troopmaster demanded a cheer for the prince. The whole force took up the cry, the swell of excitement and confidence bursting in every throat. They fought for the prince. They fought for Strath. They would win.

Nearer the rider came. The horse picked its way slowly across the fields, between the dead vineyards, apparently left by its rider to choose its own pace.

Still in the best of spirits, the prince gestured to Phelep. "Ride forward if you will and tell this peasant to move aside!"

The officer spurred his horse to a gallop and bore down on the distant figure. Meanwhile, turning his attention away from the incident, the prince issued final battle orders to his officers. The force was to divide into three brigades as discussed, planned and rehearsed in the last days. They would encircle the estate and attack on the prince's signal.

Orders were passed back to the troopmasters. The officers began to take their leave of the prince.

"Wait!" said Chaaggar, who had been watching the two riders ahead.

"They're both returning," murmured Ke Androc.

A frown had replaced the exhilaration on Osir's face. He stared hard at the two figures. In a flat, emotionless tone he asked, "Who is that?" Then before anyone could answer he said with some surprise, "It's Ke Beyil, is it not?"

As indeed it was. The king's representative in Council, swathed in heavy clothes and hat, was unmistakable by reason of both his distinctive bearing and the awkward way in which he sat his mount. Recognising him, Osir might have smiled, but his unexpected arrival here where there should only be soldiers brought consternation to his look. Suspicion, curiosity and bewilderment fought rapid skirmishes in his expression. It was obvious that he could barely restrain himself from riding forward to resolve his perplexity that instant. But honour won: he maintained the pace of the advance and allowed the two riders to come to him.

With Phelep at his side, Ke Beyil drew near. He stopped his horse, and something in this action or in the man's visage caused Prince Osir to do likewise. Officers shouted orders. The army came to a standstill.

The silence that followed was total. Chaaggar was astounded at how quiet the world was. Suddenly the tramp and thud of boot and hoof was ended. No drum filled the air. The men were still, the horses unmoving; even the land, from horizon to horizon, seemed to have shrunk in upon itself.

"Ke Beyil," Osir said in curt greeting.

Ke Beyil looked old. His face was gaunt and grey. He was not the man who had come to Mamoba six months ago. It was as if the passage of time had raced away with his life and left him clutching feebly at the world.

He had not met Osir's eye and, in a muddle of awful stammers and hesitations, responded to the prince's salutation with the utterance: "Prince Osir…"

Osir watched him narrowly.

"Prince Osir," Ke Beyil gasped once more. "I bear the most horrible news…"

At such a remark, on any other occasion, Chaaggar knew the prince would have ridiculed Ke Beyil without scruple. But the atmosphere that Ke Beyil carried with him would not allow it. There was about him a wrongness, an indescribable desolation as dark and portentous and unacceptable as the onset of pitch night at noon.

Chaaggar shivered, and made a small protective sign with his hand. Here on the boundary of Mamoba, though it was not twilight, it felt like Echrexar's horror had bled into the world.

The prince held his silence and stared at Ke Beyil, who seemed incapable of further speech, and whose eyes, haunted and agonised though they were, had locked with Osir's.

Then comprehension, abrupt and brutal as a sword blow, stripped the mask of cold arrogance from Osir's face.

At this sudden elucidation, as if released from a demon's thrall, Ke Beyil held out a crumpled letter in a trembling hand and said softly and clearly: "Prince Osir, I have a letter…the sergeant followed her. He tried to save her, but was too late. She threw herself into the cataract…"

***

His lungs burned. Cold air seared them like he was breathing fire. Down he scrambled, slithering on his legs and buttocks, taking cuts and bruises without thought. The ravine walls on this bank descended gradually, but in hidden drops and rugged tumbles of moss-covered rocks. He fell once, putting his shoulder down to take the hit and roll, but felt his sword get tangled under his arm and had to adjust, piling too much weight on his wrist and flinching in pain.

The river below surged and spat where the cataract pounded the waters, but soon it calmed, racing away north in its long meander through the vineyards and foothills to the Bay of Marshese. Kesmet found his feet again, leapt across a gap onto soft earth, brushed aside dead autumn scrub and sapling branches and glimpsed the bottom of the hill where the waters lapped up against the riverbank. He ran, and Zuse followed, and soon they reached the level ground where the annual spring flooding had carved out a wide foreshore, curving away to rise again with the contours of the hills. Stones, large round pebbles and the rotting broken trunks of waterlogged trees made a battered shoreline where the natural eddy stilled the nearest waters.

Without slowing he pulled both sword on its lanyard and crossbow bag over his head and shoulders and dumped them together with his coat, then began to jump from boulder to boulder into the freezing river. Zuse splashed his way in, seeking the unseen quarry, until the water was up to his shoulders. Kesmet had stopped, balancing on a flat boulder ten paces from the bank. He could see nothing except the racing river and the mad detonation of the torrent on the chaotic waters where the cataract descended from the heights.

There. A hunched shape, just visible on the surface, turning, turning, with the vortices generated by the inundation, and being pushed downriver. The distance was substantial, Kesmet realized with diminishing hope, at least thirty paces, widening every moment as the river carried the body away. Regardless, he stripped off his boots and threw them to the shore, then dived in, driving his arms through the icy water. Head up, he could see the distance was narrowing but not fast enough.

He slowed, called out above the din of the waterfall, "Zuse! Bring!" then returned to his fastest stroke. He did not see the dog's response. In a small fearful corner of his mind he worried that Eslin might be peering down from the heights, but it was too late for regrets. Eslin was simply a problem for later.

Another look ahead: the body was still turning slowly with the current and it was twenty paces away. Too far, too fast. Then he spotted Zuse, who must have run further downriver, cutting the angle and distance and closing fast. He was powering through the current and Kesmet began to hope. "Good, Zuse!" he shouted. "Bring!"

Zuse reached the body, took hold of the sodden clothes with his muzzle, could not get the right grip and tried again, this time with more success. Then he turned, raising his head, and paddled back towards the shore. Kesmet did the same, angling to close the gap. Soon, he was able to stand again and pushed himself along in a frenzy, water spraying in all directions as he emerged. Zuse was close, the body face down, the mass of heavy velvet clothing making a wide circle of buoyant material. It was why, Kesmet realized, the body had floated, lifted upward from the insane tumble of the waterfall. He reached out, got his arms underneath as Zuse let go, and strained with leg and back muscles to lift the body completely from the river. As he did so, the green cloak fell from one arm, dragging in the water and catching on splintered branches. He was unable to move, so he used his knee to brace the body, got his arm into a better position under the cloak and tugged. He was free. The cloak pulled from the other arm and spilled into the river, its yellow lining sinking out of sight.

Still the weight on his arms was extraordinary. It started to ease as water poured from the clothes. He stumbled over broken branches and smooth, slippery rocks to the open pasture up the bank. There he lay Che Keleu, turned her onto her side and, bent low to see if she coughed or breathed, waited a count of five heartbeats. Her lips were parted and some water drained, but not enough. Nothing. No sign of life. He cursed, rolled her onto her back, noticed the trickle of blood from her head, staining her ear and neck with bright crimson against the white of her skin. The cut was secondary. He tilted her head, gently brushed curls of soaking auburn hair from her cheek, opened her mouth and closed his own over her pale lips.

***

A troop of five Ouine lancers, accompanied by Ke Lavi and Ke Ivik, and led by Courier-sergeant Alin, had ridden madly up to the cataract. Nearby they found Che Keleu's mount, waiting patiently on the fringes of the meadow. It was near impossible to follow the river, owing to the precipitous gradient, the broken rocky outcrops and the thick undergrowth. As a consequence, they had to ride around the hill and back to the bank of the river two hundred paces downstream, a diversion five times the distance.

A young trooper found the velvet cloak. It was dragging on a waterlogged branch. Ke Ivik took it in trembling hands, folding its sodden mass and hanging it over his horse. He was in tears. One of the lancers drew attention to the tracks of a wolf or, perhaps, a large wild dog, but it meant little and the light was fading so they rode on, fruitlessly. Ke Lavi who, unlike his fellow Council junior Ivik, seemed to have mastered his shock, put questions to the courier-sergeant, in an attempt perhaps to piece together an explanation that would make more sense…or somehow make Che Keleu live again. The sergeant, whose face betrayed distress and guilt in equal measure, could add no more to the story. They had it from the stable boys anyway: the lady's insistence on a mount, her refusal to accept a bodyguard, the giving of the letter to the sergeant, and his indecision before following her. He had reached the high meadow when she jumped. At once he searched the precipice, hoping against hope, then, seeing no sign, rode at breakneck speed to the estate to summon help and give the letter to Ke Beyil.

Later, as they turned back and twilight made the flood of the river a sinuous silver-black expanse, they glimpsed, from the bank where they had earlier found the cloak, a squad of horsemen above the cataract. A single man stood on the high black rocks where they projected over the thunder of the water's descent. He was limned against the last light of the sky and he did not move.

"The Prince Osir," muttered one of the Ouine lancers. He spoke the word like a curse.

"He seeks her," Ke Ivik choked out his words, looking up with wide eyes.

"He will not find her," whispered Ke Lavi. "And then he will come at Mamoba – and destroy it."

This silenced the company. Only the courier-sergeant continued to look up at the figure, and might have been seen to shake his head, but no one noticed. After a while, with the cataract and the river an unchanging, unsympathetic presence, insensate to their mood of desolation, they headed back to Mamoba.

**

Full winter gripped the hills surrounding Mamoba. Storm-driven sleet came and went, soaking the dark soil of the vineyards. A mile distant, Osir's camp, seven days ago a sprawling mass of tents and men and horses, surrounded by a palisade of stakes, had dwindled to half its previous size. With the purple dawn more soldiers left, silently, in twos and threes, stoop-shouldered under the weight of their baggage and with hardly a glance behind. At last only the cavalry and personal guards of the nobles of Strath remained.

One morning, two days after the fortieth, Ke Chaaggar mounted his warhorse and led his men from the camp. Ke Androc walked out to meet him at the outskirts of the circle of tents. A drizzle had begun to fall, but Ke Androc was bareheaded. With him were two officers, grim-faced.

Ke Androc called out: "You're leaving us?"

Chaaggar brought his horse to a standstill. He had anticipated this but had prepared no parting words. "Aye," was all he said.

Ke Androc was not about to move. His eyes were narrow, his expression unreadable. In a flat tone he said, "We agreed to await the prince…"

Chaaggar sighed, and avoided the question implicit in Androc's challenge. "My apologies, Ke Androc. I should have informed you. I return to my estates today…"

"Then you will not wait?"

Chaaggar bowed his head. He stared long moments at the muddy ground. He was unbearably weary. His wounded arm and shoulder still hurt, the healing slow. Though he had no will for this encounter, he knew it was unavoidable. "Ke Androc," he said, meeting the other's eyes. "Che Keleu is…no more. Dead. The fortieth day is past and the prince is gone. He did not claim Mamoba when he might have. Now it is concluded. Daily the men of Strath leave this place for their homes. Should we not learn from their example?"

Androc stood stock-still. Thick grey smoke from the campfires drifted between him and Chaaggar.

"You are thirty-strong in cavalry," said Androc. "Dykal, Kesiden and I, for our part, have sixty cavalry and perhaps ninety foot soldiers. Your leaving will cut our strength."

"Why do you need my soldiers, Ke Androc?" Chaaggar responded heavily. "The prince is gone. His sister is dead. He will not return."

"And yet we might still take Mamoba. The Ta-shih are nowhere near. My outriders tell me floods delay them." Androc stepped closer and, as if he feared the traitorous ear of other men, hissed under his breath at Chaaggar, "There is only the king's representative to bear witness! We might take Mamoba and be rid of Ouine Clan!"

Chaaggar was shocked. He shook his head. "What do you say, Androc? To lift a hand against Ke Beyil!"

Androc stood close beside Chaaggar's horse. He looked up, ruddy face a brutal, desperate mask. "And yet we might! And no one be the wiser!"

Chaaggar was astounded. There was a mad logic in this. They were men of violence now. They had Ouine blood on their swords. What matter the blood of Ke Beyil and his aides?

Ke Androc gripped Chaaggar's forearm. Chaaggar noticed it with surprise and then the full horror of what Androc proposed struck him. He tore his arm away, startling the horse which shied and backed up. Androc stumbled clear.

Chaaggar waved his men forward. They passed behind him as he calmed his mount. Ke Androc, his look baleful, stood nearby.

"Return to your home, Ke Androc!" cried Chaaggar, and then with great passion: "*Honour* to you!"

***

It was a most difficult time for Ke Ivik and Ke Lavi. They were civilized young men. They were also, as both gradually came to admit, innocent of the world. Although death was not unknown to them, the violence of war was, and likewise its savage indignity. Nevertheless, they had endured these perturbations manfully and, to their credit, rose above their own troubles when Lord Mathed, bleeding in the arms of Vedarahava, had returned to Mamoba. They assisted as best they could, stayed awake through the Lady Che Keleu's sleepless vigil, remained ready upon the instant to do her smallest bidding… However, Mathed's miraculous recuperation, with all the joy that this meant for Keleu, followed by her own sacrifice – these swift, cruel changes of fortune were past bearing. For both men her death was crushing.

Of course, the daily routine of work and correspondence to which Ke Beyil had punctiliously adhered fell away like a needless memory of Chisua. Lavi and Ivik moved about the mansion like forlorn spirits, and Ke Beyil, who kept entirely to himself, wore a look of agony, as if imprisoned by doubts and self-accusations. Deep in shock themselves, this mood of the king's representative was not one for which they felt equipped. The days therefore were dark with endless waiting and tension, and no one spoke if it could be avoided. Outside there was still the threat of Prince Osir's army, but even this waned as surely as the inexorable trickle of men from his camp.

Finally, a Ta-shih detachment commander from Desdang Fortress arrived in the gloom of another rain-swept evening. With impressive despatch, and in execution of an obviously well-drilled manoeuvre, some two hundred soldiers took possession of Mamoba's environs. Cavalry thundered across the muddy ground between Osir's camp and the estate and there, even before the dim light had faded, set up a long line of lances, butts grounded in the soft earth as a symbolic warning to the two warring factions.

His forces encamped for the night, the detachment commander entered the gates of Mamoba. He enquired after Osir, and was informed by Ke Beyil that the prince had left, his whereabouts unknown. Ke Androc and the nobles of Strath remained in their camp and made no challenge.

With none to dispute the issue, Lord Mathed's overlordship in Strath was formally acknowledged. A document signed by Ta-shih, Archivists, and supervisors there present was delivered into Ke Beyil's hands, and the matter was at an end.

The remaining nobles of Strath departed Osir's camp with their cavalry. Long lines of soldiers and horses straggled out through the vineyards and fields to follow their baggage trains towards the distant blue hills around Mamoba. By noon of the following day, the only troops that could be seen were Ta-shih, solitary figures in grey, billowing cloaks who stood at intervals along the line of lances.

Two days later, his preparations complete, Ke Beyil took his leave of Lord Mathed. The young man, debilitated from his wound and, though a ten-day had passed, hardly able yet to accept the death of his bride, made the effort to attend a formal farewell. His grief, however, was plain in every shadowed hollow of his face. "I would that our parting had been on happier terms," he faltered.

Ke Beyil who, in anticipation of this moment, had made ready a suitable speech, felt suddenly the emptiness of it. Instead, with a full heart he responded, "I cannot know your grief, my lord. Forgive me then if I speak my own. I regret…I fear that in some way I missed the opportunity to act, to do something that might have prevented the sacrifice of one so dear. As to that, my penance is to witness your own sorrow and never to understand what I might have done. I came to Mamoba as one man, and I leave as another. I am glad of it only because I have known the Lady Che Keleu and, in my own poor way, have loved her."

***

It was cold. On the platform of Mamoba's keep, high above the mansion, Skava rested a shoulder against one of the stone crenellations facing south. The last of Osir's army had gone. The leaning palisade of his camp remained, like some exotic graveyard of markers.

Maki stood nearby, also watching the camp. "Touch an' go, boss," he offered.

Skava grunted. "Too fucking right." She peered forward over the edge and took in the Ta-shih soldiers below, between the keep and mansion walls. The moment they rode in and planted their spears, Skava knew it was over. Mathed was secure. The plan had worked.

"He chucked it in, boss," Maki broke into her thoughts. "Didn't think he would." He was talking about Osir.

"Hmm." She glanced sideways at Maki, one eyebrow arched. "Yes, you did."

Maki gave her a puzzled look.

"You said he had a lot to lose," she reminded him. "You said that if he was forced to choose, he'd have to make a bad choice."

Maki stared at her, and she could see things clattering into place in his head. Eventually he looked away, nodded. "Choosing," he recollected, and a shadow seemed to cross his features, "between two things you love." He was speaking, in part, about himself, about his own painful choices in years long gone.

"Yes."

"And you forced him to make a bad choice."

"Yes."

And she smiled. For the first time in ages, she smiled.

Maki was silent for the time it took the first snowflakes to start settling on the battlements. Then he asked, "But how'd you know, boss?"

It was a good question. Experience. Luck. The careful management of preparedness and opportunity. All of that. But there was also a deeper, more significant reason.

"People, Maki," she answered. "People are slaves to their own weaknesses. Sometimes you have to use it against them to save us all from being slaves. Or dead."

Maki blinked slowly and shrugged deeper into his heavy coat, flicking the wide collar up so it covered his ears. "Pity 'bout...the Lady..." he ventured.

Skava sucked in the cold soft air of the gathering snowstorm, her nostrils flaring. There was a lot she could have said in reply, but, as usual, she didn't. Instead she cocked her head at him, like a challenge, or a dare to contradict a truth. "Choices, Maki," she murmured. "She made her choices. We all make choices. All the way. Even when we choose to do nothing. All the way to the end of things. I choose to go on. What do you choose?"

Maki looked at her and, not for first time, was alarmed by the depth and intensity of her hazel eyes. It was as if there was something he could almost grasp, but it was too distant, or too deep, or too dangerous, and he averted his gaze. "I'm with you, boss," he finished, matter-of-fact, knowing it to be true. Being around Skava did not allow for any other possibility.

She grunted again, turned her face up and smiled at the snow brushing her hair and cheeks. She looked for a moment like a little girl, full of wonder and innocence, though everything Maki knew about her screamed something different and altogether huge and unreadable.

"Good," she laughed. "Don't get comfortable. We've only just started."

THE END

The Dream Murderer Cycle continues in 'Betrayer of Dreams'.